The Palgrave Handbook of the Southern Gothic

Susan Castillo Street • Charles L. Crow
Editors

The Palgrave Handbook of the Southern Gothic

palgrave
macmillan

Editors
Susan Castillo Street
Harriet Beecher Stowe Professor Emerita
Department of English Language and
Literature, King's College London
London, United Kingdom

Charles L. Crow
Professor Emeritus of English
Bowling Green State University
Ohio, USA

ISBN 978-1-137-47773-6 (hardcover)   ISBN 978-1-137-47774-3   (eBook)
ISBN 978-1-349-69333-7 (softcover)
DOI 10.1057/978-1-137-47774-3

Library of Congress Control Number: 2016947268

Cover illustration: © Jack Maguire / Alamy Stock Photo

Printed on acid-free paper

This Palgrave Macmillan imprint is published by Springer Nature
The registered company is Macmillan Publishers Ltd. London

ACKNOWLEDGMENTS

The editors would like to thank the members of the Advisory Board for their many helpful suggestions during the long process of evolving this collection: Janet Beer, Benjamin F. Fisher IV, Teresa Goddu, Richard Gray, Michael Kreyling, Barbara Ladd and Sharon Monteith.

CONTENTS

Notes on Contributors

Eric Gary Anderson is Associate Professor of English at George Mason University and director of the Native American and Indigenous Studies Program. He is the author of *American Indian Literature and the Southwest: Contexts and Dispositions* (1999) as well as chapters in a variety of books including *Faulkner and the Ecology of the South, Speak to Me Words: Essays on Contemporary American Indian Poetry*, and *South to a New Place: Region, Literature, Culture*. His essays have appeared in *PMLA, ESQ*, and *Mississippi Quarterly*. He is currently working on his next book, *On Native Southern Ground*.

Peggy Dunn Bailey is Professor of English and Chair of English, Foreign Languages, and Philosophy at Henderson State, Arkansas's public liberal arts university. Her teaching and research interests include the Female Gothic, gothic literature of the British Romantic and Victorian periods, and gothic literature of the American South(s). Recent publications on Southern Gothic texts include essays on Reynolds Price's *Kate Vaiden* (in *North Carolina Literary Review*), Dorothy Allison's *Bastard Out of Carolina* (in *Mississippi Quarterly*), and Lee Smith's *Saving Grace* (in *Appalachian Journal*).

Janet Beer is the Vice Chancellor of the University of Liverpool, UK. She is a scholar of late nineteenth- and early twentieth-century American literature. Her sole-authored books include *Edith Wharton: Traveller in the Land of Letters* (1990), *Kate Chopin, Edith Wharton and Charlotte Perkins Gilman: Studies in Short Fiction* (1997), and *Edith Wharton* (2001), and her most recent edited book is *The Cambridge Companion to Kate Chopin* (2008). With Professor Avril Horner she has written numerous articles and their most recent book, *Edith Wharton: Sex, Satire and the Older Woman*, was published in 2011.

Paula Bernat Bennett is Professor Emerita from Southern Illinois University, Carbondale. She is the author of *Poets in the Public Sphere: The Emancipatory Project of American Women's Poetry 1800–1900* (2003) and editor of *Palace-Burner: the Selected Poetry of Sarah Piatt* (2003).

Michael P. Bibler is Associate Professor of Southern Studies at Louisiana State University. He is author of *Cotton's Queer Relations: Same-Sex Intimacy and the Literature of the Southern Plantation, 1936–1968* (2009) and co-editor of the essay collection *Just Below South: Intercultural Performance in the Caribbean and the U.S. South* (2007) and a new edition of Arna Bontemps's 1939 novel of the Haitian Revolution, *Drums at Dusk*. He has also published articles in journals including *MFS: Modern*

Fiction Studies, *Philological Quarterly*, *Journal of American Studies*, *Southern Cultures*, and *Mississippi Quarterly*.

Robert H. Brinkmeyer, Jr. is Director of the Institute for Southern Studies at the University of South Carolina, as well as the Emily Brown Jefferies Professor of English and the Charles Henry Neuffer Chair of Southern Studies. A Guggenheim Fellowship recipient, Professor Brinkmeyer is the author of five books on Southern literature and culture, the most recent of which is the award-winning *The Fourth Ghost: White Southern Writers and European Fascism, 1930–1950* (2009).

Brigid Cherry is a Research Fellow in Screen Media at St Mary's University, UK. Her research is focused on cult media and fan cultures, and she has recently published work on *Doctor Who* fans' responses to the change in the series, *Twilight* and *Supernatural* fan fiction, cosplay and fan identity in the steampunk community, gothic television, the female vampire in *Daughters of Darkness*, and *Doctor Who*'s Martha as an apostolic figure. She is currently working on a book on fan handicrafting, and has published material on vampire knitting and *Doctor Who* handicrafting. Her Film Guidebook on *Horror* was published in 2009, she is co-editor of *Twenty-First-Century Gothic* published in 2011, and she had an edited collection on *True Blood* published in 2012.

Emily Clark is Clement Chambers Benenson Professor in American Colonial History at Tulane University in New Orleans. She has published four books, including the multiple prize-winning *Masterless Mistresses: The New Orleans Ursulines and the Development of a New World Society* (2007) and, most recently, *The Strange History of the American Quadroon: Free Women of Color in the Revolutionary Atlantic World* (2013). She has held fellowships from the Mellon Foundation, the American Council of Learned Societies, the Louisiana State Board of Regents ATLAS program, and the Historic New Orleans Collection.

Charles L. Crow, Professor Emeritus of English at Bowling Green State University in Ohio, now lives in California. In the gothic field, his publications include *American Gothic* (2009), *American Gothic: An Anthology* (1999, 2nd edn 2012), and *A Companion to American Gothic* (2014). He is also the editor of *A Companion to the Regional Literatures of America* (2003), and the author of monographs on Maxine Hong Kingston and Janet Lewis.

Carol Margaret Davison is Professor and Head of the Department of English Language, Literature, and Creative Writing at the University of Windsor, Ontario. Her published books include *History of the Gothic: Gothic Literature 1764–1824* (2009) and *Anti-Semitism and British Gothic Literature* (2004). She continues to publish on a wide variety of Gothic-related authors and topics, and is currently at work on a casebook of criticism of the British Gothic, 1764–1824.

Kellie Donovan-Condron is an adjunct lecturer at Babson College in Massachusetts, where she teaches literature courses on rebels in literature and urban literature, as well as first-year writing and critical thinking. Her research interests include the urban Gothic, women's writing, particularly that of Mary Russell Mitford, and the nineteenth-century novel. Her article on Charlotte Dacre's *Zofloya* appeared in the December 2013 issue of *European Romantic Review*, and an article on Black Artemis's *Explicit Content* is forthcoming from *Studies in American Fiction*.

Dara Downey is Lecturer in American Literature in the School of English, Drama and Film in University College Dublin, Ireland. As well as numerous articles on Charles Brockden Brown, Edgar Allan Poe, Henry James, Shirley Jackson, Stephen King and

Mark. Z. Danielewski, she is the author of *American Women's Ghost Stories in the Gilded Age* (2014), which was partially funded by the Irish Research Council for the Humanities and Social Sciences. She is also co-editor of *The Irish Journal of Gothic and Horror Studies*.

Sarah Ford is an Associate Professor at Baylor University, where she teaches early American, Southern, and African American literature as well as directing the undergraduate program in the English department. She is currently serving as president of the Eudora Welty society and has published articles on Welty, Zora Neale Hurston, Ebenezer Cook, and Sarah Pogson. She has recently authored *Tracing Southern Storytelling in Black and White* (2014).

Ivonne M. García is Associate Professor of English at Kenyon College in Ohio, where she teaches nineteenth-century US literature, as well as Latin@, Trans-American, and postcolonial literatures. In 2011, she received the Board of Trustees' Teaching Excellence Award, a 1-year Whiting Teaching Fellowship for research, and was given an award for her essay, 'Transnational Crossings: Sophia Peabody Hawthorne's Authorial Persona from the "Cuba Journal" to *Notes in England and Italy.*' She is currently working on her book manuscript titled 'Haunted by Cuba: U.S. Imperialism, Slavery, and the American Colonial Gothic.'

Ken Gelder is Professor of English at the University of Melbourne, Australia. His books include *Reading the Vampire* (1994), the co-authored *Uncanny Australia: Sacredness and Identity in a Postcolonial Nation* (1998), *Popular Fiction: The Logics and Practices of a Literary Field* (2004), *Subcultures: Cultural Histories and Social Practice* (2007) and *New Vampire Cinema* (2012).

Mark Graves is an Associate Professor of English at Morehead State University (Kentucky), where he teaches undergraduate and graduate courses in American and Southern literature and film. He is the co-author of *Blockbusters: A Reference Guide to Film Genres* (2006) and the co-editor of *An Encyclopedia of American War Literature* (2000). He has published articles on Ellen Glasgow, Josephine W. Johnson, John Dos Passos, and Wilfred Owen.

Richard Gray was the first specialist in American literature to be elected a Fellow of the British Academy. He has been a Professor or Distinguished Visiting Professor at several universities in the UK and USA, including Essex, Georgia and South Carolina. He is the author of more than a dozen books on American literature, including the prize-winning *Writing the South* (1998), *The Life of William Faulkner* (1994), *Southern Aberrations* (2000), *A History of American Literature* (2003), *A Web of Words* (2007) and *After the Fall* (2011). His most recent book is *A History of American Poetry* (2015).

David Greven is Associate Professor of English at the University of South Carolina. He specializes in both nineteenth-century American literature and Hollywood film. His books include *Gender Protest and Same-Sex Desire in Antebellum American Literature* (2014), *Psycho-Sexual: Male Desire in Hitchcock, De Palma, Scorsese, and Friedkin* (2013), *The Fragility of Manhood: Hawthorne, Freud, and the Politics of Gender* (2012), *Representations of Femininity in American Genre Cinema: The Woman's Film, Film Noir, and Modern Horror* (2011), *Manhood in Hollywood from Bush to Bush* (2009), and *Men Beyond Desire: Manhood, Sex, and Violation in American Literature* (2005).

Bev Hogue is McCoy Professor of English at Marietta College in Marietta, Ohio, where she teaches literature and writing classes. Her research examines the portrayal of nature and place in regional literatures. She has published articles in *Modern Fiction*

Studies, ISLE, Pedagogy, and Blackwell's *Companion to the Regional Literatures of America.*

Avril Horner is Emeritus Professor of English at Kingston University, UK. Her research interests include women's writing and gothic fiction. With Sue Zlosnik she has co-authored many articles and several books, including *Daphne du Maurier: Writing, Identity and the Gothic Imagination* (1998) and *Gothic and the Comic Turn* (2004). Her edited books include *European Gothic: A Spirited Exchange, 1760–1960* (2002). She has also written several articles with Janet Beer, with whom she co-authored *Edith Wharton: Sex, Satire and the Older Woman* (2011). She is currently co-editing, with Anne Rowe, a selection of Iris Murdoch's letters.

Michael Kreyling is Gertrude Conaway Vanderbilt Professor of English at Vanderbilt University. He is the author of several books on Southern literature, most recently *A Late Encounter with the Civil War* (2014) and *The South That Wasn't There: Postsouthern Memory and History* (2010).

Michael L. Manson is Director of Undergraduate Research at American University. He teaches in the Literature Department and the American Studies program and is the author of several articles concerning modernist poetry and poetic form, discussing Robert Frost, Sterling A. Brown, Jay Wright, Lorine Niedecker, Gary Soto, Robert Hass, and Emily Dickinson. He is co-editor of *The Calvinist Roots of the Modern Era* (1997) and contributed to the fourth edition of the *Princeton Encyclopedia of Poetry and Poetics* (2012). He has served as the president of the Robert Frost Society (2006–2007) and as the executive director of the Northeast Modern Language Association (1997–2000). In 2005, he organized a Symposium on Poetic Form for the American Literature Association.

Bill Marshall is currently Professor of Comparative Literary and Cultural Studies at the University of Stirling, and Director of the Institute of Modern Languages Research, University of London, UK. His authored works include *Victor Serge: The Uses of Dissent* (1992), *Guy Hocquenghem* (1996), *Quebec National Cinema* (2001), *André Téchiné* (2007), and *The French Atlantic: Travels in Culture and History* (2009). He has also edited books on *Musicals—Hollywood and Beyond* (2000), *Montreal-Glasgow* (2005), and a three-volume encyclopaedia on *France and the Americas* (2005).

Stephen Matterson has taught US Literature at Trinity College, University of Dublin, Ireland for over 25 years, where he is Professor of English Studies and a Fellow of the College. He has published more than 60 articles, essays and reviews and has edited, authored and co-authored 10 books, focused on poetry, US literature and nineteenth-century literature; these include the monograph *Herman Melville: Fashioning in Modernity* (2014). His teaching interests are in most areas of US literature, with special interests in Hawthorne and Melville, literature and race, modern American poetry, American autobiography, and literature of the American South.

Agnieszka Soltysik Monnet is Professor of American Literature at the University of Lausanne and author of *The Politics and Poetics of the American Gothic* (2010). She has co-edited (with Justin Edwards) *The Gothic in Contemporary American Literature and Popular Culture* (2012) and published on race and the Gothic, feminism, queer theory, war Gothic, Richard Matheson, Batman and Edgar Allan Poe.

Sarah Robertson is a Senior Lecturer at the University of the West of England, UK. Her research focuses on modern and contemporary Southern writing, and she has particular interests in capitalism and class. She has published a monograph on the Appalachian author Jayne Anne Phillips, as well as articles and chapters on writers including William Faulkner, Katherine Anne Porter and Rick Bragg.

Owen Robinson is Senior Lecturer in US Literature at the University of Essex, UK. He is the author of *Creating Yoknapatawpha: Readers and Writers in Faulkner's Fiction* (2006), as well as several journal articles and book chapters on Faulkner. With Richard Gray, he has co-edited *A Companion to the Literature and Culture of the American South* (2004). He is currently working on writing centred on New Orleans, as part of the AHRC-funded project *American Tropics: Towards a Literary Geography*. He has published several articles on New Orleans writing, and recently co-edited *Surveying the American Tropics: A Literary Geography from New York to Rio* (2013).

Éric Savoy edited, with Robert K. Martin, *American Gothic: New Interventions in a National Narrative* (2nd edn 2009). He has published widely on American Gothic, particularly on Hawthorne and James. He has essays forthcoming on Shirley Jackson and the Gothic in *Women's Studies*, and on Hawthorne's Gothic Archive in *The Canadian Review of American Studies*.

Anne Schroder is a Research Fellow in English at the University of Surrey, UK. She completed her PhD on zombification in contemporary Caribbean and US literature at the University of Essex and is currently working on a book that explores the zombie as a paradigmatic figure of Otherness. She has published on the travel writing of Jamaica Kincaid and presented papers on Jean Rhys, Don DeLillo and Erna Brodber at international conferences. She is also working on a book on the spatial dynamics in recent British and US fiction.

Matthew Wynn Sivils is an Associate Professor of English at Iowa State University. He has published numerous articles on the work of American Gothic and Southern Gothic authors, including Charles Brocken Brown, James Fenimore Cooper, John Neal, William Faulkner, Harriet Prescott Spofford, and Zora Neale Hurston. He is the editor of five scholarly editions, and a monograph, *American Environmental Fiction, 1782–1847* (2014).

Susan Castillo Street is Harriet Beecher Stowe Professor Emerita of American Studies, King's College London, UK. She has published extensively on colonial writing of the early Americas, Native American literature, nineteenth-century American literature, and the Southern Gothic. Her publications include *Colonial Encounters 1500–1786: Performing America* (2013), *American Literature to 1865* (2010), *The Literatures of Colonial America* (2001, co-edited with Ivy Schweitzer), and *American Travel Writing and Empire* (2009, co-edited with David Seed). She is also a published poet and translator.

Edward Sugden is a lecturer in American Literature at King's College London, UK. He completed his doctorate at the University of Oxford and his work has appeared in *J19* and *Leviathan*.

Sherry R. Truffin is an Associate Professor of English at Campbell University and currently teaches courses in the fields of American literature, rhetoric, and writing. She is the author of *Schoolhouse Gothic: Haunted Hallways and Predatory Pedagogues in Late Twentieth-Century American Literature and Scholarship* (2008). Among her other publications are 'Creation Anxiety in Gothic Metafiction: *The Dark Half* and *Lunar Park*' and '"Gigantic Paradox... Too Monstrous for Solution": Nightmarish Democracy and the Schoolhouse Gothic in Edgar Allan Poe and Donna Tartt' in *A Companion to American Gothic* (2013), and essays on Joyce Carol Oates, Chuck Palahniuk, James Baldwin, and *The X-Files*.

Ellen Weinauer is Associate Professor of English and the Director of Interdisciplinary Studies at the University of Southern Mississippi. She is the co-editor, with Robert McClure Smith, of *American Culture, Canons, and the Case of Elizabeth Stoddard* (2003), and the author of articles on Hawthorne, Melville, Frederick Douglass, Elizabeth Stoddard, Edgar Allan Poe, and E.D.E.N. Southworth.

Maisha Wester is an Associate Professor at Indiana University. Her research includes representations of race in American Gothic literature and horror film, African American revisions and appropriations of the Gothic genre, and constructions of race and sexuality in African American literature. She is the author of *African American Gothic Literature: Screams from Shadowed Places* (2012), and articles on gothic literature and horror film.

Christine A. Wooley is an Associate Professor of English at St. Mary's College of Maryland, where she teaches courses in nineteenth-century American and African American literature. Her essays have appeared in the *African American Review* and *Mississippi Quarterly*; currently she is working on a book-length study of the intersection of financial and inter-racial relationships in turn-of-the-century black fiction.

Tom F. Wright is a Lecturer in American Literature at the University of Sussex, UK. He is the author of *Lecturing the Atlantic: Speech, Media and an Anglo-American Commons* (2016), and the editor of *The Cosmopolitan Lyceum: Lecture Culture and the Globe in Nineteenth-Century America* (2013). He has published articles on Ralph Waldo Emerson, Thomas Carlyle, Herman Melville and the painter Richard Caton Woodville.

Nahem Yousaf is Professor of English and Chair of English, Culture and Media at Nottingham Trent University, UK. He has published books on South African, Nigerian and British writers and many essays on new immigrants to the US South, in journals including the *Journal of American Studies*, *Modern Language Studies*, and *North Carolina Literary Review*, and collections including *Poverty and Progress in the US South*, *Transatlantic Exchanges: The South in Europe*, and *The Cambridge Companion to the Literature of the American South*.

CHAPTER 1

Introduction: Down at the Crossroads

Susan Castillo Street and Charles L. Crow

The legend of blues musician Robert Johnson, selling his soul to the Devil at a crossroads in the Mississippi Delta in exchange for blues immortality, is one that will resonate with scholars working on the American South and on the Southern Gothic. Given the explosion of scholarship in this area over the last two decades, defining the South and the Southern Gothic is not a task for the faint of heart. In recent years, scholars have moved beyond traditional views of the South and of Southern literature as characterised by a strong sense of place, nostalgia for a lost past and a Lost Cause, and a history of defeat, articulated by white male writers. In her influential 2005 overview of the field of Southern studies, Barbara Ladd comments, 'At present, southern studies takes shape at crossroads,' and adds, 'Inquiry into creole and creolist discourses in the South has taken us into New World, Americas, and African studies.'

In her critical work *Playing in the Dark: Whiteness and the Literary Imagination*, and her essay 'Unspeakable Things Unspoken: The Afro-American Presence in American Literature', Toni Morrison makes a compelling case for the necessity of grounding interpretations of American literary texts in their historical and social context, and of acknowledging the uncanny presence of a non-white, Africanist presence haunting American literature. She acknowledges the central paradox underlying American identity: that the Enlightenment ideas on which the country was built accommodate slavery, in that they are defined in opposition to it. She adds that the concept of slavery enriched the country's creative possibilities, since the dramatic polarity created by skin colour allows the young nation to construct its own identity by elaborating racial difference in order to define itself by what it is not, a 'fabricated brew of darkness, otherness,

S.C. Street (✉)
King's College London, London, UK

C.L. Crow
Bowling Green State University,
Bowling Green, OH, USA

© The Editor(s) (if applicable) and The Author(s) 2016   1
S.C. Street, C.L. Crow (eds.), *The Palgrave Handbook of the Southern Gothic*,
DOI 10.1057/978-1-137-47774-3_1

alarm and desire', and by projecting this abjected darkness onto the bodies of (silenced) African slaves. Morrison continues, 'The strong affinity between the nineteenth-century American psyche and the gothic romance has rightly been much remarked.'[1] Indeed, the gothic form has enabled writers to explore the shadow cast by the uncanny, haunting presence of the nation's others.

It is in the South, though, that this shadow is most starkly defined and most darkly cast across the crossroads. Teresa Goddu states categorically:

> The American Gothic is most recognizable as a regional form. Identified with gothic doom and gloom, the American South serves as the nation's 'other', becoming the repository for everything from which the nation wishes to dissociate itself. The benighted South is able to support the irrational impulses of the gothic that the nation as a whole, born of Enlightenment ideals, cannot.[2]

She advocates the placing of American gothic texts within historical sites of haunting, and discusses the possibilities and perils of looking at texts through a gothic lens, while acknowledging the limitations of the Gothic in resurrecting and representing historical events.[3]

Indeed, the South is a region that has always been obsessed with crossroads and boundaries, whether territorial (the Mason–Dixon line) or those related to gender, social class, sexuality and particularly race. In the South, ghosts and men in white sheets are real, as are shackles and clanking chains, and the Southern Gothic is a genre that arises from the area's often violent and traumatic history.

How, then, to address the intersections between 'Southern' and 'Gothic'? Eric Gary Anderson, Taylor Hagood and Daniel Cross Turner, in *Undead Souths: The Gothic and Beyond in Southern Literature and Culture*, have recently commented on the need to move beyond the capitalised terms 'Southern' and 'Gothic', viewed as monolithic entities, suggesting that it is more productive and critically fertile to pluralise regional and generic identification 'into multiple, even contradictory forms of what counts as "southern" and as "gothic" all the while unsettling settled ideas of connections between the two'.[4] Many scholars have focused on the complex intersections between region, nation and hemisphere. Deborah Cohn and George Handley applaud the move in Southern studies away from 'nativist navel-gazing' and evoke the image of a 'liminal south, one that troubles essentialist narratives *both* of global-southern decline *and* of global-northern national or regional unity, of American or Southern exceptionalism'.[5] Martyn Bone, Brian Ward and William Link, in *The American South and the Atlantic World*,[6] similarly problematise boundaries of nation and genre in studies of the South.

There are other crossroads in Southern studies. Traditional views of class and ethnicity in the South are being challenged: given the level of racial fluidity there, John Lowe suggests, in his introduction to *Bridging Southern Cultures: An Interdisciplinary Approach*, that 'we may be moving ever closer to an all-embracing sense of southern ethnicity that is more culturally than racially defined'.[7] Race is one of the most exciting areas in which contemporary scholarship is addressing rigid binary views of racial categorisation and interaction. Previously there existed an almost exclusive focus on relations between African Americans and whites, but Eric Gary Anderson and others are exploring the presence, or indeed the absence, of Indigenous groups in Southern writing.

Another area in which traditional Southern stereotypes are being challenged is that of gender and sexuality. John Howard's landmark study *Men Like That: A Southern Queer History*[8] and Michael Bibler's *Cotton's Queer Relations: Same-Sex Intimacy and the Literature of the Southern Plantation*[9] are part of the explosion of texts focusing on the queer South. Kari J. Winter's *Subjects of Slavery, Agents of Change: Women and Power in Gothic Novels and Slave Narratives, 1790–1865*[10] and Patricia Yaeger's *Dirt and Desire: Reconstructing Southern Women's Writing, 1930–1990*[11] examine representations of Southern women and deconstruct tired stereotypes such as that of the Southern belle.

This collection is organised into five groups of chapters: on Edgar Allan Poe and his legacy; on race; on Southern Gothic spaces and places; on gender and sexuality; and on voodoo, conjure, vampires and monsters.

Poe and his Legacy

Poe's short story 'The Fall of the House of Usher' is in many ways the Ur-text of the Southern Gothic. To say that Poe casts a long dark shadow in Southern Gothic studies is a very considerable understatement. Tom F. Wright argues that situating Poe in terms of the Southern Gothic enables us not only to evaluate the extent of his influence on other writers, but also to address some of the limitations of the category itself. It has often been said that the legacy of William Faulkner, like that of Poe, looms large over subsequent writers, but it is equally true that Faulkner is the inheritor of Poe and the gothic tradition. Richard Gray, in his essay on William Faulkner, describes the ways in which Faulkner and other Southern writers use gothic conventions to subvert the triumphant narratives of American exceptionalism. Paula Bernat Bennett, in 'Dreamland: Antebellum Southern Women Poets and Poe', analyses Poe's legacy, delving into the ways in which his writing served as a template against which Southern writers could articulate concerns about the limitations placed on women in the South, the existence of domestic violence and the dangers related to slavery and slaveholding. Carol Margaret Davison picks up the motif of collapsing mansions and haunted plantation houses as a contact zone between racialised and gendered bodies, an uncanny realm where the past and present come face to face. Edward Sugden, in 'The Globalisation of the Gothic South', argues that the Southern Gothic is not about repression but about spatial compression, in that it seeks to contain and neutralise global forces into certain nodal points, adding that these points are inherently unstable, ultimately exploding Southern claims to cultural homogeneity. He adds that Poe's 'The Fall of the House of Usher' does precisely this, compressing earlier Southern globalism into its structure only to conclude with the apocalyptic image of the Usher mansion collapsing into the stagnant tarn.

Southern Gothic Space(s) and Place(s)

The second group of chapters focuses on definitions of space and place in the Southern Gothic. Matthew Wynn Sivils, in 'Gothic Landscapes of the South', traces the development of literary tropes such as the swamp in the depiction of Southern landscapes, from their origins in colonial writers such as John Smith and Garcilaso de la Vega to the present, viewing them as sites of racial and environmental haunting. Janet Beer and Avril Horner, in 'Southern Hauntings: Kate Chopin's Fiction', discuss Chopin's Louisiana as postcolonial space. Sarah Robertson, in 'Gothic Appalachia', describe gothic tropes such as the stereotypical feral hillbilly as well as environmental disasters such as strip mining in order to characterise Appalachian Gothic as a politicised genre, and Appalachia as a site of both exploitation and resistance. Nahem Yousaf, in 'New Immigration and the Southern Gothic', explores the ways in which immigrant writers and characters problematise the geographical and cultural boundaries of the Southern Gothic. Éric Savoy, in 'Flannery O'Connor and the Realism of Distance', discusses spatial and temporal distance in O'Connor's fiction. Bev Hogue, in 'Florida Gothic: Shadows in the Sunshine State', looks at the dark side of a place that is often viewed as a tropical paradise, examining the work of writers such as Francis Parkman, Lafcadio Hearn, Peter Matthiessen, Karen Russell and Jeff VanderMeer. Ivonne M. Garcia, in 'Gothic Cuba and the Trans-American South', discusses Louisa May Alcott's use of gothic conventions and tropes in order to configure Cuba as a double of the South, linking the United States and the Spanish Caribbean through the Gothic. Robert H. Brinkmeyer, in 'A Long View of History: Cormac McCarthy's Gothic Vision', suggests that what he describes as McCarthy's long view of history and its relation to the spaces in which McCarthy's fiction is sited are central to the gothicism of this work.

New Orleans has often been viewed as the archetypal city of the Southern Gothic, a liminal space where rigid racial taxonomies and norms of gender, sexuality and class are called into question. Three chapters look at New Orleans as gothic space from different perspectives. Sherry R. Truffin examines the confluence of New Orleans's geography, history and culture, highlighting its tradition of carnivalesque hedonism and excess. Owen Robinson, in 'George Washington Cable and Grace King', looks at gothic elements in the work of these two New Orleans writers and the ways in which they challenge or reaffirm the conventions of the local colour genre. Finally, Bill Marshall describes four key motifs (the house, skin colour, capitalism and the Jew, and blood) in the work of Francophone New Orleans writers Victor Sejour, Alfred Mercier and Sidonie de la Houssaye.

Race and the Southern Gothic

Given the South's history of chattel slavery, it could be said that race is a motif that underlies every chapter in this collection. A particular focus on race and racial issues, however, can be found in the third group of essays. Michael Kreyling evokes the Southern plantation as uncanny space, referring to William Styron's *The Confessions of Nat Turner*. Maisha Wester analyses gothic representations of the Haitian Revolution and Nat Turner's revolt, as well as African American appropriations of the Gothic in slave narratives. Emily Clark, in 'The Tragic Mulatto and Passing', traces the roots of this trope to eighteenth-century Orientalism and the extended Caribbean. The law, and its dramatic consequences for the lives of many Southerners, is analysed in Ellen Weinauer's 'Law and the Gothic in the Slaveholding South', in which she casts the law as gothic villain, making the case for the idea that laws concerning slaves haunt the

South, but that paradoxically they ultimately failed to erase the humanity and personhood of slaves. Christine A. Wooley, in 'Charles Chesnutt's Reparative Gothic', discusses issues of slavery and reparation, evoking Chesnutt's increasingly pessimistic vision as regards the real possibility of racial progress in the South. Agnieszka Soltysik Monnet, in 'Jim Crow Gothic: Richard Wright's Southern Nightmare', looks at gothic elements in this writer's short story collection *Uncle Tom's Children*, set in the rural South. Michael L. Manson, in 'The Turn from the Gothic to Southern Liberalism in *To Kill a Mockingbird*', discusses how the depiction of Atticus Finch in this iconic *Bildungsroman* presages the controversial vision of the same character in *Go Set a Watchman*.

It is vital to remember that African Americans are not the only group who have experienced racial oppression in the South. Eric Gary Anderson, in 'Raising the Indigenous Undead', describes the ways in which Indigenous stories of ghosts and monsters challenge European gothic conventions, with hauntings that bolster anti-colonial stances and enhance the cohesion of communities.

Gender, Sexuality, and the Southern Gothic

A fourth cluster of chapters addresses issues of gender and sexuality in Southern Gothic texts. Kellie Donovan-Condron, in 'Twisted Sisters: The Monstrous Women of Southern Gothic', discusses representations of the monstrous feminine and the female grotesque in Southern Gothic texts. Although Ellen Glasgow found many of the tropes and images associated with the Southern Gothic problematic, Mark Graves, in 'Ellen Glasgow's Gothic Heroes and Monsters', describes her use of gothic motifs in order to critique Southern norms related to gender. Dara Downey, in her study of 'The Gothic and the Grotesque in the Novels of Carson McCullers', looks at this writer's work in the context of conventional gothic plots and Bakhtinian theory, describing the social, sexual and racial tensions produced in an intolerant culture. Stephen Matterson, in '"The room must evoke some ghosts": Tennessee Williams', examines the tensions between Romanticism and the Gothic in Williams's late plays. Michael P. Bibler, in 'Truman Capote's Gothic Politics', analyses the crossroads in this writer's work where the generic conventions of the Southern Gothic on the one hand, and social and political realities related to sexual and racial oppression on the other, meet and collide.

Monsters, Vampires and Voodoo

In 'Southern Vampires: Anne Rice, Charlaine Harris and *True Blood*', Ken Gelder examines the work of these novelists in the context of slavery, plantations and the Civil War, in order to argue that the television series *True Blood* destabilises the vision of Southern whiteness as the privileged, property-inheriting norm. Anne Schroder, in 'Voodoo and Conjure as Gothic Realism', challenges traditional readings in which these African diasporic belief systems are relegated to the domain of the unreal in order to argue that the Gothic can be linked to literary realism in representations of slavery. Sarah Ford, in '"Nothing so Mundane as Ghosts": Eudora Welty and the Gothic', examines Welty's *Delta*

Wedding and the challenge that it poses to both racial and gendered norms, going on to discuss Welty's allusions to Poe's 'The Raven' and the ways in which *The Optimist's Daughter* subverts this trope of avian haunting. Peggy Dunn Bailey, in 'Talismans of Shadows and Mantles of Light: Contemporary Forms of the Southern Female Gothic', proposes three different variants of Southern Female Gothic discourses, the Supernatural, the Realistic and the Supra-natural or Romantic, in order to explore novels by Anne Rice, Dorothy Allison and Daina Chaviano. In 'Shadows on the Small Screen: The Televisuality and Generic Hybridity of Southern Gothic', Brigid Cherry analyses television programmes such as *Carnivale, True Blood, The Vampire Diaries, True Detective* and *American Horror Story Coven* and the ways in which they subvert traditional generic boundaries. Finally, David Greven, in 'The Southern Gothic in Film: An Overview', discusses the existence of pernicious, overly simplistic (and occasionally racist) stereotypes, and explores the ways in which the sub-genre resists this tendency, particularly as regards female sexuality and queer desire.

A caveat: as readers will have seen, organising these chapters into thematic clusters is an enterprise fraught with difficulty, involving diabolical bargains and trade-offs. Many could easily fit under several other designations, but that is perhaps the point. The crossroads in this volume are not isolated ones like Robert Johnson's dark midnight intersection in the Mississippi Delta, but are crossings characterised by movement across many different disciplinary axes, with occasional collisions, conflicts and contradictions, and flashes of valuable and unsettling insight.

NOTES

1. Toni Morrison, *Playing in the Dark: Whiteness and the Literary Imagination* (London: Picador, 1992), pp. 36–38.
2. Teresa Goddu, *Gothic America: Narrative, History and Nation* (New York: Columbia UP, 1997), p. 4.
3. Theresa Goddu, *Gothic America: Narrative, History, and Nation* (New York: Columbia University Press, 1997), pp. 8–10.
4. Eric Gary Anderson, Taylor Hagood and Daniel Cross Turner, *Undead Souths: The Gothic and Beyond in Southern Literature and Culture* (Baton Rouge: Louisiana State University Press, 2015), p. 4.
5. 'Uncanny Hybridities', in Jon Smith and Deborah Cohn, *Look Away: The US South in New World Studies* (Durham: Duke University Press, 2004).
6. Martyn Bone, *The American South and the Atlantic World* (Gainesville: University of Florida Press, 2013).
7. John Lowe, ed., 'Constructing a Cultural Theory for the South', in *Bridging Southern Cultures: An Interdisciplinary Approach* (Baton Rouge: Louisiana State University Press, 2005), p. 3.
8. John Howard, *Men Like That: A Southern Queer History* (Chicago: University of Chicago Press, 1999).
9. Michael Bibler, *Cotton's Queer Relations: Same-sex Intimacy and the Literature of the Southern Plantation* (Charlottesville: University of Virginia Press, 2009).
10. Kari Winter, *Subjects of Slavery, Agents of Change: Women and Power in Gothic Novels and Slave Narratives, 1790–1865* (Athens: University of Georgia Press, 1992).
11. Patricia Yaeger, *Dirt and Desire: Reconstructing Southern Women's Writing, 1930–1990* (Chicago: University of Chicago Press, 2000).

PART I

Edgar Allan Poe and His Legacy

CHAPTER 2

Edgar Allan Poe and the Southern Gothic

Tom F. Wright

Critics have for a long time talked of the 'problem of Poe': the difficulty of defining his achievement and its place within the American canon. No gothic writer enjoys a more truly global reputation, readership and influence; yet no writer has been so consistently misunderstood and excluded as an aberrant and even 'dubious' figure in the nation's literary history.[1] Underpinning this reputational uncertainty is the contentious issue of Poe's Southern identity. Few readers think of him first and foremost as a 'Southern' writer. Born in Boston, raised partly in London and associated throughout his short career with the journalistic worlds of Baltimore, New York and Philadelphia, Poe wrote almost nothing about the South, set barely any writings there, and seemed unconcerned with the topics of specific regional history, tradition and custom that form the repertoire of the Southern canon. It has been a commonplace of Poe studies for generations to fixate on the question of whether his writings bear any meaningful imprint of his regional origins, or whether his Southernness offers an illuminating framework through which to read his work.

The issue of Poe's relationship to the 'Southern Gothic' is even more unresolved. Most discussions of the genre do not find a place for his writings, for both thematic and chronological reasons. Many of the key themes of the genre – the importance of family and place, social class, religion and the tragic haunting of slavery – are treated obliquely at best in Poe's oeuvre. Chronologically speaking, it is also important to consider that he was writing just before the Civil War, a conflict that did so much to galvanise these tropes, and long before the celebrated writers of the twentieth-century Southern Renaissance whose works dominate handbooks such as this one. However, although it is tempting to dismiss the 'Southern Gothic' category as an anachronistic or imprecise route into Poe's writings, the term nonetheless retains a useful instructive value.

T.F. Wright (✉)
University of Sussex, Brighton, UK

© The Editor(s) (if applicable) and The Author(s) 2016
S.C. Street, C.L. Crow (eds.), *The Palgrave Handbook of the Southern Gothic*,
DOI 10.1057/978-1-137-47774-3_2

9

As this chapter explores, Poe's works offer a powerful gothic critique of nineteenth-century society, its values, contradictions and myths – in their spare glimpses of life below the Mason–Dixon line, but perhaps even more visibly in the seemingly placeless depictions of nightmarish aristocratic landscapes. This will be shown to be most evident in two of Poe's most peculiar and influential texts, pieces that best showcase his idiosyncratic concern with classic Southern Gothic issues of familial decay and racial fanaticism: 'The Fall of the House of Usher' (1839) and *The Narrative of Arthur Gordon Pym of Nantucket* (1838). Through ambivalent and elusive fictions such as these, Poe became a major influence on later Southern writers, and an author whose response to the South helped to construct a powerful symbolic canvas that later writers and critics would find indispensable and darkly provocative. I suggest that thinking about Poe in terms of the Southern Gothic helps to disrupt periodisation, assists us in perceiving the complex precursors to the twentieth-century Southern literary revival, and allows us to reflect on the limitations of the very term itself.

Poe's Gothic Placelessness

Poe's gothic is at once the most canonical and the most surprising in the American tradition. His tales handle all of the major themes that make up the particular texture of the gothic tradition: the concern with frontier, political utopianism and the spectre of race. Yet whereas Charles Brockden Brown, Nathaniel Hawthorne or even Washington Irving used gothic techniques as a means through which to interrogate society and the state of the nation, Poe's is a notably more inward sensibility. Rather than presenting a depiction of specific sites of historical haunting, his is the Gothic of agonised introspection, dramatising the fragility of personality and sanity, obsessively preoccupied with the ways in which the mind betrays itself and its capacity for evil.

In addressing these universal themes, Poe rarely grounded his works in specific social, political or geographical contexts. It is a commonplace that his fictions take place mostly in an invented 'otherworld', where the surreal and the illusory are the main features of the setting. The landscapes and settings of texts such as 'The Pit and the Pendulum' or the 'Tell-Tale Heart' are monstrously indistinct, and even in the case of those with specific national settings, such as the London of 'The Man of the Crowd' (1840) or the Paris of the Dupin tales 'The Murders in the Rue Morgue' (1841) or 'The Purloined Letter' (1845), the sense of place is strangely unmoored, using relatively specific locations as backdrops to intense psychological dramas.

If Poe's tales involve a sense of place at all, that is usually an abstract scene of confinement. According to Flannery O'Connor, the gothic style has at its core a sense of 'pushing its own limits outwards towards the limits of mystery'; Poe's version is one that pushes inwards, folding into tighter and tighter spaces. The gothic interiors of the London schoolhouse of 'William Wilson' (1839), the cellar of the 'Cask of Amontillado' (1846), the baronial towers of 'Ligeia' (1838) or the painstakingly delineated Paris apartment that Dupin scours in the 'Purloined Letter' are always far more the focus of events than the wider cities and landscapes in which they are set. The true topic of the Poe gothic is that morbid introversion, and the true ingredient is the ambiguously symbolist motif of enclosure.

Crucially, this 'placelessness' was in no way incidental to Poe's writings; in fact, it was central to their thematic ambitions. His apparent aim was to transcend region and nation – to strip away locale, history and geography – in search of an idealised realm of pure poetry. As the notoriously mean-spirited obituary of Poe by Rufus Griswold put it, he was 'a dreamer, dwelling in ideal realms', and it is true that Poe represented the very condition of placelessness as the gothic predicament in its purest form. He suggests that place is immaterial: that the Gothic is a state of mind, not a state of the Union.

Accordingly, for many generations critics have used Poe's claim that 'my terrors are not of Germany but of the soul' to justify taking an ahistorical approach to his work. In this view, he had little ambition to say anything of substance about the frenetic changes of the republic in which he lived; he was far more of humanist than a chronicler. This purely 'literary' approach has certainly taken Poe studies in some highly fruitful directions. T.S. Eliot and Richard Wilbur are only two of the many early twentieth-century critics who presented the author as a symbolist, and in the years since, countless articles and books have attempted to unravel the timeless psychological truths and challenges contained in his fiction.[2] Late twentieth-century high theory also found much to explore in Poe's work, most famously in the remarkable sequence of readings of 'The Purloined Letter' by Jacques Lacan, Barbara Johnson and Jacques Derrida.[3]

Another critical tradition has attempted to delve beneath Poe's deliberate abstraction and place him back into his historical context. Critics in this camp have sought to make clear how, rather than engaging purely with 'ideal realms', Poe's tales and criticism also reveal him to be, in the words of J. Gerald Kennedy, 'a sharp observer of the vehement but conflicted national culture emerging in his lifetime'.[4] Influential collections such as *The American Face of Edgar Allan Poe* (1995) have contextualised and historicised the subtleties of his writings to reveal a series of powerful insights into the market revolution, urbanisation, sectional tensions, gender politics and the crisis over slavery.[5] The result has been a growing acceptance of the fact that, as Teresa Goddu has succinctly put it, 'the terrors of Poe's tales are not of the soul but of society'.[6]

It has often proved particularly difficult to relate these texts in any meaningful way to Southern historical realities or sensibilities. Only 'The Gold-Bug' (1843) is set in the region, presenting a fragmentary image of the tidal marshlands of South Carolina. Unlike many of his antebellum Southern peers, Poe did not explicitly defend the region's social customs or heritage, seeming by contrast unattached to the Southern intellectual climate and the planter tradition. As a result, historians have tended to follow W.J. Cash's verdict in *The Mind of the South* (1941) that Poe was 'only half a Southerner'.[7] Yet the literary and political culture of Virginia was undeniably his milieu. Following an itinerant childhood as the son of travelling actors, prominent Richmond tobacco merchant Richard Allan adopted the infant Poe, and by all accounts bequeathed to his son a powerful Southern gentry identity, later funding his entry to the iconic bastion of Southern intellectualism, the University of Virginia. The South was where Poe came of age, where he first tasted success, where he began his married life and to where he returned in his final years. To his peers he was widely regarded as a Virginia man of letters, particularly identified with the world of the *Southern Literary Messenger*. In one uncommonly sentimental letter to his brother in 1839, Poe declared that 'Richmond is my home, and a letter to that City will always reach me in whatever part of the world I may be'.[8]

There are a number of ways in which these biographical facts have been seen to imprint his work. At least since the influential recovery of a decisively Virginian Poe in Allen Tate's 1949 essay 'Our Cousin, Mr. Poe', the author's Southern half has been seen to exert a great pull over his writing. As many writers have pointed out, in terms of commitment and stance Poe's reviews and journalism frequently gesture towards a recognisably Southern conservatism on issues of the past, perfectibility and progress, in his hatred of abstractions, his apparent scorn for democracy and the mob, and his belief in hierarchy. In this view, his attitudes towards race, gender, class and art can all be traced to habits of mind that aristocratic antebellum Southerners used to invent themselves. Controversies continue over his authorship of notorious anti-abolition reviews during the 1840s, and some critics such as John Carlos Rowe go as far as to claim that 'Poe was a proslavery Southerner and should be reassessed as such in whatever approach we take to his life and writings'.[9]

Some writers argue that this Southern influence was first and foremost a matter of style and aesthetics. Even if he transcends regionalism, Poe's concerns and literary techniques are identifiably Southern, in the lyricism and tendency for the lachrymose that he shared with other Southern poets. For example, fellow Virginian Ellen Glasgow recognised him as a product of his region as much through style as worldview, arguing that 'Poe is to a large extent, a distillation of the Southerner ... the formalism of his tone, the classical element in his poetry, and in many of his stories, the drift towards rhetoric, the aloof and elusive intensity, all these qualities are Southern'.[10]

Others see a powerful theme of commentary in his stories' coded or repressed treatment of issues of race and gender. In this view, although Poe might not seem to talk about Southern writerly concerns, he does so allegorically. It is a point often made that he was never more Southern than in those moments where he is offering a strident critique of the region. A number of Poe's most influential readers over the years have found him to be entirely anti-Southern. This reading emphasises the fact that Poe left the South as part of a rebellion against the values of Allan, his adoptive father. Given his complex attitudes and uniquely liminal position between class and region, he can be seen as the ideal person to deconstruct the Southern gentleman, and to lay bare the hypocrisies and pathologies on which such an ideology rested.

Both of these strands come together in perhaps Poe's most famous tale, 'The Fall of the House of Usher' (1838), a piece widely seen as one of the founding texts of the 'Southern Gothic'.

The 'House of Usher' and Southern Gentry

'The Fall of the House of Usher' (1837) is primarily a mood piece, and its plot is therefore easily summarised. A traveller arrives at the Usher family mansion to find that the sibling inhabitants are living under a mysterious family curse. Roderick Usher's senses have grown particularly acute, while Madeline has become nearly catatonic. As the visitor's stay at the mansion continues, the effects of the curse reach a terrifying climax, with both Usher siblings dead, and the mansions collapses into two pieces. This simple and haunting closet drama embraces many of Poe's signature motifs: the exploration of abnormal psychological states; an imprecise, almost Germanic, feudal setting; dark humour; violence; and a powerful sense of futility in the face of sin. Its vivid simplicity has made it one of Poe's best-known stories, and among the most anthologised gothic tales in the language. It is a paradigmatic example of a well-made gothic tale whose ambitions lie entirely within the confines of the genre itself. As with all of Poe's tales, the temptation towards a purely psychological reading is strong. Most broadly, the story can be read primarily as an allegory of the male psyche's attempts to confront the inward female.

Yet Poe's ambitions are clearly also more local and historical. This is arguably his most 'Southern' story. Set in a characteristically anonymous dreamscape, it has all the elements that would later come to characterise the Southern Gothic: great house and family falling into decay and ruin; a feverish morbid introspective hero; an ethereal heroine; implications of incest; a pervading sense of guilt propelled from the past. As Lewis P. Simpson has argued, Poe's story amounts to a recognisably 'Southern landscape of nightmare, homeland of a decadent aristocracy of slave holders, and of their descendants, prone to neurotic terrors and violence'.[11]

Above all, it is the central organising symbol of the once-great ruined mansion that strikes the most familiar Southern Gothic notes. Confronting the desolation of the edifice, the narrator explores his response to its façade of sublime decay:

> What was it – I paused to think – what was it that so unnerved me in the contemplation of the House of Usher? It was a mystery all insoluble; nor could I grapple with the shadowy fancies that crowded upon me as I pondered. I was forced to fall back upon the unsatisfactory conclusion, that while, beyond doubt, there are combinations of very simple natural objects which have the power of thus affecting us, still the analysis of this power lies among considerations beyond our depth. It was possible, I reflected, that a mere different arrangement of the particulars of the scene, of the details of the picture, would be sufficient to modify, or perhaps to annihilate its capacity for sorrowful impression; and, acting upon this idea, I reined my horse to the precipitous brink of a black and lurid tarn that

lay in unruffled lustre by the dwelling, and gazed down – but with a shudder even more thrilling than before – upon the remodelled and inverted images of the gray sedge, and the ghastly tree-stems, and the vacant and eye-like windows.[12]

As Charles Crow has argued, the 'most common site of the Southern Gothic is the decaying old plantation mansion', and in this chateau scene Poe reworks the plantation locales of John Pendleton Kennedy and Nathan Beverley Tucker into a broader source of terror and intrigue.[13] As the landscape calls up plantation images, Poe forces a contemplation of the 'old time entombed' through the mansion and the 'mystery all insoluble' it contains. The house is master – is 'alive' – so Usher insists, its grey stones and the history they contain exerting a 'silent, yet importunate and terrible influence' on this symbolic Southern family's destiny.

The symbolism of this 'Southern' edifice can also be read as central to a jeremiad that treats the dying-out of the planter aristocracy. In the 1950s, Harry Levin introduced the idea that the story was an allegory of feudal plantation culture in terminal decline, caught in the vice of inbreeding, degeneracy, neurasthenia and hypochondria.[14] In this reading, the decline of the lineage and edifice of 'Usher' can be mapped onto the disintegration of the very ideals of family and culture. Poe's decision to set his gothic exploration of the moral and mortal fate of the Southern aristocracy in an abstract and timeless landscape only magnifies the sharpness of the depiction, and its potency for imaginative allegorical treatment. In its theatrical fixation on decay and futile reconstruction, the tale becomes a lament for the threatened Southern pastoral ideal, and likewise for the fragile ideals of Southern womanhood.

Other recent readings of this tale as 'Southern' present it as a form of dark parody. In this view, the tale is really a gothic burlesque in the mode of Irving – a pastiche whose motive is not lament but satire on the decadence and inevitable decline of the Southern gentry. As many biographical critics have noted, this was a culture with which Poe maintained a complex relationship, and his ambivalent attitudes to the habits and worldview of the gentry helped drive his 1838 tale. For example, as Richard Gray has pointed out, Poe often adopted the carefree manner of the planter-gentleman, falsely assuming an air of privilege and propriety, and 'was perhaps never more of a Southerner than when he was imitating one: applying himself assiduously to the role of Virginia dandy, even when much of the historical evidence was against him'.[15] Building on these details of Poe's life, a number of critics have read the tale as a performance of gentry personae, deconstructing the 'shadow fancies' at the heart of a hollow cultural pose.

This view has been advanced most forcefully by David Leverenz, who argues that Poe played a 'trickster's role at the alienated margin of gentry culture', constantly invoking the Southern ideal of the gentleman in frequently ironic ways:

Poe inhabits and undermines gentry fictions of mastery, not least by exposing the gentleman as a fiction. Typically, he displays cultivated narrators unable to master themselves ... [and] plays with gentry specters of a debased capitalist future to put his own indulgent yet satiric spin on nostalgia for an idealised aristocracy.[16]

In a reading that also incorporates meditations on gentry themes in tales such as 'The Man of the Crowd' (1840), 'The Cask of Amontillado' and the August Dupin tales, Lerenz presents a Poe obsessed with the gentleman imperilled by modern urban settings that threaten stable hierarchies and social status. In all such stories, we might argue that the narrator's Southernness as well as his gentry identity of pretension is an unacknowledged set of themes and references. These themes are at their most vivid in 'The House of Usher', which became one of the founding texts of the Southern Gothic through its coded prophecy of the defeat of the South by the capitalist North. Poe's influence on the genre thus rested in part on his exploration of the creative possibilities of the margins of a beleaguered culture, beset by capitalism and marginalised by modernity, with tales such as 'Usher' drawing their peculiar power from their ambivalence towards a heritage both mourned and mocked.

Pym, Race and 'National Gothic'

The most obvious absence from that story, however, is the cardinal 'Southern Gothic' theme of race. As countless studies make clear, the international Gothic was in part a response to the implications of slavery. Accordingly, the American Gothic of the nineteenth century is now most commonly seen as one in which the repressions of a slaveholding democracy manifest themselves in haunting figures of blackness. One of the most important contributions to this new emphasis came in Toni Morrison's seminal essays in *Playing in the Dark: Whiteness and the Literary Imagination* (1991). In that book Morrison famously called for a more historical understanding of the American Gothic, and in particular the ways in which

> ... black slavery enriched the country's creative possibilities ... What rose up out of our collective needs to allay internal fears and to rationalise external exploitation was an American Africanism – a fabricated brew of darkness, otherness, alarm, and desire that is uniquely American.[17]

Perhaps surprisingly, Poe was placed at the dead heart of this tradition. Morrison noted that 'no early American writer is more important to the concept of American Africanism'.[18]

Morrison's revisionism was a powerful force in crystallising several generations' worth of critical thought regarding early American literature's relationship to race. Poe was far from the most obvious candidate to choose for such an endeavour, since racial themes are rarely at the foreground of his brand of Gothic. However, there are several intriguing exceptions. His tales might avoid direct confrontation of the issue of African Americans or slavery, but in their periodic stereotyped characterisations of black characters, critics from Harry

Levin onwards have seen the hallmark of the ethos of the antebellum South.[19] The late-career tale 'Hop Frog' (1849) is a usual reference point. In this, a court jester dwarf takes revenge on a sadistic king and his courtiers by dressing them up as chained gorillas, cunningly connects them to a chandelier, and sets their tarred bodies on fire in what various critics have seen as a coded depiction of Southern lynching.[20] A similarly oblique commentary has been noted in the 1845 comic short story 'The System of Doctor Tarr and Professor Fether', a tale elusively set in 'Southern provinces' that combines similarly animalistic elements with an emphasis on themes of mental health.

The work of Poe's that is most frequently analysed in terms of racial gothic is also his longest and most puzzling: *The Narrative of Arthur Gordon Pym* (1838). His only novel, published in the *Southern Literary Messenger* in two instalments, it is essentially a whimsical fictionalised travel account that follows the adventures of a stowaway who voyages through various exotic lands, meeting bizarre Indigenous populations, and ending with the characters heading towards the South Pole. As Morrison and others have shown, it offers Poe's most sustained and in many ways most perverse engagement with both race and the abstract ideas of a national and Global 'South'.

A number of incidents in the course of the voyage offer valuable insights into the author's racial worldview, and often not to his credit. A half Native American sailor is depicted in monstrous fashion, for instance, and the black cook leads 'mutiny and atrocious butchery' on board the ship *Grampus*. Most fascinating and problematically of all, Poe depicts a race of tribal black natives of the island of Tsalal, complete with black teeth, who are all repelled by the colour white. The book ends with the narrator confronted by an enormous white figure, whose whiteness causes the indigenous native Nu-Nu to perish:

> March 22. The darkness had materially increased, relieved only by the glare of the water thrown back from the white curtain before us. Many gigantic and pallidly white birds flew continuously now from beyond the veil, and their scream was the eternal Tekeli-li! as they retreated from our vision. Hereupon Nu-Nu stirred in the bottom of the boat; but, upon touching him, we found his spirit departed. And now we rushed into the embraces of the cataract, where a chasm threw itself open to receive us. But there arose in our pathway a shrouded human figure, very far larger in its proportions than any dweller among men. And the hue of the skin of the figure was of the perfect whiteness of the snow.[21]

It is a culminating scene of stark allegorical power, which Morrison summarised by noting how 'the black man dies, and the boat rushes on through the white curtain behind which a white giant rises up … both are figurations of impenetrable whiteness'.[22]

As this final scene suggests, the novel is as austere in its allegory as the most cryptic of Poe's tales. Some commentators insist on *Pym*'s status as a symbolic psychological voyage, but the more common reading is a historical one: this is a voyage to the 'perfect whiteness of an imagined South', and hence a form of pro-slavery narrative. To some readers, the Antarctica of the novel maps directly onto the geography of the United States, becoming what John Carlos Rowe calls 'a thinly disguised allegory of Poe's manifesto "Keep the South White"'.[23] The novel thereby becomes an extreme extension of both the physical and conceptual logic of a 'Southern' Gothic, once again turning on oppositions of civilisation and savagery, with its image of 'perfect whiteness' and 'terrifying blackness' standing as an emblem of an antebellum racial mindset on the verge of collapse under its own contradictions.

While these interpretations are largely persuasive, they are also potentially overly schematic. A more nuanced argument about the novel's relationship to the 'Southern Gothic' is the one made in Teresa Goddu's *Gothic America: Narrative, History and Nation* (1997) – a book that argues that our attempts to connect *Pym* to the ideas and problems of the 'Southern' Gothic are more the product of 'critical desire' than logic.[24] While Goddu concedes that the dynamics of Southern prejudice and resistance to abolition certainly run through this work, she also insists that 'by obsessively giving *Pym* a regional reading, critics have reduced Poe's complex meditation on race to a proslavery cant'.[25] She further makes the powerful claim that reading Poe in terms of the South simultaneously misses the larger 'national' critique of US society offered by his work, while tending to quarantine the idea of 'gothic' to the Southern states, so that 'race and gothic come to be identified as merely Southern problems'.[26] The desire to read Poe as an exponent of the Southern Gothic is clearly part of a wider problem. Goddu locates this problem in the obstinate refusal of many critics to admit the possibility of a truly cross-regional ideology at the heart of a racialised imagination of the type found in *Pym*. As her reading demonstrates, Poe was 'engaged with a national, not regional, discourse on race'.[27]

CONCLUSION: POE AND THE LIMITS OF THE 'SOUTHERN GOTHIC'

Although Poe's relationship with the South had been uneasy during his lifetime, during and after the Reconstruction period Southern writers and intellectuals began to reclaim him. He was in many ways a bizarre icon for his region to adopt. If he was a man without a country, then this lack of place was not thrust upon him but cultivated. Yet his work was compatible with the memorialisation involved in fashioning Lost Cause myths, and it was possible to present the values of his writings – his rejection of the ideas of perfectibility, dislike of utopianism, urbanism and intellectual abstractions – as founding 'Southern' myths. These supposed values underpinned Poe's status as a forerunner of the 'Southern Gothic'. The commitment to psychological exploration found in tales such as 'Usher' and daring works such as *Pym* helped to establish the twentieth-century genre's register and breadth in the tradition of William Faulkner, Robert Penn Warren and Flannery O'Connor, and onwards through Southern literary history.

Yet crucially, Poe also reveals the limitations of the very idea of a 'Southern Gothic'. It is a term that such an avid anti-regionalist would likely have rejected, given his belief that all art should be evaluated by global rather than local standards. It is also a term that has been used for suspect purposes. Purely in literary critical terms, far too many readers have used Poe's Southern origins as a way of excluding him from narratives of national literary emergence, and as a means of denying the darker implications of his ideas. When F.O. Matthiessen excluded Poe from *American Renaissance* (1941) as an aberrant voice, or when Leslie Fiedler concluded in *Love and Death in the American Novel* (1960) that 'it is indeed to be expected that our first eminent Southern author discovered that the proper subject for American gothic is the black man from whose shadow we have not emerged', the problem of race and gothic is bracketed as a peculiarly Southern and implicitly regional issue.

In responses to Poe, the American South has too often served as the nation's 'other' – a symbol of all that the 'nation' at large seeks to disavow. Regional stereotypes have allowed a particular racial discourse to be maintained, often at the expense of a wider recognition of the ways in which the racial scars and flashpoints too often thought of as 'Southern Gothic' permeate writings from across the early republic. As Goddu argues, 'by so closely associating the gothic with the South, the American literary tradition neutralises the gothic's threat to national identity. As a merely regional strategy, the gothic's horrifying hauntings, especially those dealing with race, came to be contained'.[28] Here is yet another example of the many ways in which re-examining the 'problem of Poe', and his dubious place within this perhaps ill-defined tradition, can shine a light that illuminates far beyond that tradition's own bounds. His writings continue to challenge our ideas of literary history, national and regional identity and the limits of the 'Gothic', enabling us to peer into the darkness even as what that darkness signifies continues to transform.

NOTES

1. Harold Bloom, 'Inescapable Poe', *New York Review of Books*, 1984.
2. T.S. Eliot, 'From Poe to Valéry', *Hudson Review*, 1949; Richard Wilbur, 'The House of Poe' (1934) in G.R. Thompson, ed. *The Selected Writings of Edgar Allan Poe* (New York: Norton, 2004).
3. These readings are collaeted in John P. Muller ed. *The Purloined Poe: Lacan, Derrida & Psychoanalytic Reading* (Baltimore: Johns Hopkins University Press, 1988).
4. Kennedy, J. Gerald, 'Poe in Our Time', *A Historical Guide to Edgar Allan Poe* (Oxford: Oxford University Press 2001), ix; for other influential historicist takes, see Shawn Rosenheim and Stephen Rachman. *The American Face of Edgar Allan Poe.* (Baltimore: Johns Hopkins University Press, 1995).
5. Shawn Rosenheim and Stephen Rachman. *The American Face of Edgar Allan Poe.* (Baltimore: Johns Hopkins University Press, 1995).
6. Teresa Goddu, *Gothic America: Narrative, History and Nation* (New York: Columbia University Press, 1997), p. 78.

7. W.J. Cash, *The Mind of the South* (New York: Knopf, 1941), p. 93.
8. Edgar Allan Poe to George W. Poe, July 14, 1839 in John W. Ostrom et al. eds. *The Collected Letters of Edgar Allan Poe, Volume 1.* (Staten Island, NY: Gordian Press, 2008), p. 185.
9. John Carlos Rowe, 'Poe, Antebellum Slavery and Modern Criticism', in *Poe's Pym: Critical* Explorations, ed. Richard Kopley (Durham: Duke University Press, 1992), p. 117. See also Dana D. Nelson, *The Word in Black and White: Reading 'Race' in American Literature 1638–1867* (New York: Oxford Univ. Press, 1992).
10. Ellen Glasgow, *A Certain Measure: An Interpretation of Prose Fiction* (New York: Harcourt, 1943), p. 132.
11. Lewis P. Simpson, *The Dispossessed Garden: Pastoral and History in Southern Literature* (Athens: University of Georgia Press, 1975), p. 80.
12. 'The Fall of the House of Usher', in G.R. Thompson, ed. *The Selected Writings of Edgar Allan Poe* (New York: Norton, 2004), p. 601.
13. Charles Crow, *American Gothic* (Cardiff: University of Wales Press, 2009), p. 96.
14. Harry Levin, *The Power of Blackness: Hawthorne, Poe, Melville* (New York: Knopf, 1958).
15. Richard Gray, 'I am a Virginian': Poe and the South' in A. Robert Lee ed., *Edgar Allan Poe: The Design of Order* (London: Vision Press, 1987), p. 183.
16. David Leverenz, 'Poe and Gentry Virginia', in Shawn Rosenheim and Stephen Rachman eds. *The American Face of Edgar Allan Poe.* (Baltimore: Johns Hopkins University Press, 1995), p. 211.
17. Toni Morrison, *Playing in the Dark: Whiteness and the Literary Imagination* (Cambridge: Harvard Univ. Press, 1992), p. 101.
18. Toni Morrison, *Playing in the Dark: Whiteness and the Literary Imagination* (Cambridge: Harvard Univ. Press, 1992), p. 101.
19. Harry Levin, *The Power of Blackness: Hawthorne, Poe, Melville* (New York: Knopf, 1958).
20. See e.g. Joan Dayan, 'Amorous Bondage: Poe, Ladies and Slaves', in Shawn Rosenheim and Stephen Rachman eds. *The American Face of Edgar Allan Poe.* (Baltimore: Johns Hopkins University Press, 1995), p. 197.
21. 'The Narrative of Arthur Gordon Pym', in G.R. Thompson, ed. *The Selected Writings of Edgar Allan Poe* (New York: Norton, 2004), p. 923.
22. Toni Morrison, *Playing in the Dark: Whiteness and the Literary Imagination* (Cambridge: Harvard Univ. Press, 1992), p. 102.
23. John Carlos Rowe, 'Poe, Antebellum Slavery and Modern Criticism', in *Poe's Pym: Critical* Explorations, ed. Richard Kopley (Durham: Duke University Press, 1992), p. 117.
24. Teresa Goddu, *Gothic America: Narrative, History and Nation* (New York: Columbia, 1997), p. 75.
25. Teresa Goddu, *Gothic America: Narrative, History and Nation* (New York: Columbia, 1997), p. 80.
26. Teresa Goddu, *Gothic America: Narrative, History and Nation* (New York: Columbia, 1997), p. 85.
27. Teresa Goddu, *Gothic America: Narrative, History and Nation* (New York: Columbia, 1997), p. 82.
28. Teresa Goddu, *Gothic America: Narrative, History and Nation* (New York: Columbia, 1997), p. 82.

Bibliography

Bloom, H. (1984). Inescapable Poe. *New York Review of Books*.

Carlos Rowe, J. (1992). Poe, antebellum slavery and modern criticism. In R. Kopley (Ed.), *Poe's Pym: Critical explorations* (p. 117). Durham: Duke University Press.

Cash, W. J. (1941). *The mind of the South*. New York: Knopf.

Crow, C. (2009). *American Gothic*. Cardiff: University of Wales Press.

Eliot, T. S. (1949). From Poe to Valéry. *Hudson Review*.

Glasgow, E. (1943). *A certain measure: An interpretation of prose fiction*. New York: Harcourt.

Goddu, T. (1997). *Gothic America: Narrative, history and nation*. New York: Columbia.

Gray, R. (1987). 'I am a Virginian': Poe and the South. In A. Robert Lee (Ed.), *Edgar Allan Poe: The design of order* (p. 183). London: Vision Press.

Kennedy, J. Gerald. (2001). Poe in our time. In *A historical guide to Edgar Allan Poe*. Oxford: Oxford University Press.

Leverenz, D. (1995). Poe and gentry Virginia. In S. Rosenheim & S. Rachman (Eds.), *The American face of Edgar Allan Poe* (p. 211). Baltimore: Johns Hopkins University Press.

Levin, H. (1958). *The power of blackness: Hawthorne, Poe, Melville*. New York: Knopf.

Morrison, T. (1992). *Playing in the dark: Whiteness and the literary imagination*. Cambridge: Harvard University Press.

Moses, M. J. (1910). *The literature of the South*. New York: Thomas Crowell and Co.

Muller, J. P. (Ed.). (1988). *The Purloined Poe: Lacan, Derrida & psychoanalytic reading*. Baltimore: Johns Hopkins University Press.

Ostrom, J. W., et al. (Eds.). (2008). *The collected letters of Edgar Allan Poe* (Vol. 1). Staten Island: Gordian Press.

Richard, W. (2004). 'The House of Poe' (1934). In G. R. Thompson (Ed.), *The selected writings of Edgar Allan Poe*. New York: Norton.

Rosenheim, S., & Rachman, S. (1995). *The American face of Edgar Allan Poe*. Baltimore: Johns Hopkins University Press.

Simpson, P. (1975). *The dispossessed garden: Pastoral and history in Southern literature* (p. 80). Athens: University of Georgia Press.

Thompson, G. R. (1988). Edgar Allan Poe and the writers of the old South. In E. Elliott (Ed.), *Columbia history of the United States*. New York: Columbia University Press.

Further Reading

Goddu, T. (1996). The ghost of race: Edgar Allan Poe and the Southern Gothic. In W. Henry (Ed.), *Criticism and the color line: Desegregating American literary studies*. New Brunswick: Rutgers. One of the more crucial modern re-interpretations of Poe's relationship to the Southern Gothic.

Shawn, R., & Stephen, R. (1995). *The American face of Edgar Allan Poe*. Baltimore: Johns Hopkins University Press. In addition to the essays cited in this work, the remainder of pieces in this excellent collection are invaluable for their historicisation of Poe's gothic within the complex cultural and political milieu in which he lived and wrote.

CHAPTER 3

Inside the Dark House: William Faulkner, *Absalom, Absalom!* and Southern Gothic

Richard Gray

Early in 1934, William Faulkner sat down at his desk and, in his characteristically spidery handwriting, wrote 'A Dark House' at the top of a blank page. It was a title that haunted Faulkner. For a while, it was the working title for the story that eventually became *Light in August* (1932), but now he was thinking of using it for another, stranger narrative. 'A plantation in the South in 1860,' begins one of the manuscript fragments that follow, 'Col. Sutpen, his daughter Judith, his son Henry. The family is well-to-do in land and slaves but still provincial: country aristocracy of that period: simple, honorable, proud, of good stock.'[1] The rest of this fragment begins to piece together the tale that would, a year or two later, become one of the great Southern Gothic novels. 'Henry attends college in a small town about 50 miles away,' Faulkner writes. 'At the college he meets a student named Charles Bon', 'about Henry's age' but, unlike Henry, 'gay … cosmopolitan, not weak so much as careless, a rich orphan.' The two young men return to the Sutpen plantation for Christmas, where Henry and his sister begin to betray signs that they are both, in their own ways, in love with the 'casual gallant' Charles. Then they visit New Orleans—or 'N.O.', as it is referred to in the manuscript—where 'Bon takes Henry to make a call.' 'The call is upon a young woman, very beautiful', who speaks to Bon in French. 'Then a small child is produced,' which Henry quickly realises is 'Bon's child'. 'He is shocked,' the manuscript tells us, 'then, … outraged'—not least, by Bon's apparently 'light and casual acceptance' of his own duplicity.

Bon has dark secrets and he evidently sees nothing wrong in keeping them secret from the young man who admires and even loves him. Slowly, fragments like these began to gather around a story that, by August of 1934, Faulkner was calling *Absalom! Absalom!*—'of a man', Faulkner explained to his editor, 'who wanted a son through pride, and got too many of them and

R. Gray (✉)
Professor Emeritus of American Literature, Essex University, United Kingdom

© The Editor(s) (if applicable) and The Author(s) 2016
S.C. Street, C.L. Crow (eds.), *The Palgrave Handbook of the Southern Gothic*,
DOI 10.1057/978-1-137-47774-3_3

they destroyed him.' However, Faulkner went on, the material was 'not quite ripe yet'; he had a 'mass of stuff, but only one chapter' that satisfied him. So he turned to writing another novel, *Pylon* (1935)—set in the New Orleans of the twentieth century—before returning in March 1935 to the story of Colonel Sutpen and his family. The process by which *Absalom, Absalom!* took shape both before and after this was gradual, accumulative, circuitous and even repetitive (to the extent that at least three or four short stories dating back as far as 1928 fed into the novel); and it foreshadowed the structure and the obsessions of what was to become the darkest of Faulkner's major novels, even though 'Dark House' was not to be its eventual title.

Elements of the Gothic

The darkest of Faulkner's major novels, *Absalom, Absalom!* is also the most seamlessly gothic. There are, certainly, elements of the Gothic in several of his fictions. One section of *The Sound and the Fury* (1929), for instance, is the impossible utterance of a wise but wordless fool; another is devoted to a fierce and febrile young man so haunted by the ghosts of the past that he has decided to commit suicide to escape them. The pivotal monologue in *As I Lay Dying* (1930) is spoken by a decaying corpse. In *Sanctuary* (1931), the character who commits the act of violence on which the narrative turns is a laconic, brutal and impotent villain described as 'the little black man'. *Light in August* reaches a dramatic climax with a ritualistic killing and castration; and the most substantial story in *Go Down, Moses* (1942) hinges on past secrets involving incest discovered in some mouldering papers.

There are also a number of short stories that are generically gothic. Notable here is 'A Rose for Emily'. The first story by Faulkner to be published in a national magazine (in *Forum* in 1930), it is the work most commonly cited when the subject is his writing and the gothic mode. One of Faulkner's boyhood friends, John Cullen, insisted that much of the tale was taken from life: specifically, from the courtship of a young Oxford woman by a Yankee who spent some time in town supervising the paving of the streets. What Faulkner wrote, Cullen claimed, was 'events that were expected but never actually happened'.[2] The tale is told by an anonymous narrator who refers to himself in the plural because he tends to identify with what he calls 'our whole town'. 'We saw' and 'we believed' are recurrent refrains; this is a story built up out of observation and guesswork. Nevertheless, the basic narrative contours are alarmingly clear.

Emily Grierson, a spinster of genteel background, appears to have lost the opportunity for marriage, not least because she can find nobody whom her family—and particularly her father—deems suitable. After her father dies, however, she takes up with Homer Barron, the Yankee foreman of a team charged with paving the local sidewalks. And then, suddenly, Homer is gone, not long after Emily has purchased some arsenic. When Emily eventually dies, after living as a virtual recluse, and her house is opened up, a 'fleshless' corpse is discovered lying on her bed—caught, as the narrator puts it, in the 'embrace' of 'the long sleep that outlasts love'. There are two pillows. One is for the corpse, which is presumably that of Homer Barron, poisoned when he tried to leave Emily. On the other there is simply 'the indentation of a head' and 'a long strand of iron-gray hair'.[3]

Sometimes, 'A Rose for Emily' is filed under the subject heading of necrophilia. Hints in that direction are certainly there, and are one reason for calling the tale gothic. What is surely more intriguing, however—and, as we shall see, helps make this a specifically Southern Gothic tale—is the intimation that Emily has done what she has done as a perverse reaction to the pressures of a stiflingly patriarchal society. Her family, her social position, her community (the 'we' of the narrator) have denied her needs and suppressed her natural feelings. She is reduced, by the gaze of her neighbours and the narrative, to object status, a figure to patronise and pity. The denial of her subjectivity (confirmed in the cruellest possible way when Homer jilts her) leads to scandal; and the extremity of her actions is, ultimately, a measure of the extremity of her condition, the degree of her imprisonment. 'A Rose for Emily' is an unnervingly gothic tale; it also offers an unerring insight into repression and the revenge of the repressed. In its darkness, a darkness that illuminates the contrived corridors and narrow passageways of a very specific, very Southern history, it offers a dress rehearsal, a preparatory sketch for what is, in the last analysis, Faulkner's greatest and most seamlessly gothic narrative.

That returns us to *Absalom, Absalom!* The darkness of Faulkner's furthest venture into the Gothic is inescapable. And the reasons for that darkness are several, ranging from the biographical to the historical to the intertextual. On the biographical level, what Faulkner referred to in one of his earliest works as 'the front door and the back door',[4] sex and death, were both in play. At the end of 1935, Faulkner went to Hollywood. There he met and fell in love with a script editor, Meta Carpenter, and began a passionate affair that lasted, off and on, for 15 years. 'I've always been afraid of going out of control,' Faulkner confided to his lover, 'I get so carried away.'[5] With Meta, perhaps for the first time in his life, he allowed to himself to let go—he experienced the sheer uncontrol of prolonged sexual abandon. That experience was not without its burden of guilt, given Faulkner's sense of duty towards his wife Estelle and his devotion to his daughter Jill; nor was it without a measure of unease, given his habit of seeing sex and death as (to use his words) 'indissolubly … associated'.

The Death of a Brother

The guilt and uneasiness the author felt at the time were, however, exponentially increased by the sudden death of Faulkner's brother Dean. Dean was nearly 11 years younger than William and their relationship was intense, intimate and deeply fraught. Dean's birth initiated a change in Faulkner's life because it took their mother's attention away from her oldest and dearest son—not least because Dean's fragile health as a baby required special attention—pushing

William into a kind of solitude. As Dean grew up, William adopted a paternal attitude towards his youngest brother, serving for a while as scoutmaster of Dean's troop and sending him affectionate letters whenever he was away. Dean, in turn, worshipped William, growing a moustache just like his oldest brother's and adding a 'u' to the family name just as big brother Bill had done. Shortly after his marriage, Dean even warned his new wife that 'Mother and Bill will always come first', and his wife Louise seems to have accepted this. Certainly, most of the family appears to have understood that there was a special intimacy between oldest and youngest brothers—Dean was the one sent in to nurse William through his regular bouts of alcoholism and depression—so it was no surprise, when Dean died suddenly in a plane that he was piloting in 1935, that William took it especially hard.

William had, in any case, particular reasons for reacting to the death in this way. It was his encouragement and example that had promoted Dean's interest in flying; it was his plane that Dean had trained in and finally bought. 'I've ruined your life,' he said to Dean's widow. 'It's my fault.' When Louise told him she had dreamed of the fatal accident one night, he replied, 'You're lucky to have dreamed it only once. I dream it every night.' Claims like this might have smacked of the theatrical, except that Faulkner took on himself the burden of looking after Louise and her child in the long term and, in the short term, took charge of the preparations for Dean's funeral. Those preparations had their own strange element: Faulkner arranged for Dean's gravestone to carry just the name and birth and death dates of the deceased together with a simple inscription: 'I bore him on eagle's wings and brought him unto me.' Some might have seen that inscription as a borrowing from the Bible, adapted from *Exodus* 19:4. Others, however, including William and Dean's mother, recognised a different source. It was the epitaph Faulkner had given another ill-fated pilot, John Sartoris in *Flags in the Dust* (published as *Sartoris* in 1929). Maud and those others did not like the inscription, regarding it, as one family member said, as 'a monument to William's grief and guilt'[6] rather than to Dean himself. It was almost as if Faulkner was taking on himself the burden of seer: as if he had prophesied his brother's death in his first Yoknapatawpha novel and was now assuming moral responsibility for the prophecy.

The most deeply unsettling events, Freud once suggested, are not those that are entirely unexpected but those that are anticipated in fantasy, those in which we have a libidinal investment. He used the term 'uncanny' to describe this phenomenon, this encounter with the realisation of one's darkest dreams. There may be doubts as to why Faulkner dreamed the death of his youngest and dearest brother. Perhaps it was to do with the rupture with his mother caused by Dean's birth and a subsequent sense of abandonment. According to this reading, William may then have played the paternal role as a way of concealing hostile feelings; not least from himself. Perhaps it was something else. There can be no doubt, however, that he dreamed it. And in particular, in his first book set in his postage stamp of native soil, he dreamed up twin brothers, Bayard Sartoris III and John, who are hauntingly like William and Dean—in their respective characters, their tangled relationship and above all in the way John's death and Bayard's reaction to it anticipate what was to happen to the author and his youngest brother some 6 years after the book was published.

John has died while piloting a plane in the First World War before the book opens, but those who knew him recall him as someone 'merry and bold and wild'. He is memorably like Dean in a number of ways: generous, exuberant, with a 'frank, spontaneous, warm and ready and generous' spirit, fondly recollected and rehearsed by friends and family alike. So close was the connection, evidently, between Dean and John Sartoris that later, when Dean's daughter sought to describe her father in a biographical study, she turned to the fictional portrait for help. Dean was, his daughter said, just like that doomed member of the Sartoris clan, with his 'warm radiance' and his possession of a character (as she put it) 'sweet and merry and wild'. Bayard Sartoris III, in turn, is just the opposite of this. Like his creator, he is an insomniac and uses alcohol to relieve physical pain; there is, other people feel, a quality of aloofness, even 'bleak arrogance' about him; and he seeks refuge from others and from his own thoughts in solitary pursuits, forays into nature and hunting.

More to the point, perhaps, Bayard remembers his dead brother as someone braver, more attractive and glamorous than him; and, despite the fact that he had nothing to do with John's death, he wrestles constantly with a sense of guilt. Sometimes, he accuses himself directly of responsibility. '*You did it*,' he tells himself on one occasion. '*You caused it all; you killed Johnny!*' At other times he goes to the opposite extreme: protesting, too much, that he has nothing for which to blame himself. 'I tried to keep him from going up there on that goddam little popgun,' are Bayard's very first words to his grandfather on his return from the war—a piece of gratuitous self-exoneration that anticipates Faulkner's own, later words to Meta Carpenter, 'I grounded Dean. I told him not to fly.'[7] Nearly all Bayard's actions in the time present of the novel seem rooted in a desire to punish himself for some guilt he can hardly articulate and, in effect, to liberate himself from his brother's death by repeating it: he dies, eventually, flying a crackpot experimental plane. It is not necessary to dip down very far into the region's of Bayard's subconscious to see that his morbid preoccupation with what happened to John, his sense of guilt and impulse towards repetition of his brother's death, spring from a sense that he *willed* the crucial event: he believes that he dreamed the disappearance of his twin, he desired it and then it was so. Nor is it necessary, either, to see that, in imagining Bayard and John and their fates, Faulkner was sublimating his own desires and enacting his own anxieties: freeing himself, for a moment, from his darker feelings about Dean by enacting them, projecting them into fiction.

The only problem for Faulkner was that, like Bayard, he then saw his scarcely acknowledged desires realised: the brother he loved and resented was destroyed in a plane crash. In his own way, like his fictional alter ego, he had tried to liberate himself by repetition; which, in turn, meant an imitation of some of the more destructive aspects of his life in his art. Tragically, life then imitated art. And Faulkner, in his own way, inscribed his recognition of this in the epitaph he chose for his brother, which, as his mother sensed, said more about the commemorator than it did about the commemorated. The recognition was devastating, certainly, and so were the grief and anxiety that precipitated it; but they were also, somehow, purgative. For Faulkner, the death of his brother was a terrible, traumatic event that, like many such events, initiated a radical emotional change by acting as a rite of passage. It shook him to his foundations but also somehow released him, perhaps perversely and precisely because it did require him to face up to his darkest fears and desires. This was and is notable, not least, in his fiction.

The theme of sibling intimacy and rivalry is a recurring one in his writing up to 1935, and in particular the idea of the dead brother rival. After that, however, it largely disappears from Faulkner's work, except for *Intruder in the Dust* (1948), where it plays a minor role. 'A book is ... the dark twin of a man,'[8] Faulkner has a character say in his second published novel, *Mosquitoes* (1927). And the 'dark twin' is both source and subject in *Absalom, Absalom!* It is a force that shapes and distorts, feeds and infects the story of the Sutpen family; it is diagnosis and symptom, there in the narrative and there behind the narrative. Coinciding with an event that, apparently, its author had feared and desired, dreamed of and dreaded, it is fired into life by Faulkner's struggle, one last time, with his own demons. In the process of being written when Dean died and then completed after his burial, it is a site of nightmare encounter and struggle: dark twins wrestle with one another both behind the narrative and in the narrative. The encounter could hardly be more fundamental and, as it turned out, cathartic: the pivotal event of *Absalom, Absalom!*, after all, is when Henry Sutpen comes home from the Civil War and, at the entrance to the 'dark house' of his father—in an act that indissolubly unites the notions of death and love—kills his 'gay' and 'gallant' half-brother.

'That's the trouble with this country,' one of Faulkner's characters says of the region, 'everything, weather, all, hangs on too long. Like our rivers, our land: opaque, slow, violent; shaping and creating the life of man in its implacable and brooding image.'[9] Slow, brooding intensity building up to a moment of storm: if there is a deep, cultural rhythm at work in the South, and so lurking there in works from and about the region, it is that. It is a regional rhythm; it is also, of course, the rhythm of the Gothic. And place, the weather of the landscape and the weather of the mind, is indelibly attached in the regional imagination to another grand obsession, the past. 'The past is never dead,' goes one of the best-known quotations from Faulkner's work. 'It's not even past.' 'No man is himself,' Faulkner admitted elsewhere, 'he is the sum of his past.'[10] That past carries a special burden in the South, for white and black Southerners alike. 'This whole land, the whole South, is cursed,' the reader is told in 'The Bear' (1942), 'and those who derive from it, whom it ever suckled, white and black both, lie under the curse.'

For white Southerners, there is what Faulkner called 'the old shame' of slavery, a regional version of Original Sin, a terrible violation of a whole race committed by some ancestor, actual or apocryphal or both; it is an inheritance of guilt and guilty knowledge that every white boy and girl must experience and accept as they grow up and enter into adulthood. For black Southerners, in turn, there is the terrible recollection of collective abuse: what the African American historian Nell Irivin Painter used the notion of 'soul murder'[11] to describe. Like any victim of historical abuse, according to this idea, the black Southerner is confronted with intolerable memories—in this case, collective rather than personal ones, a series of legacies and pathologies that hardly bear remembering. 'This is not a story to pass on,' Toni Morrison's *Beloved* (1987) concludes: this—in other words the story of slavery and its attendant violations—is a story that cannot be remembered and transmitted ('*pass* on') yet, equally, cannot be passed over or ignored ('pass *on*'). It is a story that cannot and yet must be told. So both violator and victim are caught in a landscape of nightmare. For the violator, there is the impossible memory of inherited guilt; for the victim, there is the just as impossible memory of inherited trauma, a violence inflicted on an entire race that leaves indelible scars. For both, there is a sense of being haunted, overshadowed by a past that is elusive yet somehow more tangible than the present. Landscape and character in the South are both partly material and partly spectral, substantial but also inhabited by ghosts. In such circumstances, the term 'Southern Gothic' seems almost a tautology; it is no wonder, then, that Faulkner turned to the Gothic to 'tell about the South'.[12]

The Southern Gothic

There were personal reasons, then, for the darkness of the story originally titled 'Dark House'; there were reasons to do with the history of the region; there were also intertextual reasons, a matter of dialogue with other writers. All writers talk to other writers—talk with them, talk back to them, talk sometimes against them; all literature is, as Joseph Brodsky put it once, 'all continuity, all echo'. Or, as another Southern writer, Cormac McCarthy, has expressed it rather more sardonically: 'The ugly fact is that books are made out of other books. The novel depends for its life on the novels that have been written.'[13] Faulkner and *Absalom, Absalom!* are no exceptions to this. Nor is *Absalom, Absalom!* an exception to the Bakhtinian rule that the novel is a generic hybrid. The story of the Sutpen family, as told by its various narrators, is a rich mix of genres. It is a historical novel, it is a family romance, it is a love story, it is a detective story. It is all these things, while still also being a prime example of the Southern Gothic.

And it is the Southern Gothic dimension that is at stake here. It was also a dimension that many reviewers noticed and commented on when the book was first published. William Troy, for example, in *The Nation*, suggested that *Absalom, Absalom!*, like *Wuthering Heights*, 'plunged' the reader into the 'special atmosphere' of an 'intensely personal vision' and a world characterised by 'sickness' and the 'weakness of the human soul'.[14] Kay Boyle compared Faulkner to Edgar Allan Poe: the two writers were alike, she suggested, in their common 'immunity to literary fashion, alike in their fanatical obsession with the memorable depths of mankind's vice.'[15] Malcolm Cowley, the critic who was later to help rehabilitate Faulkner and restore his reputation, took that comparison much further. In a review in the *New Republic* titled 'Poe in Mississippi', Cowley insisted that, as a writer, Faulkner was possessed by 'a daemon'. 'The daemon forces him to the always intense,' Cowley went on, 'to write in a wild lyrical style, to omit almost every detail that does not contribute to a single effect of somber violence and horror'. This was a clue, the critic suggested, to 'Faulkner's real kinship', which was with 'the "satanic" poets from Byron to Baudelaire' and with 'the "black" or "terrifying" novelists from Monk Lewis and the Hoffmann of the "Tales" to Edgar Allan Poe'. And the kinship had never been stronger, never more tangible, Cowley insisted, than in the tale of Thomas Sutpen. Sutpen is 'the lonely Byronic hero with his mind coldly fixed on the achievement of one great design'. His plantation house 'is the haunted castle that was described so often in nineteenth-century romances. Like other haunted castles, Sutpen's Hundred is brooded over by a curse.' The intimations of incest that hover around the consequences of this curse may 'suggest Byron,' Cowley tells the reader, 'but elsewhere it is Poe whose spirit seems closest to the story,' particularly 'at the end, where Sutpen's Hundred collapses like the House of Usher'. 'One might say,' the reviewer concludes, 'that Faulkner is Poe in Mississippi—Poe modernised with technical and psychological devices imported from Joyce's Dublin and Freud's Vienna.'[16]

The link with Poe that both Boyle and Cowley noted is inescapable and is one of the symptoms of just how steeped in the Gothic, and in particular the Southern Gothic, *Absalom, Absalom!* is. Thomas Sutpen may have reminded Cowley of the Byronic hero, of the kind to which Poe—as an admirer and imitator of Byron—was also drawn; he may also remind other readers unfamiliar with Southern variants of the Gothic of what Charles Crow has called 'a frequently encountered character' in gothic tales from inside and outside the South, who 'combines the roles of hero and villain'. 'Captain Ahab, the "grand ungodly god-like man",' Crow notes, 'is a model of the Gothic villain-hero',[17] and Sutpen, several critics have pointed out in turn, bears a remarkable resemblance to Ahab. As James Guetti put it in a relatively early essay on *Absalom, Absalom!*, 'the parallels between Sutpen and Ahab are so striking as to be worth detailed comment.'[18] And they range from matters of how the character is presented, as a larger-than-life man of mystery about whom endless tales are told to more fundamental issues of motive and purpose. Both men, after all, are driven by a potent mixture of revenge, pride and defiance of whatever forces appear to govern human experience; both quite explicitly reject ethical considerations—including simple human consideration, moral compunction and concern for other people—as irrelevant; and both embrace a design (to use Sutpen's chosen term) that is at once profoundly personal (and profoundly arrogant) and significantly historical (in the sense that, from one perspective, Sutpen's story is a paradigmatically Southern one just as Ahab's is paradigmatically American).

Other characters in *Absalom, Absalom!* similarly recall figures from what might be termed the cast list of mainstream Gothic. This is particularly the case with Rosa Coldfield, who appears to have borrowed the trappings of her version of the Sutpen story from two sources: the early gothic tales of Horace Walpole and Ann Radcliffe and a version of the South, largely fashioned by nineteenth-century Abolitionists, that identified the region—not, it has to be said, entirely without cause—with the landscape of a tale of terror. Rosa recalls her younger self in terms that recollect the feverish heroines of Ann Radcliffe—a type that Jane Austen was memorably to parody in *Northanger Abbey* (1817)—constantly and nervously eavesdropping (Rosa had never been taught anything as a girl, we are told, 'save to listen through closed doors'[19]), trembling on the margins of events that appear both suspicious and terrible (she was kept, Mr. Compson insists, in a 'closed masonry of females') and caught between a devouring curiosity and an equally devouring fear. It was the Abolitionist Wendell Phillips who declared that 'The South is the thirteenth and fourteenth centuries'; he was referring here not so much to an actual historical period as to an idea of feudalism that held sway in the gothic tradition, which identified it with the Dark Ages; an idea that the New England poet James Russell Lowell also had in mind when he dismissed Southern planters as 'mad knights'[20] blinded to the needs of others by their own lust for power.

'You see, I had a design in mind,' Sutpen is remembered telling General Compson, in a story handed down to the son of the General and then, in turn, to his grandson. 'Whether it was a good or a bad design is beside the point.'[21] Rosa, at least, is convinced by the time she tells the Sutpen story that it is bad, and that it is representatively so. 'Is it any wonder that Heaven saw fit to let us lose?'[22] she asks at one point; and the 'us' here identifies her not only with Sutpen, but also with her fellow Southerners who, according to this version of events, suffered a terrible punishment, retribution for embracing evil, their headlong descent 'from absymal and chaotic dark to eternal and abysmal dark'. Sentimental, hypocritical, self-righteous: these were the terms in which the North tended to be seen by the Old South, dominated as it was, as one Southerner saw it, by 'female' notions and, as another put it, by the sort of women who 'write books, patronise abolitionist societies or keep a boarding-school'.[23] Sensual, cold and overpowering: these, in turn, were the terms in which the Old South was perceived by the North. If the North through Southern eyes was a misogynist's nightmare, then the South through Northern eyes was another kind of nightmare altogether: a nightmare of patriarchy, a world of male power *in extremis* in which cruel parodies of the family were presided over by perverse versions of the father figure.

The South perceived in these terms was a version of the Gothic laced with a substantial dose of moralism; and it is that version to which Rosa turns as she remembers the man who seemed to promise to rescue her from her life on the margin of things, only to discover that he wanted her for breeding purposes. There, in the tale she tells, is the familiar, grim castle of gothic stories, a 'private hell' apparently preserved for 'some desolation more profound than ruin'.

There also is the traditional villain, Sutpen, a perpetrator of horrible deeds on innocent victims: a man who, we are told, carried his second wife off to his 'ogre-djin' and subsequently permitted her, by means of infrequent visits to church, 'to return, through the dispensation of one day only, to the world she had quitted.' Rosa herself, true to her self-appointed role of tremulous observer, is described as haunted by disembodied 'faces', 'voices', 'hands'—a frail, febrile creature who suffers a numb 'terror' at the mere suspicion that there is 'something hidden' at the top of a 'nightmare flight of stairs'. Henry and Judith Sutpen are transmuted, by Rosa's tale telling, into living ghosts, 'two half-phantom children', and the cast list is completed by a black maid Clytemnestra who—by virtue of being fathered by 'fell darkness'—has become the 'cold Cerberus' of the Sutpen mansion. Together, in this version of the fall of the house of Sutpen, all these characters seem to seal the fate of the family— helping to assure its 'doom' as the Sutpen 'name and lineage' are 'finally ... effaced from the earth.' An assault on patriarchal power, the tale that Rosa tells is marked by a sense of betrayal and the suspicion of complicity; both feelings are at once individual and collective, personal and communal. 'Our father's progenitors' and the father figure of Sutpen let 'us' down, she believes, turning her own life and that of her region into a landscape marked for retribution by 'men with valor and strength but without pity or honor'.[24]

'Sutpen was acting his role,' Mr. Compson insists as he tries to describe to his son how Thomas Sutpen gradually gained ascendancy in Yoknapatawpha, 'he was the biggest single landowner and cotton-planter in the county now.' However, Mr. Compson goes on,

> He was unaware that his flowering was a forced blooming too and that while he was still planning a scene to the audience, behind him Fate, destiny, retribution, irony—the stage manager, call him what you will—was already striking the set and dragging on the synthetic and spurious shadows and shapes of the next one.[25]

That captures something of the difference between Mr. Compson's narrative and Rosa Coldfield's. The feverish, often hallucinatory idiom of Rosa's version of things is replaced by a willed pursuit of verbal decorum, with touches of deli- cate irony and self-consciously felicitous imagery. More to the point, the dry dispassion of the style registers the terms in which Mr. Compson would seek to perceive Sutpen, not as a villain but as the hero of a decadent form of tragedy in which the noblest possible 'dream' is destroyed by the 'illogical machinations of fatality'. Like Rosa, Mr. Compson is in part seeking an explanation of his own failure as he recalls what happened to Sutpen: in his case, his failure to play the part of father adequately and to sustain the Compson family fortune and name. And, like Rosa too, that explanation of personal misfortune becomes inextricable from an account of public disaster: the story of the South and its decline, perceived through the filters of time. The difference arises from the simple fact of identification with the subject: Mr. Compson is inclined to iden- tify, or at least link, his story with those of Thomas Sutpen and the South—to see in the personal and cultural downfall he describes a mirror image, a mocking reflection of his own. Sutpen, the man who would be patriarch but whose efforts are demolished by 'destiny ... the stage manager', is not a surrogate for the narrator here, but he does offer Mr. Compson what he perceives as an ironic anticipation of his own life, as seen through a glass darkly, as well as a sad recollection of the fate of their common homeplace. As a result, the telling of his tale does tempt Mr. Compson into a romantic, simultaneously sardonic and elegiac vein.

In short, every time the story of Thomas Sutpen enters what Bakhtin would term the character zone of Mr. Compson, it takes on a peculiarly Southern colour, with Sutpen playing the plantation aristocrat, actively rehearsing himself for the role of perfect gentle knight ('He was,' Mr. Compson suggests, 'like John L. Sullivan having taught himself painfully and tediously to do the schottische'[26]). Other characters, in turn, assume appropriate accompanying roles: the plantation matriarch (Ellen Coldfield), the plantation Hotspur (Henry Sutpen) and the plantation Hamlet (Charles Bon). Instead of blame and guilt, feverish accusation and an equally feverish sense of moral complicity—which are the overriding feelings whenever Rosa Coldfield tells the story—there is a world-weary irony in play here, a sardonic sense of just how fleeting, fragile and ultimately feeble all human effort was, is and must be. So, in place of the dark gothicism of the Rosa Coldfield version of events, the reader is offered an altogether different kind of gothicism, the kind that Poe often favoured when a precious, dandified hero was at the centre of one of his tales—Dupin in 'The Murders in the Rue Morgue' (1841), say, or Prince Prospero in 'The Masque of the Red Death' (1842)—a gothicism that, in turn, both Nathaniel Hawthorne and Herman Melville picked up and played with when dealing with characters who hover at the margins of life—Hepzibah Pynchon in *The House of the Seven Gables* (1851)—or people who apparently prefer not to engage in the business of living at all—Bartleby, of course, in 'Bartleby, the Scrivener' (1853).

Absalom, Absalom! is a complexly layered tale that perhaps recalls Mary McCarthy's description of the postmodernist novel as a series of 'planes in fictive space': 'Each plane in its shadow box', McCarthy said of the typical postmodern text, 'proves to be a false bottom: there is an infinite regression, for the book is a book of mirrors.'[27] That layering not only promotes narrative instability; as Malcolm Cowley suspected, it turns the tale of Thomas Sutpen into a complex, (post)modern kind of gothic narrative, a dark tale of a dark house told by several conflicting and equally dark voices—each of which is, for its own reasons, unreliable. 'If in many of my productions terror is the thesis,' Poe famously said in the Preface to his *Tales of the Grotesque and Arabesque* (1840), 'I maintain that terror is not of Germany but of the soul.' Faulkner could have said much the same of *Absalom, Absalom!*—with the rider that the 'soul' that is the subject of *his* 'production' is multiple, fractured, divided. This is gothic without the old stable ego of character—and without even the residual belief that the terror emanating from it and then coursing into the 'soul' of the reader can ever be properly seen or spoken, let alone understood.

Versions of the Self

What complicates things still more, adding to the box of shadows, is a further narrative provided by a character who is arguably as central to the novel as Thomas Sutpen (and it is characteristic of this novel, surely, that it can be said to have two centres). Along with his roommate at Harvard, Shreve (who acts as a commentator, occasional devil's advocate and ironic summariser), Quentin Compson retells a story that seems to him to be part of the climate, inherent in the fabric of his surroundings and his past. '*I have heard too much*,' thinks Quentin, '*I have had to listen to too much, too long.*' Part of the reason why he feels he has '*heard too much*' is that he is torn between different versions of the past, the parameters of which are marked by the opposing narratives of Rosa Coldfield and Mr. Compson. Part is because he suffers an extreme case of the temptations confronting anyone who tries to recall and represent earlier times—the temptations, that is, of identity or difference—the urge either blankly to identify with the people and events of yesterday or, alternatively, to see the intervening accumulations of history as as an impenetrable barrier walling him off from an age now gone. And part—and a substantial part, at that—is because the story he is telling, of Sutpen and the South, seems to be something in himself as well, an element in his own consciousness and flesh. As Quentin himself puts it at one point:

> you knew it already, had learned it, absorbed it already without the medium of speech somehow from having been born and living beside it, with it, as children will and do: so what your father was saying did not tell you anything so much as it struck, word by word, the resonant chords of remembering.[28]

This is by way of saying that, even more than Thomas Sutpen, Rosa Coldfield or any other character in the novel, Quentin Compson is not just a gothic figure; he is a determinately Southern Gothic one. He is neurotic, imaginative, introverted, obsessed with the past and haunted by its voice—or, as this passage has it, the music played on '*the resonant chords of remembering*'—and his lineage can be traced back to Poe's Roderick Usher and forward to someone like Ashley Wilkes in *Gone with the Wind* (1936). Faulkner is playing here not only with autobiography ('I am Quentin Compson', he once claimed), but with an acutely regional character trope, a figure for the South's sense of its own distinctiveness, its separation, as white Southerners saw it and sometimes still try to see it, from the bourgeois, utilitarian norms of the nation, its impotence and apparently irreversible decline. As for so many Southerners, in fact, the reasons for this character's superiority are also the sources of his weakness: he can achieve, at best, an emotional or imaginative victory (by telling a story, perhaps, and by making that story heard)—literally, historically, he must experience defeat. What makes Quentin even more intriguing, and even more a type of a specifically Southern kind of Gothic, is his obsession with two pivotal and, in the context of both the Sutpen story and the history of the South, indissolubly united issues. Those issues receive memorable expression in an exchange between Henry Sutpen and his half-brother Charles Bon that Quentin imagines taking place right at the end of the Civil War. '*You are my brother*,' Henry tells Charles, to which comes a reply that seals the fate of both men: '*No I'm not I'm the nigger that's going to sleep with your sister. Unless you stop me, Henry.*'[29]

This imagined interchange derives much of its power from the fact that in reimagining the past, Quentin—like all the narrators—is reconstructing versions of the self. What appears to be a dialogue between two men related by blood, and by a bloody personal and communal history, is also an inner debate. Quite simply, like so many gothic heroes, and in particular Poe's Southern Gothic heroes, Quentin tends to see the other as a dark reflection of the self. Henry Sutpen and Charles Bon are mirror images, dark reflections of Quentin's own self-appointed role as protector and would-be violator of a sister's 'honour'. Henry, as Quentin imagines him, is the squire in the process of becoming knight, which is an extension of how Mr. Compson reconstructs him and also a rite of passage that Quentin would dearly like to experience for himself; Quentin, after all, cherishes a highly romanticised image of himself as the Southern gentleman exposed to a cosmopolitan education, and this only takes that image a stage further.

It is Charles Bon, Quentin's darker self-reflection in this version of things, who acts as Henry's tutor: for Henry, as for Quentin, the journey 'out' of his homeplace is also the journey 'in' to the darker, deeper recesses of identity. Henry, Quentin supposes, learns some tricks of the gentlemanly trade from Charles: 'how to lounge about a bedroom in a gown and slippers such as women wore', for instance, 'yet withal such an air of indolent assurance that only the most reckless man would have gratuitously drawn the comparison.' However, the most significant thing that he learns from his dark twin is evidently much closer to home than this: how to condone incest between Charles and their sister Judith. The feelings that Henry is imagined harbouring towards Charles are, in fact, like nothing so much as courtly love; like the knight with his lady, Henry ends, we are told, by attributing all possible graces of mind and body to Charles and then offering him 'the humility which surrenders no pride—the entire proferring of the spirit.' So, when it comes to the possibility of incest, he is recalled in the traditional posture of the courtly lover, describing various historical precedents for the liaison as a way of making 'his conscience … come to terms with his will.' 'Kings have done it,' Quentin has Henry declare, 'Even dukes! There was that Lorraine duke named John something that married his sister. The Pope excommunicated him but it didn't hurt! It didn't hurt! They were still husband and wife. They were still alive.'[30] This imagined speech is nominally addressed to Charles, but it is not difficult to see that it is really directed at Henry, the speaker, and Quentin, the narrator. The pressure of identification works here to expose and exorcise some of the darker impulses of both past and present. Incest, one of the most powerful threats latent in the Southern family romance (issuing out of the South's image of itself as a pseudo-family), and one of the deepest currents in the

Southern Gothic (Roderick Usher, we remember, dies in the embrace of his sister Madeline), is actively confronted, but it is so only as part of a strategy of special pleading—in an attempt to turn even this repressed impulse into a mark of aristocratic exclusiveness, an integral element in the closed, self-centred world of the feudal dream.

The stumbling block as Quentin rehearses the story—with a little help from Shreve—is miscegenation: '*it's the miscegenation, not the incest, which you can't bear*' is, after all, how Quentin has Charles put it to Henry. In Quentin's imagination, at least, the threat of sexual intercourse across racial boundaries is not linked to the perils of sexual relations within the family. The reason is simple. Linked they may be at the level of the Old South's notion of itself as a patriarchal 'family' incorporating both black and white. In Quentin's own mind, however, they have to be separated, because incestuous impulses are buried deep within himself in a way that the drive to inter-racial sex is not. In extenuating incest, consequently, or rather having Henry extenuate it, Quentin is (however unknowingly) defending his own position. To be more exact, he is nervously assuaging his own incipient guilt and so making it possible for him, for a while, to live with himself. And, almost as an act of over-compensation, miscegenation becomes by his reckoning the determining factor in the destruction of the house of Sutpen: not linked to the idea of use, the denial of human subjectivity, nor more specifically connected to the issues of patriarchal power and family tyranny and desire but, on the contrary, pictured as the forbidden apple in this feudal Eden—the original and the ultimate taboo. This is undoubtedly why, whenever the fact or suspicion of inter-racial sex enters Quentin's version of the tale, there is a particularly febrile, nightmarish quality to the telling, a gravitation towards types of the Gothic that recall the narrative of Rosa Coldfield.

The visit that Quentin pays to Sutpen's Hundred, for instance, in the company of Rosa the day after she has given him her account of the Sutpen history, is recalled in terms that replicate Rosa's own feverish tendencies—and that bear down, with particular obsessiveness, on the ideas of darkness and transgression. Night enveloped Quentin and Rosa, Quentin remembers, as they approached the house, which seems, as several critics have observed, to be as strange and surreal as so many haunted mansions, from the Castle of Otranto on through the House of Usher to the dark house that shadows and seems to preside over the Bates Motel in Alfred Hitchcock's *Psycho* (1960): 'It loomed, bulked, square and enormous, with jagged half-toppled chimneys. Its roofline sagging ... beneath it, the dead furnace-breath of air ... seemed to reek in slow and protracted violence with a smell of desolation and decay as if the wood of which it was built were flesh.'[31]

Inside this dark corpse of a house, Quentin and Rosa find three people, all of whom—as Quentin recollects them—tend to take on the grim colouration of their surroundings. They are Clytemnestra the housekeeper, a 'tiny gnome like creature' with a 'worn coffee-colored face'; Jim Bond, 'a saddle-colored and slack-mouthed idiot' who by virtue of two generations of illegitimacy has become 'the scion, the heir-apparent' to the estate; and a third figure lying on a filthy bed in a 'bare, stale room' whose 'wasted yellow face with closed, almost transparent eyelids' and 'wasted hands crossed on his breast' make him look 'as if he were already a corpse'.[32] The third figure is Henry Sutpen, returned from self-imposed exile and apparently haunted by his killing of his half-brother. What Quentin encounters—the virtual corpse of a man inside the virtual corpse of a house—prompts yet another echoing of Poe. 'Nevermore of peace,' Quentin reflects. 'Nevermore of peace. Nevermore Nevermore Nevermore.' Like the protagonist of 'The Raven' (1845), he is apparently condemned to rehearse, over and over again, the memory of what he has desired and perhaps lost. Desired and also perhaps destroyed.

The ironies here are multiple. Quentin has identified with both Henry and Charles to the extent that his version of the Sutpen story externalises and enacts his own inner divisions. Just as Henry's extenuation of Charles's pursuit of their sister Judith can be seen as a circuitous way for Quentin to feel good about himself and his feelings for his sister Caddy, so Henry's eventual killing of Charles can be interpreted not just as a deadly encounter with the racial taboo, but also as a projection of Quentin's (barely expressed because hardly expressible) desire to kill his own incestuous impulses. Through Henry, in short, and through Charles, Quentin both defends and destroys his repressed self. Crossing the threshold into the Sutpen house, Quentin seems set not just to identify but to immerse himself in the past. 'If we can just get to the house,' Quentin tells himself as he and Rosa approach it, 'get inside the house'—as if to get inside the house is to get inside the Sutpen story, to gain access to its inner truth and meaning. What he acquires access to, however, is not a vital organism but a living corpse: a hauntingly elusive paradigm—thanks to his history and colouration—of anxieties that are both personal and regional. Henry, to put it crudely, *is* the South's and Quentin's secret history of sex across the colour line and sex within the family.

History then speaks: which is to say that Henry responds to Quentin's questioning. The response, nevertheless, is minimal to the point of non-existence. The conversation between Quentin and his dark twin is, in effect, a conversation between ghosts:

> And you are—?
> Henry Sutpen.
> And you have been here—?
> Four years.
> And you have come home—?
> To die. Yes.
> To die?
> Yes. To die.
> And you have been here—?
> Four years.
> And you are—?
> Henry Sutpen.[33]

This is not so much a dialogue as the failure of one. Henry is a 'wasted' relic, a residual memory made flesh, while Quentin is the awe-struck novitiate, unable to venture more than the most rudimentary of questions. In a way, the gaps between speech are more eloquent than the speech itself, since they speak of silence, the emptiness across which the characters cannot reach—the plain fact that now, for all Quentin's adventures into identification with and immersion in history, the past evidently cannot talk to the present. After this, the house is burned to the ground, its flesh like wood consumed by fire. With the house that seemed constructed out of sweat and flesh goes the 'yellow' flesh of Henry and the 'coffee-colored' flesh of Clytemnestra. All the structures of the past, and by which the past might be transmitted to the present, seem to dissolve, disintegrate, bequeathing Quentin, and the reader, little more than the recollection of their loss. At the end of 'The Fall of the House of Usher', we may remember, both 'Usher' the house and 'Usher' the tale disintegrate, disappear, leaving narrator and reader alone with their thoughts and surmises. Something similar happens here as Quentin moves towards the end of his tale telling, his own encounter with his darkest impulses, urges he wants both to embrace and to destroy. His voyage into the 'dark house' of the self and the South leaves him famously with not much more than a feeling of significant absence and impotence. His final words are, in fact, the classic verbal gestures of the gothic protagonist, sounding their fear, confusion, the suspicion that they are haunted by something they cannot begin to come to terms with or even perhaps name. 'Why do you hate the South?' Shreve asks, to which comes a reply that, in its sheer negativity and repetition, enacts Quentin's entrapment: 'I dont hate it... I dont hate it... *I dont hate it... I dont. I dont! I dont hate it! I dont hate it!*'

A Secret History

It is significant and symptomatic that Quentin should voice his utter confusion in terms of what he feels about the place where he was born. The personal translates as the regional; bewilderment about the self is voiced as bewilderment about the South. This is, after all, a definitively *Southern* Gothic story, which is something of which, for all his references to 'Poe in Mississippi', Malcolm Cowley did not quite take the measure in that early review. 'Faulkner's new book falls considerably short of the powerful mood it might have achieved,' Cowley concluded. 'Possibly this is because he has failed to find a satisfactory relationship between the horror story of the foreground and the vaster theme that it conceals: the two subjects interfere with each other.' The mistake Cowley made here was to see 'horror' and history as somehow mutually exclusive, to ignore the essentially social function of the Gothic, and to neglect the particular and particularly vital role that the Southern Gothic has played in the national narrative. 'In the Gothic,' Charles Crow points out,

> taboos are often broken, forbidden secrets are spoken, and barriers are crossed.
> The key moment in a Gothic work will occur at the moment of boundary crossing

or revelation, when something hidden or unexpressed is revealed and we experience the shock of an encounter which is both unexpected and expected.[34]

It is not difficult to see how this connects with all that happens in *Absalom, Absalom!*—from the traumatic moments of crossing or not crossing thresholds that both Thomas Sutpen and Quentin Compson experience, through that sense of the uncanny that seeps through Quentin's entire version of the Sutpen story, to those key moments of revelation about the violation of both racial and familial taboos that punctuate and define the narrative. Nor is it difficult to appreciate the relevance here of something else that Crow says about the Gothic. 'The Gothic,' he suggests, 'is a literature of opposition.' 'If the national story of the United States has been one of faith in progress and success and in opportunity for the individual,' Crow adds, then the Gothic has told another, utterly different tale. It is the tale of 'those who are rejected, oppressed or who have failed'; it is a tale that disinters buried guilt, exposes hidden anxieties about what is called, at one point in *Absalom, Absalom!*, '*the eggshell shibboleth of caste and color*'[35]; it is a tale that tells of the repressed and the revenge of the repressed, as it reveals the dark corners and unearths the subterranean depths of a whole society. Horror and history do not 'interfere' with each other here, in the tale of Thomas Sutpen. On the contrary, as in so many gothic fictions, the horror is inextricable from the history; the Gothic is the means by which the secret history of a culture is told. That is why the fear we hear in Quentin's voice, in the closing pages of *Absalom, Absalom!*, is not just a fear felt by the several narrators of this strange tale and that tale's equally strange protagonists, but a fear eating at the soul of an entire region and nation. As we read, piece together and reconstruct the 'old tales and talking' that make up this novel, we are just as likely to catch the contagion; entering a 'Dark House' that is at once a geographical place, a narrative space and a matter of history, the fear that is the determining emotional feature of Gothic enters us too. And with that fear comes revelation.

NOTES

1. Manuscript titled 'Dark House,' Rowan Oak Papers, Special Collections Department, University of Mississippi Library, Oxford. See also *Faulkner in the University: Class Conferences at the University of Virginia 1957–1958* edited by Frederick L. Gwynn and Joseph Blotner (Charlottesville, Virginia, 1959), p. 36; *Selected Letters of William Faulkner* edited by Joseph Blotner (New York, 1977), p. 84. For an account of the writing of *Absalom, Absalom!* see, Elizabeth Muhlenfeld, 'Introduction' to *William Faulkner's 'Absalom, Absalom!:' A Critical Casebook* (New York, 1984); Noel Polk, 'Introduction' to vol. xiii of *William Faulkner Manuscripts* edited by Joseph Blotner et al (New York, 1987). See also, *Absalom, Absalom!: The Corrected Text* (New York, 1987).
2. Joseph Blotner, *Faulkner: A Biography: One-Volume Edition* (New York, 1984), p. 247.
3. William Faulkner, 'A Rose for Emily,' *Collected Stories of William Faulkner* (New York, 1977), pp. 119–130.

4. William Faulkner, *Soldier's Pay* (1926; London, 1964 edition), p. 246. ('Sex and death: the front door and the back door of the world. How indissolubly are they associated in us!').

5. Meta Carpenter Wilde and Orin Borsten, *A Loving Gentleman: The Love Story of Meta Carpenter and William Faulkner* (New York, 1976), p. 62. See also Blotner, *Faulkner*, pp. 347, 356, 364.

6. Blotner, *Faulkner*, p. 357. See also pp. 355–356; Carpenter Wilde, *Loving Gentleman*, p. 33.

7. Carpenter Wilde, *Loving Gentleman*, p. 33. See also William Faulkner, *Sartoris* (1929; London, 1969 edition), pp. 43, 311, 356; Dean Faulkner Wells, 'Dean Swift Faulkner: A Biographical Study,' (University of Mississippi M.A. thesis), p. 20.

8. William Faulkner, *Mosquitoes* (1927; London, 1964 edition), p. 209.

9. William Faulkner, *As I Lay Dying* (1930; London, 1963 edition), p. 38.

10. Gwynn and Blotner (eds.), *Faulkner in the University*, p. 84. See also William Faulkner, *Requiem for a Nun* (London, 1950), p. 85; William Faulkner, 'The Bear,' in *Go Down, Moses* (1942; London, 1960 edition), p. 197.

11. Nell Irvin Painter, 'Soul Murder and Slavery: Toward a Fully Loaded Cost Accounting,' in *Southern History across the Color Line* (Chapel Hill, NC, 2002), pp. 15–39. See also Toni Morrison, *Beloved* (London, 1987), p. 275.

12. William Faulkner, *Absalom, Absalom!* (1936; London, 1937 edition), p. 142.

13. Cormac McCarthy, interview with Robert B. Woodward. 'Cormac McCarthy's Venomous Vision,' *New York Times Magazine*, 19 April, 1992, p. 36. See also Luc Beaudouin, 'A Footnote to a Commentary,' translated by Jeremy Gambrell and Alexander Sumerkin, in *Rereading Russian Poetry* edited by Stephanie Sandler (New Haven, Coon., 1999), p. 84.

14. William Troy, 'The Poetry of Doom,' *The Nation*, 31 October, 1936, p. 524.

15. Kay Boyle, cited in Frederick R. Karl, *William Faulkner, American Writer: A Biography* (New York, 1989), p. 609.

16. Malcolm Cowley, 'Poe in Mississippi,' *New Republic*, 4 November, 1936, p. 22.

17. Charles Crow, 'Introduction,' *American Gothic: An Anthology 1787–1916* (Oxford, 1999), p. 2.

18. James Guetti, '*Absalom, Absalom!*: The Extended Simile,' in *The Limits of Metaphor: A Study of Melville, Conrad and Faulkner* (Ithaca, New York, 1968), pp. 69–108., rpt. in *William Faulkner: Critical Assessments* edited by Henry Claridge (Mountfield, East Sussex, 1999), III, 351.

19. Faulkner, *Absalom, Absalom!*, p. 60. See also p. 117.

20. On Northern attitudes towards the South and Northern rhetoric relating to the South, see Lorenzo Dow Turner, *Anti-Slavery Sentiment in American Literature to 1865* (Washington, DC, 1929 (see, especially, pp. 71, 196); Howard R. Floan, *The South in Northern Eyes, 1831–1861* (New York, 1958) (see, especially, pp. 24–5, 40, 57).

21. Faulkner, *Absalom, Absalom!*, p. 263.

22. Ibid., p. 20. See also p. 23.

23. Nathaniel Beverley Tucker, *The Partisan Leader: A Tale of the Future* (1836; Richmond, Va., 1862 edition), p. 69. On the 'male'/'female' equation in the South/North debate, see Richard Gray, *Writing the South: Ideas of an American Region* (Cambridge, 1986), pp. 60–1; Ann Firor Scott, *The Southern Lady: From Pedestal to Politics* (Chicago, 1970).

24. Faulkner, *Absalom, Absalom!*, p. 20. See also pp. 21, 23, 27, 136, 138, 139, 172.
25. Ibid., pp. 72–3. See also p. 102.
26. Ibid., p. 46. On character zones, see Mikhail Bakhtin, *The Dialogic Imagination* translated and edited by Caryl Emerson and Michael Holquist (Austin, Texas, 1981), p. 366. On the plantation Hotspur and the plantation Hamlet, see William R. Taylor, *Cavalier and Yankee: The Old South and the American National Character* (London, 1963).
27. Cited in Tony Tanner, *City of Words: American Fiction 1950–1970* (London, 1971), p. 34.
28. Faulkner, *Absalom, Absalom!*, pp. 212–213. See also p. 207. On the autobiographical nature of Quentin Compson, see Richard Gray, *The Life of William Faulkner: A Critical Biography* (Oxford, 1994), pp. 142–144.
29. Faulkner, *Absalom, Absalom!*, pp. 357–358.
30. Ibid., p. 342. See also p. 317. For a more detailed analysis of the relationship between Quentin Compson, on the one hand, and Henry Sutpen and Charles Bon, on the other, see John T. Irwin, *Doubling and Incest/Repetition and Revenge: A Speculative Reading of Faulkner* (Baltimore, Maryland, 1978). For a fuller discussion of the Old South's image of itself as a (pseudo-)family, see Richard H. King, *A Southern Renascence: The Cultural Awakening of the American South* (New York, 1980).
31. Faulkner, *Absalom, Absalom!*, p. 366. See also p. 356.
32. Ibid., p. 373. See also pp. 100, 366, 370. Also Bakhtin, *Dialogic Imagination*: 'the chronotope of threshold ... its most fundamental instance is as the chronotope of crisis and *break* in life' (p. 248). It is perhaps worth pointing out that almost nobody in *Absalom, Absalom!* crosses the threchold as and when they want to. Even Quentin, as the passages quoted here indicate, has to break in by an alternative entrance.
33. Faulkner, *Absalom, Absalom!*, p. 373. See also p. 378.
34. Crow, 'Introduction,' p. 1. See also p. 2; Cowley, 'Poe in Mississippi,' p. 22.
35. Faulkner, *Absalom, Absalom!*, p. 139.

BIBLIOGRAPHY

Bahktin, M. (1981). *The dialogic imagination: Four essays* (trans and ed: Emerson, C. & Holquist, M.). Austin: University of Texas Press.

Beaudoin, L. (1999). A footnote to a commentary (trans: Gambrell, J. & Sumerkin, A.). In S. Sandler (Ed.), *Rereading Russian poetry* (pp. 161–182). New Haven: Yale University Press.

Blotner, J. (1984). *Faulkner: A biography: One-volume edition.* New York: Random House.

Cowley, M. (1936, November 4). Poe in Mississippi. *New Republic.* Rpt. in Claridge, H. (Ed.). (1999). *William Faulkner: Critical assessments.* Mountfield: Helm Information, III.

Crow, C. (1999). Introduction. In *American gothic: An anthology 1787–1916.* Oxford: Blackwell.

Faulkner, W. Manuscript titled 'Dark house,' Rowan Oak Papers. Oxford: Special Collections Department, University of Mississippi Library.

Faulkner, W. (1926). *Soldiers' pay.* London: Chatto & Windus, 1964.

Faulkner, W. (1927). *Mosquitoes*. London: Chatto & Windus, 1964.

Faulkner, W. (1929). *Sartoris*. London: Chatto & Windus, 1969.

Faulkner, W. (1930). *As I lay dying*. London: Chatto & Windus, 1963.

Faulkner, W. (1936). *Absalom, Absalom*. London: Chatto & Windus, 1937.

Faulkner, W. (1942). *Go down, Moses*. London: Chatto & Windus, 1960.

Faulkner, W. (1951). *Requiem for a nun*. New York: Random House.

Faulkner, W. (1977a). A rose for Emily. In *Collected stories of William Faulkner* (pp. 119–130). New York: Random House.

Faulkner, W. (1977b). *Selected letters of William Faulkner*. New York: Random House. Ed. J. Blotner.

Faulkner, W. (1987). *Absalom, Absalom!: The corrected text*. New York: Vintage.

Floan, H. R. (1958). *The South in northern eyes, 1831–1861*. New York: McGraw-Hill.

Gray, R. (1986). *Writing the South: Ideas of an American region*. Cambridge: Cambridge University Press.

Gray, R. (1994). *The life of William Faulkner: A critical biography*. Oxford: Blackell.

Guetti, J. (1968). *Absalom, Absalom!*: The extended simile. In *The limits of metaphor: A study of Melville, Conrad and Faulkner* (pp. 69–108). Ithaca: Cornell University Press.

Gwynn, F. L., & Blotner, J. (Eds.). (1959). *Faulkner in the university: Class conferences at the University of Virginia 1957–1958*. Charlottesville: University of Virginia Press.

Irwin, J. T. (1978). *Doubling and incest/repetition and revenge: A speculative reading of Faulkner*. Baltimore: Johns Hopkins Universirty Press.

Karl, F. R. (1989). *William Faulkner, American writer: A biography*. New York: Weidenfeld & Nicolson.

King, R. H. (1980). *A Southern renaissance: The cultural awakening of the American South, 1930–1955*. New York: Oxford University Press.

McCarthy, C. (1992, April 19). Interview with Robert B. Woodward. Cormac McCarthy's Venomous Vision. *New York Times Magazine*. http://www.nytimes.com/1992/04/19/magazine/cormac-mccarthy-s-venomous-fiction.html?pagewanted=all

Morrison, T. (1987). *Beloved*. New York: Knopf.

Muhlenfeld, E. (1984). Introduction. In *William Faulkner's 'Absalom, Absalom!:' A critical casebook*. New York: Garland.

Painter, N. I. (2002). *Southern history across the color line*. Chapel Hill: University of North Carolina Press.

Polk, N. (1987). Introduction. In J. Blotner et al. (Eds.), *William Faulkner manuscripts* (Vol. xiii). New York: Garland.

Scott, A. F. (1970). *The Southern lady: From pedestal to politics*. Chicago: University of Chicago Press.

Tanner, T. (1971). *City of words: American fiction 1950–1970*. New York: Harper & Row.

Taylor, W. R. (1961). *Cavalier and Yankee: The Old South and the American national character*. New York: G. Brasilier.

Troy, W. (1936, October 31). The poetry of doom. *The Nation*.

Tucker, N. B. (1836). *The partisan leader: A tale of the future*. Richmond, 1862.

Turner, L. D. (1929). *Anti-slavery sentiment in American literature prior to 1865*. Washington, DC: The Association for the Study of Negro Life and History.

Wells, D. F. (1975). *Dean Swift Faulkner: A biographical study*. M.A. thesis, University of Mississippi.

Wilde, M. C., & Borsten, O. (1976). *A loving gentleman: The love story of Meta Carpenter and William Faulkner*. New York: Simon and Schuster.

CHAPTER 4

Gothic Landscapes: Poe and Antebellum Southern Women Poets

Paula Bernat Bennett

American gothic literature criticizes America's national myth of new-world innocence by voicing the cultural contradictions that undermine the nation's claim to
purity and equality. (Goddu 10)

This chapter examines how three antebellum Southern women poets used Poe
to gothicize (and 'deconstruct') the South's iconic image as dreamland (or
fairyland) in relation to issues around gender, violence, and slavery. Like most
poets of the slave-holding class,[1] these women were steeped in the romantic literature of fairyland and dreams that played such a key role in the literary imaginary of southern elites (see O'Brien 712–14, 721, 728, 731). Two—Susan
Archer Talley Weiss (1822–1917) and Catherine Ann Warfield (1816–77)—
published in Poe's lifetime. Weiss claims to have known Poe personally. The
third poet, Rosa Vertner Johnson Jeffrey (1828–94), started publishing only
after his death. Drawn to Poe's dark fantasy, these poets recast his material,
making it expressive of their own anxieties as upper-class women. By doing so,
they created a body of work that was not only unlike Northern women's verse
but, in its gendered critique of Southern planter culture, unlike southern men's
as well. Largely unknown today, their writing was the first to establish southern
women's peculiar affinity to the gothic and the first to use the gothic to explore
racial tensions in Southern culture from a specifically female point of view.

Susan Archer Talley Weiss and 'Dream-Land'

Information on Susan Archer Talley Weiss's life prior to the Civil War is scanty
and unreliable. Born in 1822 in Norfolk, Virginia, she descended on her
mother's side from a prominent Norfolk family. In 1830, her father, a lawyer,

P.B. Bennett (✉)
Illinois University, Carbondale, IL, USA

© The Editor(s) (if applicable) and The Author(s) 2016 41
S.C. Street, C.L. Crow (eds.), *The Palgrave Handbook of the Southern Gothic*,
DOI 10.1057/978-1-137-47774-3_4

gave up practicing for reasons of health and moved the family to a farm in Richmond, Virginia. According to Rufus Griswold and Julia Deane Freeman, both of whom included Weiss in their anthologies, she suddenly went deaf some time after this move. The anthologists disagree however when and how severely she was disabled (see Griswold 311; Freeman 313). Weiss's poems first appeared in the *Southern Literary Messenger* in the mid-1840s. Insofar as she is known today, it is not for this poetry but for two popular, although highly problematic, works on Poe: 'The Last Days of Edgar Allan Poe' (*Scribner's Magazine* 1878) and *The Home Life of Poe* (1907).

Northern ignorance about white Southern women's poetry was very much on Freeman's mind when she introduced Weiss's poems in her anthology, *Women of the South Distinguished in Literature* (1860). Like Poe before her, Freeman blamed Boston's 'literary elect' for this situation (309). But Boston snobbery was only part of the story. Like her Southern female peers, Weiss also favored poetic genres that had little purchase in the North; and this profound difference in literary taste was also responsible for her erasure.[2]

As scholars such as Joanne Dobson and Mary Louise Kete have established, antebellum Northern women poets were deeply invested in sentimental rhetoric as a medium through which to reinforce and reinvigorate communal bonds. As a result, these poets looked outward with their work. For Weiss and her slaveholding cohorts, on the other hand, many of whom were from great wealth and largely insulated from society, writing was a leisure activity, pursued for its own sake and disconnected from social needs. Unrestrained by the religio-moral commitments that led Northern women—so many of them not just middle class but missionary educated—to engage with others in their verse, elite Southern women looked inward: to the feelings and thoughts to which their own imaginations and reading gave rise. Where Northern women favored Henry Wadsworth Longfellow, Ralph Waldo Emerson, John Greenleaf Whittier, James Russell Lowell, and Lydia Huntley Sigourney—socially oriented poets all—southerners turned to Sir Walter Scott, Alfred, Lord Tennyson, and the British Romantics, Poe's early idol Byron chief among them. Enthralled by their own dreaming, and haunted by their own fears, they banished from their verse both didacticism and 'Truth' (Poe E&R 75), especially that 'Truth,' so beloved in Boston associated with moral teachings. Following Poe's lead, they made their trips through dreamland and resurrections of the feudal past barely veiled allegories for the dark side of their own lives.

Weiss was especially drawn to three kinds of poems, all immensely popular in the South: pseudo-medieval poems, most of which have gothic storylines; poems on ineffable abstractions such as beauty and light; and the darkest of her verse, poems on dreams, including dreamlands of various sorts. If Tennyson (with Scott) was the guiding genius for the first and Percy Bysshe Shelley for the second, Poe's influence unsurprisingly dominates the third. And as these poems' names suggest—'The Silent Land' (1846), 'The Spirit Land' (1846), 'The Land of Dreams' (1848)—no Poe poem on dreaming inspired Weiss more than 'Dream-Land' (1844) itself. 'The Land of Dreams' — the only dreamland poem Weiss included in her 1859 volume, *Poems* — is by far the darkest and the most complex of these works.

While Weiss was obviously deeply attracted to Poe's famous poem, she makes no attempt in 'Land of Dreams' (1848) to ape his terror-inducing imagery, choosing to present her 'land of dreams' as eerie and seductive. Dispensing with all the horrific details that make poe's 'Dream-Land' so powerful and so compelling—the 'Mountains toppling evermore/Into seas without a shore', the 'dismal tarns and pools/Where dwell the ghouls' (Poe P&T 79, ll.13–14, 29–30), she seizes on that singular moment in 'Dream Land' when Poe presents his afterlife as 'a peaceful soothing region' for those 'whose woes are legion' (ll.40, 39). Extrapolating from these lines, Weiss creates an alternate dreamland, one that, forgoing both the tumultuousness of Poe's 'Dream-Land' and the North's complaisant dreams of a Christian heaven, is based on pagan eschatology. In this 'Land of Dreams,' 'Phantom-forms' (*Poems* 37, ll.15, 29) of the dead, like the shades who inhabit the classical Hades, wander in silence, without purpose but also without woe:

> In that dim, enchanted region
> Phantom-forms for ever range,
> Pale and wan,—a shadowy legion,—
> ....
> Pale, and wan,—and silent all,
> Noiselessly their footsteps fall. (37, 38, ll.28–30, 36–7)

Neither heaven, nor hell, this dreamland is a negative space, without form, color, or sound. Hard though it is to conceptualize, it is a product of a metaphysics of nothingness, a presence that is absence. And because it is neutral and silent, it is also 'soothing' and 'peaceful' after the bruisings of life: the 'Pleasures blighted in their blooming,/Idols far too dearly cherished' (40, ll.87–8). Without '[t]imes and seasons' (37, l.16), visible boundaries (37, l.27) or pierceable 'depths,' (37, l.20), it is inhabited by dead no more substantial or aware than the shadows surrounding them. The result is a level of dematerialization that in its very alienness suggests a Gothic of a different kind: one not just without the physical accoutrements of the Gothic — poisoned chalices, feudal castles — but one having no relationship to being in any sense. Set in a 'voiceless solitu[de]' made 'real' to Weiss, one suspects, by her own deafness, it is a metaphysical Gothic, one purely of the mind (37, l.10)—and one quite as terrifying in its own 'soothing' way.

This subject—that of the interiorized Gothic, or, put another way, the Gothic that results from having to live inside one's own head—elicits from Weiss not just her darkest but her most original and probing poetry on dreams. Even had she not been deaf, Weiss, like other young women of her class, would have had only limited contact with the 'real' world; that is, the world outside her family's circle of friends and relations. Effectively imprisoned within their parents' homes with only household chores to occupy them, these women were prey, in Anya Jabour's words, to 'loneliness, boredom, and melancholy' (88). For a young woman like Weiss, who was at least partially deaf and who lived in books, dreaming was a way to get through the day. Yet as the darkest of Weiss's dream poems suggest, dreaming—like any other form of addiction—also carried its own penalties.

That Weiss was deeply troubled by her dreaming is clear from 'My Sister,' a poem in which she contrasts her sister's uninterrogated response to dreaming— 'all things seem to her as yet/A fair and fairy dream!' (Griswold 315, ll.71–2)—to the 'darker shades' that dreaming spreads over her own life (l.23). Made nothing but tranquil and happy by her dreams, her sister 'calmly plucks the flowers of life' (l.45). Not so Weiss's speaker. Because she is not satisfied, her dreams roil with emotions that oscillate between 'sudden fits of mournfulness' and 'wild and fitful glee' (ll.53, 4); and this 'bewildering strife/Beguiles [her] heart from sober truths/And wearies it of life' (ll.50–52). That is, because her dreams are as conflicted as she is, they depress her, leading to suicidal mentation. In a second poem, 'Weariness,' Weiss teases out this conundrum much more fully and precisely.

Although not based on 'Dream-Land,' 'Weariness' is similar to Poe's poem in one crucial respect: it too deals with an irresolvable dilemma, and in consequence ends—literally—where it began; that is, with the same words (Poe's with minor changes to one line, Weiss's exactly). In Poe's poem, this stasis suggests that the speaker, although he reaches Ultima Thule, never resolves whatever issues originally made him take the journey; possibly questions about the nature of the afterlife. In Weiss's poem, the issues are emotional, not intellectual. The speaker can never be what she wishes to be or have what she wants to have: that, as she says in her opening stanza, her 'soul could melt itself away,/Into its own ideal,/Or that its fair creations might become/The living real' (*Poems* 99, ll.1–4) Because she cannot, she dreams and her dreams weigh her down, deepening her isolation and unhappiness. In terms both poignant and precise, Weiss describes 'clinical depression' in the plain words of a single Southern woman who has nothing to do:

> Thought that goes dreaming through the wintry night,
> And through the summer day,
> With never words to give its meaning forth—
> With never work nor play.
> But little profit is this outer life—
> It seems not life to me,
> So slowly drag the weary days along,—and
> So slow and silently. (100, ll.9–16)

Because Weiss's speaker has no way to escape from her dilemma, carceral 'images of terror fill [her] brain' (101, ll.1, 41) and she compares herself to a 'vessel with its ghastly crew,/Locked in with icy bars' (102, ll.45–6). What she wants is not death but 'life, that flows in rapture through the heart,' and 'findeth pleasure in its own excess/Of human joy and pain' (102, ll.60, 61–2).

Captive to the South's gender expectations, what she gets instead is Jabour's 'loneliness, boredom, and melancholy' (88), a death before death.

'Weariness' suggests that Weiss knew dreaming was noxious to her. Far from bringing pleasure, it interacted with her deafness, in ways that made her all too like the silent and dematerialized phantoms populating her 'Land of Dreams,' a non-being cut off from the living, for whom others are no more than 'shadowy shapes' that 'move ever to and fro,/Like e'er returning dreams' (101, ll.27–8). For her, that is, the gothic landscape of her phantom-filled afterlives *was* 'the real,' a real unreal that, however ironically, was created out of the material conditions of her life, including her deafness. In my two remaining poets, the connection between the gothic world of their imaginations and the material world in which they lived becomes an obsessive concern, as they map on the South the 'images of terror' that fill their brains.

CATHERINE ANN WARE WARFIELD AND 'LIGEIA'

Thanks to Bertram Wyatt-Brown's archival efforts, Catherine Ann Warfield's life, unlike those of Weiss and Jeffrey, is unusually well documented; and it reads like a gothic novel. Planter, lawyer, and politician, Catherine's father, Major Nathaniel Ware, amassed a large fortune in slave-holding plantations during his lifetime. His wife, Sarah Percy Ellis Ware, a wealthy widow, claimed blood ties to one of Britain's oldest families, the Percys of Northumberland. Although Wyatt-Brown debunks this claim, he believes that Sarah did inherit something from her supposed Percy forebears; namely, a genetic predisposition to psychosis and suicidal depression. In 1819, shortly after her daughter Eleanor's birth, Sarah was institutionalized in the Philadelphia Hospital's unit for the insane, where she remained for a decade. Embittered by his wife's illness, which ended his political ambitions, Ware took to traveling, leaving his daughters' care to other family members. On January 3, 1833, Warfield, age 16, married Robert Elisha Warfield, a horse breeder from a prominent Maryland family. Eleanor, with whom Catherine co-published her two poetry volumes, died of yellow fever in 1849. After Eleanor's death, Catherine abandoned poetry for prose. Her greatest success was *The Household of Bouverie* (1860), unsurprisingly a gothic novel (Wyatt-Brown 25–7, 89–118, 334–40).

The core subjects of *Bouverie*—madness and domestic abuse—suggest that Warfield never outgrew the trauma of her mother's illness or her father's subsequent (if fitful) abandonment. Wyatt-Brown believes that Erastus Bouverie, the novel's vicious but charismatic anti-hero, is modeled at least in part on Major Ware, for whom he uses descriptors such as 'taciturn and forbidding' (101) and 'saturnine and distant' (113). And indeed, Major Ware does seem to have possessed many of the characteristics making Erastus so repellent, from his coldness and penny-pinching behavior to his determination to control all those around him. However, Warfield could have found similar inspiration elsewhere, not just in gothic novels but in the numerous planters who owned land in the Natchez area.

To understand Warfield's contribution to the Gothic one must start here: with the men whom southern patriarchy—or 'paternalism,' as Fox-Genovese would have it[3]—produced. Similar to ancient Rome's organization of family life in some respects, southern patriarchy gave men as heads of the household legal control over all their dependents—wives, children, and slaves—with potentially devastating results. Drawing on letters and other personal writings, Anya Jabour believes that young planter women not only feared marriage but had reason to do so, given their limited 'legal and cultural protections from male dominance' (90). Loren Schweninger's study of antebellum divorce statistics from across all the Southern states supports Jabour's contention. Noting that slaveholding men were especially prone to domestic violence, Schweninger suggests that slaveholding itself may have 'imbued owners with a sense of omnipotence over all in their households,' thus contributing to brutal behavior toward wives (52).

Warfield's troubled response to spousal abuse (physical and otherwise) is apparent not just in *Bouverie* but in her poetry, which is rife with controlling husbands and dysfunctional wives of just the sort that the South's gender system produced in 'real life.' In 'Geraldine,' for instance, a woman is so emotionally beaten down by her abusive husband that she continues to worship at his 'fearful shrine' long after his demise (*Indian Chamber* 98, ll.148, 147). In 'The Foe's Return,' slavery and wifedom are equated when a husband, long thought dead, returns and 'hiss[es]' in his terrified wife's 'ear,/"We've met at last, slave! dost thou fear?",' causing the woman to drop dead on the spot (*Wife of Leon*, 182, ll.79–80). While Warfield's language and situations maight seem over-the-top, the evils she depicts—verbal abuse, emotional manipulation, threats of injury, contempt—pale compared to Schweninger's list of acts of extreme violence that slaveholding men actually perpetrated on their wives: 'beating, whipping, assault, bludgeoning, poisoning, stabbing, shooting, and threats of murder' (53).

In the title poem of Warfield and Lee's second volume, 'The Legend of the Indian Chamber,' Warfield confronts domestic violence head on. In treating marriage as a hierarchical institution (like slavery) based on the putative 'natural' inferiority of the weaker partner, the Old South had mapped coverture's principles onto women's bodies, making submission their only feasible option short of divorce. (Warfield makes this point brilliantly in *Bouverie*.) At the same time, women were reluctant to divorce because, among other things, the code of ladylike behavior by which they lived and on which their reputations rested discouraged complaint both publicly and within the family (Jabour 18–19, 38–9, 44–5, 91–3). Splitting the settings and married couples of 'Indian Chamber' between Europe and India, Warfield's poem breaks this code of silence, putting the dark side of male dominance explicitly on trial.

Stripped to its barest essentials, the plot of 'Indian Chamber,' which leans heavily on Poe's 'Ligeia,' centers on wife murder occurring on two continents: in India through the ritual practice of suttee and in Europe where the poem's villainous protagonist, a nameless Norman baron, dumps his murdered bride's body in the Rhine. The poem's action occurs some time after this latter event, and takes place entirely in the 'Indian Chamber' of the baron's castle. Two of the furnishings in this sumptuous but decaying room connect the grisly murders. One is the castle's 'plumed bed of state' (*Indian Chamber* 15, l.150), whose 'long and hearse-like hangings' bespeak 'a silent history/Of departed funeral' (ll.149, 53–4). From behind these hangings, the dead bride's ghost, with 'dark and streaming hair,/And ... eyes of ghoul-like brightness' (16, ll.68–9), briefly emerges to tell the baron's servant, Basil, how she was murdered. She then predicts the baron's death that night. The second furnishing is a huge arras '[w]rought in symbols wild and weird' (13, l.88). Woven in India, this arras depicts various scenes from Indian life. By the flickering light of torches, the images waver like the 'gorgeous dreams of fever' (14, l.133)—that is, like laudanum-induced visions—'[a]ll with ghostly life imbued' (19, l.250). Among the images is a Rajah's funeral pyre, complete with wife.

In the action that follows, the Rajah's wife fulfills the murdered bride's prediction. While the baron prepares a chalice of poisoned wine for a guest, the latter, who has been studying the arras, is horrified to see the figure of the wife come alive. Referring to her as the 'victim bride' (21, l.284)—a deliberate slip on Warfield's part that fuses Indian wife and European bride into a single hybrid figure—he describes how she takes up a flaming cup, also depicted in the arras, and 'steps upon the chamber floor' (l.295). Too terrified at this point to continue, the guest stops, and the poem's narrator continues the story as the Rajah's wife metes out justice too long denied:

> Lips apart and eyes distended,
> Stood the Norman baron bold!
> High her cup the Phantom lifted,
> Flames within it seemed to roll;
> Then alone these words she uttered—
> '*Pledge me in thy feudal bowl*!'
> Chained and speechless, guest and servant
> Saw the Baron drain the draught;
> Saw him fall convulsed and blackened,
> As the deadly bowl he quaffed. (22–3, ll.308–17)

In thus melding wife and bride, Warfield makes a statement that neither woman acting alone could convey. Just as the castle's 'plum'd bed of state' (15, l.150) mirrors the Rajah's funeral pyre, so for both these women marriage is death. However, rather than submit to their fate as Warfield's other wives do, the women in 'Indian Chamber' use their shared victimhood to empower themselves. Acting jointly, they speak performatively, making their request a command, 'Pledge me in thy feudal bowl' (22, l.313)—effectively, 'kill yourself'—and undoing their vow of obedience in the process.

The many contact points between 'Indian Chamber' and 'Ligeia' hardly need stressing. The vague European settings, the river Rhine, the orientalized chamber, the arras, the flickering light that tricks the eye, the massive wooden bed, the wife-ghost with her streaming hair and unnaturally brilliant eyes, the side references to opium, and the chalice or '*feudal bowl*' (23, l.313) with its 'drop of ruby liquid' (21, l.272) are all present in Poe's story. Indeed, these, or similar props, are among the standard ones that in both senses support the Gothic genre for Poe and for High Gothic writers generally. Yet it is also here that exact similarities between Warfield's poem and Poe's tale break down. In 'Ligeia,' the eponymous heroine is many things, but unlike her alter ego, the fair Rowena, she is no Southern lady. If anything, she is the inverted nightmare of that Southern ideal, not just dark of hair and eye, but strong, autonomous, vindictive. A law unto herself, she overwhelms the narrator and Rowena both—thrusting the latter out of her body in order to possess both it and the narrator.

In having her Indian wife and northern bride honor their bond instead, Warfield shatters Poe's paradigmatic pitting of woman against woman. In the vernacular of the 1960s, these two women know who the enemy is. Transcending the ethnic and racial differences that divide them, not only do they act as one, but they establish a global context for the problem of wife abuse generally. As the poem reaches its climax, even the speaker seems exultant at the wife's imposition of justice. The poem's three males—servant, master, and guest—are immobilized. The abused woman, be she wife or bride, dark skinned or white, European or Asian, is triumphant. In the poem's apocalyptic last lines, darkness and cold wipe everything out: 'And the lofty torches warring/For a moment in the blast,/In their sconces were extinguished.'

Warfield could conceive of an alliance between Northern bride and Asiatic wife because as a southern planter woman the abusive use of power against women was a significant part of her reality, a reality whose fever-dreams were the very nightmares of revenge and apocalypse that the poem's conclusion represents. But what then do we make of Warfield, who in imagining such an alliance has effectively erased the color boundary that as a signifier of superiority gave her and her family their right to hold slaves? She, too, was the beneficiary of the power differentials that the baron and the Rajah embodied. And by that token, she could also be a target for revenge by those whom her 'rights' suppressed. Warfield does not speak directly to this possibility. Yet if her poem's subject is, as it appears to be, the evils of giving virtually limitless power to one class of persons over another, then in this poem's imaginary, Rajah, baron, and slave-holder are, finally, one and the same. And all risked suffering the same justice.

Warfield wrote her poem from the victim's point of view, but in life she was a victimizer also, one who owned by her father's fiat large tracts of land and many, many slaves, and this fact shadows her verse—the unstated raison d'être for a nightmare still in the making. What that nightmare might look like is the subject of Jeffrey's 'Hasheesh Visions,' the poem with which I conclude.

ROSA VERTNER JOHNSON JEFFREY AND 'THE ISLAND OF THE FAY'

Rosa Vertner Johnson Jeffrey was born in Natchez, Mississippi in 1828. When she was 9 months old her mother died and she was adopted by a maternal aunt, who took her to live on the Vertners' family plantation in Burlington, near Port Gibson, Mississippi. In the poem 'My Childhood' (1857), Jeffrey captures her love for Burlington in the glowing terms of undiluted nostalgia. For her, the plantation was a fairyland, and one of her favorite memories is of herself 'spread[ing] a banquet fair,/Of acorn-cup and rose-leaves bright' for the fairies to dine on (in Freeman 256, ll.55–6). To judge by her later work, moreover, in particular the novel *Woodburn* (1864), this nostalgia for planta-tion life and all its fairy dreams never fully left her, the Civil War notwithstand-ing. In 1850, 5 years after her marriage, her poems came to the attention of George Prentice, editor of the *Louisville Journal* and an aficionado of women's poetry. As was his habit with poets he admired, Prentice published her poems regularly thereafter. One of a kind both for Jeffrey and for Southern women's verse generally, 'Hasheesh Visions,' (1861), a gothic poem of extraordinary power, was among these works.

Presumably inspired by the ingestion of hashish, 'Visions' is a long phan-tasmagoric dream poem whose meaning, if it has one, is heavily encoded both in the poem's action and in the peculiar version of gothic imagery it employs. Freeman, who reprinted the poem in *Women of the South*, praises its 'crazy play and prodigality of words' (248), but leaves any possible meaning to others to discern. Lisa Day, the only scholar who has written on the poem, includes it in her 1998 dissertation on apocalypse and slavery in antebellum culture. Emphasizing the poem's striking use of color, Day describes it as 'an apocalyp-tic vision concerning the widespread practice and acceptance of slavery.' While acknowledging the poem's ambiguity, she argues that it incorporates 'implicit social messages about abolition' (91). Like Day, I think that the poem may have encoded 'messages,' but if so, they are not about abolition, although Day is probably right that Jeffrey was a gradualist (104). Rather, reading 'Visions' in relation to the three Poe works that influenced it most—'Eldorado' (1849), 'The Island of the Fay' (1841), and *The Narrative of Arthur Gordon Pym* (1837–38)—I would suggest that it is probably best understood as a tocsin. Its 'message' to Southerners: Get out of town before it is too late.

Beginning the mise en scène, the action of 'Hasheesh Visions' can be sum-marized as follows: The poem's narrator, a captive on a burning boat, breaks her '[f]iery fetters' (Bennett 164, l.1) and, hoping to take refuge among some distant 'opal islands' (l.16), throws herself into the 'crimson sea' (l.9). When after much travail she reaches the islands, 'a boiling wave' (l.32) flings her on a 'cool and polished shore' (l.37), 'the fairest in that wondrous sea' (l.36). Yet this island, whose lushness first makes it seem the 'Eldorado of [her] soul' (165, l.40), turns out to be another place of torture, with neither edible fruits nor potable water to eat or drink. Making matters worse, the island's inhabitants, 'fair forms' (167, l.156), who 'seem[ed] to glide/Beneath [its] haunted groves' (ll.156–7), only mock her cries for help. When a thick dark-ness rolls over the island, she attempts to escape by boarding a 'black' bark (169, l.233), sailed by black, ghoul-like skeletons, but ends by drowning as the sea breaks the ship apart, taking all hands with it. That is the tale the poem tells, blatantly gothic despite the poem's island location. What to make of it is another matter.

That the conclusion of Jeffrey's poem represents a demonic vision of black enfranchisement and its consequences for the South seems undeniable. By my count she uses the word black 10 times in the poem's last 56 lines. If you add the words connoting blackness such as ebon, jet, darkness, gloom, coals, raven, night, and inky, you get 22 such usages altogether. The sea, the sky, the earth, all turn black. Great shadows cover the island and the 'fruits and flowers of late so fair' turn to 'ebon cinders' (168, ll.205, 206). When the air grows cold, snow falls that is as '[b]lack as the clouds that gave it birth' (168, l.212).

> Black barks before [her] seemed to glide,
> Whose sails were *blacker* than the tide,
> Peopled by wild and frantic gholes,
> Strange skeletons, as black as coals,
> Who on those ghostly decks had met
> To quaff black blood from cups of jet. (168, ll.197–202)

Dying of thirst and overwhelmed by the feeling that all this blackness is burying her alive—an obvious tip of the hat to Poe—the narrator in desperation throws her lot in with the ghouls, 'quench[ing her] thirst at last, in *blood*!' (169, l.230). The action does not save her, however. She, the ghouls, and their black barks are all swept away '[i]nto that fathomless abyss' (l.235) where 'blind with blackness,' mid the roar/Of inky waves' she hears 'no more' (ll.241–2). Needless to say, this is *Pym*'s conclusion, with black and white figuratively and literally reversed, not as richly mysterious perhaps, but just as terrifying. A vision of the Armageddon to come, its gothic qualities are straight from Poe's playbook.

Nevertheless, the poem is also something more, namely a revision of Poe's plate article 'Island of the Fay,'[4] and this re-envisioning doubles down on the poem's gothic thematics, significantly complicating the conclusion's simplistic black/white opposition. As mentioned earlier, along with the ghouls the island is home to 'fair forms' (167, l.156). These fair forms, who glide so mysteriously through the island's groves, would be the fair folk of Celtic literature otherwise known as the fay, otherwise known as fairies. (Etymologically, 'fay' derives from the word for fairy in Middle English.) As symbolized by the lushness of the island's produce, the narrator, it seems, has landed in her beloved fairyland.

If so, however, it is a very different fairyland from the one in which she reveled as a child. That was a time, she says, before her 'trusting heart' had ever 'grieved/To find itself at last deceived' (167, ll.137–8). In this fairyland, a gothic fairyland where everything deceives, nothing can be trusted. When she sees '[p]omegranates, rare and ripe' (166, l.125), she eagerly tears them apart, only to find not 'the fruity seed/With red and luscious juice to bleed' (167, ll.131–2) but '[a] mass of rubies' 'to mock, and madden [her] despair' (ll.142, 144). So it goes with oranges, which turn out to be gold; grapes, which prove to be amethysts; and water, which turns into diamonds, leading her to cry out: 'Oh! what were *gems* to one who yearned/For water-drops' (166, ll.119–20). Topping all this off torture are the 'fair' inhabitants themselves who quaff '[f]rom crystal cups bright draughts, and laug[h]/Derisive laughter—soft and clear' (167, ll.156, 158–9).

If, as Day believes, the speaker is describing 'the far off South' (l.133) in these passages, then other, more complicated possibilities for reading the poem's conclusion become available. Yes, the poem seems to envisage black revenge and slavery's apocalyptic end. However, if so, it speaks even more profoundly to what happens to those who out of greed turn that which was animate flesh into inanimate coin, making the poem's many allusions to Midas central to its meaning. The fair folk have no interest in the narrator's plight because they are blind to it, and they are also blind to their own situation. Addicted to their luxuries, they go on eating and drinking, apparently unaware of or uninterested in the darkness in which they are complicit and which is about to overtake them as surely as blackness overtakes Poe's island of the Fay.

In a note that Whittier attached to his poem 'The Hashisch' (1854), he writes of the drug:

> A preparation of the *Cannabis Indica* or Indian hemp … is famous throughout the Eastern world for its … intoxicating qualities, producing an agreeable hallucination, or *fantasia*, and disposing the eater to all kinds of exaggeration and extravagance. The effect of the *cotton plant*, mental, moral, religious, and political, upon the people of the United States, would form a proper subject for a medico-philosophic essay like that of M. Morceau's. (173)

Looked at with Whittier's words in mind, the antebellum South's narcissistic 'fairy' dream of itself was just such a self-serving hallucination, 'a *fantasia*' such as Jeffrey's fair folk were living out on their isle. However unwittingly at the start, the South had founded its own version of Eldorado on an agricultural product that, like gold, led it to value making money over human life. To judge by 'Hasheesh Visions,' Jeffrey was terrified by the possibility of black on white violence that enfranchisement might unleash, but also, judging from this poem, she was equally terrified of living on an 'island' where those who ruled were blindly prepared to risk lands and lives for strictly material gain. Like the island's fair folk, Southern planters went on doing as they always had done, while the storm clouds of war gathered that would literally burn their lands to cinders and sweep them and their lifestyle away. Possibly taking her own warnings to heart, if indeed she saw her poem that way, Jeffrey herself gave up on fairyland at least for a while and in 1862, she and her family moved to Rochester, New York for the war's duration.

Conclusion

For all their reservations, the three poets discussed in this essay never abandoned the South: not Jeffrey, although she went north for the war and remained there well into the postbellum period; not Warfield who, unquestionably to my mind, grasped the evil of slavery most fully; certainly not Weiss, who served as a Confederate spy during the war, finally getting the adventure for which she so longed. Their connection to the land and to the way of life it spawned was simply too deep. Yet they also were not blind. And because they were not, they took advantage of the ambiguities in Poe's Gothic to develop a language through which they could address the darkness that hung over their land, distorting the lives of both its black and its white populations. For them, the Gothic became a means to deconstruct the very myths that kept their class in power. Because they did, these poets help us understand what the Old South actually was to those who lived it—apart from all the mythology, apart from the South's own, all-too-romantic dream of itself.

Notes

1. Women from other classes also wrote poetry in the antebellum period, among them the black poet Frances Harper, but slaveholding women dominated the field until the Civil War.
2. For example, Amelia Welby and Anna Peyre Dinnies, Southerners who wrote sentimental and domestic poetry, respectively, were widely admired in the North.
3. Fox-Genovese, *Within the Plantation Household*, pp. 63–4. In arguing for 'paternalism' over 'patriarchy,' Fox-Genovese seeks to soften the Southern system of slave-holding by pointing out that many Southerners viewed the Roman system, which allowed masters to kill any and all members of their household virtually at will, as 'barbaric.' While it is true that some Southerners defended slavery on these grounds, I find this a distinction without a difference.
4. Poe's brief article accompanied an etching depicting 'The Island of the Fay.'

Bibliography

Day, L. B. (1998). *"Our sufferings will come to an end": Apocalypse and slavery in antebellum American culture.* Unpublished dissertation, Southern Illinois University.

Fox-Genovese, E. (1988). *Within the plantation household: Black and white women of the Old South.* Chapel Hill: University of North Carolina Press.

Freeman, J. D. [Mary Forrest] (Ed.). (1861). *Women of the south distinguished in literature.* New York: Derby & Jackson.

Goddu, T. A. (1997). *Gothic America: Narrative, history, and nation.* New York: University Press.

Griswold, R. W. (Ed.). (1849). *The female poets of America.* Philadelphia: Carey and Hart.

Jabour, A. (2007). *Scarlett's sisters: Young women in the Old South.* Chapel Hill: University of North Carolina Press.

Jeffrey, Rosa Vertner Johnson. "My Childhood's Home." In Julia Deane Freeman, ed.. *Women of the South Distinguished in Literature.* New York: Derby & Jackson, 1861, pp. 266–67.

Jeffrey, R. V. J. (1998). Hasheesh visions. In P. B. Bennett (Ed.), *Nineteenth-century American women poets: An anthology* (pp. 164–169). Oxford: Blackwell.

Lee, E. P. W., & Warfield, C. (1844). *The wife of Leon, and other poems.* Philadelphia: D. Appleton and Company.

Lee, E. P. W., & Warfield, C. (1846). *The Indian chamber and other poems.* New York: Printed for the Authors.

O'Brien, M. (2004). *Conjectures of order: Intellectual life and the American South, 1810–1860* (2 Vols.). Chapel Hill: University of North Carolina Press.

Poe, E. A. (1984a). *Essays and reviews (E&R)*. New York: Library of America.

Poe, E. A. (1984b). *Poetry and tales (P&T)*. New York: Library of America.

Schweninger, L. (2012). *Families in crisis in the Old South: Divorce, slavery, & the law.* Chapel Hill: University of North Carolina Press.

Susan Archer Talley.' In Julia Deane Freeman, ed.. *Women of the South Distinguished in Literature*. New York: Derby & Jackson, 1861, pp. 309–313.

'Susan Archer Talley.' In Rufus Wilmot Griswold, ed.. *The Female Poets of America*. Philadelphia: Carey and Hart, 1849, p. 311

Warfield, Catherine. (1860) *The Household of Bouverie: or, the elixir of gold.* 2 Parts. N.P.: Ulan Press, 2014.

Weiss Talley, Susan Archer. "My Sister." In Rufus Wilmot Griswold, ed.. *The Female Poets of America*. Philadelphia: Carey and Hart, 1849, pp. 314-15.

Weiss, S. A. T. (1859). *Poems*. New York: Rudd & Carleton.

Whittier, J. G. (1854, February 11). The Hashish. *The Friend, 27*, 173.

Wyatt-Brown, B. (1994). *The house of Percy: Honor, melancholy, and imagination in a Southern family*. New York/Oxford: Oxford University Press.

Further Reading

Dayan, J. (2001). Poe, persons, and property. In J. G. Kennedy & L. Weissberg (Eds.), *Romancing the shadow: Poe and race* (pp. 106–126). Oxford: Oxford University Press. Noting that 'all Poe's fiction is about property and possession,' Dayan explores the consequences for Poe's women of their ambiguous status not as persons before the law, but rather as property—in much the same way that slaves were also viewed as property.

Rubin, L. D., Jr. (1989). *The edge of the swamp: A study in the literature and society of the Old South*. Baton Rouge: Louisiana State University. Anticipating Toni Morrison's argument in *Playing in the Dark*, Rubin's *The Edge of the Swamp* is an early but brilliantly insightful study of the literature and society of the Old South, with special emphasis on the impact that slavery had on Southern authors, most particularly Poe.

Warfield, C. A. W. (1875). *The household of Bouverie: or, the elixir of gold*. Philadelphia: T. B. Peterson & Brothers. Reprint edition 1923. Ulan Press OCR 2014. Indebted in equal parts to 'The Fall of the House of Usher' and 'Rappaccini's Daughter,' Warfield's novel, which depicts psychological dynamics within a single (highly dysfunctional) Southern family, is the most powerful example of the Gothic produced by a nineteenth-century Southern author after Poe.

CHAPTER 5

Southern Gothic: Haunted Houses

Carol Margaret Davison

Slavery … is dead, … [but] the spirit which animated it still lives. (Frances Harper, *Iola Leroy* [1892: 217])

One would be hard-pressed to identify a more prominent feature in the gothic literary landscape than that of the contested castle or haunted house. According to Ruth Parkin-Gounelas, since the advent of Horace Walpole's *The Castle of Otranto* (1764) the Gothic has remained fixated on anatopias, 'the repetition of other forms of … [Walpole's castle], as well as of its contents: its villains, incestuous relationships, disembodied parts, and above all, the buried secrets of its origins' (1999: 131). While Walpole's castle is haunted in that supernatural events that transpire there are connected both to Manfred's haunted consciousness and to the irrepressible sins of his fathers, transatlantic relocations of the haunted house onto American Gothic 'soil' are noteworthy in that the house becomes more than a mirror to a character's psychology or a gateway to encounters with familial history. In the American Gothic tradition, the house becomes anthropomorphised, effectively assuming a life of its own in the form of sentience and agency. As Éric Savoy has claimed, the house has served as 'the most persistent site, object, structural analogue, and trope of American gothic's allegorical turn' (1998: 9); however, as Savoy fails to note, it is regularly and variously spectrally occupied. Both north and south of the Mason–Dixon line, in text after text, from the written page to celluloid, a necropolitics is enacted in houses: occupied as they are by the unsettled undead, houses become uncanny, defamiliarised spaces, subverting the established generational power dynamic and even (dis)possessing their putative, living owners, the thematic of possession/dispossession assuming rich spiritual, psychological and material implications.

C.M. Davison (✉)
Department of English Language, Literature, and Creative Writing,
University of Windsor, Windsor, Canada

© The Editor(s) (if applicable) and The Author(s) 2016   55
S.C. Street, C.L. Crow (eds.), *The Palgrave Handbook of the Southern Gothic*,
DOI 10.1057/978-1-137-47774-3_5

In its Northern manifestations, from Charles Brockden Brown's *Wieland; or, The Transformation* (1798) through to Stephen King's *Carrie* (1974), the haunted house often assumes the role of a church, becoming a site of supernatural occupation and possession that is ultimately destroyed in a theologically inflected scene of apocalypse. In its Southern manifestations, the haunted house regularly assumes the form of the slave plantation house, a spectralised locale whose materialist substructure is exposed by way of irrepressible ghosts. True to their role as delineated by such cultural theorists as Jacques Derrida and Avery Gordon (2008: xvi), these spectres register historical traumas caused by antiquated and abusive institutions of power guilty of commodifying human beings—including, and most prominently, the peculiar institution, the backbone of the Old Southern economy—and demand reparative action. As such, as Avery Gordon argues, this haunting is 'distinctive for producing a [sense of] something-to-be-done' (xvi).

As Peter Fritzsche has noted, the haunted house is a quintessential creation of eighteenth-century modernity (2001: 1616), the apposite locale for what Terry Castle argues is a fragmented post-Enlightenment subject haunted by pre-Enlightenment certainties and belief systems (1995). This speculation goes some way towards explaining how and why haunting not only became, as Deidre Lynch rightly identifies it, 'the most favored hermeneutic metaphor of the nineteenth century' (2007: 230), but also 'the symptom of a loss—something excessive and unresolved in the past that requires an intervention in the present' (Curtis 2008: 34). In stark contrast to the secure domestic sphere of the sentimental romance, the Gothic features a house *haunted* by history, a situation represented by invisible presences that, notably, elicit desire and/or dread. Indeed, the Gothic may be said to stage various dreams and nightmarish dreads about history. Fears and fantasies about the past assume a flesh-and-blood reality in its pages.

Popularly regarded as rooted in Edgar Allan Poe's 'The Fall of the House of Usher' (1839)—a work regularly identified as the 'master text' of the genre (Savoy 1998: 12)—the Southern Gothic haunted house tale is, arguably, only first fully realised, with all of its requisite Southern socio-political ingredients and preoccupations, half a decade later, in Thomas Nelson Page's arresting short story 'No Haid Pawn' (1887). The contested, haunted plantation house featured in the Southern Gothic functions—to borrow a term from Mary Louise Pratt's work on imperial travel writing—as a fertile 'contact zone' (1992: 6). As Robert Pogue Harrison has so brilliantly stated, echoing Nathaniel Hawthorne, the house is 'in some fundamental senses mortuary ... [as it is] inhabited not only by the dead but also by the unborn in their projective potentiality' (2004: 40): 'we live'—or, at least, we did until the late twentieth century—as the suitably named Holgrave declares in Hawthorne's *The House of the Seven Gables* (1851), 'in Dead Men's houses' (1998: 183). Within its confines, historical and cultural, conscious and unconscious, collisions and collusions occur between individuals of disparate races, genders, classes, sexual orientations and generations, who 'meet, clash, and grapple with

each other, often in highly asymmetrical relations of domination and subordination' (Pratt 1992: 4). In keeping with *The Castle of Otranto*, which features
the exposure and return of undead fathers and the repressed sins associated
with them, the Southern Gothic haunted house spawns uncanny, often cataclysmic encounters between the past and the present, the foreign/imperial
and familiar/domestic, or what Homi K. Bhabha describes as 'the *heimlich*
pleasures of the hearth, [and] the *unheimlich* terror of the space or race of the
Other' (1993: 2). Perhaps most significantly for the American Gothic generally
and the Southern Gothic more specifically, the haunted house, which emblem-
atises the American ideal of property ownership and, according to some critics,
American history in general (Goddu 2007: 63), is the site of both collisions
and collusions between the American dream and the American nightmare.

By way of a cross-section of texts ranging across nearly two centuries, from
Poe's 'The Fall of the House of Usher' (1839) and Thomas Nelson Page's
'No Haid Pawn' (1887) to William Faulkner's *Absalom, Absalom!* (1936),
Toni Morrison's *Beloved* (1987) and Jim Grimsley's *Dream Boy* (1995), this
chapter examines and assesses the changing make-up of the Southern Gothic
haunted house with its generationally imbricated, (usually) bourgeois interiors. Consideration will be given to how, to what ends and with what ramifications this ghost-story setting and fertile contact zone between a variety of
bodies—living, dead, spectral, uncanny and living-dead—grant visibility and
voice to those who, as Avery Gordon maintains, are usually excluded and invisible (2008: 15). This status especially includes slaves, objectified Others who,
as Orlando Patterson has perceptively argued, have essentially experienced a
social death.

The Fall of the House of Usher

In its bizarre dramatisation of the transgressive, incestuous 'sins of the fathers'
motif that results in the decay and destruction of the house and family line,
Poe's 'Usher' replays, in an unnamed European setting, the primary traditional
British Gothic plot dynamic, while laying the figurative foundation for the
Southern Gothic tale of the haunted house. Likewise, 'Usher' reproduces the
British Female Gothic recipe that highlights a domestic sphere fatal to women,
the mortuary, carceral nature of the Usher mansion being preeminent, with the
Lady Madeline buried alive in its catacombs, the site of the old donjon-keep
(1980: 72).

Poe's manner of spacialising the self, what Eve Kosofsky Sedgwick identifies
as a key feature of the Gothic (Sedgwick 1980: 12), assumes unique proportions given his representation of the house as a figurative body. Perhaps most
importantly, Poe connects Roderick Usher's psyche to the physical space of
his mansion so that henceforth in the Southern Gothic tradition, 'psychological distress often accompanies architectural decay' (Sweeting 1999: 224). The
anthropomorphised 'melancholy house of Usher' (62) with its 'vacant and eye-
like windows' (63) affirms the connection 'in the minds of the peasantry ...

[between] the family and the family mansion' (63). Roderick Usher's malady, described as 'constitutional and a family evil' (68), signals a further aspect of the tale's inheritance theme that solidifies the conjoined fates of the house and the body. Given his incurably diseased sister and the fact that they constitute the last in their family line, Roderick is doubly haunted—by his own unavoidable demise and by that of the entire Usher family. As he informs the narrator, his mental decline is linked, in the first instance, to an oppressive belief in the house's malign influence and, in the second, to the fatal illness plaguing his 'tenderly beloved sister' (67), for whom he tellingly cries 'many passionate tears' (68). Roderick's deteriorating mental condition is exacerbated by his decision (whether unconscious or conscious) to bury Madeline alive, possibly as a form of punishment for not procreating and extending their incestuous family line that 'lay in the direct line of descent' (63).

While there are no actual ghosts in 'Usher', Roderick is a cadaverous, haunted man, 'laboring ... [under] some oppressive secret' (73), which may be the knowledge of his incestuous family history or his act of sororicide, the latter deed signalling and consolidating his moral consanguinity with his transgressive progenitors. Although this vault burial of a putatively dead sister is undertaken, as Roderick tells the narrator, to safeguard her body against inquisitive, grave-robbing medical men who would violate the sanctity of their exposed family burial ground (72), the greatest threat to the Usher family is ultimately revealed, as is often the case in early American Gothic, to lie within.

The horrifying culmination of this excessive insularity fittingly involves Madeline Usher, resembling Lewis's famous Bleeding Nun, her white robes bloody with 'the evidence of some bitter struggle upon every portion of her emaciated frame' (78), collapsing into the arms of her terrorised brother in a brilliantly choreographed operatic moment of doppelgänger death. The conjoined fates of the family and the mansion are definitively, sensationally and subsequently revealed in this climax as (divinely wielded?) lightning strikes this mansion, creating 'a rapidly widening fissure from the roof of the collapsing building to its base', followed by 'the deep and dank tarn' swallowing the fragments of the House of Usher, 'sullenly and silently', at the narrator's feet (78). Poe's magnificent use of the tarn as a feature of the dark sublime in his haunted house scenario ramps up his tale's Romantic aesthetics, in keeping with the role of beautiful but life-threatening landscapes in the Radcliffean Gothic. Thus does wild nature ultimately triumph over perverse, fragile-because-decadent civilisation.

No Haid Pawn

Published half a century after 'Usher', Thomas Nelson Page's 'No Haid Pawn' is an outstanding American ghost story, an overlooked gem of the genre that addresses that nation's slave-owning past, thus laying the groundwork for an enhanced, racially and politically charged Southern Gothic treatment of the haunted house. This ghastly, ghostly tale of terror, characterised by 'horror,

guilt, fear, and depravity' (Rubin 1974: 99), is set in the 1850s after the passing of the Fugitive Slave Act (1850), which legislated that all captured runaway slaves had to be returned to their masters, a law with which Northerners
had to comply. 'No Haid Pawn' thus transplants Poe's masterly mise-en-abîme
meditation about grotesquely insular/'incestuous' aristocracy onto Southern
Gothic soil. Page's story is an unlikely candidate for this development given
that its author was a proponent of the late nineteenth-century plantation novel,
in whose pages slavery is nostalgically idealised as a lost Golden Age and whose
enslaved subjects are portrayed as 'perfect retainers, humble, loyal, gentle, content with their lot, [and] devoted to their owners' (Rubin 1974: 99).

Signalling its indebtedness to 'Usher' and its British literary predecessors,
'No Haid Pawn' is a sedimented masterwork of literary architecture retrospectively recounted by a white narrator about a terrifying adolescent experience. The tale's centrepiece is a deserted plantation house built by slaves in the
midst of a 'primeval swamp' called No Haid Pawn. The narrator's few politically explicit comments linking the Gothic to abolitionism, fugitive slaves and
the underground railway with its emissaries—otherwise known as 'the devil'
(171)—in combination with his seemingly uninvested, offhand remark to
'[w]hatever the right and wrong of slavery' (174), are overshadowed by the
macabre details about slavery as conveyed in the two key overlapping narratives. In the first, a brutal, alcoholic slave–master transplanted from the West
Indies decapitates one of his slaves as a warning to the others, a crime for which
this 'gigantic monster' (170) is hanged during which his head is unaccountably
severed; in the second, a hulking and brutal, rebellion-fomenting 'convert' of
the abolitionists and runaway fails to be recaptured. Enhancing the terrifying
nature of the tale, the narrator notes how this former butcher-slave possesses
occult powers (172).

The story's rich rhetoric reverberates with early British Gothic and Spanish
Inquisitorial, French Revolutionary nightmares. This isolated 'fated pile',
replete with 'many mysterious rooms[,] ... underground passages' and solid
rock chambers that, according to the slaves who built them, serve as 'dungeons' (167), has a bloody, symbolically loaded history that is so terrifying,
according to the narrator, that runaway slaves opt to return to their masters
rather than traverse the dreaded plantation (164). Most grotesquely, the plantation house is literally built on black slave bodies, one of its builders being
'caught and decapitated between two of [its] ... immense foundation stones'
(167), an event, according to local slaves undertaken for ritual purposes by
their white masters, that proves how an 'evil destiny had seemed to overshadow
the place from the very beginning' (167).

Drawing on Poe's tarn, the swamp is an ambivalent, sublime setting associated with brutalised slaves. Serving on the one hand as the graveyard of those
who, suffering from malaria, were thrown into it alive and said thereafter to
haunt the locale nightly in their boat-like coffins (168), it serves on the other as
a site of potential liberation for runaways that could enable their escape. In this
latter capacity, the slave in the swamp was a signpost of rebellion and terror,

the Southern equivalent of the scalping native hidden in the forest of New England Gothic. According to William Tynes Cowan, 'Southern whites would have known of runaway bands [of slaves] living in woods and swamps, especially in eastern Virginia and North Carolina, Louisiana, and Florida, where swamplands were vast and plentiful' (2005: 3). In this latter capacity, as a site that enables slaves in their escape, the wild, dreaded landscape in 'No Haid Pawn' is the natural ally of the black slave. The lush and treacherous Southern landscape, albeit a location to which blacks were brutally and unwillingly relocated, is repeatedly and significantly described as a 'jungle' (163), transformed into an Africanised locale familiar to the slave. Thus, as the narrative evidences, do slaves, 'jungle' and the 'primeval swamp' come to emblematise the terrifying prospect in the white Southern consciousness of reverting to a state of nature/barbarism.

The reversion that transpires involves the young narrator's cherished rational belief system. Caught in a storm while hunting, he traverses the swamp to seek shelter in the 'haint'-filled plantation house. In a scene echoing the climax of Robert Louis Stevenson's masterly tale of terror, 'Thrawn Janet' (1881), published 6 years earlier, where an otherwise rational minister, his nerves fraught due to illness, sleeplessness and a series of harrowing events, falls victim to hallucination and a superstitious worldview, Page's tale limns the boundary between the rational and what is figured as the regressive and irrational 'Negro' supernatural.

In its memorable, sensational climax, the young narrator witnesses the re-enactment of the horrifying homicide perpetrated by the West Indian slave–master when he sees a 'ghastly and bloody, ... black and headless trunk' at his feet (185). Page supplies the rational explanation whereby the runaway slave is living at this plantation and has just slaughtered a pig for dinner. The sensational conclusion pays tribute to 'Usher' as the 'haunted house', dramatically destroyed by lightning, burns 'to the water's edge', where the swamp reclaims 'its secrets' (186).

The ultimate 'secret' revealed in this miniature masterpiece is that the plantation house is a mortuary born of racial violence. Despite the minor attempts to demonise the runaway slaves and their abolitionist allies, in conjunction with the implicit suggestion that a slave system operated by moderate paternalists is harmless and justifiable, 'No Haid Pawn' exposes the violence and tremendous human costs of the peculiar institution. Perhaps the greatest irony of the tale lies in the fact that the popular legend of the haunted plantation safeguards the escaped butcher-slave, rather than deterring such escapes as the dissemination of haunted plantation tales were designed to do (Martin 2002: 305).

Absalom, Absalom!

Half a century later, William Faulkner self-consciously reconfigures the haunted house formula in *Absalom, Absalom!* (1936) to craft an incisive regional—and national—allegory and lament for a 'doomed society', a 'house [racially] divided', as represented by Thomas Sutpen's 'doomed house' (1964: 375), which is built in isolation, 12 miles from the nearest town, on 100 miles of Mississippi land, otherwise known as 'Sutpen's Hundred'. In this Greek-tragedy-cum-dark-Gothic-romance, Faulkner boldly constructs a Southern house haunted by pre- and post-Civil War history, a 'fatal land cursed by God' (21). Indeed, as suggested by Rosa Coldfield, clad in her 43-year-old widow's weeds (7) and seated in what her young auditor Quentin Compson describes as 'the dim coffin-smelling gloom' (8), the entire region of 'the deep South, dead since 1865 [and] peopled with garrulous outraged baffled ghosts' (9), is figured as a type of haunted house. Jessica Hurley has cogently claimed that 'for Faulkner, ghost is a verb' (2012: 65) and *Absalom, Absalom!*

> is what we might call a metaghost story, a novel about ghosts and haunting, how ghosts are made and how we come to be haunted and what being haunted and ghosted do to us, but one in which actual ghosts are notably absent. (64)

Indeed, Faulkner's retrospectively told meta-ghost story also meditates on his writing practice, as he articulates some of the features of the Southern Gothic haunted house tale while suggesting that story-telling, of necessity, involves ghostly resurrections.

Perhaps most famously, in Miss Rosa's description of Sutpen's plantation house, Faulkner casts an eye back over the Southern Gothic tradition and artic-ulates the body–house connection whereby 'houses actually possess a sentience, a personality and character' (85). This motif is sustained throughout *Absalom, Absalom!*, serving as a signpost of the status and decline of a region and its peo-ple: Sutpen's plantation house seems to speak (142), is said to possess a 'spirit' (160) and, in the final scene before its destruction by fire, is said to 'smell of desolation and decay as if the wood of which it was built were flesh' (366).

By way of Faulkner's descriptions of Sutpen's Hundred, *Absalom, Absalom!* foregrounds the economic substructure of Southern society built on theft—land 'stolen' from a drunken Indian (301)—slave labour and human com-modification: 'the sheen on the dollar is not from gold but from blood' (250). Thus does an almost mythic Thomas Sutpen, a Gothic hero-villain character-ised by excess, pride, transgression (46) and 'ruthless speculation' (43) who seems inhumanly indestructible (305) and devoid of a soul (180), realise his grandiose but fundamentally flawed American Dream 'design' in the form of a plantation house that serves in two capacities—as a signpost of his social status as property, and as a signpost of filiation meant to ensure his symbolic immor-tality down through the generations.

The product of a 'dream of grim and castlelike magnificence' grounded in his 'fierce and overweening vanity' (38), Sutpen's plantation house is a quint-essentially gothic structure possessing Babylonian features. Drawing on the house–body connection, this mansion, the 'largest edifice in the county' (39), is horrifyingly grotesque, a type of 'cocoon … and complementary shell' born of the 'sweat of … [Sutpen's] body', like some 'suppuration of himself' (138).

As Sutpen's sister-in-law and former fiancée Rosa Coldfield suggests by way of her heavy-handed rhetoric, the settling of his plantation is essentially a rape of nature. In her words, he 'tore [it] violently' (9), 100 miles of '*virgin* land' (301; emphasis added), from '*out of virgin swamp*' (40; emphasis added). This was undertaken with the assistance of his other property, Haitian slaves purchased and brought from his previous home, where he had married and fathered a child he later abandoned after discovering his wife to be of mixed race.

Sutpen's materialist American dream is revealed to involve a deadly Faustian bargain: family values and love are exchanged for his monomaniacally danger-ous, enslaving and life-draining 'design', which is exposed to be grounded in racism, for which he sacrifices both branches of his family—its legitimate 'white' members and its illegitimate, unrecognised 'black' members who are regarded as property. Thus is Sutpen's once solid home, 'the size of a court house' (16), transformed, as a result of the 'sins of the father', into a decaying prison-house that incarcerates and ultimately destroys his family (138).

True to the Female Gothic tradition, Sutpen's Hundred becomes an espe-cially deadly carceral domain for the Sutpen women. According to Rosa, her sister Ellen was 'a blind, romantic fool' who relinquished 'pride and peace' (15) to marry Sutpen. Ironically, Ellen moved from a 'mausoleum' (60) in the form of her father's house to a 'Bluebeard's [castle where she was] ... transmogrified into a mask looking back with passive and hopeless grief upon the irrevoca-ble' (60). Southern women are all likewise transformed into ghosts (12), Rosa suggests, their fertility destroyed after the heavy death toll exacted on their male population by the Civil War.

Absalom, Absalom! remains true to the traditional British Gothic recipe with its focus on genealogy, the return of the repressed/secret sins of the fathers that haunt the family, and retribution. A house racially divided is at its centre, as played out between the two primary, racially distinct branches of Thomas Sutpen's offspring—the first involving Charles Le Bon, his son with a woman purportedly possessing some black blood; the second involving Henry and Judith, his two 'white' children with Ellen Coldfield. The depth of Southern racism is underscored by the fact that a prospective incestuous marriage between Sutpen's mixed-race son Charles and his white daughter Judith is considered acceptable until it is discovered that Charles is of mixed race. Raising the threat of dishonour, miscegenation is the deal-breaker and it costs Charles his life. Thus does *Absalom, Absalom!* engage with the 'more covert anxiety' conjured up by what has been called Lincoln's 'miscegenation proclamation' (Peterson 2007: 99), the idea that 'the spread of slavery made possible by the Dred Scott decision (1857) and the Kansas Nebraska Act (1854) would in turn lead to the spread of miscegenation' (Peterson 99), as Quentin Compson's friend Shreve prophesies at the novel's end (378).

The conclusion of *Absalom, Absalom!* sees the sins of the fathers being vis-ited upon their offspring, the nightmarish underbelly of the 'American dream' being simultaneously exposed and indicted. While Sutpen's murder occurs at the hands of the squatter Wash Jones after Sutpen rapes Wash's 15-year-old granddaughter and fathers a child on her, it is the aptly named Clytaemnestra (Clytie), a woman whom Sutpen fathers on a slave woman, who is responsible for the novel's closing apocalypse. The deliberately set conflagration of Sutpen's Hundred, like a Maroon-style slave rebellion, exacts retribution for, and liberation from, the horrors of America's slave-owning past. Given the energies at play in Sutpen's plantation house with its 'insurmountable resistance to occupancy save when sanctioned and protected by the ruthless and the strong' (95), it also signals an end to ruthless speculation and its tremendous costs. Ironically, although Sutpen successfully puts down a slave rebellion in Haiti, he is ultimately unable to defeat an uprising born of internal forces in his Mississippi home, his only remaining relative at novel's end being a now homeless, 'idiot' black grandson.

Beloved

A compelling novel with a poltergeist-occupied house as its centrepiece, Toni Morrison's *Beloved* (1987) has been repeatedly critically identified as her gothic masterpiece. Based on a historical case involving a black slave, Margaret Garner, who killed her own daughter so that she in turn would not become a slave, *Beloved* recounts the tragic history of fugitive slave Sethe, who escapes to Ohio only to be tracked down. Sethe's brutal murder of her daughter Beloved during the scene of her apprehension results in a long-term haunting—a poltergeist that takes over her house in the first instance, followed by the return of Beloved as a vampiric, embodied ghost, now grown up, some 17 years later. Sethe's mother's chilling declaration that 'Not a house in the country ain't packed to its rafters with some dead Negro's grief' (Morrison 1987: 5), in combination with Stamp Paid's identification of the voices in the house as those of 'the black and angry dead' who died as victims in white America (234), renders explicit the latent symbolism attached to Sutpen's plantation house in *Absalom, Absalom!* By locating 124 Bluestone Road, a more modest descendant of the classic Gothic's haunted house, in Ohio, Morrison also strategically transgresses the North/South divide to engage with slavery's devastating impact on the 'Sixty Million and more' to whom the novel is dedicated and on the United States as a whole. As such, Morrison makes a purposeful and political decision, giving the lie to the frequent division of the American Gothic in terms of its thematic preoccupations along both regional and racial lines. By virtue of its ideological focus and subject matter, therefore, *Beloved* is a work of the Southern Gothic.

The house at 124 witnesses the invasion of pasts upon presents, becoming the site where Sethe's horrifying act of infanticide (a personal and typically gothic family-centred crime), in combination with the greater, more national crime that motivated it—namely, that of a nation's white forefathers who sanctioned the 'peculiar institution' and the Fugitive Slave Act of 1850—are jointly exposed, explored and symbolically laid to rest following Sethe's intensive journey into guilt, retribution, self-forgiveness and healing, alongside a community-based and sanctioned ritual exorcism of 124. A liminal, maternal space that exists on the border 'between the nastiness of life and the meanness of the dead' (4), 124 is 'peopled by the living activity of the dead' (35), an apposite locale for Beloved's haunting, a location that must be made habitable for the living.

In no other American Gothic work is the house more anthropomorphised, assuming the role of a character, as it is in *Beloved*. Sethe's surviving daughter Denver considers it 'a person rather than a structure ... [, a] person that wept, sighed, trembled and fell into fits' (35), an idea with which Morrison also opens the novel ('124 was spiteful', 3) and punctuates it throughout ('124 was loud', 199; '124 was quiet', 281). The home's emotional characteristics share fitting and noteworthy echoes with babies, an aspect in keeping with Beloved's haunting presence. Like Sutpen's plantation house, 124 is repeatedly associated with women, a maternal force in all of its complexity and extremes: a force that can protect and sustain, like Sethe, but also destroy. While 124 represents the company of women to Denver's two brothers who eventually flee from it (122), Stamp Paid initially hears 'a conflagration of hasty voices' around it in conjunction with something more intimate inside—the 'eternal, private conversation that takes place between women and their tasks' (203) and, later, 'the thoughts of the women of 124, unspeakable thoughts, unspoken' (235). It is also a site of death, being a locale that when originally owned by the abolitionist Bodwins saw the deaths of various women in that family (305).

In no other work of Southern Gothic is the ghost's role as a signpost of a 'something-to-be-done' (Gordon 2008: xvi) more in evidence than it is in *Beloved*. In this house where the past never seems to go away (Morrison 1987: 43) and comes to consume Sethe the way a growing, increasingly monstrous Beloved selfishly does in dehumanising her and eradicating her sense of autonomy (283), Sethe must come back from the brink of suicide and work through her crime towards redemption and liberation into life. Riffing on the Emancipation Proclamation idea that 'A house divided against itself cannot stand', the Beloved–Sethe relationship must be healed so that 124 may be radically transformed from a gothic-style space of terror (193) into one of asylum. With the intervention of the community and Sethe's act of working through 'her unspeakable thoughts' (235) and reasserting her autonomy, 124 ultimately becomes a site where women are 'free at last to be what they liked, see what they saw and say whatever was on their minds' (235). Thus, in a redemptive, traditionally gothic narrative of ghost-busting does Toni Morrison create a singular revision of the haunted house tradition in the American Gothic.

DREAM BOY

Set against the backdrop of a spectralised plantation landscape and extending Poe's motifs of incest and the anthropomorphised mansion, Jim Grimsley's *Dream Boy* (1995) queers the Southern Gothic haunted house motif to deliberate and incisive socio-political ends. In poignant and disturbing ways, this powerful coming-of-age love story chronicles a 15-year-old's simultaneous awakening into gay identity and homophobic society. A complex mix of dread and desire is mapped onto a haunted Southern Gothic landscape as Nathan's loving experiences with the older Roy follow after Nathan's horrifying, ongoing sexual abuse by his alcoholic father, both sets of experiences exacting a strict code of secrecy. The novel's dreadful climax chronicles Nathan's fatal sexual assault and gay-bashing in a haunted plantation house, a gut-wrenching scene whose location and spectral atmospherics align with Grimsley's politically strategic racialisation of queerness that aligns racial and queer marginalisation and difference (106). Thus does this gripping narrative, in adherence to the political meaning of the ghost story, register abusive systems of power across a historical divide (Gordon 2008: xvi), granting visibility and voice to the socially excluded and invisible (2008: 15).

Dream Boy is a standout novel for its gothic atmospherics that convey the complexity of Nathan's psychic experiences against a suitably multi-layered locale; namely, the historical plantation landscape with its sedimented meaning and memories. The traditionally gothic convergence of dread and desire arising from Nathan's divergent sexual experiences—'what pleases him with Roy terrifies him with his father' (101)—is adeptly mapped onto the surrounding Southern Gothic landscape. Nathan's bedroom—a reminder of his sexual abuse—becomes a zone of terror, 'a haunted place' (104) that he initially booby-traps to safeguard himself from his rapist father (83), before eventually escaping into the nearby forest and cemetery. Thus is the traditional American Gothic locale of the forest radically altered (80–81), becoming associated with natural desire, healthy sexual exploration and safety, this last idea being Nathan's obsessive concern.

Grimsley charts the psychic Jekyll–Hyde division that men suffer within a homophobic society that enforces unnatural sexual repression: Nathan's once younger, loving father is perversely transformed into '[t]hat other Dad', an older, morally corrupt father whose body is marked by literal corruption, 'the smell of rot' (46); and Nathan's young lover Roy often becomes 'the wrong Roy' (49), who is torn between conforming to the values and demands of hetero-normative society and his homosexual desires. The impact on Nathan of this psychic fragmentation is magnified in Grimsley's pointed racialisation of queerness. As Grimsley's allusion to Ralph Ellison renders clear, Nathan becomes 'invisible during the day' (32), sitting at lunchtime away 'from Roy and his friends, at a table by the southern wall of windows, among the black kids' (32), and being 'alone in the back of the bus' on the way home from school (33).

Nathan becomes increasingly marginalised and ghostly as the narrative progresses, assuming a tragic spectrality and silence as both sexual victim and agent. As he assures Roy about their relationship, he 'can keep quiet about anything' (61). Nathan's comfort and safety outdoors among the buried dead, a position that effectively blurs the boundary between the living and the dead, serve as a social commentary that he would be better off dead, safer given the hostile homophobia of his society. This suggestion is magnified during his ominous inland forest journey with Roy and the other boys towards the ruined Kennicutt plantation when, as Nathan considers that one day the forest will reclaim everything (138), Roy recounts his ominous ghost stories. Alongside the eerie tale about the plantation master murdered and decapitated by his own slaves (136), a tale with direct echoes to 'No Haid Pawn', Roy relates that of a man murdered and lynched—castrated and left hanging upside down from a tree (115)—that evokes both racist and homophobic hate crimes. Considering that he had 'spent so much time ... among the dead Kennicutts, he feels almost at home ... among their chattel' (139), he eagerly enters the beckoning mansion (141) with its awaiting slave-ghosts, their eyes at every window (140), that breathes, waits for and touches him (142), ultimately becoming for the brutally sodomised and murdered boy a 'quiet shroud' (147).

In the disturbing penultimate scene of Nathan's sexual assault and murder, identities blur, the monstrous 'man-thing [that] molests him' (167–8) incorporating aspects of 'the shadow of Dad' (111), the repressed homosexual bully Burke who sexually assaults and kills him, and Roy. Rendered as an entry into a ghostly realm with other brothers in sorrow, the murdered Nathan is figured as a sacrificial Christ figure, an association that speaks back to the novel's numerous biblical passages cited by his father and satisfying Flannery O'Connor's claim that a distorted image of Christ is popular in Southern literature and 'better than no image at all' (1988: 859). Nathan's earlier comfort among the dead anticipates his brutal murder and in-between status at novel's end when he crosses into ghostliness, anticipating an afterlife reunion with Roy, this alongside a wish-fulfilment scene where a living Nathan and Roy, like fugitive slaves, plan their escape from the region.

Although, as Leslie Fiedler notes, 'the generation of [Thomas] Jefferson was pledged to be done with ghosts and shadows, committed to live a life of yea-saying in a sunlit, neo-classical world' (1966: 131), the repression of the 'sins of the fathers', in combination with an extreme denial of human nature, resulted in the proliferation of both crimes and ghosts. While the spectre of slavery, 'the American heart of darkness' (McDowell and Rampersad 1987: vii), infuses and informs most Southern Gothic haunted houses, other cultural wounds have been registered, wounds created by such traumas as the slaughter of natives, homophobic violence and child sexual abuse, that, as Jim Grimsley compellingly describes them, can never close (172).

BIBLIOGRAPHY

Bhabha, H. K. (1993 [1990]). Introduction. In H. K. Bhabha (Ed.), *Nation and narration* (pp. 1–7). London/New York: Routledge.

Castle, T. (1995) *The Female Thermometer: Eighteenth-Century Culture and the Invention of the Uncanny.* Oxford: Oxford UP.

Cowan, W. T. (2005). *The slave in the swamp: Disrupting the plantation narrative.* New York/London: Routledge.

Curtis, B. (2008). *Dark places: The haunted house in film*. London: Reaktion Books.

Faulkner, W. (1964 [1936]). *Absalom, Absalom!* New York: Random House.

Fiedler, L. A. (1966 [1960]) *Love and death in the American novel*. New York: Dell.

Fritzsche, P. (2001). Specters of history: On nostalgia, exile, and modernity. *The American Historical Review, 106*, 1587–1618.

Goddu, T. A. (2007). American gothic. In C. Spooner & E. McEvoy (Eds.), *The Routledge companion to gothic* (pp. 63–72). London/New York: Routledge.

Gordon, A. (2008). *Ghostly matters: Haunting and the sociological imagination*. Minneapolis: University of Minnesota Press.

Grimsley, J. (1995). *Dream boy*. New York: Scribner.

Harper, F. E. W. (1987 [1892]). *Iola Leroy, or shadows uplifted*. Boston: Beacon Press.

Harrison, R. P. (2004). *The dominion of the dead*. Chicago/London: The University of Chicago Press.

Hawthorne, N. (1998 [1851]). *The house of the seven gables*. Oxford: Oxford University Press.

Hurley, J. (2012). Ghostwritten: Kinship and history in *Absalom, Absalom! The Faulkner Journal, 26*(2), 61–79.

Lynch, D. (2007). Matters of memory: Response. *Victorian Studies, 49*, 128–140.

Martin, C. D. (2002). Ghost stories. In J. M. Flora et al. (Eds.), *The companion to southern literature: Themes, genres, places, people, movements, and motifs* (pp. 304–306). Baton Rouge: Louisiana State University Press.

McDowell, D. E., & Rampersad, A. (1987). Introduction. In D. E. McDowell & A. Rampersad (Eds.), *Slavery and the literary imagination* (pp. vii–xiii). Baltimore/London: The Johns Hopkins University Press.

Morrison, T. (1987). *Beloved*. New York: Knopf.

O'Connor, F. (1988). The Catholic novelist in the Protestant south. In S. Fitzgerald (Ed.), *Flannery O'Connor: Collected works* (pp. 853–864). New York: The Library of America.

Page, T. N. (1968 [1887]). No haid pawn. In *Ole Virginia; or, Marse Chan, and other stories* (pp. 162–186). Ridgewood: Gregg Press.

Parkin-Gounelas, R. (1999). Anachrony and Anatopia: Spectres of Marx, Derrida, and gothic fiction. In P. Buse & A. Stott (Eds.), *Ghosts: Deconstruction, psychoanalysis, history* (pp. 127–143). Basingstoke: Macmillan.

Patterson, O. (1982). *Slavery and social death*. Cambridge, MA: Harvard University Press.

Peterson, C. (2007). *Kindred specters: Death, mourning, and American affinity*. Minneapolis/London: University of Minnesota Press.

Poe, E. A. (1980 [1838]). The fall of the house of Usher. In J. Symons (Ed.), *Selected tales* (pp. 62–78). Oxford: Oxford University Press.

Pratt, M. L. (1992). *Imperial eyes: Travel writing and transculturation*. London/New York: Routledge.

Rubin, D. L., Jr. (1974). The other side of slavery: Thomas Nelson page's "no haid pawn". *Studies in the Literary Imagination, 7*(1), 95–99.

Savoy, E. (1998). The face of the tenant: A theory of American gothic. In R. K. Martin & E. Savoy (Eds.), *American gothic: New interventions in a national narrative* (pp. 3–19). Iowa City: University of Iowa Press.

Sedgwick, E. K. (1980). *The coherence of gothic conventions*. London/New York: Routledge.

Sweeting, A. W. (1999). Anxious dwellings: The rhetoric of residential fear in American realism. In N. L. Schultz (Ed.), *Fear itself: Enemies real & imagined in American culture* (pp. 224–236). West Lafayette: Purdue University Press.

CHAPTER 6

The Globalisation of the Gothic South

Edward Sugden

When I began conceiving of this chapter, I had a certain historical narrative that I wanted to test out. Within this narrative, I envisaged that what would become known as the 'South' of the United States started off as a series of local, essentially self-sustaining economies set against the backdrop of early colonialism. At this time, I expected that the cultures of the South would be regional and would exist on a small scale, to the extent that they were basically self-regulating and divorced from wider national and international cultural currents. At some point during the Revolutionary era, I had thought that these economies would grow outwards and become wedded to supralocal categories, such as the nation, race and, most importantly, the 'South', as a geographical form of identity in and of itself.

This shift, in turn, would have laid the groundwork for the sectional dramas of the antebellum era, an epoch in which to be Southern became a meaningful category of political, economic and cultural differentiation within the burgeoning United States. Then, as time went on, my sense was that this predominantly national South would link up to an international globalised marketplace that would encourage cultural and economic interchange. Within this global marketplace I had expected that the literature of the South would increasingly bear the impress of alternately intrusive and productive transnational exchanges, becoming, as each year went by, a more and more global form. After all, this is the historical narrative put forward by numerous theorists of the growth, calcification and dominance of global capitalism. For these theorists, globalisation involved a process of scale expansion ('disembedding' in Anthony Giddens's terms or in David Harvey's 'time–space compression') where locality became gradually subsumed in a wider world system, governed by the flows of goods and virtual capital (Giddens 1990; Harvey 1989; Sellers 1991).

E. Sugden (✉)
King's College London, London, UK

© The Editor(s) (if applicable) and The Author(s) 2016
S.C. Street, C.L. Crow (eds.), *The Palgrave Handbook of the Southern Gothic*,
DOI 10.1057/978-1-137-47774-3_6

69

Within this historical frame, I had thought that the Gothic South, as a recognisable, even if retroactively identified, generic mode, would emerge roughly at the point of transition from the local to the national. In this schema, the Gothic would have established a supralocal tradition for the South as a region within the United States and, because of this, a way of differentiating its literature and culture from the poetry, prose and discourse of the east coast to which it was now in cultural as well as political opposition (Greeson 2010). It would have simultaneously functioned as a vehicle for dealing with some of the traumas of this same economic and geographical transition.

The Gothic as a broad aesthetic had, in Britain at least, emerged in a similar way. Early Romantic writers, architects and painters sought to unite around a medievalist, Saxon-based national etiology to offset the twin threats of the failure of Enlightenment reason and burgeoning and untrammelled industrialisation that threated to rive the previously bucolic pastoral zones of the British countryside. There was, I felt, a broad parallelism that might be applied here given the more specific issues afflicting the South in the early to mid-nineteenth century. In the same way that the crises of the eighteenth century had created a demand for a racially distinct British genealogy, of which the Gothic was the chief aesthetic avatar, so too might the Southern Gothic have acted as a means of securing a sectional identity for the South against the dramas of slavery and Northern modernisation in the nineteenth. As James Cobb has suggested, Southern identity, as such, did not really exist until this point, as the political and economic splits began to mark it out as somehow distinct. He writes of how, at this time,

> Despite the prominent role played by southerners in rationalizing and securing American independence and in drafting the defining documents and filling the highest positions of leadership in the new nation, the slaveholding South was simply too much tied to the past, too wedded to hierarchy, and too wary of innovation and reform to make it much of a competitor as a potential role model for the nation [when compared to the North]. (Cobb 2005: 20)

By implication, the South subsequently required cultural means of differentiating itself from the rest of the Americas. Having been born of this expansion in scale, the Gothic South would then become increasingly globalised as the years passed by—the 'globalisation' of the chapter title implies, after all, a narrative of gradual, developmental-scale expansion.

However, what I actually found was the inverse. In this chapter I am going to argue that in fact the experience of globalisation in the South involved a radical *scale reduction*, with the global collapsing into the national South rather than the local growing into the global. I will make the case that the region now known as the South was, to paraphrase David Igler (2013) on the Pacific Ocean, international before it was national. That is to say that prior to the political sectionalism of the early to mid-nineteenth century, the South was, in fact, a substantially international and culturally plural entity. The debates over slavery worked to close down this international realm and replace it with a monolithically national, racially limited Southern identity aimed at facilitating the continuation of a part-feudal, part-capitalist economy (Jackson 2014). The Southern Gothic as a mode, alongside other avatars of Southern literature that gained prominence at this time, emerged at the point of this collapse from the international to the national. As such, the Southern Gothic had the impress of two competing impulses that were at cross purposes. On the one hand, it bore witness to a moment in time in which the demands made on literature of the South were increasingly about cultural and regional differentiation and distinction. However, more interestingly, the Gothic South also worked to archive an international world that was still visible, but increasingly disappearing against the demand that Southern literature should be, well, 'Southern'.

Throughout the long history of the Gothic South, we therefore discover a number of emblematic forms in which this previously global world creeps into the genre, which testify to a spatial realm that was once significantly different. Indeed, if we accept the notion that the Gothic, in various ways, tends to manifest the 'return of the repressed', whether in a psychological or historical sense, we might see this international world as the element that perpetually seeks to enter into and overthrow the everyday into radical new formations. Doing so at the very least rephrases the sectional lexicon of the Gothic South (race, slavery, incest, aristocracy) and might allow us to add some more to it (colonialism, globe, hybridity, commodity, contagion, immigrant). More radically, the avatars of the global that I have identified might in fact allow us to challenge the notion that the Southern Gothic was about repression as such, as so many of them are so evidently visible, awaiting, as it were, re-activation by a reading public aware enough to notice them (see Best and Marcus 2009). Indeed, when discussing the continuation of the global within the Gothic South, I will make the case that a process of cultural *compression* that evolved in conjunction with *repression* more accurately describes the reality of what went on.

With this argument in mind, my understanding of the Gothic South as a generic form is as one that carries with it the moment of its inception in the antebellum period in a 'residual' form throughout the rest of its development in historical time (Baucom 2001). I use 'residual' here in the way that Raymond Williams uses it in *Marxism and Literature*, which is to identify, in a culture, genre, aesthetic or whatever, that which 'has been effectively formed in the past' but 'is still active in the cultural process, not only and often not at all as an element of the past, but as an effective element of the present' (Williams 1977: 122). In this sense, I understand the Gothic South as a global rather than a regional genre, with the signifier 'South' indicating less a zoned, bordered formation than a permeable edge that allows for the access of often invisible, haunting transnational forces that recur throughout time and were compressed at its originary moment (see Dimock 2006). As such, it is a form that is anti-progressivist, alinear and anti-developmental, insofar as this global movement is transported by the genre through time, maintaining structural similarities and coherences within the form in spite of the ostensible reality of historical change. This is not to say that the genre remains static, as this international pre-history of the Gothic South instantiates temporalities that dynamically cut across, open up and collapse the form in certain ways and at certain points in time. To use Lloyd Pratt's terms about genre, the Gothic South is a 'complex archival' (Pratt 2010: 14) form that contains 'unequal but coeval orders of time' (16) that disallow the formulation of coherent identities. Yet while Pratt argues that a 'deep locality' pervades Southern literature as a result, what I want to suggest is that something like a 'deep worldliness' inflects the Southern Gothic at all times and, indeed, in all places.

The question becomes what forms this deep worldliness takes and the effects it has. In the rest of this chapter, I explore what I take to be the central structural dynamic of Southern Gothic space. My intention is not to provide a restrictive rubric here, but rather to contribute certain speculative axioms that might be built on by other scholars. I am keen that this chapter be seen as a way of opening up the Southern Gothic rather than closing it down. I express these motifs in seed form so that they act as a spur to further thought.

THE GLOBAL SOUTH

As a number of critics have made clear, nineteenth-century America is best thought of in terms of radical and jarring spatial disequilibrium (Giles 2011; Hsu 2010; Kaplan 2005): the local, the national and the global, as well as a number of smaller spatial scales interlaced in this period without any taking a dominant form. Yet, even keeping in mind this spatially uneven, transnationally disparate nineteenth-century America, the situation of the South appears particularly notable. A growing number of historians have recently deployed world systems theory to plot the development of the southern half of the North American continent from the moment of its first appropriation right through to the present day. For these historians, the notion of reading the South as somehow independent of the colonial oceanic world, with its mixing of Spanish, French, Caribbean, African, British and US Anglophone culture that preceded it and continued to shape it, is absurd. Instead, they demonstrate in a number of different ways how the South was perpetually crosscut with global flows that shaped its economic, political, social and cultural life.

In part, this interchange arose out of a constitutional preference for colonial European culture, which had occupied, and continued to occupy, Southern space. This preference took myriad forms, from the social, for instance the South's aristocratic pseudo-feudal means of organisation, through to the aesthetic. Such networks of cultural and social kinship were multi-directional and invoked relationships with any number of international cultures. In particular, these cultural networks have helped historians and critics recast the terms of sectional debate in the era, moving it beyond a predominantly North versus South national paradigm to a more international and chaotic international world. This world involved political and cultural exchanges with Britain, the

Caribbean and the Mediterranean (Hanlon 2013). As Matthew Pratt Guterl puts it,

> 'U.S.-centered' dialogue about the coming war between 'the North' and 'the South' was originally staged as a pan-American production, with rich and meaningful backdrops, global plotlines, and multiple angles of spectatorship. It took place, in short, in the American Mediterranean—the extraordinary network of rivers, seas, and waterways that served as the lifeblood of the New World, where longstanding currents and flows shaped the deeper history of slavery and freedom. (Guterl 2008: 11)

As such, then, on the level of geography we can see the 'South' as a network of colonial inheritances as well as continuing transnational overlaps.

Such overlaps were, however, not merely conceptual. Instead, they also involved the very material history of exchanges of goods and capital. At the forefront of such exchanges was cotton, a commodity that, in the wake of the invention of the Cotton Gin in 1793, revolutionised the Southern economy. Cotton farmed in the South would be picked by slaves often transported from Africa or with deep links to the West African coast. This cotton in turn would head to the port cities of the United States, from where it would be shipped over to Europe. In order to ship the cotton and to minimise risk, a complex chain of credit and insurance transformed the cotton, the land from which it came and the slaves who picked it into virtual speculative capital. The circulation of this capital would, in the end, prove perilous to investors, with a loss of confidence, financial incompetence and political scaremongering resulting in the collapse of the market in 1837. On arriving in Great Britain the cotton would then be processed in the mill towns of the north of England before, once more, being set loose on the tides of international commerce for distribution around the world. So worked what Sven Beckert has recently termed the 'empire of cotton', the dynamic, brutal catalyst through which the Western world secured imperial power on a global scale (Beckert 2014; Baptist 2013; Riello 2013).

The culture of the South is best understood in these hybrid terms, then. This was not simply a white culture, nor was it one whose cultural, political and economic life could be reduced to the more simplistic homogenising demands of nationhood. Indeed, the pre-antebellum South was a space in which various forces of international and colonial culture were foregrounded at the expense of national belonging. During this era, we can see the demonstrable influence of African, Native American, French, Spanish, Caribbean and British culture on the life of the region, an influence that often superseded the narrow demands of life in the North American continent as such. These influences took a number of forms: from religious practice, both Catholic and in the plantation fields, through to social conventions, from the dance floors of the quadroon balls to the violent gentility of the duel, right into other modes like architecture, aesthetic sensibility, song, cooking and much more besides. A historical writer like George Washington Cable is notable for having archived this world after the flood, as it were, attesting to a pre-'American' New Orleans in which the traces of a previously multiform culture are sacrificed on the altar of a new, visible and powerful national, or if not national then sectional, culture. As we will see, he was not alone in so doing.

THE COMPRESSION OF THE GLOBAL

What I hope that this necessarily very brief overview demonstrates is the existence of a very global South, formed from a mixture of the colonial, the conceptual and the material, that was extant until the early decades of the nineteenth century. This was a politically and culturally diverse world whose transnationalism created an often unrecorded international culture too, which fused Spanish, French, British and West African traditions in a melting pot of different customs. Within this frame, the 'South' as such did not exist as a bounded entity, but rather was a substantially more polymorphous geographical entity, placed, if anywhere, in relation to the multi-directional flows that surrounded this international periphery on the very edges of the colonial world system. However, as James C. Cobb and Jennifer Greeson have argued, the sectional tensions of the antebellum period, roughly from 1831 onwards with the founding of *The Abolitionist*, created the 'South' as an explicitly national entity that operated in opposition to the eastern seaboard (Cobb 2005; Greeson 2010)—or, at the very least, turned certain elements of culture in this direction. This change was characterised by a process of *repression*, insofar as a previously racially mixed heritage was directed towards the ethnic signifier of whiteness, and *compression*, as the diverse cultures in the regions beneath the Mason–Dixon line had to embody a nationally limited form of 'Southernness'. There was a collapse in space, whereby the energies of a previously spatially diverse and expansive realm were redirected towards a national space into which it could not fit. As one might expect, given the power of this structural re-organisation, this shift generated similar mutations within the cultural life of this newly national South. We see with it the first explicitly regional Southern genres emerging from this context: namely, the plantation novel, the slave narrative, the Southwestern local humour story and the Gothic South itself.

The literature of the Gothic South, from the moment of its inception and through the almost two centuries that have followed, bears the impress of this sudden process of scale reduction. It does so in particular through the representation of domestic spaces in some of its most enduring fictions. These spaces similarly compress and repress Global Southern histories, cultures and places, condensing them down into fictional realms that barely can contain them, while also seeking to occlude or hide them from view. Such a brimming spatial multitudinousness comes to define the representation of place in these fictions, as a variety of authors reflect that there simply seems to be too much space to be adequately housed within their fictional zones. Moreover, such an excessiveness will also mark the often enervated, excessive behaviour of the characters as they, as it were, come apart at the seams, pressurised by warping and conflicting cultures that run within them. Such a set-up is not sustainable, however. These mutually compressed and repressed spaces are unstable and, almost always, cataclysmically collapse, as the suppressed deep worldliness of the South explodes outwards in a catastrophic explosion of global energy. Yet the result of this explosion is an ironic one: in exploding outwards, these energies ultimately obliterate the last traces of their being, creating precisely the sort of historical and spatial carte blanche for the South to which they ostensibly were resistant and in opposition.

In what follows I concentrate on how this dynamic shapes 'The Fall of the House of Usher' by Edgar Allan Poe. This short story established a structural pattern that other authors, in the years that followed, repeated and added to. As such, in my conclusion I will suggest other authors and fictions that might be read in a similar way, as well as potential other directions this argument could take. In combining this precise reading of Poe alongside a more general cultural structure, I hope to provide more exact iterations of this structural dynamic, as well as to see how the trace of the Global South lasts, pervading the Gothic for almost two centuries after its initial inception. Ultimately, in making this argument, I am suggesting that we can see the process of scale reduction as holding something like the structural key, or occluded core, to the fictions produced within what we know as the Gothic South.

Now I want to turn to what is perhaps the originating document of the Gothic imagination in the South, Edgar Allan Poe's 'The Fall of the House of Usher', to show how these processes play out on the local scale of a single text. I will be concentrating on fleshing out the three central historical processes in the cultural logic that I have outlined above, which I see happening in relationship to the Global South, and how they manifest themselves in the text: spatial compression of the global; explosive re-emergence of the global; and final erasure of the global.

By 'compression', I mean a process whereby an excess of space is squeezed into a zone in which it does not fit. What once was substantially unbounded becomes concentrated and, through being concentrated, destabilised within a significantly smaller space. Reading Poe's story with this definition in mind, we can see that this is the prevailing logic, one that shapes his representation of architecture, his presentation of objects and his conceptualisation of character. What continues to bewilder the narrator as he anatomises the architecture, objects and denizens of the house is that there simply appears to be *too much* space to be adequately contained within its frame. Perhaps the chief avatar of this spatial excessiveness is the vapour that pervades the outside of the house, that spectral but ideal self-image of the house that strives to reach beyond its current boundaries. Yet such a logic pervades the entirety of the tale in a formal as well as conceptual sense: think, for instance, of the long hyphenated sentences that start the story, which syntactically enact a similar logic as the narrator seeks to compress his contrasting impressions of the house into a single continuous sentence; or, perhaps, of the numerous reduplicating scattered objects that lie around the house without order, packed into the dark crevices of the rooms.

The logic of the tale then operates according to a paradox: that which is spatially excessive can only be identified as such through its compression. That is to say that the evidence of there being *too much* of something is only visible through a reduction in its scale, of it becoming, temporarily at least, *too little*. Throughout the story, then, Poe sets up a series of counterpoised images that operate according to the logic of simultaneous scale reduction and strange implied expansion: Usher's repressed 'reserve', for instance, 'had always been excessive' (Poe 1984: 318); his family's charity was 'munificent', yet in spite of this largesse 'unobtrusive' (318); Usher possesses a 'breadth of nostril unusual in similar formations' and has 'inordinate expansions of the regions above the temple' (321). To state my point again: What these examples demonstrate is that there is a logic running through the tale of something larger being pushed into a repressed physical zone that it ought to exceed.

The narrator assigns to this process some explicitly global coordinates. As he observes the house, he suggests that it contains a series of diffuse world cultures that bring an aesthetic incoherence to the internal realm of the mansion. The house has an excess of aesthetic signifiers: it is linked to the gothic, the grotesque, the romantic, the sentimental, the scientific, the biblical and probably much more besides. Strewn about the house are numerous avatars of a world aesthetic sensibility that contributes to this mixing of styles: from the paintings of Fuseli to the music of Von Weber to its gothic arches. Yet perhaps the foremost avatar of this global compression is in Usher's library, where the multi-generic texts come together in the compressed form of the list. This list contains books taken from African, Italian, German, British and French traditions and, seemingly, encompasses genres that include travel narrative, science, romance, philosophy, politics and speculative fiction:

> We pored together over such works as the Ververt et Chartreuse of Gresset; the Belphegor of Machiavelli; the Heaven and Hell of Swedenborg; the Subterranean Voyage of Nicholas Klimm by Holberg; the Chiromancy of Robert Flud, of Jean D'Indaginé, and of De la Chambre; the Journey into the Blue Distance of Tieck; and the City of the Sun of Campanella. One favorite volume was a small octavo edition of the *Directorium Inquisitorium*, by the Dominican Eymeric de Gironne; and there were passages in Pomponius Mela, about the old African Satyrs and Œgipans, over which Usher would sit
> dreaming for hours. His chief delight, however, was found in the perusal of an exceedingly rare and curious book in quarto Gothic—the manual of a forgotten church—the *Vigilia Mortuorum secundum Chorum Ecclesiae Maguntinae.* (328)

A variety of international cultures, then, become compressed into a comparatively tight space of both the house and the story itself, with the list format pushing these disparate traditions into a homogenous slab on the page. As such, the list attests to the more general aesthetic tendency within the house that the narrator identifies, which is to keep a certain formal and tonal multitudinousness within 'narrow limits' (325). This aesthetic tendency, of course, participates in the wider racial field of the tale, in which Usher and his family attempt to keep their own bloodline pure, isolated and contained within the space of the house, leading to what the narrator terms a 'deficiency of collateral issue' (319).

What I want to draw attention to is the historical locatedness of this spatial pattern. I have suggested that the spatial imagination of this tale conceptualises a radical reduction in world scale at a point in time in which the denizens of the house obsess about the purity of their identity. When phrased this way, it should be evident that the story shares the logic of the moment at which it was written. In the same way that the sectional dramas of the South in the antebellum period were predicated on the notion of a homogenous white local identity that suppressed a previously rich worldliness, so too in this tale do we see a spatial logic whereby an internationalism becomes compressed, erased and rendered homogenous. Usher, after all, is one who acts with 'the constrained effort of the *ennuyé* man of the world' (321). The tale, in this sense, bears witness to the structural changes in the spatial composition of the South in this era, where the energies of sectional debate worked to render invisible a once global world. To talk of the 'globalisation' of the Gothic South, then, one first of all has to grapple with the paradox that this involved an initial reduction of global scale at a point in time at which one might expect the world to have been becoming increasingly interconnected. My sense is that the first thing critics must do in identifying the global Gothic South is, thus, to identify those points of tension in which various avatars of the world culture of the early South are repressed. The second thing, as we shall see, is to note how those energies explode outwards again.

For these global nodes are always on the point of a cataclysmic explosion outwards again. Their compression renders them increasingly unstable: like chemical molecules, increased concentration makes them more active and unpredictable. As such, the strictures placed on them buckle under the pressure of the excess space that they can no longer contain. Turning our attention back to 'The Fall of the House of Usher', we can see how this process works. For this is not only a tale that is full of artificially compressed spaces, but also one that dramatises their bursting open. Its central dynamic records how excess, compressed space explodes outwards again. Think here of the most celebrated episodes in the story: the final destruction of the house and Madeline breaking from her coffin. We could add to these a series of smaller compressions and explosions: Roderick's nervous condition, Madeline's initial entrance, the letter sent by Roderick, the sounds of the guitar, the sentience of the stones, for instance. Such forces ultimately take the form of the whirlwind, which, in its chaotic spatial multi-directionality, throwing things 'from all points against each other' (331), alludes to a South that was once similarly multitudinous and geographically indistinct.

This is an abstract argument, admittedly, but then again, Poe was an abstract thinker; indeed, we can see almost the identical logic in his late masterpiece

of philosophical thought *Eureka*. Nonetheless, there is a compelling historically embedded transformation to which the tale bears witness in all its strange
spatial abstraction. This story tells us, by implication, of the vast restructuring
of Southern space that took place in the antebellum era, where diffuse global
histories had to answer to a single 'Southern' identity and where the geography
of the region became re-oriented around a national axis. Reading the tale in
this way can, in addition, substantially alter our understanding of its central episode, the falling of the house. In the past, it might have been tempting to read
the zigzag down its middle as representing, in advance of the fact as it were,
the fissure that would sunder the nation in two during the Civil War, making it
a 'house divided'. My reading, however, does something different. The falling
of the house is not a division as such, but rather the expansion outwards of a
compressed excess of global force.

The irony is, of course, that this explosion takes everything with it. Rather
than the explosion leading to a new plural space, there is, in fact, nothing
left. The disappearance of the house destroys the landscape absolutely, erases
all trace of its presence, creating a historical carte blanche that is every bit
as totalising as the Ushers' desire to siphon off their family from the rest of
the world. Nonetheless, the spatial logic of the tale has continued, often in
a substantially more palpable and identifiable global form. To list some stories to which this dynamic of global compression and expansion applies, we
could look at George Washington Cable's 'Belles Demoiselles Plantation',
where the compressed Mississippi suddenly brims over its banks to destroy
a house and, in so doing, attests to a compressed Native American tradition;
William Faulkner's *Absalom, Absalom!*, where the house conflagrates as it cannot contain Sutpen's overbrimming Haitian genealogy; H.P. Lovecraft's *At the
Mountains of Madness*, where the buried, frozen, but visible history of a now
forgotten civilisation lies beneath the icy sheets of the Antarctic; Tennessee
Williams's *A Streetcar Named Desire*, where the small house in New Orleans
cannot fit Blanche's extravagantly francophile imaginings in the same space as
Stanley's relentless Yankee materialism; or, finally, Mark Z. Danielewski's *House
of Leaves*, where a Virginian house appears to contain one inch too much space
on its inside when measured against its outside, a fact that links to a Sudanese
event. This list exemplifies, then, not so much the 'globalisation' of the Gothic
South as the archiving of its previously international culture and how it, as a
genre, continues to bear the marks of the spatial restructurings contemporane-
ous with its emergence and codification.

In addition, my analysis invites further consideration of the specific forms
that this transnational consciousness might take: this could include exploring
the compelling presence of global commodities in tales of the Gothic South,
tracking transnational agents like contagion and immigrants, and attempting to
figure other logics by which the trace of this deep worldliness maintains itself.
Moreover, the language of 'compression' invites us to consider the extent to
which psychoanalytically inspired readings of repression hold. My sense is that

texts of the Gothic South do not work solely according to the dynamic of a suppressed Other, be it racial, sexual or whatever, but also via a logic of compression where certain forces, some global, are compressed into concentrated, only marginally visible, but structurally central forms.

BIBLIOGRAPHY

Baptist, E. E. (2013). Toxic debt, liar loans, collaterized and securitized human beings, and the panic of 1837. In M. Zakim & G. J. Kornblith (Eds.), *Capitalism takes command: The social transformation of nineteenth-century America*. Chicago: University of Chicago Press.

Baucom, I. (2001). Globalit Inc.; or the cultural logic of global literary studies. *PMLA, 116*(1), 158–172.

Beckert, S. (2014). *Empire of cotton: A global history*. New York: Knopf.

Best, S., & Marcus, S. (2009). Surface reading: An introduction. *Representations, 108*(1), 1–21.

Cobb, J. C. (2005). *Away down south: A history of southern identity*. New York: Oxford University Press.

Dimock, W. C. (2006). *Through other continents: American literature across deep time*. Princeton: Princeton University Press.

Giddens, A. (1990). *The consequences of modernity*. Cambridge: Polity Press.

Giles, P. (2011). *The global remapping of American literature*. Princeton: Princeton University Press.

Greeson, J. R. (2010). *Our south: Geographic fantasy and the rise of national literature*. Cambridge, MA: Harvard University Press.

Guterl, M. P. (2008). *American mediterranean: Southern slaveholders in the age of emancipation*. Cambridge, MA: Harvard University Press.

Hanlon, C. (2013). *America's England: Antebellum literature and Atlantic sectionalism*. New York: Oxford University Press.

Harvey, D. (1989). *The condition of postmodernity: An enquiry into the origins of cultural change*. Oxford: Blackwell.

Hsu, H. (2010). *Geography and the production of space in nineteenth-century American literature*. New York: Cambridge University Press.

Igler, D. (2013). *The great ocean: Pacific worlds from Captain Cook to the gold rush*. New York: Oxford University Press.

Jackson, H. (2014). *American blood: The ends of the family in American literature, 1850–1900*. New York: Oxford University Press.

Kaplan, A. (2005). *The anarchy of empire in the making of U.S. culture*. Cambridge, MA: Harvard University Press.

Poe, E. A. (1984). *Poetry and tales*. New York: Library of America.

Pratt, L. (2010). *Archives of American time: Literature and modernity in the nineteenth century*. Philadelphia: University of Pennsylvania Press.

Riello, G. (2013). *Cotton: The fabric that made the modern world*. Cambridge: Cambridge University Press.

Sellers, C. (1991). *The market revolution: Jacksonian America 1815–1846*. New York: Oxford University Press.

Williams, R. (1977). *Marxism and literature*. Oxford: Oxford University Press.

PART II

Space and Place in Southern Gothic

CHAPTER 7

Gothic Landscapes of the South

Matthew Wynn Sivils

From Henry Clay Lewis's moss-strewn bayous, to Flannery O'Connor's road-side nightmare of murder in the pines, to the pungent post-industrial psycho-sphere of HBO's *True Detective*, anyone with even a passing acquaintance with the Southern Gothic has encountered the region's potential for inspiring ever-verdant myrioramas of beauty and dread. This atmosphere is further enhanced by the common spectacle of abandoned, rusting or otherwise disintegrating shacks, trucks, tractors and other artefacts of a not-too-distant past, which, in their weed-wrapped embrace, seem emblematic of humanity's legacy in the South. These scenes render a well-known brand of Southern sublime, a lush-ness flecked with decay. Yet these landscapes are also aligned with a pervasive sense of the grotesque, swallowing, and at times spitting back, the virulence of humanity's ills. In considering a selection of influential Southern Gothic texts, this chapter examines how the region's landscapes function not only as sites on which atrocities occur, but also as cultural nexuses where the present is haunted by repressed apparitions from the past.

I begin with a brief consideration of the Southern Gothic landscape's origins in two seventeenth-century captivity narratives. I then move to an examination of how Lewis, Charles Chesnutt, Kate Chopin and other nineteenth-century writers popularized the image of the Southern landscape as an ambivalent realm haunted by the spectre of slavery. I end by considering how later authors have continued that tradition while also embedding within it a recognition that the trauma of environmental abuse creates a new form of Southern haunting, one in which the land preys on and even at times enacts vengeance against its human abusers. Throughout this chapter I use the term *landscape* in keeping with one of its most common definitions: 'A tract of land with its distinguishing char-acteristics and features, esp. considered as a product of modifying or shaping

M.W. Sivils (✉)
Iowa State University, Ames, IA, USA

© The Editor(s) (if applicable) and The Author(s) 2016
S.C. Street, C.L. Crow (eds.), *The Palgrave Handbook of the Southern Gothic*,
DOI 10.1057/978-1-137-47774-3_7

83

processes and agents (usually natural)' (*Oxford English Dictionary*). I veer slightly from this definition by placing emphasis on the idea that the Southern Gothic landscape functions as a dynamic, and even anthropomorphized, entity. I stress the idea that while it is often designated by its non-human characteristics, the concept of the landscape (literary or otherwise) cannot be understood without appreciating the fact that humanity—through our actions, our perceptions and our imaginings—shares in virtually every aspect of its being.

The Horror of the Landscape

Recently, critics such as Patricia Yaeger, Lee Rozelle, Tom Hillard and María del Pilar Blanco have variously argued that the literary landscape (often presented as an analogue for the natural world) deserves more attention as a source of, and emblem for, a wide range of horrors. Hillard contends, 'Since the Gothic inevitably finds its source in cultural contradictions where Gothic nature exists so too can be found competing perceptions of what that "nature" signifies' (694). Indeed, in so many gothic works the landscape represents more than just a setting; it is a threatening embodiment of the land itself, of that oft-abused supplier of our human needs. Such landscapes not only foster an important element of terror, but also represent a sort of warehouse of cultural and individual anxieties relating to the social issues in play. The cultural geographer Yi-Fu Tuan, in describing what he terms 'landscapes of fear' (6), writes,

> Every cultivated field is wrested out of nature, which will encroach upon the field and destroy it but for ceaseless human effort. … Of course, a landscape of farmstead and cultivated field does not directly evoke fear. … The farmstead is a haven, we say, but haven implies threat: one idea leads to the other. Consider now the hostile forces. Some of them, such as disease and drought, cannot be perceived directly with the naked eye. A landscape of disease is a landscape of disease's dire effects: deformed limbs, corpses, crowded hospitals and graveyards. (7)

Too often in the South the 'ceaseless human effort' was ceaseless dehumanized slave effort, and for European Americans there arose a fear not only of the cultivated landscape reverting to wilderness for lack of human dominance, but also of losing mastery over a wronged racial other. For slaves and the otherwise abused, the landscape—especially when allowed to fester into a plantation—transforms from a 'haven' into a 'landscape of disease', where slavery and institutionalized oppression produce a deceptively verdant scene of economic prosperity that is at the same time a playground for the grotesque.

Examining the concept of cultural haunting from a expansive, hemispheric perspective, María del Pilar Blanco argues that writers 'who share similar anxieties about a specific set of landscapes common to the experience of the Americas elucidate how we can establish readings of hemispheric similarities through the use of haunting' (7). Blanco further argues that instead of reading the invocation of haunting as indicative of 'past conundrums in search of closure', we should perceive 'these phenomena ... as experiments in a prolonged evocation of future anxieties and extended disquiet in multiple locations of the Americas' (7). The implication of this hemispheric approach to the poetics of haunting is that it encourages an appreciation for what are sometimes key differences between people of disparate cultural backgrounds in relation to an often violently contested landscape. This method also encourages the recognition of lines of influence that fall outside of traditional (and artificial) national boundaries. Following Blanco's pan-American approach allows for a longer literary historical timeline that reveals the deep origins of a Southern Gothic landscape that was, from the outset, marked by violence and racial oppression.

These origins can be traced to the various tragic narratives that emerged from the Spanish conquest of the southeastern portion of the North American continent. Accounts from New Spain far predate the conventionally agreed origin of the Gothic in Horace Walpole's 1764 novel *The Castle of Otranto*, but these ostensibly true stories convey elements that we now accept as firmly Southern Gothic. Racial violence, grotesque tortures and a pervasive fear of a vengeful Other are the hallmarks of these texts, which become even more recognizably gothic when we remember that they relate horrors that emerged from a dark mixture of religious dogma and greed. For example, Garcilaso de la Vega's 1605 *The Florida of the Inca* relates the testimony of three survivors of Hernando de Soto's failed expedition, and this history also includes a harrowing account of the trials of the conquistador Juan Ortiz, whom de Soto's men found living in a Timacua Indian village in what is now present-day Florida. Ortiz had been captured by an especially cruel Cacique and made to endure a number of torments. One of the most significant of these occurs when the Cacique orders Ortiz to guard the tribe's burial ground from desecration by animals, a common problem because of the tribe's practice of placing their dead in 'wooden chests that served as sepulchers' (65–6). Armed with four hunting darts, Ortiz stands guard, but that night he falls asleep long enough for a panther to abscond with the corpse of a recently deceased child. Fearing that the tribe members will 'burn him alive' (66), Ortiz chases the panther into the dark forest, where he manages to kill it with a lucky throw of a dart. This brief narrative contains a host of what have become Southern Gothic elements. There is the bewildered European, here Ortiz, who is 'haunted by the fear of death' (66) at the hands of a racial Other, and there is the ever-present, all-encompassing Florida landscape, in which Ortiz 'groped his way through the underbrush' to view 'in the light of the moon' the horror of a panther—an emissary of the wilderness itself—'feeding at its pleasure upon the remains of the child' (66).

The Swamp as Cultural Signifier

As the signature landscape of the Southern Gothic tradition, the swamp, or bayou, enjoys a particularly strong hold on the literary imagination. The swamp seems custom made to evoke feelings of gloom and hopelessness. As early as 1791, the naturalist William Bartram promoted the southern swamp as a realm alternately marked by dangerous alligators and sublimely clear natural springs. However, it was an even earlier text that first introduced English readers to the Southern swamp as a landscape of melded beauty and danger: Captain John Smith's account of his capture and subsequent release by the Pamunkey Indians. Published in 1624, 17 years after the presumed event, Smith's tale may owe some of its particulars to the Ortiz narrative, including the account of his life being spared thanks to the efforts of a chief's daughter (in Smith's account, the famed Pocahontas; Cabell 51–63). Smith's narrative is a compelling and at times bloody account of racial violence enacted within a Virginia marsh. He begins with an account of his party's attempt to reach the head of the Chickahominy River. Navigating the challenging landscape, the men make slow progress by felling the trees that block the passage of their barge. Determined to move forward, Smith, accompanied by two English companions and two Indian guides, attempts to push on in a canoe. His small party eventually makes it to the swamp that serves as the river's head, but matters take a violent turn when they are attacked by the Pamunkey Indians. With his men slain, an injured Smith takes refuge when he immerses himself 'up to the middle in an oozy creek' where the Indians—leery of approaching a man who had just killed three of their warriors and wounded several others—waited until Smith, 'near dead with cold', surrendered (87). Realizing that he must abandon the water to survive, Smith finally concedes defeat as much to the swamp as to the Pamunkey warriors. In Southern Gothic fashion, Smith's swamp is a landscape within which the European comes to blows with a subjugated racial Other.

Two centuries later, Louisiana writer Henry Clay Lewis penned stories that represented an evolution of the Southern Gothic landscape as a battleground of oppression, while also invoking the idea of the swamp, in particular, as a locale for a problematic form of wilderness-linked liberation. While his contemporary and fellow Southerner Edgar Allan Poe largely preferred ambiguous European scenes for his tales, Lewis embraced the swamp as a powerfully evocative setting. In analysing Lewis's portrayal of the Louisiana marshlands, Edward Watts writes, 'The bayous are neither land nor water: they are a constantly changing, darkening, and threatening bog. Moreover, these bayous had, before Lewis, never been described and explored as a literary device' (120).

A notable example is found in the story 'A Struggle for Life', in Lewis's *Odd Leaves from the Life of a Louisiana Swamp Doctor* (1850). As is the case with his other stories, Lewis's signature character—the racist swamp doctor Madison Tensas—serves as a decidedly unreliable and at times downright detestable narrator. In the story, a dwarf slave is charged with guiding Tensas through the swamp so that the doctor may tend to the slave owner's sick mother. As a form of pre-payment for leading him through the labyrinth of the swamp, Tensas gives the slave a drink of brandy, with the promise of more once they reach their destination. The drink proves too potent for the man, and soon Tensas realizes that the drunken slave has gotten them lost. With the hope of finding their way out in the morning, an irate Tensas makes camp on a ridge above the swamp water. He fashions a makeshift bed out of cane leaves and—in a gesture that demonstrates how the swamp environment reveals the humanity hidden behind his racism—makes a bed for the inebriated slave as well, loaning him the use of his saddle blanket. Thus the swamp of this story functions as an obstacle to physical movement and as a facilitator of otherwise impossible social interaction. However, any goodwill between the men ends when the inebriated slave, demanding another drink, attacks Tensas and all but murders him. Thinking Tensas dead, the slave releases the narrator, takes his bottle of brandy and then, in his drunkenness, accidentally immolates himself in the campfire. Tensas eventually rouses from his death-like state to find the dwarf slave's charred corpse (146–51). It is a decidedly grotesque and sophisticated tale, one that Lewis sets entirely within the ambiguously hostile landscape of a Louisiana swamp. His selection of setting is more than just the promotion of an aesthetic; the swamp affords these men the sustained social interaction necessary for their animosity to explode into a literal fight. Also, because Tensas is alone with the slave, their swamp campsite is one of the rare places where a slave might have a chance of gaining the upper hand on a white man. In the swamp, racial conventions so solidified elsewhere are malleable, even assailable. A wild landscape devoid of human settlement, the swamp exposes cracks in that fortified system of oppression.

For African American writers the swamp held a similar role as a threatening landscape that nevertheless offered a remote possibility of an escape—if only temporarily—from the horrors of slavery. The dense vegetation of the swamp coupled with its roadless, watery character made it easier for fugitives to disappear into its labyrinth of green and grey. Once absorbed into its damp security, slaves could better evade trackers and experience—for a fleeting, uncomfortable and still dangerous moment—liberation from that most white-controlled of agricultural landscapes, the plantation. One of the best literary examples of how the swamp functions as a temporary refuge from the horrors of slavery is found in Harriet Jacobs's autobiography, *Incidents in the Life of a Slave Girl* (1861). Unable to bear the continued abuses of her North Carolina slave master, Jacobs decides to flee. Fully aware that the Fugitive Slave Act makes any attempt to go north extremely dangerous, especially if she were to take her children, Jacobs's friends and family concoct a plan by which she will hide in an exceedingly unlikely place, the garret of a shed attached to her grandmother's house. While her uncle makes the necessary preparations to the ceiling of the tiny shed (where, remarkably, she spent much of the following 7 years of her life), other family members hide Jacobs in the nearby, and aptly named, Snaky Swamp.

Hiding in the swamp weighs heavily on Jacobs's physical and mental health, but she views it as far preferable to the alternative.

The heat of the swamp, the mosquitos, and the constant terror of snakes, had brought on a burning fever. … when they came and told me it was time to go back to that horrid swamp, I could scarcely summon courage to rise. But even those large, venomous snakes were less dreadful to my imagination than the white men in that community called civilized. (126)

Jacobs calls her hiding place in the garret of her grandmother's shed her 'loop-hole of retreat' (128), and just as this painfully small space in the ceiling of a shed allows her to evade a life of slavery, so too does the forbidding landscape of the swamp. Like the garret, the swamp—while fully inside the boundaries of the slave-holding South—exists beyond the notice of those who would re-insert her into that system. As Watts contends, the swamp is a landscape always at risk of succumbing to flood waters: the 'setting itself is thus quite subjec-tive. The prospect of the land's eminent inaccessibility creates the ambiguous potential for its disappearance or isolation from all external influences' (123). It is this inaccessibility that allows the garret and Snaky Swamp to serve as 'loopholes of retreat'. Jacobs may hide in either, as long as she can endure their inhospitable natures, and as long as she remains unnoticed by those in power.

The Southern Gothic swamp became so fully developed as a cultural signi-fier during the nineteenth century that it served as a form of shorthand for the various miseries of the Southern experience, especially slavery. Swamps figure significantly in Charles Chesnutt's so-called conjure tales, which relate the hor-rors of slavery as told in dialect by Uncle Julius, a former slave. In Chesnutt's 1887 story 'The Goophered Grapevine', Julius mentions a runaway slave who 'tuk ter de swamp' and whose Master 'en some er de yuther nabor w'ite folks had gone out wid dere guns en dere dogs fer ter he'p em hunt' for the man (38). Similar mentions of the swamp as a place of refuge occur in Chesnutt's 'The Conjurer's Revenge' and 'A Deep Sleeper'. Indeed, the swamp functions as the central landscape of Julius's tales. It is a realm of temporary relief from white domination, a place of healing through the procurement of medicinal plants, the secret meeting place of lovers and, in 'Dave's Neckliss', the loca-tion of 'de plantation buryin'-groun' (134). The swamp performs several of these functions in Chesnutt's 1888 tale 'Po' Sandy', a story in which the titular slave asks his lover, Tenie (who happens to be a conjure woman), to magically transform him into something free from the misery of slavery, while also allow-ing him to stay on the plantation with her. They decide that the best option is a tree. As Julius relates, 'Tenie tuk 'im down by der aidge er de swamp, not fur frum de quarters, en turnt 'im inter a big pine tree' (48). Tragically, while Tenie is away some men cut down Sandy's tree, and at the sawmill (which is also located near the swamp), they mill his tree-bound body into lumber. Since transforming him back into a man will mean his death, Tenie grieves for her lost Sandy, and his lumber is put into service over the years as the makings of various plantation-area buildings. While in this tale the swamp does not itself serve as a refuge, it is the location in which the tree-Sandy is rooted, where he—like the slave cabins that are also located in the bog—becomes a literal part of the bayou landscape.

The swamp features so largely in Chesnutt's tales because it is where those in power place the less-desirable members of the plantation population. Chesnutt's work demonstrates his understanding that the imagined landscapes of the South were ripe with gothic implications. Like Lewis before him, Chesnutt recognized how the Southern landscape becomes a foil for its characters at the same time as it works as an emblem for the social mire that encumbers their lives. No less than their Northern counterparts did these Southern Gothic writers understand that by chaining the trauma of oppression (racial and otherwise) to the land, that trauma becomes intimately associated with the larger national mind. Anxieties that haunt the land haunt the culture and, as the nineteenth century became the twentieth, other writers followed suit, employing the power of the Southern Gothic landscape to tell stories far exceeding their modest regional garb.

One late nineteenth-century writer in particular, Kate Chopin, utilized the Southern landscape in a way that served as a prevailing, and sometimes key, component of her tales. Like those of Chesnutt, her stories seem keenly aware of how the swamp represents an island of dreadful freedom. It becomes a place in which an oppressed figure (like Harriet Jacobs) might immerse herself in physical misery to shed momentarily an otherwise inescapable system of oppression. For instance, in Chopin's much-anthologized 1893 tale 'Désirée's Baby', Désirée—the young wife of Armand, a tyrannical plantation owner—gives birth to a child bearing the physical features of their slaves. Initially oblivious to the situation, Désirée (who is herself an orphan of uncertain parentage) finally notices the racial characteristics of her baby. She beseeches her husband: 'What does it mean?' Armand replies, 'It means ... that the child is not white, it means that you are not white' (192). Désirée's adoptive mother tells her to return home with her baby. Instead, she makes one of the more powerful exits of Southern fiction, when, still in her dressing gown and slippers, she walks out of the house with her baby in her arms and, as Chopin writes, 'disappeared among the reeds and willows that grew thick along the banks of the deep, sluggish bayou; and she did not come back again' (194). Chopin's swamp is similar to those found in earlier Southern Gothic texts; it is an unpleasant option for those who have run out of options. Unable to stay within the hellish confines of her near-demonic husband's plantation—ironically named L'Abri ('the shelter')—and unwilling to return to the plantation of her adoptive parents, she embraces an unlikely third option: the bayou at the edge of the plantation boundary, a realm of certain death for herself and her child.

Injustice and Degradation in the Southern Landscape

The work of Lewis, Chesnutt and Chopin presages William Faulkner's own Southern Gothic landscapes, but, unlike his nineteenth-century predecessors, he took as his project the creation of a massive fictive universe: Yoknapatawpha County, a place populated by a wealth of interconnected characters and events, where an epic story of community and family is interwoven into the larger tapestry of the South. Faulkner's landscapes often reveal a cyclical trauma, in which artefacts of injustice are buried, unearthed, mourned and reborn, so as to haunt humanity anew. In *The Sound and the Fury* (1929), he paints the legacy of human misery on the land when he describes the squalor in which the town's black population resides. It is a landscape that absorbs the human condition, melding it with desperate people who seem ever doomed to live in poverty and oppression. In one passage, Dilsey (the Compson family house-keeper) walks to church, and as she walks the narrator pans away to take in the passing scene: 'a broad flat dotted with small cabins whose weathered roofs were on a level with the crown of the road. They were set in small grassless plots littered with broken things, bricks, planks, crockery, things of a once utilitarian value' (291).

This landscape becomes a map of degradation. As the road nears the cabins where the blacks live, it transitions from pavement to dirt; the land drops on both sides until the shabby roofs are at the same level as the road. The people who live in these houses occupy a 'grassless' and eroding land, a scene that shares to some extent the looming demise that Edward Watts argues is char-acteristic of Henry Clay Lewis's swamps (120, 123). The scene is littered with 'broken things', and perhaps nothing is quite so broken as the impoverished blacks who must survive there. In the racist calculus of the tale, the blacks, like the bits of 'bricks, planks, crockery', were also 'of a once utilitarian value', but are useful now only to the extent that they are willing to perform undesirable tasks and reside in an equally undesirable landscape. In the second half of the passage, Faulkner invokes the idea that the blacks and their blighted landscape share an intimate link. He writes that the area's trees form part of 'the foul desiccation which surrounded the houses' and would 'feed upon the rich and unmistakable smell of negroes in which they grew' (291). In this landscape the plants metaphorically feed on the people, an inversion both uncanny and grotesque.

In *Light in August* (1932), Faulkner combines set-piece gothic landscapes with an anxiety about the ways in which environmental degradation, here defor-estation, serves as an indicator of a socially impoverished human community. At the opening of the novel he describes the aftermath of the timber industry at Doane's Mill: 'All the men in the village worked in the mill or for it. It was cut-ting pine. It had been there seven years and in seven more it would destroy all the timber within its reach' (4). The timber industry's impact remains apparent long after it has abandoned the area. It leaves behind a landscape of

> gaunt, staring, motionless wheels rising from mounds of brick rubble and ragged weeds with a quality profoundly astonishing, and gutted boilers lifting their rust-ing and unsmoking stacks with an air stubborn, baffled and bemused upon a stumppocked scene of profound and peaceful desolation, unplowed, untilled, gutting slowly into red and choked ravines beneath the long quiet rains of autumn and the galloping fury of vernal equinoxes. (4–5)

Environmental and human degradation ripples outwards from the dead mill's epicentre. It creates a disfigured landscape of stumps and rusted machinery that mirrors the village's sullied and decayed community.

Even in those other of Faulkner's novels in which we glimpse the forest before its degradation, we are nonetheless keenly aware of its impending doom. For example, in 'The Bear' section of *Go Down, Moses* (1942), Faulkner fashions something of a before-and-after image of the landscape of the Big Bottom, a lowland forest where young Ike McCaslin learns to hunt. This relatively unspoiled wilderness, owned by Major de Spain, is the home of a legendary bear, nicknamed Old Ben. The preservation of this wetland seems to hinge on the survival of the canny old bear, and—in one of the more sorrowful resolutions to any of Faulkner's stories—once Ben is finally killed, Major de Spain stops going on hunts and sells 'the timber-rights to a Memphis lumber company' (302).

The landscape does not always lose, and it is not always a beneficent or amoral entity. Take for example Flannery O'Connor's short story 'A Good Man Is Hard to Find' (1953), in which a band of escaped prisoners, led by an outlaw called 'The Misfit', come across a family whose car has run off a rural road into a wooded gulch. The Misfit chats with the distressed grandmother of the family as his henchmen lead the others beyond the 'dark edge' of the forest to be killed (128). Oddly enough, the landscape seems to react to the murders, even deriving satisfaction from the events. This subtle anthropomorphism emerges when the criminals lead Bailey, the grandmother's son, into the forest: 'There was a pistol shot from the woods, followed closely by another. Then silence. The old lady's head jerked around. She could hear the wind move through the tree tops like a long satisfied insuck of breath' (129). This response to Bailey's murder hints that the land is somehow more aligned with the outlaws than with their victims. After all, the gulch offers a convenient location for the crime, and as such facilitates the murders.

O'Connor's moral landscape might owe a debt to Zora Neale Hurston's novel *Their Eyes Were Watching God* (1937), in which (among several other events) a group of black field hands working in the Everglades refuse to heed the warning signs of an impending hurricane and suffer terribly as a result. Surveying the aftermath of the storm, the survivors '[s]aw the hand of horror on everything. Houses without roofs, and roofs without houses. Steel and stone all crushed and crumbled like wood. The mother of malice had trifled with men' (169). Hurston, inspired by the actual Florida hurricanes of 1926 and 1928, creates a moment of environmental vengeance. Much of the Everglades had suffered extreme environmental disturbance in the form of agricultural drainage. As Christopher Rieger argues,

> Anthropomorphizing the lake locates power, agency, and divinity in nature as it reclaims this constructed pastoral site. As the lake bursts free, it converts the seemingly stable wall of man-made dikes into a fluid boundary, similarly reversing distinctions between life and death and collapsing distinctions between humans and animals. (107)

The storm's power combines with humanity's short-sighted agricultural practice, turning Lake Okeechobee into what Hurston calls a 'monstropolous beast' that 'rushed on after his supposed-to-be conquerors' (161–2).

The hurricane ravages the human-altered landscape in such a way that the two become melded in catastrophe. The anthropogenic calamity of drainage and cultivation that erased the original Florida landscape is itself disastrously reshaped by an avenging hurricane. In a gesture akin to O'Connor's sinister wood, Hurston's hurricane-tossed Everglades landscape delights in breaking down dams, washing away houses and drowning those who dared to fetter its natural course.

The fear that permeates the Southern Gothic landscape stems from the South's long history of combining human oppression with environmental exploitation. The product of this melding is a particularly insidious amalgamation of cultural anxieties, one in which the landscape itself becomes a haunted house. Marie Liénard-Yeterian comments on this phenomenon in James Dickey's novel *Deliverance* (1970). She argues that the map the men examine at the beginning of the book (before setting out on their doomed canoeing trip in rural Georgia) 'looks like the architectural layout of a house' and that the wild landscape

> fascinates and terrorizes. It is unknown, threatening and threatened ... It connects to the past in its pristine aspect—to the days before human conquest and settlements. It is a place where you encounter the unexpected—where "accidents" happen. Going to the river, [is] like entering the haunted house. (252)

As the works of Ellen Glasgow, Eudora Welty, Zora Neale Hurston, William Faulkner, Harry Crews, Larry Brown, Daniel Woodrell, Karen Russell and so many more make clear, the same may be said for a multitude of other Southern Gothic landscapes.

Writing about the South's history of racial oppression, Farah Jasmine Griffin asserts that the 'Southern earth is fertilized with the blood of black people. ... On the surface it is a land of great physical beauty and charm, but beneath it lay black blood and decayed black bodies. Beneath the charm lay the horror' (16). As the history and culture of the South indicate, this racism mingles with a host of other horrors so that, ultimately, the landscapes of the South are haunted by the threat of a shallowly buried cultural contagion, one that threatens to expose humanity's monstrous legacy and to spread that legacy from the past to the present. That is the great fear of the Southern landscape: that its pestilence will not merely frighten us with horrors exhumed from days gone by, but that even buried those horrors continue to poison the land, as well as those who reside within its influence.

Bibliography

Bartram, W. (1996). *Travels and other writings*. New York: Library of America.

Blanco, M. d. P. (2012). *Ghost-watching American modernity: Haunting, landscape, and the hemispheric imagination*. New York: Fordham University Press.

Cabell, J. B. (1947). *Let me lie: Being in the main an ethnological account of the remarkable commonwealth of Virginia and the making of its history*. Charlottesville: University of Virginia Press.

Chesnutt, C. (1993a). Dave's Neckliss. In *The conjure woman and other conjure tales* (pp. 124–135). Durham: Duke University Press.

Chesnutt, C. (1993b). The Goophered grapevine. In *The conjure woman and other conjure tales* (pp. 31–43). Durham: Duke University Press.

Chesnutt, C. (1993c). Po' Sandy. In *The conjure woman and other conjure tales* (pp. 44–54). Durham: Duke University Press.

Chopin, K. (1986). Désirée's baby. In *The awakening and selected stories* (pp. 189–194). New York: Penguin.

de la Vega, G. (1951). *The Florida of the Inca* (trans and eds.: Varner, J. G. & Varner, J. J.). Austin: University of Texas Press.

Faulkner, W. (1990). *Go down, Moses*. New York: Vintage.

Griffin, F. J. (1995). *"Who set you Flowin'?": The African-American migration narrative*. New York: Oxford University Press.

Hurston, Z. N. (1998). *Their eyes were watching god*. New York: Harper Perennial.

'landscape, n.' *OED Online*. Oxford University Press. Web. 27 June 2014.

Jacobs, H. (2000). *Incidents in the life of a slave girl*. New York: Penguin.

Lewis, H. C. (2013). A struggle for life. In C. L. Crow (Ed.), *American Gothic: From Salem Witchcraft to H.P. Lovecraft* (2nd ed., pp. 146–151). Malden: Wiley-Blackwell.

Liénard-Yeterian, M. (2009). James Dickey's *deliverance*: When a southern house is flooded by a haunted river. *Gothic News, 1*, 251–262.

Rieger, C. (2009). *Clear-cutting Eden: Ecology and the pastoral in southern literature*. Tuscaloosa: University of Alabama Press.

Smith. (2012). The general history of Virginia, New England, and the summer Isles. In N. Baym & R. S. Levine (Eds.), *The Norton anthology of American literature, beginnings to 1820* (8th ed., pp. 83–92). New York: Norton.

Tuan, Y.-F. (1979). *Landscapes of fear*. New York: Pantheon.

Watts, E. (1990). In the midst of a noisome swamp: The landscape of Henry Clay Lewis. *Southern Literary Journal, 22*(2), 119–128.

Further Reading

Yaeger, P. (2002). *Dirt and desire: Reconstructing southern women's writing, 1930–1990*. University of Chicago Press. Yaeger focuses on a narrow selection of Southern texts, but her observations, especially those about the role of trauma and the grotesque in the South's racial politics, are applicable well beyond the book's stated boundaries. Also illuminating is Yaeger's recognition of how the landscape (and even the dirt itself) functions as a troubled contact zone between the races.

CHAPTER 8

Southern Hauntings: Kate Chopin's Gothic

Janet Beer and Avril Horner

There are no ghosts, zombies or vampires in Kate Chopin's fictions. There are, however, engagements with secrets, transgressions, the sinister, the abject, the repressed and the uncanny. In particular, the image of Louisiana as a region haunted by a complex colonial history and a very distinct legacy deriving from slavery informs many of her short stories. In this sense her work is eminently gothic: there are many reminders of former cruelties and ample evidence of continuing injustice. The uncanny intrudes into the everyday; the self merges with the Other; black and white converge; the natural and the supernatural blend into each other; and symbolic and literal borders are crossed. Indeed, boundaries are continually challenged in Chopin's work and are shown to be fundamentally unstable and unreliable. Given her skilful use of gothic effects to explore fears deriving from unresolved social questions concerning gender, class and 'race', it is surprising that so little has been written on Chopin as a gothic author.[1] Perhaps this is due to the subtlety with which she adapted the Gothic for her own purposes; or perhaps the labelling of her as a regional realist writer has obscured appreciation of her as a skilled practitioner of the Gothic. In this essay, we seek to rectify this oversight, arguing that Chopin's exploration of the cultural impact and legacy of slavery and colonisation defines her as a postcolonial writer who used gothic effects in order to convey how past horrors continue to have an impact on the present moment.

THE LOUISIANA SETTING

Louisiana's history is one of slavery and colonisation. Having first been settled by the French (1669–1763), colonised by the Spanish (1763–1800) and then briefly reclaimed by France (1800–03), Louisiana became, in law and in

J. Beer (✉)
University of Liverpool, Liverpool, UK

A. Horner
Kingston University, Kingston upon Thames, UK

© The Editor(s) (if applicable) and The Author(s) 2016   95
S.C. Street, C.L. Crow (eds.), *The Palgrave Handbook of the Southern Gothic*,
DOI 10.1057/978-1-137-47774-3_8

name, a part of the United States from 1803 through the Louisiana Purchase. However, during the last two decades of the nineteenth century—when most of Chopin's stories are set—it was a state in which boundaries, including those of supposed racial 'purity', were becoming impossible to preserve. Chopin raises disturbing questions about the physical and psychological segregation of the various populations of Louisiana: the Creoles, the Blacks, the 'Cadians, the Anglo-Americans and the Native Americans. Her fiction skilfully exploits the anxiety and fear that attended the maintenance of these boundaries and their possible dissolution. As a postcolonial gothic writer, in her tales Chopin gives us a history of Louisiana written 'to a logic of haunting' (Punter 2003: 193). Many critics have noted that the postcolonial and the Gothic have much in common. Gothic texts are characterised by fear, particularly concerning the dissolution of boundaries and borders; they evoke terror in the reader by exploring the horror and chaos resulting from the collapse of boundaries between life and death, the conscious and the unconscious, the past and the present. Such an agenda, as Alison Rudd has noted, has much in common with that of postcolonial works:

> gothic conventions and themes find a resonance with the preoccupations of post-colonial writing. Of these, in a long list, we might cite: the undermining of binary oppositions through an engagement with hybridity; ... the desire for the impossible recovery of lost origins; the re-inscription of hidden, or fragmented histories; the ethics of memory and forgetting; and the foregrounding of the notion that past systems of oppression continue well into the present. (Rudd 2010: 3)

These preoccupations articulate powerfully with Chopin's work, in which she portrays a society struggling to know itself in the post-Civil War world.

In the spirit of the Gothic, the past intrudes painfully on the present in the short story 'A Wizard from Gettysburg' (1891). The strange tramp with his long beard 'as white as new-ginned cotton' (Chopin 1997: 125), who turns up on the Bon-Accueil cotton plantation in Louisiana in the mid-1880s, is a veteran of the infamous three-day Battle of Gettysburg of July 1863, which saw the Unionists defeat the Confederate armies at a massive cost to human life. He may be flesh and blood, but he is also a disturbing reminder of America's recent bloody past and, despite the abolition of slavery in Louisiana in 1864, the failure to change the class and race system that is still firmly in place on the estate. Nuances of social status deriving from the French *Code Noir* (later, under Spanish rule, to become the *Código Negro*), which endowed slaves with certain rights, including the right to marry, to gather publicly and to rest on Sundays, further complicate the picture of life in Louisiana as portrayed by Chopin. The Code had also made unacceptable the torture of slaves and the separation of young children from their parents, as well as enforcing the education of slaves in the Catholic faith, thus implying that African slaves had souls, the same as white people. In this respect, Louisiana was in advance of and different from other Southern states, although true individual liberty remained a far-off dream.

The tension between the aspiration of the post-war American world to realise the dream of freedom in the complex social reality of Louisiana two decades later is metaphorically present in the topography of 'A Wizard from Gettysburg'. The estate, named 'Bon-Accueil'—meaning 'warm welcome'—is a territory apportioned by boundaries and hedges and is not open or welcoming to everyone. In a sudden reversal of the class hierarchy that the reader expects, the black housemaid berates 14-year-old Bertrand Delmandé for bringing a white man into the house; he has to reassure Cindy that the tired and wounded tramp he has rescued is no threat to the household or its silver. A 'great tangled Cherokee hedge' (124)—the name of the rose itself a reminder of how Native American peoples were also enslaved or displaced within Louisiana—marks the boundary line of the estate. And beyond this 'dark green hedge' that 'towered like a high and solid wall' (125) is the plantation, a 'broad, open field' where Negroes are still working the cotton and the corn. The 'openness' of the landscape is an illusion. 'Liberty and the pursuit of happiness' remain unrealised for the black workers who, although technically 'free', are very much in thrall.

Appearing to the young Bertrand as some sort of strange 'wizard', the wanderer dressed in rags turns out to be the former master of the estate, long assumed dead in battle, whose driving desire is for his son to be properly educated. However, he constantly mistakes Bertrand for St. Ange, his son (and Bertrand's father), indicating that he has somehow 'lost' 20 years or more. His wife, now 65, does not recognise him until the end of the story. Wounded in the heel and tended by his grandson, who wants to be a doctor, the man's plight evokes the story of the Fisher King, set in a Waste Land, here represented by the impoverished South and the failing estate. The land and the family cannot be healed until a representative of the coming, more mannerly age, in the shape of the grandson whose values are more humane and less trammelled by the past, can intervene. His overhearing the family talk about money troubles that would result in Bertrand leaving college prompts the old man into showing the boy where to dig for the box of gold he hid before he left for battle.

The story is full of textual as well as metaphorical hauntings. The old man has an active fear of insurrection, expressed to his grandson as he digs for the treasure in the words 'Don't let the negroes see us' (128). The buried treasure is the stuff of folk tale and the presence of the old man evokes a sort of magic; Bertrand is deeply puzzled by this stranger who walks 'in cabalistic paces', pointing 'his finger like a divining-rod'. The whole episode fills him with superstitious dread—a characteristic more usually associated with the uneducated, powerless blacks: 'It was the same feeling with which he had often sat, long ago, in the weird firelight of some negro's cabin, listening to tales of witches who came in the night to work uncanny spells at their will' (129).

Like most of Chopin's stories, this tale can be interpreted in several ways. Read as realistic regional writing, it offers a perfectly adequate explanation for the old man's appearance. The 20 years were only 'lost' to the family and the plantation. We learn that the estate owner became a wanderer after the war, working in hospitals when he could, often coming close to starvation.

His mental confusion we might today diagnose as an aspect of post-traumatic stress syndrome. However, the tale also lends itself to a gothic reading. The old man is a mysterious, almost mythic figure whose presence metaphorically conveys both the wounds and the legacy not only of the American Civil War, but also of a society that has been unable to deal with the effects of change. It is no coincidence that the estate owner fought in the Battle of Gettysburg, which took place a year before slavery was banned in Louisiana, his understanding of social and, particularly, racial boundaries having been arrested at that point.

SLAVERY AND FEAR OF INSURRECTION

The legacy of slavery also haunts Chopin's first novel *At Fault* (1890), in which she makes use of the uncanny to suggest how the past contaminates the present. Although 'mighty queer tales' circulate about the ghost of the cruel slave-owner McFarlane,[2] a man who 'can't res' in his grave fur the niggas he's killed', it is what he symbolises—inequality and exploitation—rather than the supernatural that still haunts the small society living on the Cane River saw-mill estate, Place-du-Bois, owned by the benign Creole widow Thérèse Lafirme. Ostensibly a love story in which, unusually, the lovers are mature (Thérèse is 35 years old and the hero, David Hosmer, is 40), *At Fault* is also the story of how a particular social hierarchy has evolved in this part of Louisiana and of the violence that underpins it.

The arrival of David Hosmer, a man of moral integrity and unusual empathy, who comes from St. Louis to set up a saw-mill on her estate, disturbs Thérèse's world. She finds herself falling in love with him but, on learning from his sister that he is divorced, persuades him to re-marry his ex-wife Fanny, a childish and foolish woman. Thérèse is Catholic and her renunciation of her love for David is both a decision made because of her faith (itself a legacy of French rule in Louisiana) and evidence of her major flaw or 'fault'—her belief that she knows what is best for others. The result is misery for her, for David and for Fanny, who loathes 'the South' and who quickly resumes her drinking habit. The situation is resolved only by Fanny's death when the treacherous waters of the River Cane wash away the house of Marie Louise, Thérèse's old nurse, whom Fanny was visiting in order to obtain more liquor. The story ends conventionally enough, with David and Thérèse marrying, but the narrative follows an unconventional route.

As a counterpoint to the realist trajectory Chopin draws dark shadows, for the love story of *At Fault* is set against the backdrop of a society in which racial and social tensions run high. The language that characters use to describe others betrays prejudices that belong not only to the white population. Thérèse's old Creole nurse, Marie Louise, refers disdainfully to the plantation workers as '*ces néges Américains*' (807) and 'those lazy niggers' (808). Grégoire, Thérèse's passionate and hot-headed Creole nephew, habitually refers in a derogatory way to 'niggers' and casually murders Joçint, a black estate worker. Grégoire is himself later murdered in Texas when he takes umbrage at being called a 'Frenchie' by Colonel Klayton, a white American (851). Not surprisingly, those at the lowest level become defiant: the black workers on the estate harbour a simmering resentment that is expressed in various ways. At one extreme the women who do the domestic work simply become unavailable; Thérèse tries to procure servants for Melicent, David's sister, 'but without avail' (753), and Melicent herself suspects that there is a deep motive 'underlying this systematic reluctance of the negroes to give their work in exchange for the very good pay which she offered' (753). At the other extreme, Joçint—the 'ugly' son of a black father and an 'Indian' mother—represents danger rather than mere non-compliance and with his 'retreating forehead, almost meeting the ill-defined line of eyebrow that straggled above small dusky black eyes' (756), he is anger personified. He is an embodiment of both social exclusion and rejection, bringing together as he does the two populations of Louisiana enslaved by reason of their ethnicity. Seen by Hosmer as 'treacherous' (757), Joçint does indeed threaten the social order—a constant fear for the white population in Louisiana. His resentment translates into arson when he maliciously sets fire to the saw-mill on Hallowe'en, an act that tragically results in the death of his father and himself when Grégoire shoots him at the conflagration.

However, Joçint is not the only destructive, angry and rebellious character in Chopin's fiction. The Santien boys, of whom Grégoire is one, are renowned for their lawlessness; we know from the story 'A No-Account Creole' that, while Grégoire is heading for a violent death, his brother Placide also respects no boundaries and no one else's preeminence: 'he would derail what he liked and cross where he pleased' (88). Yet they have 'the best blood in the country running in [their] veins' (84)—ironically enough, in the post-war world this is as sure a determinant of their eventual failure and violent ends as if they could lay claim to nothing other than an ancestry like Joçint's. Sanctioned by class privilege and their indisputable bloodline, the Santiens have engaged in 'mutiny and revolt' (85) wherever they go; Grégoire's murder of the unarmed Joçint is calmly described as 'a deed characteristic of any one of the Santien boys' (824). They were bred for violent, divided times and their ultimately pointless lives signal that those are passing.[3]

Set in the late nineteenth century and featuring two well-educated people as its main characters, *At Fault* is, despite this, a story full of the darkness and superstitions of previous ages. Emily Toth's claim that the tale shows us a Louisiana full of 'warmth and life, spontaneity and beauty' (Toth 1991: 188) is only partly true. In fact, the climate is uncomfortably sub-tropical and the river is prone to breaking its banks, with disastrous consequences. Ominous gothic notes sound from the beginning of the tale: 'the "Cypresse Funerall" which stands in grim majesty through the dense forests of Louisiana' (745) and from which Hosmer makes his living is a tree that has long been associated with death and mourning. Melicent and Grégoire visit old McFarlane's grave in daylight rather than at night when some have seen his 'mist-like form' … stalking 'down the hill with threatening stride' and have heard the noise of his 'blood-hounds, as the invisible pack swept by in hot pursuit of the slave so long ago at rest' (772). Even David Hosmer's sister, the urban Melicent, is wary since 'everything seems to be the sign of something down here' (763), the over-interpreted landscape—both natural and supernatural—pointing to the fact that education and power have been carefully limited to only one part of the population.

Superstitions abound, and they are more evident on specific days, such as Hallowe'en; Minervy swears that once, as her husband crossed the bayou, 'the spirits jerked him off his horse and dragged him up and down in the water, till he was nearly drowned' (818). Joçint's firing of the mill takes place on Hallowe'en when those 'restless wood-dwellers, that never sleep, were sending startling gruesome calls to each other' and bats 'were flapping and whirling and darting hither and thither' and 'the murmur of the great pine trees' was 'telling their mystic secrets to the night' (819). Joçint himself is described as 'feeling a close fellowship with these spirits of night and darkness', the blackness of the night hanging about him 'like the magic mantle of story' (820), and Thérèse suffers 'demoniac' and 'grotesque' dreams that night before waking to discover the fire (821). In what is otherwise a story told realistically and enriched by detailed and accurate observation of the speech and mannerisms of different peoples, gothic effects serve to reveal the true cause of this society's sickness: the historical fact of slavery, without which the tale would merely be a love story set against a world in which industrial methods are changing both the nature of work and the social and natural landscape. Chopin is implying that not only Thérèse Lafirme but many individuals, past and present, have been and are 'at fault': the inherited dynamic of the master–slave relationship continues to infect social and industrial relationships.[4]

MISCEGENATION AND CONCEALMENT

If the divisions of slavery and fear of insurrection haunt the plots of 'The Wizard from Gettysburg' and *At Fault*, then a contingent fear, of miscegenation, informs several other stories, including 'Désirée's Baby' (1892). The tale opens ominously, with Armand Aubigny's house described in gothic terms as 'a sad looking place', the 'roof … steep and black like a cowl', surrounded by oaks that 'shadowed it like a pall' (241). As Alison Rudd, citing Herman Rapaport, has remarked, 'In Postcolonial Gothic … any location that is freighted with unjust violent acts of the past' will be 'a "bewitched spot"' (Rudd 2010: 10).

Monsieur Aubigny, descended from the French colonisers, considers himself part of the established elite of Louisiana, and French customs and the French language are maintained in his home. A volatile man, who frequently treats 'his negroes' (241) cruelly, he married Désirée, whose origins are obscure, for her beauty. However, when it becomes clear that their 3-month-old child is developing a dark skin, he rejects his wife and child. Désirée senses this rejection before it is expressed, noticing 'something in the air menacing her peace', the 'very spirit of Satan' seeming suddenly to change her husband's temper (242), and at the same time recognises that her child looks like La Blanche's child, a small 'quadroon'. Fear grips her heart: 'The blood turned like ice in her veins, and a clammy moisture gathered upon her face' (242). Her husband pronounces that she is not white because their child is not white; unable to bear such pain and shame, Désirée takes her child and disappears. The implication is that she drowns herself and her baby. A little later, burning everything associated with his child and his wife, Armand Aubigny unearths an old letter from his mother to his father, in which she has expressed thanks to God that their son will never know that he 'belongs to the race that is cursed with the brand of slavery' (245). It is thereby revealed, in the last line of the story, that it was Armand's racial inheritance and not his wife's that influenced the colour of their child's skin; in Louisianan terms the child is, indeed, a 'quadroon'. This is the final irony in a pre-Civil War tale of multiple but unamusing ironies: Armand discovers his own mixed-race ancestry in the very act of destroying everything that might contaminate his whiteness. Chopin is clear that he cannot ever deny that discovery, as she says, unequivocally, of his mother's letter: 'He read it.' In a further irony, Désirée's home with Armand, in which she finds fear and from which she is expelled, is called 'L'Abri', meaning 'shelter' or 'refuge'. As Homi K. Bhabha has noted:

> The recesses of the domestic space become sites for history's most intricate invasions. In that displacement, the borders between home and world become confused; and, uncannily, the private and the public become part of each other, forcing upon us a vision that is as divided as it is disorienting. (Bhaba 1994: 9)

'Désirée's Baby' is only a few pages long, but it vividly and economically portrays the complete destruction of the basis for Armand's superior racial and social standing. This had been proclaimed by the racial as well as social confidence to take a 'nameless' wife, the shameless frequenting of the slave woman's cabin and the assertion of his physical as well as legal power over the slaves who work on his estate. His identity crumbles in the face of the revelation of his own ancestry and, in Bhabha's terms, the blurring of his 'home' between the big house and the slave quarters, and the open defiance of the 'world' in both the enactment and the refusal of his marriage produces an effect that will result in an irreparable division of the self. Miscegenation, read through Kristeva's theory of abjection (1982: 4), generates horror because it threatens the borders of (in this case) the 'white' self; it is the ultimate disturbance of 'identity, system, order' in a society that carefully regulates its hierarchy through gradations of skin colour. Julien-Joseph Virey's *Histoire naturelle du genre humain* (1801) identified many categories between black and white, including 'mulatto', 'griffe', 'quadroon' and 'quinteroon', and these were used to enumerate class and race distinctions in nineteenth-century Louisiana (Castillo 2008: 60). In such a society, each shift in power results in a new codification: after the Louisiana Purchase, for example, many slaves and free blacks arrived from elsewhere in America, prompting a revised hierarchy in which a 'mulatto' (a person having one white and one black parent) became regarded as 'black' and in which the status of 'free blacks' was destabilised. In such an insecure social climate, identity itself becomes, in Kristeva's words, 'a strange land of borders and othernesses ceaselessly constructed and deconstructed' (Kristeva 1991: 191). It also becomes a place in which concealment and therefore exposure or revelation are added to the list of horrors. In such a society, then, where miscegenation is both a lived reality and an imagined horror, racially based cruelty reflects a paranoia about maintaining distinct boundaries between the self and the Other, onto whom is projected all that is feared and denied in the self (irrationality, lust and superstition) and so who is perceived as monstrous, strange and threatening.

The language of 'Désirée's Baby' reflects both the careful social gradations of identity (Armand thinks that he is 'white' although he is 'dark', the nurse is 'yellow', the negro workers are 'black', La Blanche's children are 'quadroons'), yet the twist in the tale undoes those very boundaries, not least the racial categorisation of La Blanche's children if Armand is their father. The deviation from the classic story of the 'Tragic Mulatta' then becomes a deviation from the narrative of entrapment that prevailed under the system of slavery. What is unspoken even at the end of the tale, because the truth is found only in the written word of a letter, is the fact of Armand's parentage, a fact that will probably not be exposed and therefore will not subvert his ownership of slaves or the basis for his rejection of Désirée and his son. The gothic horror swallows Désirée within a rewritten narrative that, like so many other narratives in the South, is a fiction preserved by the relentless ideological drive to pretend that any kind of racial purity can exist.

The short story 'La Belle Zoraïde' covers similar territory. Using a typical gothic 'framing' device, Chopin has a black maid, Manna-Loulou, tell her white mistress, Madame Delisle, a sad old tale concerning a beautiful 'mulatta', Zoraïde, who wished to marry a handsome negro slave, Mézor, who works on the estate. Not wishing to lose her maid, Zoraïde's mistress, Madame Delarivière, refuses to give permission for the marriage and organises for Mézor to be sold 'away'. Left pregnant, Zoraïde's only consolation is the thought of the child she will bear, but her mistress tells her the child is born dead. Zoraïde's decline into abject misery prompts remorse in her mistress who, 2 years later, sends for the child—but by this time Zoraïde is so demented with grief that, still clasping the bundle of rags that has become her replacement 'baby', she refuses to recognise her daughter. 'La Belle Zoraïde' painfully reveals how the desire to engineer gradations of colour according to a white aesthetic gives rise to cruelty and trauma. It also clearly enumerates the 'privileges' of the *Code Noir* to which Zoraïde might have felt entitled—the right to spend her Sundays with Mézor, to marry, to keep her child and to lay claim to her own soul—simply and starkly in order to show that Madame Delarivière has the power to strip them away. The mistress's interventions systematically destroy any claim that Zoraïde has to agency or even full humanity—an act of destruction that sends her mad. Madame Delisle, listening to Manna-Loulou's tale 20 years or so after slavery was banned in Louisiana, seems unaware that her own black maid, although she loves her mistress, has suffered a life of restriction and has also been unable to make her own choices. The reader, however, is expected to grasp the irony and to appreciate the fact that Zoraïde, like the traditional gothic heroine, is threatened with a forced marriage to an older, physically repellent man; having had both her preferred lover and her child ripped away from her, the only relief lies in madness.

The aftermath of slavery and the effects of huge personal trauma also haunt the story 'Beyond the Bayou'. The focaliser for the story is Jaqueline, a 'large, gaunt black woman, past thirty-five' (175), who is known as 'la Folle' because she refuses to step over an imaginary line near the bayou; not a slave, she has nevertheless confined herself to a small plot of land. While this appears mad and eccentric behaviour to those on the Bellissime estate, the reader is given an explanation for it: as a child she had been traumatised—'frightened literally "out of her senses"'—by seeing P'tit Maître, a Creole of French descent, 'black with powder and crimson with blood', staggering into the cabin where she lived with her mother, 'his pursuers close at his heels' (175). Much later, P'tit Maître becomes the owner of the estate and La Folle becomes devoted to his small son, whom she calls 'Chéri'. One day the boy accidentally shoots himself while out in the woods hunting squirrels and La Folle rushes to the scene. Realising that she will have to cross the bayou to reach the estate house, she is overcome with 'the morbid and insane dread she had been under since childhood' (177). Her love for the small boy is stronger than her fear, however, and she forces herself to carry Chéri across the bayou, terror manifesting itself in her bloodshot eyes and the white foam on her lips. Falling insensible on delivering the wounded child to his father, she sleeps deeply for many hours and awakes a different woman. She is now not only physically strong, but also psychologically strong, and crossing the bayou no longer holds any fear for her. Indeed, she relishes the scents and the flowers on the other side and is able to reintegrate herself into the estate owner's household. The story closes with her watching, with deep contentment, 'the sun rise upon the new, the beautiful world beyond the bayou' (180).

'Beyond the Bayou' is, then, a story in which the gothic horrors of the past and the uncanny hauntings of the present are neutralised by the power of love. The river can be crossed; spectral terrors can be exorcised. In this sense, Chopin is what Abdul JanMohamed has called a 'symbolic' postcolonial writer: refusing to accept a Manichean division of humanity into black and white, good and bad, she constantly confuses the boundaries between them and admits 'the possibility of syncretism, of a rapprochement between self and Other' (JanMohamed 1985: 73). Those who are incapable of such rapprochement and of moving forward—such as the central character of the tale, 'Ma'ame Pélagie', whose nostalgia for the old French colonial world destroys her ability to live in the present—are also victims of the colonial system even though they are white. Ma'ame Pélagie is indeed a prime example of what Homi Bhabha, drawing on the work of Franz Fanon, describes as 'the fixity and fetishism of identities within the calcification of colonial cultures' (Bhaba 1994: 9). Chopin's ability to see that the white population of Louisiana was profoundly psychologically damaged by the legacy of colonisation was unusual.

Even more unusual was her tendency to move the Gothic beyond its customary focus into a postcolonial gothic mode where the entrapments of the past are refused or—even more bewilderingly—actively embraced in order to subvert the standardised narratives of 'race' and 'rights'. To illustrate: in 'Athénaïse', the wronged husband, Cazeau, suddenly haunted by a scene from his childhood when his father retrieved a runaway slave, determines that he will never again compel his wife to return to a marriage that she so clearly finds unendurable. For refusing the narrative of ownership of another human being, he is eventually rewarded with the return of Athénaïse, willingly and in her own good time. In 'A Dresden Lady in Dixie', a post-slavery tale, old Pa-Jeff, a trusted estate worker, confesses to something that he did not do. Moved by the plight in which the young Agapie finds herself having stolen a Dresden shepherdess from the plantation house, Pa-Jeff actively fulfils the stereotype of the untrustworthy slave when he claims that he took the ornament. He thus restores to Agapie the promise of a rich and fulfilled life in which she grows up 'to deserve the confidence and favors of the family' (351). He sacrifices his hard-won reputation for 'uprightness and honesty' (345) for the sake of Agapie; he becomes, as has been discussed elsewhere,[5] an actor in a narrative that confines him within stereotype. The poignancy of the tale lies in the fact that eventually Pa-Jeff, 'confused, bewildered, believed the story himself as firmly as those who had heard him tell it over and over for so many years' (351), so strong are those social narratives of black and white.

Another story that features the willed embrace of stereotype is 'Old Aunt Peggy', in which a different kind of faithful ex-slave plays on the sentimentality of her former masters to secure a comfortable life. She reminds them, every time she 'hobbles up to the house' (193), of all the kinship networks that they have, represented in the 'picters an' de photygraphts an' de pianny', and to which of course she, as a slave, had no right. As a result, she 'invariably returns to her cabin with a generously filled apron'. Her calculation that the reminder of the past that she provides, a past in which she was the prisoner of a system in which she had no choice of lifestyle, is sufficient to secure her position in the old narrative of slaved and unslaved. She mischievously resurrects the past in order to induce guilt in the white master and mistress and establish her own innocence in order to improve her own life.

Through such devices, Chopin reveals racism to be an irrational affliction of history, founded on spectres. Nowhere is this clearer than in the comic gothic tale 'Croque-Mitaine' (meaning 'bogey-man' or 'ogre'). Frightened by his governess from Paris, who uses tales of the Croque-Mitaine to make him obey her injunction that he must not leave his bed on the night she is to go to a local ball, P'tit-Paul decides to investigate for himself. Sitting on a bench in the dark, suddenly 'the blood chilled in his veins and the hair fairly rose on his head'. What he sees is indeed a horrific, gothic sight:

> It bore the grotesque shape of a man, but its head was that of an unfamiliar beast having great horns and wild tremendous eyes. The monster wielded a pitch-fork in his misshapen hand and Paul doubted not that in a few moments he would feel its cruel prongs piercing his own body. (201)

However, the ogre, removing his mask, turns out to be only Monsieur Alcée going to the masked ball. Such mis-seeing, Chopin implies, is the same as racism, which, through fear, turns those with a different colour of skin into gothic 'Others'. Ironically, it is the educated Parisian governess who has introduced stories of ogres and bogeymen into the household; the 'darkies knew nothing of such an existence', Uncle Juba telling P'tit-Paul, 'Don't you listen tu no sich talk' (200).

Conclusion

What we have in Chopin's gothic tales, then, is a dialectic between guilt and innocence, the 'natural' and the 'supernatural', that symbolically dismantles the oppositions between slave and master, 'good' and 'evil', the empowered and the disempowered—oppositions culturally endorsed through slavery and its aftermath. However, perhaps her most subtle strategy is her use of narrators who echo the language of the privileged white Louisianan, rendering more complex the interpretation of her work as progressive and subversive. This can be attributed to her deployment of split subjectivity or, to use gothic terminology, the adoption of a narrative alter ego. As Emily Toth has pointed out, 'like Edna in *The Awakening*, Chopin seems to have lived with an "outward existence which conforms", but with an "inward life which questions"'; having been brought up in a slave-owning family, as an adult she enjoyed meeting 'whites and blacks and Indians and people of mysterious mixed ancestry' (Toth 2008: 15, 19). It is not surprising, then, that while the language of Chopin's narrators works with the grain of Louisianan society in accepting conventional racial classifications of skin colour and identity, the stories themselves deconstruct and dissolve them, and indeed go further, showing that they imprison and destroy white as well as black characters, the Santiens and Armand Aubigny being among the most obvious. This nuanced treatment of race and class is a deliberate and subtle tactic that, through the use of a seemingly conventional narrator with conventional values, enables Chopin to hold her readers while the story itself simultaneously challenges such values. This 'split' writing self thus both textually reproduces the schisms between self and Other, yet also, through the plot itself, admits the possibility of syncretism.

Chopin's use of gothic effects in her tales not only works to offset the humour and realism of her writing, it also reminds the reader that the social and racial categories of nineteenth-century Louisiana were not absolutes, although they might have seemed so to many of her contemporary readers. Rather, they were, and continue to be, spectral boundaries redolent of past powers, ghostly echoes of colonial values and of racial segregations that can be challenged and that might, in time, be dissolved. Chopin's postcolonial gothic tales are, above all, part of a dialectical engagement in the process of enlightenment and rapprochement.

NOTES

1. Exceptions include Charles Crow who, in *American Gothic*, describes Chopin's regional realism as nurturing a 'strain of indigenous female Gothic' (67) and 'Désirée's Baby' as 'perhaps the most complex and subtle of Creole Gothic tales' (92).
2. See Susan Castillo, '"Race" and ethnicity in Kate Chopin's fiction' pp. 62–3 in Beer (2008), for two slave owners who perhaps provided the template for Chopin's McFarlane.
3. See the discussion of the role of the Santien boys in Chopin's fiction in Beer (2008), pp. 6–7.
4. See Donna Campbell's discussion of racial politics in the context of industrialisation in *At Fault* in Beer (2008), pp. 27–43.
5. See Janet Beer, *Kate Chopin, Edith Wharton and Charlotte Perkins Gilman: Studies in Short Fiction*, pp. 33–5.

Bibliography

Beer, J. (2005). *Kate Chopin, Edith Wharton and Charlotte Perkins Gilman: Studies in short fiction* (2nd ed.). Basingstoke: Palgrave Macmillan.

Beer, J. (Ed.). (2008). *The Cambridge companion to Kate Chopin*. Cambridge: Cambridge University Press.

Bhabha, H. K. (1994). *The location of culture*. London/New York: Routledge.

Castillo, S. (2008). Race and ethnicity in Kate Chopin's fiction. In J. Beer (Ed.), *The Cambridge companion to Kate Chopin* (pp. 59–72). Cambridge: Cambridge University Press.

Chopin, K. (1997). *The complete works of Kate Chopin* (2nd ed.). Ed. P. Seyersted. Baton Rouge: Louisiana State University.

Crow, C. (2009). *American gothic*. Cardiff: University of Wales Press.

JanMohamed, A. R. (1985). The economy of Manichean Allegory: The function of racial difference in colonialist literature. *Critical Enquiry, 12*(1), 59–87.

Kristeva, J. (1982). *Powers of horror: An essay on abjection* (trans: Roudiez, L. S.). New York: Columbia University Press.

Kristeva, J. (1991). *Strangers to ourselves* (trans: Roudiez, L. S.). New York: Columbia University Press.

Punter, D. (2003). Arundhati Roy and the house of history. In A. Smith & W. Hughes (Eds.), *Empire and the gothic: The politics of genre* (pp. 192–207). Basingstoke: Palgrave Macmillan.

Rudd, A. (2010). *Postcolonial gothic fictions from the Caribbean, Canada, Australia and New Zealand*. Cardiff: University of Wales Press.

Toth, E. (1991). *Kate Chopin: A life of the author of the awakening* (2nd ed.). London/ Sydney/Auckland/Johannesburg: Century.

Toth, E. (2008). What we do and don't know about Kate Chopin's life. In J. Beer (Ed.), *The Cambridge companion to Kate Chopin*. Cambridge: Cambridge University Press.

FURTHER READING

Gelder, K. (2000). Global/postcolonial horror: Introduction. *Postcolonial Studies, 3*(1), 35–38. In this brief introduction, Gelder suggests that horror's 'central trope of circulation' in popular texts from the Asia Pacific rim (South Korea, Haiti, Japan, Hong Kong and New Zealand) enables an interrogation of the borders and boundaries of postcolonialism itself—a premise explored more fully in the essays that follow.

Goddu, T. A. (1997). *Gothic America: Narratives, history, and nation*. New York: Columbia University Press. In this influential reappraisal of the American gothic novel, Goddu argues that far from being escapist, the gothic novel has always been deeply engaged with the political and cultural concerns of its time, reflecting a horrifying social reality.

Hughes, W., & Smith, A (Eds.). (2003). *Gothic studies* (5, 2). Special issue: 'Postcolonial gothic'. The editors argue that the Gothic is and has always been *post*colonial, in that it exposes the power relationships that the fictions of politics strive to conceal, a claim explored more fully in the essays that follow.

Khair, T. (2009). *The gothic, postcolonialism and otherness: Ghosts from elsewhere*. Focusing particularly on emotion, identity and the nature of terror, Khair suggests that the colonial/racial other is negotiated through gothic tropes in the work of colonial and postcolonial writers.

Punter, D. (2000). *Postcolonial imaginings: Fictions of a new world order*. Drawing on politics and psychoanalysis, Punter argues that the postcolonial is both part of the development of national imaginings and simultaneously an alibi for the emergence of a violently assertive 'new world order', committed to the management or obliteration of difference.

CHAPTER 9

Gothic Appalachia

Sarah Robertson

The ground ripped open, graves teetering on the edge of an abyss: the stage is set for a gothic enactment. Yet such scenes are not the stuff of nightmares in a place where devastated landscapes are part of daily reality. While the scene described here is specific to the fate of the Jarrell family cemetery in Lindytown, West Virginia, it is a tale familiar to many across the Appalachian Mountains. In 2013 the Jarrell family filed a lawsuit against Alpha Natural Resources in a bid to save the top of the mountain where generations of their family members are buried (Walters). Their plight is not caused by phantom ghouls, but by the aggressive processes of mountain top removal. As William Gay's character Boyd Bloodweather contemplates at the close of *Provinces of Night* (2001), the disinterment of the dead and the destruction of the natural habitat create a 'desolate moonscape of ash' that leaves people with a profound sense of 'unease' (288). In this Appalachian gothic tale, capital is cast as villain, a role it has played with gusto since settlers first encroached on the region in the eighteenth century.

For most people, though, gothic Appalachia is defined by bogey-men: hillbillies hiding behind trees with guns and toothless smiles at the ready. The script for this play is sure to include feuds, murder and moonshine set against a backdrop of menacing mountains. This is the Appalachia of the mind: a place that draws on all of the ingrained stereotypes about the region. In his 1968 review of Cormac McCarthy's *Outer Dark*, Guy Davenport claimed: 'There is a strange awfulness about Appalachia that quickens the imagination .... The world is an allegory and no violence however sickening is ever quite unexpected in the course of a day.' Davenport falls foul of the trap that Flannery O'Connor so clearly outlined when she observed that 'anything that comes out of the South is going to be called grotesque ... unless it is grotesque, in which case it is going to be called realistic' (40).

S. Robertson (✉)
University of the West of England, Bristol, UK

© The Editor(s) (if applicable) and The Author(s) 2016
S.C. Street, C.L. Crow (eds.), *The Palgrave Handbook of the Southern Gothic*,
DOI 10.1057/978-1-137-47774-3_9

From eighteenth-century travellers into the region to the local colour writers of the nineteenth century and beyond, Appalachia continues to be viewed with both fascination and repulsion. Yet, despite the work of scholars to reposition Appalachia as a region central to the economic development of the nation, culturally it remains one of America's favourite oddities: a place believed to follow different temporal paths than the rest of the nation. To engage with Appalachia, then, is to engage with long-held ideas about the region, because as Nicholson reminds us, 'we see in Nature what we have been taught to look for, we feel what we have been prepared to feel' (Nicholson 1).

However, Appalachian writing often subverts such expectations, frequently by means of gothic conventions. Appalachian literature is not without its ruins: run-down main streets, dilapidated houses and barns tell tales of loss and changing times, but the region's gothic ruins are not merely man-made structures but also the haunting vestiges of humans' aggressive pursuit of wealth. If, as Savoy suggests, 'gothic images in America ... suggest the attraction and repulsion of a monstrous history, the desire to "know" the traumatic Real of American being and yet the flight from that unbearable and remote knowledge' (169), then Appalachia's gothicism offers crucial insights into the region's socio-economic development. Ellis reminds us that the Gothic is 'a mode for the apprehension and consumption of history', and the history that emerges is a series of counter-narratives that serve to destabilise preconceptions of the region (11). In Appalachian writing gothic manifestations frequently serve to direct our attention to the stories not told, offering a 'history of the unrealized' (Gallagher and Greenblatt 57).

SINISTER LOCAL COLOUR

If history is the departure point, then the Civil War provides as much a draw for Appalachian writers as it does writers from any other part of the South. While the Civil War divided North from South, it created internal divides in Appalachian states such as North Carolina, where neighbours found themselves on opposite sides of the conflict. The mix of Northern and Southern sympathisers in one community resulted in violence as horrific as any witnessed on major battlegrounds throughout the South. Ron Rash's *The World Made Straight* (2006) examines this history through protagonist Travis Shelton's discoveries about his family's North Carolinian history under the tutelage of ex-schoolteacher Leonard Schuler. Living in the county once known as 'Bloody Madison', all Travis knows about the war is that '"Sometimes my Daddy and uncle talked about kin that got killed in Shelton Laurel during the war, but I always figured the Yankees had done it"' (29).

The Shelton Laurel massacre is a particularly dark blight in Appalachia's Civil War story, and in Rash's novel the events of the massacre continually disrupt the present when excerpts from Leonard's great-great-grandfather, a Civil War doctor, bring the horror of war to the centre of the narrative.[1] When Leonard visits the site of the 1863 massacre, on the haunted land he 'suddenly felt lighter, less substantial, as though the meadow were absorbing his very being …. Then gravity resettled on his shoulders, replanted his feet firmly on the ground' (207). In this ethereal place the fog that sweeps over the landscape is described by 'the old people' as '*Scawmy*', weather that makes the 'dead restless' (260). These ghosts bring shameful Civil War events back to the surface of the everyday, and throughout Rash's bestselling novels he utilises heavy strains of gothicism as he writes about a land as 'sinister' as those in any 'fairy tale' (*The Cove* 35).

Sinister, foreboding, threatening, intimidating and frightening: all common characteristics of the work of Appalachian writers such as William Gay and bestselling author Sharyn McCrumb. Take popular writer Laura Benedict, whose novels build a decidedly gothic image of Appalachian life. Her fiction is rife with gothic conventions, and her 2012 novel *Devil's Oven* is an Appalachian horror that opens with Ivy Luttrell sewing together 'the beautiful man whose dismembered body she had found up on' the mountain (1). In this modern-day *Frankenstein* readers encounter an Appalachia ripe with rusting trailers, murders and mountains that give life to the dead.

Benedict's Ivy completes her Frankenstein creation, Anthony, in a desperate attempt at finding companionship that resonates as much with Cormac McCarthy as it does with Mary Shelley. The intimacy with which Ivy bathes each severed part of Anthony's body before sewing him back together recalls McCarthy's *Child of God* (1973) and the tender care that Lester Ballard lavishes on the dead woman with whom he imagines setting up home. Indeed, it is Cormac McCarthy who stands as the godfather of contemporary Appalachia Gothic, with his early Tennessee novels offering up a particular slice of Southern Gothic. In the 1976 Mercer University Lamar Memorial Lectures, Walter Sullivan lamented that McCarthy was the enfant terrible of new Southern writing, producing a 'grotesque local color' that marked a decidedly gratuitous turn in Southern letters (72). While Sullivan's condemnation is reactionary, he nevertheless recognises the gothic and grotesque hallmarks of McCarthy's fiction.

Yet despite McCarthy's searing insights into humanity and societal corruption throughout his writing, he risks employing casual shorthand in his depictions of the backwoods characters in *Child of God*. In a novel where empathy is created for necrophiliac and murderer Lester Ballard, the mountain community is littered with stereotypical figures. From the dumpkeeper with his litany of oversexed daughters to the deformed child that Ballard eventually kills in a fire, this novel struggles between its use and rejection of debilitating typecasting. While the omission of these characters from James Franco's 2013 filmic adaptation of McCarthy's novel may be due to budgetary restrictions, it may also reflect the difficulty of marrying the dumpkeeper with a more subversive and empathetic approach to Ballard. If Ballard breaks the mould, then the dumpkeeper casts it in stone.

McCarthy's dumpkeeper depends heavily on ideas of the hillbilly, the figure who, although not specific to Appalachia, is nevertheless as synonymous with the region as moonshine and feuds. McKinney notes that from '1873, short story writers began to depict the mountain people in ways that led directly to the creation of the mountaineer stereotype', a stereotype that resonates as much today as it did at the end of the nineteenth century (55). The hillbilly has certainly contributed to the idea of Appalachia as a place that is 'interesting but strange and somewhat violent' (McIntyre 66).

This is most apparent in John Boorman's big-screen adaptation of *Deliverance* (1972). The film looms large in the popular imagination, since the sound of the banjo combines with male rape to consolidate an idea of Appalachian otherness and horror. While both the novel and its filmic adaptation expose the foibles of the city men and the rape scene offers a commentary on the wider environmental damage as the land is reconfigured for a dam, this cult movie is best remembered for its violent locals, who are pitted against the outsiders in a battle where the outcome is predetermined: the outsiders may fall foul of the locals, but the dam will be built, progress will not be stalled. However, beneath the stereotypical veneer of the film and indeed James Dickey's novel, a more ghostly spectre emerges that points to the battle between local communities and corporate greed.

Nixon explains that 'the primary quandary becomes how to bring into imaginative focus threatened communities and ecosystems rendered invisible by the celebratory developmental rhetoric that gushes from big dam technocrats, cabinet ministers, World Bankers, and media moguls' (160). These ignored or overlooked communities and ecosystems become part of a 'postmodern social formation [that] is still haunted by the symptomatic traces of its productions and exclusions' (Gordon 17). As I will go on to explore, this a decidedly socioeconomic haunting that resonates throughout much Appalachia Gothic fiction.

Appalachia Gothic in the Mass Media

It is useful here to consider the ways in which mass media continue to project a different form of gothic tale. A new generation of viewers are being fed hillbillies, feuds and violence through prime-time docudramas such as History's *Appalachian Outlaws* (2014–), whose success points to the contemporary desire for neatly packaged and consolidated stereotypes of the region. For Williamson, the 'public hillbilly imagery swings between foolshow and horror show' and these recent docudramas often oscillate between the two (57). *Appalachian Outlaws* contains what appear to be highly staged encounters that appeal to either the 'illiterate fool' or the 'menacing, violent aggressor' idea of the hillbilly. *History* describes the show as following 'unique characters' in a region where 'feuds last for generations'.[2] The stereotypes are manifold here: *History* plays on the long-held idea of a feuding, lawless land, but also on that of a 'unique' place and people. Indeed, these shows comfort audiences with the knowledge that as the sweep of modernity continues to shape the rest of the nation, there remain pockets where an 'authentic' life still exists.

However, the 'authentic' is a heavily packaged, consumable product in Appalachia, where local business owners and entrepreneurs are driven by economic imperatives to capitalise on the stereotypes of the region for tourist dollars. The Hatfield and McCoy feud is perhaps the most notorious example, where the actualities are blanketed in romanticised notions of lawlessness. Visitors just need to drop by Pigeon Forge, Tennessee, to take in the 'Hatfield & McCoy Dinner Show' while partaking of some 'Feudin' Fried Chick'n'. The show, with its banjo-playing revelries, turns violence into comedy as history succumbs to the need for 'good ol' times'. Across the region similar outfits trade on both the region's history and its wider typecast role as the nation's 'other'.

The clear appetite for this sanitised and often ahistorical version of the region can be seen in the success of Robert Schenkkan's 1992 Pulitzer Prize–winning play *The Kentucky Cycle* (1991), which is largely dependent on its rehashing of time-worn stereotypes. While it has met with popular approval and continues to be produced in local theatres throughout the United States, its limitations have been lamented by Appalachian scholars including Darlene Wilson, for whom the play's success 'suggests that the hillbilly-Other remains available for exploitation and expropriation by needy whit(ened) elites within the state and beyond its borders' (101).

Schenkkan's play does not merely present stereotyped hillbillies, it also portrays the land as an inherently gothic space. At the outset of the play where the greed for land acquisition is pronounced, a Native American, Dragging Canoe, warns Michael Rowen that 'Ganegedi ale gigaha gadohi. Tla yegehadehvga' [It is a dark and bloody land. You cannot live here] (28). Michael ignores the Cherokee man's advice and sets in motion a story filled with patricide, murder, feuds and revenge. Even the late turn to unionism in response to the ravages of the coal industry is not quite enough to jolt the play out of its dependency on caricature. Ultimately, it falls short of re-visioning Appalachia and its people.

COUNTER-STORIES AND CRITICAL INSIGHTS

Yet many writers are engaging in revisionist agendas that draw attention to the communities and ecosystems that are being destroyed by a never-ceasing demand for natural resources. When Glenn Taylor opens Book One of his novel *The Ballad of Trenchmouth Taggart* (2008) with a line from Cap Hatfield, 'Let any man shoot me with cannon or gun', he calls up readers' preconceived ideas of the region, only to counter them at every turn. On the surface the titular Trenchmouth is certainly one of Appalachian literature's most recent grotesques. This rich folk tale centres around Trenchmouth's life: a bildungsroman that follows a boy named after the debilitating oral disease that plagues him from birth, 'a disease that left gums eternally rotten and bloody, teeth decaying and odorous' (11). Even as a child, Trenchmouth is aware of his otherness and his ability to terrify. At one point early in the novel, as he fends off an attack he 'pulled back his forever-covering lips to reveal the mess of sores and bulges and sharp crooked calcium, and hissed. In the low light of the lantern, he made a sound reserved for mountain cats with their backs against a rock wall' (27). While Trenchmouth may appear to be destined for an isolated and violent existence, his life takes on all the characteristics of the tall tale and transcends the limitations imposed by hillbilly stereotypes.

The oral history that emanates from Trenchmouth's grotesque orifice can be usefully read in light of Gallagher and Greenblatt's work on 'outlandish and irregular' anecdotes: anecdotes that provide 'the best hope for preserving the radical strangeness of the past'. In short, they argue that 'through the eccentric anecdote, "history" would cease to be a way of stabilizing texts; it would instead become part of their enigmatic being' (51). Taylor's protagonist is highly enigmatic and his life constitutes a series of counter-narratives to the stories that people would tell about his home place.

Rather than an illiterate hillbilly, at one point in his momentous life Trenchmouth is a 'newspaper man' who wins the 'Pulitzer Prize for Local Reporting': his winning entry, 'Hill People Found a Man to Reckon With', details Senator Kennedy's 1960 Presidential Campaign visit to West Virginia. In response to claims that Kennedy bought the votes of West Virginians, Trenchmouth writes:

> John F. Kennedy did not need to buy our votes. He won them outright with his gumption. He looked us in the eye, not from a steep angle down the bridge of his nose, mind you, but straight on …. We are all shades of black, tan, and white. We come from Scotland and Ireland, Hungary and Sicily. We come from Africa by way of Georgia. (237)

In both his stint as a reporter and throughout his varied life, Trenchmouth's story is an Appalachian fable of grand, gothic proportions, but it is also a tale of the area's heterogeneous population and of its ability to transcend the type.

While Trenchmouth physically fits the bill of grotesque mountain man, he emerges as a heroic figure who chooses the hermit, mountain existence at key points in his life. In his dotage he returns to the mountains of his native West Virginia to lay claim to his land and to protect it from the companies that have already turned the hills around his home into a 'dull void' where there is '"No re-growth"' (266). This overwhelming sense of negation is mirrored throughout a number of Appalachian texts that expose the effects of mountain top removal.

Appalachian poetry leads the way with its critical insights into the desolation caused by the coal and logging industries. Rose McLarney's *Its Day Being Gone* (2014), whose very title evokes a profound sense of loss, is particularly illuminating in its concern for the land and those who inhabit it. McLarney overtly mourns the destruction of the local habitat in her poem 'Shadow Cat', in which she evokes the Appalachian myths and legends that tell of big cats prowling the hills: big cats that are believed to be either close to extinction or indeed extinct, their lives destroyed by the devastation wreaked on their mountainous habitat. In the poem, the speaker recalls walking up the mountain that was 'pure forest,/nothing fouling it, no buildings,/and no traffic either'.

However, this utopian image is disrupted by the presence of 'one man pulling a bulldozer' who whispers 'his warning,/*Careful out here alone. Big cat will get you*' (15), although the speaker realises that the real danger rests not in these tales of the cat but in the man himself, who is part of an operation '[f]orcing/new roads through trees' (16). The worker's progress ensures that 'no lion ever would/walk there again, no girl'. The pervasive negation at the close of the poem is mirrored across much of McLarney's poetry about her southern Appalachian home. Yet in the *Its Day Being Gone* collection, she also casts her glance internationally, connecting the concerns of Appalachia with global environmentalism. For Nixon, this global turn is vital to establishing 'a transnational ethics of place' that can successfully override any restrictive form of 'eco-parochialism' (242–3). McLarney's international gaze helps to position Appalachia not as uniquely 'other', but as part of a global battle against the ravages of aggressive capitalism.

Her poem 'Imminent Domain' opens out from a contemplation about current news footage of South America where people are being displaced to make way for a dam, to similar events in Appalachia where 'for one dam, thirteen hundred families/evicted, ninety cemeteries dug up' (35). The displacement of people from Appalachian land necessarily brings to mind the forced removal of Native peoples from the Appalachian region, a point to which I will return later, so that in conjunction with the 'drowned town' that lies beneath the channelled water of the dam, McLarney's poem engages with a haunted landscape, one that fellow poet Judy Jordan refers to as a 'land of ghosts and amulets' (15), in the title poem of her collection *Carolina Ghost Woods* (2000).

Jordan's poems are about the stains of history, the spilled blood that seeps into floorboards and the land, stains that continue to talk in 'worried whispers' (8). Her focus on memories, people and place creates what Turner refers to as 'heterotopic spaces, eerie and unkempt sites of irreconcilable otherness that draw forth the dissociative effects of counter-memory' (160). These counter-memories emerge through Jordan's focus on both her own family history and those of the wider communities who have lived, worked and died on the land. Patricia Yaeger's work on racial melancholia and the Southern landscape provides a useful insight into the haunted nature of Southern soil. Southern writers, she argues, commonly represent their home place as 'a world whose foundations have been built on men and women who have "worked all day" and been thrown away' (18). In Jordan's poems the ghostly voices of the dead refuse to be silenced, as the final stanza of 'Hitchhiking into West Virginia' indicates: 'Outside themselves,/the dead too,/nameless and without bound,/come closer, staking a claim' (24). The restless dead draw our attention again and again in Appalachian writing to the people and the ecosystems that are regarded as expendable by the companies whose sole drive is to extract natural resources at all costs.

In *Strange as This Weather Has Been* (2007), Ann Pancake's multi-perspectival novel about the devastating effects of strip mining in the Appalachian coal-fields, Pancake draws on research and real-life interviews with local people in West Virginia and Kentucky to rage against the environmental devastation of strip mining. This occasionally results in didacticism: take for example the 'history of slagheap disasters' that is fed through Avery, a minor character who, after surviving the 1972 Buffalo Creek disaster, becomes obsessed with the history of coal operators in the region.

Avery ruminates at length on the history of land exploitation. For him, his home place is 'so subtly beautiful and so overlaid with doom. A haunt, a film coating all of it. Killed again and again, and each time, the place rising back on its haunches, diminished, but once more alive ... Only this, Avery knows, will finally beat the land for good' (239). The utter negation caused by strip mining removes all hope of regeneration. Centuries of murdering the land have reduced it to a spectral 'haunt'. This form of haunting is intrinsic to gothic fiction, which, as Ellis explains, produces 'a kind of creative anachronism, proposing untoward, perverse connections between the deep past and contemporary life and politics' (Ellis 14). The past and present continually collide in Pancake's novel and her descriptions of the landscape are replete with the grotesque.

Floods are intensified by strip mining, leaving homes looking like 'spook-houses' (23), people are buried alive by black lung after years working underground (151), and the 'amputated' landscape casts 'shades of dead and gray' (165). Here monsters take the shape of machines that 'clawed the dirt' (165) and 'slaughtered' trees (212). Nightmares are filled not with ghosts from the past, but with distorted nature; with 'deer gone wrong' (175) and dreams of 'leaves falling as ash' (178). What scares you in this region is not the bogeyman: it is the 'slow-dying' trees, the 'goopy gray' hazardous waste secretly dumped (176–7). Rather than creepy castles, Pancake presents Appalachia as a place of hidden ruins, the 'damage that you can't see from outside: the ruined wells and dropped foundations' (211). Here satanic rituals are not carried out by locals but by the companies that 'sacrifice' the land, turning it into 'corpse-colored ground' (238–9). Here zombies come in the form of the compliant, unthinking workers who exist 'like they were in some kind of brainwashed zombie army', and open wounds are not found on the undead but on the land and in the people who have to live with the 'long, long loss' of their mountainous homes. Terrorism lies in the hands of coal companies that employ explosives, 'the same as the ones Tim Mcveigh used in Oklahoma City' (274).

This is the nightmarish, gothic-fuelled Appalachia that readers encounter in Pancake's novel, but its most resounding horror lies in its realism. Pancake's gothicism is imbued with the actual ghostly manifestations of the coal industry. Cobb notes that strip mining not only 'brought environmental and ecological ruin but many stripmine areas became virtual ghost towns where those who chose not to flee faced unemployment rates up to 30 percent' (127). Pancake's novel seethes with her knowledge of the communal and environmental fallout of mountain top removal and her novel's realism also reminds readers that, as Gordon explains, 'all these ghostly aspects of social life are not aberrations, but are central to modernity itself' (197).

There is a strong sense of foreboding throughout Pancake's novel, as characters reflect back on their lives in an increasingly impoverished and devastated landscape. Bant's observations of the landscape are full of negation as she looks around at the mountains she once knew, only to see 'nothing at all' (19). This negation and the destruction of the land are mirrored in the bodies of local people. While Bant's grandfather, a retired coal miner, dies early in the novel's chronology, his death haunts his daughter, Lace, and his granddaughter. Lace remembers his death: 'I'd hear his struggling gooey hacks, like his lungs were coming up, and coming up, pulling the rest of his guts right behind' (144). The terror-filled image of her father coughing up his insides is rendered decidedly political and becomes a form of familial haunting that is passed on through the generations. Early in the novel, Bant thinks about her grandfather's slow and horrific decline immediately after she sees aerial photographs of mountain top removal for the first time. She recalls that 'it was like dirty pictures I was seeing', that looking at the images of the stripped-back mountain was 'like looking at pictures of naked people. Like looking at pictures of dead bodies' (58).

From dead land to dead people. Bant makes her way back to a forgotten memory of her grandfather, 'wheelchair-bound and drawing breath through straws in his nose' (58). Salstrom notes that '[n]ot until 1969 did the government even acknowledge the existence of black lung disease, after many thousands of miners had already died from its slow suffocation' (80). In effect, Pap becomes one of Appalachia's ruins: a man involved in ripping coal from the earth ends up cast away and ruined inside. Stewart suggests that '[r]uined objects take on a meaningfulness or presence more compelling than the original …. Through them, a setting speaks to people, haunts the imagination, whispers an audible lamentation, trembles in expectation' (93). Pap stands as a lament for the losses inflicted by aggressive business, his gruesome death as much a by-product of the coal industry as the ravaged hills.

Despite the overbearing sense of loss, Pancake's novel does not present Appalachian people as merely passive victims. While there are those such as Jimmy who lead unquestioning lives, Lace becomes increasingly active in the resistance against strip mining. In contrast to the gun-toting hillbilly stereotype, Lace notes that violence is not an everyday occurrence in her region; for her the only threat is from the coal company. The company employee who threatens Lace does not wear a checked shirt, dungarees and a straw hat, but instead he 'was dressed up like he had an office job, tie and all, suit coat' (305). Against this dark threat, Lace comes to the understanding that 'the best way to fight them is to refuse to leave. Stay in their way—that's the only language they can hear. We are from here, it says. This is our place, it says. Listen here, it says. We exist' (314). Her stance is a challenge to the preconceptions of Appalachian people as either passive victims or willing conspirators in the brutal exploitation of the land. However, as with much Appalachian literature,

Pancake's reflections on land, belonging and loss struggle to encompass the Native peoples who were similarly dispossessed. As Cox saliently observes, 'To continue to narrate a Native absence is to enable further domination and render more generations unprepared to confront the many legacies of colonial violence' (255).

WRITING AGAINST THE GRAIN

Yet, while the forced removal of Native tribes from Appalachia is often present only through its absence, there are a number of authors writing against the grain. Tennessee-born Cherokee writer and poet Marilou Awiakta reflects throughout her work on the vibrancy of Native culture in contemporary Appalachia, as well as on the historical traumas inflicted by colonisation. Out of her contemplation of the idea that 'Sound has shaped me', Awiakta writes the following lines: 'Sound has shaped me:/mountains sending thoughts/elders telling stories/memory running in my blood/or crying out from the ground/where blood was spilled' (41). Awiakta's work brings to the surface a crucial part of the Appalachian story that contributes as much to its gothic dimensions as hillbillies, feuds or moonshine. Ultimately heterogeneity lies at the centre of her work, work that brings into sharp relief the overlooked aspects of the region.

Indeed, if Native Americans do not form part of the Appalachia of the mind, then neither do black Americans. The stereotypical mountain man is predominantly imagined to be white, even if less white than his mainstream counterpart. In response, black Appalachian poet Frank X. Walker coined the phrase 'Affrilachian' and regards it as his 'responsibility' to challenge 'the notion of a homogeneous all-white literary landscape in this region'.[3] Walker's desire to rewrite ideas of place resonates throughout the work of many of the writers included in this chapter. Certainly, if Glenn Taylor was interested in debunking hillbilly stereotypes and promoting heterogeneity in *The Ballad of Trenchmouth Taggart*, then he follows up that interest with gusto in his second novel *The Marrowbone Marble Company* (2012), which centres around the years leading up to and including the Civil Rights movement. In the novel Taylor explores both racial hatred and the desire to overcome debilitating ideas of difference and otherness. Like Taylor, many Appalachian writers suggest, in various ways, that Appalachia is not 'different' but is constituted by 'difference'.

So from foreboding mountainous terrain to sinister hillbillies, the region may manifest itself gothically in the imagination, but Appalachian writers are continually dispelling these stereotypes. Readers might easily be seduced into supposing that the sexually deviant backwoods men of *Deliverance* or Cormac McCarthy's murderous necrophiliac Lester Ballard are the greatest thing to fear, but much fiction from the region, including *Child of God*, presents outside, modernising forces as the villain of the piece. While Bayer-Berenbaum argues that '[t]he gothic imagination, like the religious imagination, reverently acknowledges awesome and terrible spiritual forces operative in the world', in Appalachia the terrible forces are far more often economic than spiritual: the

Gothic frequently draws attention to the region's ongoing battle with companies and politicians who regard states such as West Virginia as ripe for plunder, even in today's more environmentally conscious world (34).

NOTES

1. For more information about the Shelton Laurel massacre, see John C. Inscoe and Gordon B. McKinney's, *The Heart of Confederate Appalachia: Western North Carolina in the Civil War*. Chapel Hill: University of North Carolina Press, 2000.
2. Appalachian Outlaws. "About the Series," n.d. *History*. Web 28 May 2015.
3. Frank X. Walker home page. "About Frank," n.d. Web. 28 May 2015.

BIBLIOGRAPHY

Awiakta, M. (1998). Sound. In J. Dyer (Ed.), *Bloodroot: Reflections on place by Appalachia women writers*. Lexington: University Press of Kentucky.

Bayer-Berenbaum, L. (1982). *The Gothic imagination: Expansion in gothic literature and art*. London: Associated University Presses.

Benedict, L. (2012). *Devil's oven*. Gallowstree Press. http://gallowstreepress.com

Cobb, J. C. (1984). *Industrialization and Southern Society, 1877–1984*. Lexington: University Press of Kentucky.

Cox, J. H. (2006). *Muting white noise: Native American and European American novel traditions*. Norman: University of Oklahoma Press.

Davenport, G. (1968, September 29). Appalachian gothic: Review of outer dark by Cormac McCarthy. *The New York Times*. Web. 24 April 2015.

Deliverance. (1972). John Boorman. USA. Warner Bros.

Ellis, M. (2000). *The history of gothic fiction*. Edinburgh: Edinburgh University Press.

Gallagher, C., & Greenblatt, S. (2001). *Practicing new historicism*. Chicago: The University of Chicago Press.

Gay, W. (2001). *Provinces of night*. London: Faber and Faber, 2002.

Gordon, A. (1997). *Ghostly matters: Haunting and the sociological imagination*. Minneapolis: University of Minnesota Press.

Inscoe, J. C., & McKinney, G. B. (2000). *The heart of confederate Appalachia: Western North Carolina in the civil war*. Chapel Hill: University of North Carolina Press.

Jordan, J. (2000). *Carolina ghost woods*. Baton Rouge: Louisiana State University Press.

McCarthy, C. (1973). *Child of god*. London: Picador. 1989.

McIntyre, R. C. (2011). *Souvenirs of the old south: Northern tourism and southern mythology*. Gainesville: University Press of Florida.

McKinney, G. B. (2004). The civil war and reconstruction. In R. A. Straw & H. T. Blethen (Eds.), *High mountains rising: Appalachia in time and place* (pp. 46–58). Urbana: University of Illinois Press.

McLarney, R. (2014). *Its day being gone*. New York: Penguin.

Nicholson, M. H. (1959). *Mountain gloom and mountain glory: The development of the aesthetics of the infinite.* . Seattle: University of Washington Press, 1997.

Nixon, R. (2011). *Slow violence and the environmentalism of the poor*. Cambridge, MA: Harvard University Press.

O'Connor's, F. (1961). The grotesque in southern fiction. In S. Fitzgerald & R. Fitzgerald (Eds.), *Mystery and Manners: Occasional prose*. New York: Farrar, Straus and Giroux.

Pancake, A. (2007). *Strange as this weather has been.* Berkeley: Counterpoint.

Rash, R. (2006). *The world made straight.* New York: Picador, 2007.

Rash, R. (2012). *The cove.* Edinburgh: Canon Gate, 2013.

Salstrom, P. (2004). The great depression. In R. A. Straw & H. T. Blethen (Eds.), *High mountains rising: Appalachia in time and place* (pp. 74–87). Urbana: University of Illinois Press.

Savoy, E. (2002). The rise of American gothic. In J. E. Hogle (Ed.), *The Cambridge companion to gothic fiction* (pp. 167–188). Cambridge: Cambridge University Press.

Schenkkan, R. (1991). *The Kentucky cycle.* New York: Dramatists Play Service, 1994.

Stewart, K. (1996). *A space on the side of the road: Cultural poetics in an "other" America.* Princeton: Princeton University Press.

Sullivan, W. (1976). *A requiem for the renascence: The state of fiction in the modern south.* Athens: University of Georgia Press.

Taylor, G. (2008). *The ballad of Trenchmouth Taggart.* London: Blue Door, 2010.

Taylor, G. (2011). *The marrowbone marble company.* London: Blue Door, 2012.

Turner, D. C. (2012). *Southern crossings: Poetry, memory, and the transcultural south.* Knoxville: University of Tennessee Press.

Walters, P. (2013, September 7). Inside the battle over a Strip-Mine cemetery. *National Geographic.* Web. 24 April 2015.

Williamson, J. W. (1995). *Hillbillyland: What the movies did to the mountains & what the mountains did to the movies.* Chapel Hill: University of North Carolina Press.

Wilson, D. (1999). A judicious combination of incident and psychology John Fox Jr. and the southern mountaineer motif. In D. B. Billings, G. Norman, & K. Ledford (Eds.), *Back talk from Appalachia: Confronting stereotypes* (pp. 98–118). Lexington: University Press of Kentucky.

Yaeger, P. (2000). *Dirt and desire: Reconstructing southern women's writing, 1930–1990.* Chicago: University of Chicago Press.

Further Reading

Anolik, R. B. (2004). Introduction: The dark unknown. In R. B. Anolik & D. L. Howard (Eds.), *The gothic other: Racial and social constructions in the literary imagination* (pp. 1–14). Jefferson: McFarland. This is a useful introduction to the wider contexts of gothic writing.

Bell, S. E., & Braun, Y. A. (2010). Coal, identity, and the gendering of environmental justice activism on central Appalachia. *Gender and Society, 24*(6), 794–813. This study provides key insights into the nature of environmentalism in the region's coal fields.

CHAPTER 10

New Immigrants and the Southern Gothic

Nahem Yousaf

Leslie Fiedler posited in 1972, in his usual controversial style, that the dominant mode of 'the Southern' was the Gothic and it was this, Fiedler argued, that distinguished it from the Western because '[t]he real West, alas, contains no horrors which correspond to the Southerner's deep nightmare terrors' (133–5). While Fiedler's taxonomy is highly debatable given the consequences of settlement for immigrant groups, and is hardly useful in delineating historical or real differences between the West and the South, it is suggestive in defining what he called the 'Dark Sublime' or Southern Gothic mode and sensibility. Twenty-five years later, Florence King, writing as 'the failed southern lady' with tongue firmly in cheek, observed how ironic it was that the Gothic, although only ever loosely defined, remained so pervasive in literary studies and could even be cited as evidence that 'newcomers' to the region have failed to have an impact on or alter its gothic sensibility in any way at all. In this ironic formulation, 'Southern Gothic-ness' acts as 'a kind of Great White Hope', the corroboration that 'tenth-generation Anglo-Saxons can be as colourful, emotional, noisy, unruly, superstitious, unpredictable, and paranoid as everybody else' (10). Hal Crowther is similarly sardonic when he judges that the Southern Gothic has survived 'its loss of habitat and drastic reduction in the pool of decadent aristocrats who used to take its leading roles' because even when 'the last antebellum mansion has crumbled into the kudzu and the last Temple Drake or Peyton Loftis has pierced her nose', it will simply endure (12, 13). In a more measured way, Fred Hobson assesses that if by the 1970s 'savagery' in Southern literature appeared 'if not contrived, at least removed from the social base which gives rise to the fiction' (146), the 'Savage South' continues to 'exist' in the Gothic. This essay analyses the Southern Gothic

N. Yousaf (✉)
Nottingham Trent University, Nottingham, UK

© The Editor(s) (if applicable) and The Author(s) 2016
S.C. Street, C.L. Crow (eds.), *The Palgrave Handbook of the Southern Gothic*,
DOI 10.1057/978-1-137-47774-3_10

not for its southernness, but for what happens when newcomers disturb its 'Southern base'; it is extended and sometimes changed in a poetics of relation that conserves some of its most potent tropes and images, but fuses them with gothic elements grounded in other places.

Widening the scope to encompass other places can involve the translation of a Southern Gothic plot to other continents, such as French colonial Africa, in a trajectory that I trace from a trope made gothic (the Southern sheriff) to Bertrand Tavernier's 1981 Senegal-set film *Coup de Torchon* ('A Southern Sheriff's Revenge'). In the space afforded here, though, my aim is to assess the different ways in which immigrants figure in Southern fiction and to examine how new immigrant fiction deploys gothic imagery in new imaginaries. The Gothic is a hyperaesthetic mode. The tropes that can be rendered distinctively Southern are myriad and often grotesque: civil war; slavery; violent resistance to civil rights; aristocratic family feuds; bodies traumatized in war or racial violence; dismal swamps; hyperbolic and monstrous misfits of gargantuan proportions. When immigrant characters enter Southern literature, they contribute to the cultural hybridization of the gothic mode as 'troped' in these ways. Yet the most effective and intriguing of immigrant writers imagine more than a geographical extension of supposedly 'Southern' exceptionalism, whether of place or image; they intervene in the tropes themselves, in the cultural parochialism of the term 'Southern Gothic', and in the idea of distinctively Southern literature.

ALTERITY AND THE SOUTHERN GOTHIC

Incarnated as a loner, the figure of the foreign stranger in the South—and the immigrant community as reconfigured there—is typically represented as displaced and a threat to Southern cultural norms, whether those of the rural farm and labour economy as in Flannery O'Connor's 'The Displaced Person' (1954, rev. 1955) or the archetypally Southern university in Susan Choi's *The Foreign Student* (1998). In previous work, I identified a literary paradigm whereby a solitary foreigner enters the South in a bygone decade and is confined in a fictional timelock, safely historicized and largely invisible in an axiomatically black-and-white South. The paradigm is shifting in a more complex transnational and global literary culture—even in fictions that retain an individual immigrant at the centre, but engage the local and regional to explore minority and ex-centric experiences. Choi's *The Foreign Student* critiques a form of American national forgetting that wilfully occludes the Korean War, even in its immediate aftermath, and that renders refugee Chang Ahn unaccountable to those he meets in Tennessee in the 1950s. Choi's sensitive and cumulative evocation of the backstory of one Korean refugee illuminates what makes of this individual a displaced and alienated protagonist. In this novel, not only is as much space devoted to Korea as to the US South, but its nexus of temporal shifts ensures that the individual immigrant is made not only visible but knowable. Choi succeeds in no small part by deploying gothic imagery of a war elsewhere and inserting it into the domain of the University of the South and its time-honoured traditions. It is to this text that I will return in my conclusion, as a model for understanding an aesthetic of alterity that derives much from a fusion of two different imaginaries.

Alterity is a designation by which the individual is typically reduced to a subaltern or to an aberrant stranger. Barbara Ladd has summarized that in Southern literary studies, as in the United States more generally, alterity 'designates not only the submerged voices of women, minorities and the poor'—and immigrants are often all of these, of course—but also 'colonial, postcolonial, regional and national textualities obscured by cultural nationalism' (1633). In 1989 one historian of immigration to the US South characterized immigrants as pioneers on 'the nation's newest frontier', but judged that the dangers of this particular frontier emanated from long-held assumptions: 'a legacy of Old South views toward foreigners and strangers generally' (Pozzetta 203). The discourse remains ubiquitously US-centric, the metaphor of the frontier dominating and illustrating that it and such terms as the 'Old South' (or 'Solid South' or 'New South') can be left undefined when they have been so thoroughly fetishized. To unpack aspects of this formulation is to recognize that immigrants rendered 'Other' in the 'Old South' were positioned strategically in the supposedly 'Solid' South in the Reconstruction period. Thomas Muller examines how in the 1880s 'small groups of southern Italians established their own communities in the Mississippi Delta, their proximity leading to the first serious immigrant-black conflicts' when southern planters 'used the specter of immigrant labor to keep the blacks "in line"' (93). Historian George E. Cunningham illustrated how Italian immigrants were seen as a 'hindrance to white solidarity' in Louisiana, and David Roediger unpacks how another historian, Paolo Giordano, exaggerated only slightly when he asserted that black Southerners and Italian immigrants went against the social order and associated freely in Louisiana in the period (186).

The assassination of police chief David Hennessy in New Orleans in 1890, the subsequent lynching of Italian immigrants and the persecution of many more soon found a place in fiction about the city. In George Washington Cable's *Dr. Sevier* (1884), Sicilian immigrant Ristofalo succeeds in building a wholesale business out of impoverished beginnings selling bruised fruit. He rises to the rank of colonel fighting in the Civil War, and he is Cable's foil for his protagonist John Richling, whose privileged Kentucky plantation background fails to equip him to survive poverty in the same way. However, by 1909 Frances Green's *Into the Night* would be replete with gothic images of ethnic enmity and hatred: a young woman is disturbed to discover that the lawyer she intends to marry is involved in the jailhouse lynching of Italian immigrants, but is won over when he goes on to foil a 'Mafia' plot to avenge their deaths. As a literary mode, the Southern Gothic has exploited nativism, xenophobia and anti-immigrant violence as often as it has deployed immigrant characters to interrogate Southern racial norms. The South's racial history infuses gothic images of 'outsiders'. New immigrant writers extend the Gothic in the way Teresa Goddu noted in the context of African American writers; that is, by reworking 'the gothic's conventions to intervene in discourses that would demonize them' (138).

DEMONIZATION OF THE IMMIGRANT

A story that forms a model for deconstructing the discourse in which the immigrant is demonized is Flannery O'Connor's short story 'The Displaced Person', set in the aftermath of the Second World War. The Guizacs, political refugees from Poland, are caught in the net of a gothic sensibility that is held back by an overridingly moral ending in the original story in the *Sewanee Review*, but that gathers violent and twisted momentum in the version that O'Connor published a year later. O'Connor was writing in the wake of the Displaced Persons Act of 1948, which was equivocal at best in its intention to host those 'displaced' first into Nazi concentration camps, then, if they survived into refugee camps, and later, sometimes, to the United States and other countries. When an Irish priest brings the Guizacs to Mrs. McIntyre's dairy farm, lethargically run by black and white tenant farmers, they are treated as migrant workers. Their uncertain status as 'extras' who are deemed neither black nor quite white in the racialized labour hierarchy 'upsets the balance' (231). In *Caste and Class in a Southern Town* (1937), sociologist John Dollard had described the new immigrant working class as 'temporary Negroes' (93). O'Connor's inspiration was the Matisiak family working the O'Connor family farm in Georgia in 1952, and her story may be read as putting this simplification to the test and, indeed, putting it in doubt.

In 'The Displaced Person', nativist paranoia fuels the contempt of white tenant Mrs. Shortley on behalf of her husband, whose notion of 'hired help' falls into a habitual taken-for-grantedness that affords him time to keep an illicit whisky still. In the original story as focalized through Mrs. Shortley, she is so assured of her husband's superiority as the only white worker in the place that she insinuates to her employer that hardworking, thrifty and energetically competent Mr. Guizac will demand a rise in wage that will price him out of the market. However, when she puts words in the foreigner's mouth, she takes food out of her family's. She overhears that the rumour she has manufactured will be acted on: Mr. Shortley will be let go to ensure that the 'Displaced Person' will stay. Apoplectic with rage, she gathers up her family to make a midnight flit that will displace them too, but that precipitates a fatal stroke. The tale ends with Mrs. Shortley's machinations thwarted and her death.

Mr. Guizac is excised from the farm community in the revised version as a result of a violent conspiracy that damages his employer beyond recognition and leaves her farm in ruins. In an apparent explanation of the Gothic in her work, O'Connor said: 'To the hard of hearing you have to shout; for the almost blind you must draw large and startling figures' (*Mystery and Manners* 34). The revised story is cruelly caricatured and its violent ending warped and grotesque. The vile Mrs. Shortley is retained, but the imagery she conjures is amplified. The recurring memory of a newsreel according to which Mrs. Shortley visualizes the Poles is of 'a small room piled high with bodies of dead and naked people all in a heap', but in the revised version the horrific image of the Holocaust is twisted out of any understanding and all sympathy to herald her 'sudden intuition' that 'like rats with typhoid fleas' the Guizacs 'could have carried all those murderous ways over the water with them directly to this place' (196). When Mr. Guizac smiles, 'Europe stretched out in Mrs. Shortley's imagination, mysterious and evil, the devil's experiment station' (202).

The vital alteration that O'Connor makes, however, is that Mr. Guizac turns into a 'monster' (222) in his employer's eyes too when she discovers in 'shock' and 'wrath' (223) that he hopes to protect his 16-year-old cousin, orphaned in the death camp where she spent 3 years, by bringing her to the United States to marry Sulk, a black worker on the farm. It is the idea of 'race-mixing' that makes Mr. Guizac irredeemably 'Other' to Mrs. McIntyre; it suddenly renders the Poles white in her eyes and prompts her to hire back Mr. Shortley. His wife's death galvanizes in him a lethal campaign for revenge and murder: 'It's the people that run away from where they come from that I ain't got any use for' (232). When Mr. Guizac lies beneath a tractor to fix it, Mr. Shortley quickly contrives that another tractor will roll over him, breaking his back and killing the man, who is oblivious to the fear and hatred gathering around him. As Mrs. McIntyre and Sulk stand back in silence, their eyes meet Mr. Shortley's 'in one look that froze them in collusion forever' (234). Their collusion is evil and cannot be borne easily. Mr. Shortley, and Sulk who 'never felt no need to travel' (232), quit without notice and Mrs. McIntyre is afflicted with a nervous condition: her sight fails, a numbness spreads through her limbs and she loses the ability to speak. The Irish priest becomes her only visitor, intoning at her bedside the doctrines of the Catholic Church that she had disdained as irredeemably foreign and out of place in the world she has now lost. As Laurel Nesbitt argues, 'far from rehiring everyone to their initial places', Mr. Guizac's death displaces them all (160).

THE SOUTHERN GOTHIC AND MAGICAL REALISM

Struggling whites have always perceived refugees escaping to the United States in the aftermath of war, as the Guizacs do, as a threat to their livelihoods, like when fishermen-turned-Klansmen waged a war against Vietnamese fishermen on the Gulf Coast in Texas in the 1980s. Such events are yet to find more than a superficial exploration in fiction, though, and the most effective treatment remains Louis Malle's film *Alamo Bay* (1985). Malle's dramatization of racism's relationship to economics was not a box-office success and while the French director exploited and explored a shameful episode, white Southern writers have usually imagined gentler stories in which refugees secure an economic foothold in the region, as in Roy Hoffman's *Chicken Dreaming Corn* (2004), in which Mobile, Alabama sees the establishment of successful immigrant businesses between the First and Second World Wars. Augusta Trobaugh's

Sophie and the Rising Sun (2001) is intriguing both in its faint echoing of O'Connor's story and in her reworking of the Gothic. 'Mr. Oto', as he is known in Salty Creek, Georgia, is a quiet and 'unobtrusive' (27) Japanese American gardener whose foreignness 'upsets the applecart' in a 'simple town where whites and blacks know how to get along together' (20, 21). He is redefined as a dangerous alien following the Japanese attack on Pearl Harbor. Miss Anne's careless assumption that her employee must be 'a real Chinese' gardener (19) is corrected only when he fears that she will be mistaken for an 'enemy sympathizer' and assumed to be harbouring 'one of them'. She is shocked both that he is not Chinese and that this man of more than 50 who has never set foot in Japan could possibly think himself as American as her, a Daughter of the American Revolution (104–7). Nevertheless, he protects her—'If anyone asks … tell them you made me leave because I was a Jap' (108)—and she hides him like a criminal, even though a friend derides him in gothic terms as '*an ugly dried up yellow foreigner*' and now a spy (15, 86).

Miss Anne, who is telling the story of Mr. Oto's burgeoning love affair with Sophie, is awakened by an approaching hurricane on the night they disappear: 'that old devil wind … blowing so hard that it shook the whole house, and the curtains at my window whipped and fluttered out into the room like ghosts' (203). The reader cannot be sure whether Mr. Oto and Sophie come to a macabre end in the storm or at the hands of those who fear him. However, Miss Anne refuses all violent potentialities by escaping into surreal, fantastical whimsy. In the 'ending' to which she subscribes, Mr. Oto turns into a giant crane, with Sophie the Crane-Wife of ancient Japanese fable. They fly away in the form of the bird whose migration path takes in China and Russia as well as Japan, and whose symbolism is of fidelity, luck and long life.

Where a magically realist 'elsewhere' intersects with the Southern Gothic, there is freedom to experiment. In *The Minotaur Takes a Cigarette Break* (2000), Steven Sherrill creates a more sustained countercultural fantasy with its foundation in Greek myth. As Mircea Eliade asserted in his now classic *Myth and Reality* (1963), 'the possibilities for applying the mythical model are endless' (140). What Eliade described as the 'transhuman' and 'transmundane' (141) texture a bizarre fantasy in which an extraordinary character that originates in another imaginary becomes less aberrant in Southern literature precisely because gothic alienation is already an expectation and a norm. In Greek myth, the Minotaur is a punishment decreed on King Minos for having failed to sacrifice a beautiful white bull to the god Poseidon. When the gods make Queen Pasifae enamoured of the bull, she contrives an encounter that leads to the Minotaur's birth, half-bull and half-man. Minos confines the creature who feasts on blood and young Athenians in an intricate labyrinth for an eternity. Granted an afterlife in Sherrill's fiction, the Minotaur escapes his prison and his slaughter by Theseus to enjoy a quiet retirement far from Crete as an immortal. M., as he is now known, is working as a line cook at Grub's Grill in the North Carolina Piedmont and negotiating a labyrinth of personal relationships in the contemporary South. If in a new domesticated setting M. appears to transcend the monstrous appetite and monumental loneliness of legend, his representation also exemplifies almost exactly what Patricia Yaeger argued was vital to understanding the Southern grotesque: 'we must tease out its connection with the risible, the archaic, the unspeakable, the obscenely sentimental' as well as 'its brutal physicality, its propensity for somatic revulsion and rapture, its refusal to make friends with the social' (228).

M. remains iconic as the most visually conspicuous of 'newcomers' to Southern fiction, and the most nomadic because he is the least bound to the 'sense of place' that remains a shibboleth in Southern literary culture. Having no desire to settle after being imprisoned for so long, M. elects to stay for a spell in a trailer on the Lucky-U Mobile Estates. In this postmodern fiction, the fantastical and the mundane can coexist precisely because the literary South is already gothic and eccentric. The labyrinth of old is recalled only in discrete poetic inter-chapters that convey the Minotaur's bloodline and an impressionistic sense of M.'s original claustrophobia, still caught in the story that he has now escaped to wanderer in the South. As Fred Botting summarizes, the labyrinth is a crucial motif in gothic literature in novels that 'seduce, excite, confuse and disturb' (77), and the Minotaur is reconfigured in gothic idiom in a network of texts, including Jorge Luis Borges's 'The House of Asterion' (1947), in which the Minotaur awaits deliverance from the infernal labyrinth, and Mark Z. Danielewski's haunted *House of Leaves* (2000), where the Minotaur is conjured up repeatedly in red text. Sherrill succeeds in drawing North Carolina into a wider net of texts and in pushing alterity into its most bizarre formulation in an anarchic text predicated on the most exaggeratedly foreign of strangers. In returning the grotesque to its original definition of hybrid humans and animals, there is pathos too. M. is in constant pain: his purple scar from chest to waist that transitions from the deep black bull head to charcoal-grey fur and to 'moon-white human skin' remains raw:

> Sometimes this place, this division, throbs, swells, deepens, becomes a chasm within the Minotaur that he will never span, though he will spend an eternity trying … But sometimes he is able to forget it, to believe for an isolated moment that he is a singular and whole being. (36)

If Sherrill carnivalizes the Gothic in reclaiming the symbolically repressed, he also negotiates for his protagonist a safe place of mediation in the racially and ethnically mixed community of Grub's Grill. Five thousand years ago the Minotaur would have devoured the few Southerners who do tease or taunt: 'These pitifully arrogant boys and girls would have quaked at the mere mention of his name. One by one they would have been tossed into his chambered pit, oblations to rage or scapegoats to what is most base in man' (57). In Sherrill's languorous South, though, M. is slow to anger, 'knowing that each painful moment will inevitably pass away' (56). With black (JoJo and Cecie), white (David and Kelly) and Hispanic (Hernando) co-workers and friends, M. finds kindness, acceptance, familiarity and the promise of love. Even when he accidentally spears Hernando with his horn, there is no recrimination. At the end of the novel, M. is on the road again guided by his lonely star; his beloved Vega is hitched to a corndog trailer and he will roam with waitress Kelly, with whom he has bonded romantically. In an epic universe, the Minotaur exists 'out of necessity, his own and the world's' (238), but here the monstrous product of shame in classical mythology moves 'from place to place and time to time' (136). Transported to the Gothic South, M. can become a tragic hero and a 'singular and whole' character in fiction.

Sherrill's fiction is strategically divorced from Southern Gothic clichés, but they are at the core of other fictions in which immigrants feature, like T.C. Boyle's absurdist *East Is East* (1990), in which Hiro Tanaka jumps ship off the coast of Georgia to be hunted down by the Immigration and Naturalization Service that labels him an IAADA (Illegal Alien, Armed, Dangerous and Amok), despite being barely adult and pursuing a hopeless Candide-like quest to find his father and blend in. Hiro is unable to extricate himself from that most gothic of landscapes, the dismal swamp, first on Tupelo Island, which he mistakes for 'the mainrand', and then in Okefenokee: 'Was it all swamp, the whole hopeless country? Where were the shopping malls, the condos, the tattoo parlours and supermarkets? Where the purple mountains and open range?' (268). Hiro is confused with a ghost; pursued by a paramilitary racist; kept captive by a novelist as the inspiration for stories she thinks will sell; and finally, in Savannah, he commits bizarre hari-kari with a spoon sharpened while lying in a hospital bed waiting to get well enough to be arrested and deported. Stereotypes abound in this frenetic satire, loosely based, ironically enough, on an illegal immigrant's experience in 1974, and both Sherrill and Boyle's texts contain humour, satire and the 'Dark Sublime', key components of Southern Gothic fiction.

Outsiders in Southern Literature

Iranian Jewish American writer Gina Nahai's Appalachia-set *Sunday's Silence* (2001) is a lyrical novel, but it too could not have been conceived without gothic images that have hardened into stereotypes. The snake-handling motif central to Nahai's story rests on layers of sensationalism around death by snakebite and strychnine poison, what Jim Birckhead has summarized as 'truly fantastical descriptions of madness and confusion, sexuality and fanaticism, and general grotesqueness—as fitting many examples of southern Gothic writing' (171). Nahai would seem to have been seduced, at least initially, by popular media images: 'These people put their faces in blow torches and pile snakes on themselves in these religious meetings.' However, her larger aim is to explore how 'human reactions are strange and unpredictable all over the world' and that 'what happens in the West is just as sad and outrageous as what happens in the East' (Alumni interview). I have examined the novel for the way in which the region is calibrated by characters whose foreignness, or 'outsider' status, is precisely what they have in common ('The Local and the Global'), but reading it for the ways in which it engages the Southern Gothic is to underscore how Nahai embraces but then undermines the Southern exceptionalism of such rituals. There are murders, scandals, dispossession in war and displacement after it, abuse, self-hate and suicide, 'deep-bleeding' secrets and lies (*Sunday's Silence* 184), a woman maddened by snakes, a 5-year-old girl burned alive and a grandmother forcing a child to sleep with snake boxes under his bed and to watch her vomit blood and poison. Nahai forges intersecting stories with Kurdistan, Iran and Iraq, and featuring Jews, Muslims and Christians, the prismatic constellation of cultures through which she reanimates well-worn images derived from a charismatic community in Knoxville. Her Southern Gothic is caught up in a global cultural flow.

Susan Choi's *The Foreign Student* stands out, though, because the gothic imaginary makes a damaged outsider, the casualty of civil war in Korea, a complex and enduring new character in Southern literature. Chang is outwardly contained and unfailingly polite to suit his new surroundings at the University of the South, but he is arrested in moments of abject fear. His punishing nightmare of alterity is exacerbated by his attempt to suppress his past psychologically by escaping it geographically. In a place of shelter he is haunted by guilt and the spectre of his former home and self.

Detained in a South Korean prison in Pusan on suspicion of espionage, Chang is tortured to give up the location of fighters in the resistance and he betrays a man who helped him. He is tortured so intensively that he can only deduce time passing by making himself a torturer and cutting a new gash on his forearm arm each night. Chang is left so hungry that he ingests putrefying meat, cattle feed and his own vomit. His body is rendered horribly grotesque in the most abject of tautologies: 'His face washed itself with tears that were made in the same unfeeling place where his urine was made, and his blood ... He mimicked his torturers, making himself deaf to his body's cries for help' (309). Choi depicts Chang's experience as it is felt, and suffered again in nightmares, in gothic imagery of self-isolating intensity. He is left hanging by chains, bound in telephone wires and lunged at with baseball bats, until the world falls away and he is a surrogate of himself:

> He sliced through lines and wires, exploded bridges, excised his mouth and his groin, amputated his limbs ... Cast outside the boundary of itself, his body had ceased to obey any boundary between itself and the world ... he watched his hand being mangled at a great distance. He had already sawed it off. He had thrown away his body as if it were ballast, not to speed his death, but to survive. It was his body that would kill him. (310)

Chang is expected to explain himself as a newcomer in terms that are bleached clean of this experience—and of war. At the University of the South, he is perceived as 'a romantic castaway, whose presence among them confirmed everything that was best about themselves' and it is deemed 'a point of pride that he would prefer Sewanee to his home' (145). When he delivers talks in churches around Tennessee as a condition of his student bursary, he makes the lectures 'pleasant'; all Koreans are farmers 'celebrating their holidays clad in bright costumes … fond of flowers and children … unremarkable, hardly worth the trouble of a lecture' (39). Via temporal switches and by deferring the graphic description of his torture until the novel's end, Choi ensures that, finally, the reader's understanding of Chang's insertion into this Southern place must be revised.

When he arrives, the bus driver leaves Chang at the side of the road without explaining that the rest of the way is too steep to drive. He is a 'petrified figure' after a two-mile climb in the dark to the university on top of the Cumberland Plateau. The experience echoes in Chang a moment of pure fear, crystallized when, stranded by a driver who agrees to take him to Pusan but suddenly drops him near Inchon, he 'stands quaking' in the pitch dark watching the tail lights disappear and is forced to feel his way blindly through 'filthy black blasted streets' to the waterfront and to spend 3 days in 'an unlit, unventilated hold below deck with hundreds of unwashed and sick refugees' (202–3). In Sewanee, his first night's sleep is in a room without a lock ('We don't look our doors here', he is told) and he is unable to 'accept the lack of precaution as a sign he was safe' (7–8). An unlocked guest bedroom is another trigger: when North Korean forces take possession of Chang's family home, he hides from them, locked under the stairs—in an unventilated space too short to lie down and not high enough to kneel—for 3 months, the last of which he loses to oblivion. The university-town setting is undisturbed by the Gothic, except in the architecture of its handsome buildings, but Chang is trapped in a recurrent nightmare and when his encounters seem to veer into the established territory of the Southern Gothic, his experience is represented at one remove. When his college roommate invites Chang home to meet his Klansman father, a Grand Dragon, the white boy is enthralled by what he imagines will be a frisson of potential violence: if the Klan does not hang 'Orientals', he wonders if 'they might mistake him for a nigger and hang him' (57). Chang is subjected solely to a family meal. Similarly, at a gas station, when Chang is an object of suspicion in a tense moment, the threat of violence is held back and he observes, 'They don't know what to make of me' (37). Instead, in this novel, the Gothic exists in the war-torn chaos of Chang's subjectivity.

If the 'body in pain' is 'the making and unmaking of the world', as Elaine Scarry argued, in Chang the boundary between himself and the world is broken: displaced in Korea and again in the South, he occupies both places simultaneously. On New Year's Eve, for example, after drinking with the woman who will become his lover, he 'lost hold of her' (179); Katherine hears him cry out in his sleep because he is back in Inchon cowering in a hail of bullets in the dark (180–81, 216). When the couple stays on the Gulf Coast, Katherine describes a black cloud in a blue sky as they drift to sleep as 'a love tree, its trunk invisible from … our house in the middle of the ocean' (291–2). Even this romantic image is transformed for Chang into the island of Cheju, where he wanders maddened by an infestation of lice. The image of the black tree becomes the one he grinds against all night 'like a dog' and sits in all day 'numb from the cold' and when he snatches sleep it is in 'a skeleton of leaves' (295–6). From Cheju where Chang turns into 'a ghost, or a beast' (304), Choi segues finally into 'voiding black pain' (306) at the hands of the National Police, the memory that awaits him each day in the South as a nocturnal return.

CONCLUSION

The immigrant character is a displaced person even in a literary tradition in which misfits are legion. By focusing only on Southern Gothic incarnations, we may miss what gothic preoccupations mean in transnational fictions located at the shifting and ambiguous edges of 'Southern' fiction. Immigrant writers and immigrant characters enlarge the narrative space of Southern literature, pushing it beyond the region and into transtemporal and mythological fantasies too. Some writers, like Nahai, lend even the most clichéd images transcultural nuance; others, like Sherrill, use the regional as the space in which an already gothic mythical character may be re-envisioned in imaginative ways. Choi succeeds in making her migrant character knowable to himself only through his transition into the region, and she does so by carefully forging a transcultural gothic aesthetic through the kind of 'double telling' that Cathy Caruth argues is a defining feature of trauma narratives, in which the narrative oscillates between 'the story of the unbearable nature of an event and the story of the unbearable nature of its survival' (7). To know Chang is to read him back through memory triggers that unfold the horror that wrenched him out of himself and made of him a refugee; his experience is 'flattened and distorted' in his new home where he is 'unpeeled and forced on to a [new] map' (Choi 311).

BIBLIOGRAPHY

Birckhead, J. (1993). "Bizarre Snakehandlers": Popular media and southern stereotype. In K. G. Heider (Ed.), *Images of the South* (pp. 163–189). Athens: University of Georgia Press.

Botting, F. (2014). *Gothic: New critical idiom* (2nd ed.). London: Routledge.

Caruth, C. (1996). *Unclaimed experience: Trauma, narrative, history*. Baltimore: Johns Hopkins.

Choi, S. (1998). *The foreign student*. New York: Harper.

Crowther, H. (2000). *Cathedrals of Kudzu: A personal landscape of the South*. Baton Rouge: Louisiana State University Press.

Cunningham, G. E. (1965). *The Italian: A hindrance to White* Solidarity in Louisiana, 1890–1898. *Journal of Negro History, 50*(1), 22–36.

Eliade, M. (1963). *Myth and reality*. New York: Harper and Row.

Fiedler, L. A. (1972). *The return of the vanishing American*. London: Paladin.

Goddu, T. (1999). Vampire gothic. *American Literary History, 11*(1), 125–141.

Hobson, F. C. (1989). The Savage South: An inquiry into the origins, endurance, and presumed demise of an image. (1985). In G. Patrick & C. Nicholas (Eds.), *Myth and southern history: Vol. 2 The New South* (pp. 133–147). Urbana: University of Illinois Press.

King, F. (1996). In the dark. *Oxford American* special issue 'Is the South Still Gothic?' (November 1996), 10–11.

Ladd, B. (2005). Literary studies: The Southern United States, 2005. *PMLA, 120*(5), 1628–1639.

Muller, T. (1993). *Immigrants and the American city.* New York: New York University Press.

Nahai, G. (2001). *Sunday's silence.* New York: Harcourt.

Nahai, G. Alumni interview at http://www.usc.edu/dept/LAS/mpw/interview/Nahai

Nesbitt, L. (1997). Reading place in and around Flannery O'Connor's texts. *Post Identity, 1*(1), 145–97.

O'Connor, F. (1954). The displaced person. *Sewanee Review, 62*(4), 634–654.

O'Connor, F. (1970). *Mystery and manners.* Sally and Robert Fitzgerald (Eds). New York: Farrar, Strauss and Giroux.

O'Connor, F. (1990). 'The displaced person' (1955). In *The complete stories* (pp. 194–235). London: Faber.

Pozzetta, G. E. (1989). Migration to the Urban South: An unfinished agenda. In R. M. Miller & G. E. Pozzetta (Eds.), *Shades of the sunbelt: Essays on ethnicity, race, and the Urban South* (pp. 193–206). Boca Raton: Florida Atlantic University Press.

Roediger, D. (1994). Whiteness and ethnicity in the history of 'White ethnics' in the United States. In *Towards the abolition of whiteness* (pp. 181–198). London: Verso.

Scarry, E. (1985). *The body in pain.* New York: Oxford University Press.

Sherrill, S. (2004). *The Minotaur takes a cigarette break.* Edinburgh: Canongate.

Trobaugh, A. (2002). *Sophie and the rising sun.* London: Little Brown.

Yaeger, P. (2000). *Dirt and desire.* Chicago: University of Chicago Press.

Yousaf, N. (2007). The local and the global: Gina Nahai and the taking up of serpents and stereotypes. *Journal of American Studies, 41*(2), 307–330.

FURTHER READING

Anolik, R. B., & Douglas L. H., (Eds.) (2004). *The Gothic other: Racial and social constructions in the literary imagination.* Jefferson: McFarland. On the demonizing of the ethnic, racial and religious 'Other' in various contexts, including the writing of Frederick Douglass.

Bone, M. (2004). The transnational turn in the south. In Clara Juncker and Russell Duncan (Eds.), *Transnational Americas* (pp. 217–235). Copenhagen: Museum Tuscalanum. Introduction to 'the transnational' in the South with readings of Kingsolver's *Prodigal Summer* and Fink's *The Mayans of Morgantown*.

Cartwright, K. (2002). *Reading Africa into American literature: Epics, fables and gothic tales.* University Press of Kentucky. Enquiry into Senegambian literature and as comparative with African American literature, with Part 3 on the shadow of the Gothic in the slave South.

Kim, D. Y. (2009). Bled in letter by letter: Translation, postmemory and the Korean War in Susan Choi's *The Foreign Student. American Literary History, 21*, 550–589. A case for the importance of the Korean War as a watershed moment in which national and transnational histories of race converge, paying attention to Choi's historiographical context.

McIntyre, R. C. (2005). Promoting the Gothic South. *Southern Cultures, 11*(2), 33–61. Traces how travellers and tourists conceived of the region as gothic and images promoted in memoir and Southern literature.

Yousaf, N. (2007). A Southern Sheriff's revenge: Bertrand Tavernier's *Coup de Torchon*. In W. Zacharasiewicz & R. Gray (Eds.), *Transatlantic exchanges: The American South in Europe; Europe in the US South* (pp. 221–238). Vienna: Austrian Academy of Sciences. Examines a gothic motif, the corrupt southern sheriff, as cross-cultural and trans-generic and explores its relocation in French colonial Senegal.

Yousaf, N. (2013). Immigrant writers: Transnational stories of a "Worlded" South. In Sharon Monteith (Ed.), *The Cambridge companion to the literature of the American South* (pp. 204–219). Cambridge: Cambridge University Press. Argues that stereotypes about the insularity of Southern literature are untenable in myriad examples of fiction and poetry that project the regional model outwards: Monique Truong's *Bitter in the Mouth* and works by Firmat, Villatoro, Cao, Shearer and Grisham.

CHAPTER 11

Flannery O'Connor and the Realism of Distance

Éric Savoy

Much Madness is divinest Sense –
To a discerning Eye –
(Emily Dickinson, Poem 435, ll.1-2)

Late in 1961, Flannery O'Connor sent a little anecdote to her friend John Hawkes. Apparently, a woman in Texas walked into a bookstore and asked for a copy of *A Good Man Is Hard to Find*: 'The clerk said, "We don't have that one but we have another one by that writer. It's called THE BEAR THAT RAN AWAY WITH IT"' (LA 1157)[1]. O'Connor's letters, like her fiction and essays, are packed with moments that are oddly unsettling in their hilarity. Although her writing is customarily described—by herself and by her critics—as 'grotesque,' this critical term is somewhat flat, pertaining as it does to Southern literature generally and invariably. I begin, then, with an attempt at specificity. At once wry and dry, O'Connor's comic intuition is most at home in the *unheimlich*, the uncanny, which is to say that her work depends vitally on the *ludicrous*. There is always something vertiginous in O'Connor's comic scenes: they turn on an image or a detail that is grossly incongruent and out of place, and yet that 'thing' is, at the same time, ironically and inevitably *in* its place. The comic is unsettling not only because it finds itself poised between laughter and an unease that is, in her best work, not far removed from horror toward which it slides, but also because it points to the eternal human capacity for error that, as 'knowledge' long repressed by complacency, is her great subject.

The bookstore anecdote with which I began is a minor but nonetheless exemplary case in point. The clerk's error turns on a slippage between the noun 'bear' and the verb 'to bear.' Associating O'Connor with Southern literature

É. Savoy (✉)
Professor of Comparative Literature, University of Montreal, Canada

© The Editor(s) (if applicable) and The Author(s) 2016
S.C. Street, C.L. Crow (eds.), *The Palgrave Handbook of the Southern Gothic*,
DOI 10.1057/978-1-137-47774-3_11

generally, he or she conflates the verb in O'Connor's novel *The Violent Bear It Away* of 1960 with the titular noun of Faulkner's popular short fiction 'The Bear' of 1942. The clerk's ludicrously confused offer is, then, in its cultural place. The unconscious, of course, knows no chronological literary history, but the process of association that subtends the error and the consequent joke has deeper implications for the discerning eye. For the verb 'to bear' is itself divided among its primary referent, deployed by O'Connor's title, of 'to carry,' and its secondary meanings that are identical with her reiterated theme—to endure and to suffer (analogous to the French *supporter*, which, in the errant ways of etymology, provides an entirely different meaning in English)—and with her spatial poetics; that is, to travel in a certain direction toward a uncertain goal. It is not entirely unlikely, then, that the clerk spoke more than he knew, or that she knew more than she spoke. And this is precisely the kind of situation that O'Connor loved.

O'CONNOR AND THE GOTHIC

O'Connor's implication in the Gothic is not self-evident. Readers acquainted with the historical *topoi* of that genre are likely to share the bewilderment of Mrs. Flood, a minor character in *Wise Blood*, who sees that Hazel Motes's ordeal is not a matter of 'boiling in oil … or walling up cats.' Rather, she continues, 'it's like one of them gory stories, it's something that people have quit doing—like … being a saint' (LA 127). Mrs. Flood cannot name the violent essence of O'Connor's plots and situations; she can only say what it is 'like.' This essence is not a 'thing' susceptible to denomination; rather, it is a pulsion that at once subtends her fiction and is imbricated, or literalized, in her characters' *movement* across the landscape of the South toward a scarifying encounter with a possibility—the possibility that Mrs. Flood articulates as 'being a saint.' Here, in the gothic matrix of O'Connor's work, lies the uncanny and incongruent *recall* of a long-forgotten vocation, for there are no saints in the Protestant South. The progress toward the call to transcendence has several ironic dimensions. In a manner reminiscent of medieval quest narratives, O'Connor traces her characters' movement though a series of comic misadventures—generated by their willful blindness—toward a traumatic accident that is as contingent as it is inevitable. In O'Connor's scenic method, the *moment* of the encounter is paradoxically one of ascent and descent in which there is no immediately clarifying epiphany: if the violence of the *event* is interlined with the abrupt descent of what she terms 'grace,' the corresponding ascent of the subject is but a fleeting perception of a pervasive 'mystery' that remains uncanny. It is, properly speaking, a missed encounter that reveals the character's arrival at the glimpse of an understanding of something that nonetheless remains distant. O'Connor's saints, like her readers, *now* see through a glass, darkly; the full, face-to-face encounter with the sublime mystery is a matter of apolcalyptic futurity, continually deferred and pointedly disnarrated.

The gothic dimensions of O'Connor's writing are interlined with her temporal and spatial poetics, but these literary qualities are in turn shaped by her acute sense of time and place. In her lecture 'The Catholic Novelist in the Protestant South,' she argues that 'the vital strength of Southern literature'—and Southern 'identity' itself—have been 'absorbed' equally from Scripture and from a 'history of defeat and violation: a distrust of the abstract, a sense of human dependence on the grace of God, and a knowledge that evil is not simply a problem to be solved, but a mystery to be endured' (LA 861–2). It is an understatement to say that O'Connor never loses sight of where and who she is, but at the same time her commitment to 'grace' at the threshold of what must be borne as a 'mystery' entails a current of abstraction that pulsates through her work. In what sense can it be said to be present? Broadly theological rather than narrowly or pedagogically religious, epistemological rather than ontological, the framework of abstraction in O'Connor's fiction is not something to which she merely points; rather, an idea is rendered concrete through the poetics of what she would call 'incarnation.' The Incarnation represents the Christian belief that the Son of God, the second person of the trinity, took on a human body and nature and thus became both man and God. As O'Connor puts it, the possibilities of faith for the fiction writer 'are deepened less by abstractions than by an encounter with the mystery in what is human and often perverse' (LA 863). For O'Connor, as for William Carlos Williams, there was no idea but in things—or, in her case, in images and events. If O'Connor's overarching narrative method can be described as one of immanence rather than of one of accomplished transcendence, then 'idea' is conveyed through the mise-en-scène of her sharp-eyed, unsettling realism. O'Connor's Gothic, then, is a discursive field that laminates violence and the loss of everything, of life itself, to a dimension of truth beyond our understanding, yet that she insists we must accept. Theologically, this dimension is the requisite of salvation, but in modern literary culture it is the locus of horror. To the extent that O'Connor's fiction opens *out* into this dimension, into this impossible possibility, hers is a realism of the Real.

As every student of literary history knows, apologists for realism and for gothic romance traditionally articulated their projects in terms of stark and mutual difference. Flannery O'Connor's canonical status, and her peculiarity, owe a great deal to her practical deconstruction of this opposition. While her realism depends on the steady accumulation of sharp, concise, and *unkind* detail, usually of appearance or gesture—which anchors her characters in plausible reality—descriptive accuracy is not self-sufficient. In a manner reminiscent of Dickens, the visible aspects of O'Connor's personages are *pointed*, in the sense that they point to the *character* of character, which is inevitably an amalgam of the complacent and the misguided. O'Connor's imagistic placing of her characters tends to be proleptic: she sets them up for that encounter with the Christian mystery, which is a version of what Jacques Lacan conceptualized as the Real. In the 1950s, Lacan staked out the Real as that which is outside language and thus unassimilable to symbolization: it is that which menaces the coherence of the subject's fixed illusions, whether they be of the Imaginary Order (the ego's sense of its unlimited agency and its desire for fulfillment) or of the Symbolic Order (the domain of the superego in which the subject conforms to law, language, and custom). According to Dylan Evans, Lacan associated the Real with impossibility: 'The Real is "the impossible" because it is impossible to imagine, impossible to integrate into the symbolic order, and impossible to attain in any way. It is this character of impossibility and of resistance to symbolization which lends the Real its essentially traumatic quality' (160). If the Real is the site, as Evans puts it, of 'a radical indeterminacy' (160), it nonetheless makes its traumatic essence felt in the structures of everyday life, in the interstices and the gaps of the Symbolic. It is associated above all with *abjection*, with the ever-present possibility, impossible to imagine, of the utter collapse of the subject into nothingness. O'Connor's contribution to the Gothic entails the return of the impossible Real within the Symbolic contours of realism itself, not only as possibility but also as *proximity*: the Real is where everything and everyone tends. Her poetics of the Real are both small, localized, and comic, and ultimately shattering, horrifying, and apocalyptic. I shall deal with each in turn.

ABJECTION

The disquieting comedy of the abject is everywhere in O'Connor's writing. A localized effect, it is intrinsic to her economy of the visible detail—or, more precisely, to the highly selective *economy* of that economy. She takes a particular, perverse, and recurring delight, for example, in the suggestibility of images of teeth and hair. At the outset of 'The Life You Save May Be Your Own,' Mr. Shiftlet offers Lucynell Crater *mère* a piece of chewing gum, 'but she only raised her upper lip to indicate she had no teeth' (LA 173). Short on words but long on craftiness, Lucynell plots to have Mr. Shiftlet marry her mentally handicapped daughter in return for a honeymoon trip in her decrepit car, but she gets her comeuppance when Shiftlet abandons the daughter at a lunch counter. O'Connor places Lucynell not just *in* the abjection of toothlessness, and all that it signifies as synecdoche, but more immediately *by* the ludicrous gesture that she performs: the reader does not know whether to laugh or to grimace in repugnance. To be *édenté* in this story's context is indexical of an inability to perceive; constructed entirely through her grotesque body, Lucynell could not follow the (misguided) empiricism of Hazel Motes, of *Wise Blood*, to disbelieve 'anything you couldn't see or hold in your hands or test with your teeth' (LA 116). As the very mark of the Real, this image haunts the remainder of the story and persists in the gentle reader's memory by condensing the story itself. It is our encounter, in a small way, with the unimaginable.

In *Wise Blood*, teeth and hair recur with remarkable frequency, always as a sign of ugliness that has implications for the subject's limited understanding. Recall Mrs. Flood, the landlady who could not understand Hazel Motes's vocation: she 'was past her middle years and her plate was too large' (LA 124). Then there is a passing waitress, a prime example of ironically congruous incongruity: 'The waitress was a tall woman with a big yellow dental plate and the same color hair done up in a black hairnet. One hand never left her hip; she filled orders with the other one' (LA 108). It is fun to imagine O'Connor's glee as she wrote this description—and as she peopled the landscape of her novel with similar personages. Slowly and by accretion, yet suddenly and abruptly, they assault the reader's visual imagination, leaving us giddy with perverse and campy pleasure. Such characters are precarious; they seem always to be just on the point of collapse into dust and nothingness. At times, too, O'Connor's deftly ludicrous descriptions turn outward the emptiness within. Such is the case with the scoundrel Onnie Jay Holy: 'He looked like an ex-preacher turned cowboy, or an ex-cowboy turned mortician. He was not handsome but under his smile, there was an honest look that fitted into his face like a set of false teeth' (LA 83).

O'Connor's parade of the Real incarnated in the abject—uneasily at home in the Symbolic order as its necessary other—has everything to do with what Joyce Carol Oates calls 'the art of caricature.' It is in no way a lesser art than that of elevated and meditative realism, Oates insists, but its object is entirely different. Whereas the elaborate psychology of James, or the modernist intro-spection of Woolf, explores 'the *humanness* of [its] characters,' the caricaturist—'cruel, crude, reductive, and often very funny'—has no interest in *humanness* except to mock it, and to make us laugh (109–10). The poetics of caricature is indexical of O'Connor's larger project, which Oates understands as arising from her 'lifelong and variegated *irritation*':

> the two-dimensionality of cartoon art is at the heart of the work of O'Connor, whose unshakable absolutist faith provided her with a rationale with which to mock both her secular and bigoted-Christian contemporaries in a succession of brilliantly-orchestrated short stories that read like *parables of human folly con-fronted by mortality.* (111, my emphasis)

Oates's choice of critical terms to denominate O'Connor's method ('para-ble') and consistent subject (the encounter of 'folly' with 'mortality') encapsu-lates the formal contours of the *other* and overarching dimension of O'Connor's Gothic: the inexorable narrative movement toward the shattering encounter with the Real. While the violence of this encounter recalls the character to his abjection—requires him to *own* it as the precondition for transcendence—it is also, crucially, the moment of redemption, which O'Connor understands as grace. Repeatedly in her lectures, O'Connor justified the shock value of her climactic scenes against the grain of the ordinary reader's habitual compla-cency. 'The reader wants his grace warm and binding, not dark and disruptive' (LA 862), she observed in contrarian fashion, as the prelude to an anecdote. 'An old lady in California' of sentimental proclivities wrote to her to ask for something that would 'lift up [the] heart' of a 'tired reader' in the evening. O'Connor's snarky riposte suggested that 'if her heart had been in the right place, it would have been lifted up' (LA 863). O'Connor's recourse to the grammar of the conditional indicates a great deal about her staging of the Real

as a vocation: to resituate the 'heart' of the reader *in the right place* is an evangelical reformation, urgent because readers 'are all tired.' The Californian cor-
respondent is merely a synecdoche for an American malaise: 'One old lady who
wants her heart lifted up wouldn't be so bad, but you multiply her 250,000
times and what you get is a book club' (LA 863). Fiction writing, O'Connor
concludes, 'demands the redemptive act' precisely because the reader 'has forgotten the *price* of restoration' (LA 863).

Given that O'Connor's version of the Gothic approaches violence as redemption, and is addressed to 'the people who think God is dead' (LA 943), in what
sense might we understand Joyce Carol Oates's claim that the stories 'read like
parables'? To begin, Oates is pointing in the right direction, but she does not
go far enough in rendering the specific poetics of the exemplary status of the
Incarnation or of the operation of grace. The parable is the lowest common
denominator of the allegorical mode: familiar chiefly as the simple stories told
by Jesus in the Gospels, its function is to illustrate, clearly and directly, a moral
or spiritual lesson. Considering that O'Connor's goal was to solicit a complex
meditation—at once hermeneutic, theological, and spiritual—it is evident that
the elementary pedagogical status of the parable was not, to say the least, her
authentic *métier*. I would hesitate, although somewhat reluctantly, to approach
O'Connor's poetics under the exclusive auspices of allegory; reluctant, that is,
because her narrative emplotment in general coincides with at least one aspect
of the poststructuralist mapping of allegory, which I shall explain in due course.
Classical and medieval models of allegory share the parabolic impulse of revealing the truth by pointing to some underlying or anterior text; more digressive
and convoluted than parable, allegory nonetheless privileges the accessibility
of a totalizing, coherent meaning. This was the type of allegory with which
O'Connor was familiar, and she did not like it—because it was too idealiz-
ing, too 'uplifting,' and too neatly abstract in its pedagogy. Writing to Sister
Mariella Gable late in her short life, she vents her irritation with the true believ-
ers who 'ask you to make Christianity look desirable, … to describe its essence,
not what you see.' The tendency of such readers, she argues,

> is toward the abstract and therefore toward allegory, thinness, and ultimately
> what they are looking for is an apologetic fiction. The best of them think: make
> it look desirable because it is desirable. And the rest of them think: make it look
> desirable so I won't look like a fool for holding it. (LA 1182)

O'Connor's resistance to the traditional model of religious allegory is grounded
in her realism of the Real—in the gothic matrix of violence and abjection that
abuts the possibility of the 'realistically' impossible. It entails not only a scorn-
ful rejection of the beatific and the elevating but, more importantly, a profound
suspicion of an explanatory tendency that cannot be but totalizing; that is to
say, thin, abstract, reductive, and too easy. Her solution, and her method, turn
(once again) on the Incarnation: 'I know,' she offers to Sister Gable, 'that the
writer does call up the general and maybe the essential through the particular,

but this general and essential is still deeply embedded in mystery. It is not answerable to any of our formulas. It doesn't rest finally in a statable kind of solution' (LA 1182–3). At the center of the particular exemplified in the general, and the general 'embedded' in mystery, is the obscure, violent operation of grace, which requires the progress of every form of evil and horrific violence in order to emerge as both credible and necessary. This, in essence—and I offer it as a further particularization—constitutes O'Connor's realism of the Real. 'The writer,' she concludes, 'has to make the corruption believable before he can make the grace meaningful' (LA 1182).

DISTANCE AND PROXIMITY

The thorny question of the 'meaningful'—of what precisely conditions or determines O'Connor's 'meaning'—brings me to a deconstructive model of allegory with which her writing is perhaps broadly consonant. Paul de Man's account of Romantic and post-Romantic allegory explores the mechanics of the temporality of deferral, or of the absence of referential clarity in any present moment in the text. Influenced by Derrida's model of *différance*, or the endless postponement of arrival at transcendent meaning, de Man's field is narrative rather than philosophical discourse. Broadly speaking, de Man takes up the Romantic ideology of symbol, which aspires to a spatial congruence of sign and referent, in order to demonstrate its collapse into the temporality of allegory. Inevitably, he argues, 'the allegorical sign refer[s] to another sign that precedes it. The meaning constituted by the allegorical sign can then consist only in the *repetition* … of a previous sign with which it can never coincide, since it is of the essence of this previous sign to be pure anteriority' (207). A narrative that starts with an idea—which is to say, 'narrative' *tout court*—can only trace its evolving difference, as it inscribes itself in time, from that with which it began in the past, and from that which it aspires to clarify or to demonstrate in the future time of writing.

   The great benefit of this temporality of *différance* is that it is the very condition in which the particular can be elaborated; its downside, for the writer with an agenda, is that the punctual illumination of the general by the particular can only compound its elusiveness. I would argue that another word for this deManian field of difference and non-coincidence is O'Connor's 'mystery.' And it is important to recall that 'mystery' is at once the point of departure and the point of arrival in her fiction, which is to say that the *différance* of the particular, at once *from* and *with* the general, is the basic narrative contract under which she writes. A better word for O'Connor's poetics of Gothic grace—one that laminates the temporal dimension of mystery to its realistic, literal unfolding in space—is *distance*. Once again, de Man turns out to be helpful: 'Whereas the symbol postulates the possibility of an identity or identification, allegory designates primarily a *distance* in relation to its own origin, and, renouncing the nostalgia and the desire to coincide, it establishes its language in the void of this temporal difference' (207).

The deconstructive model of allegory is helpful in understanding the complex, elusive nature of theological mystery in O'Connor's fiction, as well as the indirect relation of the particular case history illustrated by a story and the transcendent and redemptive possibility (or the violent impossibility) to which it points. Yet any allegorical paradigm will take us only so far in coming to terms with O'Connor's text. The medieval template places too much emphasis on referential presence, the poststructuralist on its absence. De Man, and Derrida before him, might be said to take allegorical *différance* as the default model of *any* narrative that deals with abstract value. Although their explication of the temporal constraints of the signifer within the economy of a given text accounts for much in the *movement toward* grace that animates O'Connor's work, there is something in her larger configuration of time that allegory alone cannot comprehend. For there is an important difference in O'Connor's mapping of the world between narrative temporality, or the sequence of events leading proleptically to the violent encounter, and what she understands, theologically, as time. The critical 'something' that lies beyond the strict reach of allegory is, I suggest, the figural.

By the 'figural' I do not mean the metaphorical rhetoric of the figurative, nor do I intend anything remotely like the Transfiguration of the Gospels in which Jesus, radiant in glory and in the company of the prophets Elijah and Moses, is hailed as the Son of God. Rather, the specificity of the figural has its genesis in allegorical temporality itself: it has to do with what de Man calls an oblique 'meaning' that is constituted 'by the allegorical sign' precisely and exclusively as 'the *repetition* (in the Kierkegaardian sense of the term) of a previous sign with which it can never coincide' (207). The rise of the figural from the allegorical will require some parsing. While the 'sign' that attempts to conflate the particular with the general involves repetition, it is a very specific kind of repetition in a very specific temporality—that of Kierkegaard, who explained it (via the Book of Job) as the possibility of a *return* of a historical figure or the restoration of a previous state of grace. O'Connor's fiction, early and late, turns crucially on the figural—on the return of the prophetic figure, who emerges from the distance, or departs into the distance, bringing with him a violent, redemptive zeal that O'Connor represents as the scarifying descent of grace on the erring subject. Against the deconstructive precept of the non-coincidence of the present sign with the purely anterior, O'Connor's ultimate 'mystery' requires the alignment of the latter-day prophet, at once despite and because of his violent and corrupt nature, with the prophetic word of the Old Testament. In orienting her project toward the figural rather than the narrowly allegorical, giving narrative form to the return of the prophet is indeed a type of repetition, but whereas time binds repetition into something resembling a pattern, prophetic return binds time itself to eternity. For the prophet's function is to prophesy the fulfillment of the promise, and the explication of the mystery, in the fullness of time.

What, then, is the figural, and how does it illuminate O'Connor's poetics of time and space? It has everything to do with the character of the prophet, who appears in several guises in her fiction. For the reader who comes to *Wise Blood* and *The Violent Bear It Away* for the first time, the general uncanniness of the novels seems to arise from their literary form: they read as dark parodies, or comic retellings, of the Old Testament prophets. O'Connor situates her fanatical prophet as 'a man apart,' shaped by cultural isolation:

> for if you are a Catholic and have this intensity of belief, you join a convent and are heard from no more; whereas if you are Protestant and have it, there is no convent for you to join, and you go about in the world, getting into all sorts of trouble and drawing the wrath of people who don't believe anything much at all down on your head. (LA 1183)

The latter-day prophet and his trajectory across the fictional landscape—his career of freakish madness and volatile unreason—are the agent and the locus of what I have conceptualized as the Real, as the great disturbance in the Symbolic order. As O'Connor puts it, the prophet bears an unacceptable authenticity: 'his kind of Christianity may not be socially desirable, but it will be *real in the sight of God*' (LA 1183, my emphasis).

'Figura,' as Erich Auerbach conceptualizes it, is a mode of biblical interpretation that organizes patristics, the writings of the early church 'fathers.' Essentially, it is the attempt to demonstrate that 'the persons and the events of the Old Testament were prefigurations of the New Testament and its history of salvation' (30). While the events of the Old and New Testaments are conjoined as prophecy and fulfillment, Auerbach, following Tertullian, insists on a strict and literal realism within the economy of proleptic shadowing forth. Figural interpretation refuses the matrix of 'mere allegory,' because the Old Testament had 'real, literal meaning throughout' (30) or, in other words, historical reality. It is precisely this *claim* of the real and the actual (as opposed to the *différance* of the metaphorical), along with the narrative poetics of excoriating realism, which generates the force of O'Connor's uncanny emplotment. Haunted by a pervasive atmosphere of déjà vu (or *déjà lu*) that is never explained in parabolic fashion, O'Connor's fictions coalesce at once as familiar and strange. If she displaces the Old Testament prophetic figure by the narrative resources of Southern Gothic, she locates the contemporary fanatic within an imagistically authentic slide toward the traumatic Real, *and* within the overarching, theological temporality of eternal return. Narrative temporality, then, is necessarily a real shadowing forth, or reflection, of theological time, of the relation between prophecy and fulfillment.

It is quite likely that O'Connor absorbed this supratemporal framework from Augustine, one of her favorite writers. According to Auerbach, Augustine replaces the two poles of prophecy and fulfillment, or the strict relation between the Old and the New Testaments, with a future-oriented time that unfolds in three stages:

> the Law or history of the Jews as a prophetic *figura* for the appearance of Christ; the incarnation as fulfillment of this *figura* and at the same time as a new promise of the end of the world and the Last Judgment; and finally, the future occurence of these events as ultimate fulfillment. (41)

O'Connor's prophets, as Christ figures, endure their trials and their outcast status *in* real time, yet the obscurity of their incarnation and the violence they suffer and wreak necessarily lack completion, or closure, suspended as they are prior to the final accomplishment. While this truth in pointing subscribes to a deconstructive model of allegory, O'Connor's *figura* is better understood as a broadly anagogical vision that, as she writes in 'The Nature and Aim of Fiction,' is a method of medieval exegesis that 'had to do with the Divine life and our participation in it' (MM 72).

Squarely alongside O'Connor's fictional mediations of the prophet's return in our time is her tendency to return, in essays and letters, to a singular definition of the prophet. Initially, the prophet is defined in spatial terms: 'According to St. Thomas,' she writes to Cecil Dawkins, 'prophetic vision is not a matter of seeing clearly, but of seeing what is distant, hidden' (LA 1116). In her lecture 'The Catholic Novelist in the Protestant South,' the visual economy of spatial distance is amplified to include dimensions of uncanny temporality and gothic poetics generally. Attempting to particularize the grotesque character in, and of, the 'Christ-haunted' South, she emphasizes the strange thing that the grotesque hero sees, and what the novelist attempts to see in his very seeing:

> They seem to carry an invisible burden and to fix us with eyes that remind us that we all *bear* some heavy responsibility whose nature we have forgotten. They are prophetic figures. In the novelist's case, prophecy is a matter of seeing near things with their extensions of meaning and thus of seeing far things close up. *The prophet is a realist of distances*, distances in the qualitative sense, and it is this kind of realism that you find in the modern instances of the grotesque. (LA 860–61, my emphases)

Simultaneously eloquent and gnarled, this passage invites frequent rereading: I believe that it is the key to O'Connor's literary achievement. Although it is somewhat resistant to paraphrase, O'Connor argues that Southern realism, especially in its gothic or 'grotesque' inflection, conjoins the concrete, proximate 'near thing' to that approximate mystery, that essential human responsibility, which has been lost in the 'qualitative' distance of time.

EXTENSION OF THE MEANINGFUL

Earlier, I raised the overwhelming question of what constitutes 'the meaningful' in O'Connor's writing, considering that our grasp of meaning is never punctual. Evidently, meaning inheres for the novelist in and through the poetics of what she terms 'extension.' It is diffuse and relational rather than localized and immediate. Entirely figural, the prophet is the *figure* of that extension. If O'Connor's realism constructs the prophet in the temporality of uncanny recall and return, then her gothic turn of that return situates the figural figure in space. The prophet sees 'far things close up,' and the reader, along with the surrounding characters, sees the prophet move from the visible distance toward us, bearing with him the unpredictable volatility of the searing possibility of grace. Repeatedly, O'Connor locates this proximate distance in the prophet's eyes; as the very site of the mystery, of the 'far thing close up,' it is the often the focus of her most powerful writing. Essentially, then, 'distance' is the trope by which O'Connor may be said to literalize in the poetics of space the abstract temporality that subtends her plots. To read her at all is to be acutely sensitive to the space of the encroaching thing, the imminent and immanent touch of the Real. As the distance diminishes, we cannot avert our eyes. What is it that we see? What is it that we are capable of seeing? In 1955, O'Connor was compelled to defend 'A Good Man Is Hard to Find' from the accusation that the story is merely 'brutal and sarcastic.' She argues that, contrary to the disposition of the sentimental and the stupid, 'there is nothing harder or less sentimental than Christian realism. ... There are many rough beasts slouching toward Bethlehem to be born ..., and when I see these stories described as horror stories, I am always amused because the reviewer always has got hold of *the wrong horror*' (LA 942).

'A Good Man Is Hard to Find' requires several readings to grasp the web of ironies that frame the *right* horror. The first time I encountered the story, on a cold December morning and stricken with flu and a hangover, it was the most traumatic experience in my youthful reading life. I remember my escalating dread as the Misfit's younger companions led the traveling family, two by two, into the woods that 'gaped like a dark open mouth' (LA 146), followed by the pistol shots that resounded in the distance. Yet, even as O'Connor gives progressive turns of the screw to gothic affect, the reader cannot fail to experience a gleeful, distancing counter-turn as the fatuous grandmother and the obnoxious children meet the end that they have perversely engineered. The 'right' horror coalesces in the space between these dual narrative pulsions. For the grandmother did not want to go to Florida; she wanted to visit her relatives in Tennessee. In the course of the morning, she exchanges complacencies with Red Sam, the operator of a greasy spoon, chiefly concerning 'that criminal, The Misfit' and the fact that a good man is hard to find in these fallen times: they agree that 'there's no use talking about it' (LA 142) because it is true. Back on the road and 'outside of Toombsboro' (LA 142), the grandmother entertains the children with a description of a nearby plantation house—a gothic mansion, probably abandoned since the Civil War, with a secret panel and a cache of family silver. Predictably, the children begin to yell, scream, and whine, and their father gives in to them, turning the car down a long-disused road. The grandmother suddenly recalls that the plantation house is in Tennessee, not in Georgia—for her daydream was a Freudian wish-fulfullment—and in her violent start of consternation, the cat that she had concealed jumps on her son's shoulder, and the car winds up in a gulch. Almost immediately, they see 'a car some distance away ..., coming slowly as if the occupants were watching them.' The driver arrives and 'looks down with a steady expressionless gaze' (LA 145).

The vacant gaze is that of the Misfit, the prophet and the instrument of violent grace that arrives out of the temporal and spatial distance. The grim ironies pile up when the grandmother identifies the Misfit, who points out that 'it would have been better for all of you, lady, if you hadn't of reckernized me' (LA 147) and as she tries desperately to escape her fate by repeatedly addressing him as 'a good man' and 'not a bit common' (LA 148). The grandmother's plea invokes the precarious Symbolic order that is crumbling around her: if the fact of race and the fictions of gender and class aspiration prompt her appeal—'You wouldn't shoot a lady, would you?' (LA 147)—there is nothing in her foolish language capable of deferring her encounter with the Real. There is nothing left for her but to recognize her final abjection and to attend, if possible, to the Misfit's recall of her to her common, frail humanity. For his part, the Misfit offers a fragmented paraphrase of his own itinerant and violent life, from 'gospel singer' to being 'buried alive' in the penitentiary (LA 149). Struck dumb by terror and apprehension of her end, the grandmother wants to counsel him to pray, but can only murmur 'Jesus. Jesus' in a voice somewhere between a prayer and a curse.

The Misfit takes up this cue to zero in on a theological account of the Real, and here, like the grandmother, he finds himself suspended between the prayer and the curse. '"Yes'm" [he] said as if he agreed. Jesus thrown everything off balance' (LA 151). The Real is at once the unknowable mystery and the violence that is the consequence of unbelief:

> If He did what He said, then it's nothing for you to do but throw away every-thing and follow Him, and if He didn't, then it's nothing for you to do but enjoy the few minutes you got left the best way you can—by killing somebody or burning down his house or doing some other meanness to him. No pleasure but meanness. (LA 152)

The Misfit's 'best way' is the itinerary of 'pleasure,' but his reiterated 'nothing' points to his own arrival at nothingness: after shooting the grandmother, he confesses, 'It's no real pleasure in life' (LA 153). The 'right' horror, then, or the horror of the Real, is twofold. On the one hand, there is the Misfit's emphatic rejection of another 'way,' and his paradoxical status as both the denier of grace and its instrument. On the other, there is the grandmother's transcendent recognition: in the last moment of her life, as she reaches out and touches the Misfit on his shoulder, she claims him as 'one of my own children!' (LA 152).

Is it the case that the grandmother is brought by utter abjection to embrace the violent Real in, and as, a moment of grace? Is she finally able to glimpse the possibility of the Real thing? Or are we to understand her ultimate sentence as a final, desperate attempt to save her life? Would the life that she saved be her own? Flannery O'Connor admitted, in the wake of this story, 'I won't ever be able entirely to understand my own work or even my own motivations' (LA 944). Perhaps the hand of God touched a burning coal to the grandmother's lips in a moment of prophetic clarity—but then, the bear ran away with it.

Notes

1. References to Flannery O'Connor's writing are cited parenthetically in the text. The abbreviation LA indicates a quotation from the Library of America edition of her collected works, while the single use of the abbreviation MM indicates a quotation from *Mystery and Manners.*

Bibliography

Auerbach, E. (1959). Figura (trans: Manheim, R.). In *Scenes from the drama of European literature* (pp. 11–76). Reprint: Minneapolis: University of Minnesota Press, 1984.

de Man, P. (1983). The rhetoric of temporality. In *Blindness and insight: Essays in the rhetoric of contemporary criticism*, 2nd edn, Revised. Minneapolis: University of Minnesota Press.

Dickinson, E. (1960). In T. H. Johnson (Ed.), *The complete poems of Emily Dickinson.* Boston: Little, Brown and Company.

Evans, D. (1996). *An introductory dictionary of Lacanian psychoanalysis.* London: Routledge.

Oates, J. C. (2010). *In rough country: Essays and reviews.* New York: HarperCollins.

O'Connor, F. (1957). In S. Fitzgerald & R. Fitzgerald (Eds.), *Mystery and manner: Occasional prose.* New York: Farrar, Straus and Giroux.

O'Connor, F. (1988). In S. Fitzgerald (Ed.), *Collected works.* New York: Literary classics of the United States (the Library of America).

CHAPTER 12

Florida Gothic: Shadows in the Sunshine State

Bev Hogue

In Jeff VanderMeer's 2014 Southern Reach trilogy, he sends groups of explorers into Area X, a mysterious dystopian landscape modeled freely on northwestern Florida. Following a long line of explorers assessing Florida's resources for possession and colonization, VanderMeer's characters rely on maps that obscure as much as they reveal, and they find a landscape that mirrors their preconceived notions; seeking enlightenment, they plunge into a darkness that threatens to consume them. Although VanderMeer's fantasy veers sharply from more realistic portrayals of Florida, its mingling of sunshine and shadow exemplifies the concerns of Florida writers in the Gothic mode.

Florida has long been known as the Sunshine State, but its authors often portray it as a place where sunshine blinds unwitting characters to the presence of underlying mystery and menace. Florida has been contested terrain since the moment Europeans first touched on its shores and began the long history of battles for possession that resulted in historical traumas that many would prefer to forget: displacement and destruction of Native American tribes, slavery followed by entrenched racial injustice, and struggles for control of land and natural resources. This dark heritage shadows many Florida works, but a brief examination of five of these works will reveal common concerns of authors in the Gothic mode. Francis Parkman's *Pioneers of France in the New World* (1865) constructs the Florida landscape as a battleground where forces of good and evil clash, and Lafcadio Hearn reinforces that construction in two short works, 'A Tropical Intermezzo' and 'To the Fountain of Youth' (1911a). More recent authors drag unspeakable menace into the stark sunshine: Peter Matthiessen's *Killing Mister Watson* (1990) explores the dark forces that drive a community to murder, while Karen Russell's celebrated *Swamplandia!* (2011) shows how even sun-washed islands can be suffused with horrors that the naïve narrator

B. Hogue (✉)
Marietta College, Marietta, OH, USA

© The Editor(s) (if applicable) and The Author(s) 2016
S.C. Street, C.L. Crow (eds.), *The Palgrave Handbook of the Southern Gothic*,
DOI 10.1057/978-1-137-47774-3_12

149

cannot even name. Together with VanderMeer's *Annihilation* (2014), these works examine the troubled history of possession that haunts Florida's terrain, allowing gothic horrors to thrive beneath the searing Southern sun.

Battles on the Borderlands

Jay Ellis asserts that the Gothic mode 'continually takes us out there, below ground, and behind the door we would rather leave closed' (xvi). Florida's low-lying terrain and high water table preclude subterranean exploration, but topography does not prevent Florida writers from exploring hidden depths. Florida's long history as contested space claimed by Spanish, French, and British colonists who displaced or destroyed various Native American cultures and imported African slaves left behind what Christopher J. Walsh calls the '"dark legacy" which still informs the Southern Gothic,' a legacy that may be 'racial, political, moral, spatial and even environmental in nature' (Walsh 21). Further, Charles Crow reminds us that the Gothic is a 'literature of borderlands' that 'patrols the line between waking and dreams, human and machine, the normal and the freakish, and the living and the dead' (2). While the Gothic mode appears more frequently in recent Florida fiction, it informs earlier fiction and nonfiction accounts that explore shifting borderlands both literal and metaphorical.

Lured by legends of gold and the Fountain of Youth, early Spanish explorers found terrain so impenetrable and unfamiliar that they kept moving on, hoping for better conditions or treasure ahead. However, they eventually adapted to the sub-tropical environment and established a colony at St. Augustine in 1565. Just a year earlier, however, French Huguenots had set up a colony at Fort Caroline, in present-day Jacksonville, but the Spanish saw this as a threat and sacked the fledgling colony. Francis Parkman's *Pioneers of France in the New World* (1865) casts this frontier massacre as a mythic conflict between forces of darkness and light. Parkman's belief that French Protestant settlements were more civilized than those of the Catholic Spanish led him to characterize Spain as 'the incubus of Europe' that 'chilled the world with her baneful shadow,' while France was 'full of life,—a discordant and struggling vitality' (33). 'Day was breaking in the world,' asserts Parkman. 'But Spain was the citadel of darkness,—a monastic cell, an inquisitorial dungeon, where no ray could pierce' (83). His Spaniards are gothic villains spawned in dark, claustrophobic cloisters, 'a scourge as dire as ever fell on man' (83). If, as Parkman asserts, Florida before settlement was 'silent in primeval sleep' (15), this very silence created a blank slate on which European imagination could inscribe a treasure map that blurred the line between fantasy and reality.

Patrolling this line were European explorers who 'unveiled the secrets of the barbarous continent' (13). Parkman emphasizes the violence of this unveiling when he describes the Spaniards under Menendez marching north from St. Augustine to attack Fort Caroline: 'now hacking their way through palmetto thickets; and now turning from their path to shun some pool, quagmire, cypress swamp, or "hummock," matted with impenetrable bushes, brambles, and vines' (99). Parkman's Spaniards are constantly thrusting their way toward mastery of men and terrain with a brutality rivaled only by his description of Native Americans, who are similarly associated with mysterious, bloody rituals conducted in dark, claustrophobic settings. French colonists witness a tribal ritual when, 'immured in darkness, they listened to the howls, yelpings, and lugubrious songs' along with 'the drumming, dancing, and stamping; the wild lamentation of the women as they gashed the arms of the young girls with sharp mussel-shells, and flung the blood into the air with dismal outcries' (48). Associating both Catholic and Native American cultures with secret blood rites, Parkman portrays his hapless French Huguenots as gentle victims beset by darkness on all sides while struggling in vain to keep the light of civilization burning.

Lafcadio Hearn found similar battles between light and darkness in the same terrain long after the era of exploration and colonization. Hearn's visit to Jacksonville and voyage up the St. John's River in the early 1880s resulted in short narratives unveiling the barbarous shadows underlying the civilized state. In Hearn's short story 'A Tropical Intermezzo,' a wanderer discovers in Florida an Edenic fountain haunted by a shadow 'cast athwart the sunshine of the world' (69). While this slight but fanciful take on the Rip Van Winkle tale is haunted by artefacts of Florida's fraught history (Spanish artefacts, lost explorers, the Fountain of Youth), a nonfiction travel narrative exploring the same terrain also dabbles in the Gothic mode, emphasizing the sharp contrasts between light and shadow to construct a primitive north Florida frontier landscape as a land of sunshine obscuring deep mysteries. 'To the Fountain of Youth,' Hearn's account of a steamboat trip up the St. Johns and Ocklawaha Rivers to Silver Springs in the early 1880s, begins with the romantic hope that the journey might lead to 'those subterranean rivers, those marvelous volcanic springs haunted by dim traditions of the Fountains of Youth' (40), but this hope dims when the steamboat enters the narrow, winding Ocklawaha, where, like William Bartram before him, Hearn finds monsters battling in fluid borderlands. The Ocklawaha, he writes, is 'a narrow river undulating through the forest like some slow serpent unrolling its hundred coils of green. And, as the greater serpent devours a lesser one, so the writhing Ocklawaha swallows the shining current that flows from the Silver Spring' (43).

Hearn emphasizes the claustrophobic elements of the trip, the feeling that the Ocklawaha's banks are closing in and threatening to ensnare the boat, which is 'continually moving into fluvial recesses without an exit' (46). When darkness falls, this claustrophobic landscape 'becomes an astonishment, a revelation, an Apocalypse' as the boat seems to move 'not through a living forest, but through a world of ghosts. Forms grotesque as fetishes loom up on all sides' (51). When the steamboat whistles into the darkness, 'the deep forest laughs in scorn, and hurls back the shout with a thousand mockeries of echo—a thousand phantom thunders' (54). Although morning light 'exorcise[s] the shadowy terrors of the night' (56), Hearn continues to emphasize the subterranean mysteries that he encounters at Silver Springs, where the water is

> dark with the darkness of profundities unfathomed by the sun—the secret sources of the spring, the place of its mystic fountain-birth .... From what unilluminated caverns,—what subterranean lakes,—burst this prodigious flow? Go ask the gnomes! Man may never answer. This is the visible beginning indeed; but of the invisible beginning who may speak?—not even the eye of the Sun hath discerned it; the light of the universe hath never shone upon it.—Earth reveals much to the magicians of science; but the dim secret of her abysses she keeps forever. (58)

Here, bright sunshine is not sufficient to illuminate subterranean mysteries suggestive of haunting by unfathomed powers. Like Parkman, Hearn portrayed frontier Florida as a borderland where good and evil, civilization and savagery, knowledge and mystery come into sharp conflict that leads to a sense of irreparable loss.

Killing the Scapegoat, Spreading the Shadow

After the swamps are drained, the monsters are tamed, and the impenetrable scrub is cleared and plastered with strip malls, what mystery remains? Three more recent authors employ the Gothic mode to portray Florida as a land where sunshine blinds people to the dark forces that haunt humanity. Peter Matthiessen looks back in time to explore the frontier between personal and communal responsibility for evil, while Karen Russell situates her isolated heroine in a present haunted by thwarted desires and irresolvable conflicts. Meanwhile, Jeff VanderMeer imagines a future in which explorers once again encounter incomprehensible darkness on the border between the known and the unknown, the civilized and the savage.

Peter Matthiessen's *Killing Mister Watson* (1990) is the first in a trilogy of novels examining a still explained incident that occurred in 1910, when Edgar J. Watson, a progressive landowner and farmer on Chatham Key in southwestern Florida, was gunned down in broad daylight by a posse made up of his nearest neighbors. Carl Abbott argues that viewing the novel as an example of the Southern Gothic obscures its debt to the 'frontier/western narrative in which the driving force is the power of reinvention and escape from history' (51). Noting that *Killing Mister Watson* 'begins with a shootout, the most hackneyed trope in western fiction' (51), Abbott analyzes how Matthiessen varies the conventions of the frontier Western narrative to emphasize communal responsibility for maintaining justice rather than the individual quest to repair injustice. While he insists that 'Matthiessen constructs the *place* of Southwest Florida as *frontier West*' (Abbott 55, his emphasis), Abbott cannot overlook the ways in which *Killing Mister Watson* embodies the characteristics of Southern Gothic; he compares the novel to both *Absalom, Absalom!* and *All the King's Men*, narratives

> about the inability of individuals to escape the deeds of the past—their own pasts, those of their families, and those of their communities. The novels are therefore

constructed as historical investigations in which multiple accounts are discovered, weighed, and pieced together in an effort to cope with the power of myth and memory. (50)

Matthiessen foregrounds this power by opening the novel with a third-person prologue that reveals the central fact of the plot—Watson's death; the remaining chapters recount the perspectives of various first-person narrators, whose attempts to shed light on the murder only deepen the darkness. Watson's death thus haunts the entire novel (and, indeed, the entire trilogy), casting the Florida frontier as a postlapsarian space where characters' attempts to purge the shadows serve to spread them throughout the community. John Cooley suggests that in *Killing Mister Watson*, as in his other novels, Matthiessen takes readers on a voyage to the underworld and 'relishes rubbing his readers in the blood, feathers, and corpses that litter his rivers of Styx' (191). This process begins on the opening pages when Matthiessen, with a tone as somber as Lafcadio Hearn's, sets the scene of post-hurricane disorder: the sea birds are 'tattered,' the terns 'dirtied,' the coastline 'broken, stunned, flattened to mud by the wild tread of God' (3). In the storm's aftermath, 'a far gray sun picks up dead glints from windrows of rotted mullet, heaped a foot high,' and even the 'baleful and uneasy sky ... looks ragged as a ghost, unsettled, wandering' (3). While nature remains unsettled, the human community is reduced to debris: 'Pots, kettles, crockery, a butter churn, tin tubs, buckets, salt-slimed boots, soaked horsehair mattresses, and ravished dolls are strewn across the pale killed ground' (3).

Into this bleak scene comes a boat carrying E.J. Watson, whose approach calls the community to gather their guns. Watson's neighbors suspect him of responsibility for a number of murders (ranging from 5 to 50), but Watson has so far demonstrated a remarkable ability to escape justice—unless he is an innocent victim of circumstance or innuendo. The conflicting accounts that Matthiessen constructs emphasize the absence of certainty and thus the difficulty of pursuing justice, especially when representatives of justice are subject to the same corruption that suffuses all of Matthiessen's fallen worlds. Given a broken world in which justice remains unattainable, the community steps into the gap between civilization and savagery to purge the community of evil. To accomplish this, though, they first must abandon individuality and merge with their dark surroundings, standing 'half-hidden in the undergrowth' so that 'the postmaster can no longer make out faces beneath the old and broken hats. His neighbors seem anonymous as outlaws' (6).

While members of the posse believe that '[t]his dark day has been coming down forever' (8), they view their act as the work of civilization, quite separate from the acts of savage violence that they condemn. However, Matthiessen undermines this distinction between civilization and savagery by linking this discrete act of frontier violence with other violent acts more easily overlooked, from the plume hunting and gator hunting that devastated wildlife populations to the Disston Company's dredging, which destroyed wetlands and disrupted the course of rivers. Most notably, though, Matthiessen links all these acts of violence with the Spanish destruction of Calusa culture. While some of his characters continue the Spanish explorers' search for hidden treasure, others evoke the Calusa as an absence haunting the present and threatening to harm those who exploit Calusa places and artefacts. Watson's neighbor Richard Hamilton, for instance, fears that disturbing Calusa burial places would free the 'bad spirits' that haunt the islands (103), including, especially, the island land originally possessed by the Calusa but now farmed by E.J. Watson. Chatham Bend, says Hamilton, 'was what Indins call a power place, but it was bad power, something dark' (37). His neighbor Henry Thompson, meanwhile, constantly feels the invisible gaze of the absent Calusa, who '[w]atched us white men when we come into their country and watched us when we went away, the same way the wild critters did, the deer, the panthers, stopping at the edge of cover and looking back over their shoulder' (18). By dramatizing the brutal dispossession of the Calusa and portraying exploitation of Calusa artefacts as an ongoing endeavor, Matthiessen suggests that the shadow of trauma haunting the community has far preceded Watson's appearance on the scene and will continue after his death.

This fact does not, however, prevent the community from attempting to purge the darkness by killing Mister Watson. He first appears on the scene as an agent of progress, with plans to automate his syrup production and open up new trade routes, but the violence that accompanies Watson's enterprises becomes linked in the public mind with natural omens such as hurricanes and the appearance of Halley's Comet, 'with the scorpion tail of it curling right over us like an almighty question mark in Heaven' (280). Unanswered questions surrounding the deaths of Watson's workers and neighbors create yet another haunting absence, a gap that the suspicious neighbors fill with rhetoric about 'a great war between Good and Evil, and how that comet was a messenger of Armageddon' (280). Following quickly on the heels of these omens, the hurricane of 1910 becomes yet another sign of 'God's wrath at E.J. Watson,' inspiring the community to act as the hand of justice to fend off further disaster (280). Indeed, James J. Watson describes Mister Watson's killing as 'a symbolic act of communal sacrifice' (249), but the community soon learns that killing the scapegoat does not banish its shadow.

After the death of Mister Watson, Bill House, the putative leader of the posse, describes Watson's battered and bloated body: 'Didn't hardly look like a man, he looked like something from the ocean deep thrown up by the storm. He was scraped so raw you could not say what kind of sea monster this might of been' (331). House and his helpers bury Watson, who has become 'a thing … with legs and arms and no damn face on him,' and they drag slabs of rock on top of the grave to 'make sure this thing would not rise at dusk and come hunting the ones that turned against him' (331). Positioning Watson as an inhuman, monstrous force of evil allows members of the posse to distance themselves from their own violence and consign the murder to the forgotten past, alongside the destruction of the Calusa; however, just as Watson's neighbors fear the vengeance of the displaced Calusa, they fear that Watson's power will continue beyond the grave, haunting them in perpetuity. In life, Mister Watson serves as the community's scapegoat, the locus of darkness and evil; however, in order to purge the community of this evil, members of the posse become anonymous, blending into the darkness and erasing their own faces to escape responsibility for a monstrous act. In killing Mister Watson, they release their own murderous spirit and doom themselves to an inescapable haunting.

Journeys to the Underworld

In *Killing Mister Watson*, Jean Chevalier is a minor character, a bird fancier obsessed with finding Calusa treasure; his neighbors describe the Frenchman as looking 'like some rare old bird hisself, ... quills sticking out all over his head, beady eyes and a stiff gait' (28). Chevalier finds an echo in Karen Russell's *Swamplandia!* (2011), which is set in the same territory as Matthiessen's novel and haunted by similar historical events; for instance, the Disston Company's abandoned steam dredge, which serves as a promise of progress to the forward-thinking E.J. Watson, sits rusting near the Bigtrees' island in *Swamplandia!*— carrying, perhaps, its own ghost. Although set closer to the present day and filtered through the eyes of children, *Swamplandia!* follows Matthiessen in patrolling the border between the known and the unknown. In Russell's case, however, the shadows that threaten the stability and sanity of the main characters appear when the sunshine is at its brightest.

Russell sets up the darkness/light dichotomy in the opening pages, but frequently toys with readers' expectations. Like Matthiessen, she leads with death; the opening chapter, 'The Beginning of the End,' starts in darkness: 'Our mother performed in starlight' (3). Here, Ava Bigtree recalls her mother's performance in the family's alligator-themed tourist attraction, where by moonlight Hilola Bigtree would dive into the darkest part of a gator-filled lagoon and disappear from sight while tourists in the stands enjoyed 'the darkness of our island .... thirty-odd miles off the grid of mainland lights' (3). Russell contrasts the island's shadows and mysterious monsters with the mainland's grid of lights; however, she quickly associates the darkness with life and the mainland lights with death, portraying Hilola as most vibrantly alive in the dark lagoon while locating her death in a clean, well-lit hospital on the mainland, where the young mother succumbs to ovarian cancer (8). After Hilola's death, Ava nourishes a hatred for the mainland and cherishes those moments when her mother seemed most alive: swimming blissfully among the monsters in the dark lagoon.

The death of one parent followed swiftly by the absence of another places Ava and her siblings firmly within the tradition of adventure stories in which lost or abandoned adolescents make their way alone through a hazardous world. Russell employs many conventions of such fairytale adventures, but her repeated inversions of conventional motifs challenge the possibility that anyone can live happily ever after in a world haunted by unresolved trauma. While Ava may initially embrace fairytale thinking, she begins narrating the story with her mother's swim through darkness, leads immediately to her mother's death, and then offers readers a blunt summation of the rest of the novel: 'If you're short on time, that would be the two-word version of our story: *we fell* (Russell 9, her emphasis). Like Matthiessen, Russell places readers in a fallen world where 'one tragedy can beget another' and apparently benign characters can lead the innocent on a voyage to the underworld (9).

After her mother's death, 13-year-old Ava puts a name to the enemy that threatens to destroy her family's livelihood: a mainland theme park called The World of Darkness, which 'offer[s] things that Swamplandia! could not: escalator tours of the rings of Hell, bloodred swimming pools, boiling colas' (13). In a mainland characterized by an orderly grid of light heralding death, The World of Darkness becomes a pleasure-packed simulacrum of darkness where the most light-hearted, cartoonish plot elements take place. When Ava's brother, Kiwi, goes to work for The World of Darkness, the clueless and ill-prepared adolescent first finds himself relegated to a windowless basement cell, but soon steps into the spotlight after appearing to save the life of a girl who may or may not be drowning (233). Although Kiwi's dream of rescuing Swamplandia! from bankruptcy proves unrealistic, a series of outrageous coincidences results in his rescuing his lost sisters from disaster and reuniting the family. Throughout his experience on the mainland, Kiwi seems to inhabit a Horatio Alger tale; indeed, Sarah Graham sees Kiwi's 'triumph' as affirmation of his 'masculine role of lifeguard' and hero (603). However, the fact that this triumph is predicated on acceptance of the kind of fairytale narrative that can thrive only within the artificial confines of a theme park emphasizes the inauthenticity of this narrative, which contrasts sharply with the real dangers faced by Kiwi's sisters back on the island.

While Kiwi seeks fortune in The World of Darkness, back at Swamplandia! Ava and her sister, Osceola, encounter shadows that drive them to the borders of insanity. Bored and listless, 16-year-old Ossie explores a listing Disston dredge and projects her own private, mystical meanings onto an outdated map. '"[T]his is where the door to the underworld opens,"' she tells Ava, but the younger sister recognizes an old Calusa landmark where Grandpa Sawtooth used to go fishing (150). When Ossie falls in love with the ghost of a crewman on the Disston barge, the younger Ava sees herself as more grounded in reality than Ossie, but she admits that she resembles her sister in one regard: 'I was consumed by a helpless, often furious love for a ghost. Every rock on the island, every swaying tree branch or dirty dish in our house was like a word in a sentence that I could read about my mother' (71). Then, after Ossie 'marries' the ghost crewman and sets off with him to find the underworld, Ava realizes that she cannot rescue her lost sister without help.

Enter the Bird Man, who appears with the buzzards to lead Ava on a journey to the underworld. Like Matthiessen's Jean Chevalier, Russell's mysterious Bird Man bears a 'feathered torso' and has the ability to communicate with birds (Russell 162); '"Nobody can go to hell without assistance, kid,"' he tells Ava, and proceeds to take her there (183). Ava's eagerness to see him as a harmless friend of nature is borne of desperation, but Russell plants frequent hints of the Bird Man's dark motivations from the moment he agrees to help and then insists on sequestering Ava from the outside world and controlling her communications with others. Their voyage through the Ten Thousand Islands on a 14-foot skiff takes place in broad sunlight, but the Bird Man's malign influence over Ava imprisons her in a dungeon from which she cannot escape and subjects her to violence beyond her imagining. Although he takes cruel advantage of her trust, Ava is perhaps too eager to place her trust in a stranger because of her desire to save Ossie from the underworld—or, perhaps, to join her there. As they set out on their adventure, Ava wonders, '*What if I follow her to the underworld and find my mother?*' (Russell 196, emphasis hers).

Ava does, in a sense, find her mother again, but only after the Bird Man reveals that the underworld she seeks is a myth, and that a world of unexpected horror lies within the human heart. He rapes her in broad daylight, with Ava surrounded by pale green luminous plants and blinded by pain (329). While Kiwi's experience cleaves to the conventions of the Horatio Alger tale, Ava's rape grows 'so big and slippery inside' that she cannot 'get it to adhere to any story' and resolves to cloister her shame within herself always (331). Delivered into a mundane and very human hell, she hears her mother's voice calling and she holds to the 'brute' that lives within her breast to power her escape through sawgrass, woods, and water, wide-open space that closes in like claustrophobic walls in a labyrinthine dungeon where '[w]ater made endless mirrors and the small islands repeated themselves like a bad stutter' (337). The final chapter, 'The End Begins,' echoes the opening chapter by focusing on a deep, dark body of water that separates Ava from life while threatening to deliver her to death; like her mother in the opening chapter, Ava plunges in and swims through water darkened by her own blood before finally emerging into 'the deep bright air of our world' (383). 'I had never tasted the scattered light in the air before,' she muses. 'It felt like the sky had descended to my eye level' (383).

Florida may not be equipped with gothic ruins, castles, or dungeons, especially along its swampy southern coast; however, in Ava's journey through the underworld, Karen Russell creates gothic horrors that show themselves only in the bright light of day, when Ava, lost in the swamp, encounters ghosts of the past. Although she and Ossie are rescued and reunited with their family in the end, both girls carry the scars of their encounters with the shadows. Relocated to the mainland, Ava reckons up her losses, including her inability to draw to mind a picture of her favorite alligator: 'it feels like trying to light a candle on a rainy night, your hands cupped and your cheeks puffed and the whole wet world conspiring to snatch the flame away from you' (396). The novel that begins with a vision of vibrant life located in a dark, wet world now relegates that vision to the unrecoverable past of dream and memory, as Ava's encounter with the darkness that dwells within the human soul leaves her in a fallen world haunted by trauma and loss.

The Mirroring Monster

The gothic monster, says Stephanie Genz, 'has come to represent a figure marked for his strangeness and excess, his difference from the normality of social, cultural, moral, physical, psychological and human mores' (68). Karen

Russell's Bird Man certainly fulfills these criteria, as does Matthiessen's Mister Watson, but both monsters, despite their differences, serve to mirror the monstrousness within ordinary human nature. Jeff VanderMeer takes this mirroring one step further, creating Florida itself as a monster reflecting, mimicking, and consuming human explorers. Although set in the near future, VanderMeer's *Annihilation* (2014) echoes the experiences of the early European explorers who encountered in Florida terrifyingly unfamiliar terrain and creatures. Disoriented among bogs and thick bush, VanderMeer's explorers nevertheless find themselves reflected in 'water so dark we could see our faces in it' (5). Beauty and mystery work together to provoke a desire to possess the land and its resources, but that possession works both ways, because 'when you see beauty in desolation it changes something inside you. Desolation tries to colonize you' (6). Like early European explorers, VanderMeer's characters find evidence of prior possession, 'eerie signs of human habitation: rotting cabins with sunken, red-tinged roofs, rusted wagon-wheel spokes half-buried in the dirt, and the barely seen outlines of what used to be enclosures for livestock, now mere ornament for layers of pine-needle loam' (5). The desolation they encounter, however, proves to be a sign not of death but of the birth and growth of alien and uncontrollable life. VanderMeer upends tropes common to the literature of exploration as the explorers become the explored, the possessors the possessed.

The plot of VanderMeer's trilogy is too complicated to summarize simply, but an examination of the unusual architecture of Area X illuminates his scheme: aside from the decaying village, the bulk of the action takes place in and around two towers, one above ground (the lighthouse) and one, paradoxically, a shadowy mirror image of the lighthouse extending deep below ground. Both structures feature claustrophobic quarters and spiral staircases with messages scrawled all over the walls; the primary difference is that the below-ground tower is a living organism scrawled with graffiti formed of living fungoid flora. Both towers contain enigmatic messages such as this: '*There shall be a fire that knows your name, and in the presence of the strangling fruit, its dark flame shall acquire every part of you*' (VanderMeer 138, his emphasis). While the nature of Area X is shrouded with darkness and many who visit there succumb to unspeakable horrors, only a few characters' eyes are opened to see that the entire place—even to the depths of the subterranean tower—is aflame, burning with the light of growth and change.

Who can encounter such a place unscathed? The protagonist of *Annihilation*, known only as the biologist, first sees Area X as a place of trauma and loss, and only later comes to see that the place itself is a living mirror reflecting back what human beings carry into it; moreover, the barrier dividing Area X from the rest of the world is fluid and permeable both in space and in time, suggesting that the possessed space may eventually cross the barriers and consume the outer world. Jay Ellis reminds us that gothic narrative takes readers to subterranean depths where they can encounter, map, and contain the monstrous

Other; however, he writes, 'Beyond the normative expectations of boundaries that promise safety, but that regularly betray us, we double back only to find those boundaries are unreliable' (xxv). In *Annihilation*, that doubling back across the boundary only stretches the boundary farther, allowing the flaming darkness to consume more terrain and possess more people.

The biologist, trained to observe transitional environments with scientific objectivity, is initially befuddled by the conflicting messages conveyed by Area X, even on the cellular level. Throughout her explorations, however, she keeps seeing her surroundings as 'a blank surface that let us write so many things upon it' (VanderMeer 9). Where others see monstrous decay and savagery, she sees nature and culture merging in a kind of palimpsest, with new messages overwriting 'phantom words' constructed from 'ghost scripts' (48). The map that should provide direction instead misdirects and obscures, 'for what was a map but a way of emphasizing some things and making other things invisible?' (66). Even the journals of previous expeditions, the records of scientific experiments, measurements, and observations, turn into compost so that 'the history of exploring Area X could be said to be turning into Area X' (112). By exploring and describing Area X, she feeds the monstrous terrain the words it needs to continue growing until the observer merges with what she observes; all the expeditions become part of the palimpsest that 'creates out of our ecosystem a new world, whose processes and aims are utterly alien—one that works through supreme acts of mirroring, and by remaining hidden in so many other ways, all without surrendering the foundations of its *otherness* as it becomes what it encounters' (VanderMeer 191, his emphasis).

Like centuries of explorers encountering alien land before her, VanderMeer's nameless biologist cannot make sense of this exotic terrain, even while relying on the maps and journals of her predecessors: 'We were all in the dark, scrabbling at the pile of journals, and if ever I felt the weight of my predecessors, it was there and then, lost in it all' (117). The Gothic, writes Eric Savoy, 'registers a trauma in the strategies of representation as it brings forward a traumatic history toward which it gestures but can never finally refer' (11), and Anne Williams points out that in gothic texts 'language both mediates the unspeakable "other" and shows the impossibility of that mediation' (66). VanderMeer's befuddled biologist joins a long line of explorers patrolling the borders between civilization and savagery, known and unknown, life and death, and like others she finds in Florida a monstrous Other that mirrors her own inner darkness—a darkness thrown into sharp definition by the searing Southern sun. Florida may market itself as a state sparkling with sunshine and smiles, but these authors push aside the sunshine to peer into the shadows and tell a tale of historical trauma and loss. Whether they focus on battles for possession of land or examine human souls possessed by horrors, these works confirm that the Gothic mode endures on that tenuous borderland between sunshine and shadow.

Bibliography

Abbott, C. (2012). West by Southeast: Peter Matthiessen's Florida Trilogy as Western fiction. *Western American Literature, 47*(1), 47–64.

Cooley, J. (1994). Matthiessen's voyages on the river Styx: Deathly waters, endangered peoples. In J. Cooley (Ed.), *Earthly words: Essays on contemporary American nature and environmental writers* (pp. 167–192). Ann Arbor: University of Michigan Press.

Crow, C. L. (2009). *American Gothic*. Cardiff: University of Wales Press.

Ellis, J. (2013). On Southern Gothic literature. In J. Ellis (Ed.), *Southern Gothic literature: Critical insights* (pp. xvi–xxxiv). Ipswich: Salem Press.

Genz, S. (2007). (Re)Making the body beautiful: Postfeminist Cinderellas and Gothic tales of transformation. In B. A. Brabon & S. Genz (Eds.), *Postfeminist Gothic: Critical interventions in contemporary culture* (pp. 68–84). New York: Palgrave Macmillan.

Graham, S. (2013). Unfair ground: Girlhood and theme parks in contemporary fiction. *Journal of American Studies, 47*(3), 589–604.

Hearn, L. (1911a). To the fountain of youth. In *Leaves from the diary of an impressionist: Early writings* (pp. 35–58). Boston: Houghton Mifflin.

Hearn, L. (1911b). A tropical Intermezzo. In *Leaves from the diary of an impressionist: Early writings* (pp. 59–75). Boston: Houghton Mifflin.

Matthiessen, P. (1990). *Killing Mister Watson*. New York: Random House.

Parkman, F. (1983). *Pioneers of France in the New World*. 1865. *France and England in North America* (pp. 1–330). Vol. 1. New York: Library of America.

Russell, K. (2011). *Swamplandia!* New York: Random House.

Savoy, E. (1998). The face of the Tenant: A theory of American Gothic. In R. K. Martin & E. Savoy (Eds.), *American Gothic: New interventions in a national narrative* (pp. 3–19). Iowa City: University of Iowa Press.

VanderMeer, J. (2014). *Annihilation*. New York: Farrar, Straus, and Giroux.

Walsh, C. J. (2013). Dark legacy: Gothic ruptures in southern literature. In J. Ellis (Ed.), *Southern Gothic literature: Critical insights* (pp. 19–34). Ipswich: Salem Press.

Watson, J. G. (2004). Man writing: The Watson trilogy: Peter Matthiessen in the archive. *Texas Studies in Literature and Language, 46*(2), 245–270.

Williams, A. (1995). *Art of darkness: A poetics of Gothic*. Chicago: University of Chicago Press.

FURTHER READING

Glassman, S., & O'Sullivan, M. (Eds.). (1997). *Florida Noir: Crime fiction and film in the Sunshine State*. Bowling Green: Bowling Green State University Popular Press.

Hurston, Z. N. (1995). *Seraph on the Suwanee. Zora Neale Hurston: Novels and stories* (pp. 597–920). New York: Library of American.

Matthiessen, P. (1999). *Bone by bone*. New York: Random House.

Matthiessen, P. (1998). *Lost Man's river*. New York: Vintage.

O'Sullivan, M., & Lane, J. C. (Eds.). (1991). *The Florida reader: Visions of paradise from 1530 to the present*. Sarasota: Pineapple Press.

VanderMeer, J. (2014). *Acceptance*. New York: Farrar, Straus, and Giroux.

VanderMeer, J. (2014). *Authority*. New York: Farrar, Straus, and Giroux.

CHAPTER 13

Gothic Cuba and the Trans-American South in Louisa May Alcott's 'M.L.'

Ivonne M. García

The American Gothic is a genre 'haunted' by slavery—that is, haunted by race—as well as haunted by the intersecting racial and gender hierarchies that the institution created, depended on, and promoted.[1] As an institution and as a discursive force, slavery was not only dependent on how individual and collective bodies (white and non-white) were categorized and regulated; it also depended on the specific geopolitical landscapes in which such bodies interacted (and intersected), especially in relation to and/or against the 'body politic' of the US nation. It is at the three-pronged intersection of race, gender, and geographical location that this examination of the relationship between the US South and the Caribbean begins. Intersectional theory explains why we should pay attention to how and when racial and gender constructs connect, and I want to explore how a similar intersectionality functioned in nineteenth-century literary representations of slavery in relation to two specific geopolitical locations: the US South and Cuba.[2]

Within the context of gothic representations of the South, this chapter explores how and why Cuba became one of the variables in what I describe as a 'representational equation.' This equation, a literary 'action of making equal,' depended on independent variables that, when brought together as a sum, produced racialized cultural codes used to represent the island (and its associated Spanish and African cultural traits) as a stand-in, or double, for the US South.[3] In making meaning within the context of US slavery, this representational equation drew its persuasive power from the discursive intersection of race, gender, and location, establishing slave bodies as 'human territories' within the US imperial project in which Cuba was a prime geopolitical landscape.[4]

I.M. García (✉)
Kenyon College, Gambier, OH, USA

© The Editor(s) (if applicable) and The Author(s) 2016
S.C. Street, C.L. Crow (eds.), *The Palgrave Handbook of the Southern Gothic*,
DOI 10.1057/978-1-137-47774-3_13

Within the framework of nineteenth-century US literary history, two colonial locations in the Caribbean hold primary significance as gothic figurations: Haiti (also known by its French colonial name of Saint Domingue, or 'San Domingo') and Cuba. Although significant work has been done on gothic representations of Haiti, not as much has been written about how and why Cuba was gothicized as it became a double for the US South in nineteenth-century literary representations.[5] In texts that did so, Cuba is represented as a source of fear over the possibility of slave insurrection and black rule, an American (in the hemispheric sense) version of what the Haitian Revolution meant for France. Against that backdrop, I explore how and why Louisa May Alcott, one of the most important nineteenth-century US women writers, used Cuba as a gothic signifier in her fiction, specifically in her story titled 'M.L.' In several of her pieces, including her first novel *Moods*, and in at least two of her best-known short stories, Alcott used the representational equation that established a correspondence of meaning between Cuba and the US South through conventions of the Gothic, specifically by representing race (through slavery) as a source of fear and abjection. Alcott was one of the many authors who wrote about Cuba in the nineteenth century, but she is one of only a few writers who drew on gothic tropes to convey a sense of the island's peril to the United States.

A Guide to Cuba

Throughout the nineteenth century, Cuba was the subject of dozens of published travelogues and accounts written by increasingly large numbers of visitors, from both the North and the South, who flocked to the island from the United States. Some traveled to Cuba as part of the 'invalid trade,' the part of the tourism business that catered to US Americans who were ill (often with tuberculosis) and sought a warm climate to recuperate.[6] Others went to Cuba as curious tourists, especially after mid-century, and wrote popular travelogues.[7] The popular interest in travel literature about Cuba reflected an equally strong US colonial desire for the island, articulated early on by Thomas Jefferson when he advocated for the acquisition of Cuba in 1823 as fulfilling 'the measure of our political wellbeing.' Similarly, John Quincy Adams categorized Cuba and Puerto Rico as 'natural appendages,' and Cuba, specifically, as being of 'transcendent importance' to the United States.[8] After the Latin American revolutions against Spain exploded in the 1820s and Cuba and Puerto Rico remained 'ever faithful' to the old empire, the United States advocated for their continuation as Spanish colonies to prevent them from being acquired by Britain or another competing imperial power.[9]

The relationship between 'the island colony and the budding empire' continued to grow as the United States colonized and consolidated territory within the North American continent, fashioning itself politically and culturally as an 'empire of liberty.'[10] By the end of the 1840s, when the United States' size doubled after it annexed Texas, acquired Oregon, and took half of Mexico's territory, 'U.S. expansionists saw Cuba as a prize waiting to be taken.'[11] Between 1845 and 1861, three presidential administrations—those of James Polk, Franklin Pierce, and James Buchanan—unsuccessfully attempted to purchase Cuba from Spain.[12] Also within that time period, a number of filibustering expeditions, launched from the United States, attempted to take Cuba from Spain by force.[13] Interest in acquiring Cuba abated during the US Civil War and then regained momentum between the 1870s and 1880s, cul- minating by century's end in the Spanish-American War of 1898, when both Cuba and Puerto Rico were invaded by US forces.

Rodrigo Lazo has categorized most of the nineteenth-century travelogues about Cuba as a genre that he calls the 'Cuba guides.' In doing so, he has noted how such texts combined 'political observation with practical informa- tion on travel' and tended to offer 'a gamut of information about accommo- dations, history, politics, and flora and fauna, with additional ruminations on slavery, gender conventions, and Catholicism.'[14] However, there is a smaller group of texts that differ from the prolific number of travel books about Cuba by deploying the Gothic to raise the alarm about colonial acquisition of the island.[15] The sentiments toward Cuba expressed in these few outlier texts— letters, novels, short stories—diverge markedly from the Cuba guides, and range from ambivalence to ambiguity and even toward outright rejection of the island as a potential colony. For a small group of authors, which included Martin Robinson Delany, Mary Peabody Mann, and Alcott, Cuba was not only a site of colonial fascination and desire, but also a place of inherent duplicity and potential toxic contamination for the United States.

These texts reveal that when the Gothic—in its American expression—came into contact with the Caribbean, specifically with Cuba, it became obsessed with the intersection of race and gender on which slavery depended (for one, the *partus sequitur ventrem* doctrine mandated that the black woman's body conveyed slave status), and with the island itself as a racialized geopolitical landscape.[16] In Alcott's fiction, specifically, intersectionality connects with geo- politics to support a representational equation that translates Cuba into the US South and vice versa to articulate anxieties about the future of a nation riven by racial fault lines. Because the Gothic as a genre is inextricably connected to the violent history of colonialism and slavery in the Americas, it was ideally suited for writers like Alcott who wished to sound the alert of how the US South and Cuba functioned as doubles of each other. In that way, most writers who drew on the Gothic sought to caution against the acquisition of the island. In Alcott's case, however, she also used Cuba as a stand-in for how reconciliation with the slave South might be achieved.

The imbrication of race and slavery on the American Gothic has been long recognized and examined, especially after Leslie A. Fiedler famously argued that American literature is 'a gothic fiction ... a literature of darkness and the grotesque in the land of light and affirmation' (29). Coming at this 'darkness' from another vantage point, Toni Morrison has underscored the significance of what she termed a 'dark, abiding, signing Africanist presence,' one through and against which a national literary 'whiteness' was constructed (5, 9). In this vein, Morrison argues for our understanding of the Romance and the Gothic as foundational genres in American literature, not because these genres seek to evade history but because they express 'the head-on encounter with very real, pressing historical forces' and the inherent contradictions they create (36). Both Fiedler and Morrison underscore the power of the Gothic simultaneously to exploit and to collapse the binary oppositions that structure the myths of US national formation, and they point us to why race becomes a foundational signifier in gothic romances.

Following in Morrison's wake, Teresa A. Goddu argues that the American Gothic has been mostly associated with the US South, which 'serves as the nation's "other," becoming the repository for everything from which the nation wants to disassociate itself' (3–4). Insisting 'on the gothic's intimate relation to the romance,' Goddu categorizes American literature as 'haunted' by history, specifically the history of slavery (8, 10). In particular, she notes how 'American gothic literature criticizes America's national myth of new-world innocence by voicing the cultural contradictions that undermine the nation's claim to purity and equality' (10). Notwithstanding the genre's potentially disruptive characteristics, Goddu adds that the Gothic 'can also work to coalesce [national] narratives [by serving] as the ghost that both helps to run the machine of national identity and disrupts it' (10). As we see in Alcott's work, the Gothic functions as a kind of dialectical catalyst, pitting one idea against its antithesis to produce a synthesis that enables opposites to operate in tandem, thereby creating a narrative of national reconciliation.

Given the Gothic's significance in constructing a US literary identity in the nineteenth century, it is equally important to recognize that the American Gothic is not limited to US borders, but is also inextricably linked to US imperial ambitions in the Americas.[17] The colonial, imperial, Caribbean, and postcolonial Gothics have been broadly identified and theorized in British literature, but less so in nineteenth-century US literature.[18] To contribute to an examination of the colonial Gothic in US texts, this chapter focuses on how Alcott's gothic romances—or her 'race melodramas,' as Sarah Elbert has described them—are gothic precisely because they conjure the 'dark abiding presence' of race. Furthermore, by establishing a representational equation that assumes Cuba as a double of the US South, Alcott shows us the trans-American nature of Morrison's Africanist presence. In the case of Cuba, a trans-American Africanism becomes embodied in the desired colony, which is always already a racialized geography and a gendered location. Cuba's gothicized representation is then not only linked to the 'dark, abiding presence' to which Morrison points us, but also occurs at the intersection of race, gender, and the project of US empire.

The repeated literary figurations of Cuba in Alcott's sensationalist and gothic fictions, most of them published anonymously or pseudonymously, have been read as 'political allegory,' whereby Cuba would have been understood by Northern readers 'less as a tropical paradise than as a potential slave state'

(Williams 101). Because Cuba was desired primarily by the antebellum South for its slave economy, Susan S. Williams has suggested that Alcott—who described herself as a 'fanatic' abolitionist and racial integrationist—would have likely viewed the 'would-be slave state [as] a stand-in for the Confederacy' (Elbert x; Williams 102). In writing about Cuba before and during the Civil War, Alcott addressed concerns that many of her (mostly Northern) readers would have had about the impending conflict and its outcome, and about the issues of racial mixing (then more commonly known as 'amalgamation' or 'miscegenation'), as well as the intersecting vectors of race and gender foundational to slavery. Because they evoke similar anxieties, Cuba and the US South become nearly synonymous cultural denominators in the representational equation that we find in Alcott's fictions.

Race and the Gothic in 'M.L.'

Although Alcott became a famous and beloved author after the publication of *Little Women* (Part 1 in 1868 and Part 2 a year later), she wrote and published many short stories that Elbert describes as 'abolitionist interracial romances' (x). Alcott submitted 'M.L.' in 1860 to the *Atlantic Monthly*, a renowned journal that published many well-known writers of the time, including Nathaniel Hawthorne. That journal, however, refused to publish the story because, as Alcott wrote in a letter, '"it is anti-slavery and the dear South must not be offended"' (Elbert x). 'M.L.' was finally published in 1863, in serial form, in Boston's anti-slavery weekly newspaper, *Commonwealth* (x). Although the story does not directly mention the Civil War, Alcott believed that the *Atlantic* editors were concerned that its clear anti-slavery and racial intermixing message would 'offend' Southerners even before the war had begun. That is despite the fact that 'M.L.,' like Alcott's 'Pauline's Passion and Punishment' and the original version of her first novel, *Moods*, is not about the US South but about Cuba. Notwithstanding that, the strength of the representational equation in which I am interested was such that the *Atlantic* editors were not fooled by Alcott's attempt to pass one for the other in 'M.L.'

Alcott's 'M.L.' utilizes race as its primary Gothic element to tell the story of Claudia, a white, upper-class American woman who falls in love with a supposed 'Spaniard' of 'swarthy skin,' named Paul Frere. Elbert includes 'M.L.' in her edition of Alcott's stories as one of the many 'abolitionist interracial romances' that preceded *Little Women* (x). Because it is written right after the attack on Harpers Ferry by John Brown in 1859, Elbert also argues that 'M.L.' is a story that shows 'Alcott as a writer whose art was consciously in the service of her political commitments' (xxvi). Further, Alcott's representation of the intersection of race and gender contributes to the way in which Elbert says the author sought 'to amend literary and cultural conventions that mandated representing *rebellious* black and biracial men as predatory beasts or, alternatively, portraying black or biracial men as patiently enduring earthly bondage as emasculated souls' (xl). By crafting an interracial love story, Alcott challenged one of the greatest anxieties—for both Northerners and Southerners—about emancipation without repatriation: the fear of what was first called 'amalgamation' and then 'miscegenation,' or the mixing of races (Elbert xxxii).

In addressing this fear, Alcott constructs clearly regionalized and racialized gender binaries. Within the New England social context in which 'Spaniard was frequently a code word for black,' Alcott at first establishes an opposition based on race and gender between her heroine, Claudia, and the story's hero, whose name, as Elbert notes, translates to 'Brother Paul' (Elbert xxxv). Where Claudia is 'white' and 'pale,' shining with 'cold brilliancy' and occupying a 'Mont Blanc of cool indifference,' Paul is 'the dark man with melancholy eyes' whose '[b]lack locks streaked an ample forehead, [and whose] black brows arched finely over southern eyes as full of softness as of fire' (Alcott 5, 6). While there are no apparent contradictions to Claudia's representation—she is clearly a Northern ice maiden—Paul is a study in contrasts, whose gaze, regionalized as 'southern,' reveals quick mood changes between opposite and opposing feelings. Even though he is supposedly European because of his 'Spanish' blood, Paul is associated by the narrator with the stereotypical representations of the South ('southern eyes'), thereby initially racializing his character as an archetype that would be easily intelligible to Alcott's audience.

While working with stereotypical racial representations of white, cold purity (as the North) and dark, temperamental passion (as the South), embodied by Claudia and Paul, respectively, Alcott also inverts such preconceptions. Her heroine, for one, is no damsel in distress. Despite being orphaned and standing 'alone in the world,' Claudia is 'a woman of strong character and independent will, gifted with beauty, opulence and position' (7). Because she has not known 'true love,' and because 'the master had not come,' Claudia has turned down many suitors and refused to marry for convenience or to assuage her solitude (7). Like Claudia, Paul also breaks with narrative conventions because, while he is racialized as a 'Spaniard,' he also is a music teacher, described by Claudia's companion, Mrs. Snowden, as devoted to 'books and art.' Further, he is a 'handsome soul' who makes 'pale-faced gentlemen look boyish and insipid to a mortifying degree,' according to Mrs. Snowden (5). Paul's masculinity is not represented as a sexualized threat; on the contrary, because he is courteous and a good listener to women, he is highlighted as a better man—even 'heroic' in Claudia's eyes, because of his honesty. Instead of the sexually threatening mixed-race male, Paul exemplifies what to Claudia is 'real manliness' because, despite not being a 'scholar erudite and polished by long study or generous culture,' Paul has been taught by adversity, which has 'been his college' (6). By subverting racial and gender preconceptions, Alcott suggests that the North–South binary might be too simplistic a way to understand the larger national conflict.

In addition to representing Claudia as a single woman of power and means, with an important standing in her social circle, Alcott also fashions her heroine as a sexual being. On hearing Paul sing, she feels her blood deeply 'stirred,' and the narrator describes how, in listening to his music, passion 'thrilled along her nerves like south winds full of an aroma fiery and sweet,' while the 'melody devout and sweet as saintliest hymn' connected all who listened to 'that diviner self' (3, 4). This exposure to a Southern influence, which 'sway[s] her like a wizard's wand,' shows us a woman who is moved by the racial 'Other,' but one with the self-control and will for self-improvement that prevent her from being victimized by her desire (3). Moreover, Alcott represents Paul as a man (as opposed to a boy) whose strong masculinity eclipses that of the white American men whom Claudia and Mrs. Snowden know, but not as one who would exploit that power. In this way, both the heroine and hero—although set up as racial antipodes—are similarly connected to desire bounded by strong aesthetic and moral principles.

Race and the Gendered Gaze

In describing the relationship between Paul and Claudia, Alcott establishes the gendered gaze as one that inevitably intersects with race. By 'the gaze' here I mean the gender structure created by the subject who looks (usually male) and the object being looked at (usually female).[19] Alcott, however, complicates the representation of gender in the story when Claudia gazes at Paul and recalls a painting 'of a tropical island, beautiful with the bloom and verdure of the South,' which she saw as a child (5). Thereby, Alcott establishes a link between the US South and not only the Old World (because Paul is believed to be a Spaniard) but also the Caribbean. Given that Cuba was commonly discursively paired with the US South, Alcott connects the United States to the Caribbean as two geographies that, while separate, share a similar 'tropical' landscape, thereby producing similar aesthetic and emotional responses. Here, also, it is Claudia with her gaze (as a woman) who surveys Paul, actually intuiting (although she will not know it until later) the concealed truth of his racial background.

The narrator provides further details of the picture in Claudia's mind, one where the sky is 'ardent,' the air is 'fervid,' and the luxuriance is 'rank,' creating a feeling of fevered disease and corruption inherent to the island's beauty.

> An ardent sky, flushed with sunrise canopied the scene, palm trees lifted their crowned heads far into the fervid air, orange groves dropped dark shadows on the sward where flowers in rank luxuriance glowed like spires of flame, or shone like stars among the green ... But looking nearer, the eye saw that the palm's green crowns were rent, the vines hung torn as if by ruthless gusts, and the orange boughs were robbed of half their wealth, for fruit and flowers lay thick upon the sodden earth. Far on the horizon's edge, a thunderous cloud seemed rolling westward, and on the waves an ominous wreck swayed with the swaying of the treacherous sea. (5)

Claudia's gaze (both physical and inward in her recollection) is drawn initially to what seems like a landscape of boundless nature. On more careful examination, however, she notices that this is a place destroyed by a storm, likely a hurricane, which has caused a ship to 'wreck,' suggesting a resulting

loss of human life. This 'looking nearer' that the narrator encourages is necessary for Claudia to 'see' what at first appears concealed so that she can understand the implied 'ominous' message of 'treachery.' In being associated with
this troubled island (which later information will lead us to presume is Cuba),
Paul is also connected to a place where the aesthetic pleasure produced by
the landscape actually conceals the true 'nature' of an enticing but potentially
deadly threat.[20] This is clearly a place that necessitates that we 'look' more carefully for clues that something may be troublingly amiss.

When Claudia recalls this picture as she gazes on Paul while trying to decipher his character, she also notes how 'as in the picture, the tempest seemed
to have gone by, but though a gracious day had come, the cloud had left a
shade behind' (5). The notion that Paul is concealing something dangerous
is suggested, along with the sense that whatever happened in his past marked
his character with darkness. Further, Claudia has the sense that, as with the
picture, 'a vague unrest still stirred the air, and an undertone of human woe
still whispered through the surges' song' (5). Whether the 'human woe' in the
picture is related to the loss of life in the shipwreck, perhaps because the ship
was a slaver, carrying captured souls from Africa, we are not told. However, it
is this sense of Paul's past sufferings, as represented in the narrative suggested
by the painting that Claudia remembers, that first hints to the fact that Paul's
'minstrelsy,' a word used to describe his talent for music, is not just related to
his musical performance but also to some kind of racial impersonation.

In suggesting that Claudia's 'master' had yet to arrive, Alcott utilizes the
discourse of slavery to associate marriage with a master/slave relationship in
her heroine's mind, providing a reason why strong-minded Claudia has chosen
to remain single. To that discourse, which naturalizes marriage as an asymmetrical power relationship, Alcott adds the language of kingship and royalty.
As the narrator states, 'In "plain Paul Frere," Claudia found her hero, recognized her king, although like Bruce he came in minstrel guise' (8). Seemingly
recalling Robert the Bruce, the Scottish king, Alcott uses the word 'minstrel'
to signify Paul as impersonating a servant or lower-class person, or a trouba-
dour, but in the US context the word very much suggests the act of minstrelsy
or racial impersonation (more commonly known as blackface). Claudia's figuration implies that she is willful and strong only because she has not met her
'master' or 'king,' whose masterly role will be to bring her within the folds
of 'normalized' subservient womanhood. However, because Alcott has associated Paul with minstrelsy, specifically in the sense of racial performance, the
implication is that such normalization will not and cannot be achieved. If Paul
is himself some kind of 'counterfeit' (a word that Alcott used in her stories to
describe escaped slaves), then he will not be able finally to domesticate Claudia.

Indeed, through the intervention of Mrs. Snowden, Claudia's widowed
companion, who resents Paul for choosing Claudia instead of herself, Paul is
forced to confess to Claudia that he is an escaped Cuban slave. Once his racial
passing is revealed by Mrs. Snowden (who, quite interestingly, is described as
having 'gipsy blood'), Paul confesses that he was born to 'a Cuban planter' and
a mother who was 'a beautiful Quadroon, mercifully taken early out of slavery

to an eternal freedom' (17).[21] As Paul tells it, he lived for 15 years as 'a happy child' with a loving father, forgetting 'that I was a slave' and sharing his life with 'a sister, heiress of my father's name and fortune' (17). When Paul's father dies without freeing him, however, his sister Nathalie 'goes to her guardian's protection,' but he goes 'to the auction block' (17). Paul explains that his 'father's kindness proved the direst misfortune that could have befallen me, for I had been lifted up into humanity and now I was cast back among the brutes. I had been born with a high heart and an eager spirit ... now they were to be crushed and broken by inevitable fate' (17–18). In Alcott's figuration, Paul's nature—as a mixed-race man—distinguishes him from the 'brutes' (ostensibly black slaves), and it is his whiteness, both racial and cultural through his father's influence, that sets him apart and makes slavery untenable for him.

During his years as a slave, Paul tries to escape and to contact Nathalie, but she 'had learned to look on me in another light,' by which Alcott again inserts the notion of the gaze within the context of race. Nathalie, the narrator suggests, changes her feelings for her brother once she had to 'look' on him as a slave, and she no longer concerns herself with him. The power dynamic of the master/slave relationship alters the sibling connection and she cannot feel the same toward Paul, despite the fact that he 'could not change my nature though I were to be a slave forever' (68). Here, Alcott suggests that while Paul very much feels like a free man inside, and despite the fact that he does not even actually look like a slave, his condition as a slave changes the way he is looked on—meaning that any power relations in which he is engaged must perforce shift because of his status. The story proposes that the joining of nature and nurture—the merging of white and black blood and cultures—is stronger than either one of those forces acting separately. They are stronger in their connection than either the 'nature' notion that 'one drop' of African blood doomed people of mixed race as a 'tragic mulatto/a,' or the 'nurture' of years as a slave that cannot 'educate' Paul into being submissive or accepting his subordination. Even though Nathalie eventually leaves the plantation and he loses touch with her, during her visit to Paul's master years later he surreptitiously finds a way to get into her room and persuade her to take pity on and free him. Thereby, Alcott suggests that while all his years as a slave give Paul a tragic air, they do not turn him into a 'tragic mulatto' by divesting him of agency.

Ostracism and Sacrifice

In the same way that the gaze functions to establish a power structure in gender relations, Alcott shows how race functions as a force that may not be 'seen' (as is the case with Paul's passing) but that, when admitted to, transforms the object that is known to be a slave into a figure of abjection.[22] When speaking of his mixed race, Paul describes his non-white legacy as 'the black blight' and his heritage as 'a curse,' as he explains that the scar on his right hand—about which Claudia has asked in the past but he has not wanted to discuss—used to be 'the initials of a name—"Maurice Lecroix."'[23] A decade before, Paul confesses to Claudia, 'he was my master, I his slave' (17). Right after Paul says this, the narrator states that '[i]f Paul had raised his strong right arm and struck her, the act would not have daunted [Claudia] with such a pale dismay, or shocked the power more rudely from her limbs' (17). Why does Alcott represent this moment with words that describe a physical blow and a near fainting spell for Claudia? This is, after all, the man she has known and loved, confiding in her the horrible sufferings of having been a slave. Yet, as the narrator notes, Claudia 'shudders' when Paul mentions how he 'learned to be a slave' and pleads with her to 'give her abhorrence to the man who dared to love you, but bestow a little pity on the desolate boy you never knew' (17). What Alcott suggests by this scene is that it is Paul's race, as it intersects with gender within the context of Cuban slavery, that reveals him to be something horrible; and, by extension, it is Paul's race that produces Claudia's 'shudder' and that makes this story a gothic romance.

Because she can no longer 'look' on him in the same way (that is, the power balance between them is forever changed by his having made race visible), Claudia, 'true woman through it all, covered up her face and cried: "Go on, I can hear it, Paul!"' (17). Claudia may be a 'true woman' in her courage, but the shift here from looking to hearing must be noted. The fact that she can no longer look at Paul reveals the altered symmetry between them. Before knowing his racial status, Claudia gazed on Paul (as in the scene with her recalling the painting) as an equal with the goal of understanding him, albeit intuiting that there was something more beneath the surface. However, now, once he has revealed his nature as a Cuban slave, she is visibly disgusted and is now clearly superior to Paul. Alcott reveals how racial codes, intersecting with gender, invert the power relations between a 'black man' and a white woman. At the moment when Claudia accepts Paul, as he cries in gratitude, the narrator states that 'Paul was the weaker now,' which to Elbert signals the way in which Alcott 'restores the sentimental racial hierarchy common to the works of antislavery women writers' (xxxix). In this way, Claudia's whiteness is redefined at the same time that it is revalued, suggesting that her coming in contact with Paul has made her not only a better woman but a better white woman, reaffirming the dominant racial hierarchy.

Such a narrative of improvement and futurity, within the implied context of miscegenation, is the moral of the story. The engaged couple contends, as Paul warned Claudia would happen, with the rejection of her friends and with becoming social outcasts. On a sleepless night, Claudia struggles with having been ostracized and losing her social position, and in the only oblique reference to the Civil War the narrator describes how 'good and evil spirits compassed her about, making that still room the battle-field of a viewless conflict between man's law, and woman's love' (23). In a story in which the gaze has been central to defining power dynamics between characters, Alcott describes this moment of self-doubt as a 'viewless conflict,' one in which looking is no longer a factor because what was viewed had actually failed to reveal the truth. Tempted 'to forget the lover in the slave,' Claudia instead decides to be like the 'young knights' who 'came forth eager for heroic deeds,' and 'with valiant soul' she decides to devote 'herself to the duty which would bring her life's defeat or victory' (23).

By casting Claudia's role as Paul's wife as a 'heroic' sacrifice, Alcott recognizes that any futurity for the nation depends on the ability of the different races—like the North and the South themselves—to move beyond affect toward the duty of accepting each other, and thereby allegorizes the future reunified nation.

In the most direct reference to the US South in the story, the narrator notes how Claudia's determination to sacrifice her desire for social acceptance in favor of their marriage makes Paul 'a happier, more *contented* slave than those fabulous captives the South boasts of, but finds it hard to show' (Alcott 24, her emphasis). In this way, Alcott shifts the master/slave relationship from the context of slavery to the context of marriage and then takes a swipe at the claim by pro-slavery Southerners that their slaves were happy. As her life with Paul continues, Claudia begins to 'realize the emptiness of her old life, for now she looked upon it with a clearer eye,' and the narrator adds that marrying Paul 'was the lesson she had needed' (26). Alcott describes the change in Claudia as a 'new world,' where she 'found a religion that welcomed all humanity to its broad church' (27), suggesting that transformation is possible through new understanding and a truly Christian outlook. The story ends with the narrator noting how Claudia 'had found her place' and Paul had 'found a country,' looking forward to a transformed nation unified in its rejection of slavery. In that future nation, white women find their calling, and erstwhile 'black' men are accepted as part of the body politic.

Although Alcott uses the representational equation that doubles the South as Cuba, she also uses Cuba because, as a variable in this equation, the island establishes a distance that makes the interracial romance more palatable for her audience (after all, Paul is not a US slave). And while she initially represents Paul's race as a source of gothic horror for Claudia, it is a fear that her heroine eventually overcomes through a profound sense of Christian 'duty' and purpose. In this way, Alcott proposes that the threat of race can be diffused and that what seems like the worst of times becomes, as Claudia herself states, the necessary lesson for reconciliation and futurity. Claudia, as the white woman protagonist, embodies the US nation, representing both its vulnerability (the 'battlefield' on which her love and her prejudices fight) and its heroism (the acceptance of a higher, divinely ordained mission). By having Claudia become 'the braver of the two' for her sacrifice, as Paul remarks toward the end of the story, Alcott suggests that, like her heroine, the suffering, embattled nation can recalibrate its priorities to find its true superiority (24). In that way, Alcott reinscribes the racial hierarchy that reifies whiteness, but does so by inverting the intersections of gender and race that stereotyped white women as victims and black or mixed-race men as predators.

Conclusion

Ultimately, Alcott's 'M.L.' shows one way in which the Gothic was used in the representational equation established between the US South and Cuba in nineteenth-century American literature. Further, Alcott articulates what we could describe as a kind of 'trans-American South,' one that connected the US South and the Spanish Caribbean through racialized and geopolitical forces.[24] Within this trans-American context, Alcott foregrounds the significance of race, gender, and location as cultural codes in our understanding of how and why these regions create a larger trans-American South that can be represented in these ways. Within this context, Alcott's story functions as an allegory of the US nation, engaged in a Civil War over race, slavery, and geography, in which whiteness becomes redefined and revalued through Christian sacrifice. Through this redefinition/revaluation of whiteness, one through which the 'black blight' of a slave past can be erased and a Cuban identity assimilated, Alcott argues for a transformative change from the Old to the 'New World,' from the individual to the community, and from the nation engulfed in a war about race to one in which race loses its power to produce horror and abjection. What begins as a gothic romance, made gothic precisely because of the 'race melodrama' at its core, concludes as a narrative of reconciliation, one that proposes an acceptance of 'miscegenation' as the future of a truly united nation. Moreover, through the assimilation of a 'Cuban' slave, the story suggests that such a unified nation will be finally poised to become a true 'empire of liberty.'

NOTES

1. Goddu, *Gothic America*, 3.
2. See Vivian M. May's *Pursuing Intersectionality* for a recent history of intersectionality.
3. Matthew Pratt Guterl suggests that by the 1850s, 'Cuba and the South had long enjoyed a special relationship as two of the largest and closest remaining slave-holding societies in the New World,' and that while the island was often set in opposition to the United States, it 'could also serve to distinguish "the North" from "the South"' (100).
4. In discussing the 'shifting analogies among peoples of color, women, and workers consistently colonized *within* the United States' and 'a variety of "foreign" peoples successfully colonized by the United States *outside* its territorial borders,' John Carlos Rowe collectively identifies such bodies as 'human "territories" colonized by the United States' (8).
5. For recent examples see Edwidge Danticat's edited collections *Haiti Noir* and *Haiti Noir 2*.
6. Lazo, *Writing to Cuba*, 9.
7. Louis Pérez notes that 'visitors to Cuba were among the most prolific contributors to this genre.' Pérez, *Slaves*, xxv. See also Harold Smith's bibliography on books on Cuba written prior to 1900.
8. Gordon S. Wood notes how 'Jefferson had had his eye on not only all the rest of the Floridas but also Cuba, Mexico's provinces, and Canada.' Jefferson believed that the United States was destined to become an 'empire for liberty' (376).
9. Staten, *History of Cuba*, 21. See also Gott, *Cuba*, 52. Gott argues that most of Cuba's 'economic elite was conservative, fearful of the economic and social consequences of a break with the colonial motherland.' Further, Gott notes that fear of the African-descended population among the white Cuban *criollos* served to curb separatist ambitions.

10. Lazo, *Writing to Cuba*, 2.
11. Ibid, 8.
12. Ibid, 9.
13. Ibid, 5.
14. Lazo, 'Against the Cuba Guide,' 181.
15. In my book manuscript titled 'Haunted by Cuba,' I analyze texts by Alcott, Martin R. Delany, and Mary Peabody Mann, who used gothic representations of Cuba as a way to address US colonial desire toward the island.
16. Sally L. Kitch has proposed the terms 'racialized gender' or 'genderized race' to describe the ways in which the institution of slavery was adapted in the American colonies.
17. Johan Höglund argues that 'the American imperial gothic is concerned with the maintenance of the racial, sexual, cultural, political and territorial borders that have helped this form of culture to explain and even justify colonial expansion and the maintenance of empire' (3).
18. Patrick Brantlinger argues that the imperial Gothic served to articulate national anxieties about Britain's declining imperial power (227, 230). Lizabeth Paravisini-Gebert connects the Gothic and colonialism to argue that the Caribbean became 'the premier site of the colonial and postcolonial Gothic since the early nineteenth century' (233). In the US context, Jesse Alemán describes the 'trans-American gothic' as emerging in the 1830s in a romance that appropriates the hemispheric space of Mexico and turns it into a 'trans-American gothic space haunted by the specters of empire' (408, 410).
19. Laura Mulvey's discussion of 'woman as image, man as bearer of the look' defined the field of gender studies through the concept of the gaze (442).
20. Elbert notes how the fictional painting in the story 'is identical to the illustration in the Alcott's family edition of Longfellow's *Poems on Slavery*,' published in 1842 (xxxvii).
21. Mrs. Snowden, whom Alcott will describe as a 'cat' transformed into a woman, notes that she has 'gipsy blood in [her] veins,' which suggests that while Alcott may not have perceived racial mixture as a problem in men, she more stereotypically represented racially mixed women as dangerous.
22. In defining abjection, Kristeva notes: 'what is *abject*, … the jettisoned object, is radically excluded anddraws me toward the place where meaning collapses. A certain "ego" that merged with its master, a superego, has flatly driven it away. It lies outside, beyond the set, and does not seem to agree to the latter's rules of the game. And yet, from its place of banishment, the abject does not cease challenging its master' (2).
23. Although Cuban, Paul Frere, his father, and his 'hard' master, Maurice Lecroix, all have French names. This appears rhetorically aimed at connecting Haiti and Cuba in another kind of representational equation.
24. Anna Brickhouse suggests that examining 'the transamerican and multiligual literary practices of these American arenas' enables a reconsideration of nineteenth-century literary history within the practice of what she calls 'literary transamericanisms' (27–8).

Bibliography

Alcott, L. M. 'M.L.' *Louisa May Alcott on Race, Sex, and Slavery*. Ed. Sarah Elbert. Boston: Northeastern University Press, 1997. 3-28. Print.

Alemán, J. (2006). The other country: Mexico, the United States, and the Gothic history of conquest. *American Literary History, 18*(3), 406–26. Web. 9 June 2015.

Brantlinger, P. (1988). *Rule of darkness: British literature and imperialism, 1830–1914.* Ithaca: Cornell University Press. Print.

Brickhouse, A. (2004). *Transamerican literary relations and the nineteenth-century public sphere.* Cambridge, UK: Cambridge University Press. Print.

Danticat, E. (2011). *Haiti Noir.* New York: Akashic Books. Print.

Elbert, S. (1997). Introduction. In S. Elbert (Ed.), *Louisa May Alcott on race, sex, and slavery.* Boston: Northeastern University Press. Print.

Fiedler, L. A. (1960). *Love and death in the American Novel.* Champaign: Dalkey Archive Press, 2008. Print.

Goddu, T. A. (1997). *Gothic America: Narrative, history, and nation.* New York: Columbia University Press. Print.

Gott, R. (2004). *Cuba: A new history.* New Haven: Yale University Press. Print.

Guterl, M. P. (2007). An American Mediterranean: Haiti, Cuba, and the American South. In C. F. Levander & R. S. Levine (Eds.), *Hemispheric American studies* (pp. 96–115). New Brunswick: Rutgers University Press. Web. 9 June 2015.

Höglund, J. (2014). *The American imperial gothic: Popular culture, empire, violence. Farnham.* Surrey: Ashgate Publishing. Print.

Kitch, S. L. (2009). *The specter of sex: Gendered foundations of racial formation in the United States.* Albany: State University of New York Press. Print.

Kristeva, J. (1982). *Powers of horror: An essay on abjection.* (trans: Roudiez, L.S.). New York: Columbia University Press, Print.

Lazo, R. (2005). *Writing to Cuba: Filibustering and Cuban exiles in the United States.* Chapel Hill: The University of North Carolina Press. Print.

Lazo, R. (2006). Against the Cuba guide: The 'Cuba Journal,' *Juanita* and travel writing. In M. M. Elbert, J. E. Hall, & K. Rodier (Eds.), *Reinventing the Peabody sisters* (pp. 180–95). Iowa City: University of Iowa Press. Print.

May, V. M. (2015). *Pursuing intersectionality: Unsettling dominant imaginaries.* New York: Routledge. Print.

Morrison, T. (1992). *Playing in the dark: Whiteness and the literary imagination.* New York: Vintage Books. Print.

Mulvey, L. (1997). Visual pleasure and narrative cinema. In R. R. Warhol & D. P. Herndl (Eds.), *Feminisms: An anthology of literary theory and criticism.* New Brunswick: Rutgers University Press. Print.

Paravisini-Gebert, L. (2002). Colonial and postcolonial Gothic: The Caribbean. In J. E. Hogle (Ed.), *The Cambridge companion to Gothic fiction.* New York: Cambridge University Press. Print.

Pérez, L. (1992). *Slaves, sugar, and colonial society: Travel accounts of Cuba, 1801–1899.* Wilmington: Scholarly Resources. Print.

Rowe, J. C. (2000). *Literary culture and U.S. imperialism.* New York: Oxford University Press. Print.

Smith, H. F. (1966). A bibliography of American traveller's books about Cuba published before 1900. *The Americas, 22*(4), 404–412. Web. 9 June 2015.

Staten, C. L. (2003). *The history of Cuba.* Wesport: Greenwood Press. Print.

Williams, S. S. (2006). Revising romance: Louisa May Alcott, Hawthorne, and the Civil War. In *Reclaiming authorship: Literary women in America, 1850–1900.* Philadelphia: University of Pennsylvania Press. Print.

Wood, G. S. (2009). *Empire of liberty: A history of the early Republic, 1789–1815.* New York: Oxford University Press. Print.

CHAPTER 14

A Long View of History: Cormac McCarthy's Gothic Vision

Robert H. Brinkmeyer Jr.

At the heart of what we might call Cormac McCarthy's gothic imagination—an imagination haunted by a frightening vision of destruction and waste—lies a long view of history that stretches far back to the origins of humanity and far forward to its apocalyptic future. It is the shadow of this long view that adds a startling and terrifying dimension to McCarthy's work, one that seems somehow simultaneously pre- and post-human. Commenting on *Blood Meridian*, perhaps the touchstone for understanding McCarthy's gothic vision, Dana Phillips writes that McCarthy 'is not a writer of the "modern" or "postmodern" eras, but of the Holocene, with a strong historical interest in the late Pleistocene and even earlier epochs' (452), while Charles McGrath, drawing a line from *Blood Meridian*, argues that the novel's world is 'straight out of the "The Road Warrior"—an end-of-the-road stretch in which "the ragged flames fled down the wind as if sucked by some maelstrom out there in the void, some vortex in that waste apposite to which man's transit and his reckonings alike lay abrogate"' (180). From the perspective of this long view of history, the significance of the human and of the humane is at times all but erased, canceled out by overwhelming forces of darkness and devastation. While there are a few quiet heroes throughout McCarthy's work who make their stands amid the destruction, grounding the novels in the here-and-now rather than in McCarthy's vast historical timeline, these figures seem tiny stays against the confusion and chaos that otherwise reign.

McCarthy's Historical Timeline

While McCarthy's timeline of historical destruction is most fully present in his fiction set in the West (established most clearly in *Blood Meridian*), its presence

R.H. Brinkmeyer Jr. (✉)
Institute for Southern Studies, University of South Carolina, Columbia, NY, USA

© The Editor(s) (if applicable) and The Author(s) 2016
S.C. Street, C.L. Crow (eds.), *The Palgrave Handbook of the Southern Gothic*,
DOI 10.1057/978-1-137-47774-3_14

175

begins appearing in his earlier novels set in Tennessee, particularly in *Outer Dark* and *Child of God*. In *Outer Dark*, for instance, frightening backdrops of death and waste, seemingly mythic in dimension, repeatedly tower over the wanderings of Holme and Rinthy, not unlike the way in which aspects of the eternal suddenly burst forth in Flannery O'Connor's fiction. Near the end of *Outer Dark*, for instance, Holme walks a road that dead ends in a swamp whose description pushes toward framing the novel in a span from earthly creation to earthly (and spiritual) annihilation: 'Before him stretched a spectral waste out of which reared only the naked trees in attitudes of agony and dimly hominoid like figures in a landscape of the damned. A faintly smoking garden of the dead that tended away to the earth's curve' (242). Shadowing Holme and Rinthy throughout the novel are three mysterious and murderous figures laying waste to the countryside, performing 'a nameless black ballet' (3) that can be understood as an orchestration of the primal and destructive principle that is always at work in McCarthy's world.

Lester Ballard's exile from his community in *Child of God* is likewise framed in a timeline stretching far back to the origins of life, suggesting that humanity's violence is eternal and unchanging and that, within the novel, humanity's inner darkness is made visible in Lester's outer darkness, his plunge into savagery and violence. 'Were there darker provinces of night he would have found them' (23) opens one chapter, in a comment about Lester that also suggests the provinces into which McCarthy's imagination itself descends, here and in his other novels. In losing his farm and place within the community, Lester begins a rapid descent into the primal, devolving into a literal and figurative caveman as he moves deeper into the wilderness, finally settling into an underground grotto. On this spiral downward, which carries him into murder and necrophilia, he is described variously as a 'sullen reprobate,' 'some crazy winter gnome,' and a 'crazed mountain troll' (56, 107, 152); when he carries one of his victims down a hill he looks as 'a man beset by some ghastly succubus, the dead girl riding him with legs bowed akimbo like a monstrous frog' (153). Lester's pursuit of victims is mirrored in the ferocious fight that he observes between a wild boar and a roiling mass of pursuing hounds, a passage that recalls 'the nameless black ballet' of *Outer Dark*: 'Ballard watched this ballet tilt and swirl and churn mud up through the snow and watched the lovely blood welter there in its holograph of battle, spray burst from a ruptured lung, the dark heart's blood, pinwheel and pirouette, until shots rang out and all was done' (69).

Musings by the narrator and by characters in the novel suggest that Lester's fall from—or perhaps better, fall into—fundamental humanity is best understood as not being aberrant but representative of the human condition, once the cultural constructions of everyday life, most of which affirm humanity's fundamental goodness, are stripped away. Lester, the narrator tells us, is 'a child of God much like yourself perhaps,' a point underscored by a character's later observation that rather than being more evil in the past, 'people are the same from the day God made one' (4, 168). Further underlining Lester's representative status are the many parallels in the novel between his acts of violence and those sanctioned by custom or law. The sheriff, for instance, is as enthusiastic a voyeur as Ballard in trolling the town's lovers' lane; and the medical students who dissect Lester's body at the end of the novel, turning it into slushy bags of detritus, appear to treat it with less respect than Lester treats the bodies of his victims. Indeed, the parallels between Lester's and the medical students' handling of bodies are striking: both work underground, both lay out their bodies on pallets, and both follow strict rules of conduct. In developing these correspondences, McCarthy suggests that social systems are perhaps at heart as violent as the 'savages' against which they define themselves, their social structures similar to those found in the Mexican prison in *All the Pretty Horses*: 'Underpinning all of it like the fiscal standard in commercial societies lay a bedrock of depravity and violence where in an egalitarian absolute every man was judged by a single standard and that was his readiness to kill' (182).

The Added Dimension

The readiness to kill appears as well to be the standard structuring the world of *Blood Meridian*, McCarthy's most gothic novel, at least in the terms I am using to define his particular gothic vision. Voicing this standard is the satanic Judge Holden, who throughout the novel repeatedly articulates a philosophy of war that takes the commitment to kill to its limits. For the Judge, war is the fundamental state of nature and humanity, a life-and-death battle that trivializes, if not voids, all other issues and concerns. 'Decisions of right and wrong, of what shall be and shall not, beggar all question of right,' he pronounces. 'In elections of these magnitudes are all lesser ones subsumed, moral, spiritual, natural' (250). After telling one of his followers that it makes no difference what people think of war, the Judge adds: 'War endures. As well ask men what they think of stone. War was always here. Before man was, war waited for him. The ultimate trade awaiting its ultimate practitioner. That is the way it was and will be. That way and not some other way' (248).

The Judge's words here voice the defining element of McCarthy's gothic vision, the contextualizing of events in a timeline stretching from pre- to post-history. That perspective is announced even before the novel opens, in one of the epigraphs, a newspaper report that a 300,000-year-old skull had been found showing evidence of being scalped, a clear signal to the reader to connect the actions of the novel's nineteenth-century scalp hunters with those of our very distant ancestors. Within the novel itself, this extended timeline becomes visible in the many descriptions of the Judge's marauders that appear to locate the men less in the nineteenth century than in some primordial era. One such description, for instance, looks back to the Cambrian period (540–485 million years distant, when multi-celled life began first to appear):

Spectre horsemen, pale with dust, anonymous in the crenellated heat. Above all else they appeared wholly at venture, primal, provisional, devoid of order. Like beings provoked out of the absolute rock and set nameless and at no remove from their own loomings to wander ravenous and doomed and mute as gorgons shambling the brutal wastes of Gondwanaland in a time before nomenclature was and each was all. (172)

One effect of such descriptions, as Dana Phillips has discussed, is to locate the reader in a world perceived by 'optical democracy,' a perspective in which all things, inanimate and animate, stand on the same level of significance. The term and the perspective that Phillips identifies come specifically from this passage in the novel:

> In the neuter austerity of that terrain all phenomena were bequeathed a strange equality and no one thing nor spider nor stone nor blade of grass could put forth claim to precedence. The very clarity of these articles belied their familiarity, for the eye predicates the whole on some feature or part and here was nothing more luminous than another and nothing more enshadowed and in the optical democracy of such landscapes all preference is made whimsical and a man and a rock become endowed with unguessed kinships. (247)

By voiding the orders by which people typically judge themselves and the world (religious beliefs, social customs, legal structures, etc.), optical democracy confounds and disorients, providing what Flannery O'Connor called an 'added dimension' for contextualizing the events of the narrative. For O'Connor that dimension was the divine mysteries; for McCarthy, in stark contrast, that dimension is the vast, empty reaches of time and space, perhaps best represented in the novel by the desert wastelands, what McCarthy calls at one point 'the bloodlands of the west' and that at another he describes this way:

> If much in the world were mystery the limits of that world were not, for it was without measure or bound and there were contained within it creatures more horrible yet and men of other colors and beings which no man has looked upon and yet not alien none of it more than were their own hearts alien in them, whatever wilderness contained there and whatever beasts. (138)

In terms of the immense reach of time, *Blood Meridian* for the most part looks backward to the distant past rather than forward to the uncharted future—until the end, that is, where two scenes of dancing (recalling McCarthy's previous evocations of a 'black ballet') swing the perspective unswervingly into the time yet to come. In the novel's closing scene, the Judge, having characterized war as a dance that will never ends, is himself dancing naked, singing out that he never sleeps and will never die, declarations that look frighteningly forward to the conflagrations, large and small, that the world will soon be suffering from in the next century and beyond. The novel's epilogue, describing a posthole digger at work on a plain filled with bone gatherers, even more explicitly points to the coming terrors in the twentieth century. The digger's work, in which 'he enkindles the stone in the hole with his steel hole by hole striking the fire out of the rock which God has put there' (337), looks forward to the twentieth century's splitting of the atom and the development of nuclear weapons—and to the horrifying destruction that they wreak. The seemingly choreographed movements of the bone gatherers suggest a dystopian, totalitarian future in which people have been all but crushed into mindless automatons. The bone gatherers 'move haltingly in the light like mechanisms whose movements are monitored with escapement and pallet so that they appear restrained by a prudence or reflectiveness which has no inner reality' (337). Recalling the Judge's words on war's eternal dance (as well as Samuel Beckett's *Endgame*), the posthole digger and the bone gatherers work their way across the plain in orchestrated steps: 'He strikes fire in the hole and draws out his steel. Then they all move on again' (337).

The Military-Industrial Complex

By the time of the Border Trilogy (comprising *All the Pretty Horses*, *The Crossing*, and *Cities of the Plain*), the 1940s and 1950s, the atom has been split and the atomic bomb detonated, a point underscored at the end of *The Crossing*, when Billy Parham witnesses the false dawn created by the Trinity Test's detonation on July 16, 1945. Although not the killing fields of *Blood Meridian*, the West of the Border Trilogy is nonetheless in many ways shaped by the war and violence that the Judge prophesized, suggesting that the Trilogy's historical context is *Blood Meridian*'s—McCarthy's timeline of eternal conflict. And while there is no figure similar to the Judge, no unequivocal prophet of eternal war in the three novels, perhaps the Trinity explosion itself, its very name suggestive of the title given to McCarthy's three linked novels, stands as the Trilogy's image of eternal war and its never to be forgotten menacing threat (as the mushroom cloud has stood in the American consciousness since the end of the Second World War). The misshapen dog that Billy encounters the night before the Trinity test makes visible the atomic bomb's terrifying power to disfigure and destroy. When the dog first appears, shaking itself off and turning around three times before lying down (another detail suggestive of the linkage of Trinity/Trilogy), McCarthy describes it as being 'wet and wretched and so scarred and broken that it might have been patched up out of parts of dogs by demented vivisectionists,' adding that it is the 'repository of ten thousand indignities and the harbinger of God knew what' (423, 424). As these words suggest, the grotesque dog looks far back to an extended history of violence as well as far forward to a coming apocalypse. McCarthy describes the dog's bellowing, a fanfare of the world's endless suffering, as 'something not of this earth. As if some awful composite of grief had broke through from the preterite world' (424).

Embedded within the Border Trilogy's expansive time frame of eternal violence is the more focused timeline of the military-industrial complex's takeover of the West. A frightening sense of loss and insecurity hovers over people's lives resulting from this takeover and its destruction of traditional values and culture. 'People dont feel safe no more,' John Grady Cole's father comments in *All the Pretty Horses.* 'We're like the Comanches was 200 years ago. We dont know what's going to show up here come daylight. We dont even know what color they'll be' (25–26). 'Somebody can wake up and sneeze somewhere in Arkansas or some damn place and before you're done there's wars and ruination and all hell,' Rawlins says to John Grady in that same novel, speaking of the uncertainty unmooring the structures of everyday life. 'You dont know what's going to happen' (91–92).

As the Border Trilogy unfolds, the military's annexation of the West becomes progressively widespread, both materially and culturally, including a transformative reconfiguration of language and its referents. When late in *The Crossing* a border guard asks Billy Parham if he is returning to the United States in order to join an outfit—that is, to join the military—Billy misunderstands, thinking he is being asked if he is seeking work as a ranch hand. Billy soon discovers that in the militarized West the defining figure is not the cowboy but the soldier. 'Once the proving ground for the American hero,' as I have written elsewhere, the West is now 'the proving ground for missiles and bombs. Hawks have become hawk missiles; Indian reservations, military reservations; open ranges, firing ranges' (Brinkmeyer 47). When Billy is rejected for military service because of a heart defect, thereby losing his place within the new order, he finds himself adrift, without identity and purpose. 'He seemed to himself a person with no prior life,' McCarthy writes, describing Billy's feelings as he aimlessly wanders about on his horse, ever the cowboy. 'As if he had died in some way years ago and was ever after some other being who had no history, who had no ponderable life to come' (*The Crossing* 382). '"The world will never be the same," a man whom Billy meets says. "Did you know that?" "I know it,"' Billy responds. '"It aint now"' (420). By the time of *Cities of the Plain*, the early 1950s, the sense of dislocation and disorientation has become endemic. The coming annexation, by the Alamogordo Air Force base, of the ranch on which Billy and John Grady work looms large in the novel, emphasizing the military-industrial complex's unstoppable expansion. Few places are left untouched. The future is uncertain. 'We'll all be goin somewhere when the army takes this spread over,' John Grady says, but neither he nor anyone else knows where that somewhere will be. What they do know is what Mr. Johnson suggests is the hardest lesson of the world: 'when things are gone they're gone. They aint coming back' (126).

Such knowledge of a world passing even more piercingly haunts Sheriff Bell, the protagonist of the next novel in McCarthy's Western sequence, *No Country for Old Men*, set some 25 years after the events of *Cities of the Plain* (aside from the concluding pages that spin forward into Billy's old age). Sheriff Bell is an aging lawman, decent and upstanding in his small-town traditionalism (a believer in family, honor, community, etc.), who is totally out of place in a West given to drug trafficking violence and widespread mayhem. We are not quite back in the blood-drenched world of *Blood Meridian*, but almost, as the landscape is filled with roving gangs of hit men and drug dealers, armed to the teeth, turning once quiet communities into war zones. As he witnesses his world collapsing, trying all the while to stay true to his ideals and to perform his duties, Sheriff Bell repeatedly ponders the future in apocalyptic terms, invoking the type of cosmic timeline found in McCarthy's other works. 'Somewhere out there is a true and living prophet of destruction,' Sheriff Bell says early in the novel, adding later that he often finds himself waking up at night, pondering the dark days he sees coming, knowing 'as certain as death that there aint nothin short of the second coming of Christ that can slow this train' (4, 159). When he finds his wife reading the Apocalypse of Saint John, Sheriff Bell asks her if there is anything in it that can help explain the breakdown going on around them—where else to turn for answers to explain the scale of the horror and bloodshed that the Sheriff sees overtaking the world?

The military-industrial complex's threat to traditional order, developed so fully in the Border Trilogy, has been replaced in *No Country* with a new menace, what might be called the military-industrial-narcotic complex, a configuration of drug cartels, corporations, and governments spanning national borders that is spreading its tentacles into all areas of life. This new superpower is not merely undermining traditional patterns of culture, but is transforming the traditional West into a modern-day Wild West, a lawless space where everyone, those involved in the trade and those who are not, are at risk. Violence is everywhere—in the desert, on the highways, in homes, in storefront businesses, in corporate offices, on the streets of towns and cities. 'Dead bodies in the street,' the sheriff of Eagle Pass says to Sheriff Bell, after a horrific shootout a block from the county courthouse. 'Citizens' businesses all shot up. People's cars. Whoever heard of such a thing?' (134). Although not responding here, Sheriff Bell has in fact heard of such a thing and knows the type of warfare he faces. Those realizations had come earlier in the novel, when one of his deputies had commented on the carnage from a shootout in the desert, saying that 'it must of sounded like Vietnam out here.' Sheriff Bell had then responded simply and ominously, 'Vietnam' (75). In fact, the Vietnam War haunts *No Country*, the drug wars of the West presented as a variation of the war in Southeast Asia, particularly in that war's blurring of the lines between civilian and combatant, as well as in the breakdown of civil order resulting not only from the war itself but also from the massive corruption in the government and marketplace. It is not insignificant that two of the primary characters in the novel, Llewelyn Moss and Carson Wells, served in Vietnam and that Llewelyn's father, in an extended discussion with Sheriff Bell, observes that the Vietnam War highlighted the undermining of national belief and purpose that had long been at work in public life. That undermining, Llewelyn's father concludes, was a contributing factor to the mayhem of contemporary times.

The physical embodiment of this mayhem, the prophet of destruction that Sheriff Bell fears, is the satanic Anton Chigurh, a figure who recalls the Judge in *Blood Meridian* in his almost unworldly skill at killing and evading capture, as well as in his total commitment to his trade. If the Vietnam War contextualizes *No Country* in the immediate past, Chigurh's ghostly presence, together with the Sheriff's commentary about him, places the tighter context within

McCarthy's long view of history. 'He's a ghost,' Sheriff Bell says of Chigurh, after an FBI database search of his fingerprints had yielded nothing. 'But he's out there. You wouldnt think it would be possible to just come and go that-away' (248). At the end of the novel, having been severely injured in a car acci-dent, Chigurh puts his crushed arm in a makeshift sling and disappears before the police arrive, not to be seen again—at least in the novel. There is no sense that he will die anytime soon or that he will step away from his work. Indeed, McCarthy makes clear throughout the novel that Chigurh—or at least his spirit and what it represents—will never die, that (like the Judge in *Blood Meridian*) he will be forever performing his satanic dance. Chigurh's connection with this earlier figure, it might be speculated, also comes in his very name, which sounds a little like a slurred version of 'the Judge.'

An Ever-Darkening World

The apocalyptic future to which much of McCarthy's fiction points, a key dimension of his gothic vision, is fully realized in *The Road*. Set sometime in the future, after an unidentified disaster has destroyed civilization and covered the world in ash, *The Road* at the same time harks back to *Blood Meridian*, particularly in its descriptions of a desolate waste land peopled by roving bands of marauders. If, as we've seen, McCarthy links the scalp taking of *Blood Meridian* with humanity's ancestors from 300,000 years ago, the widespread cannibalism of *The Road* extends that timeline back much more, to the time of *Homo antecessor*, some 800,000 years ago, when, as recent discoveries sug-gest, cannibalism was prevalent. And in fact the novel appears to look back even further, to the Earth's origins, chronicling (until its final pages) a world seemingly devolving to the fundamental elements of existence. 'Perhaps in the world's destruction it would be possible at last to see how it was made,' observes the father, one of the novel's unnamed protagonists. 'Oceans, moun-tains. The ponderous counterspectacle of things ceasing to be. The sweeping waste, hydrotopic and coldly secular. The silence' (230–31).

The main tension of the novel, aside from the basic matter of whether the father can keep himself and his son alive, is whether the son can keep his father's human-ity alive; that is, can he stop his father from devolving into a state of savagery, as almost all of the other survivors have done. That general process of devolution, most evident in the ravaging marauders, is also chronicled in the father's flash-backs discussing the progressively deteriorating conditions since the catastrophic event. 'Within a year there were fires on the ridges and deranged chanting,' the father remembers, thinking back to the time immediately after the cataclysm. 'The screams of the murdered. By day the dead impaled on spikes along the road' (29). Over time, as food and supplies had grown scarcer, the killing and mayhem had dramatically increased. For many people all matters of existence had become reduced to the basic matter of staying alive, a situation, recalling the Judge's observations (from *Blood Meridian*), in which 'decisions of life and death, of what shall be and what shall not, beggar all question of right' (250).

That logic, as the novel progresses, becomes more prominent in the father's thinking; indeed, in his efforts to protect his son, he comes to commit acts that approach the savagery of those against whom he fights, shedding moral concerns in the face of life-and-death struggles. He does not question any of this. How could he? He is driven by only one concern: keeping his son alive, at whatever cost, including his own humanity. His son, however, sees what his father is becoming and fears what he sees. Acting as his father's conscience, he repeatedly challenges his father, particularly when he refuses to help people in need whom they come across—a little boy in a town, a man struck by lightning, the people imprisoned (and being held for food) in the basement of a plantation house. 'Are we still the good guys?' the son repeatedly asks, his appeals growing more urgent as his father's acts become more desperate. So frightened is the boy about his father's actions that after his father has abandoned those chained in the plantation basement, the son asks in complete seriousness, 'We wouldn't ever eat anybody, would we?' (109).

One of the verbal signals that the father and son use to confirm that they are not the 'bad guys' is that they are still 'carrying the fire,' an expression that suggests that they are keeping alive the small flame of human decency and charity in the ever-darkening world. The image harks back to the ending of *No Country for Old Men*, to Sheriff Bell's dream about his father. In that dream, a youthful Bell is riding a horse through a mountain pass when his father gallops past him,

> carryin fire in a horn the way people used to do and I could see the horn from the light inside of it. About the color of the moon. And in the dream I knew that he was goin on ahead and that he was fixin to make a fire somewhere out there in all that dark and all that cold and I knew that whenever I got there he would be there. (309)

As in *The Road*, the image of carrying the fire, keeping it alive and passing it on to others, suggests the individual's simple and yet profound commitment to civility and decency, in a world where such values no longer appear operable. Sheriff Bell's dream sheds light on understanding his decision to step aside from being sheriff: rather than an act of cowardice, Sheriff Bell's retirement might be read as an act of strength, as a commitment to keep himself and his own small world—his marriage and his ranch—free from the bedlam that everywhere else reigns. Not as a lawman, but simply as a good man, Sheriff Bell hopes to keep alive the virtues of hope and charity, and to pass them along to anyone who still recognizes their value.

At the end of *The Road*, a similar passing along occurs when a couple welcomes the boy, now by himself with his father dead, into their family. Their act of kindness and generosity might at first glance appear small, even insignificant, in light of the catastrophic destruction of the world, as well as the vast timeline that structures this and other of McCarthy's novels. Yet in McCarthy's dark and forbidding world, such small acts of goodness are in fact grand acts of heroism, the fundamental means by which humans stay humane in the face of the terrifying, gothic dangers that always threaten. Indeed, throughout

McCarthy's fiction there are a number of characters who selflessly, and at times at great risk, offer kindness and succor to those in need—the group of workers who load Boyd Parham into their truck and the doctor who tends to him in *The Crossing*; the Judge who counsels John Grady Cole near the end of *All the Pretty Horses*; the woman who takes the aged Billy Parham into her care at the conclusion of *Cities of the Plain*; the wife of Sheriff Bell who looks after the incarcerated in *No Country for Old Men*; and many others, often nameless but never insignificant. In fact, one could say that these caregivers, even in their small roles, are the heroes of McCarthy's fiction, tiny beacons of light in the vast darkness, signaling the way for McCarthy's seekers.

'What I need most is to learn charity,' says Ben in McCarthy's play *The Stonemason*. 'I know that small acts of valor may be all that is visible of great movements of courage within' (131). In their small acts of heroism and charity, McCarthy's quiet heroes, at least momentarily, collapse the vast historical timeline that lies at the heart of McCarthy's gothic imagination and that structures most of his novels. Their actions represent a different type of optical democracy—not one that, because of the vastness of its scope, reduces all existence to the same level of (in)significance, but one that, because of its intimate focus on human interaction and fellowship, grounds humanity in a lived-in place where goodness is possible, rather than in the empty reaches of space.

Bibliography

Brinkmeyer, R. H., Jr. (2000). *Remapping southern literature: Contemporary southern writers and the west*. Athens: University of Georgia Press.

McCarthy, C. (1968). *Outer dark*. New York: Vintage. 1993, print.

McCarthy, C. (1973). *Child of God*. New York: Vintage. 1993, print.

McCarthy, C. (1985). *Blood meridian: Or the evening redness in the West*. New York: Vintage. 1992, print.

McCarthy, C. (1992). *All the pretty horses*. New York: Vintage. 1993, print.

McCarthy, C. (1994a). *The crossing*. New York: Vintage. 1995, print.

McCarthy, C. (1994b). *The stonemason*. New York: Ecco Press. 1995, print.

McCarthy, C. (1998). *Cities of the plain*. New York: Vintage. 1999, print.

McCarthy, C. (2006a). *No country for old men*. New York: Vintage. 2005, print.

McCarthy, C. (2006b). *The road*. New York: Knopf. Print.

McGrath, C. (1994, June 27). Lone rider. *New Yorker*, pp. 180–185.

Phillips, D. (1996). History and the ugly facts of Cormac McCarthy's *Blood Meridian*. *American Literature, 68*(2), 433–460.

FURTHER READING

Arnold, E. T. (1999). *Perspectives on Cormac McCarthy*. Rev. ed. Jackson: University press of Mississippi. An expanded edition of the important collection of essays that appeared in 1993.

Arnold, E. T., & Luce, D. C. (Eds.). (2001). *A Cormac McCarthy companion: The border trilogy*. Jackson: University Press of Mississippi. The first collection of essays to examine *All the Pretty Horses*, *The Crossing*, and *Cities of the Plain* as a trilogy.

Cooper, L. R. (2011). *No more heroes: Narrative perspective and morality in Cormac McCarthy.* Baton Rouge: Louisiana State University Press. Focuses on the quiet presence of the humane and the ethical in McCarthy's violent world.

Cremean, D. N. (Ed.). (2013). *Critical insights: Cormac McCarthy.* Ipswich: Salem Press. A fine overview of the important issues and themes in McCarthy studies.

Frye, S. (2009). *Understanding Cormac McCarthy.* Columbia: University of South Carolina Press. A splendid introduction to and overview of McCarthy's career.

Frye, S. (Ed.). (2014). *The Cambridge companion to Cormac McCarthy.* Cambridge: Cambridge University Press. A wide-ranging collection of essays on McCarthy's work from many critical perspectives.

Hall, W. H. (2002). *Sacred violence: Cormac McCarthy's western novels.* El Paso: Texas Western Press. A companion to the volume on McCarthy's Appalachian works, this collection, by some of McCarthy's finest critics, focuses on his Western fiction.

Hall, W. H., & Wallach, R. (Eds.). (2002). *Sacred violence: Cormac McCarthy's Appalachian works* (2nd ed.). El Paso: Texas Western Press. An important collection of essays on McCarthy's fiction set in Tennessee.

Holloway, D. (2002). *The late modernism of Cormac McCarthy.* Westport: Greenwood. Rather than from regionalist perspectives, Holloway explores McCarthy's fiction in the context of modernist discourses.

Lilley, J. D. (Ed.). (2014). *Cormac McCarthy: New directions.* Albuquerque: University of New Mexico Press. A very fine sampling of sophisticated critical readings of McCarthy.

Lincoln, K. (2009). *Cormac McCarthy: American canticles.* New York: Palgrave MacMillan. Focuses on McCarthy's overall vision, with a particular focus on McCarthy's post-Tennessee fiction and its interrogation of the cultural myths of the United States.

Luce, D. (2009). *Reading the world: Cormac McCarthy's Tennessee period.* Columbia: University of South Carolina Press. A reading of McCarthy's early fiction by one of his finest critics.

CHAPTER 15

New Orleans as Gothic Capital

Sherry R. Truffin

America may lack a medieval past, but it has never wanted for a gothic imagination, and since the Civil War the South has been America's primary 'arena
for terror' (Fiedler 474). With its aristocratic pretensions, its ghastly abuse
of slaves, and its ruined monuments to an unenlightened past, the South is
America's analog to the barbaric European medieval.

Within the South, it is difficult to imagine a city with more potential as a
gothic site than New Orleans, Louisiana. A typical gothic setting is an unsafe,
physically isolating space in which a past characterized by archaic authority
structures, religious superstition, and/or transgressive excess is experienced as
omnipresent, threatening, seductive, or maddening (Baldick xix–xx; Botting
1–17). The geography, history, and culture of New Orleans, considered in light
of this definition, combine to make the city a 'gothic capital.'

Excess and Disorientation

Like much Southern Gothic, imaginative representations of New Orleans focus
on social and racial boundaries and their attendant anxieties, the 'ruins' of
the past, and the general 'otherness' of the place. However, more than other
Southern cities, New Orleans appears as an unreal or alien space associated with
a foreign Catholic heritage, the chronic transgression of sexual and social taboos,
the replacement of moral with aesthetic values, a loss of control that is simultaneously frightening and liberating, and madness. It is a city of excess, masquerade,
trickery, and disorienting juxtapositions: the beautiful and the monstrous, the
refined and the crass, the sacred and the profane, the living and the dead. It is
simultaneously multi-cultural and provincial, crowded yet isolating, and it is a

S.R. Truffin (✉)
Campbell University, Buies Creek, NC, USA

© The Editor(s) (if applicable) and The Author(s) 2016
S.C. Street, C.L. Crow (eds.), *The Palgrave Handbook of the Southern Gothic*,
DOI 10.1057/978-1-137-47774-3_15

site of frightening transformation or dark self-discovery. It is resilient but cursed, perpetually poised for environmental or cultural apocalypse.

Geographical isolation, environmental vulnerability, and man-made peril all contribute to New Orleans' gothic image. Waterlocked until the mid-nineteenth century, New Orleans is surrounded by swamps, oppressively humid, and weather-beaten. Its history is replete with hurricanes, floods, fires, and plagues of yellow fever, and its dead are buried above ground because most of the city is at or below sea level. Early on, it served as a French 'penal colony' (Sublette 52), and an Ursuline nun who arrived in 1727 grimly declared, 'the devil here possesses a large empire' (qtd in Dawdy 1). Since then, New Orleans has been notorious for heavy alcohol consumption, organized crime, and ineffective or corrupt government and law enforcement.[1]

The exotic 'otherness' of New Orleans also marks it as a place of gothic fear and fascination. New Orleans has been called 'the most foreign of all North American cities' (Holditch 63) because of its unusual colonial history: Louisiana was French, then Spanish, then briefly French again before the Louisiana Purchase made it American. New Orleans was named for a 'notorious womanizer and drinker,' Regent Philippe II, Duc d'Orléans, who gave control of Louisiana to 'professional gambler' John Law in 1717 without properly funding Law's scheme to make New Orleans a regional commercial center (Sublette 46–8). France did, however, supplement the colony's population of 'Creoles' (residents born in the colonies) through so-called 'Louisiana slavery' by emptying prisons and deporting criminals and prostitutes (53).

Louisiana saw significant development and diversification during the Spanish colonial period. Its power in the region waning, France gave Spain the Louisiana Territory in 1762, partly to keep it from the British, and the Spanish made New Orleans 'a political appendage of Havana,' infusing Cuban culture into city life (98). Under Spanish control, Louisiana also saw an influx of Acadians ('Cajuns'), Catholics expelled from British Canada in 1755, as well as refugees from the Saint-Dominigue slave uprising (1770s and 1780s). The Spanish regime rebuilt areas decimated by fire, creating a French Quarter with decidedly Spanish architecture. After Louisiana began to cultivate sugar cane, Napoleon re-acquired the territory in 1801, hoping to develop a new empire around the Caribbean sugar trade, then sold it to the United States in 1803 after French forces failed to take back Saint-Dominigue (196).

The considerable cultural diversity of New Orleans was augmented by a heterogeneous African slave population that experienced periods of relative freedom and of inhuman degradation. The first slaves in Louisiana were Native American sex slaves (Sublette 40), and the French imported African slaves from Senegal, Ouidah (present-day Benin), and Cabinda (present-day Angola; 57), among them skilled laborers who would create a 'culture of artisanship' (59) in Louisiana. The Spanish brought new slaves from the Kongo-Angola region (107), but eased punishments and allowed slaves to own property, marry, and purchase their freedom (97). Slaves could also congregate, play music, and dance on Sunday afternoons in Congo Square (now Louis Armstrong Park), named after Louis Congo, a slave freed to serve as executioner (58). After sugar cultivation began in the 1790s, however, Louisiana planters replicated the brutal conditions of similar plantations in Saint-Domingue, and violent uprisings there and in Haiti prompted Louisiana planters to become increasingly repressive. When importing slaves became illegal, privateers diverted slaves bound for Cuba to New Orleans (265), helping to make New Orleans the largest slave market in the United States (219).

The unique black culture that developed from the diversity and relative freedom of New Orleans' slave population accounts for the city's associations with foreign superstitions and black power, both historically frightening to whites. Many Louisiana slaves practiced a 'composite' religion that blended traditional African religious practices with Christian or Muslim ones (141). Catholics had already nominally Christianized the Kongo, and many Kongolese 'disguised their spirits' as Catholic saints (68), while Senegal is in a more Islamized area of Africa, explaining why 'gris-gris,' charms of Muslim origin, were part of early Louisiana slave culture (60–61). Many slaves from Ouidah practiced voodoo, a 'creolized' religion derived from Haitian 'vodou' (61), which involved ritualized drumming, dancing, and worship of a deity or spirit in the shape of a snake. When fears of slave rebellion led to increased repression, the practice of voodoo became clandestine (285). White fears of slave practices beyond their understanding or control were exacerbated by the fact that by 1810, New Orleans was a black-majority city (260).

Free people of color represented 29% of New Orleans' population in 1810 (113) and contributed significantly to the city's 'otherness' within the South and America as a whole. During Spanish rule, free blacks served in militias (113) and played in military bands (100–1); in fact, Louisiana was the only North American colony that permitted blacks to play drums (104), associated in the minds of whites with revolt (73). Many free women of color represented a property-owning 'courtesan class' (259) who entered into contracts of 'plaçage' or concubinage with wealthy white men through a system of elaborate 'quadroon balls' (244). Although free blacks experienced considerable discrimination and were subjected to various segregation measures (102, 126), this population had a measure of liberty and power unthinkable for most African Americans, particularly in the nineteenth century.

New Orleans is, in sum, a place of environmental vulnerability and linguistic, historical, and religious hybridity. It is a place in which distinct neighborhoods and the socio-economic and racial boundaries they represent carry considerable weight: to this day, life in Tremé (formerly the site of prostitution hub Storyville) or the Lower Ninth Ward remains very different from life in the Garden District or the French Quarter. At the same time, however, social and racial boundaries have been difficult to police and constantly, often violently, transgressed. It is not hard to see why New Orleans has produced literature rife with gothic themes.

New Orleans Literature

Scores of writers of varying degrees of reputation and success were born in, settled in, or temporarily made a home in or near New Orleans, and many visitors have written about the city. Nancy Dixon identifies war as the central topic of New Orleans literature before the Louisiana Purchase and slavery and racism as the key topics thereafter, although the latter were always present (12). Early literature was primarily written by and about wealthy white classes of the city, but New Orleans also produced the first anthology of African American literature in 1845 (13). The 'golden age' of New Orleans literature, the late nineteenth century, encompasses the work of George Washington Cable, Grace King, Alice Dunbar Nelson, and others (16). Doomed love is a recurring theme throughout the city's literature, and other prominent topics include the Catholic Church, voodoo, carnival, drink, dance, and violence, as well as the Mississippi River, which Joshua Clark describes as 'a colossal metaphor' for hidden depths of meaning (13).

Most important for our purposes, ghosts are omnipresent in New Orleans literature (Dixon 14), emphasizing the inescapability of the past. Jeanne deLavigne's 1946 volume *Ghost Stories of Old New Orleans* describes encounters with the restless spirits of priests, witches, pirates, thieves, gamblers, slaves, and unrequited lovers, many of whom, particularly those based on historical persons, often appear in New Orleans literature. One of them, 'The Haunted House of the Rue Royale,' involves the infamous Madame Lalaurie,[2] who lived in New Orleans from 1831 until 1834, when a house fire deliberately set by the cook prompted the discovery of horrifically maimed and disfigured slaves, some alive, some dead. Lalaurie escaped with her husband to Paris, leaving the ghosts of frightened, fleeing slaves to haunt the Lalaurie manor. George Washington Cable's earlier, more famous, and more dramatically embellished version of the haunted Lalaurie house, based on Harriet Martineau's 1838 account, was featured in *Strange True Stories of Louisiana* (1890). Ghosts also frequently appear in Lafcadio Hearn's New Orleans writings, including 'The City of Dreams,' which suggests that New Orleans residents who walk the city muttering to themselves talk about and to the dead.

The ghost story and the gothic tale may be separate genres (Baldick), but ghosts regularly appear in gothic fiction. Mollie Evelyn Moore Davis's tale 'At La Glorieuse' (1897), for example, tells of a visitor to a plantation near New Orleans who becomes enthralled, with the help of a mysterious ring, by the ghost of a beautiful but 'soulless' woman of Greek origin (287), the wife of his father's best friend, his father's would-be seducer, and the mother of the orphaned young lady he is courting. The man abandons New Orleans and restlessly travels until he loses the ring in the cleansing surf of the Atlantic Ocean and is freed from the curse. He rushes to New Orleans to find his paramour, but discovers her in a cathedral taking vows, entering 'another and mysterious world into which he could not follow' (291). Since the Gothic is a traditionally Protestant form that regards the Catholic Church with both fascination and suspicion (Fiedler 144), New Orleans' Catholic culture contributes to the city's gothic atmosphere.

The image of the city as haunted lends a gothic sensibility to many works about the city and its surroundings. S. Frederick Starr argues that Lafcadio Hearn 'invented' New Orleans, or the common conception of it, in the late nineteenth century, although Holditch makes a similar claim about George Washington Cable (65). Botting contends that while the Gothic ceased to be a dominant literary form after the nineteenth century, one continues to find 'a diffusion of Gothic traces among a multiplicity of different genres' (13), and much New Orleans literature fits this description. While works by Cornel Woolrich, Walker Percy, John Biguenet, Jarret Keene, Anne Rice, and Poppy Z. Brite (now Billy Martin) are decidedly gothic, most New Orleans Gothic is hybrid. Social realism and journalism mix with local color, historical romance, and the Gothic in the writings of Cable and Hearn, respectively. Tennessee Williams's 'poetic realism' and John Kennedy Toole's picaresque *A Confederacy of Dunces* feature characters who are isolated, haunted, and/or mad, lending these works a gothic sensibility. Valerie Martin, best known for *Mary Reilly,* a retelling of Stevenson's *Dr. Jekyll and Mr. Hyde* from a servant's perspective, writes New Orleans novels that mix social/psychological realism and the Gothic. Andrew Fox offers gothic parody, and three notable post-Katrina novels are hybrids: Mary Robison's *One DOA, One on the Way* is realism infused with gothic tropes, while Louis Maistros offers gothic magical realism in *The Sound of Building Coffins,* and Alys Arden mixes fantasy with the Gothic in *The Casquette Girls.*

Significantly, New Orleans literature by African American writers generally eschews the Gothic in favor of realism, perhaps because verisimilitude supplies sufficient horrors. The nineteenth-century writings of Armand Lanusse, a free Creole of color, implicate the Catholic Church and others in the peddling of young black women into prostitution through plaçage. Tom Dent's *Ritual Murder* (1967) considers structural inequities in New Orleans that condemn black youth to lives of hopelessness and violence, while Fatima Shaik's 'Climbing Monkey Hill' (1987) examines the tensions and violence surrounding integration in 1960s New Orleans through the eyes of an African American teenager. Charles Johnson's historical novel *Middle Passage* (1990) has elements of superstition and mystery, but its protagonist, a newly freed slave, abandons New Orleans at the outset, and its real setting is the slave ship on which he stows away. Countering the realist tendency is the carnivalesque postmodern fiction of Ishmael Reed (1960s and following), in which New Orleans voodoo and Southern hoodoo,[3] sources of gothic horror for white writers, become resources for black identity and agency, as they do in Zora Neale Hurston's New Orleans writings from the 1920s and 1930s.

Work by white writers, however, frequently depicts New Orleans as a gothic space. George Washington Cable's *The Grandissimes* (1880) presents early nineteenth-century New Orleans as a mysterious, alien culture cursed by its racism. Its central figure is Joseph Frowenfeld, a German immigrant, apothecary, and abolitionist who has lost his family to yellow fever. His friendship with Honoré Grandissime helps draw him into disputes concerning age-old family feuds and pressing tensions over race and caste, some involving Honoré's half-brother, a free man of color shunned by most of his white Creole brethren. The novel also incorporates the story of Bras-Coupé, a maimed fugitive slave based on a historical figure who was eventually lynched. In Cable's version, Bras-Coupé curses those who have disfigured him and kept him from his love, Palmyre, a voodoo practitioner. For Frowenfeld, New Orleans is a place of 'shadows ..., hints, allusions, faint unspoken admissions, ill-concealed antipathies, ... mistaken identities and whisperings of hidden strife' (96). At the end, the chief antagonist, Honoré's uncle Agricola, dies, 'the aged high-priest of a doomed civilization' (324).

Cable's portrayal of New Orleans as cursed by its violent history extends into contemporary gothic works like John Biguenet's 'A Plague of Toads' (2001). An unnamed city comparable to New Orleans is menaced by the scourge of the title, perhaps in retribution for aggressive attempts to Christianize indigenous tribes while sacrificing their lands to city development. The narrator, a journalist, draws this conclusion after finding an underground room in City Hall containing chronicles of the city's history written by Franciscan friars, one apparently insane. The narrator believes that a previous plague ended when city leaders made offerings to an indigenous god figure called 'the Emperor' (72). In the end, the state capital has been relocated due to the toads' toxic slime, and the narrator, a devoted follower of the Emperor like the 'mad friar' before him (72), is trapped in an insane asylum in Philadelphia. The city has an apocalyptic reckoning with a past that condemns its historians to madness.

Curses from the city's racist past inform two representative voodoo-themed tales that emphasize white exploitation and black retaliatory power. Cornell Woolrich's 'Dark Melody of Madness' (1935) is the story of struggling white jazz musician Eddie Bloch, who happens upon a barbaric voodoo ceremony depicted in a stereotypically racist fashion as 'a roomful of devils' (120) dancing 'in a jungle frenzy' (123). When discovered, he pretends to be an initiate, then steals the voodoo music and successfully transforms it for popular (white) audiences, but is cursed and begins wasting away. He eventually murders the voodoo leader and turns himself in to the police, who imprison voodoo practitioners while covering up Bloch's crime. Bloch begins to recover, but when he performs his voodoo song on stage, he falls down dead. Jarret Keene's 'Conjure Me' (2003) takes place during an antebellum yellow fever outbreak and focuses on Josephine, a slave in a sexual relationship with her master, 'the Good Doctor' (291). Josephine tries to kill the doctor's wife with voodoo, but he discovers her malevolent talisman. The doctor's friend Tallant,[4] a drunken health warden, rapes and apparently murders Josephine, dumping her corpse among yellow fever victims and nonchalantly shooting slaves who report a missing body. Josephine crawls to a voodoo ceremony, realizes she has had a 'monster' inside her since arriving in New Orleans, asks voodoo congregants to 'conjure' her into a 'Zombi' (302), and returns for Tallant, whose violence has made him 'one with the city' (303). He laughs at distant sounds of voodoo rituals until he feels the blade of Josephine's machete on his neck.

New Orleans also functions as a gothic site because its culture of carnival and masquerade promulgates deception and danger. Laura Lippman's 'Pony Girl' from *New Orleans Noir* (2007) resembles Amiri Baraka's 'Dutchman' in reversing stereotypes, presenting black men as victims and white women as predators. The narrator, a New Orleans man, points out that 'people do odd things, especially when they's masked' (70), and recalls a Mardi Gras in which an attractive young white woman and her friend dress and dance provocatively at a bar in the mostly black neighborhood of Tremé, drawing lascivious stares from the men, including the dangerous Big Roy, whom they spurn and mock. Roy follows them from the bar and attacks 'Pony Girl,' at which point the girls batter and slash him 'like a piñata' and drink a 'geyser' of his spurting blood 'like greedy children, as if it were a fire hydrant ... on a hot day' (75). The girls become folkloric 'white devils' who 'go dancing on Mardi Gras, looking for black men to rob and kill' (77). The narrator points out that a man who won't pursue 'a demon or a witch' might 'be lured into a dark place by a fairy princess ... or a Cowgirl and her slinky Pony Girl' (77), emphasizing that masks create threats along with thrills.

Predatory scam artists who find a home in New Orleans' carnivalesque culture are Truman Capote's subject in 'A Tree of Night' (1945). Young Kay leaves her uncle's funeral in New Orleans to return to college in Alabama and finds herself on a gothic train, a 'relic with a decaying interior' (447), forced to sit with a grotesque-looking woman and her mute male companion. The woman reveals herself as a former New Orleans fortune teller and bullies Kay into drinking gin; the man stares disconcertingly at Kay, pressuring her to buy a strange love charm. In her anxious, inebriated mind, he becomes the fabled 'wizard man' who eats children (453). She buys the charm out of fear, then faints from alcohol and exhaustion, and the woman steals her purse and coat, which she pulls over the girl's head 'like a shroud' (453), linking New Orleans with trickery and menace.

The Gothic Other

Much twentieth-century New Orleans Gothic does not, however, present this menace from the perspective of a victim or bystander. Instead, it exemplifies the contemporary trend of embodying the perspective of the 'other,' forcing the reader to identify with a marginal, often monstrous point of view (Punter 178). And instead of being terrified by the gothic space of New Orleans, the monster, although often lonely, feels right at home.

Walker Percy's *Lancelot* (1977) is a first-person narrative chronicling the descent of a New Orleans man into psychopathy and murder, a transformation that he regards as an awakening. Lancelot Andrewes Lamar is a bored attorney living in a 'dream state' at Belle Isle (50), an old family estate outside New Orleans, when he happens upon proof of his actress-wife's infidelity and embarks on an ultimately homicidal quest for the nature of evil. Angry that the city and country are being overrun by 'pornographers' (204), he secretly videotapes his wife and her colleagues (ironically becoming a pornographer himself), then murders them in Belle Isle, which he sets ablaze during a hurricane and leaves a gothic ruin. Now an inmate in a 'Center for Aberrant Behavior' in New Orleans, Lancelot admits to finding 'nothing at the heart of evil' (237) and plots a 'Third Revolution' (203) that will herald a newly chivalrous world. He regards his time staring at Lafayette Cemetery from a cell window as revelatory: 'the narrower the view the more you can see' (1), embracing violence and madness as components of a larger apocalyptic epiphany.

The perspectives of monsters dominate the horror novels of Anne Rice and Poppy Z. Brite, in which vampires and serial killers hail from or find a home in New Orleans, where they blend into the carnivalesque atmosphere; find an endless supply of targets; enjoy art, culture, and constant stimulation; and vie with disease and natural disaster for victims. Rice's vampires are sensualists and aesthetes in love with 'barbaric' New Orleans (*Vampire Lestat* 465). Louis, the brooding, guilt-ridden protagonist of *Interview with the Vampire*, describes New Orleans as a 'magical and magnificent place' in which a 'vampire ... might attract no more notice ... than hundreds of other exotic creatures' (40). Throughout his self-imposed exile in Europe, he misses 'desperately fragile' New Orleans (203), where he never had to conceal 'the kill,' since 'the ravages of fever, plague, crime ... competed with us always, and outdid us' (170). In *The Vampire Lestat* (1985), Louis's antagonist becomes the protagonist, a vampire who sees the world as a lovely but 'savage garden' (465) that renders moral categories meaningless (131). He embraces the decadent New Orleans of the decadent 1980s and becomes a rock star, reveling in the theatricality and excess of that life. Andrew Fox's *Fat White Vampire Blues* series (2003 and following) parodies Rice's novels with its obese vampire protagonist Jules Duchon, a New Orleans cabbie whose existence is much less romantic and erotic than Louis's or Lestat's.

The monsters of Poppy Z. Brite's fiction relate to New Orleans as Rice's protagonists do, although their sexual practices and murderous acts are rendered in more graphic detail. *Lost Souls* (1992) focuses on a vampire named Nothing born in New Orleans, the child of a vampire father and a human woman who died in childbirth, but raised by human parents in suburban Delaware. New Orleans is a 'garden of Eden' for vampires (39), where alcohol makes victims tastier, and streets have 'magic talismanic names' (276). When the teenaged Nothing abandons his northeastern home and heads south to 'follow his whims' (93), he becomes sexually involved with a vampire who turns out to be his father and travels with him to New Orleans, where 'every ancient brick' seems to belong to him (277). Meanwhile, a psychic named Ghost tries to rescue a friend from the vampires and finds himself overwhelmed by the voices of 'greedy' spirits speaking from 'every street corner' (302) of the city. Brite's *Exquisite Corpse* (1996) focuses on the partnership between Andrew, an escaped serial killer from England, and Jay, a serial killer, necrophiliac, and cannibal modeled after Jeffrey Dahmer. Jay is from a prominent New Orleans family whose name and wealth give him the means, privacy, and deference to get away with horrific crimes, as well as a family mansion with old slave quarters where he keeps his dead and dying victims. New Orleans is Jay's 'womb' (208), and, like Rice's vampires, Jay and Andrew blend into a city 'where robbery and murder [are] as common as afternoon rainstorms' (42), a city that provides endless 'offerings' in the form of passive victims (79).

While New Orleans represents home to the gothic 'other,' it cannot ensure freedom from loneliness, which causes Lestat to make Louis and Claudia, makes Louis eternally restless, keeps Nothing in a sexual relationship with his own father, and prompts Andrew and Jay to become killing partners. Before loneliness became a constant refrain for Rice and Brite's monsters, however, it was thematized in much New Orleans literature. Tennessee Williams's 'Vieux Carré,'[5] while not explicitly gothic, is full of damaged, haunted characters stricken with loneliness in a world of transgression and violence. A semi-autobiographical play from 1977 based on Williams's 1943 story 'Angel in the Alcove,' 'Vieux Carré' designates its protagonist only as 'writer,' a New Orleans newcomer living in a boarding house beset by bats, peopled with misfits, and managed by a mentally unbalanced woman. He is seduced into his first homosexual experience by a dying artist, then visited by a spirit that he associates with his dead grandmother. Life in the seedy French Quarter bleeds him emotionally, teaching him the bitter lesson that 'there's a price for things' and making him feel 'overdrawn, depleted' (418). Still, he admits that there was no 'better place' to 'encounter [his] true nature' (427), marking New Orleans, once again, as a place of dark self-discovery. At the end, he sees the ghosts of his tortured housemates and hears a 'cacophony of sounds' representing 'the waiting storm of his future – … racking cries of pain and pleasure' (445). Comparatively subtle gothic elements of Toole's satiric tragicomedy *A Confederacy of Dunces* (1980) include its corpulent hero's mysterious anatomy (his pyloric valve has prophetic powers) and his obsession with the medieval. Like other New Orleans protagonists, Ignatius Reilly is fated to alienation, madness, and confinement.

The gothic-inflected New Orleans novels of Valerie Martin emphasize disturbing transformations and juxtapositions, explore the terrors and pleasures of transgressing boundaries, and focus on the darker aspects of history. *The Great Divorce* (1994) weaves together the stories of three women, two contemporary, one antebellum. Ellen, a veterinarian at the New Orleans Zoo, copes with her husband's infidelity and abandonment, while her assistant Camille, an emotionally abused and sexually exploited young woman, experiences intense fantasies in which she becomes the large predatory cats from the zoo. The antebellum woman, the subject of Ellen's historian husband's research, is the 'Catwoman of St. Francisville,' a wealthy Creole woman trapped in an oppressive marriage who is executed for murder after claiming that she became a black leopard and tore her husband limb from limb. Racist ideologies equated blacks with animals (and black women with 'breeders') to justify and perpetuate slavery, but the white women in Martin's novel, perhaps constrained by notions of Southern white femininity, find the idea of transforming into animals liberating. The zoo's black panther dies, and Camille reflects that 'everything was too close together, ... beauty to ugliness, death to life' before committing suicide (285), while Ellen's husband wonders whether history is 'merely the record of how vicious the human animal has always been' (317). Martin's novel *Property* (2003), the first-person narrative of another antebellum Creole woman bound to a husband she hates, equates slavery with monstrous transformation. Its narrator, haunted by the memory of a father she worshipped who had been consumed by problems of effective slave management to the extremity of suicide, is herself obsessed with controlling Sarah, a slave who has borne her husband a child. Although the narrator feels as 'as if an iron collar ... used to discipline field women' has been affixed to her own 'skull' (182), she takes pleasure in the subjection of others. When her husband dies and Sarah escapes, she spares no cost in recovering her human 'property.' She is mistress and slave, captor and prisoner, monster and victim in one.

Since 2005, New Orleans literature has reckoned with the devastation caused by Hurricane Katrina and its horrific aftermath, extending the gothic emphasis on death and haunting. Mary Robison's *One DOA, One on the Way* (2009) is narrated by Eve, a New Orleans movie location scout married (of course) to Adam, a man slowly wasting away from Hepatitis C, a twin from an old, wealthy New Orleans family. This novella reads like minimalist noir fiction but is permeated with Southern Gothic tropes: an ancient family estate, family secrets, incest, madness. Eve conducts an affair with her husband's dissipated twin, whose wife has tried to kill him, prompting Eve to steer her into a mental institution. She punctuates her story with facts about the relative usability of different gun holsters and dispiriting statistics about the city's high crime and incarceration rates, devastated infrastructure, and the like. Eve's job ensures her intimate familiarity with the city's geography, but New Orleans remains 'full of meanings' that she cannot fathom (72). The city's devastation compounds the family drama, leading to a deadly confrontation at the fountain where Adam's sister drowned herself years before.

Other post-Katrina novels end with affirmations of New Orleans' resilience while maintaining the city's gothic image. Louis Maistros's *The Sound of Building Coffins* (2009) focuses on an earlier hurricane in New Orleans history, 1905. This magical realist novel begins in 1891, covers a 15-year period, and features fictionalized versions of iconic figures from the city's history, including voodoo priestess Malvina Latour and jazz cornetist 'Buddy' Bolden. Its focus is the Morningstars, an African American family whose patriarch named his children after attractive-sounding diseases (Diphtheria, Malaria, etc.) to remind them that death is close and beautiful. Characters are vexed by 'shoe-doves' ('should've's' or regrets; 234), dark family secrets, voodoo curses, and demon possession, while the souls of aborted fetuses are magically 'rebirthed' in an ever-present 'Spiritworld' accessible from and through the Mississippi River. Conflicts build to a climax as a deadly hurricane hits the city, and the narrator remarks that 'life is short the world over, but the truth is more acute here and so life is lived as if endless' (336). The novel ends with visions of rebirth.

Hope of restoration can also be found in Alys Arden's *The Casquette Girls* (2013), a young adult fantasy novel set in the immediate aftermath of Hurricane Katrina, where returning citizens resemble 'post-apocalyptic zombie victims' (14). The title refers to eighteenth-century women sent from France to New Orleans, along with caskets of clothing and dowry items, to be educated by Ursuline nuns until finding husbands. The teenage protagonist of Arden's novel, Adele, discovers that she is the descendent of a casket girl, that she has supernatural powers, and that the fury of 'The Storm' has helped to unleash vampires, former casket stowaways, on the already traumatized city. An apocalyptic battle between vampires and a newly formed coven of good witches takes place on a Halloween night featuring a moving display of sheets representing the ghosts of Katrina's victims. After the battle, Adele and her coven walk the streets singing, inspiring her with faith that the city will recover.

And so the specters of Hurricane Katrina join the already considerable assembly of specters found throughout New Orleans lore. New Orleans may be 'The City That Care Forgot,' but its literature suggests that its past refuses to be ignored. Although post-Katrina rebuilding has involved ever more commercialization and homogenization of the city, its foreignness lingers. New Orleans has been described as 'less a place than an idea,' the antithesis of everything normally considered modern or American (Starr ix), a place where, as Lancelot puts it, 'dead Creoles [are] more alive than … Buick dealers' (Percy 233). Even now, New Orleans remains an imaginative space of greedy spirits, exotic traditions, transgressive excess, dark epiphanies, and seductive madness. It is a gothic capital where the pursuit of pleasure is inextricable from the pursuit of terror.

NOTES

1. See Asbury's *The French Quarter: An Informal History of the New Orleans Underworld* (Basic Books, 2003) and Moore's *Black Rage: Police Brutality and African-American Activism from World War II to Hurricane Katrina* (Louisiana State University Press, 2010).
2. Madame Lalaurie is frequently referenced in New Orleans literature and even appears as a character played by Kathy Bates in the third season of the television series *American Horror Story* (2013), which features a coven of witches whose ancestors had been expelled from New England and found a home in New Orleans.
3. African American folkloric magic syncretized with Protestant Christianity rather than with Catholicism, as in voodoo.
4. Named after Robert Tallant, who wrote a largely discredited but still popular study of New Orleans voodoo in 1946.
5. The original name of the French Quarter.

Bibliography

Arden, A. (2013). *The Casquette Girls*. FortheARTofit. New Orleans
Baldick, C. (1992). *The Oxford book of gothic tales*. Oxford: Oxford University Press. Print.
Biguenet, J. (2001). A plague of toads. In *The torturer's apprentice* (pp. 59–79). New York: Ecco.
Botting, F. (1996). *Gothic*. London: Routledge. Print.
Brite, P. Z. (1996). *Exquisite corpse*. New York: Scribner. Print.
Brite, P. Z. (1992). *Lost souls*. New York: Dell. Print.
Cable, G. W. (1988). *The Grandissimes*. New York: Penguin. Print.
Capote, T. (2013). A tree of night. In D. Nancy (Ed.), *N.O. Lit: 200 years of New Orleans literature* (pp. 447–453). New Orleans: Lavender Ink. Print.
Clark, J. (2003). *French Quarter fiction: The newest stories of America's oldest bohemia*. New Orleans: Light of New Orleans Publishing. Print.
Davis, M. E. M. (2013). At La Glorieuse. In *N.O. Lit: 200 years of New Orleans literature* (pp. 278–291). Lavender Ink: New Orleans. Print.
Dawdy, S. L. (2008). *Building the devil's empire: French colonial New Orleans*. Chicago: University of Chicago Press. Print.
deLavigne, J. (2013). The Haunted House of the Rue Royale. In *Ghost stories of old New Orleans* (pp. 248–258). Baton Rouge: Louisiana State University Press. Print.
Dixon, N. (2013). *N.O. Lit: 200 years of New Orleans literature*. New Orleans: Lavender Ink. Print.
Fiedler, L. (1966). *Love and death in the American novel*. Normal: Dalkey Archive Press. Print.
Hearn, L. (2001). The city of dreams. In S. Frederick Starr (Ed.), *Inventing New Orleans: Writings of Lafcadio Hearn* (pp. 134–136). Jackson: University of Mississippi Press. Print.
Holditch, W. K. (1992). South toward freedom: Tennessee Williams. In R. S. Kennedy (Ed.), *Literary New Orleans* (pp. 61–75). Baton Rouge: Louisiana State University Press. Print.
Keene, J. (2003). Conjure Me. In J. Clark (Ed.), *French Quarter fiction: The newest stories of America's oldest bohemia* (pp. 291–303). New Orleans: Light of New Orleans Publishing. Print.
Lippman, L. (2007). Pony Girl. In J. Smith (Ed.), *New Orleans noir* (pp. 68–77). New York: Akashic Books. Print.
Maistros, L. (2009). *The sound of building coffins*. New Milford: Toby Press.
Martin, V. (1994). *The great divorce*. New York: Doubleday. Print.
Martin, V. (2003). *Property*. New York: Vintage Contemporaries. Print.
Percy, W. (1977). *Lancelot*. New York: Ivy Books. Print.
Punter, D. (1996). *The literature of terror, vol. 2: The modern gothic* (2nd ed.). London: Longman. Print.
Rice, A. (1976). *Interview with the vampire*. New York: Ballantine Books.
Rice, A. (1985). *The vampire Lestat*. New York: Ballantine Books.
Robison, M. (2007). *One DOA, another on the way*. Berkeley: Counterpoint. Print.
Starr, S. F. (2001). *Inventing New Orleans: Writings of Lafcadio Hearn*. Jackson: University of Mississippi Press.
Sublette, N. (2008). *The world that made New Orleans: From Spanish silver to Congo Square*. Chicago: Laurence Hills Books. Print.

Williams, T. (2013). Vieux Carré. In N. Dixon (Ed.), *N.O. Lit: 200 years of New Orleans literature* (pp. 403–445). Lavender Ink: New Orleans. Print.

Woolrich, C. (1987). Dark melody of madness. In *Nightmares in Dixie: Thirteen horror tales from the American South* (pp. 105–139). Little Rock: August House. Print.

Further Reading

Dixon, N. (Ed.). (2013). *N.O. Lit: 200 years of New Orleans literature.* New Orleans: Lavender Ink. Dixon's anthology of New Orleans literature features a diverse range of works selected to illuminate the city's history and culture.

Kennedy, R. S. (Ed.). (1992). *Literary New Orleans.* Baton Rouge: Louisiana State University Press. These 'essays and meditations' examine New Orleans' impact on the life and work of writers like Grace King, Kate Chopin, William Faulkner, and Walker Percy.

Kennedy, R. S. (Ed.). (1998). *Literary New Orleans in the modern world.* Baton Rouge: Louisiana State University Press. This sequel to *Literary New Orleans* emphasizes local New Orleans literary history and extends the work of the first volume to include modern writers like John Kennedy Toole and Shirley Ann Grau.

Starr, S. F. (Ed.). (2001). *Inventing New Orleans: Writings of Lafcadio Hearn.* Jackson: University of Mississippi Press. The impressions, sketches, editorials, and studies of New Orleans from journalist Lafcadio Hearn (1877–88) contributed much to the city's image as a place of authenticity, mystery, beauty, and decay.

Sublette, N. (2008). *The world that made New Orleans: From Spanish silver to Congo Square.* Chicago: Laurence Hills Books. Sublette's history of New Orleans' first century explores the colonial conflicts and world revolutions that shaped the city, emphasizing the development of a unique Afro-Louisiana culture.

CHAPTER 16

George Washington Cable and Grace King

Owen Robinson

By the 1880s, when George Washington Cable and Grace King locked literary horns over New Orleans' Creole population, that city had seen its fair share of conflict over its identity and soul, arising from its complex colonial history and the even more complex politics of race that resulted. The writers' dispute is an intriguing example of two figures addressing many of the same materials and coming to very different conclusions. Similarly interesting is that they also employ many of the same means to do so, resulting in a blend of local colour and gothic elements and techniques employed to sometimes opposing ends.

Two of the most well-known exponents of the local colour branch of New Orleans writing, Cable and King's respective fictions and essays frequently portray the relations between the city's Creole establishment – by the 1880s greatly diminished after eight decades of 'Americanisation' – and its black and mixed-race populations: broadly speaking, Cable was deeply critical of Creole history and society, and in particular its treatment of slaves and free people of colour as well as Native Americans, while King portrayed the same social milieu in more positive terms. In so doing, both writers vividly depict the idiosyncrasies of New Orleans' site, climate, and architecture, as well as the rich folk cultures that developed between the cracks of its stratifications of race, gender, and class. This chapter will look at some examples from key works by Cable and King in comparison, examining their respective employment of certain tropes in their analyses of New Orleans social codes and depiction of place.

New Orleans has, of course, become a renowned site for an idiosyncratic take on Southern Gothic themes and tones – idiosyncratic partly because the city's own status as a Southern place is notoriously slippery. Louisiana was a French and then a Spanish colony from its founding in 1718, only becoming part of the United States – and therefore part of that nation's 'South' – with

O. Robinson (✉)
University of Essex, Colchester, UK

© The Editor(s) (if applicable) and The Author(s) 2016
S.C. Street, C.L. Crow (eds.), *The Palgrave Handbook of the Southern Gothic*,
DOI 10.1057/978-1-137-47774-3_16

the Louisiana Purchase of 1803. It was already, and remained, an important part of the wider American tropical world largely to *its* south, a region based in colonial policies, power shifts and positioning, plantation economies and slavery, stretching from northern South America, through the Caribbean and Central America, to the southerly parts of North America. The decades following the Purchase provide a particularly fascinating coming together of various sometimes clashing populations and mindsets, with New Orleans' identity politics becoming ever more complex and ambiguous. It shares with other sites in the wider region a rich and often discussed tradition of zombie imagery and mythology, tied in with its voodoo heritage. Similarly, representations of vampires are widespread in New Orleans' popular literature. Perhaps inevitably, much of this feeds into commercialised and profitable outlets, and the French Quarter is full of tourist-trapping voodoo shops and 'Haunted New Orleans' tours, while the city's cemeteries, its 'cities of the dead', remain among its greatest draws for visitors. As with many other facets of its past and present, there is a romantic exuberance to much of New Orleans' engagement with death and deathliness, which sits in intriguing ways with the macabre, at times horrific subject matter.

George Washington Cable (1844–1925) and Grace King (1851–1932) are not among the writers who necessarily come to mind straight away when one thinks of New Orleans Gothic, not least because of the hugely popular and more explicitly genre-bound work and culture that have been produced in recent decades. However, they can be seen as part of a rich body of nineteenth-century writing from and about the city that uses gothic figurations to register its shifting, nebulous, delicate place in the Americas. Much of this work does not necessarily set out to be part of a gothic tradition in particular, but whether through authorial temperament or the peculiarities of New Orleans itself, elements that can usefully be considered in gothic terms frequently become paramount. For instance, numerous European and American travellers to the city in the period after 1803 give colourful, gothic-tinged accounts of their arrival and experience in a place at once beguiling and forbidding, seemingly isolated at the edge of the world and confused as to its existence and status, surrounded on all sides by swamps and treacherous bodies of water, and troubled by vaguely defined but powerful threats of violence and pestilence from outside as well as enemies within (Robinson, forthcoming). All of these facets are present in Cable and King's respective work across a number of literary modes – short and long fiction, history, journalism – and are among their most powerful qualities even when they seem to be at odds over the value of what is being described. For all their political differences over the history and culture of their city and region, and the resonances of that history in their contemporary culture, Cable and King are similarly possessed of skilful eyes and ears for local and regional nuance, and are both adept at capturing and evoking the multi-levelled narratives that can be read in and onto the city-, land- and waterscapes of New Orleans and its surrounds.

The two writers, on the face of things, surely have a great deal in common. Their lives and careers spanned the late nineteenth and early twentieth centuries, but their work usually concentrated on earlier periods in the city's history, particularly the decades following the Louisiana Purchase and the US Civil War (1861–65), while powerfully addressing their own times. They both enjoyed a degree of fame and success in the 1880s and 1890s, both locally and farther afield, before dropping from view somewhat as literary tastes and interests changed, eventually to be re-evaluated through more recent critical perspectives. Both wrote novels that often read as loosely linked sets of stories, and collections of short fiction that are somewhat novelistic in cumulative effect, as well as stylised, unashamedly partisan volumes on Louisiana history. And both were from Anglo-American backgrounds, but frequently took New Orleans' Creole community as their subject – and it is on this point that they most famously diverge. In our own time, this purported divide can look like something of a straw man given the far greater number of things that unite them as writers, but their respective positions regarding Creole conduct and culture had great resonance for them and their contemporary reception. Here, I will examine key gothic-infused elements of some of their most important work. I will not attempt to account for any of their texts in their entirety, but will rather consider how particular modes of description, interrogation and evocation play a crucial part in their respective engagements with the idiosyncrasies of the Crescent City.

Historical Narratives

The two authors' most celebrated respective works of history serve as a useful foundation. Both Cable's *The Creoles of Louisiana* (1884) and King's *New Orleans: The Place and the People* (1895) present sweeping narrative histories of the city and its people and surroundings that usefully mark both their authors' similarities and their differences as artists as well as thinkers on their place. Both are indebted to the pioneering research and writing of Charles Gayarré, the Creole historian whose massive *History of Louisiana*, published through the 1840s and 1850s, is a touchstone of romantic history of the region. Indeed, both these volumes by Cable and King, and indeed much of their work ostensibly in other disciplines, operate at meeting places of romanticism and social realism that are in part indicative of the time of their writing and its prevailing literary moods, and in part in keeping with the narrative traditions of New Orleans itself. While one might suggest that, free from the fiction writer's obligations towards plot and character, these books present their authors' most straightforward views on the city's history and culture, this would be to understate the importance of narrative construct in their versions of that history, as well as the degree to which much of each of their fiction is thinly disguised socio-political and socio-cultural comment riding on some sometimes creaky plot and character wagons. While presented, more or less, as factual accounts of the city from before its founding in 1718 to the writers' 1880s and 1890s present, neither Cable nor King really makes much attempt at pretending to be objective. There is inevitably a large amount of overlap in the material covered, and as such the differences and similarities in tone are fascinating.

Broadly speaking, while both offer enthusiastic although critical pro-US stances, King is far more complimentary towards the city's Creole history than Cable, and as such her book is somewhat more boosterish and positive in tone. Cable, indeed, is apt to make rather extreme generalisations about Creole indolence and ignorance, for instance, which had much to do with his effectively being drummed out of the city into New England exile soon after this book's publication. One might suggest, indeed, that their respective positions in this regard denote their differing positions on the slide rule between realism and romance that can also be discerned in their fiction: although the two manifest both, again broadly speaking King is more ready to embrace her romantic inclinations as a writer.

Both books, however, give accounts of the city and region's topography that are at once geographically accurate and romantically stylised, as well as troubling and disturbing. Cable's narratives of the eighteenth-century development of New Orleans are full of descriptions of a 'gloomy wilderness' (*Creoles* 14) filled with 'the rank growth of a wet semi-tropical land' (24), in which a 'disorderly and squalid' (23) city struggles to assert itself in the face of a constant threat of destruction from this inhospitable environment as well as neighbouring Native American nations and rival colonial powers. It is a city seemingly surrounded by death or the threat of death on all sides, and it is here in this fetid, diseased, isolated place, 'amid the willow-jungle of the Delta's wet forests, [that] the Louisiana Creole came into existence – valorous, unlettered, and unrestrained, as military outpost life in such a land might make them' (52). Figured like this, Cable has the Creoles effectively emerging from the deadly swamps, to be torn between often confused European loyalties and conditioning by the fearful particularities of their immediate environment. King, for her part, describes the journey of the Ursuline nuns from the mouth of the Mississippi at Belize up the river to New Orleans as infinitely harder than the horrors and difficulties of their transatlantic crossing (*New Orleans* 64–5). Given the importance with which King goes on to present the Ursulines as a force for good in the city, this really is a depiction of noble female missionaries struggling against all environmental and human odds to reach the thus far benighted inhabitants of a distant, isolated outpost.

King's and Cable's histories are full of ghosts, and again their presentation of this aspect marks similarities and differences. King, indeed, begins the first chapter of *New Orleans* with a statement on the inextricability of place and people through and across the city's history:

> In the continuity of a city which has a historical foundation and a historical past, there is much secular consolation for the transitoriness of human life. To the true city-born, city-bred heart, nothing less than the city itself is home, and nothing less than the city is family; and, more than in our hearts, do we look in the city for the memorials that keep our dead in vital reach of us .... Through these streets they were carried in their nurses' arms; through these streets they were carried in their coffins. These stars, passing over these heavens, passed so for them; and

these seasons, by local promises and disappointments so personally our own, sped by the same for them .... As we walk along the banquettes, our steps feel their footprints, and even the houses about us, new and fresh, and ignoble heirs as we hold them to be of respected ruins, with kindly loyalty to site, still throw down ancestral tokens to us .... [T]he youngest baby-hand of to-day can clasp its way back to its first city parent, to the city founder, Bienville himself. (1–2)

To walk these city streets, then, is to walk with the dead, at least if one is a true local, and this applies to both human and built components of New Orleans' history. King describes here something beyond a simple reflection that things have happened in the place we currently inhabit, to suggest effectively that those things, those lives and deaths, are *still* happening, in part through our active engagement with them. Indeed, while the ghosts of the past are present, the agency required to realise them is ours, as we map onto the streets and houses and even the stars the lives that have been lived and lost here before ours.

This principle is shared by Cable, whose work is suffused with stories perpetually being told and retold, lives perpetually being lived and lost and relived and lost again. Perhaps the most notable example of this in Cable comes in his rendition of the horrific events that took place in the house of Madame Lalaurie, whose murderous, sadistic treatment of her slaves was already the stuff of local legend by the time Cable recorded them in 'The Haunted House in Royal Street', in his history–folklore hybrid collection *Strange True Stories of Louisiana* (1888). Cable describes his own visit to the house's 'belvedere' and the extraordinary widescreen view over the city, old and new, that it affords. He provides a lengthy description of New Orleans' various sections from this vantage point in space and time, which effectively becomes a Bakhtinian chronotope of the Crescent City, its histories meeting here in the consciousness of our guide, whose experience now intersects with our own (197–9). The city being laid out before us spatially and temporally in this way, Cable then reads and writes the terrible story onto it, both establishing narrative history and anticipating his own narrative of the story to come. He points out the street down which the house's murderous mistress fled/will flee, as well as the courtyard where the young slave girl plunged/will plunge to her death. The story both has happened and is going to; these places will always be partly constituted of these told events, and will in turn always constitute them. Cable's own role as narrator and guide is crucial, as it renders the city as a work of art to be studied, a work whose own depicted characters relate to it in more immediate and fleeting but paradoxically just as conceptually influential ways.

Walter Benjamin tells us that 'a man who concentrates before a work of art is absorbed by it .... In contrast, the distracted mass absorbs the work of art' (241).[1] New Orleans' buildings and streets are here at once subject both to the 'concentrated' reception that Benjamin notes as essential to a work or a place's 'aura', in the attentive, 'absorbed' perception of our narrator, and to the narratively perpetual 'distracted' reception of the story's protagonists that destabilises that aura. If the narrator's absorption risks fixing the work's meanings, then the necessarily unfixed engagement of those who inhabit it continually opens up the meanings anew. Even as the account attempts to authenticate the city-work laid out before us, all that is authenticated is the movement, temporal and spatial, that absorbs it in turn; as such Cable, the reader, previous tellings of the story, and the unfortunate, distracted characters all contribute to the strange truth somewhere to be found in these inextricable dynamics.

The Narrative Voice

Although he is probably best known today for his first novel, *The Grandissimes* (1880), Cable is arguably at his best as a writer of short stories and sketches. In *Old Creole Days* (1879, 1881), the component pieces are frequently sharp, focused and often much more complex than they initially seem, their comparative brevity both heightening the dramatic (often melodramatic) action and boldly registering their political points. The opening passages of many of Cable's stories are microcosms of the tensions that will pervade the stories as a whole, the narrative voice often leading us through a section of the city towards the site of the tale's beginning, and effectively back through time to its setting. For instance, before we meet the protagonists of 'Madame Delphine' (originally published separately in 1880 but included in subsequent editions of *Old Creole Days*), we are taken from the noisy clamour of Canal Street 'into the quiet, narrow way which a lover of Creole antiquity, in fondness for a romantic past, is still prone to call the Rue Royale':

> You will pass a few restaurants, a few auction-rooms, a few furniture warehouses, and will hardly realize that you have left behind you the activity and clatter of a city of merchants before you find yourself in a region of architectural decrepitude, where an ancient and foreign-seeming domestic life, in second stories, overhangs the ruins of a former commercial prosperity, and upon everything has settled down a long sabbath of decay .... Many great doors are shut and clamped and grown gray with cobweb; many street windows are nailed up; half the balconies are begrimed and rust-eaten, and many of the humid arches and alleys which characterize the older Franco-Spanish piles of stuccoed brick betray a squalor almost oriental. (1–2)

This, of course, is what is now referred to as the French Quarter, the site of the original settlement. The sense of decay circa 1880 that Cable describes here has long since been commodified into tourist-trapping tours of a now somewhat gentrified although still vibrant area, but at the time of Cable's writing it was genuinely falling into something like ruin, as he describes here. There is an important movement of space and time in a passage like this, the cobwebs, rust and grime that barricade and rot these buildings both testifying to their obsolescence, since the Creole quarter has been overtaken by 'American' activity on and beyond Canal Street, and seemingly encasing the way of life and thinking that they once hosted as icons of a bygone age. They also continue to

accumulate and entrap the buildings and their occupants ever more wholly –
smothering them, really – unless and until effort is made to clear them away,
to move forward. That we move so starkly – and physically, within the narrative – from 'clatter' on Canal to 'a long sabbath of decay' on Royal is telling in
itself in suggesting that Creole life in the city is dying in the face of irresistible
Americanisation. Cable overtly orientalises the quarter, exoticising it as 'ancient
and foreign-seeming' to the American mainstream that has stolen its thunder.
That it was once mighty in itself is suggested alongside the extent of its fall,
and one might say that the manner in which it got from one state to the other
is essentially the central investigation, or agenda, of much of Cable's fiction.
The story itself quickly moves back 'sixty years ago and more' to the period just
after the city and its mostly reluctant population had been delivered into US
ownership, when this now decrepit section *was* the city, and when 'Americans'
were the 'foreign-seeming' element to be viewed with suspicion and fear. That
a point only 60-odd years ago is rendered 'ancient', alien and antiquated in
itself speaks volumes about the volatility of change in the Americas, a sense as
disorienting and disturbing as the decay that is being more overtly discussed.

   In her first novel, *Monsieur Motte*, Grace King's narrative voice evokes comparable relationships between past and present centred on the physical spaces
that present and contain them. The key difference, however, is that while
Cable's story takes place in the past although being told from the perspective
of a much-changed present, with this movement charted in the physical decay
of the buildings, King's for the most part remains in the post–Civil War era,
with the past forcing its way into the present through memory and the very
fabric of the built environment. In the section 'The Drama of an Evening',
the 'square of the city' is depicted as a 'once fashionable neighborhood, now a
quartier perdu given over to coffee-houses, oyster-stands, mattress-makers, and
chambres garnies suspects' (183). The evening concerned is focused upon an

> old gray stucco building, – a by no means insignificant theatre of social festivities
> in that celebrated time long past, to which even a reference now is monotonous.
> As night fell, the venerable mansion arose through the darkness, glittering with
> light, shedding a stately radiance over the humble roofs opposite, and shaming the
> social degradation of its whilom intimates and neighbors on each side. (183–4)

The state into which the *vieux carré* has fallen is emphasised more in moral(istic)
terms than Cable's physical ones, the quarter having succumbed to vice against
which the old mansion stands literally as a beacon of light. Yet while this may
seem a straightforwardly nostalgic image of a bastion of purportedly better
times holding firm against the depravities and deprivations of the present, the
portrait becomes rather more complex as it continues and heads indoors:

> The antique gilt chandeliers festooned with crystal drops lighted up the faded, as
> they had once lighted up the fresh, glories of the spacious rooms …. Old mag-
> nificences, luxuries, and extravagances hovered about the furniture, or seemed to

creep in, like the old slaves at the back gate, to lend themselves for the occasion; even in a dilapidated, enfranchised condition, good, if for nothing else, to propitiate present criticism with suggestive extenuations from the past. (196)

This is a space that has remained resolutely of its time, regardless of the changing world around it. Beginning with a fairly simple juxtaposition of contemporary shabbiness with the splendour of the same articles in times gone by, that purportedly glorious past is then figured as 'hovering' in the room as a rebuke to the present. Handsome and worn furniture coexist here, the contrasting states of the same items encompassing decades of social, political, economic, and cultural change. These ghosts, and the changing times and resistance to them, are given corporeal form as the ball proceeds: 'Out in the hall was the punch-bowl, and out in the hall were the fathers and uncles, and all the old, old gentlemen who are neither fathers nor uncles, but who come to balls simply because they cannot stay away' (207–8). Vainly attempting to relive their own former glory, these slightly comic, slightly sinister, seemingly immovable spectres 'were eager to fall in love again – with one another's grand-daughters', a comment both on their refusal or inability to move with the times or even to develop personally, and on the incestuous, inward-looking attitude of upper-class Creole society. Like the furniture with which they have grown old and intransigent through a lifetime of such parties, they are out of place and time, but they nonetheless suggest a history that is continually present, a society that is hidebound by its idealised past.

'The old slaves at the back gate' are also present at the ball, ready to serve in the past and mark in their 'dilapidated' freedom the disorder and asserted failings of the present. And just as the honoured ghosts are granted human form, so are these 'back-door guests':

> Like shadows they crept out on tiptoe from their hiding-places to hang over the banisters and look down on the exalted, God-favored world below, their eager eyes catching the light and shining strangely out of the darkness of their faces .... What did they not know of the world in which destiny had placed them in the best of all positions for observation? What had been too low, dim, or secret for them as slaves to crawl into? From their memory or experience, as they sat there, what private archives of their city might not have been gathered, – the snarls and tangles, the crossings and counter-crossings of intrigue, the romances dipped in guilt, the guilt gilded with romance, the tragedies from the aspiring passions of some, the degrading passions of others, and all the impurities from common self-indulgence, with indestructible consequences to stalk like ghosts through the pleasant present! (211–12)

King skilfully uses this anachronistic ball to give a detailed social portrait of both past and present and across the decades. These former slaves, or their forebears, have witnessed and even participated in the goings-on of the 'old, old gentlemen' in the past, and witness their consequences now that both youth and slavery are over. On the one hand, this can all seem like a fairly harmless exercise in going through the social motions one more time; on the other, and scarcely hidden beneath the surface, it is testament to the damage still being done by past activities and attitudes that are being maintained by the charade in play, 'stalk[ing] like ghosts through the pleasant present!' While the narrative tone remains mostly affectionate, the 'ghosts' are vibrant enough, their 'private archives' eloquent and voluminous enough, to disrupt the surface picture and the official narrative with unbidden but undeniable problematic voices, destabilising the comforting fiction that the hosts and guests are trying to maintain.

Journeys Towards Houses

Both writers also give compelling accounts of houses, or journeys towards houses, in the watery hinterland surrounding New Orleans. The physical treachery of the city's environs is richly evoked in what is otherwise a rather slight tale from King's *Balcony Stories* (1892), 'The Story of a Day'; indeed, the first-person narrator opens with the qualifier, 'It is really not much, the story; it is only the arrangement of it, as we would say of our dresses and our drawing-rooms' (69).[2] The narrator even seems self-conscious of her 'poor poetry' as she describes setting out in the early morning in a skiff, 'silvered with dew, waiting in the mist for us, as if it had floated down in a cloud from heaven to the bayou' (69); this mode is continued into the flowery description of a seeming paradise that she explicitly terms 'an Elysium' (72). Yet the tone changes as 'the rising sun made revelations' about the half-land, half-water world through which she is travelling, as grazing cattle find themselves 'bogged ... buried alive' (72). The previously charmed travellers watch in horror as several cows stray from the relatively solid ground into the treacherous, lily-hidden depths. Different modes of death are witnessed:

> And such a pretty red-and-white heifer, lying on her side, opening and shutting her eyes, breathing softly in resignation to her horrible calamity! And, again, another one was plunging and battling in the act of realizing her doom: a fierce, furious, red cow, glaring and bellowing at the soft, yielding inexorable abysm under her, the bustards settling afar off, and her own species browsing securely just out of reach. (73)

Some of the cows face their doom with fatal acceptance, others rage futilely against the inevitable while scavengers wait to reap unearned rewards – the parallels with the human inhabitants of this region and its city are hard to resist, at least in King's romantic mode, particularly as story ends with its absent male centre drowned without trace in the same bayou-swamp netherworld.

In describing another representative and heavily symbolic, but this time more rural house, a further Cable story, 'Jean-ah Poquelin', is more acerbic, even sarcastic in its opening evocation of the immediately post-Purchase situation 'in the first decade of the present century', in which the relation between the time of setting and the time of writing and contemporary reading is again foregrounded. We are told of Creole disgust at 'such vile innovations as the trial by jury, American dances, anti-smuggling laws, and the printing of the Governor's proclamation in English', and fear of 'the Anglo-American flood that was presently to burst in a crevasse of immigration upon the delta [which] had thus far been felt only as slippery seepage which made the Creole tremble for his footing' (*Old* 179). The United States clearly being posited as a crucial modernising force here, it then becomes clear that this opening set of jibes is effectively a reflection en route to 'an old plantation-house half in ruin', standing 'a short distance above what is now Canal Street'; that is, just outside the city limits at the time of the Purchase (179). The house itself is a classic Southern Gothic pile, as described, although it should be noted that it has only just become 'Southern' as such:

> It stood aloof from civilization, the tracts that had once been its indigo fields given over to their first noxious wildness, and grown up into one of the horridest marshes within a circuit of fifty miles.
>
> The house was of heavy cypress, lifted up on pillars, grim, solid, and spiritless, its massive build a strong reminder of days still earlier, when every man had been his own peace officer and the insurrection of the blacks a daily contingency .... Around it was a dense growth of low water willows, with half a hundred sorts of thorny or fetid bushes, savage strangers alike to the 'language of flowers' and to the botanist's Greek .... Two lone forest-trees, dead cypresses stood in the centre of the marsh, dotted with roosting vultures. The shallow strips of water were hid by myriads of aquatic plants, under whose coarse and spiritless flowers, could one have seen it, was a harbor of reptiles, great and small, to make one shudder to the end of his days.
>
> The house was on a slightly raised spot, the levee of a draining canal. The waters of this canal did not run; they crawled, and were full of big, ravening fish and alligators, that held it against all comers. (179–80)

Powerful enough as a description of the house and its situation in its own right, this also has striking parallels with many accounts of New Orleans and its environs overall, both in the settlement's earliest years and up to Cable's own time. A forbidding place on a slightly raised spot, surrounded by treacherous swamp teeming with dangerous beasts and dense, mysterious foliage too strange even for science, there is a strong sense here that those who do not belong will and must perish or be driven away. This works on an individual level, as the house's owner, Jean Poquelin, is doing everything in his diminishing power to resist American incursion onto his 'land' as the city seeks to expand, and more widely, given the city's fragile, unforgiving position between the Mississippi, Lake Pontchartrain, and the swamps and wetlands between and around them.

The story goes on to depict the once wealthy indigo planter and slave trader Poquelin living in apparently complete isolation, denying the right of the now American-owned city to his property before eventually being defeated by both the city's power and the Creole community's own wider feeling that his obstinacy is holding them back, and dying. At the funeral, there suddenly appears 'the living remains – all that was left – of little Jacques Poquelin, the long-hidden brother – a leper, as white as snow' and 'dumb with horror, the cringing crowd gazed upon the walking death' (209). The story ends with the half-dead Jacques and the brothers' 'African mute' slave disappearing into the swamp with the coffin, never to be seen again (209). The story works as a genuinely chilling tale, with a distinctly Poe-esque quality to its physical horror and deeply unsettling air of mystery and unknowability, but it also stands as a barbed rebuke to intransigence and cultural isolation, along with the implicit sense that the leprous brother has been damned for their engagement in the brutalities of the transatlantic slave trade. Cable's contemporary local readers, and others then and since with an understanding of New Orleans history and geography, will be keenly aware that Poquelin's plantation stood where the Faubourg Ste. Marie was soon to be built, the 'American' section across the purported dividing line of Canal Street from the original Creole city that was to become dominant as the nineteenth century progressed.

A Theatre of Death

Perhaps more than any other element, however, both Cable and King register New Orleans as a place of pervasive death, crucially sited in an inhospitable part of the transnational world of the American tropics, through its regular succumbing to the horrors of yellow fever. Other, more academic historical sources are more reliable in terms of the specifics and statistics of this disease that blighted the city through the long nineteenth century, but few register it in such chilling, impressionistic terms. Throughout the pre–Civil War years of comparative plenty, King tells us in *New Orleans*, 'there was at the rout and feast not any conventional, suggestive *memento mori*, there was Death itself, Death, as palpable, visible, audible, as a stolid official executioner; and not as a fleeting presence but functioning steadily, regularly for days, weeks, months, year after year' (280). She gives numerous stories of individual suffering, and ends up listing Death's exploits as a terrifying catalogue of horror:

> A hospital being found deserted, physicians, nurses, attendants all dead or run away, and the ward filled with corpses, – the mayor had the building and contents burned. Persons of fortune died unattended in their beds, and remained for days without burial. In every house there were sick, dying, and dead in the same room, often in the same bed …. Multitudes who began the day in perfect health were corpses before night; carpenters died on their benches; a man ordered a coffin for a friend and died before it was finished. A bride died the night of her marriage, and was buried in her veil and dress cast off a few hours earlier …. Corpses were found all along the streets, particularly in the early morning. (283–4)

Small wonder, then, that 'a thick, dark atmosphere hung over the city, neither sun, moon, nor stars being visible' (284). This is given tangible explanation through the barrels of tar being burned in the streets in futile, misguided attempts to smoke out the disease, but it further contributes to the sense of a city descending into absolute terror, deprived even of the stars that keep it connected in some way to other places and times. This is a powerful, unashamedly heartrending and frightening process of effect-by-accumulation, the bodies literally piling up in such numbers that the narrative cannot contain them. And these lives, these deaths, must also be figured among the ever-present ghosts with which King begins her history, discussed earlier.

In *The Creoles of Louisiana*, Cable gives us a similarly sickening account of the 'theatre of horrors' that New Orleans became in 1853, the year of the very worst of the city's epidemics (299). On top of the sheer scale of the death and suffering from yellow fever itself, the city descends into lawlessness, and the always dangerous weather compounds matters even further. 'Despair now seemed the only reasonable frame of mind,' we are told. 'In the sky above, every new day brought the same merciless conditions of atmosphere. The earth below bubbled with poisonous gases. Those who would still have fled the scene saw no escape' (301). Cable makes clear that, alongside the waterlogged noxiousness of the ground at the best of times, here it is made all the worse by being wholly overfull of poorly buried corpses. Death, again, seems almost absolute, and impossible to cheat.

Cable also gives a brief but powerful fictional treatment of the fever in his novel *Dr Sevier* (1882), in which the titular doctor accurately predicts, when the signs of an outbreak start appearing, that the city will immediately barricade itself behind a catastrophic screen of denial. The authorial voice allows himself an undisguised comment on the complicity with the disease for which the population must accept responsibility:

> We call the sea cruel, seeing its waters dimple and smile where yesterday they dashed in pieces the ship that was black with men, women, and children. But what shall we say of those billows of human life, of which we are ourselves a part, that surge over the graves of its own dead with dances and laughter and many a coquetry, with panting chase for gain and preference, and pious regrets and tender condolences for the thousands that died yesterday – and need not have died? (3316 of 5504)

In many ways, Cable's depiction of the disease is similar to King's, but it differs primarily through its *anger*. He likewise, in both these books, gives us a scene of utter horror, in which death is all-pervasive and chaos reigns, but he is much more willing than King to point a finger of blame at city authorities and private citizens for their own part in the extent of the devastation. He gives us a city seemingly suicidally driven towards its own destruction, a masque of the yellow death that gruesomely links it to the wider fever-ravaged Caribbean world around it while trying to close itself off behind a wall of hedonistic insularity.

New Orleans has expanded exponentially by the late nineteenth-century point at which Cable and King are writing, and its once outlying cemeteries have become 'enisled in the dwellings of the living' while suburbs grow around them (King, *New Orleans* 399). As King puts it in the closing pages of *New Orleans*, 'the festival of the dead might be called the festival of the history of the city' (399). If King is more prepared to indulge in the dark romanticism of this point than Cable, they both nevertheless provide, in the various ways I have discussed and in others, a strong sense of the isolation and treacherousness of the city's position, the related complexities of its codes of race, class and demography, and of the full horror that flows once the always latent threat is made manifest through such events as yellow fever epidemics. King and Cable were at odds with regard to the qualitative legacy of their city's history and culture, with Cable's reformist zeal, particularly concerning race, giving him a somewhat bleaker view, but in their work they often account for the city's gothic idiosyncrasies in some strikingly similar ways. Ultimately, as we are not reading them with contemporary responsibilities and allegiances to attend to or disregard, we need not feel too bound to fall on one side or the other of such debates, or to see this as the defining point of comparison between them. What they provide us with, both individually and in relation, are rich, detailed, multi-layered depictions of a deeply complex place, a city that seems to revel in its ongoing dance with death, and in the stories that keep being told about it.

NOTES

1. Mike Savage provides a valuable discussion of the paradoxes of Benjamin's theories of aura in relation to cities in 'Walter Benjamin's Urban Thought: A Critical Analysis', in Mike Crang and Nigel Thrift (eds.), *Thinking Space* (London and New York: Routledge, 2000), pp. 33–53.
2. Something similar might be said of most of the tales in the *Balcony Stories* collection, the stories of which are often so negligible as to render them merely sketches, such power as they have coming from the 'arrangement' of their elements.

Bibliography

Benjamin, W. (1970). *Illuminations: Essays and reflections* (Ed. Arendt, H., trans: Zohn, H. London: Jonathan Cape. Print.

Cable, G. W. (1897). *Dr Sevier* [1882]. New York: Charles Scribner's Sons. Kindle.

Cable, G. W. (1997). *Old Creole days* [1879, 1881]. Gretna: Pelican. Print.

Cable, G. W. (1999). *Strange true stories of Louisiana* [1888]. Gretna: Pelican, 1999. Print.

Cable, G. W. (2000). *The Creoles of Louisiana* [1884]. Gretna: Pelican. Print.

Cable, G. W. (2001). *The Grandissimes* [1880]. Gretna: Pelican. Print.

Crang, M., & Thrift, N. (Eds.). (2000). *Thinking space.* London: Routledge. Print.

King, G. (1888). *Monsieur Motte.* New York: A. C. Armstrong and Son. Print.

King, G. (1902). *New Orleans: The place and the people* [1895]. New York: Macmillan. Print.

King, G. (1968). *Balcony stories* [1892]. Ridgewood: Gregg Press. Print.

Robinson, O. (2016). "The head-quarters of death": Early nineteenth-century New Orleans as gothic nexus. In J. D. Edwards & S. G. T. Vasconcelos (Eds.), *Tropical gothic in literature and culture: The Americas.* New York: Routledge. Print.

Further Reading

Castillo, S. (2004). Violated boundaries: George Washington Cable's "Belles Demoiselles Plantation" and the Creole gothic. *Litteraria Pragensia, 14*(28), 50–56. Print. A superb reading of the Gothic in another story from Cable's *Old Creole Days*.

Kelman, A. (2006). *A river and its city: The nature of landscape in New Orleans.* Berkeley: University of California. Print. A geographical and historical study of the relationship between New Orleans and the Mississippi, including a valuable chapter on yellow fever.

Ladd, B. (1996). *Nationalism and the color line in George W. Cable, Mark Twain, and William Faulkner.* Baton Rouge: Louisiana State University Press. Print. A comparative study of the three authors, placing Cable in more exalted company than he often is, and particularly valuable for considering his work in transnational contexts.

Petry, A. H. (1988). *A genius in his way: The art of Cable's Old Creole days.* Cranbury: Associated University Press. Print. A close study of the component sections of *Old Creole Days*.

Simpson, C. M., Jr. (1974). Grace King: The historian as apologist, review of Robert Bush. *Southern Literary Journal, 6*(2), 130–133. Print. A useful brief summation of King's political and cultural positions as a historian.

Taylor, H. (1989). *Gender, race, and region in the writings of Grace King, Ruth McEnery Stuart, and Kate Chopin.* Baton Rouge: Louisiana State University Press. Print. A fine comparative study of these three writers.

Turner, A. (1956). *George W. Cable: A biography.* Durham: Duke University Press. Print. A dated but still valuable source of information regarding Cable and his contexts.

CHAPTER 17

Francophone Gothic Melodramas

Bill Marshall

If, in Teresa Goddu's description, the American South is 'the nation's "other",
becoming the repository for everything from which the nation wants to disassociate itself' (Goddu 1997: 3), then the nineteenth-century francophone culture
of Louisiana, centred on New Orleans, has suffered a double marginalisation.
A very under-researched (outside Louisiana) but rich literary corpus extends
from 1779 to 1918; that is, from the period of Spanish rule to the eve of ban-
ning the speaking of French in state schools. Despite the influx of anglophone
Protestant Americans from the time of the Purchase in 1803, New Orleans
remained a majority Francophone city into the 1830s and 1840s. In addition
to the Creoles, descendants of settlers from the periods of French and Spanish
rule, there were the 'foreign French', migrants from metropolitan France, particularly the south and west, among their ranks a large number of political exiles
fleeing regime changes there. To these are to be added the large influx from
Saint-Domingue that began in the 1790s. This culminated in 1809–10, when
Joseph Bonaparte's usurping of the throne of Spain led to war and the expulsion of exiles from Cuba, which doubled the French-speaking population of the
city. These arrivals swelled the ranks of the francophone merchant and professional classes, and contributed much to the cultural dynamism of the following
decades, educational attainment and even literacy among the white Creoles
being initially low, despite the *ancien régime* pretentions of the upper-classes.
There was thus an established readership for literary production in the French
language, which reached its peak in the city between 1840 and 1850.

Thus, in addition to the '(dark) othering' of the anglophone South by
Enlightenment-based narratives of US identity, a terrain of struggle has for long
extended into popular and scholarly historiography. This poses the question of

B. Marshall (✉)
University of Stirling, Stirling, UK
Institute of Modern Languages Research, University of London, London, UK

© The Editor(s) (if applicable) and The Author(s) 2016   215
S.C. Street, C.L. Crow (eds.), *The Palgrave Handbook of the Southern Gothic*,
DOI 10.1057/978-1-137-47774-3_17

how to place – how to assimilate – Louisiana and especially New Orleans into that master national American narrative, and tends to respond with a (thus double) peripheralisation and exoticisation outside the New England mainspring of 1776 and the manifest destiny of westward expansion. Examples abound of the latter (the northern gaze on Congo Square, voodoo, the quadroon balls, as we shall see) and of the former, where we can here single out the complete absence of translations into English that are contemporary to this nineteenth-century literary output, and its extremely limited nature thereafter. Before the late 1970s, the sole examples of English translations of French Creole work were those by the African American poet Langston Hughes. In 1958, he included in his *Langston Hughes Reader* two poems from the 1845 anthology *Les Cenelles: Choix de poésies indigènes*, which is the first such work written by Americans of African descent. A bilingual English–French version was produced in the 1970s (Latortue and Adams 1979) and a wider collection of poetry from the whole nineteenth-century corpus published in 2004 (Shapiro 2004). Yet apart from translations of Victor Séjour's *Le Mulâtre/The Mulatto*, which we shall discuss, and of two of his Parisian plays (Séjour 2002, 2006), that is it. The diligent and indeed remarkable work since 2003 of the Editions Tintamarre (based at Centenary College in Shreveport) in re-publishing texts from the period (often re-assembled from serialised newspaper forms) has not yet been accompanied by translation projects. The winds of change blowing from paradigmatic shifts such as the re-centering of New Orleans and Louisiana through the lens of Atlantic Studies and the 'Atlanticisation' of American history (Bailyn 1988, 2005; Bond 2005; Hall 1992), or the renewed focus on the multi-lingual realities of US literary culture (Lauret 2014; Rosenwald 2008), may yet impel new attention and dynamics here.

Questions thus arise not only as to what manifestations of the Gothic – what hauntings, monstrosities, irrationalisms and bloody excesses – can be found in this large and varied corpus, but what specific francophone influences and migrations contribute to this circulation of gothic motifs and, moreover, in what ways these motifs articulate meanings in relation to politics, to the profound class and racial divisions of the period. A preliminary point to be made is that the presence of the Gothic is part of a wide circulation of literary tendencies and fashions that is mediated at several degrees. The well-known narrative of English gothic novels spreading their influence through continental Europe is here complicated by the fact that Louisiana literature partakes of a transatlantic, indeed French Atlantic, movement of influences that is interdependent and multi-directional, indebted to metropolitan French forms but not determined by them. Indeed, much Louisiana writing was inspired by Parisian developments, such as takes on Eugène Sue's *Les Mystères de Paris* (1842–43): *Les Mystères des bords du Mississippi* (1843–44) by Charles de la Gracerie and *Or et fange ou les mystères de la Nouvelle-Orléans* (1852–53) by the French émigré Charles Testut (1818–92). However, the main influences were Romanticism and melodrama, audiences flocking to the two francophone theatres in the city, especially in this period the Théâtre d'Orléans, and tropes from both these genres played a major role in prose fiction in general, and its gothic elements in particular. What is termed in France *romantisme noir* is associated with a current in French Romanticism that not only distances itself from the Enlightenment and *lumières* through sensibility, emotion and subjectivity, but cultivates an aesthetic of the strange, mysterious, pre-modern, horrific and fantastic. This current may be said to include the Marquis de Sade and elements in Victor Hugo, the work of Charles Nodier (who among other outputs adopted Polidori's story *The Vampire* for the stage in France in 1820), right through to the stirrings of a more modernist sensibility with the poet Charles Baudelaire. In addition, the massive popularity of a writer such as Alexandre Dumas (himself a mixed-race Creole, his grandparents being a white French nobleman and an African slave on Saint-Domingue) wrote some heavily gothicised novels that contributed to these circulations (*Pauline* 1838; *Le Château d'Eppstein* 1843).

The full florescence of melodrama on the Parisian stage in the early nineteenth century, in parallel with the Romantic theatre's demolishing of classical rules, is also relevant here. For, as Peter Brooks has argued, melodrama and the Gothic may be seen as adjacent, since they both represent responses to 'desacralisation': 'melodrama starts from and expresses the anxiety brought about by a frightening new world in which the traditional patterns of moral order no longer provide the necessary social glue', in which sacralisation can now be conceived only in personal terms, with new symbolic potency bestowed on the family, and the family house. As with the gothic novel, Brooks continues, melodrama 'is equally preoccupied with nightmare states, with claustration and thwarted escape, with innocence buried alive and unable to voice its claim to recognition. Particularly, it shares the preoccupation with evil as a real, irreducible force in the world, constantly menacing outburst' (1976: 20).

There is no slavish following of Parisian fashion. Rather, Louisiana literature in its diversity can be read as a tension between forces – of mimicry and 'authenticity', and of the transatlantic and the local – negotiating through Romanticism and melodrama particular articulations of the personal and collective via, for example, tropes of emotional loss that spoke to the historical itinerary of the Creole people. Occupying overall a position that plays on the cultural capital represented by the centripetal pull of Paris – to which they also rushed, in spirit or for their offspring's education, as they sought both to catch up with and distinguish themselves from the American newcomers – the Creoles sought a balance between an identitarianism associated with the French language and even (elements of) the French Revolution and republicanism, but also, as Clint Bruce puts it, an adherence to 'Jacksonian democracy' that ultimately implied and impelled support for the confederacy (Bruce 2012). The Civil War, Reconstruction and the period after 1877 meant that most saw no choice but a necessary 'rush to whiteness' and absorption into the violent polarisations of American racial politics.

In what ways do forms of the Gothic articulate these issues and contradictions in the Louisiana literary corpus? While there are examples of what has been called 'frontier gothic' ('best defined by its cultivation of often-unstable border zones, of hazy demarcations between self-reliance and self-delusion, between the humane and the monstrous'; Wynn Sivils 2014: 93), as in Jacques de Roquigny's 1849 short story 'Le Soulier rouge' (*Contes et récits* 2008) set during French colonial rule, we shall concentrate here on three of the most prominent writers in the corpus and on the four most salient motifs: the house; skin; the wandering Jew/capitalism; and blood.

THE HOUSE

We have already noted the importance of the family, indeed of the family house and all that it implies in terms of secrets and patriarchal right, in both the Gothic and in melodrama. A notable instance of the encounter between this motif and a free writer of colour who unambiguously invokes the memory of both the French and Haitian Revolutions to argue a passionately abolition-ist position is Victor Séjour (1817–74) and his short story *Le Mulâtre/The Mulatto*, published in 1837 in the anti-slavery Parisian journal *Revue des colonies*. Séjour was born in New Orleans. His father was a shopkeeper born in Saint-Marc, Saint-Domingue, in 1787 to a white man and a free woman of colour, and his mother was a local free woman of colour: Victor's baptismal record is as 'free quadroon'. *Le Mulâtre/The Mulatto* is set in his father's home town in pre-revolutionary Saint-Domingue, 'now known as Haiti/aujourd'hui la république d'Haïti', the text reminds us (Séjour 1995/1837); it is unclear whether the scene of narration by the 'vieux nègre/old negro' is before or after 1804. It recounts the revenge of mixed-race slave Georges, whose wife Zélie refuses the advances of Alfred the slave master, accidentally striking him and thus condemning herself to death according to article 33 of the *Code noir*. The master refuses to spare her, despite the fact that Georges had previously saved his life from bandits and been wounded in the process, and he and his own wife are killed by Georges, just as the latter learns that Alfred is in fact his biological father. *Le Mulâtre/The Mulatto* is an outstanding example of the way in which European cultural forms, in this case domestic melodrama, are adapted and transformed – *détournés* indeed – in the transatlantic crossing to slave-owning societies. Dramas of patriarchal right, and hyperbolic investments in moral polarities of good and evil, virtue and villainy, are about investing the family with new symbolic potency; that is, as the site and origin of all symbolic order or instability. In the context of Saint-Domingue and Louisiana, and in *Le Mulâtre*, the symbolic crisis of the Law of the Father and of social legitimacy is lived literally and viscerally. The colonial family romance here really means killing the father, as the conflict between slave and slave master is, so often, a family drama too. As Anna Brickhouse puts it: 'In the father's name, the story suggests, lies the security of representation as manifested both in the ostensible racial purity of the biological bloodline and in the ostensibly unshakeable polit-ical predominance of the *patrie* or paternal colonial power itself' (Brickhouse 2004: 12). Georges begs Alfred for the word that will spare Zélie, but it does not come; the password is 'Afrique et liberté'. After Georges waits in a *marron* camp, outside the law/Law, for Alfred to marry and produce a cherished (legitimate) son, the last word of the father, 'pè...re', is fractured as his severed head rolls on the ground.

Le Mulâtre/The Mulatto is thus full of reversals. The potentially threatening forest just beyond the plantation – 'ces forêts épaisses, qui semblent étreindre le nouveau-monde/those thick forests that seem to hold the new world in their arms' (although *étreindre* can also imply a close embrace in a struggle) – also contains the *light* represented by the maroon camp: 'cette espèce de joie qui brille dans ses yeux/the joy that shone in his eyes'. While Alfred is tormented by 'des songes affreux et terribles/hideous, frightful dreams' that the night and darkness bring, Georges's promised final, vengeful actions in the house's bedchambers are recounted in violent detail:

'I poisoned her ....'
   'Oh!'
   'Do you hear those cries ... they're hers.'
   'The Devil ....'
   'Do you hear those screams ... they're hers.'
   'A curse ....'
   ...
   'Alfred ... help ... water ... I'm suffocating,' shouted a woman, as she threw herself into the middle of the room. She was pale and disheveled, her eyes were starting out of her head, her hair was in wild disarray.
   'Alfred, Alfred ... for heaven's sake, help me ... some water ... I need water ... my blood is boiling ... my heart is twitching ... oh! water, water ...'

Moreover, Georges understands his actions in terms of a Faustian pact: 'j'aurais vendu mon âme à Satan, s'il m'avait promis cet instant/I would have sold my soul to the Devil, had he promised me this moment', as this time the master is held in an iron grip: 'Georges le retenait de son poignet de fer, et ricanant comme un damné/Georges held him fast with an iron hand. Laughing like one of the damned.' Uniquely then, Séjour's gothic plantation house melodrama envisages collective, political negations – guiltless and even diabolical – as a consequence of the exploration of ethical choices in what is an ambiguously domestic space, but in fact much more. The final, literal beheading of the father/master/patriarch/'king' re-enacts a melodramatic mode set in motion by the French Revolution. This is indeed 'a world where the traditional imperatives of truth and ethics have been violently thrown into question, yet where the promulgation of truth and ethics, their instauration of a way of life, is of immediate, daily, political concern'. Thus the Revolution's manichean narrative of virtue or terror argues a 'logic of the excluded middle', and images 'a situation ... where the word is called upon to make present and impose a new society, to legislate the regime of virtue' (Brooks 1976: 15).

Skin

Another famous Louisiana literary plantation house almost bookends this period of literary history. *L'Habitation Saint-Ybars* (1881) is a family saga bestriding the Civil War period that musters French republicanism and science, along with commemoration of Francophone Creole culture, in what amounts to a valediction to that culture marked by death, ruins, and a line of flight out towards Europe. Its author was Alfred Mercier (1816–94), a white Creole who had trained as a doctor in Paris, and indeed practised medicine there during the Civil War. In 1876 he founded the *Athénée louisianais*, which with its regular *Comptes-rendus* attempted in by that time rearguard fashion to promote francophone literary activity. Other works by Mercier are more explicitly gothic in their approach.

A short story by Mercier, '1878', published in 1883 in the *Comptes-rendus de l'Athénée louisianais*, is set during the yellow fever outbreak of that year (in which 13,000–20,000 people died in the Lower Mississippi valley). It begins by conveying the city's preoccupation with death – frantic funeral activity, morbid children's games with dolls or playing the sick: 'un silence de nécropole/ the silence of a necropolis' (my translation, and following) invades a whole district. With the coming of a rainstorm – the low, threatening clouds are said to weigh on the city like 'une voûte de marbre noir/a vault of black marble' (*Contes et récits* 2006: 120) – an unnamed *passant*/passerby shelters under the portico of the Opera and is allowed into the theatre. Sitting in his habitual seat there, he daydreams of past spectacles, audiences and beautiful women, all in an ambiance of light and dark created by the lightning. Falling asleep after a few minutes, he seems to hear a strange clicking noise that turns out to be 'le grincement d'os arides frottant les uns contre les autres/the grinding of dry bones rubbing against one another'. Still referred to as 'the sleeping man', he sees skeletons coming into the auditorium, with wigs and teeth. The first is a person beside whom he used to sit, a Don Juan figure, Lovelace, who asks him when he died and how. The sleeping man denies that he is dead, but Lovelace replies in return:

> Bah! … You are too modest, because the worms have not yet removed your flesh. Rest assured, it won't be long: when they have cleaned you well and good and you are shining like ivory, you will be among the most beautiful of us all. (121)

A dialogue between the two ensues, in which Lovelace explains the subtle passage from sleep to death, and presents a parade of personages from the sleeper's past life, including a former lover who died young with her illusions intact; the disfigured realities behind the appearances kept up when people were alive. The central event is a *danse macabre*, a performance by the skeletal troupe of the famous balletic section of the third act of Giacomo Meyerbeer's 1831 opera *Robert le diable*. Here Gothic and melodrama meet once more, in a medieval setting where nuns who have broken vows, in a cloister filled with tombstones, rise from their graves in an attempt to seduce the eponymous hero. Lovelace, mirroring in more benign fashion the machinations of Bertram (the devil, Robert's father) in the opera, continues to attempt to persuade the sleeper that he is fact dead from yellow fever, analogous for him with Helena, the principal diabolical seductress (and former Abbess) in the scene: 'Elle [la mort] s'est prise de belle passion pour votre métropole, cet été. Elle a revêtu un costume jaune qui lui sied à ravir/She [death] has taken a great fancy to your city this summer. She has put on a yellow suit which suits her beautifully.' For someone to be hers, 'il suffit qu'elle passe près de lui et le frôle du bout de sa robe/it's enough for her to brush past with the edge of her dress' (131), as had occurred to the sleeper a few days previously.

It has been argued in connection with the anglophone Southern Gothic that yellow fever and other critical disease outbreaks are 'figuratively linked' to social and political issues in a context of US nation-building (Gessner 2013: 220). Thus the 1793 Philadelphia outbreak, the subject of Charles Brockden Brown's *Arthur Mervyn* (1799), has been linked to questions of contagion, of radical political ideas from the terroristic phase of the French Revolution, or of imported slaves and corruption. Race is never far away here, with anxieties surrounding black people's supposed immunity to the disease, and the breakdown of racial hierarchies risked when whole cities are emptied or turned upside down by the epidemic. What is happening in Mercier's '1878' is subtly different. Certainly, a fantasmagoria of colour and race is present. The dramatic, contrasting blacks and whites of the lightning effects not only remind us of the way in which such gothic codings inescapably point to race, Mercier as a doctor[1] would have been well aware of the black bile that is a symptom of the disease's closing stages (hence the Spanish name for it, *vómito negro*).

However, we have also seen that the whitest element in the story is associated with death; namely, the 'shining ivory' of the human skeletons. How revealing, then, are two of the last exchanges. Lovelace's final gambit is to tell the sleeper to look in the mirror, 'vous verrez que le citron le plus fraîchement importé de Sicile n'est pas d'un plus beau jaune que vous/you'll see that the most freshly imported lemon from Sicily is not of a more beautiful yellow than you' (*Contes et récits* 2006: 131). Yet, having awoken from his slumber and on his way out of the theatre, he is reassured by his friend who let him enter that he does not have yellow fever, describing the indigenous New Orleans Creole, 'un Créole pur sang tanné au soleil de la ville, où tu as toujours vécu/a pure-blooded Creole tanned by the sun of the city, where you have always lived.'[2] The text is therefore polyvalent, and mixes French *romantisme noir* (meaning and beauty in death and dying), musings on appearances and the fleetingness of life, scientific fascination, and moreover a reflection on the destiny of the Creole people of Louisiana, drawn to every coding of colour and visibility but black, and unsatisfactorily at that. Whiteness (to which, as we have seen, the Creoles have rushed) equals death, anything less (yellow, light brown – really because of the sun rather than *métissage*?) is fraught with anxiety and ambiguity, like the still mysterious 'resolution' of the story itself. Like *L'Habitation*

Saint-Ybars, Mercier's entertainment is both lucid about the changes under-gone, and melancholic about the movement of travel.

THE WANDERING JEW

Hénoch Jédésias (1892), sometimes subtitled *Les Mystères de New York*, is Mercier's final novel, and the most gothic. It is set an imprecise number of decades in the past. The first-person narrator, Benjamin Patrick, is employed by the eponymous Jewish usurer to find out where his amassed fortune is gradu-ally disappearing every night, from a heavily fortified vault beneath his home: 'Et comme ils sont sûrs de leurs coups, ils l'emportent peu à peu, comme des vampires qui vous sucent le sang à petites gorgées/And since they are sure of what they are doing, they remove it gradually, like vampires sipping at your blood' (Mercier 2009: 23; my translation, and following). Patrick discovers that Jédésias, inhabited by the 'demon' of avarice (169), likened several times to a ghost and spectre (34), is sleepwalking and removing barrels of gold and other treasures from the vault to a mortuary chamber beneath the tomb of a Spanish nobleman buried there in the eighteenth century, and over which the New York house was built. Jédésias's other nighttime activity there is to write his memoirs, and not without placing two human skulls on the desk. Patrick promises to reveal the truth to Jédésias on condition that he bequeaths his fortune to him. He reads Jédésias back the usurer's memoirs, a narrative of his past life in Europe that takes up nearly half the novel and recounts his adop-tion of and then marriage to a young girl, Noémi, and his jealous poisoning of her and her lover Randal. Jédésias's vengeance is complete when he reveals his presence and holds a mirror up to the lovers' faces as they die from a poison 'qui rend hideux/which makes its victims appear hideous': 'voyez ce que j'ai fait de vous/see what I've done to you' (133). Two years later, Jédésias (named Eliphaz in the flashback) is approached by the coffin-maker friend of his dead father with a proposition to exhume the deceased parents in order to obtain the gold secreted in the coffin. This leads to the novel's other pit, a depot where the coffins can be dismantled. Accompanied by thunder and lightning outside, the father's semi-mummified body

> seemed to be taking part in the activity; the flickering light of the lantern played on the desiccated features and made them appear alive. The skin pulled back from the mouth revealed long white teeth, simulating a silent anger. The gusts rushing into the hearth made the corpse swing back and forth. (152)

And indeed, the body is blown on to the perpetrators, and its 'phalanges sèches et crochues/dry and hooked fingers', 153) get caught in their hair. Jédésias/Eliphaz dispatches his accomplice with a mallet and hurls him into the pit, grabs the gold, and dumps his parents' bones in Lake Geneva. He dumps his second wife financially and heads for New York with his new name. In the present, Jédésias learns of his sleepwalking and makes attempts to rectify it, but his home is invaded by an Irish criminal gang who torture him to reveal the whereabouts of his riches and open it. Jédésias dies under a pile of gold and the gang eventually meet a sorry end.

Chains, creaking doors, pits, vaults, crypts, opened graves, coffins, horrible deaths, a spatial and metaphorical mapping of the conscious and unconscious mind ('vous vivez d'une vie contraire à celle du jour/you live an opposite life from that of the day', admonishes Patrick, 163): all these elements conspire in the gothic flavour of the tale(s), not least in that the real denouement – Jédésias's realisation that he is his own tormentor – fits Eve Sedgwick's description of the real horror in the Gothic lying in release or unblocking (Sedgwick 1986: 22). The influence of Poe is palpable; Billy's speech to Jédésias as the gang threaten to bury him alive in the subterranean space (Mercier 2009: 207) is straight out of *The Pit and the Pendulum*, and it is known that Mercier had in his library a copy of Baudelaire's translation of the *Extraordinary Tales*. Barbey d'Aurevilly's short story collection *Les Diaboliques* (1874) is no doubt also an important intertext.

Strikingly, *Hénoch Jédésias* also fulfils a key gothic approach to time, as Anna Powell puts it 'a loop or a series of interlinked planes rather than a linear progression', marked by 'overlay, the over-riding of present time with the past' (Powell 2009: 91). Even before the discovery of the loop that he is in, Jédésias is described at the outset as living a 'uniform' time, flat and unpunctuated (Mercier 2009: 9), lacking progression. Even Patrick, preoccupied by the brevity of life and the necessity to live it well, is thus haunted by the arithmetic that brings the past so much closer (63). The palimpsest, the equal presence in the text of a very contemporary New York of finance and immigration and of a very Old World, *ancien régime* Europe (the Paris sequence is explicitly set in the Bourbon Restoration period 1814–30), contributes to an enmeshing of past and present from which the whole text, and not just Jédésias, attempts to break.

To what use is the Gothic being put here? The central Jewish character might at first be seen to prolong the familiar gothic trope of the Wandering Jew that emerged out of Matthew Lewis and then took several avatars (Tichelaar 2012), including the benign guardian angel(s) of Eugène Sue's novel of 1844–45, *Le Juif errant*, the antagonists of which are the Jesuits. The monstrousness of Jédésias's crimes, the all too familiar archetype of the grotesque Jewish usurer and the lurid workings of his unconscious mind would seem, however, to point to the dominance in the text of an alarming ethnic caricature. Nevertheless, this reading is obviated not only by the fact that (Irish) Catholics emerge badly as well (Mercier's anticlericalism was deep rooted), but by the relations that the novel is clearly exploring between nation (it opens as Patrick traverses New York during the 4 July celebrations), finance and capitalism. After all, the widowed Jédésias's ethnicity and religion prove no obstacle to his eligibility for the unmarried women of early nineteenth-century Geneva (Mercier 2009: 156). For Jédésias's avarice echoes the accumulative Protestant ethos but decisively stops short of capitalism, which of course through credit conjures something out of nothing, capital begetting capital and remorselessly, often monstrously, transforming the world as it does so, as well as incurring bankruptcies and ruin. Jédésias's concern is that nothing is being conjured out of something, in other words his disappearing treasure. An early exchange between himself and Patrick makes clear that he likens this mysterious disappearance to the ruinous workings of the credit market, governed by a 'puissance mystérieuse/mysterious power' and 'principe occulte/secret principle' (22). Patrick in fact finds him later in the novel sleepwalking through the city and even rowing out into the East River to dump his own treasure overboard, believing that he has robbed bank vaults and is getting rid of the banks' money. So his sleepwalking is not just about personal guilt, it is about an imaginary relation to a changed economic, financial, social and indeed cultural epoch.

The narrator is, perhaps, some kind of centred voice of reason in the novel, asserting that he sees money as a means to an end (travel, culture), rather than an end in itself (31). He also promotes the idea of philanthropy in the context of a *society* in which the idea of charity diminishes the greater the wealth possessed: society is like a high mountain range, 'la chaleur est en bas, la glace au sommet/warmth is down below, ice at the summit' (69). There is a revealing diatribe from Patrick as he addresses Jédésias about the latter's activities and their impoverishment of his poor debtors:

> So, secure in this house, *like a baron in his feudal castle of old*, you hold the people to ransom with impunity …. Through the power of money, you have achieved a form of slavery worse than that endured by the negro; the law protects, *up to a certain point*, the negro against the master's malice; but for you the law is your friend, your accomplice, and even your agent of persecution. (162; my emphases)

Jédésias allows Patrick the chance to face and oppose a territorialised capitalism, with the New York house a contemporary version of a feudal castle. However, this is itself a contradiction in terms, for all the philanthropy in the world would not correct the inequalities engendered by a law that, he makes clear later in his speech, renders property sacrosanct (including, at the time the novel is set, the ownership of other human beings). We may see the forces of tension in the narrator's discourse regarding money and capitalism as part of a whole structure within the novel, where scientific discourses (for example on somnambulism, 37) coexist with lurid appeals to affect and horror. For Mercier, a rationalist, a progressive Romantic but pro-Confederacy, valedictory in later life to the fast disappearing if not lost Creole francophone world, the profoundly deterritorialising effects of post-bellum capitalism – and immigration – on that world are themselves able here to generate incoherence about the Law and, from the perspective of 1892, at the very least a complex ambivalence about the Creole cultural and political heritage. The Gothic is here as much a repository of those contradictions as it is of those of Jédésias.

BLOOD

Mercier turned to blood rather than skin in another very gothicised short story, 'L'Anémique', published in 1871, in which a young anaemia patient falls victim to a charlatan who persuades him that the cure lies in drinking the blood of a captured child. However, we shall concentrate here on the chronologically final works in our corpus selection, by the most important woman writer of the period, Sidonie de La Houssaye (1820–94). Les *Quarteronnes de la Nouvelle-Orléans* is a serial novel in four parts, *Octavia, Violetta, Gina* and *Dahlia*, published in 1892–94. It looks back on the period after the Purchase when laws prohibiting marriage between the races produced the phenomenon of *plaçage*, in which young women of colour were kept as mistresses in a contractual arrangement with white, often married, men, liaisons launched at the 'quadroon balls' that were such a source of fascination for outsiders such as de Tocqueville (1957: 192).

For example, Octavia's story is one of revenge. She is the mistress of a lawyer, Alfred D., but he rejects her when, having been made a judge, he decides to lead a respectable life and marry his cousin, the appropriately named Angèle, who bears him first a son, Léonce, and then a daughter, Mary. Octavia, apparently pregnant (she had in fact bribed neighbours to collude with the deception), kidnaps Mary and leaves New Orleans for Havana, bringing the girl up as her own. Returning to New Orleans 16 years later, Octavia arranges for Léonce to fall passionately in love with Mary. Octavia reveals her plot to Alfred, and that she has made Mary 'la courtisane la plus vile qui puisse se rencontrer dans la fange/the most vile courtesan to be found in the mire' of New Orleans (de La Houssaye 2006: 136; my translation, and following). Alfred surprises the siblings having sex and shoots himself and Mary; the revelation drives Léonce insane.

While on one level the text condemns the moral failings of the quadroons, in familiar terms from Christian (*diablesse*, serpent), pagan (*démon*) and classical myth and history (Circe, Medea, the sirens, Messalina), it nonetheless seduces in the same way as its subjects, portraying its beautiful, charismatic and diabolical protagonists as generating important power reversals (in this example, it is the white girl Mary who is 'sold') and invariably casting and describing them in terms of light and brilliance (jewellery, white skin). It is clear, however, that for all the bling of seduction and the chameleon-like duplicity, the women's strategy unfolds on a battleground of profound and even violent racial and gender inequality. The rules of the appearance game, which the women master, are in fact controlled by white men, because its artifices count as nothing in relation to what *does not appear*; namely, the invisible portion of 'black blood' that is decisive in American racial codifications. These works, then, play on, and disturb, questions of visibility.

Gina has at its centre the wealthy, virtuous household of Léontine Percy Castel and her family's complex relations with her former *soeurs de lait*, now freed quadroons: the fundamentally saintly Gothe/Althéa and the diabolical Jeannette/Adoréah. The latter is the mistress of a wealthy doctor, but wreaks havoc with her debauchery and extravagance, typically, in a novel that emphasizes performance, disguising herself as Léontine's aristocratic (and rather gothically ugly) British relative in order to frame someone else for a jewellery theft, and on one occasion beating a slave to death. The visibility of blood is here a constant threat, as the Percy family are congenitally affected by tuberculosis: the 18-year-old Alice dies with an 'écume sanguinolente/bloody foam' covering her lips (de La Houssaye 2009: 57), as does the younger Percy (492). Adoréah, suffering a delirium after the failure of her machinations, utters in her death agony cries that 'glaçaient d'effroi/made the blood run cold' (459) of those around her as she expires from a haemorrhage: 'Et jetant un second cri, un cri qui retentit dans toute la maison, Adoréah la quarteronne tomba de tout son long sur le tapis de son studio, rendant par la bouche un torrent de *sang noir*/And with a second scream that echoed throughout the house, Adoréah the quadroon collapsed on the rug of her studio, a torrent of *black blood* pouring out of her mouth' (454, my emphasis). While de La Houssaye is employing a metaphor of the blackness of blood that has its origin in classical vocabulary, we have seen that, in the context of the Southern Gothic, questions of colour, and of light and dark, have no innocence.

NOTES

1. In fact he wrote a scientific booklet about yellow fever, *La Fièvre jaune, sa manière d'être à l'égard des étrangers à La Nouvelle-Orléans et dans les campagnes, quelques mots sur son passé et son avenir en Europe*, published in 1860.
2. It should be noted that *tanner/tanné* in standard French does not principally mean to be sunburned, but can indicate a 'tan' colour, or even convey the idea of tanning leather, so that a face becomes 'leathery' with the sun.

BIBLIOGRAPHY

Bailyn, B. (1988). *Voyagers to the West: A passage in the peopling of America on the eve of the revolution*. New York: Random House.

Bailyn, B. (2005). *Atlantic history: Concept and contours*. Cambridge, MA: Harvard University Press.

Brickhouse, A. (2004). *Transamerican literary relations and the nineteenth-century public sphere*. Cambridge: Cambridge University Press.

Brooks, P. (1976). *The melodramatic imagination: Balzac, Henry James, Melodrama and the mode of excess*. New Haven: Yale University Press.

Bruce, C. (2012). Caught between continents: The local and the transatlantic in French-language serial fiction of New Orleans' *Le Courrier de la Louisiane*, 1843–1845. In P. Okker (Ed.), *Transnationalism and American serial fiction* (pp. 12–35). New York: Routledge.

Bond, Bradley G. (ed). 2005: *French Colonial Louisiana and the Atlantic World*. Baton Rouge: Louisiana State University Press.

De La Houssaye, Sidonie. 2006: *Les Quarteronnes de la Nouvelle-Orléans, I: Octavia et Violetta*. Shreveport, LA: Editions Tintamarre.

De La Houssaye, Sidonie. 2009: *Les Quarteronnes de la Nouvelle-Orléans, II: Gina.* Shreveport, LA: Editions Tintamarre.

de Tocqueville, A. (1957). *Voyage en Sicile et aux Etats-Unis, t.5.* Paris: Gallimard.

Gessner, I. (2013). Contagion, crisis and control: Tracing yellow fever in nineteenth-century American literature and culture. In C. Birkle & J. Heil (Eds.), *Communicating disease: Cultural representations of American medicine* (pp. 219–242). Heidelberg: Universitätverlag Winter.

Goddu, T. A. (1997). *Gothic America: Narrative, history and nation.* New York: Columbia University Press.

Hall, G. M. (1992). *Africans in colonial Louisiana: The development of Afro-Creole culture in the eighteenth century.* Baton Rouge: Louisiana State University Press.

Ham, M. (Ed.). (2008). *Contes Et Recits de La Louisiane Creole, Tome II.* Shreveport: Editions Tintamarre.

Hughes, L. (1958). *The Langston Hughes reader.* New York: George Braziller.

Latortue, R., & Adams, G. R. W. (Eds.). (1979). *Les Cenelles: A collection of poems by Creole writers of the early nineteenth century* (translated by editors). Boston: G.K. Hall.

Lauret, M. (2014). *Wanderwords: Language migration in American literature.* London: Bloomsbury Press.

Mercier, A. (2009). *Hénoch Jédésias.* Shreveport: Editions Tintamarre.

Owens, A. (Ed.). (2006). *Contes Et Recits de La Louisiane Creole, Tome I.* Shreveport: Editions Tintamarre.

Powell, A. (2009). Duration and the vampire: Deleuzian gothic. *Gothic Studies, XI,* 86–98.

Rosenwald, L. (2008). *Multilingual America: Language and the making of American literature.* Cambridge: Cambridge University Press.

Sedgwick, E. K. (1986). *The coherence of gothic conventions.* London: Methuen.

Séjour, V. (1837). Le Mulâtre. *Revue des Colonies,* mars, 376–392. http://www.centenary.edu/french/textes/mulatre.html

Séjour, V. (2002). *The Jew of Seville* (trans: Shapiro, N. R.). Champaign: University of Illinois Press.

Séjour, V. (2006). *The fortune-teller* (trans: Shapiro, N. R.). Champaign: University of Illinois Press.

Séjour, V. *The Mulatto* (trans: Barnard, P.). http://www.southernspaces.org/2007/seeds-rebellion-plantation-fiction-victor-s%C3%A9jours-mulatto#section8

Shapiro, N. R. (Ed.). (2004). *Creole echoes: The francophone poetry of nineteenth-century Louisiana* (translated by the editor). Champaign: University of Illinois Press.

Tichelaar, T. R. (2012). *The gothic wanderer: From transgression to redemption.* Ann Arbor: Modern History Press.

Wynn Sivils, Matthew. 'Indian Captivity Narratives and the Origins of American Frontier Gothic', in Crow, Charles L. (ed), *A Companion to American Gothic.* Hoboken, NJ: Wiley Blackwell, 2014. (pp. 84-95).

PART III

Race and Southern Gothic

CHAPTER 18

Uncanny Plantations: The Repeating Gothic

Michael Kreyling

Gothic texts are not realistic.[1]

The Gothic is a repetitive literary condition; at certain moments a fixed genre, at others more fluid, almost an iteration of the perennial debate about the nature of literary representation: mirror or lamp?[2] The historical collision of the Gothic and new world plantation forms of race and labor has proven to be the Gothic's most definitive repetition, collapsing the difference between mirror and lamp.

Begin, for example, with Northrop Frye's underestimation of the Gothic in *Anatomy of Criticism* (1957). For Frye, 'Gothic' is so far from realism as to be a lesser form of romance, a form of secession from (or weakness in the presence of) the real. He relegates Gothic to one of his taxonomic hold-alls, The Mythos of Spring: Comedy. Frye writes:

> In this kind of comedy, we have finally left the world of wit and awakened critical intelligence for the opposite pole, an oracular solemnity which, if we surrender uncritically to it, will provide a delightful *frisson*. This is the world of ghost stories, thrillers, and Gothic romances, and, on a more sophisticated level, the kind of imaginative withdrawal portrayed in Huysmans' *A Rebours*. (185–6)

For Frye and many who might still subscribe to his view, 'the Gothic' brands an inventory of weak ('uncritical') effects most commonly found in sub-genres like 'ghost stories, thrillers, and Gothic romances.' Frye's Gothic provides 'surrender' from the rigors of mature intellection: wit, critical intelligence, engagement with the world rather than 'withdrawal' from it. Effeminate rather than feminist.

In his recent introduction to a comprehensive assessment of the British Gothic, Fred Botting continues Frye's line: 'Not tied to a natural order of

M. Kreyling (✉)
Vanderbilt University, Nashville, TN, USA

things as defined by realism, gothic flights of imagination suggest supernatural possibility, mystery, magic, wonder and monstrosity' (2). On the other hand, Gothic's latter-day revisionists acknowledge its guilty pleasures, but resist relegating them to the category of diversions from realism. George Haggerty argues that the erotic terror, sexual violence, vicarious thrills of enclosure and escape—the frisson-inducing aspects of the Gothic—have had to wait at least a century for a proper reading. 'Gothic fiction emerged from a dream [Horace Walpole's dream that produced *The Castle of Otranto* in 1764] and subsided into infamy' until new reading and writing communities (postcolonial, feminist) emerged to re-territorialize 'the world' that Frye was so confident the Gothic had departed (Haggerty 262).

A Reversal of Realism

Views of the Gothic as adaptable ('repeating') suggest that changing 'communities change the gothic by, in extreme cases, reversing its antipodes of escape and engagement.' In one community, 'an absence of the light associated with sense, security, and knowledge' (Botting 2) is not a 'flight' away from 'realism' and its putative power to define a 'natural order of things,' but a compelling, if unwilled, return to it: the dark enclosure being Legree's haunted plantation in *Uncle Tom's Cabin* or the dank prison cell in which Nat Turner narrates slavery in both Thomas Gray's and William Styron's *Confessions*.

Teresa Goddu, among many critics who study the discourse of US Gothic, has pioneered this reversed path. The shared revisionist assertion is that the fact of Negro slavery in the United States and in adjacent plantation economies bonded with traditional, literary Gothic to generate a dynamic, hybrid genre that forecloses 'withdrawal' from experience at the same moment that it challenges the limits of representation. Negro slavery upsets the neat gothic binary of real and wondrous, natural and monstrous, calling the Gothic back into a contested relationship with a 'natural order of things' that incorporated the brutalities of Negro slavery as given. In '"To Thrill the Land with Horror": Antislavery Discourse and the Gothic Imagination,' Goddu ventures to the threshold of proclaiming the realistic/gothic reversal. Her argument is that nineteenth-century compilers of the actual cruelty of plantation slavery found themselves in a conundrum of representation—if they were too 'realistic' in their depictions of the horrors of slavery, they risked eliciting the common, protective response to the Gothic: withdrawal by their readers to a protective distance where they could not be tainted by the evil they might witness in reading about plantation 'monstrosity' (82). A reader of a ghost story or thriller can always close the book if the gore becomes too intense; but those closed books are exactly what ex-slave and abolitionist authors did *not* want. In Goddu's reading of the plantation Gothic, the reality of slavery does not entirely disappear, and yet it is not fully represented either. Some horrors are not too real to be suffered, but might be, ironically, too real to be narrated. In Goddu's reading, the plantation gothic text is always on the verge of revealing itself as more realistic than the formal properties of the genre can manage.

The reversible relationship between realism and the Gothic continues in another contemporary view of the plantation: Elizabeth Christine Russ's *The Plantation in the Postslavery Imagination* (2009). For Russ, the plantation functions as a narrative mode that subsumes the Gothic, becoming (in the US South, Caribbean, and Brazil) the crucial narrative mode of the 'postslavery' era of the 1940s through the turn of the twenty-first century (6). Russ begins her book by proposing two axes: history and representation.

> The displacement and extermination of native populations, the forced exile and enslavement of millions of Africans, the tragedy of the Middle Passage, the ravaging of peoples and lands: these form the irreducible core of the legacy of the slaveholding plantation of the Americas, an institution that produced seemingly infinite riches for Old and New Worlds alike, and helped to fund the imperial projects of Europe and, later, of the United States. The present study proposes a model by which to evaluate the development, over the course of the twentieth century, of a trans-American poetic imaginary that has emerged from this brutal, dehumanizing past. (3)

Russ's 'trans-American poetic imaginary' is a repetition of the Gothic in a postmodern, perhaps even posthistorical, era in which what happens (the first sentence of the quotation) and the narrative forms that communities use to communicate what happens (the second) are equally 'real.' In formulating her position, however, Russ returns to the basics of the new world or Anglo-American Gothic: the tortuous relationship between a history of actual brutality and its 'image' in a 'poetic imaginary' that transforms a 'brutal, dehumanizing past' into conventions for narrative. It is not the brutal suffering that she wishes to recover and publish, but rather the poetic forms that have solidified around representations of it and, in elusive ways, embody the pain. The distinction is important, for it brings *The Plantation in the Postslavery Imagination* into the orbit of gothic repetitions. 'As a great many historians and cultural critics have noted, the voices of those whose exploitation and loss were most intense under the plantation regime have, more often than not, been silenced or marginalized by the official archives of history' (Russ 3). Other writers outside the 'archives of history'—the novelists, poets, and essayists whose work Russ studies—have utilized the 'trans-American poetic imaginary' to defeat the silencing and marginalization.[3]

THE UNCANNY PLANTATION

The plantation, then, while historically a form of agricultural capitalism, is also a construction of words whose genome is gothic. As Goddu advises in 'The African American Slave Narrative and the Gothic,' the art and act of representing plantation slavery are rife with mutualities: 'Slavery, then, is a central historical content that produces the Gothic and against which it responds' (Goddu 2013: 71). Slavery did not need the Gothic to supply content: 'Represented as a house of bondage replete with evil villains and helpless victims, vexed bloodlines and stolen birthright, brutal punishments and spectacular suffering, cruel tyranny and horrifying terror, slavery reads as a Gothic romance' (72). Yet the Gothic made representation of slavery problematic. The Gothic could, by virtue of its generic weight, persuade readers that they were encountering 'representations' and not the historical record. Goddu's reading of Poe's *Arthur Gordon Pym* takes due note of Poe's usage of 'formalistic effects' (light and dark imagery, for example), but stresses the 'need to locate the gothic's effects in history' (Goddu 1996: 230).

The plantation must be read *both* as an evasion of history and as the return of the history that it aims to avoid. This complex alternating current often, if not invariably, disturbs the generic tranquility claimed by definitions such as Northrop Frye's. In Charlotte Brontë's *Jane Eyre*, the madwoman in the attic represents remnant guilt for the Caribbean slave economy (invisible in the novel) that finances Rochester's social status and erotic appeal; she must not be read as a diversion of mere 'effects,' but as a surreptitious intrusion of history into the Gothic. The figure of Heathcliff draws on the same deposit of guilt in human capital and erotic power in Emily Brontë's *Wuthering Heights*. In Hawthorne's *The Scarlet Letter*, the 'black man' whom Little Pearl spies in the forest is not only the sable-clothed Dimmesdale, but also the 'ghosts' of African slaves who haunt 'The Custom House' prologue to the novel. For all the 'imaginative withdrawal' that Frye laments, then, plantation Gothic— extended to the Yorkshire moors or the New England forest—pulls the reader back into the nightmares of history with the very effects that, from a different vantage point, seem to propel us away.

Far from being 'delightful,' I want to suggest that the repeated frisson integral to plantation Gothic is the touch of history distanced or denied. Freud gave us the model. The touch of the unexpected yet familiar is the jolt that he described as proceeding from repressed shames, and, using his own analytic technique, manifests as much in our languages as anything else. The Salem of *The Scarlet Letter*, for example, whose part in the slave trade is confined to a truncated reference in the quasi-historical 'The Custom House,' or the moors of the Brontës' novels, whose proximity to the slave trade through Liverpool—as Maya-Lisa von Sneidem reminds us—is elided in Heathcliff's or Rochester's offstage histories, function as sites of the Freudian uncanny where consciousness drowsing in 'The Mythos of Spring' is prodded to wakefulness by a forceful reminder of history.

At its most narratively fundamental, the uncanny derives its frightening power from the sense that it has been here all along, yet unconsciously repressed: like the familiar household slaves who, in Mary Boykin Chesnut's experience, 'suddenly' become assassins. In Freud's basic formula, this rhythm begins with the familiar, *heimlich*, and becomes its inversion, finally coinciding with its opposite, *unheimlich*. 'The uncanny is that species of the frightening that goes back to what was once well known and had long been familiar' (Freud 124). Freud uses an example from one of E.T.A. Hoffman's tales, 'The Sand-man,' in which a young man named Nathaniel becomes erotically obsessed with the automaton-daughter, by name Olympia Spalanzani, of a heartless scientist.

Nathaniel's obsession with Olympia overshadows a 'normal' and therefore approved relationship with Clara, a distant relative whom he has known for most of his life. Clara is *heimlich*, Olympia *unheimlich*. Hoffman's Nathaniel is only weaned of his sensuous urge for difference when he sees Olympia's maker-father and a rival scientist pull her apart piece by piece. Madness ensues, from which, nevertheless, Nathaniel wakes up under Clara's tender gaze. Thus the narrative arc is from sameness (Clara) to its other (Olympia) and back to the familiar again. Yet Nathaniel's fevered desire for Olympia returns in an intimate moment with Clara, and he comes close to throwing her over a roof parapet until Clara's brother rescues her and, in the process, knocks Nathaniel from the roof to his death.[4] Freud, characteristically, situates the uncanny narrative within the family romance. It is just as deeply emplotted in the plantation narrative and its repetitions.

Freud located the source and energy of the uncanny in sexual urges felt by sons and forbidden by fathers. Hoffman's Olympia serves his paradigm well, for she is bodily possessed by two fathers before she is made available to the son. In its universal inclusion of themes of sexual threat and predation, the plantation Gothic retains the power of patriarchal control over female bodies, adding white control of the black body as labor. The plantation Gothic thereby controls what the reader may encounter of the material, historical basis of its existence, adding psychological anxiety to sexual. Freud writes:

> In the first place, if psychoanalytic theory is right in asserting that every affect arising from an emotional impulse—of whatever kind—is converted into fear by being repressed, it follows that among those things that are felt to be frightening there must be one group in which it can be shown that the frightening element is something that has been repressed and now returns. (147)

Apparitions of the uncanny, Freud's formulation suggests, resemble interpellations, hailings, in which the white subject confronts (him)self as an object. As the nexus of pastoral perfection and morbid anxieties incubated by repression of its sexual and materialistic underpinnings, nothing but the Gothic could narrate it.

Harriet Beecher Stowe framed *Uncle Tom's Cabin* (1852) as a narrative with vestiges of the uncanny plantation. In Chap. IV, Stowe depicts the first of many scenarios in which *heimlich* and *unheimlich* trade places. The *heimlich* Shelby plantation is uncomfortably doubled by the household of slaves Chloe and Tom. Tom and Chloe's habitation might be robed in climbing blossoms, but the 'rough logs' of which it is built still register a 'vestige' (30) of its aberrant, unseen, disruptive historical situation and origins. Its slave inhabitants, as much as they seem contained by the white household, are still movable chattels in a more comprehensive economy. Inside Chloe and Tom's cabin, the slave family lives in one room; no privacy or intimacy is presumed as part of the slave's consciousness. And, although Stowe gives Chloe high marks for her domestic skills (the one room is spotless and the food efficiently cooked and delicious even though there is no separate kitchen), the first consumer of her housekeeping acumen is the white son of the master, 13-year-old George Shelby, whom Chloe feeds before tending to her own children (37). White patriarchy—even its youthful deputy—controls all products of the bodies under its ownership. Two households, then, occupy the same frame, one *heimlich* and the other *unheimlich*. In the genre of the plantation Gothic, it is never easy to say which depends on the other, for, coexisting in the same narrative frame, their doubling produces distortion, rendering the slave and slavery both the same and the other.

The Shelby plantation functions as a fault-lined simulacrum of proper domesticity; it literally houses both the delightful withdrawal or escape from the real (its claim to pastoral as norm) and its uncanny antithesis. Mr. Shelby, under the pressure of debt, is in one room, reserved for males and business, haggling with the slave trader Haley over the sale of Tom, Eliza, and her son. Mrs. Shelby is in another room assuaging Eliza's justified suspicions and then facilitating her escape. Riven as it is with uncanny reminders that, as much as Stowe is invested in the sanctity of maternalized domestic space, slavery is nevertheless an anti-domestic capital market haunting the same spaces, *Uncle Tom's Cabin* repeats the Gothic on the uncanny's schedule.

Legree's Red River ruin is the full gothic inversion of the domestic or *heimlich*. Readers approach with the full panoply of frisson-inducing scenery:

> It was a wild, forsaken road, now winding through dreary pine barrens, where the wind whispered mournfully, and now over log causeways, through long cypress swamps, the doleful trees rising out of the slimy, spongy ground, hung with long wreaths of funereal black moss, while ever and anon the loathsome form of the moccasin snake might be seen sliding among broken stumps and shattered branches that lay here and there, rolling in the water. (447)

Poe might have written Stowe's description of one of Legree's rooms: 'There was a small window there [in the side of the garret], which let in, through its dingy, dusty panes, a scanty, uncertain light on the tall, high-backed chairs and dusty tables, that had once seen better days. Altogether, it was a weird and ghostly place' (519). Stowe seems as diverted by gothic paraphernalia as she is concerned with the slave experience itself. Cassy, the mulatto woman who presides over the Red River plantation's domestic situation so inverted by Legree, has been, Stowe tells us, reading a book 'of stories of bloody murder, ghostly legends, and supernatural visitations, which, coarsely got up and illustrated, have a strange fascination for one who once begins to read them' (523). Driving Legree to disintegration by literally becoming the return of his repressed memory of the black woman he had, earlier, locked up in the aforementioned garret and abused in unspecified ways, Cassy uses a fundamental version of Freud's theory of the uncanny to, ultimately, drive Legree deeper into his morbid anxieties rather than retrieve him through therapy. The house itself is no longer animated by the white plantation mistress but rather by the ghost of 'a negro woman, who had incurred Legree's displeasure, [and] was confined there for several weeks. What passed there,' Stowe demurely warns us, 'we do not say' (520). The madwoman in the attic returns, but there is no Eyre to save Legree.

A Terrorist Gothic

In *Postmodernism, or, The Cultural Logic of Late Capitalism* (1991), Fredric Jameson hints at one of the pitfalls of using 'the Gothic' as a hermeneutic—as I just did. The Gothic can become, he claims—perhaps chastising Frye even though he repeats the latter's feminizing of the genre—a 'boring and exhausted paradigm ... where—on the individualized level—a sheltered woman of some kind is terrorized and victimized by an "evil" male' (289).

> Certainly the gothic mobilizes anxieties about rape, but its structure gives us the clue to a more central feature of its content which I have tried to underscore by means of the word *sheltered*. ... Gothics are indeed ultimately a class fantasy (or nightmare) in which the dialectic of privilege and shelter is exercised: your privileges seal you off from other people, but by the same token they constitute a protective wall through which you cannot see, and behind which therefore all kinds of envious forces may be imagined in the process of assembling, plotting, preparing to give assault. (289)

Jameson's evocation of a terrorist Gothic preserves the frisson as a virtual or touristic experience, placing not actual rape but 'anxieties about rape' at its hub. When the 'sheltered woman of some kind' is, in fact, the master's human property, then the word 'evil' forfeits its scare quotes. Stowe observed the restraint that Jameson (erroneously) imputes to 'Gothics': 'What passed there, we do not say ....' Saying the plantation Gothic, however, is William Styron's mission in *The Confessions of Nat Turner* (1967).

Its predecessor Thomas Ruffin Gray's *Confessions of Nat Turner, the Leader of the Late Insurrection in Southampton, Virginia* (1831) might stand as the primary terrorist Gothic, rooted in and repeating through the white subconscious of the plantation imaginary. Much has been written about Gray's ventriloquizing version of the slave Nat Turner's voice and persona, most notably as the original text relates to Styron's attempt to expand and 'correct' it in his novel. The 1831 text bears an interesting relationship to contemporary slave narratives that, in turn, according to Goddu and others, relate uneasily to the Gothic. In language echoing the vocabulary of the Gothic, Gray juxtaposes the pastoral myth of the plantation society against an ominous undercurrent embodied by Turner. Gray foreshadows his prison account of an interview with Turner:

> It will thus appear that whilst every thing upon the surface of society wore a calm and peaceful aspect; whilst not one note of preparation was heard to warn the devoted inhabitants of woe and death, a gloomy fanatic was revolving in the recesses of his own dark, bewildered, and overwrought mind, schemes of indiscriminate massacre to the whites. (14)

Writing from a 'calm,' 'peaceful' 'surface of society' that he assumes, albeit now uneasily, to be the norm, Gray (serendipitously surnamed) proposes to delve into whiteness's (Gothic) Other where 'gloomy fanatic[s]' 'revolv[e]' 'schemes of indiscriminate massacre' in the 'recesses of [their] own dark, bewildered, and overwrought mind[s].' And, it must be added, these 'fanatics' do so in the carceral 'recesses' of white society's prisons as well as their own minds. Jameson's concept of *'sheltered'* thus finds its uncanny complement: walls confining the gothic subject ominously repeat the confines of the slave mind, which have been set by whites' preconceptions. Without doubt Gray controls the Turner confession, accentuating several acts of execution of planter families—men, women, children, infants—and just as significantly swerving away from Turner's own narrative of his young life as a prodigy who developed a definite, and problematic, charisma among the slaves whom Turner himself called 'the negroes in the neighborhood' (18) as if he were not integral to either race. Styron recovered these slivers of autobiographical confession (for example, Turner's alienation from the other black people among whom he lived) and tried, eventually to his pain, to explore and exploit them. Gray's Turner, however, is leveled to the archetypal bogeyman, a darker spot among 'the negroes in the neighborhood': 'It [the revolt] will be long remembered in the annals of our country, and many a mother as she presses her infant darling to her bosom, will shudder at the recollection of Nat Turner, and his band of ferocious miscreants' (Gray 15). Again, the frisson. Lost, in fact probably willfully jettisoned as incompatible with 'the annals of our [white] country,' is the Turner who, in his miraculous literacy—he boasted to Gray that he could not locate a moment when he could not read (18)—and in his biblical Christianity was uncannily *like* the whites who were slaughtered in his revolt. For ultimate cultural *heimlich*, Turner had to be stuffed into the gothic persona of the gloomy, dark, bewildered, and overwrought fanatic bent (without motive save for a thirst to do harm) on massacre. Here we might see the Gothic and the uncanny working toward the same goal, for the person (Turner) who is *like* the narrating (white) subject, the possessor of 'our country,' must be, in the vehicle of the Gothic, driven beyond the pale into radical otherness. 'I looked on him,' Gray himself states as the transcript concludes, 'and my blood curdled in my veins' at the vision of the other's combination of innate intelligence and his opting for rampant and apparently cold-blooded violence (28). Styron's Turner begins here, for Styron does not 'look on' Turner but outward from him to the whites who have 'gothicized' him.

Gray's utilizing of gothic tropes, then, functions narratively as a means of sequestering Turner's likeness to the white master inside the 'function' of villain. Beyond the convenient adaptability of the dark/light tropes of the Gothic to the racial binary of the plantation, the suspension of realism feeds into the genre as well, for Gray can omit the possibility that Turner's experience as a slave in the white world might have anything to do with his motivation. Motivation is reserved, as is subjectivity, to the white narrator and his white readers.

The Gothic's Effects on History

The complex assemblage of narrative tropes, durable character profiles, and cultural landscape constituting the plantation Gothic takes on perhaps its most anguished and problematical incarnation in Styron's *The Confessions of Nat Turner*. The achievement of Styron's novel has been overtaken by the controversy of its reception; as Ashraf Rushdy has shown, the tangled racial deceptions of the novel penetrate deeply into its structure. My purpose here is not to recuperate Styron's *Confessions*, but simply and carefully to position it at a certain moment in the history of the uncanny plantation. As Goddu insists, we must 'locate the gothic's effects in history,' and Styron's project requires as much.

In a decade (the 1960s) inaugurated by a flawed attempt to commemorate the centennial of the Civil War, Styron's narrative project was particularly apt; for whatever else it is, *The Confessions of Nat Turner* is a wrecking ball on an arc toward the plantation edifice. Leaving aside, if possible, Styron's controversial inhabiting of Nat Turner's mind and body, the novel annihilates 'realism' claims in the plantation imaginary. The white body, male and female, is transformed, in Styron's acidic depictions, from ideal to grotesque. Styron's Thomas Gray debuts with 'discolored blotches on his flushed' alcoholic's face (22). Another white man for whom Turner works 'towered over [him], sickly, pale, and sweating, his nose leaking slightly in the cold' (63). Still another itinerant white possesses a 'cruelly pockmarked face' (119). Yet another assumes white racial privilege in spite of being 'a knobby-limbed benighted illiterate, filthy of tongue, blasphemous, maladroit even at such unskilled tasks as the ploughing and hoeing and wood-chopping' (274). We must see these white bodies as authorial acts of uncanny demolition of the white narrative, and hear them in a black voice, for Styron attributes each and every word to Turner.

The beauty and virtue of the belle fare no better. One plantation mistress, according to Hark, Turner's lieutenant, emits a smell '"like an ole catfish somebody lef' three days up on a stump in July .... Even de buzzards fly away from ole pussy like dat"' (43). She suffers from blocked sinuses, breathes through her mouth as a result, and applies a 'poultice of lard' to her cracked and bleeding lips (43). Another, Emmeline Turner, attached to the family from whom Nat Turner derives his name, begins as the boy Nat's idol of purity and feminine virtue, only to bring down the whole myth when he eavesdrops on her copulating with her cousin outside an evening fete. To finish off his destruction of the belle, Styron adds that Emmeline had been working the streets of Baltimore as a prostitute (177–83).

Other accessories to the pastoral are likewise undermined or destroyed. The site of the narrative is no principality in the cotton empire, but rather a scattering of small and medium-sized farms struggling to grow tobacco on exhausted soil (45). Turner is sold when his owner's 'plantation' can no longer make expenses (220). As he waits for the white man who has bought him, the Turner plantation undergoes a darkening transformation from pastoral haven to haunted gothic shell. Styron's vocabulary is unmistakable. Turner feels an 'overall sense of ominousness, the spidery disquietude and perplexity which, like the shadows of vines creeping up a stone wall in descending sunlight, began to finger my spine' (230). Insignificant sounds gradually become deafening in the 'ominous hush and solitude' (230). In a familiar gothic trope, a 'crack[ed] and bluish' mirror comes alive with reflections of 'the vanished portraits of Turner forebears' (231). Echoes of Stowe's evocation of Legree's hellish plantation are not out of place, the difference being that what Stowe would not say, Styron enunciates with melancholic exactitude. For example, the white man who comes to take possession of Turner is not only a minister, the Reverend Eppes, but a minister with a prurient curiosity as to Turner's penis: "'I hear tell your average n_____ boy's got a member on him inch or so longer'n ordinary. That right boy?'" (238).[5]

More historically interesting in Styron's version, however, is his attempt to re-imagine Turner as a man who suffered the physical and psychological brutality of plantation slavery, but possessed the verbal, intellectual skill to narrate his experience. Indeed, it is important to remember that, *pace* charges of appropriation by many black critics, Styron intends Turner to create or evoke the world that he narrates while incarcerated. In the 1960s, Styron had models, if he chose to consider them, of Turners whose reality was significantly, and sometimes almost exclusively, behind prison bars: incarcerated black radicals like George Jackson, Eldridge Cleaver, and Malcolm X before them. Although Styron confined Turner to reading the Bible, the black prison intellectuals of the decade read more widely. More importantly, the incarcerated black intellectual of the decade educated himself into a particular subject who could stand outside the gothic type—Thomas Gray's invocation of a fanatic propelled by a 'dark, bewildered, and overwrought mind … [to] massacre … the whites' (Gray 14)—by which he was controlled and, like Malcolm Little, used correspondence courses and the prison library (Malcolm X and Haley 247, 248, 251) to transform himself into Malcolm X. Or, like George Jackson, to fill in the intellectual spaces left vacant by an abortive parochial and public school education with 'Marx, Lenin, Trotsky, Engels, and Mao' (Jackson 16). Or like Eldridge Cleaver, whose prison education included Bakunin, Machiavelli, and 'A MAO MAO, A MAO MAO, A MAO MA' (Cleaver 31, 38).

George Jackson, who lived the decade of the 1960s in prison and died there in 1970, shot (like his gothic avatar Tom Robinson in *To Kill a Mockingbird*) by a prison guard in an 'escape attempt,' saw his situation vis-à-vis his white overlords quite clearly:

> There are still some blacks here [Soledad Prison] who consider themselves criminals—but not many. Believe me, my friend, with the time and the incentive these brothers have to read, study, and think, you will find no class or category more aware, more embittered, desperate, or dedicated to the ultimate remedy—revolution. The most dedicated, the best of our kind—you'll find them in the Folsoms, San Quentins, and Soledads. (26)

If, as the black writers said who chastised Styron for (what they saw as) his flagrant appropriation of the persona of black masculinity in his rendering of Turner, Styron's novel is an elaborate 'strategy of containment' (Rushdy 80), it nevertheless acknowledges that 'containment' as a blind seam in the white myth of black masculine consciousness. In his problematic attempt to use the 'postslavery [white] imagination' to penetrate black male consciousness, its experience of incarceration, the forging of sexual and gendered identity through brotherhood, Styron portrays the plantation as real wreckage rather than untainted ideal. In his *Confessions*, it is always already the carceral order and, inasmuch as it is, Styron provides the link from the Gothic as literary genre to what Michelle Alexander, in a contemporary repetition of the Gothic, terms an 'eerily familiar' age of mass incarceration linking plantation slavery to Jim Crow, and thence to the present 'Age of Colorblindness.' Alexander draws an unbroken line from the plantation through post–Civil War Jim Crow to what many critics, expanding on Michel Foucault in *Discipline and Punish* (1975), call the carceral state. Alexander's premise is important to a retrospective reading of Styron's *Confessions*, and to the repetition of the Gothic in the present:

> This larger system, referred to here as mass incarceration, is a system that locks people not only behind actual bars in actual prisons, but also behind virtual bars and virtual walls—walls that are invisible to the naked eye but function nearly as effectively as Jim Crow laws once did at locking people of color into a permanent second-class citizenship. The term *mass incarceration* refers not only to the criminal justice system but also to the larger web of laws, rules, policies, and customs that control those labeled criminals both in and out of prison. (12–13)

The Gothic has been, certainly in its connection with the new world plantation, a system and set of customs of control by metaphor, repeated over time and adaptable to changing 'realisms.' Thomas Gray, in his original prison interview with Nat Turner in 1831, sought to impose such control—albeit retroactively, over events that had just recently occurred. He employed the Gothic with do-it-yourself crudity, resisting all cues to hear the man present and talking to him, instead typing him as the hackneyed villain of a bloody and dreadful story. To be sure, Gray could be confident that in short order Turner would be hanged and therefore incapable of speaking his own reality. Styron's intervention was twofold (at least). First, he obliterated the white fantasy of the beneficent plantation, collapsing the real and imaginative distance between white bodies and black so that his novel has a feeling of moiling physicality on the surface of which 'race' is just one of the shames of the human body, along with stink, pockmarks, and knobby joints. Second, he sought to transform Nat Turner from gothic mannequin into prison intellectual. Styron writes in his 'Author's Note' to the novel: 'The relativity of time allows us elastic definitions: the year 1831 was, simultaneously, a long time ago and only yesterday.' I would add that the repeating Gothic facilitates the 'elasticity' of time by connecting what happened then with what happens now by means of the continuity of narrative mores that human communities (contoured by race, class, gender, and historical moment) use to construct justifying stories. Michelle

Alexander, in fact, adumbrates the central plot of such a repeating control strategy when she connects '[r]umors of a great insurrection terrif[ying to] whites' with 'current stereotypes of black men as aggressive, unruly predators' (Alexander 28). And she strongly suggests that, at least in new world Gothic, dark chambers and enclosed spaces, sexual threat and frisson, and sudden transgressive violence lacking apparent motive are much more than metaphor; they are the uncanny projections of a reality too disturbing for representation without some form of control.

NOTES

1. Fred Botting (2013) 'Introduction: Negative Aesthetics' in *New Critical Idiom: Gothic*, 2nd edn. (New York: Routledge), p. 12.
2. M. H. Abrams (1953) *The Mirror and the Lamp: Romantic Theory and the Critical Tradition* (NY: Oxford).
3. Sven Beckart, in his *Empire of Cotton* (Cambridge, MA: Harvard UP, 2014), chronicles such silencing and marginalization as the slaves who toiled on plantations worldwide became dehumanized as 'labor.'
4. Readers will of course immediately note the similarity to *Nathaniel* Hawthorne's tale of male obsession and female victimization, 'Rappaccini's Daughter.' The plot is most durable, reappearing in Alfred Hitchcock's *Vertigo* (1958) and most recently in Alex Garland's film *Ex Machina* (2015), and always carved to fit the times.
5. I have opted not to repeat the n-word in this quotation; Stryon does use it.
6. Note: Any cursory look at a research library's holdings under the general subject area of 'the Gothic in literature' will produce myriad titles. Nearly every literary period from medieval to postmodern provides its take on 'the Gothic.' There are works of the Gothic inflected by race, nationality, sexual identity, and class. The Gothic truly is the indispensable genre to the voices of reading and writing communities. What follows is a severely truncated list of suggestions.

Bibliography

Abrams, M. H. (1953). *The mirror and the lamp: Romantic theory and the critical tradition*. New York: Oxford.

Alexander, M. (2010). *The New Jim Crow: Mass incarceration in the age of colorblindness*. New York: The New Press.

Botting, F. (2013). Introduction: Negative aesthetics. In F. Botting (Ed.), *New critical idiom: Gothic* (2nd ed.). New York: Routledge.

Clarke, J. H. (Ed.). (1968). *William Styron's Nat Turner: Ten black writers respond*. Boston: Beacon.

Cleaver, E. (1992). *Soul on ice* (Preface by Ishmael Reed). New York: Delta.

Cook, R. J. (2007). *Troubled commemoration: The American Civil War Centennial, 1961–1965*. Baton Rouge: Louisiana State University Press.

Foucault, M. (1975). *Discipline and punish: The birth of the prison* (trans: Sheridan, A.). New York: Vintage, 1977.

Freud, S. (1919). *The Uncanny* (trans: McLintock, D.). London: Penguin, 2003.

Frye, N. (1957). *Anatomy of criticism*. Princeton: Princeton University Press. 2000.

Goddu, T. A. (1996). The ghost of race: Edgar Allan Poe and the Southern Gothic. In H. B. Wonham (Ed.), *Critics and the color line* (pp. 230–250). New Brunswick: Rutgers University Press.

Goddu, T. A. (2013). The African American slave narrative and the Gothic. In C. L. Crow (Ed.), A companion to American Gothic (pp. 71–83). Somerset: Wiley.

Goddu, T. A. (2013). To thrill the land with horror: Antislavery discourse and the Gothic imagination. In M. Savoianen & P. Mehtonen (Eds.), *Gothic topographies in language, nation building and 'race'* (pp. 73–85). Burlington: Ashgate.

Gray, T. R., & Turner, N. (1831). *The confessions of Nat Turner, the leader of the Late Insurrection in Southampton, Virginia*. Chapel Hill: University of North Carolina Press. 2011.

Haggerty, G. (2012). Gothic success and gothic failure: Formal innovation in a much-maligned genre. In R. L. Caserio & C. Hawes (Eds.), *The Cambridge history of the english novel*. Cambridge: Cambridge University Press.

Jackson, G. (1994). *Soledad brother: The prison letters of George Jackson*. Foreword by Jonathan Jackson, Jr. Chicago: Lawrence Hill Books.

Jameson, F. (1991). *Postmodernism; or, the cultural logic of late capitalism*. Durham: Duke University Press.

Malcolm X. With the assistance of Alex Haley. (1965). *The autobiography of Malcolm X*. New York: Penguin, 2001.

Rushdy, A. H. A. (1996). Reading Black, White, and Gray in 1968: The origin of the contemporary narrativity of slavery. In H. B. Wonham (Ed.), *Critics and the color line* (pp. 63–94). New Brunswick: Rutgers University Press.

Russ, E. C. (2009). *The plantation in the postslavery imagination*. New York: Oxford.

Stowe, H. B. (1852). *Uncle Tom's cabin; or, life among the lowly* (Introduction by David Bromwich). Cambridge, MA: Harvard University Press. 2009.

Styron, W. (1967). *The confessions of Nat Turner*. New York: Random House.

von Sneidem, M.-L. (1995). *Wuthering heights* and the Liverpool slave trade. *ELH, 62*, 171–196.

FURTHER READING [6]

Abrams, M. H. (1957). *A glossary of literary terms*. (New York: Rinehart). This is the first edition; there have been at least six subsequent editions.

Andrews, W. L. (1986). *To tell a free story: The first century of Afro-American autobiography, 1769–1865*. Urbana: University of Illinois Press.

Andrews, W. L. (2011). *Slave narratives after slavery*. New York: Oxford University Press.

Beville, M. (2009). *Gothic-postmodernism: Voicing the terror of postmodernity*. Amsterdam: Rodopi.

Crow, C. L. (2014). *A companion to American Gothic*. Hoboken: Wiley.

Goddu, T. A. (1997). *Gothic America: Narrative, history, and nation*. New York: Columbia University Press.

Kristeva, J. (1982). *Powers of horror: An essay on abjection*. New York: Columbia University Press.

Marcus, G., & Sollors, W. (Eds.). (2009). *A new literary history of America*. Cambridge, MA: Harvard University Press.

Martin, R. K., & Savoy, E. (Eds.). (1998). *American Gothic: New interventions in a national narrative*. Iowa City: University of Iowa Press.

Morrison, T. (1992). *Playing in the dark: Whiteness and the literary imagination*. Cambridge, MA: Harvard University Press.

Townshend, D. (2015). *Terror and wonder: The Gothic imagination*. London: British Library.

CHAPTER 19

Slave Narratives and Slave Revolts

Maisha Wester

Nineteenth-century pro-slavery texts and newspapers often used gothic tropes to discuss slave rebellion, cultivating a terror of the unrestrained black body. Such depictions betray a latent anxiety of the incompleteness of white authority over blacks. While slavery supporters presented images of the happy slave and the master's benevolent paternalism, the specter of the rebellious slave served as a doppelganger, haunting romantic narratives via newspaper accounts of rebellions and adverts for runaway slaves.

In contrast, slave narratives like Charles Ball's *Slavery in the United States* (1837) mobilized the genre to portray slavery itself as a horror-generating institution. While numerous ex-slave narratives are replete with scenes of slaves' brutal tortures and afflictions, Ball's text is intriguing for the ways it uses the Gothic in scenes of slave resistance and 'crime.' His narrative manipulates several depictions of the savage and powerful slave; however, unlike pro-slavery papers, which produced such images to argue black monstrosity, Ball's text undermines the power of the idea of 'savage' slaves and focuses on the horror of their punishments.

Slave Revolts

While popular genres like the Plantation romance relied heavily on depictions of happy, naïve slaves serving under gentle masters, representations of runaway slaves and the punishments meted out to slaves depict a very different picture. The severity of the punishment for slaves who attempted to escape or failed to meet their master's command suggests an over-determination to stifle all sense of agency in slaves. Texts like *The American Slave Code* (1853) reveal the

M. Wester (✉)
Indiana University, Bloomington, IL, USA

© The Editor(s) (if applicable) and The Author(s) 2016
S.C. Street, C.L. Crow (eds.), *The Palgrave Handbook of the Southern Gothic*,
DOI 10.1057/978-1-137-47774-3_19

master's control to be limited and imperfect (Freeburg 17). Agency in slaves, and the inevitable drive toward self-determination, directly undermined the sanctity of the master's (way of) life. Therefore, moments of slave insurrection inspired horror.

Slave rebellions were consequently narrated through a gothic frame. The Haitian Revolution was especially constructed as a gothic event—termed 'the horrors of St. Domingo'—in a variety of socio-political and fictional texts. Accounts depicted the rebels as mercenaries at best, but mostly monstrous, cannibalistic fiends delighting in the torture of white victims and promising disastrous influence if not quarantined. At the revolution's start, *The Gazette of the United States*, a Philadelphia newspaper, claimed that slave rebels slaughtered 'all the Whites, men, women, and children, and burned all the plantations for 60 miles round' (qtd in Matthewson). Leonora Sansay *Secret History; or The Horrors of St. Domingo* (1808) depicts the Haitian Revolution as scene upon scene of violent crime perpetrated by subhuman fiends 'thirsting after blood, and unsated with carnage' (123). Sansay particularly emphasizes stories of white womanhood imperiled by black menace, suggesting that rape and force in interracial sexual relationships were part of the slave revolution. Likewise, Bryan Edwards's non-fictional *Historical Survey of the French Colony in the Island of St. Domingo* (Edwards 1797) sensationally proclaims that 'upwards of one hundred thousand savage people, habituated to the barbarities of Africa, avail[ed] themselves of the silence and obscurity of the night, and [fell] on the peaceful and unsuspicious planters, like so many famished tigers thirsting for human blood' (63). He details their monstrosity, describing how rebels nailed a police officer to his plantation gates, hacking off his limbs while he still lived; sawed a carpenter in half; gang raped women, reserving some for further violation and killing others or, worse, scooping out their eyes with knives; and used impaled infants as standards (74–5). Despite describing violations in graphic detail, accounts often turned toward the unspeakable, claiming that the revolution's true horrors defied representation; these turns imply that the terror of the slave revolution lay elsewhere, beyond bodily violation.

Newspaper depictions of Nat Turner's rebellion echo these reports, and Turner's insurrection reads as a Haitian Revolution in America. Periodicals extensively described the insurrectionists' bloody violence, marking how 'whole families, father, mother, daughters, sons, sucking babes, and school children, [were] butchered, thrown into heaps, and left to be devoured by hogs and dogs, or to putrify on the spot' ('Extract' 51). One letter invokes gothic romantic pathos in relating how its author, 'struck with [more] horror, than the most dreadful carnage in a field of battle could have produced,' discovered a single survivor, 'a little girl about 12 years of age, looking with an agonized countenance, on a heap of dead bodies lying before her' ('Letter' 96–97).

Like the Haitian revolutionaries, Turner and his rebels were positioned as gothic villains, reduced to 'banditti' at best, stalking the local woods. Their attacks were characterized as 'horrible ferocity' perpetrated by wraiths who 'remind one of a parcel of blood-thirsty wolves rushing down from the Alps; or rather like a former incursion of the Indians upon the white settlements' ('Banditti' 43). Turner, reduced to a 'fanatic preacher' both in newspaper accounts and in his own confessions, receives the worst of the representations. Deemed 'a monster of iniquity' (Old Virginia 144), editorials employed gothic tropes in describing his character. Turner 'is of a darker hue, and his eyes, though large, not prominent—they are very long, deeply seated in his head, and have a rather sinister expression' ('Banditti Taken' 137). He seems a calculating sociopath that 'betrayed no emotion, but appeared to be utterly reckless in the awful fate that awaited him and even hurried his executioner in the performance of his duty' (*Norfolk Herald* 140). Even Thomas Gray's account of Turner's confessions uses gothic affect. In his introduction to what is supposed to be Turner's text, Thomas explains:

> whilst not one note of preparation was heard to warn the devoted inhabitants of woe and death, a gloomy fanatic was revolving in the recesses of his own dark, bewildered, and overwrought mind, schemes of indiscriminate massacre to the whites. Schemes too fearfully executed as far as his fiendish band proceeded in their desolating march. No cry for mercy penetrated their flinty bosoms. No acts of remembered kindness made the least impression upon these remorseless murderers. Men, women and children, from hoary age to helpless infancy were involved in the same cruel fate. Never did a band of savages do their work more unsparingly. (14)

Thomas's introduction casts Turner as a merciless villain, effectively denying him and his followers the roles of rational people motivated to rebellion by slavery. Rather, their violence is dismissed as proceeding 'in consequence of the absence of all true religious feeling, ... being given up to the natural lusts and passions of their depraved and wicked hearts' (Old Virginia 144–5). Since he is reduced to a heartless, fiendish fanatic, any word that Turner might utter in the text that follows is already defined as monstrous.

Accounts consistently undercut all signs of humanity in the slaves. For instance, when the rebel Billy Artis committed suicide, papers remarked that he 'wept like a child, but having once tasted blood, he was like a wolf let into the fold' ('Letter' 97). Such remarks recall antebellum distinctions between civilized and savage warfare. Civilized men engage in righteous violence and murder to defend their lives and their freedom, protect their family, avenge a suffered wrong, and/or defend the honor of a loved one. In contrast, 'proslavery authors alleged that once they had gotten a taste for blood, black men ... would revel in killing for its own sake' (Roth 220). The contradiction between Southern ideals of justified (white) violence and representations of (black) insurrectionists as unjustifiable monstrosities is significant. Fighting for one's life and freedom is high on the list of reasons for the civil man to commit violence; given the rebels' enslaved positions, these are logically the primary motives for their insurrection. Yet commentators repeatedly refused meditations on this possibility, preferring to mystify the mental processes of the rebellious slaves who are 'artful, impudent and vindictive,' and who 'without any cause or provocation' go about 'knocking on the head, or cutting the throats of their victims' ('Banditti' 44). Because they disrupt the social order and its notions of racial subjection, agency (or lack thereof), and power, slave rebels are necessarily pre- and over-determined as gothic monsters. Artis, although repentant, is doomed to be a wolf.

The punishments of the slave rebels read like gruesome horror storylines. Several were beheaded, their heads 'stuck up on poles, ... a warning sign to all who should undertake a similar plot. With the same purpose, the captain of the marines, as they marched through Vicksville on their way home, bore upon his sword the head of a rebel' (Tragle 17). The road leading to the location where the slaves first fought the militiamen 'became known after the revolt as Blackhead Signpost because the head of a black man, killed in the aftermath of the revolt, was fixed to a stake at that point' (7). Thus while the newspapers explicitly used gothic tropes to convey the horror of slave insurrection, accounts of 'justice' and restored peace prove grotesque texts whose horror stems from cheerfully narrated abuses of slaves. This is a trend that slave narratives reproduce as gothic scenes.

Inevitably, white residents agreed that the area would remain haunted—literally and figuratively—by the violence of the events. Writers predicted that '[i]n future years, the bloody road, will give rise to many a sorrowful legend; and the trampling of hoofs, in fancy, visit many an excited imagination' ('Letter' 97). Generations after slavery's end, local residents recalled the history with a shudder:

> We well remember the thrill of horror which shot through the veins of the community when news of the massacre reached home. ... In the few days that this murderous band held their carnival of death .... White families were mercilessly butchered and infants were killed by dashing their brains against the walls'. (*Petersburg Index* 154)

Such narratives insist on re-presenting the slaves as mythic villains offering psychological violence to new generations of innocent whites. The region's haunting stems from the slaves' violent disruption of social order; there is no room allotted for the possibility of the wronged slaves, abused and/or killed by vigilantes in response, returning to bewail the violence done to them. No headless slave stirs to demand justice in these narratives.

Yet the real horror of the insurrection was not merely its violence. As debates after the event show, profound unease stemmed from what such violence by black hands signified. Editorials, which repeatedly asked 'why' while proving incapable of producing a satisfactory rationale for the rebels' violent resistance, expressed anxiety about the overall (il)legibility of the slave. The few explanations for the revolt were that the rebels 'are mad—infatuated—deceived by some artful knaves, or stimulated by their own miscalculated passions' (*Richmond Compiler* 37). Yet such explanations register a gothic turn in their insistence on 'madness' and 'miscalculated passions' in attempts to understand and manage the slave rebel. Assumptions that the slaves were 'deceived by artful knaves,' typically read as Northern abolitionists, prove equally problematic, for they suggest regional infiltration by contaminating ideologies; further, both explanations fail to account for the slaves' abilities to perform contentedness and submission preceding the moments of revolt.

Unsurprisingly, the later reports suggest dissatisfaction with the insurrection's presumed culmination: the capture and execution of the slave rebels. Rather, after Turner's capture, editorials continued to ruminate on the unfathomable nature of the slave psyche. Papers published debates that defined blacks, free and enslaved, as a contaminating 'evil' and an 'unhappy and degraded race … whose presence deforms our lands' (O.P.Q. 120). Commentators postulated the end of slavery and exile of freed blacks as the only solution, not because of black humanity but because of the unidentifiable, uncontrollable nature of black monstrosity; they worried 'what stay to this impending and horrible evil do you propose? Will you wait until the land be deluged in blood, and look alone to the fatal catastrophe' (122). Thus the notion of black insurrection took on an apocalyptic significance for whites, whose social order depended on racial power and authority over black subjects.

Gothic fictions built on these two events and the general quandary of slave insurrection. For instance, Herman Melville's 'Benito Cereno' (1855) may be read as a staging of both the Haitian Revolution—given the ship's name, *Santo Domingo*, and the date of the events, 1799—and the Turner insurrection. The story conveys excessive anxiety over slaveholders' 'power to make objects of their slaves only to show that in the slaves' revolt and performance of their own subjection, this work of objectification is not complete: Masters cannot fully transform humans into objects. … the slave's performance [is] *a ruse of objectification* that renders all narratives of absolute power incoherent' (Freeburg 95). Like editorials after the Turner insurrection, the text's victim, Cereno, is haunted beyond the successful capture and execution of the slave rebels, claiming that 'the negro' casts a shadow over him. 'The negro' assumes a manifold effect, as a mediator of 'the very idea of New World slavery and social totality itself … which encompasses everything from racist opinions that can be changed to unalterable facts of contingency that forever haunt the social field of human interaction and conflict' (Freeburg 94); therefore slave rebellion proves catastrophic.

Southern writers take up the discourse quite frequently. Charles Crow explains that Henry Clay Lewis's 'A Struggle for Life' (1850) 'begs for interpretation as a fantasy of slave rebellion …. The grotesque dwarf seems to arise directly from the subconscious of the doctor, compounded of all the repressed guilt and terror of his class' (35). Poe's novel *The Narrative of Arthur Gordon Pym of Nantucket* (1838) proves explicitly evocative of the Haitian Revolution and Turner rebellion. The novel presents two moments of black insurrection. The first occurs amid the mutiny on the *Grampus*; Turner's supposed blood-thirsty fanaticism reverberates in the black cook's unfathomable rage and irrational violence. The second moment, which concludes the book, is the prolonged and far more successful attack staged by the black inhabitants of the southern island of Tsalal. In their assault, the natives effectively destroy a group of white explorers who represent the possibility of white colonization of a southern island. The revolt echoes the final consequences of the Haitian Revolution: the destruction and dispossession of whites on the Caribbean island.

Thus the nightmare of slave rebellions and their significance for American social and racial order proved fitting subjects for gothic literature across the country. For slavery to remain the fitting image of the Plantation romance, slaves had to 'appear happy, content and respectful; at least, they wear a mask that conveys this, and never speak their true thoughts' (Crow 35). Yet part of the gothic nightmare of slavery stems from the very question of slave seemingness. Any slave might seem happy—the terror was the impossibility of truly knowing which slave was happy, which not; which would run, which would stay; and which would revolt. Teresa Goddu significantly concludes that '[r]epresented as a house of bondage replete with evil villains and helpless victims, vexed bloodlines and stolen birthrights, brutal punishments and spectacular suffering, cruel tyranny and horrifying terror, slavery reads as a Gothic romance' (72). While Goddu rightfully focuses on the institution itself as inherently gothic, it is also important to remark on the moments when slavery became nightmarish for the slaveholders.

Slave Narratives

The use of the Gothic by former slaves was a complex manipulation. The genre, given to using blackness to signify moral degeneration and consequently depicting the monstrous and fiendish as 'black,' inherently coded the black body as inhuman and inferior. Ex-slaves used the genre to argue for their innate humanity and to portray the warping effects of slavery as an institution. Slave narratives functioned as a form of resistance, emphasizing the incompleteness of white domination; as such, the former slaves' very determination to speak produced horror for slave masters. This peculiar production of horror is significant when contemplating slave appropriation of the genre: the ex-slave narrator uses gothic tropes in order to articulate the profound terrors of slavery and betray the dehumanizing effects of the institution, only to have those tropes turned back against him for daring to speak. The ex-slave narrator is thus in danger of being caught in a peculiar web in which he can be rendered monstrous by the very genre—already (over)loaded with racial anxieties—that he uses in hopes of rendering himself human.

Yet the popularity of the Gothic made it a worthwhile vehicle for ex-slave narrators to risk using. The antislavery movement particularly pushed ex-slave narratives toward the genre, seeing the Gothic as an easy way to portray slavery's atrocities and 'arouse a moral response in their audience and prompt them to vigorous action. ... Antislavery's success in demonizing slavery depended on forging a seamless connection between the Gothic and slavery—to make slavery comprehensible through and inseparable from the Gothic's conventional scenes of cruelty' (Goddu 74). Further, awareness of a marketplace rife with Plantation romances impelled blacks to present a corrective demystifying the 'chaotic, violent, and reprehensible' system behind the Southern romance; as such, the slave narratives are products of a 'process [which] involved political awareness and shrewd calculations in a literary marketplace' (Schermerhorn 1010). In former slaves' uses of the Gothic, terror shifts from mere effect and product of a nightmarish imagination; slavery becomes a lived nightmare whose horrific nature produces gothic plots and affect.

Slave narratives utilize a number of gothic tropes but revise their associations. For instance, narratives rewrite the hero/victim/villain position to imagine the slave as both victim in his tortured enslavement, and as hero for daring to break free from a system that criminalizes him for defending himself and his family, and for fleeing. The battle scene between Covey and Douglass in *Narrative of the Life of Frederick Douglass* (1845) illustrates such a revision. Not only does Douglass emphasize Covey as villain, but in choosing to fight back Douglass suggests that previous subjugation at Covey's hands has rendered Douglass an innocent victim. In prefacing the fight, Douglass declares: 'You have seen how a man was made a slave; you shall see how a slave was made a man' (Douglass 75). Given the ramifications of any resistance in a slave and slavery's tendency to portray such behavior as monstrous, Douglass's moment reclaims the rebellious slave from dehumanizing narratives, insisting instead that rebellion is not only heroic, but also constitutive of (masculine) subjectivity.

While Charles Ball's text uses the Gothic in ways typical to many slave narratives, his tale is significant because of how he uses gothic tropes in depictions of the 'savage' and 'criminal' slave. While these tropes in pro-slavery texts were used to convince whites to read 'black men as a dangerous threat to the security of white society and to the preservation of the American republic' (Roth 210), Ball's depictions undercut the power attributed to such bodies. In recounting the sale of his father, Ball complicates the trope of the American black male slave as savage and powerful to reveal the truth of the man: a father and husband traumatized by loss. Because his 'father was a very strong, active, and resolute man,' the slave catcher and constable deem it dangerous to seize him 'even with the aid of others … as it was known he carried upon his person a large knife' (Ball 19). While his father illustrates the physical prowess associated with the savage slave, Ball emphasizes how his father has been irreparably wounded by slavery. The reason that his father is no longer useful is because of the emotional suffering he has endured as a slave: the man never recovered from the sale of his family, becoming depressed and forlorn as a consequence. Thus, while he is physically powerful, he is nonetheless incapable of preventing his family from being stolen from him. Further, savagery stems from willingness to commit (extreme) violence; while Ball's father is equipped to do violence, his immediate and lasting reaction—depression—is not merely nonviolent, but harms only himself. The 'savage slave' is a victim, not a villain.

When slaves are guilty of violent crime, Ball explains their behavior as a consequence of their master's influence. For instance, the crime that the two mulatto slaves David and Hardy commit proves gruesome and gothic in its perpetration. Lusting after a young mistress visiting the plantation with her brother, the two slaves successfully kidnap her by surprising the siblings in the woods as they ride home one evening, knocking the woman from her horse and dragging her screaming into the woods. The two try to pin the crime on Ball, but he successfully defends himself and later discovers their hiding place and captive. While the story is interesting in terms of the men's violence, their betrayal of another slave, and the torture that Ball consequently suffers, what is more peculiar is the explanation that Ball gives for such horrible criminality even before he relates the tale. American-born slaves, who tend to be pessimistic about their futures and desires as a whole, 'borrow' notions 'of present and future happiness, from the opinions and intercourse of white people' (219). In this brief sentence, Ball represents slaveholders' idealizations as the contaminating influence that guides black criminality. And while Ball explains that the mind of the American slave is 'bent upon other pursuits … his discontent works out for itself other schemes' that are non-rebellious, the example of Hardy and David reveals how 'schemes' may allude to violent but significantly less widely destructive ends.

While Hardy and David's crime proves gothic in plot, Ball's chosen points of emphasis suggest that the real horror stems from slavery's gruesome punishments. Ball's account of the woman's suffering is generally brief, limited to an occasional sentence without additional commentary. In contrast, he lingers over the violence that Hardy and David suffer. Hardy, tracked by bloodhounds, is mangled as the dog had 'torn a large piece of flesh entirely away from one side of his breast, and sunk his fangs deep in the side of his neck' (256). Ball likewise extensively describes their execution: already wounded, they are stripped and tied down to the earth, their mouths stuffed so they cannot scream, and left 'to be devoured alive by the carrion crows and buzzards' (256–7). Ball amplifies the horrid effects of the scene by noting: 'The buzzards, and carrion crows, always attack dead bodies by pulling out and consuming the eyes first. They then tear open the bowels, and feed upon the intestines' (257). Ball's choice to linger on the tortured death of the two slaves—criminals that they are— requires us to consider where the real terror lies. Like Turner's insurrectionaries, Hardy and David commit horrible crimes, but the consequent punishment they receive proves even more villainous.

While readers may desire to rationalize the criminals' horrible execution as an emotional response to their assault on and the consequent death of an innocent woman, other innocent slaves suffer equally horrendous torture. Ball, falsely accused of the crime, endures one such encounter. His master ties him down to be skinned alive. The doctor responds:

> it would not do to skin a man so full of blood as I was. I should bleed so much that he could not see to do his work; and he should probably cut some large vein,

or artery, by which I should bleed to death in a few minutes; it was necessary to bleed me in the arms, for some time, so as to reduce the quantity of blood that was in me, before taking my skin off. (225–6)

The scene plays on the grotesque in two ways: first, the determination to skin Ball alive presents an inherently gruesome prospect; secondly, the calm and measured tones in which the torture is discussed prove incongruent with the horror of the activity. In recounting the weird gap between voice and action, Ball's narrative evokes the cheerful tones in which newspapers and white masters narrated the brutalization of (rebel) slaves.

Another moment of slave torment is overly inscribed with gothic effects; it is also a moment that repeats Hardy and David's torture with a difference: this time the slave's only crime was seeking freedom. Finding himself in the Murderer's woods—so renamed for Hardy and David—and hearing the sound of mysterious bells approaching, Ball is seized by horror when he beholds

> the form of a brawny, famished-looking black man, entirely naked, with his hair matted and shaggy, his eyes wild and rolling, and bearing over his head something in the form of an arch, elevated three feet above his hair, beneath the top of which were suspended the bells …. It slowly approached within ten paces of me, and stood still. (326)

In sensationalist fashion, the text delays recognition of the seemingly monstrous, mysterious black body confronting Ball: 'My heart was in my mouth; all the hairs of my head started from their sockets; I seemed to be rising from my hiding place into the open air, in spite of myself, and I gasped for breath' (326). Ball thus positions himself as the horrified witness, performing gothic affect for the reader.

Yet in a twist recalling the story of his 'savage' father, he reveals the 'monster' to be a victim. By extending the gothic scene, Ball invites us to ponder the nature of this silent, seemingly deranged specter as the 'apparition' kneels for a drink:

> The forest re-echoed with the sound of the bells … as their bearer drank the water of the pond, in which I thought I heard his irons hiss, when they came in contact with it. I felt confident that I was now in the immediate presence of an inhabitant of a nether fiery world, who had been permitted to escape, for a time, from the place of his torment, and come to revisit the scenes of his former crimes. I now gave myself up for lost. (326–7)

While in a traditional gothic text this would prove a climactic scene of confrontation with a demon, Ball relocates the horror of the scene and the damnation that the figure signifies. The oddly attired man rushes into the water and begs Ball 'in a suppliant and piteous tone of voice, to have mercy upon him, and not carry him back to his master' (327). The would-be monster is a victim, named

Paul, so helpless that even a slave proves a threat to him, and so brutalized by whippings that his back is covered in a mass of white and flesh-colored scars.

The encounter illustrates how slavery literally creates the monstrous, disfigured bodies that populate gothic nightmares. The sound of the iron, so hot that it hisses when it touches water, augments the extreme nature of the slave's torment: Paul must wear the excessively hot iron cage against his skin. Ball's reading of Paul as a resident of hell proves a fitting metaphor as the poor man is literally burned; slavery, as the source of this 'fire,' becomes hell. Ball's sense that Paul has 'escaped for a time' touches on the truth since Paul is a runaway slave; consequently, Ball's modifying phrase 'for a time' proves the real source of horror as it implies his recapture. Lastly, Paul is familiar with the area, having been there during a previous escape. Thus even Ball's statement that he is 'revisit[ing] the scene of his former crimes' is accurate; however, in revealing the actual nature of Paul's crime—running away—the monstrosity of the figure is dissolved and rightfully displaced onto the institution that actually produces the nightmare.

The description of Paul's death is equally replete with nightmarish imagery. Ball returns some nights later to help Paul, shuddering as he passes the place of David and Hardy's demise in a scene that echoes narratives of strolls through haunted graveyards. Ball observes the scattered and whitening bones of the men, and remarks on their grinning skulls while crows flock above his head and wolves howl in the nearby brush as they gnaw the dry bones (331–3). The prolonged description of Ball's trip through the nightmare region is followed by the discovery of Paul's body hanging from a tree in an apparent suicide. While Ball again extends gothic description to the scene, noting the buzzards and ravens peopling the tree from which Paul hangs while crows cloud the air, the description of what has happened to Paul's body proves more important. Paul's corpse has been devoured by the birds in a manner similar to the description that Ball provides for Hardy and David. Like them, Paul is never buried but is left hanging in the tree 'until the flesh fell from the bones, or was torn off by the birds' (337). In the same way that Ball passed David and Hardy's unburied bones on the way to see Paul, now he sees Paul's 'bones hanging in the sassafras tree more than two months afterwards' (337), still wearing the iron collar and arch of bells. Thus all of the slaves, villains and victims, are marked only through slavery in death—in the former case, the place where they were tortured by masters; in the latter case, the instrument of torture itself becomes the sign. Slavery's failure to distinguish between good and bad slaves, or even between violently criminal and mildly resistant slaves, invariably proves the supreme horror for Ball. An important element of the damnation that Paul offers is the possibility that Ball will become him. Consequently, Ball determines not to return; the swamps are haunted not by ghosts but by slavery's horrors. Yet the whole South is grotesque, marked by slaves, 'moving skeletons' (82), laboring on the blighted land. Ball thus renders the region cursed, the 'abode of the spirit of ruin' (48) peopled by the living dead.

Unsurprisingly, slave narratives tend to end on notes of unease, remarking the incompleteness of their freedom in light of laws like the Fugitive Slave Act. Narrators explain that they can be dragged from their peaceful lives in the North back into the hell of the South. Harriet Jacobs, for instance, exhibits absolute paranoia at the end of her text, remarking on her hypervigilance, lest slave catchers surprise her unawares. James Williams's tale betrays a similar anxiety, revealing how 'slavery's Gothic shadow encompasses the whole nation'; Williams 'can never fully escape its cruel grip' but can only 'resist slavery's Gothic conspiracies' (Goddu 79). Ball's narrative repeats this trope to a dramatic extreme. Having escaped from slavery twice—remarrying and having children with his new wife after the first escape—Ball discovers on finally reaching Pennsylvania that his wife and children, all of whom were born free, have been falsely taken into slavery. His life ends in dread as 'even yet it may be supposed, that as an article of property, ... [he is] worth pursuing in [his] old age' (Ball 517). There is no true, stable happiness for the runaway slave, deemed criminal by Southern law and therefore subject to horrible punishments. Even more troubling, just as slavery fails to distinguish between good and bad slave, so too does it fail to recognize rightfully free blacks.

Slavery proves a lasting curse, for both free and enslaved blacks, and free whites. In much Southern Gothic literature the decaying plantation house is a stock feature of the Southern landscape. Slave narratives like Ball's predict this feature. In describing the Virginia landscape, Ball notes how the once magnificent estates—home to powerful, wealthy, and proud families—have 'fallen to decay, ... occupied by the descendants of those who erected it, still pertinaciously adhering to the halls of their ancestry' (51); such plantations maintain a meager stable of slaves while the descendants stubbornly hold fast to a lost era, 'vain of their ancestral monuments, and proud of an obscure name, contend with all the ills that poverty brings upon fallen greatness, and pass their lives in a contest between mimic state and actual penury ... too spiritless to sell their effects' and leave the estate (51–2). William Faulkner's Southern landscapes evoke similar imagery, populated by dying aristocracy and angry, impoverished, industrialized white laborers. Decaying plantations become the abodes of characters like Miss Emily; thus Crow's reading of 'A Rose for Emily' proves equally relevant to Ball's comments. Noting that Emily stubbornly refuses 'to acknowledge change, time or loss,' Crow concludes, 'Like Miss Emily, many Southerners clung to memories of the past, and to faded symbols of the dead. She is an extreme example of a common theme, in a culture that was collectively haunted' (125). The writings of other Southern writers illustrate similar racial hauntings, as characters are forced to replay the dramas, oppressions, and rebellions of the slave past. In a landscape that tortured slaves into an existence marred by social death, families are cursed and destroyed by problematic inheritances, and the houses doomed to ruin. Yet the terrible question left by the slave narratives is: When will the black body cease to be h(a)unted?

Bibliography

(1971). *The Petersburg Index* (Petersburg, VA) 1 Oct. 1869. In H. I. Tragle (Ed.), *The Southampton slave revolt of 1831: A compilation of source material* (pp. 153–154). Amherst: University of Massachusetts Press.

(1971). *The Richmond Compiler* (Richmond, VA) 24 Aug. 1831. In H. I. Tragle (Ed.), *The Southampton slave revolt of 1831: A compilation of source material* (pp. 36–38). Amherst: University of Massachusetts Press.

(1971).*The Norfolk Herald* (Norfolk, VA) 14 Nov. 1831. In H. I. Tragle (Ed.), *The Southampton slave revolt of 1831: A compilation of source material* (p. 140). Amherst: University of Massachusetts Press.

Ball, C. (1837). *Slavery in the United States: A narrative of the life and adventures of Charles Ball*. New York: John S. Taylor. Web. *Documenting the American South*.

Crow, C. L. (2009). *History of the Gothic: American Gothic*. Cardiff: University of Wales Press.

Douglass, F. (1993). *Narrative of the life of Frederick Douglass, as American slave*. Boston: Bedford Books of St. Martin's Press.

Edwards, B. (1797). *A historical survey of the French colony in the island of St. Domingo*. Cambridge, UK: Cambridge University Press.

Extract of a letter from the Senior Editor. (1971). *The Constitutional Whig* (Richmond, VA) 29 Aug. 1831. In H. I. Tragle (Ed.), *The Southampton slave revolt of 1831: A compilation of source material* (pp. 50–52). Amherst: University of Massachusetts Press.

Freeburg, C. (2012). *Melville and the idea of blackness: Race and imperialism in nineteenth century America*. New York: Cambridge University Press.

Goddu, T. A. (2013). The African American slave narrative and the Gothic. In C. L. Crow (Ed.), *A companion to American Gothic* (pp. 71–83). Somerset: Wiley.

Gray, T. R. (2011). To the public. In *The confessions of Nat Turner, the leader of the late insurrection in Southampton, Virginia*. Chapel Hill: University of North Carolina Press.

Letter. (1971). *The Constitutional Whig* (Richmond, VA) 26 Sept. 1831. In H. I. Tragle (Ed.), *The Southampton slave revolt of 1831: A compilation of source material* (pp. 90–99). Amherst: University of Massachusetts Press.

O.P.Q. Letter. (1971). *The Constitutional Whig* (Richmond, VA) 26 Sept. 1831. In H. I. Tragle (Ed.), *The Southampton slave revolt of 1831: A compilation of source material* (pp. 119–123). Amherst: University of Massachusetts Press.

Old Virginia. "To the Editors of the Enquirer." (1971). *The Richmond enquirer* (Richmond, VA) 25 Nov. 1831. In H. I. Tragle (Ed.), *The Southampton slave revolt of 1831: A compilation of source material* (pp. 143–150). Amherst: University of Massachusetts Press.

Roth, S. N. (2010). The politics of the page: Black disfranchisement and the image of the savage slave. *The Pennsylvania Magazine of History and Biography, 134*(3), 209–233.

Sansay, L. (2008). In M. Drexler (Ed.), *Secret history: Or, the horrors of St. Domingo and Laura*. Toronto: Broadview Editions.

Schermerhorn, C. (2012). Arguing slavery's narrative: Southern regionalists, ex-slave autobiographers, and the contested literary representations of the peculiar institution, 1824–1849. *Journal of American Studies, 46*(4), 1009–1033.

The Banditti. (1971). *The Richmond Enquirer* (Richmond, VA) 30 Aug. 1831. In H. I. Tragle (Ed.), *The Southampton slave revolt of 1831: A compilation of source material* (pp. 43–46). Amherst: University of Massachusetts Press.

The Banditti Taken. (1971). *The Richmond Enquirer* (Richmond, VA) 8 Nov. 1831. In H. I. Tragle (Ed.), *The Southampton slave revolt of 1831: A compilation of source material* (pp. 136–138). Amherst: University of Massachusetts Press.

Tragle, H. I. (1971). Introduction. In *The Southampton slave revolt of 1831: A compilation of source material* (pp. 3–25). Amherst: University of Massachusetts Press.

FURTHER READING

Anolik, R. B., & Howard, D. L. (2004). *The Gothic Other: Racial and social constructions in the literary imagination*. Jefferson: MacFarland and Comp.

Crow, C. (2013). *A companion to American Gothic*. Somerset: Wiley.

Edwards, J. (2003). *Gothic passages: Racial ambiguity and the American Gothic*. Iowa City: University of Iowa Press.

Wester, M. (2012). *African American Gothic: Screams from shadowed places*. New York: Palgrave Macmillan.

Winter, K. J. (1992). *Subjects of slavery, agents of change: Women and power in Gothic novels and slave narratives, 1790–1865*. Athens: University of Georgia Press.

CHAPTER 20

The Tragic Mulatto and Passing

Emily Clark

The tragic mulatto is among the most recognizable figures in American literature. This character's first appearance in fiction dates to the late 1830s, but many of the features associated with the popular stereotype appear decades earlier in journalism and travel accounts, some of them associated with places far beyond the borders of the American South and North America. This makes the trope of the tragic mulatto a slippery one. Although it undoubtedly runs through many works that can be classified as Southern Gothic, it is not easily bounded by the parameters of the genre. The standard narratives developed around this literary archetype do the typical work of exposing and interrogating the social and cultural mores of the American South and the legacies of slavery, but some of its historical and discursive roots lie in eighteenth-century Orientalism and the Caribbean. The cultural and political work advanced by the figure's literary deployment in America was not static. Although many character elements and plot points have remained in play from the figure's debut in the nineteenth century to its less frequent appearances in the twenty-first, the narrative arc has changed to reflect shifting values and popular preoccupations.

Passing, usually a minor element in antebellum tragic mulatto tales, became central in the twentieth century. Emancipation, white supremacy, the Great Migration and the racial uplift movement that climaxed in the Harlem Renaissance converged to raise popular fascination with those whose physical appearance allowed them to elude the racial categories of black and white. Passing provoked critiques from both whites and African Americans, feeding a rich literary output that spilled over into the new medium of film.

The first part of this chapter excavates the transnational career of the tragic mulatto, paying particular attention to connections with Haiti and Orientalism. Discursive and historical phenomena linked to these two influences emerged

E. Clark (✉)
Tulane University, New Orleans, LA, USA

© The Editor(s) (if applicable) and The Author(s) 2016
S.C. Street, C.L. Crow (eds.), *The Palgrave Handbook of the Southern Gothic*,
DOI 10.1057/978-1-137-47774-3_20

in the eighteenth century and unfolded in the first decades of the nineteenth, shaping and imprinting the familiar trope that emerged in the antebellum United States. The second section traces the evolution of the 'classic' tragic mulatto in American fiction and effectively sketches out a periodization for the figure and the literary production that deployed it.

The colour label *mulatto* was coined in the late sixteenth century to describe people of mixed race. By the eighteenth century, elaborate racial classification schemes developed that specified a mulatto as a person of one half European ancestry and one half African. Médéric Louis Elie Moreau de Saint-Méry's charts and descriptions, published in 1797, were among the most elaborate and best known (Moreau de Saint-Méry 71–90). The typical nineteenth-century tragic mulatto is a female of mixed race living in the antebellum US South. In much of the literature, the figure is not labelled a mulatto/mulatta, but is designated a quadroon, meaning a person of three-quarters European and one-quarter African ancestry, or octoroon, to denote someone of seven-eighths European and one-eighth African ancestry. The term tragic mulatto thus refers not to a character of specific racial admixture, but to those mixed-race literary characters who share a common set of characteristics, including their role in standard narrative lines and plot points. Since the figure is nearly always a woman, the feminine variant of *mulatto*, *mulatta*, is, strictly speaking, more apt when discussing the trope and is used in this chapter.

The literary tragic mulatta is sometimes enslaved, sometimes free, but always doomed by her racial liminality, which denies her a niche in a rigidly bi-racial world. This alienation asserts itself most clearly in the realm of marriage. Whether a mulatta falls in love with a white man or a black man, a happy marriage is beyond her reach. She is forbidden by law from marrying a white man, by the hierarchy of race from marrying a black. Sex, love and marriage are almost always at the heart of the narrative variations in the genre and are often connected to a dramatic revelation that leads to tragedy.

The Transnational Tragic Mulatta

The figure of the tragic mulatta does not depend solely on the American South for its makeup. Orientalism finds its way into much of the antebellum literature, particularly that featuring New Orleans free women of colour, commonly known as quadroons. In Joseph Holt Ingraham's novel *The Quadroone*, the Spanish cavalier Don Henrique awakens in a room decorated like a seraglio after being wounded in a skirmish in colonial New Orleans. His eye falls on a beautiful woman. Thinking that he must have died in battle, Henrique exclaims in wonder, 'Surely this is Paradise; and this is an Houri!' The Catholic Castilian cavalier is welcomed to heaven not by an angel, but by a houri, 'a nymph of the Muslim Paradise', a being of incomparable beauty and sensuality thought to welcome virtuous Muslim men to the afterlife (Ingraham 1841, 141–142).

The earliest of the fictional tragic mulatta short stories, Ingraham's 'The Quadroon of Orleans', likewise evokes an Orientalist description of the quadroon

Emelie by highlighting her use of a veil, the signature garment of women of the harem. When Baron Championet spies Emelie at prayer in St. Louis Cathedral, she 'wore no bonnet, but instead, a black veil, that fell from a gold comb set with precious stones, down to her feet' that 'fell in thick folds and hid her face, which, if in harmony with the exquisite symmetry of her figure could not be less than beautiful'. As she departs the cathedral, conscious of the Baron's eyes on her, the veiled woman tantalizes him with a series of movements that gestured towards the Ottoman east: 'Hastily wrapping her veil about her head, she passed him with a stately, undulating motion, and by a side door, hitherto concealed by a curtain, left the cathedral' (Ingraham 1839, 259).

The Orientalist influence is less explicit in other antebellum fiction featuring the tragic mulatta, but is present nonetheless. Xarifa, one of the doomed mixed-race women in Lydia Maria Child's short story 'The Quadroons', was named for the Moorish heroine in a popular song of the era, 'The Bridal of Andalla'. The Xarifa of the ballad faces the same heartbreak as Child's quadroon when her lover abandons her to marry someone else.

Some tragic mulattas, especially the quadroon women sketched by Ingraham, wore sumptuous, exotic clothing reminiscent of the attire of the grand vizier's wife described by Lady Mary Wortley Montagu in her *Turkish Letters*, who wore 'a *caftan* of gold brocade, flowered with silver', over pantaloons and embroidered slippers. Azèlie wore a vest 'of the finest lawn, with large and loose sleeves, open at the neck and breast, embroidered with gold, and ornamented with little diamond buttons' and pantaloons that took the place of a skirt, 'of the finest linen, deeply bordered with lace, and around her waist' (Ingraham 1841, 82).

These Orientalist features typify the tragic mulatta narratives set in New Orleans and Louisiana in which the mixed-race women are nearly always identified as quadroons. Other sites in America, including Virginia, New York and Massachusetts, sometimes served as the setting for tales of the antebellum tragic mulatta, but most were set in New Orleans and Louisiana or had heroines with connections to this locale. The tragic mulatta characters in this large subset of the literature were identified as quadroons. The complex explanation for this is explored more fully elsewhere, but two of the reasons for the entanglement of the New Orleans variety of the tragic mulatta with Orientalist discourse are directly relevant to the historical evolution of this phenomenon.

The Louisiana Purchase of 1803 and the Barbary Wars fought between 1785 and 1815 converged to encourage the association of New Orleans free women of colour with the exotic Muslim East. The Purchase brought Anglophone Protestants into contact with the Catholic culture and the large population of free people of colour in New Orleans, both of which were alien to English-speaking migrants—and authors—who wrote about the city after it became part of the United States. At the same time, Americans were awash in accounts about the Muslim world of which the Barbary Coast was a part. Lady Montagu's *Turkish Letters*, published in 1763, brought the sequestered female space of the Ottoman Empire to life for American readers. At the turn of the nineteenth century, her account and others that appeared in the early 1900s resonated powerfully in the American imagination in the midst of the Barbary Wars and found their way into descriptions of New Orleans free women of colour as a familiar index of the exotic.

The '[l]ong spangled robes, open in front, with pantaloons embroidered in gold and silver', worn by the ladies of the seraglio according to Edward Daniel Clarke's 1813 account, can easily be compared to the attire of Azèlie in Ingraham's *The Quadroone*. Even more striking is the similarity between Thomas Ashe's description of the headgear of New Orleans free women of colour and that offered by Lady Montagu. Ashe observes of New Orleans quadroons, 'Their most general head-dress is either a handkerchief of gold-gauze braided in with diamonds, or else chains of gold and pearls twisted in and out through a profusion of fine black hair, which produces a pleasing effect' (Ashe 343). The headgear of the grand vizier's wife is described by Lady Montagu as 'a rich Turkish handkerchief of pink and silver, her own fine black hair hanging a great length in various tresses, and on one side of her head some bodkins of jewels' (Montagu 1:196).

Ashe may, in fact, never have visited New Orleans, but there was a model for the sartorial extravagance of the free women of colour that he claimed to see there not only in the accounts of Lady Montagu and others, but in the lines that Médéric Louis Elie Moreau de Saint-Méry penned to describe the typical *mûlatresse* of Saint-Domingue before the Haitian Revolution. According to him, the free women of colour of Saint-Domingue relentlessly pursued luxury, especially in their sartorial display. Their dresses, liberally decorated with lace and jewellery, were made from 'the most beautiful things that India produces, the most precious in muslins, in handkerchiefs, in fabrics and linens' (Moreau de Saint-Méry 93).

The account that Karl Bernard, Duke of Saxe Weimar, wrote of the free women of colour that he encountered in New Orleans in 1825 focuses more on the social than the sartorial: 'A quadroon is the child of a mestizo mother and a white father. The quadroons are almost entirely white: from their skin no one would detect their origin; nay many of them have as fair a complexion as many of the haughty Creole females.' Bernard observes that marriage 'between the white and coloured population is forbidden by the law of the state. As the quadroons on their part regard the negroes and mulattoes with contempt, and will not mix with them, so nothing remains for them but to be the friends, as it is termed, of the white men. The female quadroon looks upon such an engagement as a matrimonial contract.' The preference for white men and apparent whiteness of the mixed-race women that Bernard saw and documented became a common component in fictional tragic mulatto narratives and persisted well into the twentieth century (Bernard 61–2).

It was the English intellectual Harriet Martineau, however, who actually published the first accounts of New Orleans quadroons that furnish two clear prototypes of the tragic narrative arc that became fixed in fiction. Martineau's source for the first of these variations is apocryphal. It tells of a man from New

Hampshire who migrated to Louisiana to acquire and run a plantation. Once in Louisiana, he 'followed another custom there; taking a Quadroon wife: a mistress, in the eye of the law'. The two lived together happily for 20 years, but the woman was not free, and she implored the man to formally manumit the three daughters they had together. Mother and father died in quick succession, leaving their three teenaged 'beautiful girls, with no perceptible mulatto tinge', to the mercy of the auction block to settle their father's debts. The girls are shocked to learn of their slave status, but neither they nor a sympathetic uncle from New Hampshire can prevent their being 'sold, separately, at high prices, for the vilest of purposes' (Martineau 2:114–116). The revelation of enslaved status and sale into sexual slavery subsequently became standard in numerous works of fiction featuring the tragic mulatta, including Lydia Maria Child's short story 'The Quadroons' and Dion Boucicault's play 'The Octoroon'.

The second of Martineau's quadroon accounts is presented as fact, the fruit of her visit to New Orleans in the early 1830s. 'The Quadroon connexions in New Orleans are all but universal, as I was assured on the spot by ladies who cannot be mistaken,' she explains. Martineau repeats the standard assumption that quadroon women would have no relations with mixed-race men, reporting their response to the prospect as 'ils sont si degoutants!' (They are so disgusting!) According to Martineau, the relationship with the white lover 'now and then lasts for life: usually for several years', but most ended in tragedy: '[W]hen the time comes for the gentleman to take a white wife, the dreadful news reaches his Quadroon partner, either by a letter entitling her to call the house and furniture her own, or by the newspaper which announces his marriage.' Their abandonment for a white wife ended the quadroon's life, figuratively and sometimes literally: 'The Quadroon ladies are rarely or never known to form a second connexion. Many commit suicide: more die broken-hearted' (Martineau 2:326–7). The inevitable abandonment that most quadroons experienced at the hands of their caddish white lovers that Martineau introduced as fact was to become a standard plot point in tragic mulatta fiction.

Both Martineau and Bernard visited New Orleans at a time when liaisons between white men and mixed-race women were particularly numerous and visible. In 1809, some 10,000 refugees of the Haitian Revolution poured into New Orleans. A third of them were free people of colour, most of these women and children. Refugee and refugee-descended women who arrived without partners or resources lacked the security that most New Orleans–born free women of colour enjoyed. In the 1820s, they were as likely to marry as white women were, the legacy of a deeply rooted tradition of sacramental marriage among the city's free people of colour. The hundreds of entries in the St. Louis Cathedral marriage register documenting the marriages between free men and women of colour contradict Bernard's observation that 'the quadroons on their part regard the negroes and mulattoes with contempt, and will not mix with them'. However, relatively few refugee and refugee-descended women found the security and respectability that marriage conferred. The city's free men of colour married women from New Orleans, whose resources and social connections offered far more than a refugee could bring to a marriage (Clark). Bernard may have misapprehended the reasons for what he observed, but his assurance that 'nothing remains for them but to be the friends, as it is termed, of the white men' may have reflected a sad truth that inspired more than a little the fictional figure of the tragic mulatta that would soon emerge in antebellum American literature.

The Classic Tragic Mulatto

The fictional American tragic mulatto made its debut and enjoyed its first heyday in the nineteenth century, both before and after the Civil War. Antebellum writers used the figure of the light-skinned tragic mulatto to expose the evils of slavery and arouse the sympathies of white readers, who were less likely to be stirred to outrage by the suffering of darker-skinned protagonists with whom they could less easily identify. After the Civil War, the trope served to depict the persistence of racism and to illuminate the way in which it distorted American values and society, especially in the South.

Lydia Maria Child introduced a prototype of the tragic mulatta in 'Joanna', published in 1834 in the anti-slavery journal *The Oasis*. The piece is a compilation of extracts from the journal of Anglo-Dutch soldier John Gabriel Stedman, interleaved with commentary and exegesis by Child. Joanna was a 15-year old mulatto slave girl in Suriname who became Stedman's sexual partner in the 1770s. Stedman lacked the funds necessary to buy Joanna's freedom, but he pledged his fidelity to her in a religious ceremony and fathered a child on her. He was sent back to England before he could save the money to liberate her and while he was there, she died. Child drew on Stedman's diary to craft a morality tale about the evils of slavery tied to sexual exploitation and the impossibility of marriage and respectability for women of colour.

Child may have introduced the standard narrative of doomed love and tragedy to American audiences, but it was popular author Joseph Holt Ingraham who first made the United States the setting for the tragic mulatta narrative with the publication of his 1839 short story 'The Quadroon of Orleans'. While at prayer in St. Louis Cathedral in New Orleans, Emelie catches the eye of Baron Championet, a young French aristocrat who has come to the United States to flee the French Revolution. The Baron is surprised to learn that the beautiful, fair-cheeked woman who has stolen his heart is a quadroon, but he courts her nonetheless and establishes her as his mistress. He is called back to France, but settles a generous income on Emelie and promises that he will send for her. He does not, but the tragedy does not end there. When Emelie gives birth to Championet's daughter, Louise, she vows that the child will never know about her illegitimacy or her race. Emelie and her daughter move to Paris, where both pass as white and become the toast of the town.

Emelie, her vow and her daughter are, nonetheless, all doomed. Louise catches the eye of young Baron Caronde while at prayer in Notre Dame Cathedral. The two become engaged and proceed smoothly to their wedding.

Baron Caronde's father, who has been away at war, makes his way into the sanctuary as the ceremony ends. He is none other than Emelie's former lover and Louise's father, Baron Championet. Realizing the incestuous catastrophe that has just taken place, Emelie falls to the floor dead. Louise is sent to a nunnery, and Championet and his son meet their deaths soon afterwards in battle.

Emelie tried to forestall the inevitable fate of her mixed-race daughter, but other mothers of tragic mulatta figures surrendered to the inevitable course of their daughters' love lives and hoped for the best. The nameless protagonist of Armand Lanusse's 1843 short story 'Un Marriage du Conscience' is dispatched by her mother to a New Orleans ballroom frequented by white men. There she meets and falls in love with Gustave, who promises fidelity at a secret religious ceremony, a 'marriage of conscience'. Nevertheless, Gustave proves a cad and informs her that he plans to marry a white woman. The heartbroken mulatta is trampled by the horses bearing Gustave and his wife through the streets of New Orleans before she can tell the white wife who she is.

Lydia Maria Child's 1842 short story 'The Quadroons' is often recognized as the first example of the American literary tragic mulatta narrative, although it essentially recapitulates the tragic arc and character development that Ingraham introduced in his 'Quadroon of Orleans'. Child's story is set in Georgia, where the quadroon beauty Rosalie and the young white bachelor Edward fall in love. Rosalie agrees to live with Edward in an unofficial conjugal arrangement in a little cottage near Columbus, Georgia. In due course a daughter, Xarifa, is born and the family enjoys a decade of happiness. Then Edward abandons his secret family to marry a white woman whose influential father can help him realize his political ambitions. Rosalie soon dies of a broken heart. Descendants of Rosalie's owners claim Xarifa as their property and auction her off as a sex slave. Xarifa subsequently succumbs to insanity and dies.

The anti-slavery critique of the tragic mulatta reaches its most explicitly political expression in William Wells Brown's 1853 *Clotel*. An escaped mixed-race slave himself, Brown attacks slavery and the sexual exploitation of enslaved women without restraint. Set in Natchez, New Orleans and Richmond, *Clotel* features multiple figures who qualify as tragic mulattas: Currer, the mistress of Thomas Jefferson, and her daughters, Clotel and Althesa. Clotel lives happily with her white lover and bears him a daughter, but like the feckless Edward of Lydia Maria Child's short story, he abandons Clotel to marry a white woman. The white bride discovers the existence of Clotel and demands that she be sold on. Clotel commits suicide by jumping into the Potomac.

The climactic appearance of the tragic mulatta came in 1859 with the staging of Dion Boucicault's melodrama 'The Octoroon'. Like others before her, the heroine Zoe allows herself to fall in love with a white man, George. Their love is thwarted not only by her race, but also by the lascivious scheming of the overseer, M'Closky. Zoe is mistaken as white by George who, when Zoe reveals her race in response to his proposal of marriage, declares that he will elope with her to a foreign country. Before George can execute his plan, M'Closky unearths documents that prove that a debt of Zoe's deceased father nullifies her manumission and requires that she be sold to satisfy the creditor. In a fraught auction scene that sees the demure Zoe placed on the block for a packed room to ogle, M'Closky succeeds in outbidding her lover George. In New York, where the play debuted, Zoe takes poison and dies rather than subject herself to M'Closky's sexual predations, adhering to the standard tragic mulatta narrative arc. When the drama was performed in London, where mixed marriages were legal, the play ended happily with the marriage of Zoe and George.

Stock plot elements inform these and other antebellum tales of the doomed mixed-race woman. A young woman grows up knowing that she is of mixed race but allows herself to fall in love with a white man anyway. He pledges eternal fidelity in a relationship sanctified by their love and often blessed by a religious ceremony, but soon opts for respectability and marriage to a white woman. Heartbreak and suicide ensue. Or the white suitor remains faithful, but is unable to save his beloved from enslavement.

The messages that these narratives convey are consistent. Slavery makes it impossible for women of African descent to enjoy the safety and security guaranteed to white women through marriage. They are subject to men's basest desires and destined either for a life of sexual bondage or death. The effectiveness of tragic mulatta stories as anti-slavery literature depended on a shared ideal of respectable womanhood that turned on sexual continence. For women of the emergent middle class in antebellum America, North and South, sex outside of marriage vitiated their position as the family's moral anchor and the lodestar of the nation's virtue. Free married white women could fulfil their role as brake and censure on their husbands' baser instincts, ensuring the nation's survival as a paragon of freedom.

The tragic mulatta did not disappear from American literature after the Civil War. The figure was taken up by both those who championed racial reconciliation and those who reasserted white supremacy and segregation in the wake of emancipation. The sexual exploitation of black women and the Oedipal tragedy that ensued when white fathers and mixed-race children failed to recognize one another often figure prominently in the plots of postbellum works, and passing and incest become more frequent themes.

Lydia Maria Child's novel *A Romance of the Republic* sketches a prescription for the re-unification of the nation through racial mixing. The protagonists of this 1867 work are Rosa and Flora Royal, beautiful and cultivated young women who discover on their father's death that their mother was a slave, making both of them slaves and mulattas. Gerald Fitzgerald, a white man, pledges fidelity to Rosa in the kind of unofficial wedding ceremony familiar from antebellum narratives. Fitzgerald follows a typical trajectory by taking a legal white bride. Both women bear Fitzgerald a son at the same time and Rosa switches the infants. Her biological son enjoys the upbringing of a white man and Fitzgerald's white son grows up as a man of colour and marries a mixed-race woman. Both Flora and Rosa eventually marry white men, but Rosa's peace of mind is temporarily disturbed when her biological son begins to court the daughter she has borne her white husband. The kind of incestuous catastrophe that ended Ingraham's 'The Quadroon of Orleans' looms. It is conveniently averted when Rosa's biological son is informed of his true parentage and race. He not only aborts his plans to marry Rosa's daughter, but also joins the Union army and dies in the Civil War.

George Washington Cable's novella *Madame Delphine* likewise deployed an exchange of babies and passing to illustrate the immorality of those who insisted on absurd racial distinctions and the futility of policing procreation across the colour line. The eponymous protagonist bears a daughter to a white man. He dies abroad and she sends the infant to his family, who take her in despite her mixed race. When they die, Delphine takes back her daughter, Olive. The white father, Capitaine Lemaitre, in fact did not die and returns to New Orleans under a different surname. Without disclosing his identity to Madame Delphine, he promises her that he will find a suitable white husband for Olive. The white father effectively returns from the grave to re-write the story of his own doomed love for Delphine. He succeeds in finding a willing husband, but when his family discovers that Olive is not the white woman she appears to be, Delphine is driven to construct a lie that ensures her daughter's happiness even as it dooms her to heartbreak. She calls on the family of the groom and shows them pictures of Capitaine Lemaitre and his sister, to whom Olive bears a striking resemblance, claiming that they are the young woman's true parents. The ruse works. Olive marries the white suitor and Madame Delphine, heartbroken, goes into seclusion.

In the twentieth century, the central tragedy attaching to the tragic mulatta is her inability to reconcile herself to her African ancestry and her futile attempt to become white by passing. The prominence and proliferation of passing as a theme were in part a consequence of the sensational Rhinelander case of 1925, which introduced a broader American public to the phenomenon and its potential to engender misfortune for mixed-race people who attempted it. Leonard Rhinelander, the scion of a prominent New York family, married Alice Jones, a mixed-race woman, in 1924. He initially proclaimed, 'We are indeed very happy. What difference does it make about her race? She's my wife, Mrs Rhinelander.' Family protest quickly led Rhinelander to reverse course and seek an annulment based on his claim that Jones had hidden her true racial background from her husband and allowed him to think that she was white. At court, Jones was effectively tried for passing, and although she eventually won the suit, the spectacular coverage of the trial turned it into an opportunity for Americans to be reminded of the case for and against sex across the colour line and the moral implications of passing at a time when these were matters of renewed interest. The Great Migration that brought thousands of African Americans from the South to the cities of the North after 1900 and the violent white supremacy movement that prompted it combined to draw Americans from all parts of the country into debates about race.[1]

African American author Nella Larsen references the Rhinelander case in her 1929 novel *Passing*. Set in New York, this follows two mixed-race women, Clare and Irene. Clare, who passes for white, encourages her friend Irene to attempt to do so too. Irene resists, marries a black man and makes a life in Harlem. Clare seeks her out and becomes increasingly drawn to the African American community of which Irene is a part. Clare's white husband is ignorant of her racial ancestry, and Irene warns her that as she becomes more involved with the African American community she raises the risk of her husband discovering her secret. The white husband, who has already revealed himself to be a racist, in due course does discover his wife's racial background. In a confrontation at a party hosted by a dark-skinned woman, he confronts Clare as she sits at an open widow. She falls, or is pushed, through the window and falls to her death.

Other tragic mulattas of the 1920s and 1930s who attempt to pass meet similar fates. Julie, the heroine of Edna Ferber's 1926 novel *Show Boat*, despairs when she discovers that she is of partial African ancestry. Although her white husband ritually makes himself 'black' by cutting her hand and sucking her blood, Julie is never reconciled to her new racial identity and descends into hopeless alcoholism. Solaria in Vara Caspary's 1929 novel *The White Girl* passes for white, but her racial secret is betrayed by the arrival of her dark-skinned brother, and her life ends, like that of many antebellum tragic mulattas before her, in suicide.

The male tragic mulatto, who barely makes an appearance in antebellum literature, figures more frequently in racist postbellum plots, but usually as an agent of tragedy rather than its victim. Silas Lynch, in Thomas Dixon's white supremacist novel *The Clansman*, is portrayed as a lascivious, self-serving man with ideas above the racial station assigned him. Dixon presents his desire to marry a white woman as terrible proof of what can happen when white men give in to their own sexual craving and father sons who will grow up to desire and rape their white daughters, sisters and wives.

William Faulkner's compelling and disturbing *Absalom, Absalom!* is the most artful twentieth-century Southern Gothic novel built around the standard themes and plot points of tragic mulatta literature, although the protagonist, Thomas Sutpen, is a white man. Passing, incest, madness and tragic death weave their way into the convoluted narrative, twisting, wounding and ending the lives of a large cast of characters. Among these are two mixed-race characters: Charles Bon, the son borne to Sutpen by a free woman of colour in Saint-Domingue, and Clytie, Sutpen's daughter by one of his slaves. Both Bon and Clytie travel the tragic mulatto's well-worn path to disaster. Bon is spared from making an incestuous marriage, only to be murdered by his half-brother. Clytie dies in a fire she sets in a doomed effort to save the last remnant of Sutpen's white family. In an ending baldly evocative of Edgar Allen Poe's gothic short story 'Fall of the House of Usher', Sutpen's white supremacist dynastic dreams die in the literal destruction of the family mansion by Clytie's fire.

After the Second World War, the mixed-race woman continued to surface as a protagonist, and while her fate does not invariably lead to tragedy, some of the standard plot points of the tragic mulatta tale persisted. In Robert Penn Warren's 1955 novel *Band of Angels*, Amantha Starr, the daughter of a plantation owner in antebellum Kentucky, grows up believing that she is white and free. When her father dies, she discovers that her mother was his slave and that she is now to be auctioned off to the highest bidder. Her white buyer falls in love with her, and after the trials and dangers of the Civil War, the two find happiness together in the North.

Twenty-first-century fiction continues to conjure the features of the tragic mulatta, but often provides a happy ending. In Isabel Allende's 2009 novel *Island Beneath the Sea*, the mixed-race daughter and white son of a sugar planter find one another in New Orleans after the Haitian Revolution and fall in love. Rosette and Maurice discover that they share the same father, but they thumb their noses at the incest taboo that doomed earlier tragic mulatta characters and announce that they will marry and move to Boston. At their wedding a friend raises a toast: 'To this symbolic couple of the future, when races will be mixed and all human beings will be free and equal under the law' (Allende 432).

Notes

1. Miriam Thaggert,. 'Racial Etiquette: Nella Larsen's "Passing and the Rhinelander Case" '. *Meridians* 5:2 (2005): 1–29, provides an excellent discussion of the Rhinelander case, its historical context and its influence on literature.

Bibliography

Allende, I. (2010). *Island beneath the sea* (trans: Peden, M.S.). New York: Harper Collins. Originally published as *La Isla Bajo el Mar*. Barcelona: Random House, 2009.

Ashe, T. (1808). *Travels in America performed in 1806, for the purpose of exploring the rivers Alleghany, Monongahela, Ohio, and Mississippi, and ascertaining the produce and condition of their banks and vicinity*. London: R. Phillips.

Bernard, K. (1828). *Travels through North America, during the years 1825 and 1826*. Philadelphia: Carey, Lea & Carey.

Boucicault, Dion. n.d. The Octoroon; A play, in Four Acts. In *Dicks' London acting edition of standard English plays and comic dramas*. New York: De Witt Publishing House.

Cable, G. W. (1881). *Madame Delphine*. New York: C. Scribner's sons.

Caspary, V. (1929). *The white girl*. New York: J.H. Sears & Company.

Child, L. M. (1834). Joanna. In *The oasis* (pp. 65–104). Boston: Benjamin C. Bacon.

Child, L. M. (1842). The Quadroons. In *Liberty bell* (pp. 115–141). Boston: Massachusetts Anti-Slavery Fair.

Child, L. M. (1867). *A romance of the Republic*. Boston: Ticknor and Fields.

Clark, E. (2013). *The strange history of the American Quadroon: Free women of color in the revolutionary Atlantic World*. Chapel Hill: University of North Carolina Press.

Clarke, E. D. (1813, January). Spirit of magazines. Description of the Seraglio of the Grand Signior. From Clarke's Travels, Part 2. In *The Analetic Magazine* 1, American Periodicals, 48.

Faulkner, W. (1936). *Absalom, Absalom!* New York: Random House.

Ferber, E. (1926). *Show boat*. New York: Grosset & Dunlap.

Ingraham, J. H. (1839). The quadroon of Orleans. In *The American lounger, or tales, sketches and legends gathered in sundry journeyings* (pp. 255–271). Philadelphia: Lea and Blanchard, Successors to Carey & Co.

Ingraham, J. H. (1841). *The Quadroone; or, St. Michael's Day*. New York: Harper & Brothers.

Larsen, N. (1929). *Passing*. New York: Knopf.

Martineau, H. (1837). *Society in America* (Vol. 2). London: Saunders and Otley.

Montagu, M. W. (1763). *Letters of the right honourable lady M--y W---y M----e]: Written during her travels in Europe, Asia and Africa*. London: T. Beckett & P. A. de Hondt.

Moreau de Saint-Méry, Médéric Louis Elie. (1797). *Description Topographique, Physique, Civile, Politique Et Historique De La Partie Francaise De l'Isle Saint-Domingue. Avec Des Observations Generales Sur Sa Population, Sur Le Caractere & Les Murs De Ses Divers Habitans; Sur Son Climat, Sa Culture, Ses Productions, Son Administration, &c*. Philadelphie: Chez l'auteur.

Thaggert, M. (2005). Racial Etiquette: Nella Larsen's "Passing and the Rhinelander Case". *Meridians*, 5(2), 1–29.

Warren, R. P. (1955). *Band of angels*. New York: Random House.

FURTHER READING

Brown, S. A. (1937). *The Negro in American fiction*. Washington, DC: The Associates in Negro Folk Education.

Brown, S. A. (1933). Negro character as seen by white authors. *Journal of Negro Education, 2*, 179–203.

Brown's early analyses of African Americans in literature are foundational to the study of the tragic mulatta and remain useful.

Gross, A. J. (2008). *What blood won't tell: A history of race on trial in America*. Cambridge, MA: Harvard University Press.

Legal historians have recently been especially active in the deconstruction of race, miscegenation and passing. Gross's study has been very influential in historical studies of legal racial discourse that shaped both the lives of mixed-race people and the literary fiction about them.

Raimon, E. A. (2004). *The 'Tragic Mulatta' revisited: Race and nationalism in nineteenth-century antislavery fiction*. New Brunswick: Rutgers University Press.

This sophisticated analysis investigates the cultural and political work that the literary tragic mulatta advanced in the intersection of race and nation-making.

Sharfstein, D. J. (2011). *The invisible line: Three American families and the secret journey from black to white*. New York: Penguin Press.

Like Ariella Gros, Sharfstein is a legal historian. He explores the phenomenon of passing via the family histories of mixed-race Americans.

Sollors, W. (1997). *Neither black nor white yet both : Thematic explorations of interracial literature*. New York: Oxford University Press.

This study by one of the most distinguished analysts of the role of race in American literature is packed with brilliant analysis and offers an exhaustive catalogue of works featuring mixed-race people.

Wald, G. (2000). *Crossing the line: Racial passing in twentieth-century U.S. Literature and culture*. Durham: Duke University Press.

A series of imaginatively analysed case studies explores the social and psychological project of making racial identity in a changing historical context.

CHAPTER 21

Law and the Gothic in the Slaveholding South

Ellen Weinauer

A brief glance at laws regarding enslaved persons and cases brought before various Southern courts offers up a catalogue of real-life horrors that eclipses those that we might find in any gothic narrative. Whether involving prohibitions against civic and civil rights (literacy, property ownership, representation in court, marriage), punishments for alleged crimes, or the practical lack of genuine recourse against cruel and inhumane treatment, the laws that governed the institution of slavery and those held within its grasp demonstrate the kind of terrifying 'no exit' with which readers of the Gothic would have been familiar.

Let us take, for example, the (increasingly elaborate and restrictive) penal codes that developed across slave-holding states in the eighteenth and nineteenth centuries. Since imprisonment was both redundant and counterproductive – slaves were already denied personal freedom, and a prison sentence would simply deprive the owner of the slave's labor – and since the vast majority of slaves lacked the wherewithal to pay fines, such codes typically laid out extreme physical punishments for slaves convicted of acts deemed criminal. According to laws in both Virginia and Mississippi, for instance, a slave who gave 'false testimony' would have first one ear and then the other nailed to the pillory for an hour, 'then have both ears cut off, and receive thirty-nine lashes' (Farnham 185). A North Carolina statute specified that a slave convicted of hunting on his master's property 'is subjected to a whipping of thirty lashes' (qtd in Goodell 313). In Mississippi, similar punishments would be meted out to slaves convicted of keeping a dog or riding on horseback without the master's permission; and in Maryland, slaves could be whipped, cropped, or branded with the letter 'R' for riding on horseback in the daytime or for 'rambling, riding, or going abroad in the night' (Stroud 104–5). In the words of anti-slavery activist William Goodell, who published an important compendium of slave

E. Weinauer (✉)
University of Southern Mississippi, Hattiesburg, MS, USA

S.C. Street, C.L. Crow (eds.), *The Palgrave Handbook of the Southern Gothic*,
DOI 10.1057/978-1-137-47774-3_21

codes in 1853, the slave 'is under the *control* of law, though *unprotected by* law, and can know law only as an enemy, not as a friend' (309). Excessive, often unpredictable, and arbitrary, the law functioned to create a real-life universe for enslaved persons that had its fictional parallels in the dark, twisting labyrinths, locked rooms, blocked exits, colluding despots, and gory tortures of the popular Gothic. As Teresa Goddu asserts, 'the African-American experience' in slavery 'resembles a gothic narrative'; the Gothic, therefore, offers 'a useful vocabulary and register of images by which to represent the scene of America's greatest guilt: slavery' (131, 133).[1]

While ever mindful of the dangers of relying on fictional tropes to make urgent political and moral arguments,[2] anti-slavery writers appeared willing to make use of this ready vocabulary early on. Indeed, gothic conventions and figures inform a wide body of anti-slavery literature, from works of fiction such as Stowe's *Uncle Tom's Cabin* (1852), William Wells Brown's *Clotel* (1853), and Hannah Crafts's *The Bondwoman's Narrative* (ca. 1850s) to slave narratives such as Douglass's 1845 *Narrative* and Jacobs's *Incidents in the Life of a Slave-Girl* (1861).[3] Nor is the use of such conventions to describe the realities of slavery solely the province of anti-slavery writers. In *The Confessions of Nat Turner*, for example, an allegedly confessional account of 'the origin, progress and consummation' of the rebellion that terrorized Southampton County, Virginia in 1831, Thomas Gray – Turner's interlocutor and the editor of the confession – presents Turner as a bloodthirsty gothic villain, the 'diabolical' leader of a 'fiendish band' of 'remorseless murderers' actuated by 'hellish purposes' (Gray 428, 427). Turner describes the pleasure he takes in his murderous acts – 'I … viewed the mangled bodies as they lay, in silent satisfaction, and immediately started in quest of other victims' – and, in a statement that could as well come from the mouth of one of Radcliffe's confessing antagonists as from that of a slave rebel, declares his intentions: 'it'twas my object to carry terror and devastation wherever we went,' he proclaims (437).[4]

While I am intrigued by the differing purposes that the Gothic could serve in antebellum texts about slavery, I am particularly interested in how anti-slavery texts work to expose the role that the law plays in crafting slavery's gothic story. In such texts, the law itself becomes a kind of gothic villain, exerting a seemingly absolute and inescapable control over the lives of the enslaved. Yet even as anti-slavery texts – along with such other texts as legal treatises, laws, and judicial decisions – register and record the law's suffocating power, they also simultaneously recognize the ways in which, in the words of Leslie Moran, law becomes 'a living archive through which the present may be haunted by a specific past as a logic of evil acts, corruption, monstrosity, dread and terror' (105). Despite – or, perhaps more accurately, because of – the efforts to contain and control slave agency, the antebellum Southern present is one always already haunted by the 'evil acts' performed in slavery's name, the 'dread and terror' that the institution visits on the 'free' as well as the enslaved.

THE HAUNTED SOUTHERN PSYCHE

In *Democracy in America* (1835), Alexis de Tocqueville offers a gothic rendition of the effects of slavery on the American psyche: 'The danger of a conflict between the white and the black inhabitants of the Southern states of the Union,' he writes, 'perpetually haunts the imagination of the Americans, like a painful dream' (376). According to Tocqueville, this danger – 'which, however remote it may be, is inevitable' – has differential effects: while the 'inhabitants of the North make it a common topic of conversation':

> In the Southern states the subject is not discussed: the planter does not allude to the future in conversing with strangers; he does not communicate his apprehensions to his friends; he seeks to conceal them from himself; but there is something more alarming in the tacit forebodings of the South, than in the clamorous fears of the North. (376)

While Tocqueville here recognizes how slavery subjects the American imagination to a kind of generalized haunting, he also notes the ways in which fears of slave insurrection might affect the Southern slaveholding mind in particular: unspoken but ever present, repressed but never fully quelled, the 'apprehension' of slave revolt produces what the prescient Tocqueville renders as a 'haunted' Southern psyche, tormented by an 'all-pervading disquietude' (376) that must be denied but cannot be escaped.

Tocqueville also recognizes the tools deployed in the South to manage this irrepressible 'disquietude,' among which is a legal system that 'betray[s] the desperate position of the community in which that legislation has been promulgated' (379). The law serves as a marker of secreted fears, a daylight eruption of nighttime terrors. While to some extent traceable specifically to efforts to quell slave insurrection – as might be expected, instances of organized slave revolt often resulted in new, more repressive legislation – by and large, as Henry Farnham observes, such laws 'had their real justification in the institution of slavery itself and were practically universal' (188) across the slave states. In the words of legal historian Lawrence Friedman, 'Slave law ... had its own inner logic. Its object was repression and control. Everything tended toward this end. Every door was shut to Negro advancement' (201). A quick look at some of the chapter titles from Goodell's *American Slave Code* reveals a variety of such shut doors: 'Slaves Can Possess Nothing,' 'Slaves Cannot Marry,' 'Slaves Cannot Constitute Families,' 'Unlimited Power of Slaveholders,' 'The Slave Cannot Sue His Master,' 'No Power of Self-Redemption or Change of Masters,' 'No Access to the Judiciary,' 'Subjection to All White Persons,' 'Education Prohibited,' 'Free Social Worship and Religious Instruction Prohibited' (Goodell, 'Contents' iii–ix). Nor can this stunningly totalizing depiction of the law's effort to render the slave powerless be attributed simply to Goodell's anti-slavery sensibility. Evidence for these prohibitions, liabilities, and disabilities abounds in the law itself, as legal treatises and histories of

American law, both early and late, attest. There is, in short, abundant evidence for Tocqueville's claim that 'The legislation of the Southern states with regard to slaves presents at the present day such unparalleled atrocities as suffice to show that the laws of humanity have been totally perverted' (379).

THE FORCE OF THE LAW

Many anti-slavery texts are fuelled by moments of recognition of the law's twisted and absolute force in the lives of enslaved people – and many of those moments are also rendered in gothic terms. This should come as no surprise since, from its origins and earliest developments, the Gothic has been 'obsessed with the law, with its operations, justifications, limits' (Punter 19).[5] In *Uncle Tom's Cabin*, for example, Cassy offers a speech rich in gothic vocabulary to the whipped and wounded Tom about the ghastly prison that Legree's plantation has become. Ministering to Tom's injuries in the 'old forsaken room of the gin-house, among pieces of broken machinery, piles of damaged cotton, and other rubbish,' Cassy counsels Tom to 'give up' all thought of resistance and surrender to Legree, for he is 'in the devil's hands' (Stowe 1852, 510–11). Rendered faithless by the five years she has spent under Legree's despotic rule – 'body and soul, under this man's foot' (512) – Cassy sees no possibility of relief, whether human or divine:

> Here you are, on a lone plantation, ten miles from any other, in the swamps; not a white person here, who could testify, if you were burned alive, – if you were scalded, cut into inch-pieces, set up for the dogs to tear, or hung up and whipped to death. There's no law here, of God or man, that can do you, or any one of us, the least good. I could make any one's hair rise, and their teeth chatter, if I should only tell what I've seen and been knowing to, here, – and it's no use resisting!' (512)

Cassy will, of course, go on to resist. Abetted by Tom and inspired by both his otherworldly sacrifices and a latent maternal impulse, she orchestrates an escape plan for herself and the young female slave Emmeline that, famously, involves all manner of gothic devices: haunted tokens, mysterious passages through locked doors, ghostly visitations, unexplained footfalls.[6] Her escape notwithstanding, Cassy's remarks provide a trenchant analysis of the law's creation of a gothic existence for the slave, pointing as they do to the ways in which the law not only fails to protect the enslaved, but indeed positively ensures that the slave owner can abuse with impunity.

To be sure, most states had laws on the books that restricted cruel punishment and ill treatment of slaves; but such protections, as Cassy is well aware, were hardly worthy of the name, for enforcement was rare, and loopholes and constraints were plentiful. According to Louisiana law, for example, a white person could be prosecuted for the 'mutilation, severe ill-treatment, or killing of a slave' (Schafer 30). Moreover, since slaves were largely prohibited from testifying against whites in court, as Cassy acknowledges in her remarks to

Tom, the law included a provision designed to protect the slave in the absence of white witnesses to such abuses. In this instance, in order to be acquitted of criminal violence, the slave owner had to offer proof of innocence. That proof, however, was not hard to come by, since a slave owner 'prosecuted under such circumstances could clear himself "by his own oath"' (Schafer 30). Friedman provides a useful gloss on the ways in which the law offers with one hand what it takes away with the other: 'The rights of slaves were narrow, and not often invoked,' he explains. 'These rights gave Southern law the appearance of justice, without upsetting the real social order. Had these rights been widely used, or used beyond the limits of Southern toleration, they would not have survived, even on paper' (199). Cassy's declaration to Tom that 'I could make any one's hair rise, and their teeth chatter, if I should only tell what I've seen and been knowing to, here, – and it's no use resisting!' (512) can thus be read in multiple ways. Of course, she is referring here to the 'true' gothic stories that she could tell about the particular brutality of life for slaves on Legree's plantation. However, the law plays a key role in these gothic stories, entrapping the slave by offering 'protections' that not only fail to protect, but also remind the slave over and over again, precisely through that failure to protect, that 'it's no use resisting.'

While they may be based in fact (as Stowe's *Key to Uncle Tom's Cabin* took pains to assert), Cassy's gothic stories are just that – stories, fictionalized accounts. By contrast, the 'teeth-chattering' and 'hair-raising' tales that Harriet Jacobs relays in *Incidents in the Life of a Slave-Girl* are, as Jean Fagan Yellin long ago established, autobiographical. Like Cassy (and Stowe, working behind her), Jacobs – using Linda Brent as her pseudonymous narrator – draws on the Gothic to tell her story; but unlike Cassy, Jacobs must repeatedly remind the reader that she is 'a person rather than a character' and work to resist the 'gothic's dematerializing effects' (Goddu 149, 148). Along the way, Jacobs offers a searing indictment of the role that the law plays in slavery's gothic story. As is well known, *Incidents* brings to light the sexual depredations at the heart of the slave experience, recounting the drawn-out, depraved, but legally sanctioned sexual assault to which Dr. Flint subjects Linda Brent. As Flint initiates that assault – Jacobs depicts him as a relentless and nearly inescapable villain, Linda as a feisty, resourceful, eminently capable gothic heroine – Linda reflects, as does Cassy, on the closed door of the law:

> My soul revolted against the mean tyranny. But where could I turn for protection? No matter whether the slave girl be as black as ebony or as fair as her mistress. In either case, there is no shadow of law to protect her from insult, from violence, or even from death; all of these are inflicted by fiends who bear the shape of men. (Jacobs 27)

In the absence of legal protections, Linda understands the value of living in a 'town not so large that the inhabitants were ignorant of each other's affairs. Bad as are the laws and customs in a slaveholding community, the doctor, as a professional man, deemed it prudent to keep up some outward show of decency' (29). Yet if Linda is shielded to some extent by the nature of her community and the prominent role that her grandmother has played in it, this protection is arbitrary, unreliable. The community may protect her, should it choose to do so, but the law certainly will not.

Jacobs goes out of her way to document the capricious unreliability of community sanction in a chapter entitled 'Sketches of Neighboring Slaveholders.' Providing a sort of catalogue of slavery's ghastly cruelties, this chapter is famous in part for the strong editorial role played in it by Lydia Maria Child. Child advised Jacobs to take the 'savage cruelties' scattered throughout *Incidents* and consolidate them into one chapter, 'in order that those who shrink from "supping on horrors" might omit them, without interrupting the thread of the story' (qtd in Sorisio 77). Horrors indeed abound in what Jacobs calls the 'cage of obscene birds' (Jacobs 52), from whippings and starvation to exposure and rape. Jacobs's flat declaration that '[c]ruelty is contagious in uncivilized communities' (47) serves not only to qualify the idea that her community can offer her protection (if that community is 'uncivilized,' how much protection can it actually offer?), but also to impugn the legal system that is supposed to serve as a distinguishing hallmark of a 'civilized' society.

To both these ends, Jacobs describes 'Mr. Litch,' a planter who lives 'not far from us' on a large plantation: 'There was a jail and a whipping post on his grounds; and whatever cruelties were perpetrated there, they passed without comment. He was so effectually screened by his great wealth that he was called to no account for his crimes, not even for murder' (46). Yet while the community fails to call Litch to 'account,' Jacobs uses her narrative to do so, insisting on a power of witness, and indeed of judgment, that the law would deny her. Saidiya Hartman has noted the ways in which 'the quotidian terror of the antebellum world made difficult the discernments of socially tolerable violence vs. criminal violence. How did one identify "cruel" treatment in a context in which routine acts of barbarism were considered not only reasonable but also necessary?' (97). By defining Litch's actions as 'crimes' and the deaths of slaves on his plantation as 'murder,' Jacobs certainly presents herself as an able discerner. More significantly, however, here she also rejects the perverse legal logic of slavery. From early on, David Punter observes, gothic writers were 'absorbed' by the 'problem of how the criminal can be distinguished from the wielder of unjust but legalised power' (39). In the world of the Gothic, Punter goes on, punishments are often meted out by 'a system of laws too stringent for human wellbeing'; those who 'suffer under these deadly systems become deeply confused about their own legality' and begin to feel 'criminalised regardless of the innocence of [their] actions' (39).

While Linda Brent feels shame because of Flint's predation – and struggles with the moral implications of her decision to have sex with another white man, Mr. Sands, in order to elude her predator – she is never 'confused' about her own 'legality.' In fact, she rejects categorically the system of laws that governs her, and therefore dismantles the ostensible difference between 'socially tolerable violence' and 'criminal violence.' Indeed, for Linda/Jacobs, the very idea that there is a 'socially tolerable violence' – an idea central, as we have seen, to the workings of the slave system – reveals the corruption at the institution's heart. In Jacobs's rendition, the violence (both verbal and physical) enacted on the slave by the slave owner is *always* criminal, based as it is on the fundamental denial of slave humanity. Using the ready justification of what the laws of slavery allow, Flint reminds Linda over and over again that 'I was his property; that I must be subject to his will in all things' (Jacobs 27).

Linda recounts a particularly humiliating encounter with Flint, 'whose restless, craving, vicious nature roved about day and night, seeking whom to devour' and who had recently been filling her ears 'with stinging, scorching words; words that scathed ear and brain like fire' (18). Noting the violence of Flint's speech act, she goes on to defy his right to inflict it on her: 'When he told me that I was made for his use, made to obey his command in *every* thing; that I was nothing but a slave, whose will must and should surrender to his, never before had my puny arm felt half so strong' (18). In a dizzying act of mental defiance, Linda refuses the 'deadly system' of slavery, a circular system that would first deny her humanity, and then enforce that denial through an elaborate legal code from which (given the first proposition) there is no recourse, exit, or escape. In an essay treating 'Law and the Gothic Imagination,' Leslie Moran takes note of a key 'manifestation of law' in gothic literature: 'law as a form of violence through which the social order is made possible' (88). Jacobs's gothic treatment of legal failures in *Incidents* – the law fails to protect the slave; further, and deeper, the law redefines as 'socially tolerable' the criminal violence enacted on enslaved persons – reveals her incisive critical awareness of the law as itself a 'form of violence,' one on which the very 'social order' of slavery depends.

STATE V. MANN

Perhaps no judicial decision exemplifies the perversity of a system that requires legally sanctioned violence – or, perhaps more precisely, that obviates entirely the possibility of 'criminal' violence in the context of slavery – as well as *State v. Mann* (1829), a case brought before the North Carolina Supreme Court that, interestingly, had its origins in Jacobs's own community of Edenton, North Carolina. John Mann, a sailor living in Edenton, had been found guilty by a jury of assault and battery on a slave named Lydia, whom Mann had hired from Elizabeth Jones. Mann sought to discipline Lydia by whipping; when she resisted and ran away, he shot her in the back, leaving her injured. At Mann's trial, the judge instructed the jury to bear in mind that, as a hirer rather than an owner, Mann had only a 'special property' in the slave and therefore more limited rights with regard to discipline and punishment. Mann was found guilty, but the North Carolina Supreme Court overturned the conviction. Writing for the majority, Judge Thomas Ruffin first did away with the standard distinction between slave owner and slave hirer – 'the hirer ... in relation to both rights and duties, is, for the time being, the owner' (*State v. Mann* 221) – and then went on to offer a devastating and notoriously bald justification for granting absolute power to the slave owner: 'The power of the master must be absolute, to render the submission of the slave perfect' and thus to keep the institution functioning (222). Professing his discomfort with this statement – 'I most freely confess my sense of the harshness of this proposition, I feel it as deeply as any man can' – Ruffin insists that the court must base its decision not on the 'principle of moral right' but rather, and only, on 'the actual condition of things' (222–3). And in light of the 'actual condition of things,' the master's authority must be unconditional and total: 'The slave, to remain a slave, must be made sensible, that there is no appeal from his master; that his power is in no instance, usurped; but is conferred by the laws of man at least, if not by the law of God' (223).[7]

Ruffin's decision is notable in part for its 'tell it like it is' rendition of the legal necessities that follow from the institution of slavery itself; in light of that system, might may not make right, but it certainly *must* make law. Thus, Ruffin flatly observes, 'The end [of slavery] is the profit of the master, his security and the public safety; the subject, one doomed in his own person, and his posterity, to live without knowledge, and without the capacity to make any thing his own, and to toil that another may reap the fruits' (222). No 'moral considerations' can make this proposition palatable or true; it is folly, Ruffin suggests, to try to convince the slave that he should 'labour upon a principle of natural duty, or for the sake of his own personal happiness' (222). Rather, 'such services can only be expected from one who has no will of his own; who surrenders his will in implicit obedience to that of another. Such obedience is the consequence only of uncontrolled authority over the body. There is nothing else which can operate to produce the effect' (222). This is, Ruffin notes, a 'harsh' proposition, but in slavery, 'it must be so. There is no remedy. This discipline belongs to the state of slavery' (223).[8]

There is much to be said about this case and about Ruffin's decision, of course. While abolitionists deplored the court's findings, they also found the decision helpfully stark in its assertion that there was no higher law argument for slavery. In *A Key to Uncle Tom's Cabin*, for example, Harriet Beecher Stowe quotes at length from Ruffin's decision, citing the 'deep respect for the man and horror for the system' and expressing special admiration for Ruffin's 'straightforward determination not to call a bad thing by a good name, even when most popular, and reputable, and legal' (78–9).[9] For the purposes of this chapter, however, I am particularly interested in the bleak and terrifying – indeed, the gothic – features of the legal prison that Ruffin outlines for the slave. As in the Table of Contents in Goodell's *American Slave Code*, negatives proliferate in Ruffin's decision: the slave can have 'no will'; there is 'no appeal' from his master; the master's 'power' can be 'in no instance, usurped'; there 'is no remedy.' Those negatives point to the grim existential reality that slave law is meant to enforce. As Friedman explains with devastating understatement, 'the law dispensed with many niceties in exposing the slave to social control' (200).

Although *State v. Mann* is one of the most notable decisions outlining the legal mechanisms of the slave system, Ruffin's bleak limning of the 'impassable gulf' between 'freedom and slavery' – 'a greater [gulf] cannot be imagined,' he opines – did not stand alone. Drawing a similarly stark picture of the slave condition, the Louisiana 'Black Code' stipulated: 'The condition of a slave being merely a passive one, his subordination to his master and to all who represent him, is not susceptible to any modification or restriction, ... he owes to his master, and to all his family, a respect without bounds, and an absolute obedience' (qtd in Schafer 8). And in an 1847 South Carolina case, Justice J. L. Wardlaw insisted that, even in the absence of a statutory prohibition, a slave could be criminally prosecuted for 'insolent language and actions.' A 'freeman would have a right to demand that the law should be pointed to, which provides for the punishment of the act for which he is to be tried,' Wardlaw emphasized, but the slave has no such right or expectation: 'a slave can invoke neither *magna charta* nor common law.' The slave, then, must do the law's bidding – even when the law's stipulations are unspoken – for, '[i]n the very nature of things' the slave 'is subject to despotism. Law is to him only a compact between his rulers, and the questions which concern him are matters agitated between them' (qtd in Strobhart 42–3). In statute after statute and case after case, then, the law tells the slave 'No Exit'; by definition, the condition of enslavement means that all avenues for redress and protection are closed, all signs point to utter powerlessness. At every turn and in often mind-bogglingly disturbing ways, the enslaved is reminded that the law is 'an enemy, not ... a friend' (Goodell 309). In this light, slavery might well be understood as the classic gothic chamber, locked from the outside, with the law as the keeper of the key.

CONCLUSION

As the antagonists in virtually any gothic narrative recognize, their power is never failsafe. Indeed, the repressive disciplinary technologies of the Gothic point to the anxiety surrounding the exercise of absolute power (whether legal or otherwise), the chinks and gaps through which the objects of such power might escape and exercise agency. In this light, we might consider what Hartman calls the 'selective recognition of slave humanity' (80): the fact that in the domain of criminal law, the slave became, suddenly and paradoxically, a willful person. As Goodell notes,

> the slave, who is but '*a chattel*' on all *other* occasions, with not one solitary attribute of personality accorded to him, becomes '*a person*' whenever he is to be *punished! He* is the only being in the universe to whom is denied all self-direction and free agency but who is, nevertheless, held responsible for his conduct and amenable to law. (309, emphasis in the original)

Even as it is enlisted to quell the 'all-pervading disquietude' provoked by slavery in the white Southern mind, in other words, the law points to slave personhood and to the agency with which the enslaved are endowed. Such agency emerges intriguingly in *State v. Mann*, where Ruffin's insistence that the slave must be compelled to 'surrender' his will to the master's absolute power indicates, of course, that the slave has a will to surrender in the first place. Indeed, Ruffin essentially derides the idea that the slave might be convinced that it is a 'principle of natural duty' to serve whites; all but the 'most stupid must feel and know' that this 'can never be true' (*State v. Mann* 222), he states unequivocally. The absolutism and brutality of slave law, in other words, not only 'betray the desperate position of the community in which that legislation has been promulgated' (Tocqueville 379), but also betray that community's awareness that the effort to exorcise slave agency is doomed to be a futile one, for the slave's humanity can only be repressed – it cannot be denied. And in this way, the slave at law can be seen to possess a kind of haunting power. Harriet Jacobs acknowledges precisely this in her treatment of the savage Mr. Litch. Insisting again on her jurisdictive authority, Jacobs turns the law's gothic powers against its creators: 'Murder was so common on his plantation,' she asserts of Mr. Litch, 'that he feared to be alone after nightfall. He might have believed in ghosts' (47). While indicting Litch's savagery in particular, and the savagery of slaveholders in general, Jacobs at the same time repeatedly bears witness to the law's inability to hold her and her fellow slaves fully in its grasp. Like Tocqueville's perpetually haunted Southerners, Litch is right to fear the 'ghosts' that the laws of slavery produce, for those ghosts are not products of the imagination but are, rather, made of righteous flesh and blood.

NOTES

1. Although recognizing the ways in which slavery can be represented in a gothic register, in a recent study Siân Silyn Roberts takes issue with what she calls the 'guilt thesis' of American Gothic. That thesis, she asserts, 'succumbs to the mimetic fallacy that the gothic reflects deeply embedded social and political anxieties that precede their articulation in writing' (23). Roberts wants instead to grant the Gothic a more fully productive function, to recognize it as 'an important cultural site for the *formation* rather than merely the *reflection* of phobic categories' (22).
2. For a treatment of the 'dematerializing' and dehistoricizing risks of deploying the Gothic for anti-slavery purposes, see Goddu 134–7.
3. For critics who discuss such texts and their use of the Gothic, see, in addition to Goddu, Winter, *Subjects of Slavery, Agents of Change*; Marshall, *The Transatlantic Gothic Novel*; and Roberts, *Gothic Subjects*. Marshall focuses on the ways in which the law functions in gothic literature in both the United States and England.
4. More complicated in terms of motivation is the treatment of Turner from *The Liberator*, which in 1832 represented Turner as a 'sable fiend' who stands gloating over the corpses of a 'babe' whose 'bruised lips' are 'dashed with blood' and an 'unripened virgin' who lies on 'the cold hearth stone' (qtd in Sundquist 53). For my treatment of the complexities of Turner's legacy for the mainstream anti-slavery movement, see Weinauer, "Writing."

5. For other critics who document the Gothic's obsession with the law, see Further Reading.
6. For a thoughtful treatment of Cassy's gothic effects, see Goddu; and DeWaard. The latter offers an incisive analysis of the ways in which Stowe's treatment of Cassy denies her meaningful agency and 'reinforces the racialized violence of law' (5).
7. See Crane, *Race, Citizenship, and Law*, for an examination of the ways in which nineteenth-century writers and legal thinkers engaged and critiqued the positive law argument by drawing on a 'higher law constitutionalism.'
8. For treatments of *State v. Mann* specifically and the role of the judiciary in the slavery debate, see Tushnet; and Cover.
9. Ruffin and his decision in *State v. Mann* serve as key elements of plot and character in Stowe's 1856 novel, *Dred: A Tale of the Great Dismal Swamp*. For discussion, see Brophy; Korobkin; and Crane, 'Dangerous Sentiments.'

BIBLIOGRAPHY

Brophy, A. L. (1998). Humanity, utility, and logic in Southern legal thought: Harriet Beecher Stowe's vision in Dred: A tale of the Great Dismal Swamp. *Boston University Law Review, 78*, 1113–1161. Print.

Cover, R. M. (1975). *Justice accused: Antislavery and the judicial process.* New Haven/ London: Yale University Press. Print.

Crane, G. D. (1996). Dangerous sentiments: Sympathy, rights and revolution in Stowe's antislavery novels. *Nineteenth-Century Literature, 51*(2), 176–204. Print.

Crane, G. D. (2002). *Race, citizenship, and law in American literature.* Cambridge, UK/New York: Cambridge University Press. Print.

de Tocqueville, A. (1966). *Democracy in America* (trans: Reeve, H.). New York: Alfred A. Knopf. Print.

DeWaard, J. E. (2006). 'The shadow of law': Sentimental interiority, gothic terror, and the legal subject. *Arizona Quarterly, 62*, 1–30. Print.

Farnham, H. W. (1938). *Chapters in the history of social legislation in the United States to 1860.* Washington, DC: Carnegie Institution of Washington. Print.

Friedman, L. M. (1973). *A history of American law.* New York: Simon and Schuster.

Goddu, T. (1997). *Gothic America: Narrative, history, and nation.* New York: Columbia University Press. Print.

Goodell, W. (1853). *The American slave code in theory and practice.* New York: John A. Gray. Web. 15 June 2015.

Gray, T. R. (2000). *The confessions of Nat Turner.* 1831. In R. S. Levine (Ed.), *Clotel, or the president's daughter* (pp. 427–443). Boston/New York: Bedford St. Martins.

Hartman, S. V. (1997). *Scenes of subjection: Terror, slavery, and self-making in nineteenth-century America.* New York/Oxford: Oxford University Press. Print.

Jacobs, H. (1987). In J. Yellin (Ed.), *Incidents in the life of a slave girl.* Cambridge, MA/London: Harvard University Press. Print.

Korobkin, L. H. (2007). Appropriating law in Harriet Beecher Stowe's *Dred. Nineteenth-Century Literature, 62*(3), 380–406. Print.

Marshall, B. M. (2011). *The transatlantic gothic novel and the law, 1790–1860.* Farnam/ Surrey/Burlington: Ashgate. Print.

Moran, L. J. (2001). Law and the Gothic imagination. In F. Botting (Ed.), *The Gothic.* Cambridge, UK: D.S. Brewer. Print.

Punter, D. (1998). *Gothic pathologies: The text, the body, and the law.* New York: St. Martins. Print.

Roberts, S. S. (2014). *Gothic subjects: The transformation of individualism in American fiction, 1790–1861.* Philadelphia: University of Pennsylvania Press. Print.

Schafer, J. K. (1994). *Slavery, the civil law, and the Supreme Court of Louisiana.* Baton Rouge/London: Louisiana State University Press. Print.

Sorisio, C. (2002). *Fleshing out America: Race, gender, and the politics of the body in American literature, 1833–1879.* Athens: University of Georgia Press. Print.

State v. Mann. (1999). In W. R. Lee (Ed.), *A documentary history of slavery in North America* (pp. 220–224). Athens: University of Georgia Press. Print.

Stowe, H. B. (1852). *Uncle Tom's cabin.* New York: Penguin, 1981. Print.

Stowe, H. B. (2015). *A key to Uncle Tom's cabin.* Boston: John P. Jewett and Company. Print.

Strobhart, J. (1848). *Reports of cases argued and determined in the court of appeals and court of errors of South Carolina, on appeal from the courts of law* (Vol. II). Columbia: A.S. Johnston. Web. 27 June 2015.

Stroud, G. M. (1827). *A sketch of the laws relating to slavery in the several states of the United States of America.* Philadelphia: Kimber and Sharpless. Web. 25 June 2015.

Sundquist, E. (1998). *To wake the nations: Race in the making of American literature.* Belknap: Cambridge, MA. Print.

Weinauer. (2005). Writing revolt in the wake of Nat Turner: Frederick Douglass and the construction of black domesticity in 'the heroic slave'. *Studies in American Fiction, 33,* 193–202. Print.

Winter, K. J. (1992). *Subjects of slavery, agents of change: Women and power in gothic novels and slave narratives, 1790–1865.* Athens/London: University of Georgia Press. Print.

FURTHER READING

DeWaard, J. E. (2006). 'The shadow of law': Sentimental interiority, gothic terror and the legal subject. *Arizona Quarterly, 62,* 1–30. Focusing on the figure of Cassy in *Uncle Tom's Cabin,* this essay offers a rich reading of the ways in which 'sentimental and gothic discourses ... work together to critique legal injustice' while simultaneously attempting to 'manage the bodies of others.'

Hoeveler, D., & Jenkins, J. D. (2007) Where the evidence leads: Gothic narratives and legal technologies. *European Romantic Review, 18,* 317–337. With a unique, if not exclusive, focus on non-canonical texts, this essay examines 'how and why the gothic novel explored a number of contested legal issues and evolving legal technologies' in the late eighteenth and early nineteenth centuries.

Marshall, B. M. (2011). *The transatlantic gothic novel and the law, 1790–1860.* Farnam/Surrey/Burlington: Ashgate. Examining such writers as Godwin, Shelley, Charles Brockden Brown, and Hannah Crafts, Marshall offers a transatlantic exploration of how, why, and in what ways the Gothic is 'haunted' by legal themes.

Moran, L. J. (2001). Law and the Gothic imagination. In F. Botting (Ed.), *The Gothic.* Cambridge, UK: D.S. Brewer. Interested more in judicial and juridical context than in literary texts, this essay argues that 'the Gothic and law are intimately connected institutions and sets of practices through which the sense and nonsense of past and present, stability and change, tradition and modernity are made and unmade on a day-to-day basis.'

Punter, D. (1998). *Gothic pathologies: The text, the body, and the law*. New York: St. Martins. Surveying a heterogeneous body of works by a wide range of writers, Punter's book offers a theoretically dense reading of the relationship between law and the Gothic that spans continents and centuries.

Wein, T. (1997). Legal fictions, legitimate desires: The law of representation in the romance of the forest. *Genre, 30*, 289–310. Identifying a conservative strain in the Gothic, Wein argues for the ways in which trials function to make the author the 'representative of the law, rightfully withholding from the prying eyes of a public secrets it cannot benefit them to know.'

CHAPTER 22

Charles Chesnutt's Reparative Gothic

Christine A. Wooley

Critical attention to Charles Chesnutt's work often begins by contrasting his conjure stories to the plantation fiction written by Joel Chandler Harris and Thomas Nelson Page. Understanding Chesnutt's relation to the Gothic benefits from a similar attention to contrasts, and so this chapter will begin with a brief reading of Page's short story 'No Haid Pawn', first published in the 1887 collection *In Ole Virginia*. In this tale, the narrator recounts his fright on spending a stormy night in a deserted plantation house located near the pond of the story's title. From the beginning, he takes care to note that this 'ghostly place' (162) is 'as much cut off from the rest of the country as if a sea had divided it' (163); it is surrounded by 'simple swamp and jungle' (166) and 'unhealthy beyond all experience' (167). The unknown owners of this place at the time of the narrator's terrifying night are 'aliens' (163), but the original owners were too: '[t]he house had been built many generations before by a stranger in this section … [and] no ties either of blood or friendship were formed with their neighbors' (166). The local slaves add far more frightening details: they claim that dungeons form the foundation of the house, and that 'one of the negro builders had been caught and decapitated between two of the immense foundation stones', perhaps 'in some awful and occult rite' (167).

This originating violence is duplicated by more recent events at No Haid Pawn, when the property is taken over by a man 'more gloomy[,] more strange, and more sinister' (168). A West Indian who speaks only 'a *patois* not unlike the Creole French' (169), his 'personal characteristics and habits' are seen as 'unique in that country' (168); he is a 'blot upon civilization' believed to drink human blood (169). After he is executed for beheading one of his slaves, rumours abound that both the murderer and his victim haunt No Haid Pawn, investing it 'with unparalleled horror' (171). Meanwhile, the local planters

C.A. Wooley (✉)
St. Mary's College of Maryland, St. Marys, GA, USA

© The Editor(s) (if applicable) and The Author(s) 2016
S.C. Street, C.L. Crow (eds.), *The Palgrave Handbook of the Southern Gothic*,
DOI 10.1057/978-1-137-47774-3_22

285

deal with horrors of their own: the discovery that the Underground Railroad is operating in the vicinity, and the arrival of a 'negro … without either superstition or reverence' (172) who eventually escapes, much to the relief of the white slave-owning population. It is after this escape that Page's narrator finds himself forced to weather a bad storm in the abandoned house at No Haid Pawn. He collapses in fright when he encounters what he believes to be the ghosts of the West Indian planter and his victim. We know – although Page does not emphasize the connection for us – that the narrator may have seen the escaped slave instead. When he returns the next day, the house has burned to the ground; now 'the spot with all its secrets lay buried under [No Haid Pawn's] dark waters' (186).

Or maybe not so buried. In ways that might surprise readers of Page's 'Marse Chan' or 'Meh Lady', 'No Haid Pawn', with its emphasis on slaves' vulnerability to cruel masters, acknowledges a form of slavery that is far from the idealized paternalism typical of Page's plantation stories. At the same time, however, the story insistently quarantines the brutality that its plot exposes. This site of horrors – and Page links them not just to a particularly violent master's actions but to the more mundane work of building and operating a plantation – is cut off from the community by both geography and custom. The house is surrounded by swamp and marshes, and its proprietors are insistently described as wholly unlike the local community of slave holders: they are aliens who do not speak English; they are vampiric monsters whose cruelty towards 'negroes' is implicitly contrasted with the presumably kinder treatment of the narrator's friends and family. To the extent that this same site of horrors is also linked to potential rebellion through the spectre of Caribbean slave rebellions raised by the cruel owner's identity as a Creole-speaking West Indian, through the escape of a recalcitrant slave and through the rumoured presence of the Underground Railroad, Page gives an account of slavery and abolition that transforms the reality of exploitation (the most obvious reason a slave would seek to rebel or escape) into a set of isolated incidents, contained geographically and temporally. It is, after all, the narrator's past experience at No Haid Pawn with which we are asked to identify. It is his 'mind [that is] … enchained by the horrors of [his] situation' (182) as he sleeps in a house with 'blood-stained foundation stones' (181), not that of the slave – or that of the African American struggling under Jim Crow. Unintended irony aside, if 'No Haid Pawn' suggests that something about slavery haunts the narrator – and by extension the South, both before and after the Civil War – it is the result of singular actions taken by unknown outsiders whose experiences of slavery are distinct from those of familial devotion and the natural, mutually beneficial hierarchy that supposedly defined the peculiar institution.

Chesnutt's plantation stories, published primarily between 1887 and 1900 and in the 1899 collection *The Conjure Woman*, are well known for countering generous accounts of Southern slavery such as those offered by Page. His work unsettles the ideological détente between North and South that romanticized accounts of the Old South promoted in the post-Reconstruction era.

The gothic tropes that he employs are central to this project, for as Teresa Goddu writes of both Harriet Jacobs and Toni Morrison, such a use of 'the gothic serves as a mode of resistance' that 'reclaim[s] ... history instead of being controlled by it' (155). Chesnutt's Uncle Julius stories – populated by ghosts, conjurers and the insane, and depicting an animistic world in which any escape from violence and subjugation is tentative and often incomplete – reverse the quarantine attempted by a story like 'No Haid Pawn'. While the isolation of Page's haunted plantation works to contain the disruption caused by acknowledging the slave's vulnerability to both mundane dehumanization and the violent whims of masters, Chesnutt uses gothic tropes to reconfigure the Southern landscape and imbue it with a history of exploitation that shapes conditions in the present. If we see in Page an uncanny return of repressed knowledge concerning the injustice of slavery, in Chesnutt's fiction this uncanny rupture becomes the defining structure of his literary representations of slavery and its aftermath.

In this chapter, I begin with critical accounts that explore this gothic strain in Chesnutt's work. I then present his 1888 story 'Po' Sandy' as an exemplar of how, as Eric Sundquist writes, Chesnutt's use of 'conjure ties the violent, painful ancestral world of slave culture to the precarious world of contemporary African America' (377). In my reading of 'Po' Sandy', particularly its representations of ghosts and haunting, I suggest that Chesnutt's Gothic also models responses to such history in order to show how his postbellum readers should react to stories of trauma: with material remedies. I then turn to the final novel published in Chesnutt's lifetime, 1905s *The Colonel's Dream*. I read the conclusion of this novel, in which the philanthropic colonel abandons his attempts to modernize the Southern town of his birth, as a stinging rejection of the ethical possibilities figured in the Uncle Julius tales. This shift reflects Chesnutt's deepening pessimism concerning racial progress, and it is revealed not by a ghost, but by a body: that of the colonel's former slave, disinterred from a white cemetery and left as a protest on the colonel's front porch. While 'Po' Sandy' and other stories from *The Conjure Woman* use ghosts to reveal history as an explanation – and to inspire potential remedies – for the socio-economic inequality that African Americans faced in the late nineteenth century, the most gothic moment in *The Colonel's Dream* insists on the materiality of the former slave's body as a symbol for the impossibility of economic and moral progress in the South.

CRITICAL ACCOUNTS

Discussions of Chesnutt's Gothic typically begin with Robert Hemenway's essay from 1974, 'Gothic Sociology: Charles Chesnutt and the Gothic Mode'. Although Hemenway ultimately suggests that Chesnutt is 'not a Gothic writer at all, even though the subject matter of conjure would seem ready made for Gothic effects' (119), his analysis recognizes that '[t]he terror in Chesnutt's tales comes not from transformations of nature, fears of night, the irrationality of supernatural force, but from what men do to each other in the name of race' (112).

As a result, Hemenway argues, redress must necessarily come from animism and other forms of occult power that exceed the logics of race and reason – the very discourses that have defined blacks as inferior. To the extent that such structures are seen as products of the Enlightenment, recognizing the gothic strain in Chesnutt's work links him to earlier gothic texts in both the United States and England that present the contradictions and inconsistencies within western discourses of freedom and progress. For example, critic Ellen J. Goldner argues that Chesnutt's conjure stories use the Gothic to critique the immorality of an 'overly rationalist economic discourse' that justifies both slavery and capitalism. Similarly, Hyejin Kim's analysis suggests that 'Julius uses gothic strategies against John's logic and reason to conjure the abject' (414), a kind of haunting back that functions as resistance by 'resurrect[ing] the unvoiced ghostly presence of African Americans in official American history' (411).

While much of the attention to Chesnutt's gothicism has quite understandably focused on the conjure stories, critics have also explored the impact of his gothicized accounts of racial violence and racialist ideologies in his novels. In these readings, they recognize a use of the Gothic that influences our perception of events in the novel, rather than the structure of its plot. Gerald Ianovici's essay on *The Marrow of Tradition* (1901) argues that gothic tropes shape our understanding of the tangled, hidden history of Olivia Carteret's inheritance as well as the spectres of black dominance and inter-racial mixing that motivate her husband and his allies; the instability of the self within racial binaries likewise occupies Justin Edwards in his reading of *The House Behind the Cedars* (1900). Working with the little-known *Mandy Oxendine* (rejected for publication in 1897), Joanna Penn Cooper similarly contends that in this novel, Chesnutt 'mirrors and defamiliarizes the horror of post-Reconstruction-era racism and violence against African Americans ... [through] literary analogues for the personal and cultural hauntings engendered by unspoken racial trauma' (120).

It is easy to see the critical appeal of attending to the Gothic in these and other works by Chesnutt: the critic's attention shows the mobility of literary figures to great effect. We are presented with powerful examples of how gothic plots and tropes are re-configured by writers in new contexts; this gothicism exposes histories that are ignored or re-written in order to reinforce structures of social, political and economic inequality. Such readings put the critic in league with the writer: together, they reveal not just unspoken histories, but the means by which they become heard. Yet the Gothic, I would suggest, is most powerful when its forms present us with a conundrum, a contradiction that cannot be easily resolved or addressed. In what follows I contrast the work of the Gothic in Chesnutt's early story 'Po' Sandy' and that which emerges in his last published novel, *The Colonel's Dream*. This contrast, I argue, reveals the tension between two poles of the Gothic's literary effects: that which brings the unknown to light in order to resolve what has haunted us, and that through which similarly repressed histories remain disturbingly and stubbornly unassimilated. Such a change tracks with Chesnutt's increasing pessimism concerning the position of African Americans in the United States.

'Po' Sandy'

'Po' Sandy', the second of Chesnutt's conjure stories published in the *Atlantic Monthly*, traces the attempts of Sandy and his second wife Tenie to circumvent the power of the slave holder. Early in the story, we learn that Sandy is tired of being loaned out to other families, and thus he asks Tenie – who has revealed that she is a conjure woman – to turn him 'inter sump'n w'at'll stay in one place' (47). Tenie turns Sandy into a tree, returning him to human form every once in a while so that he can stay connected to her and hear news of his surroundings. Sandy's tribulations continue, however. As a tree, he is assaulted by woodpeckers and used as a source of turpentine – injuries that leave scars in his human flesh as well as his arboreal form. Given these problems, Tenie decides to transform herself and Sandy into foxes so that they can run away, but before she can do so, she is ordered to tend to a sick woman on another plantation. While she is gone, her master decides that he wants to build a new kitchen and, with a great struggle, Sandy the tree is cut down and taken to the sawmill to be cut up into boards for the new building.

Meanwhile, Tenie returns home and discovers that the tree that was Sandy has been cut down. She rushes to the sawmill, hoping to turn the tree back into Sandy to tell him that she is sorry before he dies, but the mill hands grab her and tie her to a post; she witnesses the saw's 'mighty hard wuk; fer of all de sweekin', an moanin', en groanin', dat log done it w'iles de saw wuz a-cuttin' thoo it' (51). The new kitchen is built and Tenie is driven crazy by her grief; rather than send her to the poorhouse, however, her master puts her to work watching the slave children. The new kitchen is quickly pronounced haunted: the slaves say '[d]ey could hear sump'n moanin' en groanin' 'bout de kitchen [and] dey could hear sump'n a-hollerin' en sweekin' lack it wuz in great pain en sufferin'' (52). Soon only Tenie will willingly occupy the kitchen, and so the building is dismantled and re-assembled as a schoolhouse. Tenie spends her nights there until one morning she is found dead.

All of this, as readers of Chesnutt's conjure stories know well, is recounted by Uncle Julius as he seeks to convince his postbellum employer, John, and John's wife, Annie, not to use the wood from the schoolhouse to build their own new kitchen. Julius, we find out, has plans to use the schoolhouse for a splinter group from the local church. After hearing Julius's tale and assessing its intended effect, John is unmoved, but Annie decides that she wants new wood instead of the schoolhouse wood for her kitchen. And when Julius asks to use the schoolhouse for meetings, she agrees, and makes a donation to the new congregation as well.

Sundquist writes of this resolution that, just as the schoolhouse lumber will be haunted until it crumbles, 'the ghosts of slavery will haunt the South (and America) until its last remains have disintegrated'; moreover, he continues, Julius's use of the wood demonstrates that he 'has a right to the created property of slavery – produced by his own labor and that of his ancestors – while John does not' (376). This reading is all the more compelling given the ways in which the Gothic – the transformation of a man into a tree by occult means, the forced captivity of Tenie as she watches the destruction of 'Sandy', the new building haunted by both Sandy and the now mad Tenie – literalizes the dehumanization on which the system of slavery relied and through which the labour of slaves created the plantation and its products. The figurative work of 'Po' Sandy' reveals that the plantation and its products are made of slaves' bodies, bodies that have, as Sandy's story shows us, suffered profoundly. Chesnutt's tale makes this constitution vividly clear, as Sandy 'is turned into a material part of the plantation' (Sundquist 376). Sandy does not so much haunt the kitchen as be the kitchen.

Notably, however, the character who shows the reader how to react to these revelations is not John or Julius but Annie. It is her choice, not John's, to relinquish the schoolhouse and make a donation to the new church. These choices model for the reader the right response to encountering the knowledge that the story of Sandy and Tenie reveals. As Heather Tirado Gilligan has argued, Annie offers an 'alternate model of reading' that both returns to and revises the responses constituted by antebellum sentimental discourse (211). How Annie comes to embody such a corrective to John's hard-hearted rationality, however, is not just a matter of sentiment and sympathy, but a function of the Gothic. This function tells us that the nation is haunted by the histories it ignores, but significantly, it also tells about the impact of such histories on individuals. This might seem to be an obvious point, but Chesnutt's use of the Gothic to represent different versions of this experience deserves our attention. Indeed, to say that Tenie is haunted by the ghost of Sandy is itself a simplification, for what Chesnutt describes is that Sandy's ghostly presence alienates the other slaves but draws Tenie inside the haunted building. Tenie, haunted by Sandy, joins Sandy in haunting the new kitchen that she believes was built from his wood. In this sense, the spectre-like presence of Tenie, much like Sethe in Toni Morrison's *Beloved*, shows us what it might mean to live among the buildings, the fields, the crops and the profits that are created by the labour of exploited slaves and still be a slave.

Furthermore, to the extent that Annie and the reader come to recognize that plantation spaces are haunted, they do so by sympathizing with Tenie. 'What a system it was … under which such things were possible!' Annie exclaims, to John's dismay. 'Poor Tenie!' she concludes ('Po' Sandy' 53). With these statements, we see that Annie's focus is less on Sandy than on one who must live through the experience of trauma, however difficult it is: Tenie. This is the insight that leads to Annie's decision to use new wood and donate money to the church; through Tenie's story, she recognizes Julius's right to the building, but also the impact of the kind of temporal upheaval – that is, the experience of being haunted – that trauma creates in certain spaces for certain individuals. Moreover, her donation signals that although she is not directly responsible for Tenie and Sandy's traumas, she is moved by them to do something that benefits those who, like them, were slaves: Julius and his church fellows. Chesnutt shows us that Annie's actions and Julius's claim embody communal claims and shared responsibilities; thus, it is Julius and his congregation, not the departed

Sandy and Tenie, who will benefit from Annie's relinquished claim on the spaces constructed by slave labour, and it is Annie, a Northern invalid not a former slave master, who acts to repair these injustices. At a moment when the limits of Reconstruction in altering the socio-economic status of former slaves has become vividly clear, 'Po' Sandy' uses the Gothic to uncover an argument for reparations, albeit one writ small, in the relationship between a carpetbagger's wife and an elderly former slave.

To the extent, then, that Chesnutt's story – and others, perhaps most notably 'Dave's Neckliss' – counters romanticized postbellum representations of the institution of slavery, emphasizing exploitation and trauma through gothic tropes and figures, his work also seeks to address the impact of the past that he has exposed on the present in which he lives. If we are unsettled by Chesnutt's stories – and we should be – we are also offered a path towards resolution, in the sense that Chesnutt shows us how this history should be used and responded to. Julius certainly uses it: widely recognized as a 'trickster' figure, he recounts stories of the antebellum South to his employers John and Annie in order to improve postbellum working and living conditions for himself and those close to him. Meanwhile, Annie's choices both recognize and repair, however modestly, past injustices. We as readers similarly come to understand the relationship between the antebellum past and the current conditions of African Americans through the gothicism that shapes Chesnutt's tales. Such an understanding suggests that the gothic storytelling that Chesnutt employs highlights contradictions in order show how best to address them. The history of slave experience brought to light in *The Conjure Woman* may remain unsettling in its brutality, but we are quite settled in the sense that we understand what it means and what Chesnutt thinks we should do about it.

This account of Chesnutt's conjure stories brings together gothic content and what, following Gilligan, we might call sentimental reading. Such a conjunction reflects Chesnutt's literary ambitions: to be an author, a 'wish to write [that] is never separable from the will to a certain sort of social mobility', as Richard Brodhead has argued (191), but also to write in such a way that will re-shape the socio-political milieu in which his stories circulate.[1] Annie models for us how such a re-shaping will occur: not just by altering individual knowledge and feelings, but by taking action based on these affective and intellectual revelations. If Chesnutt structures an ethical, material response to the socio-economic and political inequality that African Americans continued to suffer after the Civil War, he does so in a way that harks back to the ideal reader of *Uncle Tom's Cabin*. Furthermore, as we have seen, this reader's transformations are mediated by the Gothic.[2]

THE COLONEL'S DREAM

Such mediations collapse in the final novel that Chesnutt published, *The Colonel's Dream*. Like *The Marrow of Tradition*, this focuses on the kinds of issues – inter-racial violence and distrust, the retrenchment of white supremacy, the limited efficacy of racial uplift – that prompted William Dean Howells to say of *Marrow* that 'it would be better if it was not so bitter' (456). The plot begins with echoes of John and Annie's migration south in the conjure stories: needing a healthy climate for himself and his son, a successful Northern businessman, Colonel French, returns to the Southern town of his birth, the fictional Clarendon. Finding that the place satisfies his sentimental memories of the antebellum era and presents a number of opportunities to exercise his beneficent, charitable impulses, he elects to stay.[3] The colonel's work, however, quickly creates conflict in the town. His efforts, consistently characterized as driven by paternalistic but enlightened principles and a democratic belief in equal opportunity, run afoul of the aptly named Mr Fetters, who, in the wake of the Civil War, has risen from poverty to control most of the town's economic institutions. Fetters and his allies capitalize on white resentment of the colonel's willingness to pay local blacks an equitable wage and to give them jobs usually reserved for whites. These conflicts culminate in two losses for the colonel. One occurs when, after the colonel's son (Phil) and his former slave (Peter) die in a freak accident and are buried side by side in the whites-only cemetery, Peter's casket is disinterred and left on the colonel's porch. The other happens when a man to whom the colonel had promised the protection of the law is lynched by a mob encouraged by Fetters's allies.

The violence of this lynching is described only after the fact, and in language more notable for its powerful understatement than any gothic excess: 'A rope, a tree – a puff a smoke, a flash of flame – or a barbaric orgy of fire and blood – what matter which? At the end there was a lump of clay, and a hundred murderers where there had been one before' (*Colonel's Dream* 290). However, such understatement, along with the novel's stylistic debt to realism and its emphasis on the colonel's sentimental motivations, makes the 'ghoulish' (295) quality of Peter's disinterment all the more marked. Moreover, it is this ghoulishness – not the actual deaths of Phil, Peter or the lynching victim – that ultimately deters the colonel from his plans to rehabilitate Clarendon. Indeed, Chesnutt takes great care to show us that despite these deaths, and other setbacks to his plans to advance economic and social progress in Clarendon, the colonel remains committed to his work. Chesnutt writes that after Phil and Peter are buried:

> The colonel was beaten but not dismayed. Perhaps God in his wisdom had taken Phil away, that his father might give himself more completely and single-mindedly to the battle before him. Had Phil lived, a father might have hesitated to expose a child's young and impressionable mind to the things which these volcanic outbursts of passion between mismated races might cause at any unforeseen moment. Now that the way was clear, he could go forward ... in the work he had laid out. He would enlist good people and demand better laws ....
>
> Diligently he would work to lay wide and deep the foundations of prosperity, education and enlightenment, upon which should rest justice, humanity and civic righteousness. In this he would find a worthy career. Patiently would he await the results of his labours, and if they came not in great measure in his own lifetime, he would be content to know that after years would see their full fruition. (292)

Here, the colonel contemplates his own willingness to work hard for what might, in the end, be only modest progress towards his most idealistic goals. Although elsewhere in the novel Chesnutt's portrayal of Colonel French dramatizes the limits of his progressive impulses, at this moment the emphasis on the 'foundations' required for a more just and humane society is a sincere articulation of what Chesnutt most values. As we see at the end of the novel, he pins his hopes on the idea that 'a new body of thought, favourable to just laws' is 'slowly ... but visibly, to the eye of faith ... growing' (309). The emphasis on both justice and prosperity reminds us that the colonel's actions earlier in the novel were intended, in however flawed a fashion, to remedy the economic injustices perpetrated by the slave system and continued in the South, in different and various forms, after the Civil War.

Nonetheless, *The Colonel's Dream* is ultimately the story of a failed dream of progress, and while the colonel's paternalism and somewhat conservative approach to race and reform are certainly part of the problem, the climactic moment of the novel gives us a darker and more complex reason for his failure, one that literally interrupts his dream of a new South. The colonel is asleep when:

> Shortly after dawn there was a loud rapping at the colonel's door:
> 'Come downstairs and look on de piazza, Colonel,' said the agitated voice of the servant who had knocked. 'Come quick, suh.'
> There was a vague terror in the man's voice that stirred the colonel strangely. He threw on a dressing gown and hastened downstairs, and to the front door of the hall, which stood open. A handsome mahogany burial casket, stained with earth and disfigured by rough handling, rested upon the floor of the piazza, where it had been deposited during the night. Conspicuously nailed to the coffin lid was a sheet of white paper, upon which were some lines rudely scrawled in a handwriting that matched the spelling:
> *Kurnell French:*
> *Take notis. Berry yore ole nigger somewhar else. He can't stay in Oak Semitury. The majority of white people of this town, who dident tend yore nigger funarl, woant have him there. Niggers by there selves, white peepul by there selves, and them that lives in our town must bide by our rules.* (*By order of* Cumitty. (294))

This event puts before the colonel the dead body of his former slave. Peter's coffin, removed from a site of sentimental fulfilment and promise – the integrated burial plot shared, however briefly, by the white French family and their former slave Peter – now literally blocks the colonel's pathway to the public space of the town in which he sought to promote reform. The figurative meaning of this blockage quickly becomes apparent: the colonel decides to abandon his philanthropic work and return to the North.

What should we make of this obstruction and its gothic representation? Although gruesome and unsettling enough to warrant the label 'gothic', it is not a moment of haunting and, unlike Annie in 'Po' Sandy', the colonel does not come to understand the impact of past traumas on African Americans so much as he now sees the entanglement of the past with the present as an insurmountable obstacle. While the presence of the body is certainly indicative of racist ideologies and class divisions that ossify Southern socio-political and economic institutions in the years after the Civil War, the portrayal of this obstacle through the Gothic shows us the affective component of this barrier. The colonel now recognizes an impenetrable difference in feeling between himself and those who would remove a body from a grave and embark on the 'ghoulish' work of delivering it to his house in the dead of night. The presence of the body on his porch thus represents a radically different relation to the blackness of Peter's body, living or dead. In response, the colonel abandons his progressive agenda for Clarendon and returns to the North, taking Peter's and Phil's bodies with him.

If in 'Po' Sandy' the hauntings spawned by Sandy's death ultimately create a clearer understanding of the past, as well as a greater likelihood of ethical choices based on this understanding, at the end of *The Colonel's Dream* the material presence of the dead and the colonel's choice to return to the North signal a very different kind of impact of the past on the present. The Gothic links the resistance to social and economic progress that the colonel encounters in Clarendon to a history of racial injustice and the intractable nature of white racism that cannot be productively addressed or meaningfully altered. This impasse, the note on the coffin suggests, comes from a difference in feeling as well as ideas and education: those who were so agitated as to remove Peter from the white cemetery 'dident tend yore nigger funarl', whereas for the colonel, the fact that '[a]ll the people, white and black, had united to honour his dead' is an event that 'would be beautiful to remember all the days of his life' (289). By using a gothic figure to show us these differences, however, Chesnutt teaches us how to react to such an impasse: with horror. This horror signals a form of pessimism that, despite the novel's concluding affirmation of the inevitability of progress (however slow), reflects worsening socio-political conditions for African Americans in the early twentieth century. Through Annie's reaction to Julius's tales and the gothic eruptions of trauma that structure them, Chesnutt imagines the affective conditions for the material improvement of African American lives. In *The Colonel's Dream*, the Gothic exhumes a material body – the dead freed slave – and suggests that its treatment by white Southerners reflects a willingness to humiliate and terrorize such bodies, living and dead, that we also see in the extreme acts of violence against African Americans and the everyday acts of segregation that defined the Jim Crow era. To the extent that we understand that this desire for desecration is implacable and unresolved by the novel's conclusion, *The Colonel's Dream* leaves us in the midst of a nightmare.

NOTES

1. In a frequently referenced journal entry from 1880, Chesnutt notes that 'I shall write for a purpose, a high, holy purpose .... The object of my writings would be not so much the elevation of the Colored people as the elevation of the Whites, – for I consider the unjust spirit of caste which is so insidious as to pervade a whole nation, and so powerful as to subject a whole race and all

connected with it to scorn and social ostracism – I consider this a barrier to the moral progress of the American people' (139–40).
2. Goddu writes that 'the gothic intrudes into the sentimental in order to register the full horror of slavery' (142). Focusing on the details that Cassy gives to Tom about the Legree plantation, Goddu states that '[t]his section of the novel shows how the event of slavery is structured in gothic terms' (143).
3. Francesca Sawaya notes that these impulses are shaped by the colonel's immediate and more distant experiences: as a businessman, his charitable acts are shaped by the conservative rationality of corporate capitalism (151); as a Southerner, he is limited 'by his residual Southern high-mindedness' and an evasion of 'questions of justice' when the answers to such questions are too intrusive or difficult (152). Perhaps most significantly, his efforts to reform the town evince the kind of paternalism through which, Susan Ryan argues, 'benevolent hierarchies and racial hierarchies were mutually constitutive in U.S. culture' (47).

BIBLIOGRAPHY

Brodhead, R. H. (1993a). *Cultures of letters: Scenes of reading and writing in nineteenth-century America*. Chicago: University of Chicago Press.

Chesnutt, C. (1993a). *The conjure woman and other conjure tales*. Ed. R. H. Broadhead. Durham/London: Duke University Press.

Chesnutt, C. (1993b). *The journals of Charles W. Chesnutt*. Ed. R. H. Broadhead. Duke University Press: Durham.

Chesnutt, C. (2005). *The Colonel's dream*. New York: Harlem Moon.

Cooper, J. P. (2009). Gothic signifying in Charles Chesnut's *Mandy Oxendine*. *MELUS, 34*(4), 119–144.

Edwards, J. D. (2003). *Gothic passages: Racial ambiguity and the American gothic*. Iowa City: University of Iowa Press.

Gilligan, H. T. (2007). Reading, race, and Charles Chesnutt's "Uncle Julius" tales. *ELH, 74*, 195–215.

Goddu, T. (1997). *Gothic America: Narrative, history, and nation*. New York: Columbia University Press.

Goldner, E. J. (1999). Other(ed) Ghosts: Gothicism and the bonds of reason in Melville, Chesnutt, and Morrison. *MELUS, 24*(1), 59–83.

Hemenway, R. (1974). Gothic sociology: Charles Chesnutt and the gothic mode. *Studies in the Literary Imagination, 7*(1), 101–119.

Howells, W. D. (2002). A psychological counter-current in recent fiction. In N. Bentley & S. Gunning (Eds.), *The marrow of tradition*. Boston: Bedford/St. Martins.

Ianovici, G. (2002). "A living death": Gothic signification and the Nadir in the marrow of tradition. *MELUS, 27*(4), 33–58.

Kim, H. (2014). Gothic storytelling and resistance in Charles W. Chesnutt's the conjure woman. *Orbis Litterarum, 69*(5), 411–438.

Page, T. N. (1991). *In ole Virginia*. Nashville: J. S. Sanders & Company.

Ryan, S. (2003). *The grammar of good intentions: Race and antebellum culture of benevolence*. Ithaca: Cornell University Press.

Sawaya, F. (2014). *The difficulty art of giving: Patronage, philanthropy, and the American literary marketplace*. Philadelphia: University of Pennsylvania Press.

Sundquist, E. (1993). *To wake the nations: Race in the making of American literature*. Cambridge: Belknap Press of Harvard University Press.

FURTHER READING

Bentley, N. (2009). *Frantic panoramas: American literature and mass culture 1870–1920*. Philadelphia: University of Pennsylvania Press.

Bentley's section on Chesnutt (in the chapter 'Black Bohemia and the African American Novel') situates his critique of realism within his awareness of the power of spectacle. While her focus is not on the Gothic, her argument that 'the real role for the black person in public' is 'to perform his own nonexistence as a black citizen' (199) aids gothic readings of dead black bodies, lynchings and minstrelsy, particularly the representation of such in mass culture.

Clymer, J. A. (2013). *Family money: Property, race, and literature in the nineteenth century*. New York: Oxford University Press.

Clymer's chapter 'The Properties of Marriage in Chesnutt and Hopkins' shows how Chesnutt's fiction assesses the impact of anti-miscegenation law on the economic rights of African Americans, making inter-racial marriage a site through which to see the possibilities, and limits, of inheritance as a form of redress.

CHAPTER 23

Jim Crow Gothic: Richard Wright's Southern Nightmare

Agnieszka Soltysik Monnet

African American author Richard Wright's interest in crime writing and hard-boiled pulp fiction is well known to readers and critics, as is his use of horror elements in his major novels, such as *Native Son* (1940) and *The Outsider* (1960). However, by far the most gothic work he wrote is the collection of short stories set in the rural South of his youth, *Uncle Tom's Children* (1938). Wright, born and raised in Mississippi, published this volume just 2 years after Margaret Mitchell's *Gone with the Wind* (1936), but painted a very different portrait of the American South. Instead of white plantations and colourful balls, he depicts a dark landscape shaped by fear, violence and moral monstrosity. Each story conveys an oppressive sense of dread that inevitably ends in a scene of violence, exposing the brutal reign of terror that enforced Jim Crow legislation in the first decades of the twentieth century.

Published in 1945, the autobiographical *Black Boy* provides another layer to this picture of the South as hell for blacks, corroborating and fleshing out some of the details in *Uncle Tom's Children*, but also complicating the narrative with anecdotes of Wright's ordeal as a child of poverty, including abandonment, lack of education, religiously fanatical female relatives, and a mother who is abusive and helpless by turns, instilling in him an intense ambivalence towards women that appears throughout his fiction. *Black Boy* also reveals how Wright's interest in literary gothicism began, with his electrifying early exposure to stories like *Bluebeard and His Seven Wives* and later his fascination with horror pulp fiction. Together with the later *The Long Dream* (1958), these publications represent key texts of a strain of Southern Gothic that we could call Jim Crow Gothic, focused specifically on the South as a land permeated by racial fear and white violence against black selfhood.

A.S. Monnet (✉)
University of Lausanne, Lausanne, Switzerland

© The Editor(s) (if applicable) and The Author(s) 2016   297
S.C. Street, C.L. Crow (eds.), *The Palgrave Handbook of the Southern Gothic*,
DOI 10.1057/978-1-137-47774-3_23

Susanne B. Dietzel points out that critics have been slow to recognize the use of popular genre forms by African American writers (156). Nevertheless, critics have discussed the rather explicit gothic elements in Wright's later works (see for example Brodziok, Dow and Bryant). *Native Son* (1940) is structured into sections titled 'Fear', 'Flight' and 'Fate', while *The Outsider* (1960) has equally gothic-sounding chapters, such as 'Dread', 'Descent' and 'Despair'. William Dow observes that *The Outsider* is 'filled with allusions to what might be called the topoi or landmarks of the gothic: premonitions, curses, the subterranean, confinement, doubles, conspiracies, and premature burial' (142). A key incident in the novel is an underground train wreck that allows the protagonist to shed his identity and begin a new life without attachments (or so he thinks). In order to escape the burning train, he must step on the body of a young woman, his feet sinking into her chest as he does so. The novel is permeated by a sense of claustrophobia and horror as Cross finds himself again trapped in his new life, both by circumstances and his own crimes, just like Bigger Thomas in *Native Son*.

Generically, Wright's later work is characterized by a hybridity in which the darkness and violence of urban crime fiction are blended with the moral and epistemological complexities of the Gothic. The result is a sensational exploration of the nightmare world that is specific to African American experience of the mid-century metropolis as urban ghetto. Wright's influence on later African American urban crime fiction has been enormous – one can think of Chester Himes, Iceberg Slim and Walter Mosley – but his connections to the Southern Gothic have been less explored by scholars, even though his Southern childhood is indisputably at the origin of his attraction to the gothic mode. This chapter examines Wright's Southern writing in order to demonstrate that his work constitutes a crucial piece of the Southern Gothic puzzle. In contrast to the Southern Gothic of white authors that often approaches race obliquely, through minor characters, family secrets, haunted houses and ghostly reminders of past crimes, Wright's gothicized fiction reveals the terror and violence that lie at the heart of the Southern Gothic as a whole. His South is a landscape drenched in fear, the mutual fear of blacks and whites, and terror, or more specifically 'the white terror', which is another word for lynching and its variations. No survey of Southern Gothic could be complete without Wright's work, because no other writer exposes so clearly and so powerfully the racial violence that has shaped the American South.

Uncle Tom's Children

The first and most important work in this regard is *Uncle Tom's Children*. Had Wright published nothing else after this collection of stories, his legacy as a Southern Gothic writer would still have been assured. The five short stories and one autobiographical sketch that constitute this powerful collection paint an indelible portrait of the South in the first decades of the twentieth century as a land so permeated by the threat of lynch-mob violence that even the white houses and neat hedges of a white Arkansas suburb become an 'overarching symbol of fear' for the black narrator. The first piece, a sketch called 'The Ethics of Living Jim Crow', shows the protagonist, ostensibly Wright himself as a young man, learning the strict and humiliating rules of Jim Crow–shaped interaction with Southern whites. In a series of vignettes, Wright describes his 'education' in the ways of subservience and self-effacement.

The sketch opens with a description of a childhood battle between a group of black boys and a group of white boys that ends with Wright hit on the cheek by a broken bottle. Instead of tending to his wounded face and pride, his mother reacts with fury, stripping the young Wright naked and beating him 'till I had a fever of one hundred and two' (*Uncle Tom's Children* 4). The subsequent illness is accompanied by delirious visions of 'monstrous white faces suspended from the ceiling, leering at me' (5). This incident serves as the reader's gateway into the often bewildering world of the Jim Crow South for the young Wright, and is charged with many layers of meaning. First of all, the incident is told very differently in Wright's autobiography, *Black Boy*, where the beating and subsequent illness are prompted by him setting his family home on fire. Here Wright transposes the beating to an incident that makes his mother's reaction seem not only disproportionate but perversely unjust, underscoring the fear that grips the black population, so distorting normal human emotions that a mother whips her son to teach him a potentially life-saving lesson rather than tend to his injuries, and also infusing the incident with a strange sexual charge. His mother strips him 'naked' to beat him, adding a layer of shame, which then expresses itself in the boy's feverish vision of being 'leered' at by the white faces hovering near the ceiling.

This mixing of sexuality and violence is typical of Wright's work, although it is fairly muted in the stories of this collection, appearing more forcefully in his later *Native Son* and *The Long Dream*. Why does he inject a sexual layer into this story of childhood in the Jim Crow South? The reasons become more apparent when reading these later novels and they go beyond the simple observation that social subordination exacts a symbolic castration of black men, although this is also true. For Wright, the fear that the Jim Crow legislation created produces a complex set of taboos that become perversely intertwined with sexual anxiety, shame and a desire to transgress, leading to situations that reveal the violence that gives the South its uniquely terrifying atmosphere.

In 'The Ethics of Living Jim Crow', for example, the price for sexual transgression appears in vignette VII, the shortest of all, which tells of a bell-boy at the hotel where the narrator worked. Discovered in bed with a white prostitute, the young man is castrated and run out of town. This is presented to the other bell-boys and hall-boys as both a 'lucky' break (presumably because he is not killed) and a warning, since the hotel would not be responsible for the lives of other 'trouble-making niggers' (12). In this, the shortest of the anecdotes he recounts, Wright's narrator evokes the darkest kind of white violence against black men in the South: mutilation and murder for any hint of sexual contact, whether real or imagined, between black men and white women. The reverse situation, white men sexually using and abusing black women, has not only been an open secret of Southern society since the earliest slave times, but is also represented as an ongoing source of danger to black men. The vignette that immediately follows the castration of the bell-boy is an incident in which a white man slaps a black maid on the backside in front of the narrator, who is ordered at gunpoint to say that he does not mind (12). The man is apparently known for having killed two black men. The narrator is not only forced to accept the humiliating harassment of the black woman in his presence – and he is too 'ashamed to face her' after the incident – but has to pretend that he approves, an assault on his dignity and manhood that leaves him feeling intensely violated.

'The Ethics of Living Jim Crow' also establishes another aspect of Wright's gothicism that recurs throughout his work and is quite striking in its pointed revision of Southern Gothic code; namely, the reversal of the symbolic meaning of black and white. If the conventional use of blackness is to align it with fear and mystery, Wright consistently inverts this code, attributing both horror and uncanniness to the colour white. In the incident mentioned earlier, the narrator's childhood illness is rendered terrifying not by black shadows in his room, but by the 'monstrous white faces' floating horribly above his bed. In *Black Boy*, the terms 'the white terror' and 'the white-hot face of terror' recur on a number of occasions, sealing the association between whiteness and fear in the young black boy's mind (*Black Boy* 53, 52). In *Uncle Tom's Children*, danger and horror are also repeatedly described in terms of whiteness. When a boy is hiding from a lynch mob in a kiln full of snakes, he imagines the snakes preparing to strike him with their 'long *white* fangs' (42, my emphasis). When he sees another boy being burned by the mob, the narrator repeatedly describes the tar-drenched body as a 'writhing *white* mass' and the feathers that have been brought to tar and feather the boy rise in a 'widening spiral of *white* feathers into the night' (49, my emphasis). Conversely, the kiln that protects the boy from the mob is described as 'black' and a bird that he watches from his hiding place and that calms him is 'a spot of wheeling black against the sky' (42).

In general, Wright's use of colour is seeped in symbolic weight and takes on an almost expressionist intensity. The other important colour in *Uncle Tom's Children* is red, often associated with fire and blood, both linked to the South in general. In a story titled 'Fire and Cloud', an African American preacher who has been beaten by whites tells his congregation that they live in a kind of hell: not a Puritan hell of brimstone burning away their sinfulness, but a modern hell of racial injustice requiring an act of collective resistance and civil disobedience:

> Wes gotta git together. Ah know whut yo life is! Ah done felt its *fire!* It's like the fire that burned me last night! Its sufferin! Its hell! Ah cant bear this fire erlone. Ah know now whut to do! Wes gotta git close t one another. (178)

In this passage, Wright paints a livid portrait of life in the South as defined by almost constant violence troped as hellfire. In 'Long Black Song', the fire is literalized when a black man named Silas, who has shot a white man for sleeping with his wife, allows himself to be burned to death in his home, defiantly refusing to surrender to the 'white terror'. Instead, he is consumed by the 'eager plumes of red' that devour his house and everything for which he has worked (128). In succumbing to the rage and death that are so often produced by encounters with white men, Silas is described as joining 'that long river of blood' that flows through the South, fed by the history of killing between blacks and whites. Red rivers of blood and red plumes of fire: this is the colour of the violence that erupts regularly from the monstrous white faces that haunt the black South.

BLACK BOY

With his autobiographical *Black Boy* (1945), Wright returns to the South of *Uncle Tom's Children*, elaborating on his portrait of the white South and reflecting on it with the critical tools that would make him one of the great social analysts of the twentieth century. Like that of W. E. B. Du Bois or Franz Fanon, Wright's work attempts to probe the painful recesses of Jim Crow and the psychology of social subordination. Heavily influenced by Freudian psychoanalysis as well as the ambient misogyny of his time, like many modernists were, Wright often used sexualized metaphors for his experience of horror. A striking example is the return of the incident of beating and illness at the beginning of 'The Ethics of Living Jim Crow', which also opens *Black Boy* but with significant differences. As already mentioned, Wright is beaten for setting the house on fire instead of fighting with white boys, revealing that he had felt free to alter and exaggerate details of his childhood in *Uncle Tom's Children* to make the violence of Jim Crow more explicit and striking. This recalls the words of another Southern Gothic writer, Flannery O'Connor, who explained that she used the Gothic and especially the grotesque in her fiction because writing for an audience that does not share the writer's view of the world requires the use of hyperbole and heightened dramatization:

> When you can assume that your audience holds the same beliefs you do, you can relax a little and use more normal ways of talking to it; when you have to assume that it does not, then you have to make your vision apparent by shock – to the hard of hearing you shout, and for the almost blind you draw large and startling figures. (34)

Similarly, in writing for an America of the 1930s where Jim Crow–style practices and laws, both explicit and implicit, existed in nearly every state, Wright had felt obliged to emphasize the excessive violence of his mother's desire to inculcate these rules. Hence, the scene of his mother beating him unconscious for being injured in a fight is meant to shock the reader with the palpable injustice of the narrator's experience. In *Black Boy*, on the other hand, published at the end of the Second World War – a war fought in order to eradicate fascism from Europe and Asia – Wright feels freer to complicate the dynamics of race that he has established in the earlier work with details of his individual circumstances as a boy raised by strict and religious women, a problematic relationship to a remote and finally absent father, and a growing sense of alienation from his relatively illiterate community as a black teenager hungering for the pleasures of language and narrative. The incident remains securely rooted in a gothic vocabulary and framework, but its racial resonance is complemented by sexual and familial overtones.

As an example of how Wright revises and complicates the incident of the feverish illness haunted by 'monstrous white faces', in *Black Boy* the white faces are not described as faces at all, but as 'huge wobbly white bags, like the full udders of cows, suspended from the ceiling above me' (5). The fear is still coloured white, although the material shape of the fearful object is no longer white faces but white 'udders', threatening to drench the child with 'some horrible liquid' (5). Since it is his mother who has beaten him to unconsciousness, it is his mother who becomes his first symbol of terror, before he is even aware of white people, and this is figured in the text with transparently feminine images. The boy's helplessness transforms the mother's face into a more remote and therefore acceptable object, a cow's udder, but the paragraph ends with his explicit naming of the mother as the source of fear when he writes that he felt 'chastened' for a long time, remembering that his 'mother had come close to killing him' (5).

The autobiography further explores the gothic dynamic of Wright's own typically Southern family – his sharecropper father and his deeply religious mother, aunt and grandmother – with an incident about a kitten that reveals how violence begins early and at home. Wright remembers his father as a forbidding and tyrannical presence, often tired from work and requiring silence from his children in order to rest. On one occasion, when Wright and his brother find a stray kitten and bring it home, the father orders them to keep the animal quiet, shouting at them to kill it. Although he understands that his father does not really mean what he says, Wright's hatred and resentment of his father lead him to apply the command literally, as a form of irreproachable rebuke to the verbal violence. He believes that he cannot be punished for following the letter of his father's command, even though he knows full well that he is wilfully misreading its real intent. His mother finds the strangled kitten and torments Wright with the 'moral horror' of what he has done, harassing him with 'calculated words which spawned in my mind a horde of invisible demons bent upon exacting revenge' (10). She orders him to go outside into the night and dig a grave for the kitten, further terrifying him, and eggs him on with an eerily 'floating' and 'disembodied voice' as he gropes towards the dead animal in the dark (12).

In this way, Wright prepares for his later discovery of the 'white terror' with an account of a Southern childhood already laced with violence and fear. O'Connor again offers a useful point of comparison, arguing in *Mystery and Manners* that childhood offers plenty of material for a lifetime of writing by virtue of its inherently unequal power structure and many opportunities for subtle and overt violence (84). Wright's relationship with his mother provides an excellent example of this power dynamic and its equally troubling inversion. If children are initially overwhelmed by their parents' early power over them, this structure often proves to be reversible in later life, with children controlling and dominating their elderly and more and more helpless parents. O'Connor's work is full of such relationships – as is the Southern Gothic in general, since many generations often live together in the rural communities typical of the South. In *Black Boy*, Wright's mother, so powerful and terrifying in his early chapters, later suffers a stroke that leaves her incapacitated and ill, cared for by her religiously fanatical mother and sister, who also raise Wright. He frequently finds himself in conflict with his puritanical grandmother and occasionally discovers that his increasingly helpless mother approves of his defiance. When he wins an argument with his grandmother, his mother – now a powerless and grotesque figure in the household – 'hobbles' over to him 'on her paralytic legs' to kiss him (144). The woman who once beat him unconscious is now scarcely able to stand upright, an object of pity and guilt.

In addition to his troubled and tumultuous early years, Wright's autobiography offers two more sources for his lifelong fascination with the gothic genre. The first is his discovery of the pleasures of narrative fiction, at the hands of a schoolteacher who boards with his grandmother. The story that this woman 'whispers' to the child is that of *Bluebeard and His Seven Wives*, and Wright's response is powerful and life altering. He is not only mesmerized but transformed by the tale: 'As she spoke, reality changed, the look of things altered, and the world became peopled with magical presences' (37). He describes feeling 'an almost painful excitement' and his first experience of a 'total emotional response' (38). Wright describes his initial contact with fiction – in the form of a violent folktale, one of the most gothic modern fairy tales – almost like a sexual experience. The story produces in him a 'thirst for violence ... for intrigue, for plotting, for secrecy, for bloody murders'; for more gothic narrative, in other words (38). 'No words or punishment' can make him doubt or abandon his craving for such stories, which he describes as 'life' itself for him from that moment on. At this point, Wright has not even had enough schooling to be able to read, but now he 'burned to read novels' and 'tortured his mother into telling me the meaning of every strange word I saw ... because it was a gateway to a forbidden and enchanting world' (39).

The anecdote is interesting for the great power that it attributes not only to storytelling in general, but specifically to dark and bloody stories, which awaken in the young Wright a lifelong thirst for sensational fiction. The particular tale that captures his imagination is also intriguing for its focus on violence against women, something to which Wright's fiction itself often gives great prominence, sometimes disturbingly so. The best example of this is the murder of Mary Dalton in *Native Son*, an accidental murder but one over which Bigger Thomas gloats proudly, and which Wright inscribes in a long tradition of gothic murders of women with several overt references to Edgar Allan Poe's 'The Black Cat', except of course that the cat tormenting Bigger is white.

Wright's fondness for the Gothic, awakened by *Bluebeard*, is further fuelled by stories that he discovers as a teenager working as a delivery boy for a Chicago-based newspaper. Ill edited and cheap, the newspaper targets 'rural, white Protestant readers' and features a magazine supplement consisting of lurid pulp fiction and mystery stories. Once more, Wright finds himself completely seduced by this material, and spends all his time reading the magazine, hungering for 'the next instalment of a thrilling horror story' as he builds up a subscriber base among people who know him in the area (*Black Boy* 128–9). After several weeks, a man comes to ask him if he realizes what kind of magazine he has been convincing his African American neighbours to buy. Wright had been so absorbed by the magazine instalments that he had never even looked at the newspaper itself. He realizes to his horror that the magazine is a racist vehicle of Klu Klux Klan doctrines, including the advocacy of 'lynching' as a 'solution to the problem of the Negro' (131). When he reads the paper for the first time he discovers that it features articles 'so brutally anti-Negro that goose pimples broke out over my skin' (131). With brilliant conciseness and irony, the incident demonstrates that while the young Wright had been absorbed in the fictional horrors of the magazine supplement, the real horrors lay in the newspaper's racial politics. The 'goose pimples' that he gets while reading these articles allow him to understand at last that the reality of black life in the United States is far more terrifying than anything he can read in a fictional narrative.

As in *Uncle Tom's Cabin*, the underlying theme of Wright's story of his childhood is the threat of white violence – against him and against other black people – that determines social relations and shapes subjectivities in the South. When Wright is 9 years old, his uncle is shot by white people for running a business that was too successful, and Wright realizes that the 'white terror' can reach into any black home and pluck anyone from their family (53). By the time he is 10 he has developed a 'permanent dread of white people', whom he knows can 'violate my life at will' at any moment and he would be powerless to prevent it (71). This threat takes on a demonic life of its own in his imagination and fantasies and becomes an overwhelming force in his daily life: 'I had never in my life been abused by whites, but I had already become as conditioned to their existence as though I had been the victim of a thousand lynchings' (72). He finds himself 'continuously reacting to the threat of some natural force whose hostile behaviour could not be predicted' (72). As Brian Massumi has argued about threat, 'fear is the anticipatory reality in the present of a threatening future. It is the felt reality of the nonexistence, loomingly present as the *affective* fact of the matter' (Massumi 54). In other words, threat exists materially in the present as affect, and Wright's *Black Boy* is eloquent testimony to the power of threat as mental reality.

Later in the book, a friend of Wright's is lynched for sleeping with a white prostitute, probably the event that inspired the vignette about the bell-boy at the hotel in 'The Ethics of Living Jim Crow' (*Black Boy* 172). In the earlier work, the only thing that is said is that nothing was said: 'We were silent'

(*Uncle Tom's Children* 12). In *Black Boy*, Wright describes his world 'crashing' and his body becoming 'heavy' as the anxiety and depression accompanying a threat take over (172). The result is a 'paralysis of will and impulse' and a kind of nervous breakdown, all the more terrible – and gothic – for concerning something imagined rather than personally experienced:

> The actual experience would have let me see the realistic outlines of what was really happening, but as long as it remained something terrible and yet remote, something whose horror and blood might descend upon me at any moment, I was compelled to give my entire imagination over to it, an act which blocked the springs of thought and feeling in me, creating a sense of distance between me and the world in which I lived. (173)

The crisis continues, and soon the young Wright feels his self crumbling under the weight: 'My personality was numb, reduced to a lumpish, loose, dissolved state. I was a non-man, something that knew vaguely it was human but felt that it was not' (196). In this manner, he documents with an extraordinary first-person narration the deadening and distorting effects of Jim Crow legislation on black subjectivity. He finds that just as his inner world collapses, he must keep performing the role of a mindless, unfeeling menial for the whites around him in order to survive. To do so, he presents to them what he calls a 'dead face' (240). This gothic strategy – wearing an expressionless mask instead of a human face – is his most important form of self-defence in the permanently hostile environment that is the Jim Crow South. The trouble is that he has come to feel dead inside as well and sees himself drifting towards crime or oblivion, suggesting that moral monstrosity is the natural outcome of life under such conditions, which the narrator describes as 'one long, quiet, continuously contained dream of terror, tension and anxiety' (255). This line comes nearly at the end of the book, just before Wright escapes from the South by getting on a train heading North.

The Long Dream

The same year that *Black Boy* was published, Wright moved to Paris and settled in France, where he lived until his death in 1960. In 1958, after 13 years of French residence, he published one more work set entirely in the American South, a novel that took an image from the just-quoted line for its title: *The Long Dream* (1958). In fact, nothing in the novel explains the title as clearly and explicitly as this quotation from *Black Boy*. The 'long dream' is actually a nightmare of endless terror: life in the South before the reforms slowly brought on by the Civil Rights movement. Drawing on the insights articulated in *Black Boy*, *The Long Dream* focuses on the moral deformities that are produced by Jim Crow, on both whites and blacks. If white men become bloodthirsty monsters, then black men become corrupt and deceptive sycophants. The former transform slowly into fiends and the latter gradually sink into abjection. Just as power corrupts, Wright's novel suggests, so does powerlessness. The result for both sides is a loss of humanity.

The focus of *The Long Dream* is a boy named Fishbelly and his father Tyree Tucker, a prominent mortician in a Southern town. Although the main arc is a coming-of-age story, concerned with Fishbelly's racial and sexual self-discovery, the novel is almost equally concerned with Tyree's complex negotiations of black manhood and fatherhood, as well as his ambiguous compromises with the white authorities in the town. Although Tyree's official business is undertaking, he also runs a brothel and pays bribes to the police chief. In exchange for being allowed to prosper as a brothel owner, on occasion Tyree renders services to the police chief, such as fixing lynch victims' bodies so that the violence of their death is camouflaged. Fishbelly's maturation is achieved through a series of discoveries, rejections, reconciliations and arrangements with his powerful yet occasionally abject father.

As in the earlier work, the Southern setting for this novel is a moral land-scape dominated by mutual fear between whites and blacks. The fact that white people fear the African American population in their midst is made explicitly clear to Fishbelly by his father, who explains that 'white folks is scared to death of us!' (*Long Dream* 143) and that this is the reason why 'a white man always wants to see a black man either crying or grinning' (142). That the threat of lynching lies at the heart of this relationship is established by Wright early in the novel with an incident that is based on the same murder of a friend caught with a white prostitute that appears in *Uncle Tom's Children* and *Black Boy*. In *The Long Dream*, an older boy named Chris is tortured, killed and mutilated so savagely that 'not only had the whites taken Chris' life, but they had robbed him of the semblance of the human ... The mouth, lined with stumps of bro-ken teeth, yawned gapingly, an irregular, black cavity bordered by shredded tissue that had once been lips' (75). The destruction of the boy's human-ity focuses on his face, a conceit that recurs throughout the novel as Wright describes the way in which Tyree and other African Americans have to present an 'act' – like the 'mask' evoked in *Black Boy* – to white people to survive. At one point, Fishbelly watches with horror and loathing as 'a change engulf[s] his father's face and body' when he performs a perfect caricature of the abjectly obsequious Southern 'nigger' for the town mayor (126).

The deformation of African Americans by the terror of Jim Crow is a larger issue for which Chris's facial mutilation serves merely as synecdoche. Wright's novel develops the theme initiated in *Black Boy* of how terror and helpless-ness deform and mutilate Southern blacks psychologically, even if they escape actual lynching. Just as the younger Wright felt himself becoming dead and void inside, he shows Fishbelly slowly hardening as a result of his exposure to white cruelty. This process begins when Fishbelly is picked up by police and threatened with castration, which makes him faint, amusing his white torment-ers so much that over and over again they jab at his crotch with a knife. If Chris is literally castrated and killed, the young Fishbelly is humiliated, symbolically castrated and made to efface himself in self-protection, repeatedly. He is so frightened by this episode that he fails to help a wounded white man dying in a car wreck on the way home, because his terror of the police causes him to ignore the man's pleas. By the time he is a teenager, he has developed the kind of hatred for whites that makes him precisely the dangerous and gothic enemy in their midst that they fear.

In short, Wright uses the Gothic in *The Long Dream* as a way to underscore and exaggerate the mechanisms of psychological and social destruction that he sees in the South. A final example is the fire that burns down the brothel that Tyree runs, killing Fishbelly's girlfriend just after he has made plans to start a new life with her. The fire is the result of both white corruption and black neglect of fire regulations, complicating the issue of guilt, and it kills around 50 people. Wright's description of the fire is seeped in a gothic register that goes far beyond the needs of the plot in its gruesomeness and horror. The people in the bar are asphyxiated while those on the upper floors are trapped and *cooked*, producing a distinct smell of roasting flesh (221). They have stuck their black arms and legs through the wooden slats on the upper floor in an unsuccessful effort to escape, and onlookers are horrified to see that the charred limbs appear to be moving and still *alive* (218). Although the movement is just an illusion of the heat and flames, Wright's portrait of the African American victims of the fire as uncanny figures, abject, burned to death and reduced to their body parts – hovering in a space between life and death, humanity and thingness – alludes to the way in which African Americans become uncanny and terrifying in a context where their humanity is consistently denied, and resonates with the earlier tropes of the South as a hell where African Americans *burn*.

Conclusion

We have seen that Wright's sustained engagement with the Gothic begins in his earliest childhood and permeates all his published work. Drawing on the codes of the genre to describe the process by which both whites and blacks become monstrous in the Jim Crow South, Wright explores the psychological damage that the reign of terror inflicted on everyone within its geographical and mental range. In *12 Million Black Voices* (1941), he explicitly writes the history of the African American in the United States as a gothic tale:

> We black men and women in America today, as we look back upon scenes of rapine, sacrifice, and death, seem to be children of a devilish aberration, descendants of an interval of nightmare in history, fledglings of a period of amnesia on the part of men who once dreamed a great dream and forgot. (27)

Here Wright comments on American identity and myth by claiming that African American history is not a record of collective memory, but of national forgetting, and anticipates Malcolm X's reversal of King's image of a dream into an American nightmare (in speeches such as 'The Ballot or the Bullet'). Maisha L. Wester has suggested that 'Southern Gothic can be understood as a genre that is aware of the impossibility of escaping racial haunting' (25). Wright's fiction certainly emerges from a sense of this impossibility, and therefore deserves a key place in our understanding and repertoire of the Southern Gothic. It is like a piece of the puzzle without which racial haunting remains truly spectral and undefined. However, precisely because Wright's work is not so much about haunting as about violence, mental and physical, cyclical and retributive, in the present of the narrative and not the past, it could also be called Jim Crow Gothic and be recognized as a specific subset of the Southern Gothic.

BIBLIOGRAPHY

Brodziok, J. (1988). Richard Wright and Anglo-American gothic. In *Richard Wright: Myths and realities* (pp. 27–42). New York: Garland Publishing. Print.

Bryant, C. G. (2005). "The soul has bandaged moments": Reading the African American gothic in Wright's "Big Boy Leaves Home", Morrison's "Beloved", and Gomez's "Gilda". *African American Review, 39*(4), 541–553. Print.

Dietzel, S. B. (1984). The African American novel and popular culture. In M. Graham (Ed.), *The Cambridge companion to the African American novel*. Cambridge: Cambridge University Press.

Dow, W. (2014). Pulp gothicism in Richard Wright's The Outsider. In W. E. Dow, A. Craven, & Y. Nakamura (Eds.), *Richard Wright in a post-racial imaginary* (pp. 141–160). London: Bloomsbury. Print.

Massumi, B. (2010). The future birth of the affective fact: The political ontology of threat. In M. Gregg & G. J. Seigworth (Eds.), *The affects reader* (pp. 52–68). Duke University Press: Durham. Print.

O'Connor, F. (1969). The fiction writer and his country. In *Mystery and manners: Occasional prose*. New York: Macmillan. Print.

Wright, R. (1965). *Uncle Tom's children* (1936). New York: Harper and Rowe. Print.

Wright, R. (2000a). *The long dream*. Boston: Northeastern University Press, (originally 1958). Print.

Wright, R. (2000b). *Black Boy* (1945). London: Vintage. Print.

Wright, R. (2008). *12 million black voices* (1941). New York: Basic Books. Print.

Wester, M. L. (2012). *African American gothic: Screams from shadowed places*. New York: Palgrave. Print.

FURTHER READING

Bain, J. G. *Disturbing signs: Southern gothic fiction from Poe to McCullers*. Unpublished dissertation, University of Arkansaw. ProQuest. http://search.proquest.com/docview/750371293. Web.

Hakutani, Y. (1996). Richard Wright's the long dream as racial and sexual discourse. *African American Review, 30*(2), 267–280.

Walker, M. (1988). *Richard Wright: Daemonic genius*. New York: Amistad Press.

CHAPTER 24

To Kill a Mockingbird and the Turn from the Gothic to Southern Liberalism

Michael L. Manson

I would like to leave some record of the kind of life that existed in a very small world. ... This is small-town middle-class southern life as opposed to the Gothic ... In other words, all I want to be is the Jane Austen of south Alabama. (Harper Lee, 1964)

It is hard to square Harper Lee's ambition to write Austen-like novels of manners with the Southern Gothic elements of *To Kill a Mockingbird*, which features the 'malevolent phantom' Boo Radley, a town's collusion with the scandalous conviction of Tom Robinson for an impossible rape, a barely avoided lynching, a man's incest with his daughter, his later attempt to murder two children, and a morphine-addicted Confederate patriot who curses a man for defending African Americans and spends her final days reading *Ivanhoe*, which Mark Twain held indirectly responsible for the Civil War. And yet a reading attentive to genre reveals that *To Kill a Mockingbird* is governed less by the Gothic than by the *Bildungsroman*. It is a curiously shortened *Bildungsroman*, since Scout is only 9 when the novel concludes and since Lee makes a point at the end of how much more experience Scout needs. Still, *To Kill a Mockingbird* is first and foremost a *Bildungsroman*, depicting the education of two children, especially Scout, into a particular Southern and liberal worldview.[1] The Gothic is one phase of Scout's education, one that she must reject in order to grow in insight. From Atticus, Maudie, and Calpurnia, Scout learns the tenets of Southern liberal segregationism, but she also develops her own critical assessment of her society, discarding the racialism she has learned from Atticus and paving the way for the mature Jean Louise met in *Go Set a Watchman*, who believes in integration and can now turn a more critical eye on her father's politics.

M.L. Manson (✉)
American University, Washington, DC, USA

THE GOTHIC AS SOCIAL CRITIQUE

The Gothic influences only the first quarter of *To Kill a Mockingbird*. Gothic elements appear in its opening pages when Scout orients the reader, describing the geography of the neighborhood and the Radley Place, which 'jutted into a sharp curve' as if to interrupt the normal flow of traffic and force the passers-by to linger, exposing not just the porch but the side of the lot (9). Like so many gothic edifices, the Radley Place is decaying. White clapboard has become 'slate-gray,' the shingles are 'rain-rotted,' and the veranda—site of so much Southern conviviality—is no longer inviting but has become 'caves.' In a moment of fine local color, Scout describes the 'swept' yard as overgrown. In this touch, Lee replaces the plantation that has figured in so much Southern Gothic with something closer to most readers: the middle-class household. The middle-class home is expected to be neat, orderly, and modest, but the white picket fence that usually enforces bourgeois boundaries only 'drunkenly guarded the front yard.' The Radley Place represents the gothic decay of the middle class, and readers are certain from this point forward that the novel will involve some suspense, that the climax will reveal the identity of the house's 'malevolent phantom,' and that the plot will expose something usually not discussed about the characters' or the society's repressed reality.[2]

The gothic elements of *To Kill a Mockingbird* expose Southern society as riven by gender binaries, patriarchal abuse, class division, and racial animosity. Scout struggles to create an identity outside Southern womanhood, and Dill's games try to force Boo to 'come out,' making homosexuality visible for those with the eyes to see it. The novel features no functioning and complete nuclear families. The fathers in the Radley and Ewell families are revealed as abusive and incestuous.[3]

Like many a Southern Gothic tale, the social critique expressed in *To Kill a Mockingbird* involves race and scapegoating. The paragraph following the description of the Radley Place relates a long list of things that 'people' blamed on Boo, from cold snaps to small crimes:

> Once the town was terrorized by a series of morbid nocturnal events: people's chickens and household pets were found mutilated; although the culprit was Crazy Addie, who eventually drowned himself in Barker's Eddy, people still looked at the Radley Place, unwilling to discard their initial suspicions. (9)

No small-town idyll, the novel presents a town haunted by suspicion and incrimination. The 'mutilated' chickens and pets recall the mutilated bodies of the lynched that are never explicitly mentioned, while the suicide of Crazy Addie recalls the desperation underlying Southern violence. The 'malevolent phantom' will turn out to be not Boo but the townspeople, who will turn their groundless suspicions on another innocent, Tom Robinson, before returning to their routines.

At some point or another in the first half of the novel, we encounter a range of gothic effects, from horror to decay and from the perverse to the grotesque. The most poignant and central gothic scenes, however, feature the uncanny. After the frightening scene in Chapter 1 in which Jem slaps the side of the Radley house, the children find gifts that may or may not be benevolent. In Chapter 4, Scout discovers chewing gum in one of the Radleys' live oaks and later 'the kind of box wedding rings came in' (38). These gifts are mysterious and could point in multiple directions, from true offers of friendship to something creepier. The chapter also ends with the uncanny: Scout's secret that she heard someone laughing in the Radley house the day she rolled up to its porch in a tire (45).

ANTI-GOTHIC HUMANIZATION

These gothic moments are short-lived, nevertheless. Chapter 5 begins the project of humanizing the Radley story and extricating it from the gothic plot in which it has been embedded. Maudie is the first to satisfy Scout's desperate curiosity about why Boo stays in the house, explaining that the Radleys are foot-washing Baptists who 'think women are a sin by definition. They take the Bible literally, you know' (50). Her explanation replaces the haunted psychological explanations preferred by the Gothic with societal ones. Maudie gives Scout her first lesson in feminism, connecting how people treat others to their ideas about people. Maudie takes one step further, pointing out that ideology explains only part of behavior. The rest is personality: Maudie's 'voice hardened. … sometimes the Bible in the hand of one man is worse than a whiskey bottle in the hand of—oh, of your father.' Like Atticus, Maudie teaches Scout to never treat someone as merely a member of a group. When asked whether the things said about 'B—Mr. Arthur' are true, Maudie says plainly, 'No, child, … that is a sad house' (51). The move from a gothic to a social and realistic understanding of the world is signified by a change in names as Boo becomes humanized into Mr. Arthur, someone worthy of respect, and when the house becomes sad, not haunted. The lesson is solidified in the second half of the chapter when Atticus instructs the children to 'stop tormenting that man' (54). Boo is a man, not a ghost who says 'boo.'

The anti-gothic humanization of Boo begins in earnest after the climax in Chap. 6 of Dill's attempts to see Boo, when the children glimpse a shadow at the Radley Place reach out toward Jem and then as they run away, someone shoots at them. Readers begin to speculate in Chap. 7 that Boo has sewn up Jem's pants and placed gifts in the live oak for the Finch kids. The uncanny turns here from threatening to intimate when Jem realizes that his sewn-up pants reveal something deeper about his relationship with Boo:

> Jem shuddered. 'Like somebody was readin' my mind … like somebody could tell what I was gonna do. Can't anybody tell what I'm gonna do lest they know me, can they, Scout?'
> Jem's question was an appeal. I reassured him: 'Can't anybody tell what you're gonna do lest they live in the house with you, and even I can't tell sometimes.'
> We were walking past our tree. In its knot-hole rested a ball of gray twine. (66)

Jem's gothic shudder is caused by the fear that Boo has penetrated his mind, and yet readers realize that Arthur's motive is warmer and friendlier when the next paragraph answers Jem's appeal: the gifts bestowed in 'our tree.' The twine is the first of a series of gifts that, when they come to a stop at the end of the chapter, leave Jem crying out of Scout's hearing. The intimacy so threatening at the beginning of the chapter has become tender, the uncanny changing from the fear of a 'malevolent phantom' who can read Jem's mind to the certainty of a benevolent gift giver. This transformation is completed in Chap. 8 when Scout is the last to realize that it was Arthur who placed a blanket around her while Maudie's house burned down. With 21 chapters and 241 pages left to go, this is the last time before the climax that Arthur appears. Although the Radley story looms large in readers' and especially film viewers' memories, the trajectory of that narrative is wrapped up by Chap. 8. The novel becomes much more than the gothic Radley story.

Toward a *Bildungsroman*

While the Gothic shapes much of *To Kill a Mockingbird*, it is not the primary genre expectation. As we have seen, the Gothic quickly becomes tamed as Scout learns to appreciate Arthur's humanity through the tutelage of adults, Atticus and Maudie. While other Southern novels explore the gothic nature of the Southern experience, Lee resolutely sets *To Kill a Mockingbird* on the path of the *Bildungsroman*, making the novel primarily a portrait of Southern maturity—what one gains from the liberal education that the South could offer at the time, including a triumph over racism.

The narrative structure of a *Bildungsroman* is usually episodic, each episode contributing to the education of the protagonist. Thus the Radley story is only one part of Scout's education. Even Chap. 8, an unusually rich chapter in which Arthur is revealed as Scout's guardian, is largely about other issues: the nostalgia that Southerners feel for the first great snowstorm ever seen and for the community spirit of small towns responding to a fire; a psycho-racial narrative discovering something suggestive in the 'morphodite' snowman, black on the inside and white on the outside; and, for the *Bildungsroman* narrative, the education that Scout receives from the example of Maudie's good humor in the face of disaster. Other chapters address different parts of Scout's education, many of which are quite far from the Gothic. In Chap. 9, Scout learns to navigate the family dynamics presented by Uncle Jack, Aunt Alexandra, and Cousin Francis. Chapter 10 incorporates elements of the Western genre with the revelation that Atticus is the 'deadest shot in Maycomb,' ensuring that readers see Atticus as heroic even before the Robinson trial. The effect of these episodes is to subsume the Gothic in the *Bildungsroman*.

Nowhere is the novel's subsumption of the Gothic more keenly felt than in the conclusion of Part I. Chapter 11 is the stand-alone story of Mrs. Dubose, so divorced from any larger narrative that it could be cut without losing any information that forwards the plot, and yet the episode is among the novel's most memorable. The chapter clarifies that the Gothic is a mode of understanding that Scout must grow out of if she is to achieve the mature wisdom that Atticus and Maudie possess. Rather than revealing the nature of the South, the Gothic obscures the humanity of outsiders by turning them into phantoms or grotesques.[4]

Lee fronts the gothic elements of the Dubose story. Gothic decay oppresses both the house and Dubose's face. The house is 'all dark and creepy' with 'shadows and things on the ceiling,' while Dubose's face is 'horrible,' the 'color of a dirty pillowcase' (121). The Gothic transforms the life-giving force of water into a force of rot, from the smell of 'rain-rotted gray houses' to the 'glacier'-like 'wet' around Dubose's mouth. This gothic scene is Southern in its poverty, a constant reminder of defeat in the Civil War: the smell of 'coal-oil lamps, water dippers, and unbleached domestic sheets.' The horror increases when Dubose stops listening to Jem's reading and her mouth develops a 'private existence of its own,' a detached doubling of Dubose herself. The insults regularly flying out of Dubose's mouth become physically manifest in the saliva forming a 'vicious substance coming to a boil.' The sight of her mouth as a 'clam hole at low tide' working 'out and in' moves into the uncanny realm of gothic imagery, vaguely sexual, laden with disgust, and suggesting a realm of activity beyond the conscious mind.

If *To Kill a Mockingbird* were primarily gothic, it would explore that unconscious realm, but its primary structure is as a *Bildungsroman*, and so it moves the scene out of the Gothic and into the education of Scout. Rather than providing more revelations from the unconscious, visits to Mrs. Dubose are punctuated with lessons. Atticus teaches them that '[w]hen people are sick they don't look nice sometimes' (123) and that Dubose's favourite term of abuse for Atticus is

> just one of those terms that don't mean anything—like snot-nose. It's hard to explain—ignorant, trashy people use it when they think somebody's favoring Negroes over and above themselves. It's slipped into usage with some people like ourselves, when they want a common, ugly term to label somebody. (124)

The novel demonstrates Atticus's explanation falling far short of the truth. Dehumanizing terms for African Americans and their white supporters do in fact 'mean' something: these terms lead to the jury's conviction of Tom Robinson and thus his death. And Atticus's conviction that racism spreads from lower social classes to higher ones reveals a class blindness that Scout does not have. Yet *To Kill a Mockingbird* is about Scout's education, and Atticus trains her here to rise above one form of racism. Jem, meanwhile, receives his own education, learning to respond to the woman's insults by gazing 'at Mrs. Dubose with a face devoid of resentment' (126).

Instead of concluding with some gothic revelation of misdeeds, the chapter ends with a revelation more suited to the social realism of the *Bildungsroman*. Dubose remains a crazed racist, but she is also an example of 'real courage,' the 'bravest person' Atticus ever knew. She chose to die in pain but free of her morphine addiction. Atticus believes that she would have suffered no dishonor had she continued to take morphine: 'when you're as sick as she was, it's all right to take anything to make it easier' (127). Nevertheless, Dubose lived by a higher code, more in keeping with traditional Southern values. She wanted 'to leave this world beholden to nothing and nobody.' The values of the Old South live on in Dubose, who knows a Lost Cause when she sees one: 'It's when you know you're licked before you begin but you begin anyway and you see it through no matter what' (128). In explaining Dubose, Atticus also explains his defense of Tom Robinson. More importantly, he describes the South's post-Reconstruction understanding of the Civil War as a Lost Cause: the South standing for principle without regard to the unlikelihood of success. Dubose, racist scold and defender of segregation, and Atticus, champion of humanity against prejudice, are both products of this South. Their courage when facing doomed matters of principle is their Southern heritage. It is what Scout can be proud of even when she learns how deeply racist the citizens of Maycomb are. Atticus's statement 'She was the bravest person I ever knew' bookends the chapter and closes Part I of the novel. The chapter had opened with Atticus's gracious response to Dubose's abusive speech and Scout's conclusion that '[i]t was times like these when I thought my father, who hated guns and had never been to any wars, was the bravest man who ever lived' (116). Over the course of the chapter, Scout learns the nature of true bravery. Atticus's Southern graciousness in the face of his town's abuse is brave, but braver still is the Southern willingness to take on Lost Causes, whether it be the Civil War, a fight against morphine addiction, or the attempt to save Tom Robinson from certain conviction.

At the conclusion of Part I, in a literally central chapter, Scout learns which part of her Southern heritage is most important in motivating her father. Although the novel is remembered most for the lesson of learning to walk in another's skin, Lee has also found a way of taking pride in the South, depicting its character as Jane Austen might. The South is built on the bravery necessary for pursuing principle even when success is unlikely. Without the Dubose scene, the novel would have no strong case for Southern virtue.[5] The novel would have only the shame of racism.

SOUTHERN LIBERALISM

The Gothic excels at exposing the hypocrisy festering underneath cherished ideals, articulating long before Walter Benjamin that every document of civilization is also a document of barbarism, whether it is Maycomb breeding a murderous racism under its placid surface or the children's discovery of the uncanny in Boo—their simultaneous attraction to and horror of the story of a young man who dared rebel against the social order and stab his father only to be locked away in his father's house, never to see the light of day again. The *Bildungsroman*, however, requires a different sort of social analysis, asking what a young person must learn in order to fit in with and perhaps change a particular social order. Scout receives her education in empathy most famously from Atticus, but Maudie teaches her about the existence of sexism and instructs her in seeing how personality is more important than ideology. Maudie also models a successful form of Southern womanhood that is independent and ambiguously gendered. Calpurnia provides a third source of knowledge and guidance. One of her chief lessons is in code-switching, teaching Scout the skill of speaking differently in different social situations.

Together, Scout's three teachers instruct her in the era's Southern liberalism.[6] The Southern liberals that Lee portrays still view the Civil War as a struggle over states' rights and still look with suspicion on Northerners, even Northern Alabamans, and yet they support New Deal measures such as the National Recovery Act. Because Scout's liberal mentors value empathy, human dignity, and the rule of law, they oppose racism, supporting African Americans in their struggle to be treated respectfully. And yet they retain racialist theories and remain committed to segregation. Maudie teaches Scout that Atticus is not alone in his fight for Tom Robinson. Several members of the white elite support Atticus, from Judge Taylor, who appointed him to the case, to Link Deas, the grocery store owner who employed Robinson, defending him in court while still calling him 'boy' (222). Best illustrating the complexity of Southern liberalism is Braxton Underwood, the publisher who 'despises' African Americans (178) but assists the case at key moments, including covering Atticus with a shotgun during the attempted lynching. Underwood believes in the rule of law, but he also believes that African Americans are a lesser race. Illustrating the difficulty of living as an integrationist is Dolphus Raymond, whose complete lack of standing suggests that, at this point in history, the South is capable of creating only varieties of segregationists. Raymond pretends to be a drunkard in order to live as he wants: integrated with African Americans.

The reader learns about Southern liberalism along with Scout, acquiring a more complex understanding than outsiders are used to having of the South, especially through the Southern Gothic. Outsiders learn in *To Kill a Mockingbird* that few Southerners are either Klansmen or integrationists; most are segregationists. Some segregationists believe in the fundamental dignity of African Americans, despite holding firm racialist theories. A range of genders and religions are possible in the South—Scout, Maudie, and Calpurnia live out alternatives to Southern womanhood as Dill, Atticus, and Raymond live out alternatives to Southern manhood. Maycomb is home to Jews as well as Methodists and foot-washing Baptists. There is outrage toward Hitler's persecution of the Jews, even among those who persecute blacks. The South is not solid: northern Alabama tried to stay in the Union during the Civil War and is still home to Republicans and new ideas. The divide between rural and urban pertains even in small-town Maycomb, town folks not always comprehending country ways or town and country conflicts. Southern society is marked not just by decay, hypocrisy, violence, and racism, but also by acts of graciousness and bravery. Most importantly, outsiders learn that there is a culture of liberalism using Southern ways and goals to move Southern society forward.[7]

A Racialist Worldview

Scout, however, is not merely a blank slate on which her instructors write. She does not only receive education but applies a native insight, taking her beyond her instructors' teaching, including that of Atticus.[8] Atticus holds a lightly racialized worldview. He believes in races, breeds, sets of people, and hierarchies of class. His belief in the dignity of all humans runs deep and strong, and he sees greater variation within categories, but he continues to divide the world into race and class hierarchies. Readers widely misunderstand Atticus because Lee so often contrasts him with others. Lee makes a point of distinguishing Atticus from crude racialism in Chap. 13, which is almost entirely devoted to the contrast between Atticus and Aunt Alexandra. Alexandra's 'preoccupation with heredity' leads her to divide society into 'tribal groups,' each of which 'had a Streak' (147). Atticus explicitly mocks the idea of streaks when he asks whether 'the Finches have an Incestuous Streak.' Scout's response to Alexandra's typically Southern concern with family and heredity is more direct: 'Somewhere, I had received the impression that Fine Folks were people who did the best they could with the sense they had.' The 'somewhere' is obvious; Scout has been listening to her father, who does not speak in terms of heredity. Consequently, when he later encourages his children to 'live up to your name' because they are 'the product of several generations' gentle breeding,' the children are perturbed (151). Scout thinks, 'This is not my father. My father never thought these thoughts. My father never spoke so. Aunt Alexandra had put him up to this, somehow.' Scout and Atticus see individuals, not family breeds. Alexandra is a thorough-going racialist. Her racism does not extend as deeply as Ewell's, but she would have Atticus quit his case. She supports the racist order.

Atticus is not entirely free of racial thinking either. He is at his worst during the trial when he describes the code against miscegenation: 'She has committed no crime, she has merely broken a rigid and time-honored code of our society, a code so severe that whoever breaks it is hounded from our midst as unfit to live with' (231). He believes that separate can be equal. When Cecil Jacobs asks Scout whether Atticus is a radical, Atticus says that he is as 'radical as Cotton Tom Heflin,' a contemporary US senator from Alabama who was an outspoken racist and segregationist (287). Atticus is clearly more humane than Heflin, but he supports the racial order that Heflin had helped create. In 1901, Heflin had helped draft the notorious Alabama state constitution, which had disenfranchised poor whites and all blacks, the constitutional convention opening with the President's statement that the intention of the convention was to 'establish white supremacy in this State.' By associating himself with Heflin, Atticus indicates his support of segregation even though he fights for the recognition of the dignity of African Americans.

Atticus's belief in breeding is less rigid than Alexandra's, but it does appear, and breeding implies a racial theory of humanity. Atticus distinguishes between 'ignorant, trashy people' and 'people like ourselves' who will sometimes stoop to using 'a common, ugly term to label somebody' (124). People like the

Finches are higher than the 'common' and the 'trashy.' This is less a matter of behavior than the difference between people who should know better and those—the 'ignorant'—who do not. How they should know better is unstated, probably a matter of race, class, education, and personality.

Atticus's racism is more fully described in *Go Set a Watchman*. What get more attention in *To Kill a Mockingbird* are his failures to understand the depth of racism in his community. In an impassioned moment, Atticus explains:

> 'As you grow older, you'll see white men cheat black men every day of your life, but let me tell you something and don't you forget it—whenever a white man does that to a black man, no matter who he is, how rich he is, or how fine a family he comes from, that white man is trash.'
>
> Atticus was speaking so quietly his last word crashed on our ears. I looked up, and his face was vehement. 'There's nothing more sickening to me than a low-grade white man who'll take advantage of a Negro's ignorance. Don't fool yourselves—it's all adding up and one of these days we're going to pay the bill for it. I hope it's not in you children's time.' (252)

This is one of Atticus's memorable anti-racist moments, but he also mischaracterizes the problem, which is not 'ignorance' but power. Tom Robinson is not ignorant. He has not been 'cheated.' Ewell and then the jury act out of the confidence of racial privilege. They know that they will get away with their crimes because and only because of race. There is nothing Robinson needs to *know* so that he can protect himself. His knowledge or ignorance is not the issue. The issue is the power of whites to define race and to act on the privileges they have given themselves.[9]

Scout quietly replaces Atticus's racialist worldview with a more sociological one.[10] For example, Scout reveals the sociological forces at work when she describes Gates's class exercise in current events. She is skeptical of the exercise's goals, its fight against the 'evils' of bad posture and poise (279). She believes that its real goals are to make each student feel 'more than ever anxious to return to the Group.' Education in Maycomb is about conformity, not critical thinking or liberation. Furthermore, Scout realizes that the sociological realities of Maycomb prevent reform: 'The idea was profound, but as usual, in Maycomb it didn't work very well.' Rural poverty breeds class resentment: few 'rural children had access to newspapers, so the burden of Current Events was borne by the town children, convincing the bus children more deeply that the town children got all of the attention anyway.' When rural children do try to participate, they use the Grit Paper, which 'was associated with liking fiddling, eating syrupy biscuits for lunch, being a holy-roller, singing Sweetly Sings the Donkey and pronouncing it dunkey, all of which the state paid teachers to discourage' (280). Scout sees education as a state agent of class repression, promoting some class values over others, from eating habits to cultural taste and even religion. When Little Chuck Little brings an advertisement rather than a newspaper article, Gates stops and corrects him, but Scout sees more deeply, understanding that Chuck is 'a hundred years old in his knowledge of cows and their habits.' School exercises make the otherwise knowledgeable Chuck look ignorant and contribute to the rural/town tensions that fuel the resentment and violence of the Cunninghams and the Ewells. While Atticus and other townsfolk see the sordidness of working-class families as a result of bad 'breeding,' Scout sees sociological forces at work.

The contrast between Scout's sociological analysis and Atticus's racialist analysis appears earlier in another education scene. Like Gates, Caroline uses education to enforce conformity. She tells Scout that she is too young to read and to write cursive and insists that Atticus stop teaching her. Caroline would, of course, be scandalized to learn that Calpurnia, not Atticus, has been teaching her to write cursive, so Scout does not mention that. On her first day of class, Scout learns to work under the radar, away from surveillance. And she knows that Caroline, like Gates, does not understand the lives of country folks. Unlike Scout, Caroline cannot read Walter Cunningham's face to see that he has hookworms and therefore cannot afford either shoes or lunch, much less repay any loan. In fact, Caroline is so far removed from understanding country ways that she might not understand Southern ways, even though she is from Alabama. Atticus has explained to Scout:

> If he held his mouth right, Mr. Cunningham could get a WPA job, but his land would go to ruin if he left it, and he was willing to go hungry to keep his land and vote as he pleased. Mr. Cunningham, said Atticus, came from a set breed of men. (23)

Once again, Atticus has a racialist worldview, thinking in terms of 'set breeds,' but he also uses his famous empathy to understand the perspectives of others, in this case Cunningham's rejection of the New Deal. Cunningham rejects not only the loss of land but also the loss of political freedom, which includes not just how he votes but what he says. He finds coercive the freedom from want that the New Deal offers. It is not clear whether Atticus agrees with Cunningham, but he admires the principled stand. Like Mrs. Dubose and like Atticus, Cunningham stands by his convictions regardless of whether they result in a Lost Cause. This spirit as well as his love of the land and political freedom make Cunningham a Southerner.

Scout brings her sociological awareness to bear on Caroline as well as the Cunninghams. Caroline is not just a teacher; she is from Winston County, and 'every child' knew that Winston had seceded from Alabama when it seceded from the Union and now is 'full of Liquor Interests, Big Mules, steel companies, Republicans, professors, and other persons of no background' (18). There is mockery of Southern prejudices in this list, and readers learn once again that Scout and other children have absorbed these prejudices from their parents, but the action of the chapter demonstrates that outsiders like Caroline do not understand the rural South. The passage suggests that the South is much more complicated than it appears from the outside. It might be worthwhile walking in the skins of white Southerners as well as those of African Americans and outcasts like Arthur Radley. And Scout even suggests that readers empathize with the Ewells, explaining that Maycomb's charity failed truly to reach out to the poor as equals: 'Maycomb gave them Christmas baskets, welfare money, and the back of its hand' (257). While Atticus champions empathy and principled convictions, he is trapped in racialist thinking. It is Scout who uses empathy to grasp a richer history and sociology. The novel even suggests that Scout learned some of her more sociological approach from Maudie, who teaches Scout to have 'enough humility to think, when they look at a Negro, there but for the Lord's kindness am I' (270). Some readers have taken Maudie to mean that Scout should pity African Americans (McElhaney 217), but in the context of the trial, what makes Robinson less fortunate is not so much his race as how whites treat his race, from the murderous racism of Bob Ewell to the cowardice of most white townsfolk whom Maudie castigates in this passage. Maudie, like Scout, points toward systematic racism.

CONCLUSION

Under the tutelage of Atticus, Maudie, and Calpurnia, Scout has grown out of the Gothic, its insights being too limited for understanding the South. Yet Scout has also transformed her father's lessons in empathy, expanding them further than he has been able to because she has moved beyond his racialist thinking. When this *Bildungsroman* ends, Scout's education is far from complete. She will need to learn more than either she or her father understands. In pursuing her ambition to become the Jane Austen of south Alabama, Harper Lee has made the Gothic just one of the customs she depicts in her novel of manners. The Gothic is part of the South, but it falls far short of explaining the region or its people. In *To Kill a Mockingbird*, Harper Lee uses the Southern Gothic and the *Bildungsroman* not just to portray the South, but to map out how the South can change from within. Atticus, Maudie, Judge Taylor, Sheriff Tate, Link Deas, and Braxton Underwood, among others, are already fighting for the dignity of African Americans by appealing to Southern values. Lee hoped that *To Kill a Mockingbird* would inspire further action and greater understanding. She succeeded.

NOTES

1. Murray argues that the novel is more about Jem's education than Scout's and describes the numerous misreadings occurring when critics focus on Scout's growth.
2. In the first extended study of the novel, Johnson argues that it is a gothic work describing 'the confrontation of the unknown Alien or Other in the process of self-definition, and the power and significance of legal boundaries in the life and mind of the community' (39). Despite the many gothic elements in the novel, I would argue that the Gothic is primarily defined by its effect on the audience. Readers must feel dread, horror, terror, or the uncanny for a tale to be

gothic (Crow 2). One must want to say 'Don't open that door' (Ellis xvi). Such moments are rare, making primary the *Bildungsroman* and the novel of manners. Petry observes that the novel was first praised for its difference from 'other, less savory southern texts,' quoting the *Times Book Review*'s approval of the novel's avoidance of the 'current lust for morbid, grotesque tales of Southern depravity' (viii). The best guide defining and describing the genre is Leitch.

3. Johnson has exhaustively catalogued the gothic elements of the novel and described how they cross social boundaries between self and Other. See also Blackford's queer reading of the novel. Blackford's larger subject is the novel's use of nineteenth-century literary forms and twentieth-century techniques.

4. Murray describes this chapter as evidence of the 'forced transformation of genre' occurring when Lee turned her short-story collection into a novel (77). I would observe that the *Bildungsroman* is often episodic.

5. For an opposite view, see Seidel, who argues that Scout's 'central problem is that she is in danger of becoming a southerner' for she 'embodies all of the faults of the Old South when we first meet her' (81). Scout must journey 'from a code of honor to a code of law.' I would argue that Scout learns to bring one part of her Southern heritage against another. Seidel describes a positive Southern heritage when she explains how Atticus reflects the Ciceronian tradition of the South (84).

6. For a description of Southern liberalism, see Gladwell.

7. Lee says little about the roots of this liberalism in the Christianity so central to Southern identity. She satirizes the Methodist church of her youth as well as foot-washing Baptists and even the AME. Atticus speaks more about the law than about God, but the centrality of his faith is clear when he explains that he 'couldn't go to church and worship God if I didn't try to help that man' (120). Not all Southern liberals are religious. Neither Tate nor Underwood attends church, but Atticus does (167–68).

8. Fine is one of the first to suggest Scout's awareness of Atticus's limitations, his 'subtle but unquestionable tolerance of sexism, racism, and incest' (72).

9. Discussions of Atticus's weaknesses have grown recently. Pryal is especially sharp about his failure to empathize.

10. Jay places the novel in the context of the novel of racial liberalism, which emphasizes sympathetic understanding over economic interpretations of racism. He goes on to argue that the novel's depiction of race thus fails and becomes less interesting than the sexual space it opens up. I argue, however, that the novel does open up space for economic interpretations. It is a small space, but many Southern liberals struggled to imagine a way out of personal and institutional racism that did not require massive disruption. *Mockingbird* and *Watchman* reflect one writer's evolving attempt to understand and promote change. Although much of the initial reaction to *Watchman* focused on the revelation that Atticus is racist, Scout already fights his racism in *Mockingbird*, and Shields had described Lee's father's evolution from segregationist to integrationist (120–26). The novel's effect on readers also needs to be considered. See, for example, Engar's multi-faceted description of *Mockingbird*'s effect on lawyers. Wood provides a more spirited defense of Atticus's practice of law.

WORKS CITED

Blackford, H. (2011). *Mockingbird passing: Closeted traditions and sexual curiosities in Harper Lee's novel*. Knoxville: University of Tennessee Press.

Crow, C. L. (2009). *American gothic* (Gothic literary studies). Cardiff: University of Wales Press.

Ellis, J. (2013). On Southern gothic literature. In *Southern gothic literature* (Critical insights). Amenia: Grey House.

Engar, A. *To kill a mockingbird*: Fifty years of influence on the legal profession. *Meyer*, 66–80.

Gladwell, M. (2010). The courthouse ring: Atticus Finch and the limits of Southern liberalism. In M. J. Meyer (Ed.), *Harper Lee's to kill a mockingbird: New essays*. Lanham: Scarecrow.

Jay, Gregory. 'Queer Children and Representative Men: Harper Lee, Racial Liberalism, and the Dilemma of *To Kill a Mockingbird*'. *American Literary History* 27.3 (2015) 487–522. Print.

Johnson, C. D. (1994). *To kill a mockingbird: Threatening boundaries* (Twayne's masterwork studies). New York: Twayne.

Lee, Harper. Interview with Roy Newquist. *Counterpoint*. By Roy Newquist. London: George Allen, 1965. Print.

Lee, H. (2001). *To kill a mockingbird 1960*. New York: Harper Perennial.

Leitch, T. (2002). *Crime films* (Genres in American cinema). Cambridge: Cambridge University Press.

McElaney, H. (2010). "Just one kind of folks": The normalizing power of disability in *to kill a mockingbird*. In M. Meyer (Ed.), *Harper Lee's to kill a mockingbird: New essays* (pp. 211–230). Lanham: Scarecrow.

Murray, J. (2010). More than one way to (mis) read a mockingbird. *The Southern Literary Journal, 43*(1), 75–91.

Petry, A. H. (2008). *On Harper Lee: Essays and reflections*. Knoxville: University of Tennessee Press.

Pryal, K. R. G. (2010). Walking in another's skin: Failure of empathy in *to kill a mockingbird*. In M. J. Meyer (Ed.), *Harper Lee's to kill a mockingbird: New essays* (pp. 174–190). Lanham: Scarecrow.

Seidel, K. L. Growing up Southern: Resisting the code for Southerners in *to kill a mockingbird*. *Petry*, 79–92.

Shields, C. J. (2006). *Mockingbird: A portrait of Harper Lee*. New York: Holt.

Wood, J. B. (2010). Bending the law: The search for justice and moral purpose. In M. J. Meyer (Ed.), *Harper Lee's to kill a mockingbird: New essays* (pp. 81–99). Lanham: Scarecrow.

CHAPTER 25

Raising the Indigenous Undead

Eric Gary Anderson

Native American and Indigenous writers in the South as elsewhere make occasional, not extensive, forays into the Gothic. However, this is not for a lack of paranormal activity in Native literatures, which are highly populated with ghosts, spirits, and other entities that the Oklahoma Cherokee storytellers who collaboratively created *Cherokee Stories of the Turtle Island Liars' Club* (Teuton et al.) describe as Ulvsgedi (The Wondrous). The continuing vitality of Indigenous ghost stories points up the continuing presence as well as the diverse functions and motives of Indigenous ghosts. As Renée L. Bergland rightly observes (even as her remarkable study largely sidesteps the South), 'Indian ghosts are everywhere in the pages of American literature' (19). These ghosts also crop up with some regularity in other domains, from the highly local places where many of them were forged in colonial genocide and violence to the seemingly ubiquitous 'Indian burial ground' that characters in non-Native mass market horror stories so frequently make the mistake of disrespecting. Yet I am most concerned here with how Indian ghosts, monsters, and other avatars of the Wondrous work within Indigenous American literatures, particularly those associated with the US South.

Of course, in storytelling circles that now extend to the ethereal realm of Facebook, an inter-tribal 'Native Ghost Stories' community page with over 74,000 'likes' sets out 'to deliver Stories from Native Americans From All of North America or where ever there are Native Americans with creepy, chilling, eerie, goose bumping stories.'[1] Southern Native ghosts and hauntings are active, but far from alone, within this larger Indigenous context. However, Facebook harbors more localized Southern groups, too, such as 'Lumbee Ghost Stories, Legends, and Lore,' created by Nancy Strickland Fields (Lumbee), who is working on a book that 'will not only document these very fascinating stories,

E.G. Anderson (✉)
George Mason University, Fairfax, VA, USA

© The Editor(s) (if applicable) and The Author(s) 2016
S.C. Street, C.L. Crow (eds.), *The Palgrave Handbook of the Southern Gothic*,
DOI 10.1057/978-1-137-47774-3_25

but also reveal how integral they have been to preserving Lumbee culture for hundreds of years.' This group's nearly 3600 members share both stories and photographs of supernaturally afflicted houses, backyards, public spaces, and people. Fields explains:

> These stories have empowered the Lumbee and challenged this tribe to learn in depth, who we are as Lumbee people, as well as how interconnected we are as a people. Personally, these stories also made me feel proud that I belong to a strong, distinct, ancient, indigenous culture that has spanned for hundreds if not thousands of years. ('Lumbee Ghost Stories')

Building on her comments, I argue that Native Southern ghost and monster stories typically eschew or downplay Euro-American gothic conventions—and, surprisingly often, fear itself—in favor of haunts that foster anti-colonial critique as well as Indigenous community.

INDIGENOUS HAUNTINGS

From the Cherokee monster Spearfinger—who stalks through stories, thrilling small children and other listeners—to the ghosts of Indian female ancestors who float through Chickasaw writer Linda Hogan's late twentieth-century Florida Everglades novel *Power* and instill not fear so much as a powerful, mysterious sense of kinship in Omishto, the book's teenage protagonist, Indigenous hauntings raise the Indigenous undead in ways that acknowledge difficulty, tension, uncertainty, trauma, and loss. Yet they also attempt to resettle the sites of this trauma, console and heal the wounded, exorcise the demons, and improve if not resolve troubled and troubling situations. As Coll Thrush observes, 'examining ghost stories can be a sort of place-based methodology, in which hauntings gesture toward salient conflicts and patterns in the history of conquest. A ghost, in effect, is a place's past speaking to its—and our—present' (58). Haunted places are audible and legible; they speak 'salient conflicts and patterns' through their ghosts; and while they are certainly capable of instilling fear, ghosts tell other stories, too, not all of which are generated by conquest, lodged in a past that returns primarily to plague the present, or patterned in ways that follow the expectations of non-Native horror genres, including the Gothic.

Admittedly, Spearfinger *is* terrifying and seemingly unvanquishable—until, in Cherokee storyteller Kathi Smith Littlejohn's telling, a little boy, with the help of a small bird, vanquishes her and becomes a hero. As Woody Hansen points out in a *Cherokee Stories of the Turtle Island Liars' Club* conversation about Spearfinger, 'There is a darkened nature about some things and some people' (239); the monster helps remind people to be aware of this potential, witchy darkness. Nevertheless, the four spectral women in *Power* never inspire out-and-out chills. They first appear to Omishto 'walking slightly above the ground as if they are gliding and have no feet' (24); she tells us, 'They remind me of ghosts' (25). Her Aunt Ama does not answer when Omishto asks who they are: 'She closes her eyes and there's a look on her face I can't name, like she has seen something terrible and beautiful at one and the same time' (26). At the end of the novel Omishto accepts the women's invitation and walks with them to Kili Swamp, the Taiga's home place. Spectral as they seem to be, they help her navigate the complexities she faces and they guide her to the place where she needs and wants to be. Indian ghosts in Indigenous literatures often do this kind of work; they are therefore less scary and less likely to appear in 'gothic' trappings than are their non-Native-generated counterparts. As the 'Ghost Stories' section of the UNC Lumbee History website explains:

> to Lumbees, ghost stories are not narratives told to children simply to scare them, or for entertainment[;] ghost stories often provide a connection to the past, or a way to remember ancestors. ... Ghost stories of family members who have passed away are often pleasant and viewed as a comforting event. These family stories help to pass on the connection to family members after they have left this world. This is a manifestation of the importance of family ties and helps form a part of identity and outlook on the world for Lumbees.

Such stories reanimate the dead—or, perhaps more accurately, reaffirm the living presence of the dead—to strengthen Indigenous familial and tribal connections and to help solidify their presence and encourage their continuation. While these spectral returns to loved ones and significant places do not entirely cancel out the traumas of removal, dispossession, and other forms of violent departure, they open up spaces for re-considering, re-interpreting, and re-claiming colonized land. They are a conduit and a portal; they suggest Indigenous counternarratives and/or they decenter settler colonial narratives, presenting *them* as counternarratives.

The Problem with the Gothic

Yet why do Indigenous raisings of the Indigenous undead sideline rather than embrace the Gothic? What is the problem with the Gothic? In the first sentence of her essay 'Is There an Indigenous Gothic?' Michelle Burnham remarks, 'The simplest way to answer the question posed in the title of this chapter might simply be to say no, there is no Indigenous Gothic' (225). As she suggests, maybe non-Native genres, with their accompanying non-Native forms, expectations, and boundaries, constrict and misrepresent Indigenous experiences.[2] Jennifer Andrews elaborates on this point when she explains that Jodey Castricano's work on the novel *Monkey Beach* by Haisla writer Eden Robinson

> probes the relevance of applying the term Gothic—and the Eurocentric materialist context that frames it—to a Native-authored text such as *Monkey Beach* ... [which] ultimately undermines Western tendencies to use the Gothic as a means of normalizing or at least pathologizing what is perceived as primitive or 'Other.' (206)

Even when they partake of European strains of the Gothic some of the time, to some extent—indeed, even when the word 'gothic' appears in the title of an Indigenous novel, as in Curve Lake First Nations writer Drew Hayden Taylor's *The Night Wanderer: A Native Gothic Novel*—Indigenous writers meld 'gothic' elements into an Indigenous context that is understood to be larger than what it imports from Europe, as well as more central to the world of the novel. They see the Gothic as something like a small tributary that occasionally trickles into a larger Native body of water.

Put another way, the problem with the Gothic lies in its complicity with settler colonial operations. For example, American Indians in a host of nineteenth-century Euro-American gothic narratives are typically cast as howling 'savages' who live in the wilderness, violently attack white people, and otherwise threaten a tenuous social order at its physical/architectural and metaphorical thresholds. Yet the Gothic also ventilates other Euro-American fears, doubts, and troubles, many of which extend into the twentieth and twenty-first centuries. Charles L. Crow explains:

> the Gothic is a counter-narrative, an alternative vision, recording fear, failure, despair, nightmare, crime, disease, and madness. The Gothic is that which is left out. ... [It] is thus the natural medium for expression of our great national failures and crimes, such as the enslavement of Africans and the displacement and destruction of indigenous peoples. (xviii)

As Crow's phrasings suggest, the Gothic is a useful venue for telling uncomfortable and at times outright disturbing truths, for confronting and articulating grievous national anxieties and unsettlements. In the Gothic, a need or desire to remember and express some sort of repressed or otherwise secret knowledge tangles with the difficulty of expressing, and thus acknowledging, buried truths. This in turn helps to produce and propel arresting narrative tensions and ambivalences along with highly symbolic, richly atmospheric 'gothic' settings. Renée Bergland finds a different, although related, tension:

> the interior logic of the modern nation requires that citizens be haunted, and that American nationalism is sustained by writings that conjure forth spectral Native Americans. In American letters, and in the American imagination, Native American ghosts function both as representations of national guilt and as triumphant agents of Americanization. (4)

Bergland contends that '[w]hen Indians are understood as ghosts, they are also understood as powerful figures beyond American control' (5). However, as she points out, 'beyond American control' is predicated on ruthless centuries-long impositions of American control. All in all, the gothic mode is, by both design and inclination, well suited for giving shape and voice to Euro-American fears, desires, anxieties, and ambivalences. Although Indigenous fiction writers such as Stephen Graham Jones (Blackfeet) and Drew Hayden Taylor have explored the

Gothic and other Euro-American popular genres in fresh ways, the Gothic as a general rule gives Indigenous people less. Indeed, as Jodi A. Byrd (Chickasaw) observes of Jones's novel *Demon Theory*, 'Jones constructs a story with no American Indian characters. … The absence of Indians within [his] text is entirely the point—how does the disappeared colonial contexts of horror's functioning continue to influence the genre's obsession with flight and fright?' (356).

A NATIVE SOUTHERN GOTHIC

Shifting from a largely non-Native US context (as in Bergland and Crow) to an Indigenous one changes the terms significantly and helps explain why Indigenous narratives about ghosts, monsters, hauntings, and undeadness are neither particularly gothic nor particularly frightening. As I have begun to suggest, these Indigenous narratives are not driven by the Gothic; they are not primarily about the feelings of white settlers, although they are happy to note the irony of residual settler guilt. Instead, Indigenous hauntings challenge borders and border crossings in other ways, opening up possibilities for a more richly and pointedly Indigenous tapping into the power of ghosts, haunts, and various other incarnations. Byrd argues:

> For American Indian writers the borders and boundaries of genre are infinitely transgressible and permeable as the trans- itself—understood here as crossing, movement, and change—becomes the site of aesthetic production within American Indian reimaginings of what popular genres are and can be. (347)

In a similar vein, Native oral stories are flexible containers well equipped to re-imagine what stories are and can be, as in the transcribed story 'Formula against Screech Owls and Tskilis [bad spirits],' told by Robert Bushyhead (Cherokee). One of this story's key points is that Cherokee witchcraft is not 'evil' as witchcraft is often understood today; in fact, it was used to help people become good hunters and to confer 'the ability to change [themselves] into another figure spiritually' (Duncan 176). Yet, laments the storyteller, humans all too often take 'a good thing … [and] make evil out of it' (177). For example, he acknowledges:

> I was very superstitious when I heard the screech owl:
>> that was somebody, and he was there to do us harm.
> And I was very superstitious when I heard it screech. (177)

However, his mother cures this by teaching him the differences between real owls and witches. She also teaches him a formula to chase the owl away. Translated from Cherokee, this formula basically tells the owl that 'a lot of non-Indians' are coming to catch and kill you. Amusingly, the storyteller teaches this formula in turn to a non-Indian, a Scout leader, who uses it and reports that it works. Indeed, this is what the story affirms: *it works*. With lightly sketched 'gothic' trappings—references to witchcraft and brief mentions of nocturnal screech owls—that turn out to be not terribly 'gothic' after all, the story delivers an anti-colonial point, as the formula that a non-Indian is invited to intone cautions that non-Indians 'are going to cut your head off with a lot of swords' (178). 'You just say it to yourself,' the Cherokee storyteller helpfully tells the non-Native Scout leader (178). And in the end, everyone is witch free and happy.

As I began to suggest earlier, similar challenges and complications obtain when it comes to identifying, or considering the possibility of, a Native *Southern* Gothic. Particularly in the wake of New Southern Studies, which came to prominence in Southern literary studies either just before or just after the beginning of the twenty-first century, depending on who you ask, region came to be considered a less solid, more porous, and altogether less reliable explanatory paradigm than it had previously been. Southernists today are much more inclined to read 'the South' as multiple 'Souths,' entangled in complicated ways with the nations and nationalisms that suffuse and define them, and also global in their reach, their circulation. As Coleman Hutchison explains, the New Southern Studies

> constellates southern localities in relation to a number of non- or extra-national cultural configurations such as the global South, the native or indigenous South, and Greater Mexico. This has allowed, in turn, issues of empire, diaspora, immigration, cosmopolitanism, and cultural exchange to come to the fore. (694)

Like the Gothic, region is complicated in its own right and complicated, in somewhat different ways, when considered in relation to historical and contemporary Indigenous cultures. Whether imagined as impermeable or porous, as helping to confer Southern exceptionalism or aiding in exceptionalism's dismantling, region is a Euro-American form invented for particular audiences and purposes. As Jennifer Greeson observes, 'intellectual and cultural historians of the southern states generally have agreed that their residents did not self-identify as "southerners" particularly allied to one another until the rise of sectionalist politics around 1820' (50). Yet while the Gothic is an overtly literary and covertly political form that opens up conduits for expressing otherwise inexpressible anxieties and troubles, region is an overtly nationalist political concept that plays out in literary and other venues and enables interested parties to define and defend their lifeways, practices, and home places oppositionally, against other regions, and never more oppositionally than US South/US North.

Moreover, region takes hold as a category of identity and a political and cultural paradigm at around the same time that the Indian Removal Act was passed and signed into law in 1830, accelerating the forced dispossession of Native people from their homelands in the southeast. However, as evidenced by the contours of Greeson's argument about a predominantly black-and-white South on a largely North–South axis, these large processes of region formation and sectionalism are still often described as if they took place without Indians. In a sense, Indians are the third race in a bi-racial South; they are the ghosts in the nation- and section-making colonial machine, the removed, the specters that, in Bergland's formulation, demonstrate settler colonial triumphs and activate settler guilt. Moreover in a larger sense, 'Native Southern' is simply not an Indigenous construct, let alone an Indigenous self-representation, and to this day Indigenous writing in and of the South does not accept let alone embrace 'the South' as comfortably as non-Native Southern writers often do. In what follows, I want to begin to give a sense of the range and variety of Indigenous literary raisings of the Indigenous undead in Southern places. Each is grounded in some significant way in the US South, but each places undeadness in Native contexts; collectively, this gathering of brief examples points the way toward a counternarrative to the Gothic's counternarrative. As in Robert Bushyhead's story, Native texts associated with the South also offer their own oppositional critiques and assert their own claims to land, home places/homelands, and much more.

The Indigenous Undead

Edna Chekelelee (1930–1995) 'grew up speaking Cherokee in a very traditional family in the Snowbird community, part of the Qualla Boundary lands located in Graham County, North Carolina' (Duncan 125). As Virginia Moore Carney (Cherokee) writes, 'Having spoken Cherokee all her life, Chekelelee was determined to keep the language alive, and she devoted her life to teaching traditional arts and crafts, as well as Cherokee songs and dances, to as many children as possible' (130). In her 'Santeetlah Ghost Story,' which Duncan reports that she 'first heard Edna tell to elementary school children at Halloween' (127), the young first-person narrator and her family leave their house around 8 pm to sit up with a relative who has just passed on. As the storyteller describes them walking the trail, 'climbing up the hill./And nothing but laurel bush and moonlight' (133), she confesses that 'I was always afraid of the dark' (133)—which immediately prompts her to remember a scary ghost story that the old people used to tell while sitting on the porch. This ghost story of course intensifies her nervousness; but her strong memory of the story as well as the place where she heard it and the old people she heard it from delivers a message about how stories work to build and sustain connections between tribal people in and on their home places.

More immediately pressing, though, there is a thing—'something white'— behind them as they walk to the dead person's house:

> and it would go
>   [heavy breathing] like that.
>   And I peeped,
>   opened my eyes like that,
>   and I saw nothing but a

sheer
white
cloth
looked like a clinging curtain,
and it didn't have no head,
no shape over the head,
all I saw was the shoulders. (Duncan 134–135)

The storyteller tells us that her Daddy stands this unnerving apparition down by saying 'You've scared my children enough,' telling it that 'I just about know who you are,' and asserting that 'I don't care about you' and 'I'm not going to hurt you' (135). After he utters these four strong statements, the entity 'go[es] up in the air,' climbs up the laurel bushes, and fades away (135). The storyteller reports that she's 'still afraid of the dark,' but happily, 'ever since then I felt much better about being in the dark' (135). While this story shares certain atmospherics with the conventional Gothic—night, moonlight, a genuinely frightening ghostly apparition, and fear so powerful that it makes you alternately close your eyes and peep—its concluding point is distinctly counterintuitive to the Gothic's working mechanics: 'if you're not afraid,/A ghost can't hurt you' (135). Compare David Punter's searching argument that

> The theory of the Gothic is always a theory of origins; of beginnings which have been obscured, written over, overwritten, and which therefore invite us as readers into the fiction of a return, of a set of moves which might (at last) make the inheritance clear, might reveal that behind the dust and cobwebs of age-old, disputed (and frequently mangled) texts there may be a purer writing, a title deed, which will give us the keys to the castle and enable us to set about our necessary work of modernizing it and rendering it fit for presentation within the ideological boundaries of modernity. (23)

Mixing familiar gothic images and theoretical propositions, Punter in a lengthy single sentence evokes the Gothic's energy, its impulse to pack a great deal into a single built structure, its habit of layering and parenthesizing and at once seeking and dreading that one elusive official document or key. Alongside Punter's sentence, the proposition that 'if you're not afraid/a ghost can't hurt you' offers a strikingly different 'theory of origins,' one that suggests that the fear packed inside gothic forms can be unpacked, or neutralized, or bypassed altogether, in the interests of sharing, and centering on, Indigenous knowledge in an Indigenous context. As Duncan says, this 'is a personal story with a positive moral ending'—a statement that the majority of non-Native gothic writers, and readers, would be hard-pressed to echo.

Gothic manifestations gain much traction in isolated, lonely settings, whether the place is an old dark mansion cordoned off from the world or a hardscrabble moor or a backcountry graveyard that you probably do not want to walk by, let alone through, after the sun sets. Although not gothic, Edna Chekelelee's ghost story gains power because she sets it in a rural and fairly remote area. Yet cities harbor the Gothic, too, as they also host strains of undeadness that do not patch into gothic fabrics. In her early collection *She Had Some Horses* (originally published in 1983, reissued in 1997), Joy Harjo (Muscogee) includes several urban poems, with individual poems moored to a single city, whether it be Anchorage, Chicago, Albuquerque, Kansas City, or someplace else. In a variety of ways, the speakers of these urban poems are haunted by personal and historical trauma; however, Harjo does not activate gothic conventions in order to articulate or explore these traumas.

Indeed, Craig Womack (Creek/Cherokee) observes that Harjo's poem 'New Orleans' is interesting for something typically quite far afield from the Gothic: 'the way tribal specificity and pan-tribal experience intersect' (226). More, the poem exemplifies

> Harjo's … collapse of constructed boundaries that separate time, space, myth, and personal experience. The larger meaning of the poem is also familiar turf in Harjo's poetic landscape—America's legacy of violence and greed, and the lack of consciousness of explorers like de Soto. (226)

Of course, this legacy is not limited to a single US city, state, or region. Nevertheless, particular places inflect it in particular ways, and Harjo's consideration of different situations in different cities gradually brings into view a map of urban Indigenous America that proposes connections between cities as well as between Indians who live, grieve, remember, and survive there. 'New Orleans' begins:

> This is the south. I look for evidence
>   of other Creeks, for remnants of voices,
>   or for tobacco brown bones to come wandering
>   down Conti Street, Royale, or Decatur. (42)

As the poem unfolds, however, the speaker shifts from seeking 'evidence/of other Creeks' to claiming and asserting her own Creek-centered knowledge. Harjo, like her Creek ancestors and predecessors, places De Soto in Creek contexts; he does not appear until very deep inside the poem, and when he does appear, he is dead and his burial place is unmarked. Instead of leading with Spanish (or other European) colonial versions of history, let alone assuming that De Soto and company won, the speaker remarks, 'He should have stayed home.' In fact, 'Creeks knew of him for miles/before he came into town,' and further, they 'knew he was one of the ones who yearned/for something his heart wasn't big enough/to handle.' The Creeks eventually 'drowned him in/the Mississippi River/so he wouldn't have to drown himself' (43).

In a potentially gothic gesture, the speaker intones: 'My spirit comes here to drink./My spirit comes here to drink./Blood is the undercurrent' (42). Yet again, the frame is Creek, rather than European. This is not blood in a Stephen King sense (liquid tons bursting out of the elevator of the Overlook Hotel);

instead, 'blood is the undercurrent' of relations, of family, of tribal nation, of 'ancestors and future children.' Blood also links Oklahoma and the French Quarter:

> I have a memory.
>   It swims deep in blood,
>   a delta in the skin. It swims out of Oklahoma,
>   deep the Mississippi River. It carries my
>   feet to these places: the French Quarter,
>   stale rooms, the sun behind thick and moist
>   clouds. (42)

Although the Creek Nation's homelands are primarily in Georgia, Creeks were involved in diplomatic, trade, and other transcultural relations in much of the South and beyond; the site of present-day New Orleans was of course also well known to Indigenous people who lived and worked in the area. This west-to-east, Oklahoma-to-New Orleans movement is a return, not a removal. As with Chekelelee's ghost story, so too with Harjo's poem: elements that could, in a different context, be gothic—here, the grappling with historical trauma and the seeking of difficult knowledge, including the exact place where the body is buried—make for a different kind of mix, one driven by, as Womack says, 'the poet's willingness to use her imagination to convert New Orleans to a place of meaning for Creeks' (227). While gothic narratives often quarantine or smother or distort memories, making them difficult to retrieve and at times terrifying to raise up from their subterranean depths, 'Harjo refuses to allow the submergence of memory' (Womack 228). Instead, she honors her ancestors' anti-colonial work and, in so doing, she raises the Indigenous undead.

So, too, do a host of other Native Southern texts. There are the Mississippi swamps, restless Choctaw haunts, and serial killer settlers of Choctaw/Cherokee writer Louis Owens's novels, especially *The Sharpest Sight* and *Bone Game*. There are the eighteenth-century Choctaws who return, embodied in their late twentieth-century descendants, in Choctaw writer LeAnne Howe's novel *Shell Shaker*. Perhaps nearest to traditional Gothic of them all, there is the old, untenanted plantation house in Tiya Miles's *The Cherokee Rose*, with its ghosts and secrets in conversation with the strong black and Indigenous women who converge on this Cherokee slave holder's house in the present and who find it necessary to work against both past and present Southern power structures in order to form empowering inter-racial and/or same-sex relationships. Although she does not herself claim Native identity, Miles has written a novel that significantly expands Native Southern studies and is very much of a piece with her scholarly studies *Ties That Bind: The Story of an Afro-Cherokee Family in Slavery and Freedom* (2005) and *The House on Diamond Hill: A Cherokee Plantation Story* (2010). Lastly, there is 'Back End of the Canal,' a wonderfully evocative non-fiction piece by Chitimacha writer Roger Emile Stouff, a newspaper columnist and outdoorsman from Louisiana. In this short piece, Stouff and his undead ancestors share '[a] world of twilight, where the margins of the present and the past, the dividers separating this world from the next and that which has come before, are feeble, thin' (321). He still sees them in this home place where they once lived and he now lives. 'I … feel I should roll cast to a corner of their resting-place to make sense of the world' (321); as I have argued, Native writers often raise the Indigenous undead for precisely this reason. Yet Stouff also sounds an elegiac note: 'When a people fade into the darkness at the back end of shallow canals, they take their monsters with them' (322). For him, raising the Indigenous undead ultimately cannot really counterbalance all that has been lost. For all of these writers and storytellers, the Gothic and horror are forces to be entertained, however briefly, and then set aside, not to raise Indian dead in the form of ghosts as these Euro-American genres so frequently do, but to raise the Indigenous undead in Indigenous contexts, and for Indigenous purposes.

In Judith Richardson's apt summation:

> ghosts, those apparently insubstantial emanations from the past, are produced by the cultural and social life of the communities in which they appear. Ghosts operate as a particular, and peculiar, kind of social memory, an alternate form of history-making in which things usually forgotten, discarded, or repressed become foregrounded, whether as items of fear, regret, explanation, or desire.

With Indigenous ghosts, this inclination toward the 'particular, and peculiar' specificity of the haunting—the reasons why *this* ghost manifests in *that* Southern location—must be counterbalanced by an acknowledgment of a generally shared Native trauma. As Jace Weaver (Cherokee) observes:

> When Natives are removed from their traditional lands, they are robbed of more than territory; they are deprived of numinous landscapes that are central to their faith and their identity; lands populated by their relations, ancestors, animals and beings both physical and mythological. A kind of psychic homicide is committed. (38)

Many of these psychic crime scenes are still fresh today. They are among the most powerful places where Indigenous hauntings happen.

CONCLUSION

Indigenous undeadness duly reflects and represents the traumatic histories that Weaver discusses; it also participates in the burying and unburying of 'things' that Richardson describes. However, perhaps most importantly, Indigenous undeadness works to recontextualize social memories. The ghost stories and other hauntings I have discussed understand storytelling itself as a vital cultural force, a conduit that carries scary stories from a horrifying past toward a still imaginable future. While an account of Indigenous hauntings in the South must acknowledge all the various places and texts from which Indians continue to be removed, the more important Indian ghost stories insist on Native presences and staying power even as they also mark losses of land, blood, language, and people. To raise the Indigenous undead is to unsettle *and* to re-settle, to re-enter and re-claim old home places.

NOTES

1. The number of likes, and the number of members in the Lumbee-focused group also discussed, are current as of 6 August 2015.
2. Readers interested in a more extended discussion of the problem of genre in Indigenous American literatures might consult my essay "Situating American Indian Poetry: Place, Community, and the Question of Genre," in *Speak to Me Words: Essays on Contemporary American Indian Poetry*, eds. Dean Rader and Janice Gould (Tucson: University of Arizona Press, 2003), 34–55.

BIBLIOGRAPHY

Andrews, J. (2009). Rethinking the Canadian Gothic: Reading Eden Robinson's *monkey beach*. In S. Cynthia & T. Gerry (Eds.), *Unsettled remains: Canadian literature and the postcolonial gothic* (pp. 205–227). Waterloo: Wilfrid Laurier University Press.

Bergland, R. L. (2000). *The national uncanny: Indian ghosts and American subjects*. Hanover: University Press of New England.

Burnham, M. (2014). Is there an indigenous gothic? In C. L. Crow (Ed.), *A companion to American gothic* (pp. 225–237). Chichester: Wiley.

Bushyhead, R. Formula against screech owls and tskilis. *Duncan*, 176–178.

Byrd, J. A. (2014). Red dead conventions: American Indian transgeneric fictions. In J. H. Cox & J. Daniel Heath (Eds.), *The Oxford handbook to indigenous American literature* (pp. 344–358). New York: Oxford University Press.

Carney, V. M. (2005). *Eastern band Cherokee women: Cultural persistence in their letters and speeches*. Knoxville: University of Tennessee Press.

Chekelee, E. Santeetlah ghost story. *Duncan*, 132–136.

Crow, C. L. (2014). Preface. In C. L. Crow (Ed.), *A companion to American gothic* (pp. xvii–xxii). Oxford: Wiley Blackwell.

Duncan, B. R. (Ed.). (1998). *Living stories of the Cherokee*. Chapel Hill: The University of North Carolina Press.

Ghost Stories. Lumbee History: UNC's 'Native American Tribal Studies' Course. Web. Accessed 8 Aug 2015.

Greeson, J. R. (2010). *Our South: Geographic fantasy and the rise of national literature*. Cambridge: Harvard University Press.

Harjo, J. (1997). New Orleans. In *She had some horses 1983* (pp. 42–43). New York: Thunder's Mouth Press.

Hogan, L. (1998). *Power*. New York: Norton.

Howe, L. A. (2001). *Shell shaker*. San Francisco: Aunt Lute Books.

Hutchison, C. (2014). 'The brand new southern studies Waltz'. In 'Forum: What's new in southern studies—And why should we care?' Ed. Brian Ward. *Journal of American Studies, 48*(3), 694–697.

Littlejohn, K. S. Spearfinger. *Duncan*, 62–66.

Lumbee ghost stories, legends, and lore. Facebook group. Web. Accessed 8 Aug 2015.

Miles, T. (2015). *The Cherokee Rose*. Winston-Salem: John F. Blair.

Native ghost stories. Facebook group. Web. Accessed 8 Aug 2015.

Owens, L. (1992). *The sharpest sight*. Norman: University of Oklahoma Press.

Owens, L. (1994). *Bone game*. Norman: University of Oklahoma Press.

Punter, D. (2014). Gothic, theory, dream. In C. L. Crow (Ed.), *A companion to American gothic* (pp. 16–28). Oxford: Wiley Blackwell.

Richardson, J. (2005). *Possessions: The history and uses of haunting in the Hudson valley*. Cambridge, MA: Harvard University Press.

Stouff, R. (2010). Back end of the canal. In H. Geary, M. A. Janet, & W. Kathryn (Eds.), *The people who stayed: Southeastern Indian writing after removal* (pp. 320–323). Norman: University of Oklahoma Press.

Teuton, C. B. with Shade, H., Still, S., Guess, S., Hansen, W. (2012). *Cherokee stories of the turtle island liars' club*. Chapel Hill: University of North Carolina Press.

Thrush, C. (2011). Haunting as histories: Indigenous ghosts and the urban past in seattle. In C. E. Boyd & T. Coll (Eds.), *Phantom past, indigenous presence: Native ghosts in North American culture and history* (pp. 54–81). Lincoln: University of Nebraska Press.

Weaver, J. (1997). *That the people might live: Native American literatures and Native American community*. New York: Oxford University Press.

Womack, C. S. (1999). *Red on red: Native American literary separatism*. Minneapolis: University of Minnesota Press.

FURTHER READING

Anderson, E. G., Taylor, H., & Daniel Cross, T. (Eds.). (2015). *Undead Souths: The gothic and beyond in southern literature and culture*. Baton Rouge: Louisiana State University Press. This collection explores and expands traditional notions of Southern Gothic, moving across historical periods and genres to reveal a wide-ranging Southern 'undeadness.' Sustained discussions of Native Southern undeadness can be found in "Burying the (Un)Dead and Healing the Living: Choctaw Women's Power in LeAnne Howe's Novels" by Kirstin L. Squint, "The Indigenous Uncanny: Spectral Genealogies in LeAnne Howe's Fiction" byAnnette Trefzer, and "Crossin' the Log: Death, Regionality, and Race in Jeremy Love's *Bayou*" by Rain Prud'homme C. Gómez (Choctaw-Biloxi, Louisiana Creole, and Mvskoke).

del Pilar Blanco, M. (2012). *Ghost-watching American modernity: Haunting, landscape, and the hemispheric imagination*. New York: Fordham University Press. Although not specifically about the US South, this study brilliantly reconceptualizes how ghosts, hauntings, and by extension the Gothic work in space and place.

Thrush, C., & Boyd, C. E. (Eds.). (2011). *Phantom past, indigenous presence: Native ghosts in North American culture and history*. Lincoln: University of Nebraska Press. A well-conceived collection that complements and supplements Bergland's work.

PART IV

Gender and Sexuality in Southern Gothic Texts

CHAPTER 26

Twisted Sisters: The Monstrous Women of Southern Gothic

Kellie Donovan-Condron

The archetypal monstrous female of Southern Gothic literature is, unexpectedly, neither explicitly monstrous nor explicitly Southern. When Madeline Usher briefly appears midway through Edgar Allan Poe's 'The Fall of the House of Usher' (1839), her previous absence might seem attributable to dark causes, but the medical and familial discourse about her puts her strange behavior and isolation in a human rather than a supernatural context. Although Madeline and Roderick are twins, the story's patriarchal social structure makes clear that she is subordinate to him rather than his equal, a sibling dynamic made all the more necessary because she suffers from, and seems to succumb to, a more attenuated version of her brother's extreme constitutional delicacy. Roderick even frames Madeline's terrifying return from the grave in the story's denouement as the actions of one who was buried alive rather than re-animated. Context likewise deflects the story's presumed Southern-ness. The titular building and the family line in 'Usher' are ancient, and the mansion, set by a tarn,[1] includes a vault that was formerly used as a 'donjon-keep' in 'feudal times.' Combined with Roderick's preference for European intellectuals and artists, Poe's setting connotes a European heritage rather than a family line rooted in the United States' earliest colonial period. Both the woman and the location seem to be unlikely progenitors of a genre with such specific regional ties.

Yet Madeline epitomizes the monstrous belle of Southern Gothic precisely because personal, social, and geographical history are inextricably bound in Poe's story. Roderick, believing that the stones of their ancestral home have a degree of consciousness but that his sister is dead, cannot maintain categorical distinctions. Madeline, who actually is not quite dead when Roderick places her in the vault, destroys the mansion's foundation in the course of her ferocious escape and brings about the near-simultaneous collapse of the family

K. Donovan-Condron (✉)
Babson College, Wellesley, MA, USA

© The Editor(s) (if applicable) and The Author(s) 2016
S.C. Street, C.L. Crow (eds.), *The Palgrave Handbook of the Southern Gothic*,
DOI 10.1057/978-1-137-47774-3_26

line and their home. As the narrator flees, the tarn 'sullenly and silently' sub-
merges the building and its corpses, leaving no trace that either had existed.
The Ushers' relationships with each other and with their land illustrate how
history, both personal and national, haunts Southern Gothic (Marshall 14;
Punter 23; Savoy 167; Wester 26). Teresa Goddu observes that Southern settings, in turn, function as a 'safety valve' to vent the unacceptable, or even just
the merely unpalatable, aspects of the American national story (76). Jay Ellis
asserts that the region is the designated gathering point for attitudes that have
been banished from 'otherwise proper audiences' (xxxii). If the South bears
America's historical and societal sins, Southern characters embody the consequences of those sins.

The prominence of history in Southern Gothic deepens the overall genre's
long association of femininity with fear, excess, and the non-normative. E. J.
Clery has noted the centrality of 'extremes of feeling' and situations 'well beyond
the normal range of experience' in gothic literature written by women (13),
while Juliann Fleenor points to the 'nightmare' for women 'in conflict with
the values of [their] society and [their] prescribed role' (10), a 'devalued' role
that Karen Stein argues leads women to 'accentuate their perception of themselves as monstrous' (126). America's particular history heightens what Kari
Winter calls 'the terrifying injustices at the foundation of the Western social
order' at the center of female gothic and slave narratives (2), and what Allan
Lloyd-Smith sees as 'the unvoiced "other" … in a predominantly masculin-
ist culture' (28). Although Lloyd-Smith's analysis could productively include
Roderick's effete demeanor in an expanded range of 'monstrous feminine,'
such a reading is beyond the scope of this chapter. Additional approaches to the
Gothic in America connect the genre to economics and gender (Goddu 94–6)
and see monstrousness as 'deviation from a white, able-bodied physical ideal'
(Weinstock 44). If it is true that '[o]n the ruins of the house of Usher, Poe lays
the foundation of a Southern Gothic' (Moss 179), the genre's patriarchal social
structures have long seen women as—and have caused women to become—
abnormal, abject, perverse.

Madeline ends the ancient Usher line, but she spawns a diverse array of
twentieth-century descendants. As Charles L. Crow indicates, 'The American
South, with its legacy of profound social and economic problems, became a
major focus and source of American literature in the twentieth century, and the
principal region of American Gothic' (124). Among these problems, slavery,
'the master trope' of American Gothic (88), and its after-effects remain a bedrock theme of Southern Gothic. Wester describes the genre as one 'that is aware
of the impossibility of escaping racial haunting and the trauma of a culture that
is not just informed by racial history, but also haunted and ruptured by it' (25),
and Goddu likewise asserts that the genre is 'haunted by race' (7). A slight
misquotation from Faulkner's *Requiem for a Nun*—'The past isn't dead …
it isn't even past'—becomes Lloyd-Smith's 'motto for American Gothic itself
as it explores the tensions between a culturally sanctioned progressive optimism
and an actual dark legacy' (118). For Patricia Yaeger, the demands of various

modern social and political movements cause 'change [to erupt] abruptly, via images of monstrous, ludicrous bodies' (4), while Susan V. Donaldson cites 'regional anxiety about rapidly changing gender roles in the first half of the twentieth century' as a particular threat in Southern Gothic. Simultaneously grappling with past and present, twentieth-century Southern Gothic situates women at the vortex of churning cultural issues deeply tied to geography.

MISS EMILY GRIERSON

Faulkner's Miss Emily Grierson is the doyenne of monstrous femininity in Southern Gothic literature. Her funeral at the opening of the short story 'A Rose for Emily' (1930) illustrates the grotesque results of fusing person and place. Although the town's men attend out of respect for her and the women go in order to see the inside of her long shut-up house, these motives overlap far more than the narrator suggests; the town always thinks of her and her house together, the latter a metonym for the former (Palmer 123). Miss Emily is a 'fallen monument' on her death, a description that parallels the town's belief that she had become a fallen woman engaging in a sexual relationship with Barron before marriage ('Rose' 1). So thoroughly is Miss Emily linked to her house that when neighbors insist that a town leader do something about the rank odor emanating from her property, he responds as if asked to attack the woman herself, 'will you accuse a lady to her face of smelling bad?' (2). Furthermore, the narrator's details about the house embody Miss Emily's past and present; heavy and over-ornamented in a way once deemed fashionable, its decay is both 'stubborn and coquettish' (1). If Miss Emily as a young woman had comprised with her father a 'tableau ... framed by the back-flung front door' (2), she virtually barricades herself behind that door for the latter half of her life. Miss Emily and her house are each the last of their kind, the last hold-outs of an antebellum generation that would concoct—and believe—a barely plausible lie about taxes to preserve a genteel woman's self-image and dignity.

Were Miss Emily merely very attached to her house and set in her ways, she would be eccentric but not especially monstrous. Her conflation of body and place crosses into perversion because it represents the other ways in which she flaunts binaries and refuses to stay on the side of the line assigned by her father and her community. Miss Emily's neighbors are most unnerved by her elision of two particular categories: they are repulsed by the excesses of her body and flummoxed by her rejection of others' expectations of her after her father dies. Miss Emily's body is monstrous because it collapses distinctions. She is obese despite, or, as the narrator suggests, because of, her 'small and spare' bone structure, and her hair comes to have the 'vigorous iron-grey ... of an active man' (1, 4). Physically manifold, Miss Emily's behavior is singular in both senses of the word. She takes just one perspective on any issue—her own, social expectations notwithstanding—and neighbors view her actions as decid-edly odd. She refuses to acknowledge that she owes taxes, insisting that a long-ago arrangement remained in effect. She will not allow street numbers to be

attached to her house, nor will she comply with the legal requirement to spec-
ify her intention for the arsenic she purchases. She is equally defiant regarding
social niceties, declining to receive visits from the town's ladies in the period
following her father's death, keeping company with Homer Barron despite his
Yankee origins and lower-class status, and saying something so upsetting to the
Baptist minister that he refused to return to her house. In her body and in her
actions, Miss Emily transgresses the norms of her culture.

Whatever the facts of Miss Emily's bodily condition and behavior, however, the narrator and townspeople are equally complicit in casting her as an
unacceptable freak, sharing the excesses that they would foist on her alone.
Margie Burns's argument that the Southern Gothic 'mark[s] the sites of *social*
dislocations' (108) and Marshall's assertion that Miss Emily is as much a victim of 'restrictive gender and social roles' as a villain of the tale (11) emphasize the town's co-responsibility for what Faulkner's character has become. It
is the community's prurient focus on Miss Emily's Sunday rides with Barron
that establishes as 'fact' that he is courting her: 'it's really so. ... What else
could ...,' an alternative so unspeakable that the narrator trails off without
finishing the implication ('Rose' 3). Repeated laments of 'poor Emily' convey
both pity for her lack of familial guidance after her father's death and judgment
for the sexual relationship that they assume she is having. Not content to talk
behind Miss Emily's back, the community routinely take her matters into their
own hands. Unwilling to confront her about the smell from her house, a small
group of men furtively spread lime on her property, going so far as to break into
her basement. Unwilling to ask directly about her relationship with Barron, the
town's ladies compel the Baptist minister to speak to her about her supposedly
lapsed morality, and the minister's wife subsequently writes to Miss Emily's
estranged relatives to summon them to Jefferson to address the affair. By the
time the narrator discloses the irrefutable evidence of Miss Emily's acts of murder and necrophilia, she is so thoroughly vilified that the story simply ends;
there is nothing left to say.

A Trio of Monstrous Women

Although the full range of Faulkner's gothicism is discussed elsewhere in this
volume, the trio of central women in *Absalom, Absalom!* (1936) are notable
for their compounding of feminine monstrosity in Southern Gothic. Miss Rosa
Coldfield, Judith Sutpen, and Clytemnestra ('Clytie') Sutpen join Miss Emily
in what Donaldson terms 'a rogues gallery of women who have stepped out of
line, transgressed the boundaries of their traditional roles, and served as disruptive forces in male narratives or perhaps even threatened to usurp narratives in
general.' The women are able to destabilize the novel's many narratives because
each has an intimate connection with Sutpen's Hundred, the plantation that
family head Thomas Sutpen built from nothing on his arrival in Jefferson. Half-
sisters Judith and Clytie are both born at Sutpen's Hundred, and both die
there. Rosa, their aunt, is bound by her dying sister's plea to take care of her

children, and very nearly becomes their stepmother and the plantation's second mistress until a grievous insult from Thomas causes her to return to her own home. However, the women's relationships with the land are over-determined, fraught with complications that disrupt their relationships. At 19 years old, Rosa is quite a bit younger than her ostensible charges, and Judith became a widow before she was wed. Clytie, born out of wedlock to one of Thomas's African American slaves, is accepted at Sutpen's Hundred even as Thomas repudiates Charles Bon, his son by his first wife whom, he discovers, has racially mixed heritage. Individually and collectively, these women unsettle the plantation that Thomas struggled so hard to establish and then restore after the Civil War.

Miss Rosa is a gothic belle because of the power of her narrative, which opens the novel and immediately connects the land and those on it with destruction. Thomas Sutpen 'tore violently a plantation,' she says, with terrible repercussions for the family he later built there: 'they destroyed him or something or he destroyed them or something' (*Absalom* 4). Eager to tell her story to Quentin before he leaves Jefferson for Harvard University, her bitter account of Thomas Sutpen's ruination of her family provides the novel's first view of the patriarch, painting a vicious portrait of a nasty man. Rosa's story is not the only one, since later tellings by Quentin's father, Quentin himself, and Quentin's Harvard roommate fill in missing details with facts and speculation that humanize Sutpen through sympathetic detail about his childhood and early life, but it is the ur-text to which all subsequent versions respond. As Sutpen becomes a more fully developed figure, the gaps in Rosa's perspective grow more prominent. Significantly, the combination of precision and vagueness at the outset of the novel generates subsequent versions of the past, each building on the other, none of them complete. If, as Philip Goldstein argues, '[t]he conflicting multiple narratives of *Absalom, Absalom!* emphasize the speculative character of its history' and are one of the novel's distinguishing gothic characteristics (134), then Miss Rosa's story is the font of the novel's gothicism; her version is simultaneously the one that revises history, and that is revised by others, the most. Quentin's father makes listening to Rosa seem like a polite social obligation, but the strength of her account belies his patronizing attitude. He says, 'we in the South made our women into ladies. Then the War ... made the ladies into ghosts. So what else can we do, being gentlemen, but listen to them being ghosts?' (*Absalom* 6). Rendered irrelevant and invisible by the social changes following the Civil War and left a spinster by Sutpen's crude comments, the doubly marginalized Rosa commits the monstrous act of refusing to remain quiet or to moderate her view of the Sutpen story. Furthermore, because Rosa is blatant about her animus, her invective subverts the reliability of any of the novel's subsequent male-authored narratives; their accounts may seem more objective than hers, but their conjecture makes their versions even less stable than her eye-witness testimony.

Judith and Clytie, who live at Sutpen's Hundred for their entire lives, become as closely affiliated with their house as Miss Emily does with hers, perversely embracing their roles as caretakers of the house even after their father tacitly abandons it, and them. Just after the crucial moment in which Judith's brother Henry murders her fiancé and permanently binds her to her childhood home, the house seems to subsume both women's voices. Rushing into the house, Rosa describes first Clytie's voice and then Judith's as being that of the building itself. Clytie's is 'an echo ... which was not mine but rather that of the lost inevocable might-have-been which haunts all houses, all enclosed walls erected by human hands' (109); the house ventriloquizes Judith later in the same scene, 'not Judith, but the house itself [was] speaking again, though it was Judith's voice' (112). The murder pre-empts Judith unwittingly committing incest and miscegenation, shifting her monstrosity from that of shattering patriarchal social relationships to that of excessive attachment to her father's house. Confined by patriarchal and racist social structures to Sutpen's Hundred—Judith left with no additional marriage prospects because of her brother's scandalous act, Clytie because she is bi-racial in an as-yet-unReconstructed South—the women exist in stasis while they wait with Rosa for Thomas to return from the Civil War. Rosa describes their condition as 'an apathy that was almost peace,' until Sutpen would inevitably 'sweep [them] with the old ruthlessness whether [they] would or no' into 'the Herculean task which [they] knew he would set himself' of attempting to rebuild Sutpen's Hundred (124, 126). Judith and Clytie care for the house and each other, bound to the only location each had ever known. As with Madeline and Miss Emily, the fate of the house is concomitant with the fate of the women who inhabit it.

The final act of monstrous femininity in *Absalom, Absalom!* centers on Clytie. Rosa, having discovered that Henry had secretly returned to Sutpen's Hundred to await his apparently imminent demise, brings an ambulance to the plantation in an attempt to save his life; Clytie, however, intervenes before Rosa can reach the house. Reminiscent of Bertha Rochester, Clytie sets the house on fire, killing Henry and herself. Although she is not kept as a literal prisoner, a shameful madwoman in the attic, Clytie's action does respond to the racist and classist social structures that have so severely constricted her life. Removing Henry from the house eliminates her function as caretaker, a further marginalization tantamount to social death. By immolating the house, her half-brother, and herself, Clytie ends her narrative as she alone determines. Because her incendiary action brings Rosa's discussion with Quentin, and therefore the novel as a whole, to a close, Clytie's final moments are subject to the least amount of the speculation, re-interpretation, and re-telling that have characterized the rest of the text. Lloyd-Smith links Faulkner's gothicism in *Absalom, Absalom!* to his intricate language, seeing in the style an always failing effort to communicate fully (117–18). Fittingly, then, the novel's most iconic gothic scene is also non-verbal. The burning of Sutpen's Hundred is as close as the novel comes to a moment of narrative unity about what happened, yet no one can explain Clytie's motive. It is an act of tremendous destruction of all that patriarchy stands for, by its most disenfranchised member.

WOMEN OUT OF PLACE

In counterpoint to Faulkner's exploration of women made monstrous by a too-close affiliation between person and place, Eudora Welty explores the grotesqueries that befall women when they are separated from their own places. The eponymous figures in the short stories 'Clytie' and 'Keela, the Outcast Indian Maiden,' both from *A Curtain of Green and Other Stories* (1941b), are all-too realistic portrayals of the consequences to women for being out of place and out of time. Faulkner's Clytie is bound so closely to her home that she destroys it and herself in order to preserve her own narrative, but Welty's Clytie has no such autonomy within the home to which she is similarly tied. Instead, she is disassociated from her own body and mind, a kind of automaton whose monstrousness stems from the vacuum in which she functions. Keela is an abject Other, a carnival freak-show performer whose utter inhumanity and incompatibility with civilized society are the very point of her display; 'she' is also a fraud, a kidnapped African American man forced to play a grotesque role over and over again. Welty may have rejected any identification of her work with Southern Gothic (Donaldson), but her engagement with the body, the home, and the terrifying things that happen to both situates her squarely in the genre.

A member of the same once-elite but now ruined and irrelevant class as Miss Emily Grierson, Miss Clytie's life has constricted to the needs of her household. Her disabled father, alcoholic brother, and insane sister, whose 'monumental voice' ('Clytie' 178) evokes Miss Emily's body and house, treat her like a servant rather than a family member. She scurries to cook, clean, and fetch for them, while barely tending to her own needs. She furtively opens windows, welcoming the fresh air but fearful of Octavia's intolerance of the 'prying from without' that it might bring, and she bolts her food like an animal, quickly, alone, 'bit[ing] the meat savagely … and gnaw[ing] the little chicken bone' (164, 171). Her family's imperious attitude and various dysfunctions minimize Clytie's humanity, and the resulting impairment of her mental faculty renders her a grotesque shell of a woman. The faces of her family have obtruded on Clytie's ability to perceive others, particularly the 'face that had looked back at her' when she was a young woman (168). Compelled to search for this face that she can no longer recognize, Clytie leaves her house at approximately the same time every day, unable to function in the present while she looks for her past. This mental task so thoroughly overtakes her awareness that townspeople have to tell her to get out of the rain. A further sign of her mental deterioration is her involuntary stream of invective when she is in the garden, a pouring forth stopped only when she sees her sister looking at her from inside the house. In her wordless searching and socially unsanctioned cussing, Clytie illustrates Donaldson's argument that 'Welty's gothic heroines … [are] hysterics whose bodies provide expression in the absence of appropriate language.' If Clytie is losing her mind, as her neighbors speculate, then her body is all that she has left, however tenuous her control of it.

Body and mind, self and family, the inside and outside of the house collide in a fateful moment of re-integration when Clytie goes to fetch rainwater from a barrel for her father's shave and finally realizes that her own reflected face in the water is the one for which she has been searching. This bittersweet moment brings her to a full awareness of the depravity into which her life has sunk. Crow's observation about the importance of 'distortion to the point of the monstrous' in the Gothic and the grotesque (129) suggests why this scene is crucial. The reflected face is distorted in the 'slightly moving water,' the face itself 'wavering' ('Clytie' 177), although the narrator does not make clear whether Clytie recognizes her reflection because of, or in spite of, the image's uneven quality. Shocked that 'the half-remembered vision had finally betrayed her' (177), she will not comply with yet another insistent demand from her 'monumental' sister. In this moment, Clytie feels the full weight of what Sarah Gleeson-White calls 'the burden of a simultaneously idealized and detested womanhood' (49); it is a freeing moment that Donaldson argues provides an opportunity for Welty's gothic women to redefine their options. Suicide, 'the only thing she could think of to do' ('Clytie' 178), is Clytie's first and last independently chosen act. Her willful demise on recognition of her grotesqueness suggests that femaleness in Southern Gothic is implicitly monstrous, and is a state that cannot, should not, be borne.

While Clytie might be a metaphorical savage for 'gnaw[ing] the little chicken bone,' Keela is presented as a literal one, a creature whose main draw at the carnival is the spectacle of watching her eat a live chicken. Keela is multiply monstrous, trapped in narratives that mislabel her true body and emphasize her staged social dislocation. Everything about the title 'Keela, the Outcast Indian Maiden' is a lie, a script designed to attract an audience by triggering then soothing its worst fears. Because 'the human freak … served as a "not-me" figure embodying features considered undesirable or dangerous by the dominant order,' as Ladislava Khailova demonstrates, Keela represents the denigrated opposite of the Southern white woman (Khailova 276). Caged like an animal, ordered only to grunt if approached, clothed in a red dress whose color evokes her ersatz race, gender, and sexuality, and referred to as 'it' by Steve the carnival barker, Keela's surface presentation is overloaded with qualifiers that would be unnecessary if the show's sole purpose were to repulse its viewers. After all, witnessing an African American man eating a live chicken would be equally disturbing and the ensuing disgust could easily tap into racist, 'not-me' views. However, in an era that saw the first tentative steps toward civil rights for African Americans, Little Lee Roy's actual subject position is insufficiently taboo. Khailova (280) shows how Native Americans were still seen as 'unacceptably transgressive' even after the Indian Citizenship Act of 1924, which is why Little Lee Roy is made monstrous by being mis-gendered, mis-raced, and dehumanized.

As the first of his untruthful labels highlights, Little Lee Roy's geographical place, or lack of it, plays a significant role in the horrors that happen to him. Kidnapped as suddenly as if swept up in a tornado, Little Lee Roy is forced to join a traveling carnival, in a kind of permanent homelessness intensified by the cage that confines him at all times. The roadshow takes him far from anyone in his community who might recognize him. His liberation comes after a Texan repeatedly views Keela's act over several days, a sort of short-term residency, which allows this particular spectator to see through the disguise. Only the most normative representative of patriarchal culture—a white, hyper-masculine Texan who is savvy about the law, a 'hero' in Steve's eyes ('Keela' 80)—can rescue this 'maiden' in distress and restore 'her' to a rightful home. The gender politics of a man rescuing a man are quickly and quietly subsumed by Little Lee Roy's other marginalized statuses: black, crippled, and poor. The Texan's actions become civil justice rather than a romance plot. So integral is place to identity that Steve cannot recognize Little Lee Roy away from the carnival, even when standing right in front of him. At least for Steve, the perverse 'Keela' identity effectively re-writes Little Lee Roy's actual position, so much so that Steve continues to refer to Little Lee Roy as 'it' even after he knows that 'Keela' was a fraud. That Welty's story takes place on Little Lee Roy's front porch, a liminal space between inside and outside, further illustrates the centrality of home and the ways in which place is the locus of the 'slippery world of shifting boundaries, roles, and genders' (Donaldson) in Southern Gothic.

ACCOMMODATING MONSTROSITY

These gothic belles demonstrate a wide swath of the feminine experience. They have the power to destroy bloodlines as well as buildings, embody the otherness of ethnicity, gender, and sexuality, and expose the consequences of patriarchy's association of women with domestic spaces. Yet none of these women has given birth. The closest mother figure is Rosa, whose charges are older than her.[2] Furthermore, except for Ellen in *Absalom, Absalom!*, none of these women's mothers is present in their text nor is reference made to them. A key aspect of these women's monstrosity, then, is their motherless, unmothering social position. Tethered to a past they did not shape, they are bereft of a future of their own making, literally and metaphorically. Unlike the work of the other authors discussed here, Toni Morrison's novel *Beloved* (1987) explicitly connects the major themes of Southern Gothic—slavery, history, and the relationship between past and present, individual, familial, and social relationships, ties between bodies and property—to the monstrousness of motherhood. Morrison has called *Beloved* a 'ghost story' (qtd in Horvitz 93), an apt if minimalist description of a novel that features haunting by a murdered infant's incorporeal, and then embodied, form, whose presence requires an exorcism to banish fully. Because the institution of slavery confounds property and parenting, the central mother and daughter in *Beloved* are inherently monstrous. The challenge of the novel, then, is to find a future that accommodates rather than resists or ignores this reality, a solution found through integration in community (Goddu 155).

Beloved opens with the monstrous feminine, starkly announcing that the house at 124 Bluestone is haunted by an angry, sad baby. Although the novel unspools the details of what happened slowly and in fragments, Sethe knows from the outset that the spirit is that of her older daughter who died as a toddler, named Beloved on her gravestone from the words of her funeral service. Beloved's spirit harasses 124's inhabitants, moving furniture and ruining food, but she is particularly threatening to males. Her disturbances drove away her brothers when they were young teens, and she is especially hostile to Paul D, whom Sethe had known at the Sweet Home plantation years ago and who begins a relationship with Sethe at the outset of the novel. As much of a nuisance as Beloved's spirit is, she is far more threatening when she shows up in corporeal form. Paul D realizes that there is '[s]omething funny'bout that gal' (*Beloved* 55) shortly after her arrival, and that the discomfort he feels in the house, which causes him repeatedly to change where he sleeps, is 'involuntary,' that 'he wasn't being nervous, he was being prevented' (115). Despite Paul's wariness of Beloved, he is unable to resist her seduction.

Beloved is likewise a threat to Sethe and Denver, Sethe's younger daughter, although the nature of her harm to them is initially more difficult to discern. Beloved feeds on stories of the family's past, insatiable for details about Sethe's 'diamonds' (57) or Denver's birth during Sethe's flight from Sweet Home. Because mother and (living) daughter take comfort and pleasure in telling their stories to Beloved, her presence seems positive, a vehicle for productive 'rememory,' as Sethe calls it (36). However, the spirit-Beloved chokes Sethe in the Clearing under the guise of soothing her neck pain, and Denver feels helpless to stop whatever further harm Beloved has planned for her mother because of her own 'unrestricted ... need to love another' (104). Denver's desperate need for love causes her to form an unhealthy attachment to, even sense of territoriality about, Beloved. Late in the novel, Beloved takes the best, the most food to nourish her pregnancy, while Sethe wastes away. Only an intervention by the community's women, in which they prevent Sethe from committing a second act of murder, succeeds in permanently banishing Beloved from 124.

For all of her evil, Beloved is not born a monster, but becomes one through her mother's actions. Having sacrificed so much to escape from Sweet Home, Sethe will not let herself or her children go back when Schoolteacher comes to retrieve them. She intends to murder her children to keep them safe; although she only completes the act with Beloved, her infanticide does, indeed, protect her other children when Schoolteacher decides that they are not fit to return to Sweet Home. The horrific murder spawns a second perverse act, as Denver's urgent need to nurse before Beloved's blood is cleaned from Sethe's breasts means that she ingests both life and death. Sethe's fierce love of her children and desperation to protect them enact a deeply twisted version of gothic belles' attachment to their property. As slaves, Sethe and her children are another's property, and she has no legal right to determine what happens to them; her assertion of her right as a mother rejects the ownership of slavery, which Wester identifies as the novel's 'real source of terror' (190). *Beloved* blurs the distinction between monster and mother (Decker 257) to critique the institution that made Sethe's choice inevitable.

Like their kinswomen across Southern Gothic, Beloved and Sethe are monstrous not only for what they do, but for the ways in which their actions—their very lives—cross, refute, and re-write the categorical distinctions by which patriarchal society would control them. Individually and collectively, the gothic belles demonstrate how power warps those who wield it and those whom it subjects.

NOTES

1. Although 'tarn' now describes small mountain lakes across the globe, in Poe's time the word referred only to bodies of water in Northern England. *Oxford English Dictionary*.
2. In the way that she takes care of her father and siblings, Welty's Clytie might be considered a mother figure, although their brusque treatment of her aligns her more with the role of servant.

BIBLIOGRAPHY

Burns, M. (1991). A good rose is hard to find. In D. B. Downing & S. Bazargan (Eds.), *Image and ideology in modern/postmodern discourse* (pp. 105–123). Albany: State University of New York Press. Print.

Clery, E. J. (2000). *Women's Gothic: From Clara Reeve to Mary Shelley*. Tavistock: Northcote House in association with the British Council. Print.

Crow, C. L. (2009). *History of the Gothic: American Gothic*. Cardiff: University of Wales Press. Print.

Decker, S. (2013). In J. Ellis (Ed.), *'Anything dead coming back to life hurts': The Double Murder of Beloved* (pp. 243–262). Ipswich: Salem Press. Print.

Donaldson, S. V. (1997). Making a spectacle: Welty, Faulkner, and Southern Gothic. *Mississippi Quarterly: The Journal of Southern Cultures* 50(4) (1 September 1997), n. pag. Web. 18 May 2015.

Ellis, J. (2013). On southern Gothic literature. In J. Ellis (Ed.), *Critical Insights: Southern Gothic Literature*. I apologize for that oversight. (pp. xvi–xxxiv). Ipswich: Salem Press. Print.

Faulkner, W. (1990). *Absalom, Absalom!* New York: Random House Inc. Kindle file.

Faulkner, W. (2013). A rose for Emily. *Internet Archive*. 9 February 2013. Web. 2 May 2015.

Fleenor, J. E. (1983). Introduction. In J. E. Fleenor (Ed.), *The female Gothic* (pp. 3–28). Montréal: Eden Press. Print.

Gleeson-White, S. (2003). A Peculiarly Southern Form of Ugliness: Eudora Welty, Carson McCullers, and Flannery O'Connor. *Southern Literary Journal*, 36(1) (Fall 2003), 46–57. Web. 28 May 2015.

Goddu, T. A. (1997). *Gothic America: Narrative, history, and nation*. New York: Columbia University Press. Print.

Horvitz, D. (1998). Nameless ghosts: Possession and dispossession in beloved. In B. H. Solomon (Ed.), *Critical essays on Toni Morrison's beloved* (pp. 93–103). New York: G. K. Hall & Co. Print.

Khailova, L. (2007). Ethnic freaks, white ladies, and the dissolution of southern patriarchy: Eudora Welty's critical commentary on sideshow practices in "Keela, the

Outcast Indian Maiden". *Mississippi Quarterly: The Journal of Southern Cultures*, 1 March 2007, 273–287. Web. 27 May 2015.

Lloyd-Smith, A. (2004). *American Gothic fiction: An introduction*. New York: Continuum. Print.

Marshall, B. M. (2013). Defining southern Gothic. In J. Ellis (Ed.), *Critical insights: Southern Gothic literature* (pp. 3–18). Ipswich: Salem Press. Print.

Morrison, T. (1987). *Beloved*. New York: Random House Inc. Kindle file.

Moss, W. (2014). The fall of the house, from Poe to Percy: The evolution of an enduring Gothic convention. In C. L. Crow (Ed.), *A companion to American Gothic* (pp. 177–188). West Sussex: Wiley. Print.

Palmer, L. (2007). Bourgeois blues: Class, whiteness, and southern Gothic in early Faulkner and Caldwell. *The Faulkner Journal*, Fall 2006/Spring 2007, 120–139. Web. 12 May 2015.

Poe, E. A. (2010). The fall of the house of Usher. *Project Gutenberg*, 15 December 2010. Web. 14 May, 2015.

Punter, D. (2014). Gothic, theory, dream. In C. L. Crow (Ed.), *A companion to American Gothic* (pp. 16–28). West Sussex: Wiley. Print.

Savoy, E. (2002). The rise of American Gothic. In J. E. Hogle (Ed.), *Cambridge companion to Gothic fiction* (pp. 167–188). Cambridge: Cambridge University Press. Print.

Stein, K. L. (1983). Monsters and Madwomen: Changing female Gothic. In J. E. Fleenor (Ed.), *The female Gothic* (pp. 123–137). Montréal: Eden Press. Print.

Weinstock, J. A. (2014). American monsters. In C. L. Crow (Ed.), *A companion to American Gothic* (pp. 41–55). West Sussex: Wiley. Print.

Welty, E. (1941a). Clytie. In *A curtain of green and other stories* (pp. 158–178). New York: Harcourt, Brace and World, Inc. Print

Welty, E. (1941b). Keela, the outcast Indian maiden. *A curtain of green and other stories* (pp. 74–88). New York: Harcourt, Brace and World, Inc. Print.

Wester, M. L. (2012). *African American Gothic: Screams from shadowed places*. New York: Palgrave Macmillan. Print.

Winter, K. J. (1992). *Subjects of slavery, agents of change: Women and power in Gothic novels and slave narratives, 1790–1865*. Athens: University of Georgia Press. Print.

Yaeger, P. (2000). *Dirt and desire: Reconstructing southern women's writing, 1930–1990*. Chicago: University of Chicago Press. Print.

Further Reading

Mallonee, S. M. (2005). A summer to Pardon: Southern Gothic and the family in Janis Owens's Myra Sims. In *Women of Florida fiction: Essays on twelve sunshine state writers* (pp. 93–100). Print. An examination of a contemporary writer whose title character's madness reflects the social and civil unrest in the South.

Moers, E. (1976). *Literary women*. New York: Doubleday. Print. The foundational text of feminist Gothic studies.

Showalter, E. (1991). *Sister's choice: Traditions and change in American women's writing*. London: Clarendon. Print. An important study linking American women's writing with feminism and with the Gothic.

CHAPTER 27

Ellen Glasgow's Gothic Heroes and Monsters

Mark A. Graves

In her memoir, *The Woman Within* (1954; henceforth *WW*), Ellen Glasgow recounts her earliest discernible memory, an impression so lingering that it seemed to shape her relationship with the world she portrayed as an artist:

> I open my eyes and look up at the top window panes. … I see a face without a body staring in at me, a vacant face, round, pallid, grotesque, malevolent. Terror—or was it merely sensation?—stabbed me into consciousness. Terror of the sinking sun? Or terror of the formless, the unknown, the mystery, terror of life, of the world, of nothing or everything? One minute, I was not; the next minute, I was. I felt I was separate. I could be hurt. … And I had discovered, too, the universe apart from myself. (3–4)

Although Glasgow literally portrays here fleeting, fragmented memories that her infant consciousness could not re-arrange coherently, the sensation of stark awareness in combination with a dream-like state of unknowing and the resulting terror also resembles a gothic moment, a time of heightened sensitivity, an awareness of an imperceptible, ominous, and menacing burden hanging over one's head, and the uncanny.

Later episodes in Glasgow's life similarly echo the Gothic, especially the suicide of her older brother Frank and brother-in-law Walter McCormack, and the death of her mother. The author must have felt both extraordinary sympathy for her sister Cary and the loss of McCormack's faith in Glasgow's own intellectual abilities when he checked into a New York hotel under an assumed name and shot himself, whether because of financial or health-related difficulties or threatened exposure by a woman to whom he may have been engaged or a homosexual tryst gone wrong. Equally tragic, the naturally introspective

M.A. Graves (✉)
Morehead State University, Morehead, KY, USA

© The Editor(s) (if applicable) and The Author(s) 2016   351
S.C. Street, C.L. Crow (eds.), *The Palgrave Handbook of the Southern Gothic*,
DOI 10.1057/978-1-137-47774-3_27

Frank Glasgow suffered considerably under the high expectations of their father, and education at a military academy and the lingering illness and death of their mother led to Frank eventually shooting himself (*WW* 65–7). As perhaps living examples of the traditional gothic heroine and hero-villain, the match between Anne Jane Gohlson's Tidewater gentility and Francis Glasgow's rural Scots-Irish Calvinism made for disastrous outcomes, at least for their matriarch. Because of his sternness, Glasgow disavowed any legacy from her father beyond her blue eyes and a share in a trust fund, but ironically, her characters' admirable fortitude—the 'vein of iron' that shares its name with one of her best-regarded novels—she drew from her father's dour Presbyterian worldview. Whether exacerbated by multiple pregnancies circa the Civil War or her husband's alleged infidelity with a black mistress or all factors, Anne Glasgow died of typhoid in 1893, and for Frank and her three youngest children—Cary, Ellen, and Rebe—the world crumbled (83). Even Glasgow's depiction in her memoir of her alleged clandestine love affair with an older married man whom she called 'Gerald B—' reads like the pastiche of a gothic romance (153–68).

Her biography aside, what more conclusively aligns Glasgow with gothic imperatives is her 1935 *Saturday Review of Literature* commentary entitled 'Heroes and Monsters,' in which she makes the first recorded reference to the term 'Southern Gothic' in print (Crow 134). Critically, Glasgow has been counted among the first Southern realists, and she prided herself on her earnest efforts to rebel against the sentimental 'evasive idealism' of late nineteenth-century Southern writing in favor of the 'blood and irony' that she believed Southern literature sorely lacked, but she clearly took issue with the 'multitude of half-wits …, whole idiots …, nymphomaniacs …, paranoiacs, and rakehells in general that populate the Modern literary South' (*A Certain Measure* 69; henceforth *CM*). The violence and depravity indicative of the Southern realists' subject matter of the late 1920s and 1930s—the 'Raw-Head-and-Bloody Bones' that she assigns to such fiction—she considered acceptable topics for literature, provided they be treated rightfully, with a recognition of their suitable place as romance or as fable, rather than masquerading as the real. In fact, Glasgow questions the possibility of a true Southern school of realism at all, given the 'incurably romantic' nature of the South, writing: 'Only a puff of smoke separates the fabulous Southern hero of the past from the fabulous Southern monster of the present' ('Heroes' 163).

Yet what of a middle ground in Southern writing, somewhere between romance and history and the 'disordered sensibility' of fiction influenced by James Joyce? For as much as Glasgow styled herself as a rebel against the past, she objects to the crop of historically immature Southern realists dining on a 'stew of spoiled meat' who emphasize the degenerate and barbaric, rather than the whole of human existence, which, Glasgow agrees, may include the doomed, the despairing, the 'moral and physical' disintegration revealed by Modern experience (165–6). Ultimately, Glasgow begrudges the Southern Gothicist his or her claim of practicing realism. 'The Gothic as Gothic, not as pseudo-realism, has an important place in our fiction …,' she implores.

'All I ask him is to deal as honestly with living tissue as he now deals with decay, to remind himself that the colors of putrescence have no greater validity for our age, or for any age, than have ... the cardinal virtues' (167). In separating the Gothic from the real, Glasgow hopes to preserve the vibrancy of literature. Her concern: '[T]he literature that crawls too long in the mire will lose at least the power of standing erect' (166).

A PREOCCUPATION WITH THE GOTHIC

Although Glasgow largely eschewed the authors now considered part of the Southern Gothic tradition, she nonetheless indulged in the Gothic herself, with Edgar Allan Poe as her self-confessed inspiration.[1] Glasgow's stories of the supernatural published in her collection *The Shadowy Third and Other Stories* (1923), along with another in the collection, 'Jordan's End,' all rely on a concentrated first-person narration in the vein of Poe and Henry James in *The Turn of the Screw*, designed to achieve '[a] thickness in the human consciousness that entertains and records, that amplifies and interprets it' (qtd in Meeker 15). For her narrators, the author often chooses lawyers, doctors, or nurses to bear witness to the unexplainable events taking place, frequently told in retrospect, since through the lens of their (implied, at least) rational, professionally trained perception, inexplicable occurrences cannot be dismissed as mere hallucination. Moreover, Glasgow replaces the conventional terror-inspiring castles, abbeys, dungeons, or prisons with the Southern home, often an isolated, decaying plantation mansion symbolizing a dying set of values and the class or family that valiantly tries to uphold them. Historic, sinister resonances reverberate from the South's legacy of slavery, violence, war, romantic and sexual betrayal, and racial and gender oppression, imbuing the Glasgow domicile with unresolved frustrations and rage.

Marking the 1916 revival of the author's short fiction career, 'The Shadowy Third' merits particular consideration here, both because Glasgow highlighted it in the title of her short fiction collection and because her portrayal of spectral unresolved history is representative. Told in the first person 'in the fevered style' of James's governess, the saga of a widow haunted by the ghost of her daughter, an heiress, whom she could not save from her second husband's greed is conventionally read as a tale of projection and revenge (MacDonald 321). With a nod to Ellen Moer's seminal work *Literary Women* (1977), Matthews claims that Glasgow's connections between female selfhood and gendered identity, or 'other,' as she puts it, classifies Glasgow's ghost stories as both clearly gothic and gothic in the female sense (109). In addition, Matthews asserts that Glasgow transforms the conventional gothic plot of the isolated female into the female Gothic by providing her with assistance from another woman. She does this in 'The Shadowy Third' through the inclusion in the Maradick household of Margaret Randolph, a young Richmond nurse, quickly torn between her hero worship for the great surgeon, Dr. Roland Maradick, and her compassion for his invalid wife, the young widow who lost daughter Dorothea two months earlier. Since then, Margaret's charge has been tortured by the appearance of her ghostly child whom she fears Maradick murdered and a belief that he seeks her own death as well to acquire and share her wealth with another woman. From the outset, Margaret's fascination with the doctor problematizes her role as narrator. Apropos of the Gothic, 'He was …,' she remarks, 'born to be a hero to a woman' ('Shadowy' 53), and Margaret must caution herself against reading any ulterior motive into Maradick's request for her professional services, despite rationalizing: 'I suppose it was my "destiny" to be caught in the web of Roland Maradick's personality' (54).

In the context of Mrs. Maradick's ultimate fate, imprisoned on the third floor of her own home with only an open window and a secluded garden providing freedom, her husband's incarnation as both gothic hero and villain progressively emerges. When a celebrated alienist recommends that Mrs. Maradick 'rest' in the country—a guise, even the patient knows, for her commitment to an asylum where she will perish separated from her child—Margaret witnesses the ghostly Dorothea open the door in response to her mother's hysterical outburst and run to Mrs. Maradick. Margaret's spontaneous utterance, '"After this can you doubt?,"' repeated by the alienist, assumes dual significance in this moment of gothic convergence. To her own horror, Margaret realizes that everyone else in the room merely sees a desperate woman pantomime the embrace of an immaterial figure (68).

After Mrs. Maradick does indeed die mysteriously in an asylum, Margaret wonders if the doctor has retained her as his office nurse in hopes of containing any gossip surrounding his wife's demise, or if he wishes 'to test the power of his charm over [her]' (68). In time, she comes to exonerate him for any past misdeeds toward his dead wife, but a rapid reversal sends Margaret into, as she puts it, 'a perpetual dizziness of imagination' on news of Dr. Maradick's impending marriage to the original woman of his desire one year to the day after news of Mrs. Maradick's death (69). With Margaret's unconscious recitation of poetry often uttered by Mrs. Maradick, the ghostly Dorothea appears in the garden, but vanishes before Margaret can seek answers about the mystery of her death. The ring of the telephone beckoning the doctor to an emergency shakes Margaret out of her sense of doom, merging with images of a coiled child's jump rope, her automatic reach for the light switch, and Maradick's fatal downstairs tumble. Consistent with the sustained narrative voice throughout, Margaret has the last word on Maradick's fate: 'Something … it may have been as I am ready to bear witness, an invisible judgment—something had killed him at the very moment when he most wanted to live' (72).

Glasgow's conventional gothic ending here points to Maradick's death as an act of revenge from beyond the grave, but in an alternative reading of the story, the change in Margaret's disposition, what might be called obsession with the doctor, combined with his immunity to her presence and her own tendency to romanticize attachments, suggests a rage on her part leading to the suppression of her deadly deed at the end. One clue to the last-minute switch in Margaret's mindset is her waning interest in a romantic novel that interested her before the appearance of Dorothea, but then seemed tedious afterward, a reminder of the possible crimes committed in the house. Symbolically, then, her romantic visions torn asunder, Margaret more clearly perceives the dynamics in the household. Her continual denial of her hero's culpability in the moments between Dr. Maradick's arrival home from dinner with his fiancée and his call to return from upstairs, the phrase 'There can't be a bit of truth in it' that she repeats three times, each time more frantically, followed by her admission 'For the first time in my life I knew what it was to be afraid of the unknown, of the unseen …,' prompts an interpretation with Margaret as the aggressor and the spectral occurrences under question (70–71).[2]

In her ghost stories Glasgow relies on supernatural elements to convey the bizarre, but 'Jordan's End' reveals the author's skill in creating the Gothic using the conventions of realism. The title references both the decaying Jordan plantation mansion situated in the chilly November woods, reminiscent of 'grim tales of enchanted forests filled with evil faces and whispering voices,' and also the fate of a once-great Virginia family burdened by hereditary insanity ('Jordan's' 206). When called to the house the doctor discovers Alan Jordan's beautiful, charming wife Judith among the detritus of this hereditary scourge. Narratively, the unanswered questions surrounding the death of physically robust Alan Jordan, stricken by the family disease, link the realism of 'Jordan's End' to the ghost stories. Undoubtedly, when summoned to confirm Jordan's demise, the young doctor recognizes all the elements of a mercy killing, principally on the mantle the uncorked, empty vial of the opiate left to soothe the patient. Committed to aiding the now-widowed Judith Jordan, he has a lingering nagging doubt in the back of his mind: 'How had it happened? Could she have killed him? Had the delicate creature served her will to the unspeakable act? It was incredible. It was inconceivable. And yet …' (215). The ellipsis here reflects the doctor's conflict between believing in Judith's will to perform euthanasia versus his infatuation for a woman he considers incapable of any immoral or unkind act. The possibility, however, that Alan, in a lucid moment, ingested the drug himself forces the doctor to waiver in his opinion once again. Although technically freed by the death of her husband, Judith's enduring commitment to the remaining Jordan legacy, literally embodied by her 10-year-old son, Glasgow pits against the overwhelming forces of entropy facing the South. Aware that her desperate gasp 'He was my life …' places Judith, as Glasgow phrases it, 'beyond all consolation and all companionship,' the doctor fears that some incidental movement will reveal the truth of Alan Jordan's death before they can part with his idealized memory of her intact (215–16). MacDonald views Judith Jordan's last gesture, dropping her shawl as she turns back toward Jordan's End, as a nod to an uncertain future, symbolic for the author of sloughing off a dead past (330–31).

Whereas the origins of the Gothic in America have been amply theorized—fears of what lurks in the dark forests of a new America and the violence of slavery, among others—Glasgow's gothic stories lean more toward biographical than broadly historical readings, a conclusion supported by both Matthews and Dominguez-Rué. As a case, the moldering plantation mansion, Whispering

Leaves, in Glasgow's story of the same name evokes Jerdone Castle, Glasgow's childhood summer home that offered a sense of security under the loving care of her own nurse. This conclusion is reinforced by the narrative of an alienated young boy rescued time and time again by the ghost of his mother, Mammy Rhody, a name reminiscent of Annie Gholson Glasgow's own childhood caregiver, Mammy Rhoda (Matthews 143). More universally, the story speaks to a yearning for solace in a chaotic and uncertain environment, a description for Glasgow's own yearning during this period. In his analysis of Glasgow's short fiction as evidence of the mounting influence of Jung and Freud on American fiction, for instance, Julius Rowan Raper locates her short stories within the context of 'Glasgow's search, during her decade of emotional and aesthetic crisis for a language to express the invisible world that had very nearly wrecked her life and career,' including the lexicon of the Gothic ('Invisible' 67). While publishing in magazines the stories later collected as *The Shadowy Third* (1923) proved lucrative, Glasgow also turned to short fiction because the chaos presented by her romantic entanglement with Romanian Red Cross Commissioner and Virginia lawyer Henry Anderson, wrapped up in the politics of the impending First World War and then its aftermath, as well as the death of her father and the debt resulting from his last illness—what Glasgow called her 'Slough of Despond'—distracted her from painting on the large canvases, as Richard Meeker described them, that her novels often became (6).

In fact, Glasgow's conception of the war in horrific terms connects her mindset with her preoccupation with the Gothic. Glasgow recounts how her psyche conjured up 'an allegory of doom' as she entered a dream world of the trenches where the dead and dying entered into a swirling *danse macabre* above the battlefields. Every night, she imagined 'the gangrened flesh on barbed wires, the dead, stiffened in horror, the eyeless skulls and the bared skeletons, the crosses and the poppies, the edge of the universe' (*WW* 233). More apropos of events on the home front, Glasgow biographer Stanley Godbold reads the haunting of the second Mrs. Vanderbridge in the gothic-infused 'The Past' by the apparition of her husband's first wife as expressing the author's frustration with then fiancé Henry Anderson's infatuation with Queen Marie during his tenure as a Red Cross wartime commissioner in Romania (127). Similarly, in 'Dare's Gift' Lucy Dare betrays her Northern fiancé to Confederate forces in the name of a blind Southern nationalism, with the resulting shockwaves absorbed through time to the present day by the eponymously named house. Often read as women's search for their own voice, Glasgow also seemingly critiques the jingoism in initial calls for American involvement in the First World War, given the date of the story's composition.

Social Critique

Of the importance of Glasgow's short fiction, Julius Rowan Raper asserts, 'We may safely conclude that without the short stories we would never have known Glasgow's major phase' ('Invisible' 90), resulting in the acclaimed *Barren*

Ground (1925), *The Sheltered Life* (1932), and *Vein of Iron* (1935). Despite her ambivalence toward the transference, her earliest works of long fiction chronicle the demise of the residual aristocracy in favor of the rising middle class, and through them she explores the social problems often encountered by the non-aristocratic whites decades before Faulkner, Erskine Caldwell, or other writers considered Southern Gothicists. In *The Voice of the People* (1900), for example, a young Nick Burr aspires to transcend his humble origins, declaring "'There ain't nothin' in peanut-raisin'. ... It's jest farmin' fur crows. I'd ruther be a judge'" (39). Aided by a kindly, yet self-serving, aristocrat, Nick defies the odds to become Virginia's governor through honest political means, but a lynch mob bent on vigilante justice kills him on the eve of his probable election as Virginia's junior senator. Analogously, in Glasgow's Civil War romance *The Battle-Ground* (1902), aristocratic Dan Montjoy and poor white Pinetop unite in defense of the South, but, chancing upon the mountaineer struggling with words in his first primer, Dan realizes for the first time how his genial plantation life had condemned lower classes to ignorance, 'overlook[ing] the white sharer of the negro's wrong' (384). Anticipating the Southern Gothic mode's potential for exposing violence and social injustice, Glasgow reveals the obstacles that extant class prejudices in the defeated South foretold even in her own generation.

Two additional works from Glasgow's earlier canon anticipate the later potential of the Southern Gothic mode to offer social critique with more traditional gothic settings and themes of exploitation, violence, and entrapment. Both *The Deliverance* (1904) and *The Miller of Old Church* (1911) evoke the South's agricultural heritage and notions of class privilege in replacing the castles and dungeons of traditional gothic iconography with the plantation mansions, tobacco sheds, and utilitarian architecture indicative of an agrarian economy once dependent on chattel slavery. With her portrayal of Christopher Blake in *The Deliverance*, Glasgow sought 'to test the strength of hereditary fibre when it has long been subjected to the power of malignant circumstances,' certain that 'environment more than inheritance determines character' (*CM* 34). Either squandered by ancestors or stolen, the Blake's loss of their family holdings underlies the gothic theme of revenge in the text. The events surrounding their former overseer's 'purchase' of the Blake home and vast property for only $7,000 remains a mystery, since the plantation ledgers conveniently burned near the time of the sale. Did Fletcher embezzle the funds from the Blakes, preventing the payment of debts, or had the Blake ancestors frittered away the family fortune over the years, one spiked punch bowl at a time? In either case, Fletcher acquires the Blake plantation in hopes of shaping his grandson, Will, into a gentleman, but all such efforts drive a wedge between the two. Christopher exploits the boy's desire to stand on his own, cunningly realizing that "'the way to touch the man is through the boy ...'" (*Deliverance* 184). Having set in motion a sequence of events, Christopher watches as young Will Fletcher indulges in self-destructive behaviors that include expulsion from college and marrying a lower-class woman of limited intellect and character. In a rage sparked by the news that his grandfather has disinherited him in favor of his sister Maria, the young man strikes his patriarch and kills him. Recognizing himself as 'a man debased by ignorance and passion to the level of the beasts,' Christopher confesses to the crime as a form of atonement for his manipulation of Will and serves five years in prison (427, 535). On his release, Christopher marries Maria, and he regains Blake Hall and his heritage despite his ambivalence about both.

Corresponding elements of aristocratic decadence exhibited by the Blake ancestry manifest themselves in the Gays in *The Miller of Old Church*. Although the title refers to Abel Revercomb, an enterprising middle-class man, the novel ultimately focuses on the circumstances of Molly Merryweather's birth and its implications for the neighboring social strata. Molly's story begins with old Jonathan Gay's purchase of the Jordan family plantation, Jordan's Journey, at which time he entered into a sexual liaison with his overseer's daughter, Janet, and fathered Molly. Nearing her 21st birthday during the expanse of the novel, Molly learns of her parentage and the $10,000 annuity bequeathed to her in old Jonathan Gay's will, provided she live in the mansion with her widowed aunt by marriage, Angela, and Angela's hideous sister Kesiah. Old Jonathan and Janet become aligned, then, with the hero-villain and benighted heroine of more traditional gothic texts, with Janet atoning for her sexual impropriety by dying insane and old Jonathan dead by an assassin's bullet. Witnesses saw Janet's fiancé, Abner Revercomb, Abel's older brother, trekking away from the spring with a gun on the morning of the murder (*Miller* 101).

The same class and emotional conflicts replicate themselves in the next generation with the appearance of Angela Gay's son, young Jonathan, whose own actions, in combination with a tarnished family history, do nothing to dispel attitudes about lingering aristocratic decadence indicative of the Southern Gothic, such as his intention to marry Molly after she inherits, despite Abel's widely known love for her. Unknown to all, he had already succumbed to the natural appeal of Abel's niece, Blossom Revercomb, and made her his wife (74). Abel's own marriage to a lower-class white woman takes on distinctly gothic overtones as his wife pines away in the throes of her own impossible love for the minister. History repeats itself in the demise of young Jonathan Gay, whose wounding in the same location as his uncle, the spring known as the Haunt, concludes the gothic subplot of aristocratic debauchery, since Jonathan resists naming as his murderer Blossom's father Abner, seen once again carrying a gun in the region of the crime.

Dorinda Oakley's discharge of a firearm serves as a precipitating factor in Ellen Glasgow's personal favorite, *Barren Ground* (1925). Dorinda hails from the union of a devoutly Calvinist mother whose raison d'être dissolves with the death of her missionary fiancé and a hard-working, 'poor white' farmer whose only appeal when the more cultured Eudora Abernathy had the instinct to marry was his proximity. Such combined attributes make for a stoic existence eking subsistence out of the depleted soil of southwestern Virginia around Pedlar's Mill and little emotional or spiritual hope, particularly for women.

Indicative of both the naturalist and gothic elements in the text, Dorinda often felt 'caught like a mouse in the trap of life. ... held fast by circumstances as by invisible wires of steel' (*Barren* 57), so when she falls in love with Jason Greylock, a doctor returned home from New York City, '[t]he powers of life had seized her as an eagle seizes its prey' (29). On the eve of her wedding to Jason, delight and optimism rapidly turn to disappointment and disgust when Dorinda learns of Jason's 'shotgun' marriage to a wealthier neighborhood farmer's daughter. Jason's alcoholic father tells her this in the impossible-to-overlook gothic setting of the Greylock brick farmhouse on Five Oaks farm, despite its size and architectural detail a hovel full of cobwebs and trash. Driven by the type of temporary psychosis experienced by her mother on the loss of her own fiancé and a bloodthirstiness indicative of an ancestor's search for religious renewal hitherto never understood by Dorinda, in the moonlight barn she confronts her errant lover, who cowers on her spontaneous discharge of a rifle found propped against a barrel. Inhibited by her muscles from firing again, Dorinda realizes that Jason betrayed her for the worst reason, weakness. Desperate to leave her disappointment behind, she arrives in New York City, only to miscarry Jason's child after she is struck by a cab. She physically recovers, but emotionally denounces any prospects of future romantic intimacy. A debilitating stroke suffered by her father compels her to return to the family homestead, Old Farm, and she conquers the barren soil more successfully than her arid spirit.

Glasgow's labeling of subdivisions in the novel 'Broomsedge,' 'Pine,' and 'Life Everlasting' after Virginia's indigenous flora are apt descriptors also for Dorinda's states of being. Most relevant for interpreting the Gothic, broomsedge, a species of invasive natural grass, symbolizes the overwhelming sense of fatalism that results from meager, if not failed, harvests for years on end. As an old sage in the neighborhood of Pedlar's Mills observes, '"Broomsage ain't just wild stuff. It's a kind of fate"' (4). Ravaged by the Civil War and antiquated horticultural practices, the farms that Dorinda and her generation inherit easily succumb to whatever scant vegetation will sink roots into nutrient-deprived soil. For some, like Dorinda's father, tradition drives them to fight back against the fast-growing broomsedge and scrub pine and oak, 'struggling inarticulately against the blight of poverty and the barrenness of the soil' (40), while others, like Dorinda's mother, cling to the tenets of Calvinism and hard work to combat 'the feeling that the land contained a terrible force, whether for good or evil' (38), as Dorinda perceives Old Farm.

In the preface to the Virginia Edition of the text, Glasgow vowed that she had set out to reverse the predicament of the traditional jilted woman, and the remainder of Dorinda's saga attests to the author's success (*CM* 160). For Dorinda, the longer she remains in Pedlar's Mill, the more she is galvanized by the neighborhood maxim, '[Y]ou've got to conquer the land in the beginning, or it'll conquer you before you're through with it' (*Barren* 16). She is partnered in business as in daily life with shopkeeper Nathan Pedlar, with whom she enters into a celibate marriage, and the two prosper through a combination of innovative farming practice and animal husbandry, purchasing the Greylock farm, overgrown but still occupied by the eremitic Jason whom she nurses until his death from alcoholism. Success and emotional frigidity have rewarded Dorinda with a careworn appearance, but she knows that her youth and the idealism lost by Jason's betrayal will not be returned by inflicting a revenge thirty years overdue.

As in *Barren Ground*, a shooting exerts a gothic influence on the narrative of *The Sheltered Life* (1932), another of Glasgow's ambivalent social critiques of lingering 'evasive idealism.' In the years leading up to the First World War, the once-elegant older homes on Queenborough's Washington Street, like crumbling gothic edifices, have rapidly disappeared under the demands of industrial expansion, but octogenarian General Archbald has vowed to stay in the neighborhood as long as the legendary Eva Howard Birdsong remains, her beauty an enduring monument to the ideals achievable by humanity.

If assessments of the grotesque as an instrument of social critique accurately describe the function of such figures in the Southern Gothic—as the work of Flannery O'Connor and Carson McCullers suggests—then the idealized women in this text qualify, switching emotional for physical malformation. For example, Eva's illusions of marriage tell her to overlook her husband George's multiple infidelities because he loves only her (*Sheltered* 81), but her failure to acknowledge the moral failings of men from her pedestal manifests itself in a feminine malady requiring life-saving surgery that Eva would prefer kill rather than merely disfigure her. Such feminine idealization proves damaging to Jenny Blair Archbald as well, beginning with a roller-skating accident that exposes the 9-year-old to George Birdsong's affair with Memoria, the neighborhood's mixed-race laundress. As Glasgow biographer Susan Goodman observes, for Jenny to inherit her role in 'the sheltered life' of the Southern family community, she must bury 'the truth of her own experience' in acknowledging this episode, or more accurately to keep and romanticize for over a decade the promise that she makes the adult George to remain discreet about Memoria, a bond sealed by his flattery ('Memory' 41). The principles of 'the sheltered life' that shield Jenny from such historical and sexual realities prevent her from consciously understanding the ramifications of her romantic attachment to another woman's husband until too late, culminating in an episode replete with Southern Gothic overtones. After George returns from a duck-hunting trip with 25 fine specimens, bound in pairs with green ribbons that Jenny recognizes as discarded from an old dress of Eva's, blood clotting on their beaks, she cannot help but observe 'He was never so happy … as when he had killed something beautiful,' a statement layered with meaning. George's reckless behavior has destroyed her own romantic innocence, his wife's well-being, and, most important, his wife's ideals, with no concern for or even apparent awareness of the detritus left in his path (*Sheltered* 382). After witnessing her husband's tell-tale embrace of Jenny, Eva shoots George, putatively to keep him from ruining Jenny, the world seemingly crashing down around all of them as a thunderstorm approaches. Like the ducks strewn throughout the Birdsong library, Jenny knows that the next time she sees George '[h]e will have blood on him' (393). With the neighborhood committed to believing that George's death resulted from an accident on his part, Jenny's cry, '"Oh, Grandfather, I didn't mean anything. ... I didn't mean anything in the world!,"' becomes a telling commentary on the pitfalls of saddling the young with antiquated illusions long after their era has surpassed them (395).

Conclusion

True to her word that subjects such as deep-seated aristocratic revenge, sexual immorality, and class and racial mixing merit literary portrayal, Glasgow explored these taboos using the gothic mode, presumably in the style that she recommended others follow. If she is a hypocrite, then, relevant Glasgow works might best be described as embodying the Gothic in Southern literature rather than the Southern Gothic. Yet beyond her criticism of Southern Gothic aesthetics, Glasgow resented that Southern Gothic writers refused to credit her pioneering efforts to salvage Southern literature from the bathos of the plantation school, paving the way for their own achievements.[3] Some writers of the Southern Renaissance whose works overlap with or embody the Southern Gothic at its best considered Glasgow's efforts most favorably as anachronistic and, at worst, horrid. For a writer who continually sought recognition, her inability to admire the works of many younger Southern writers, such as Katherine Anne Porter and Faulkner, likely resulted from her anxieties about remaining in the mainstream of Southern letters during her lifetime.[4] Unfortunately, then, Glasgow became a sort of 'hereditary obligation,' as Faulkner would describe Emily Grierson in 'A Rose for Emily,' a figure not to be discounted more for her longevity than her continuing relevance (Goodman, *Ellen Glasgow* 216–17).

Notes

1. See Rouse 352.
2. This reading draws partially on Raper, *From the Sunken Garden* 67–8.
3. As Goodman asserts, Faulkner and Julia Peterkin owe to Glasgow 'her challenge to contemporary views of history' and 'her frank treatment of race' (*Ellen Glasgow* 183–4).
4. Although he would grow to appreciate Glasgow, initially Allen Tate wrote, 'I am of the opinion that she writes an abominable prose style, and that she is one of the worst novelists in the world' (qtd in Caldwell 210).

Bibliography

Caldwell, E. (1984). Ellen Glasgow and the southern agrarians. *American Literature*, *21*(2), 203–213.

Crow, C. (2009). *American Gothic*. Cardiff: University of Wales Press.

Dominguez-Rué, E. (2004). Madwomen in the drawing-room: Female invalidism in Ellen Glasgow's Gothic stories. *Journal of American Studies, 38*(3), 425–438.

Faulkner, W. (1995). A rose for Emily. In *The collected short stories of William Faulkner* (pp. 119–130). New York: Random-Vintage.

Glasgow, E. (1904). *The deliverance*. New York: Doubleday, Page, & Co.

Glasgow, E. (1911). *The miller of Old Church*. New York: Hurst & Co.

Glasgow, E. (1929). *The battle-ground*. Garden City: Doubleday, Page & Co.

Glasgow, E. (1932). *The sheltered life*. Garden City: Doubleday, Doran & Co.

Glasgow, E. (1943). *A certain measure: An interpretation of prose fiction*. New York: Harcourt, Brace, and Co.

Glasgow, E. (1954). *The woman within*. New York: Harcourt, Brace, and Co.

Glasgow, E. (1963a). Dare's gift. In R. K. Meeker (Ed.), *The collected short stories of Ellen Glasgow* (pp. 90–118). Baton Rouge: Louisiana State University Press.

Glasgow, E. (1963b). Jordan's end. In R. K. Meeker (Ed.), *The collected short stories of Ellen Glasgow* (pp. 203–216). Baton Rouge: Louisiana State University Press.

Glasgow, E. (1963c). The shadowy third. In R. K. Meeker (Ed.), *The collected short stories of Ellen Glasgow* (pp. 52–72). Baton Rouge: Louisiana State University Press.

Glasgow, E. (1963d). Whispering leaves. In R. K. Meeker (Ed.), *The collected short stories of Ellen Glasgow* (pp. 140–164). Baton Rouge: Louisiana State University Press.

Glasgow, E. (1972). *The voice of the people*. New Haven: College & University Press.

Glasgow, E. (1985). *Barren ground*. New York: Harvest-Harcourt.

Glasgow, E. (1988). Heroes and monsters. In J. R. Raper (Ed.), *Ellen Glasgow's reasonable doubts: A collection of her writings* (pp. 162–167). Baton Rouge: Louisiana State University Press.

Godbold, S. E. (1972). *Ellen Glasgow and the woman within*. Baton Rouge: Louisiana State University Press.

Goodman, S. (1996). Memory and memoria in *The Sheltered Life*. *Mississippi Quarterly* 49/2 (Spring 1996), 241–254.

Goodman, S. (1998). *Ellen Glasgow: A biography*. Baltimore/London: The John Hopkins University Press.

MacDonald, E. (1996). From Jordan's end to Frenchman's bend: Ellen Glasgow's short stories. *Mississippi Quarterly* 49/2 (Spring 1996), 319–332.

Matthews, P. (1994). *Ellen Glasgow and a woman's traditions*. Charlottesville: University of Virginia Press.

Meeker, R. (1963). Introduction. In R. K. Meeker (Ed.), *The collected short stories of Ellen Glasgow* (pp. 3–23). Baton Rouge: Louisiana State University Press.

Raper, J. R. (1977). Invisible things: The short stories of Ellen Glasgow. *The Southern Literary Journal* 9/2 (Spring 1977), 66–90.

Raper, J. R. (1980). *From the Sunken garden: The fiction of Ellen Glasgow, 1916–1945*. Baton Rouge: Louisiana State University Press.

Rouse, B. (1958). *Letters of Ellen Glasgow*. New York: Harcourt, Brace and Co.

FURTHER READING

Carpenter, L. (1991). Visions of female community in Ellen Glasgow's ghost stories. In L. Carpenter & W. K. Kolmar (Eds.), *Haunting the house of fiction: Feminist perspectives on ghost stories by American women* (pp. 117–141). Knoxville: University of Tennessee Press. In her exploration of feminine bonds in her ghost stories, Glasgow offers a powerful critique of heterosexual love and marriage.

Haytock, J. (2002). Gender, class, and ghosts: Ellen Glasgow and the single woman. *The Ellen Glasgow Newsletter* Iss. 49 (Fall 2002), 3–5. As individuals outside the web of gender, class, and race inherent in a gender economy involving marriage, Glasgow's single female protagonists in her short fiction can see what other married women (and men) cannot, namely 'ghosts,' or deeply ingrained aspects of society that can only be resisted by those able to recognize their existence.

King, A. (2008). Matrilineage, mythology, and fable in Ellen Glasgow's 'whispering leaves', *The Ellen Glasgow Journal of Southern Women Writers* 1/2 (Spring 2008), 47–68. The power of matrilineal bonds of both blood and association in Glasgow's tale, often portrayed in mythic terms, offers an alternative to patriarchal constructions of the past.

CHAPTER 28

The Gothic and the Grotesque in the Novels of Carson McCullers

Dara Downey

According to Carson McCullers, the 'Gothic School' in Southern writing that emerged during the middle decades of the twentieth century drew its unsettling effects not from the 'romantic or supernatural', but from 'a peculiar and intense realism'. Such fiction, she asserted, involved the 'juxtaposition of the tragic with the humorous, the immense with the trivial, the sacred with the bawdy, the whole soul of a man with a materialistic detail' ('Russian Realists' 258). Born in Georgia, and spending much of her life in the South with brief stints in New York, McCullers consistently produced fiction that was very much a part of this movement. Her work conjures up an image of the American South as a gothic, haunted locale, but through largely realist prose that images fully fleshed out social worlds that rarely, if ever, stray into the realm of the symbolic or the supernatural. Indeed, this very commitment to social realism is precisely what renders McCullers's work gothic, or, to use the term most frequently applied to Southern fiction of this kind, 'grotesque'—that is, focused on the odd, the eccentric, and the physically or sexually atypical.

In McCullers's fiction, society is made up not of an integrated community of those who resemble and support one another, but merely of a collection of alienated, disconnected individuals. From *The Heart Is a Lonely Hunter* (1940) and *Reflections in a Golden Eye* (1941), through *The Member of the Wedding* (1946) and *The Ballad of the Sad Café* (1951), and up to her final novel, *Clock without Hands* (1961), the reader is presented with an entire society made up of outsiders, as the result of various combinations of class difference, sexuality, physical attributes, or ideology and worldview. This is a fictional world in which everyone is warped in some way; indeed, her fiction implies that the potential exists for her characters to unite in their shared experience of otherness. However, as a result of the South's nostalgic longing for a past founded

D. Downey (✉)
School of English, Drama and Film, University College Dublin, Dublin, Ireland

© The Editor(s) (if applicable) and The Author(s) 2016
S.C. Street, C.L. Crow (eds.), *The Palgrave Handbook of the Southern Gothic*,
DOI 10.1057/978-1-137-47774-3_28

on intolerance and sectarian hatred, it in fact divides them irreducibly and tragically, to the point at which each individual feels at once far stranger and far more normal than everyone else. Unable or unwilling to comprehend or acknowledge their common oddity, McCullers's characters experience social fragmentation at best, mutual misunderstanding, hatred and violence at worst.

This chapter therefore focuses on the concern in McCullers's fiction with the fault-lines between a societal drive towards 'the normal' and individuals who are classed as 'freaks' and grotesques. As Melissa Free puts it, 'McCullers makes abnormality the norm', to the extent that 'it is the normal that hovers around the edges of the unusual' (443). Indeed, in fictional spaces where oddity and eccentricity seem to characterise a large proportion of the population of small, barely modernised Southern towns, 'normality' is depicted as an external, often depersonalised and overtly gothic regulating force. Consequently, those characters struggling against the norm feel themselves to be confronted by a two-pronged threat, taking the form of both a fear of the freakish (self) *and* a fear of the social structures created to suppress and deny it. In other words, McCullers's characters are portrayed as terrorised simultaneously by their own abnormality and by the looming social threat of judgement and ostracism, creating an inescapable atmosphere in which gothic foreboding and unease pervade the quasi-rural environments they inhabit, attacking individuals both from within and from without.

Southern Gothic, as employed by McCullers, can be seen as taking the basic premise and conventional plots of the Gothic and reconfiguring them within the 'peculiar' (to use the euphemistic adjective often used to describe the institution of Southern slavery) socio-cultural, historical and geographical milieu of the mid-century American South. As Kate Ferguson Ellis argues, the Gothic encodes 'in the language of aristocratic villains, haunted castles, and beleaguered heroines, a struggle to purge the home of licence and lust and to establish it as a type of heaven on earth' (xii). In the most familiar and conventional gothic plot by eighteenth-century writers in English like Ann Radcliffe and Clara Reeve (and continued in America by Charles Brockden Brown, Louisa May Alcott and their inheritors), the heroine performs this cleansing of the home by exposing the terrible deeds perpetrated by the villain at some point in the novel's pre-history. She is therefore tasked with running around draughty corridors and gloomy forests in an effort not to be abducted, or worse, frequently encountering other women, their bodies or their ghosts, who have fallen prey to his reign of terror. This situation is only ended when the heroine pokes into enough dusty corners and crumbling manuscripts that she reveals what has happened to make the imprisoning structure at the heart of the narrative so dirty and dangerous, discovering an appalling crime that has been covered up—generally that some innocent person was wrongly imprisoned, seduced, killed or disinherited; Alcott's *A Whisper in the Dark* (1889) follows this formula very closely. Doing so allows the heroine to reconcile the present with a past that has been haunting it, because that past has been forcibly hidden by those in power (Ellis 37, 50). As critics like Leslie Fiedler and

Eugenia C. DeLamotte have explained at length, the heroine's continued 'resistance' to the villain's wiles, machinations and violent coercion, combined with her successful discovery of his unutterable misdeeds, is ultimately 'rewarded' with a happy marriage and with either a cleaner version of the previously perilous castle, or a totally new, more appropriately middle-class home.

Onto this basic plot structure, Southern Gothic literature (of the kind produced by McCullers, O'Connor, Capote and their ilk, working from a model established by William Faulkner) superimposes the particularities of Southern life, post–Civil War but pre–Civil Rights, but also those of an alienated and alienating modernity. In the process, that plot is both repeated and altered. In McCullers's work in particular—although also in Capote's *Other Voices, Other Rooms* (1948), which can fruitfully be paired with *Clock without Hands*—the virginal heroine becomes a slightly androgynous teenage boy or girl, while villain and haunted castle both disappear as physical entities, only to resurface as social and cultural structures, embodied in but not reducible to powerful leaders of the community such as *Clock without Hands*' Judge Clane, or simply in that community itself. Consequently, the 'happy' ending of conventional Gothic becomes rather trickier to locate, not least because the protagonist positioned as gothic heroine is, like all of the characters in McCullers's novels, fundamentally isolated and powerless, to an extent that it becomes impossible for him or her fully to understand the evils that are perpetrated by the society in which he or she lives. Deprived of a villain to accuse or a gothic castle to clean, McCullers's young protagonists go some way towards uncovering the abuses that are depicted as endemic to Southern culture, but succeed only in redeeming themselves, while society at large remains unchanged.

Matters are further complicated by the literary convention that associates all things Southern with the grotesque. Mikhail Bakhtin's theorisation of it as fundamentally linked to pre- and early-modern carnival sees the grotesque in literature and culture as democratic, generative of bonds within a community, across classes and factions. In McCullers's fictional vision of the mid-century South, however, community ties function only to foment and cement mutual hatred and bigotry. Depicting the South as a region potentially carnivalesque in its multifarious mingling of race, class and sexual orientation, but also as one where the forces of normativity are all the more brutally imposed in the face of this disordering multiplicity, McCullers positions her youthful, idealistic but socially ineffective protagonists, particularly in *The Member of the Wedding* and *Clock without Hands*, as caught precisely between these two opposing sociocultural trajectories. Freaks and grotesques themselves, they nonetheless fear this aspect of themselves, while all the time straining against the narrow confines of the normal, which seeks to prevent progress and change. With this in mind, this chapter begins by briefly exploring the troubled and troubling continuation of an imagined past in the Southern present at mid-century, and the effect that this has on the region, economically and culturally. It then moves on to examine the ways in which this has resulted in a preoccupation in Southern writing with the grotesque and the 'freak'. Finally, by illustrating the ways in which McCullers's novels engage with this cultural environment, it demonstrates the extent to which the South's idealisation of tradition and convention alienates her characters from one another and causes them to fear their own rebellious impulses, to the point at which they are unable or unwilling fully to uncover the past horrors that render the present eerie, dangerous and gothic.

THE OLD SOUTH

The changes brought about by the two world wars, industrialisation and modernisation more generally produced a strong backlash among conservative Southern intellectuals, who bewailed the loss of the 'old ways', primarily those of an agricultural economy and a system of paternalistic, quasi-aristocratic land ownership (Bradbury 8, 17, 200; Holman 1; O'Brien 26; Gray 122–3). The American South was a region that, for some people at least, was characterised by its defeat in the Civil War, by the knowledge that it had been forced to abandon a way of life (based on slavery, perceived as a public and individual good) in which it still believed, and by the poverty that resulted from the loss of its primary source of income—unwaged labour (Holman 9, 92). As C. Hugh Holman elaborates, while the world, and indeed much of the South, was moving into a new era during the early decades of the twentieth century, 'the old order ... lingered in the memory and the heart of the region after the social fact of the order itself had been demolished, and which together formed a powerful myth of a way of life' (191–2; see also O'Brien 124–5; Gray 139, 141). In essence, the South 'was old, and good because it was old' (Gray 154). Consequently, as Alan Tate famously announced in 1940, 'With the war of 1914–1918, the South reentered the world—but gave a backward glance as it stepped over the border: the backward glance gave us the Southern renascence; a literature conscious of the past in the present' (545–6). While many critics now challenge Tate's all-encompassing vision, it remains true that much of the literature from the middle decades of the twentieth century depicted the Southern past as continuing to haunt the Southern present. The present was therefore not the present as such, but a form of continuous past (Gray 179–80). As Gavin Stevens remarks in Faulkner's *Intruder in the Dust*:

> For every Southern boy fourteen years old, not once but whenever he wants it, there is the instant when it's still not yet two o'clock on that July afternoon in 1863, the brigades are in position, the guns are laid and ready in the woods and the furled flags are already loosened to break out ... and it's all in the balance, it hasn't happened yet, it hasn't even begun yet.... (187–8)

The result was a society that was looking in two directions at once, and that suffered for it. As William Van O'Connor puts it, 'the old agricultural system depleted the land and poverty bred abnormality; in many cases people were living with a code that was no longer applicable, and this meant a detachment from reality and loss of vitality' (343). In effect, Southern infrastructure was modernised long before the mindset, beliefs and customs of the region moved beyond a sense of failure that was the legacy of the South's defeat in the Civil War, and beyond its adherence to casual racism, paternalism and a quasi-aristocratic, highly traditional form of social organisation (Gray 124; O'Brien 162), one based in a romanticised, European-inspired feudalism. As Mark Twain noted in 1883, the French Revolution had performed 'great and permanent services to liberty, humanity, and progress' by ensuring that in Europe, 'crowned heads' are seen as 'only men … and can never be gods again, but only figure-heads'. However, in the Southern states, progress was not so linear, something that he blames on the region's mania for the work of Walter Scott, which he claims

> checks this wave of progress, and even turns it back; sets the world in love with dreams and phantoms; with decayed and swinish forms of religion; with decayed and degraded systems of government; with the sillinesses and emptinesses, sham grandeurs, sham gauds, and sham chivalries of a brainless, and worthless long-vanished society. (467)

Consequently, 'practical, common-sense, progressive ideas' became 'mixed up with the duel, the inflated speech, and the jejune romanticism of an absurd past that is dead', and the Southern love and reverence for 'rank and caste' (468–9). Indeed, he also blames Scott for the fact that the Capitol building in Baton Rouge is an 'ungenuine' mockery of a medieval castle, 'with turrets and things' (416–17). This devotion to anachronistic architecture and manners was directly manifested in the plantation novel genre, such as John Pendleton Kennedy's *Swallow Barn* (1832), which 'portray[ed] the plantation as a bulwark of benevolent paternalism overseen by provincial but good-hearted gentlemen and ladies and attended by their deferential and contented black "servants"', a setting where 'men and women, white and black all know their place almost instinctively; the tranquillity of the patriarchal order is tested at times but never seriously disturbed' (Andrews et al. 8).

This nostalgic fantasy was violently dismantled by Faulkner and his inheritors, in novels such as *The Sound and the Fury* (1929), *Sanctuary* (1931) and *Absalom, Absalom!* (1936). However, the Southern plantation house, the gothic castle of the South, is notable for its absence in McCullers's work, and had been gradually sliding out of the frame in Southern writing during the middle decades of the twentieth century. In Capote's *Other Voices, Other Rooms*, for example, the genteel but decaying Scully's Landing, where much of the action takes place, and the once-bustling, now-derelict Cloud Hotel are depicted as part of this legacy, as is a house in the centre of Noon City where three beautiful virgin sisters were supposedly murdered during the Civil War. These architectural structures are but ruins punctuating the landscape, relics that gesture towards but only figuratively perpetuate the unequal social structures that they once upheld. Flannery O'Connor and Tennessee Williams further reduced the plantation house to mere memories of lost homes, in the form of Blanche DuBois's hazily evoked Belle Reve in Williams's *A Streetcar Named Desire* (1947); and the 'threadbare elegance' of Julian's great-grandfather's house, which he has never seen, in O'Connor's 'Everything That Rises Must Converge' (409). However much symbolic weight they might hold as diegetic elements, these buildings are peripheral, and lost forever to the characters who mourn for them. In McCullers, these structures have disappeared completely, and remain only as habits of mind. As Fiedler writes, the atmosphere of Southern Gothic reflects 'the Faulknerian syndrome of disease, death, defeat, mutilation, idiocy, and lust [which] continues to evoke in the stories of these writers a shudder once compelled only by the supernatural' (475). Eschewing the gothic castle and its spectral phantasmagoria, McCullers's brand of the Southern Gothic nonetheless rebuilds it as a function of lingering social intolerance and conservatism.

This is particularly evident in her final novel, *Clock without Hands*, via the figure of Judge Clane, a once powerful member of the legal profession who, even in old age and infirmity, remains a strong voice within the community, laying down the law in matters of opinion, particularly when it comes to the 'race question'. His obsession with reinstating the defunct Confederate currency, of which he has a vast but now worthless fortune, and with which he hopes to return the South to what he sees as its former, pre-war glory, is extricable from his loudly expressed, regressive attitudes towards African Americans. While describing his plans to his grandson, Jester, he announces that he has once been in New York, where he saw a 'white girl' sharing a table with a 'Nigra man'. In his account, 'something in [his] bloodstream sickened' and he fled the city in horror, never to return (*Clock* 40). Although the conversation comes about because Jester challenges his grandfather's views, announcing that he '"question[s] the justice of white supremacy"', when the Judge asks him whether he would consider marrying an African American woman Jester finds himself thinking of the family cook, Verily, and '[h]e could not answer immediately, so much did the image appal him' (32, 39). What this implies is that it is not only the Judge whose actions and emotions are determined by what should be an obsolete set of attitudes—even his vocally rebellious grandson, who strives to break free of the intolerance represented by the Judge and his circle of 'cronies', is caught up in the cycle of hatred and disgust that is part of his heritage, both familial and social, and that modernisation and liberalisation do not appear to be able entirely to erode.

What is most troubling about Jester's latent racism is that he himself by no means matches up with the strictly demarcated norm that his grandfather preaches and embodies. Consumed by adolescent longings—first for a boy in school and then for Sherman, an African American boy with blue eyes whose singing lures Jester out of the Judge's house in the middle of the night, but also for his English teacher, Miss Pafford—his desires are not merely homosexual, but rather polymorphous, difficult to pin down. While these yearnings remain purely private, it rapidly becomes clear that others recognise that he does not fit neatly into the charmed circle of what is considered normal in Milan, Georgia, the small town where the novel is set. J. T. Malone, a pharmacist who functions as a sort of everyman figure in the novel, finds Jester '"strange"', thinking 'he had never been a Milan boy. He was arrogant and at the same time over-polite. There was something hidden about the boy and his softness, his brightness seemed somehow dangerous' (25).

THE GROTESQUE AND THE CARNIVALESQUE

McCullers's fiction is full of characters, like Jester, who do not quite fit in (Gleeson-White 111). *The Heart Is a Lonely Hunter* is populated almost entirely by outsider figures: Singer, a deaf-mute around whom the other characters revolve; Antonapoulos, his overweight, half-mad soulmate; Jake Blount, an alcoholic, itinerant manual labourer, who preaches Marxist politics to unheeding men; Dr Copeland, an African American medical doctor whose violently expressed ideas about racial equality drive his family away and cannot even find a comprehending audience in Blount; Biff Brannon, a thoughtful café owner with a penchant for his dead wife's clothes and perfume; and Mick, a musically talented teenager who smokes to stunt what she sees as her unnatural growth spurt. Frankie Addams in *The Member of the Wedding* also believes herself to be freakishly tall and fundamentally out of kilter with girls her own age, to the point where she wants her brother and his new wife to make her a 'member' of their wedding and their subsequent married life. Her companions are Berenice, an African American servant with one blue glass eye, and John Henry, a little boy who likes to dress up in Berenice's clothes and shoes (see Adams 5) and who feels 'that people ought to be half boy and half girl' (*Member* 116). The cast of *Reflections in a Golden Eye* include a frustrated homosexual army major; his unfaithful, quasi-animalistic wife; her lover's wife Alison, a seriously ill woman who has cut off her own nipples; and Anacleto, Alison's diminutive, decidedly camp Filipino servant. *The Ballad of the Sad Café* features Miss Amelia, a bar owner who dresses for the most part in men's clothing, and Cousin Lymon, a 'dwarfed', dapper hunchback, with whom Miss Amelia seems to enjoy an asexual but satisfying domestic arrangement, until her former, conventionally masculine, overtly violent husband arrives and steals Cousin Lymon's affections.

It is the high incidence of physically, sexually and racially marked characters in her work that has earned it the label of 'grotesque', a form of Southern writing that William Van O'Connor has described as a 'reaction against the sometimes bland surfaces of bourgeois customs and habits'; a genre in which 'the sharp division between tragedy and comedy has broken down' and where 'the sublime sometimes lurks behind weirdly distorted images' (342). This sense of the grotesque as a form of resistance to the normative is taken up by Free, who remarks that McCullers's 'plethora of grotesque imagery', particularly in relation to gender and sexuality and to distorted, painful bodies, marks 'a disruption—not of the sexually aberrant body, but of the social body that silences and condemns deviance' (429). Similarly, Sarah Gleeson-White sees

McCullers's work as closely related to Bakhtin's notion of the carnivalesque, which she reads as a 'strategy of resistance' (110).

The carnivalesque is, for Bahktin, the 'temporary suspension ... of hierarchical rank' that 'created during carnival time a special type of communication impossible in everyday life'—specifically, communion between those who social structures would usually divide from one another (10). Referring to pre-seventeenth-century literature that made use of carnivalesque tropes, in the form of revels and jokes, dwarfs, giants and ambiguously gendered individuals, which he calls 'grotesque realism', Bahktin stresses that this entails an emphasis on the materiality of the body, and specifically on bodily functions and forms usually excluded from the literary (18). Doing so creates a strong sense of community, since '[t]he unfinished and open body (dying, bringing forth and being born) is not separated from the world by clearly defined boundaries; it is blended with the world, with animals, with objects' (26-7). However, such grotesque bodies, deformed, decayed or exaggerated in terms of their material functions as they tend to be, only remain part of the carnival spirit as long as they are associated with community—when isolated and individualised, they take on far more negative and destructive overtones (23). Bakhtin asserts that this occurred in later centuries, when carnival was transformed into mere extensions of state power and control, so that it lost its truly communal and democratic functions and effect (33). At the same time, in Romantic literature, the carnivalesque was being transformed into a purely individualistic vision of otherness, producing 'a terrifying world, alien to man' and revealing the chaos beneath the apparently secure, ordered universe, rather than embracing and celebrating a generative form of misrule and disorder (37–9).

McCullers's Southern Gothic is far closer to the Romantic version of the grotesque. According to Fiedler, her work is populated by 'images created out of the homosexual's conviction of the impossibility of love; and they move ... through a society in which passion leads only to thralldom and suffering' (478). Similarly, for Bradbury, McCullers's 'partiality for grotesques' cannot be disentangled from her 'concern for the lonely and the loveless', as well as for 'failures of communication and self-betrayal', conjuring up a world in which brotherhood and love are equally impossible (110, 112). Hers is a fictional universe marked by 'isolation without hope of communication' (Emerson 17), a status quo that she herself described as a 'moral isolation' that 'is intolerable' to 'the weak, lonely self' ('Loneliness' 265). As the narrator of *The Ballad of the Sad Café* puts it, 'every lover ... feels in his soul that this love is a solitary thing. He comes to know a new, strange loneliness and it is this knowledge which makes him suffer' (216).

What prevents McCullers's freaks and outsiders from forming the kind of community that Bakhtin describes is an intractable combination of modernist alienation and the intolerance of normative South society, depicted as a place where community is both impossible and ubiquitous (O'Brien 2, 26). As Faulkner's Gavin Stevens remarks, when Southerners defended what they saw as the good old Southern lifestyle, they were 'defending not actually our politics or beliefs or even our way of life, but simply our homogeneity' (*Intruder* 149). Within this context, McCullers's 'grotesque' but sympathetically portrayed characters *should* act as powerful disordering forces, disrupting such homogeneity from within. For Rachel Adams, 'Freaks and queers suffer because they cannot be assimilated into the dominant social order, yet their presence highlights the excesses, contradictions, and incoherencies at the very heart of that order' (552). Indeed, as *The Member of the Wedding* makes clear, the freak-as-spectacle was very much a part of Southern society at mid-century. The novel details Frankie Addams's lonely summer following rejection by her peers, a fracture that is positioned as coeval with her sudden growth spurt, which she feels renders her a 'freak', and which causes her to experience the kitchen where she spends most of her time, and the town more generally, as somehow dark, eerie and threatening, despite its bright, sunny, summer weather—that is, as Gothic. The passage detailing her memories and feelings in relation to this unpleasant change of circumstances comes immediately before a description of the annual Chattahoochee Exposition, a fair featuring carnival rides and sideshows, including 'the House of the Freaks'. This is a tent that houses a 'Giant', a 'Fat Lady', a 'Midget', a 'Wild Nigger', a 'Pin-Head', of whom John Henry is especially enamoured, and a 'Half-Man Half-Woman, a morphidite and a miracle of science' (*Member* 25–7). The latter is described in some detail:

> This Freak was divided completely in half—the left side was a man and the right side a woman. The costume on the left was a leopard skin and on the right side a brassiere and a spangled skirt. Half the face was dark-bearded and the other half bright glazed with paint. Both eyes were very strange. Frankie ... was afraid of all the Freaks, for it seemed to her that they looked her in a secret way and tried to connect their eyes with hers, as though to say; we know you. She was afraid of their long Freak eyes. ...
> 'I doubt they ever get married or go to a wedding,' she said. 'Those Freaks.' (27)

Far from identifying potential kindred spirits in the 'freaks', then, Frankie (whose hair is cut short and who wears boy's shorts and a vest, rendering her an equally visually ambiguous figure) here rebels not against the norms of femininity and adolescence into which she is failing to fit, but against the freakishness in herself, setting this up against her brother's impending wedding (which she sees as her ticket out of small-town claustrophobia) and the possibilities for communion and belonging that it seems to hold out to her. As a marker of this new identity, she begins to call herself F. Jasmine, a decidedly more feminine name than the androgynous Frankie. She is, in other words, trying to solve her own ostracism by an appeal to heternormativity (Adams 560). Similarly, in *Clock without Hands*, reading the Kinsey Report on the varieties of American sexual preferences and practices, Jester 'worrie[s] terribly' because he 'was afraid, so terribly afraid, that he was not normal and the fear corkscrewed within him. ... he had never felt the normal sexual urge and his heart quaked with fear for himself, as more than anything else he yearned to be exactly like everyone else' (*Clock* 85). As Adams points out, 'the irony of Jester's longing "to be exactly like everyone else" is that nearly "everyone else" in McCullers's fiction is plagued by queer tendencies that cannot be classified within a system of normative heterosexuality', not least because the positioning of the Kinsey Report within *Clock without Hands* implies that freakishness is now general all over America (Adams 565–6).

Adams therefore argues that both Frankie and Jester ultimately accept their own oddity within a more rounded and coherent but in no way normative identity. In both novels, however, matters are rather more ambiguous than Adams would have it. At the end of *The Member of the Wedding*, the mother of Frankie's new female friend, Mary Littlejohn, forbids her and Mary from visiting the House of the Freaks, a moment that Adams read as a recognition that freaks are everywhere (575–6). After the convulsions of the previous episodes, however, during which Frankie is nearly raped by a soldier, causes a terrible scene at her brother's wedding and is kept away while John Henry dies screaming from meningitis, her decision to settle into a sorophilic, adolescent friendship seems closer to an acceptance of social norms (which relegate sexuality and even the mixing of the sexes to adulthood and marriage) and a repression (rather than an exorcism) of her troubled past. She does ultimately abandon the assumed name F. Jasmine, but nonetheless settles on Frances, which is feminine in spelling if not in pronunciation, indicating a less oppositional identity choice.

Similarly, Jester might argue with his grandfather over the racial integration of Southern schools, and even plan to become a lawyer like his socially progressive father Johnny (who killed himself after a disastrous court case in which he failed to defend an African American for the murder of a white man) when he grows up, but the narrative never encompasses such redemptive scenes within its frame. Moreover, Jester fails, or indeed refuses, to see his grandfather's complicity in Sherman's murder. Sherman spends much of the novel acting as the Judge's secretary, but leaves in anger once he learns of the Judge's plans to redeem the Confederate currency, and that the Judge has been concealing his knowledge of Sherman's parentage (his father was the man whom Johnny Clane had defended). In an act of audacious defiance, Sherman rents a house in a 'white' area of Milan, and the Judge, smarting from the boy's rejection of his patronage, calls a town meeting to decide who should bomb Sherman's house. Jester overhears the men plotting, warns Sherman but is ignored, and later invites Sammy Lank (who throws the bomb) for a spin in his private plane, planning to shoot the man, but cannot go through with it, and Lank is brought safely back to earth, unaware of the danger that he has been in.

The point here is that, like Frankie seeing the sideshow 'freaks', rather than the cultural norms that have restricted and ostracised her, as the enemy, Jester lashes out against the wrong target. Lank is merely the weapon—his grandfather is Sherman's real murderer. In Ellis's formulation, the function of the gothic heroine is to redeem a troubled and troubling past, having made public the horrors of patriarchal, aristocratic rule (48–9). Caught in the trap of the South, Jester's putative rebellion against the Judge's outmoded values leads not to the discovery and release of the traumatic, gothic past, but instead to further (threatened) violence and misappropriation of blame. McCullers's vision is not, however, completely pessimistic, and while wrongs may not be revealed or righted, both Frankie and Jester as individuals appear to escape the gothic atmosphere that has been oppressing them. Frankie, or rather Frances, is initially 'visited' by the ghost of John Henry, and Berenice's foster brother is unfairly imprisoned for burglary, but the novel ends, rather abruptly, with the advent of winter, a sign that the stifling heat of the summer, which Frankie associates with restriction and rejection, is finally over. Even more optimistically, Jester's attempt to avenge Sherman's murder is derailed by a story that Lank tells him. Lank and his wife, who is abnormally prone to producing twins and triplets, believe that they would be made rich and famous if they had quins, and so effectively bankrupt themselves with one multiple birth after another. We are told:

> The grotesque pity of the story made Jester laugh that laughter of despair. And once having laughed and despaired and pitied, he knew he could not use the pistol. For in that instant the seed of compassion, forced by sorrow, had begun to blossom. Jester slipped the pistol from his pocket and dropped it out of the plane. (*Clock* 201)

While this is by no means a 'happy ending', it does imply that, while Frankie might have partially capitulated to the norm, Jester, in McCullers's final novel, goes some way towards forging the kinds of social ties, particularly among the odd and the outcast, that Bakhtin saw as essential to the carnivalesque. The gothic doom overlaying her work in general may not have been fully exorcised, and Sherman's murder remains unavenged, but Jester has succeeded in altering the mode of the novel, from the frightening modernist grotesque to something that resembles, even in its sadness and despair, the rather more liberating and celebratory grotesque that is founded in community, and in a shared experience of common strangeness.

Bibliography

Adams, R. (1999). "A mixture of delicious and freak": The queer fiction of Carson McCullers. *American Literature, 71*(3), 551–583. Print.

Alcott, L. M. (1977). A whisper in the dark. In M. B. Stern (Ed.), *Plots and counterplots: More unknown thrillers of Louisa May Alcott*. London: W.H. Allen. Print.

Andrews, W., et al. (1998). *The literature of the American South*. New York/London: W.W. Norton and Co. Print.

Bakhtin, M. (1984). *Rabelais and his world* (trans: Iswolsky, H.). Bloomington/ Indiana: Indiana University Press, Print.

Bradbury, J. M. (1963). *Rethinking the south: A critical history of the literature, 1920–1960*. Chapel Hill: University of North Carolina Press. Print.

Capote, T. (1988). *Other voices, other rooms*. London: Pan Books. Print.

DeLamotte, E. C. (1990). *Perils of the night: A feminist study of nineteenth-century Gothic*. New York/Oxford: Oxford University Press. Print.

Ellis, K. F. (1989). *The contested castle: Gothic novels and the subversion of domestic ideology*. Urbana/Chicago: University of Illinois Press. Print.

Emerson, D. (1962). The ambiguities of clock without hands. *Wisconsin Studies in Contemporary Literature, 3*(3), 15–28.

Faulkner, W. (1960). *Intruder in the dust*. London: Penguin.

Fiedler, L. (1984). *Love and death in the American novel*. Harmondsworth: Penguin. Print.

Free, M. (2008). Relegation and rebellion: The queer, the grotesque, and the silent in the fiction of Carson McCullers. *Studies in the Novel, 40*(4), 426–446. Print.

Gleeson-White, S. (2001). Revisiting the southern grotesque: Mikhail Bakhtin and the case of Carson McCullers. *Southern Literary Journal, 33*(2), 108–123.

Gray, R. (1986). *Writing the south: Ideas of an American region*. Cambridge: Cambridge University Press. Print.

Holman, C. H. (1972). *The roots of southern writing: Essays on the literature of the American South*. Athens: University of Georgia Press. Print.

McCullers, C. (1998). The ballad of the sad café. In *Collected stories of Carson McCullers*. Boston/New York: Houghton Mifflin. Print.

McCullers, C. (2008a). *Clock without hands*. London: Penguin. Print.

McCullers, C. (2008b). *The heart is a lonely hunter*. London: Penguin. Print.

McCullers, C. (2008c). *The member of the wedding*. London: Penguin. Print

McCullers, C. (2008d). *Reflections in a golden eye*. London: Penguin. Print.

McCullers, C. (2008e). The Russian realists and southern literature. In *The mortgaged heart* (pp. 258–264). London: Penguin. Print.

McCullers, C. Loneliness … An American Malady. In *The Mortgaged Heart*, London: Penguin, 2008. 265–267. Print.

O'Brien, M. (1993). *Rethinking the south: Essays in intellectual history*. Athens/London: University of Georgia Press. Print.

O'Connor, F. (1971). Everything that rises must converge. In *The complete stories of Flannery O'Connor*. New York: Farrar, Straus, and Giroux. Print.

Tate, A. (1968). The new provincialism. In *Essays of four decades*. Chicago: Swallow Press. Print.

Twain, M. (Samuel Clemens). (1883). *Life on the Mississippi*. Boston: James R. Osgood and Company, Print.

Van O'Connor, W. V. (1959). The grotesque in modern American fiction. *College English, 20*(7), 342–346.

FURTHER READING

Gleeson-White, S. (2003). A peculiarly southern form of ugliness: Eudora Welty, Carson McCullers, and Flannery O'Connor. *Southern Literary Journal, 36*(1), 46–59. Print. Discusses Southern womanhood and the body.

O'Connor, F. (1970). Some aspects of the grotesque in southern fiction. In Sally & R. Fitzgerald (Eds.), *Mystery and manners: Occasional prose* (pp. 36–50). London: Faber and Faber. Print. O'Connor's vision of the Southern grotesque.

Richards, G. (2002). "With a special emphasis": The dynamics of (re)claiming a queer southern renaissance. *Mississippi Quarterly, 55*(2), 209–229. On homosexuality in Southern writing, including *Clock without Hands*.

Thurschwell, P. (2012). Dead boys and adolescent girls: Unjoining the Bildungsroman in Carson McCullers's *The Member of the Wedding* and Toni Morrison's Sula. *English Studies in Canada* 38:3/4 (Sept-Dec 2012), 105–128. On the relationship between adolescent girls and younger boys in *The Member of the Wedding* and *The Heart Is a Lonely Hunter*.

CHAPTER 29

'The room must evoke some ghosts': Tennessee Williams

Stephen Matterson

In a recent interview, the great theatre director Peter Brook recalled his first meeting with Tennessee Williams, prior to Brook's Paris production of *Cat on a Hot Tin Roof* in 1956. The two got on well together from the start. Over lunch, Brook recalled, their talk had been general. Then Williams said that he would like to ask Brook a few questions:

> 'Do you have many, many, nights of anxiety?'
> I said, 'no.'
> 'But are there times when you wake up during the night feeling tortured and shaking?'
> 'No.'
> 'Don't you wake up with a feeling of horror that it's a new day that you now have to live through?'
> And I said, 'no.'
> And when he had finished this question he looked at me, with deep affection and understanding, and said: 'Well man, then you're really in very bad shape!' (Brook)

Amusing as it is in Brook's interview, the recollection captures something of Williams that is part of his personality as well as being a trait that he invests in some of his major dramatic characters. Anxiety, corrosive loneliness, tortured feelings of dislocation, frustration, restlessness, and a sense of the 'horror' of life are all part of Williams's vision, at the core of his work and of his repeatedly staged version of Southern Gothic. As he wrote in his Preface to *The Rose Tattoo* (1950), 'Fear and evasion are the two little beasts that chase each other's tails in the revolving wire-cage of our nervous world' (*Plays 1937–1955* 650). In his work there is an intense interrogation of what we think of as 'normal' as

S. Matterson (✉)
Trinity College, University of Dublin, Dublin, Ireland

© The Editor(s) (if applicable) and The Author(s) 2016
S.C. Street, C.L. Crow (eds.), *The Palgrave Handbook of the Southern Gothic*,
DOI 10.1057/978-1-137-47774-3_29

he looks underneath the surfaces that characters present to the public, typically locating deep personal divisions and anxieties in that inner 'nervous world,' as well as shaping a stagecraft through which he could show these being acted out before us. His plays include rape, murder, fractured families, revenge plots, and quite possibly cannibalism. As the strapline for Williams's interview for *Playboy* in 1973 asserted, he was 'the man we pay to have our nightmares for us' (Jennings 69).

A Driven Writer

Williams's sense of personal dislocation has varied origins: in his acute aware-ness of his socially unacceptable sexuality, in the dynamic of his family, notably the conflicts between his parents, and in their treatment of his slightly older sister, Rose. However, this sense of dislocation was certainly exacerbated by his ambivalent relation to the South, and it is this ambivalence that informs a major portion of his creative output. Thomas Lanier Williams, known as 'Tom,' was born in Columbus, Mississippi in 1911. (He adopted the 'Tennessee' in 1938, primarily with reference to the home state of his paternal family.) However, the family was very soon on the move due to the father's restless employment. After periods spent in Nashville, in St. Louis and again in Mississippi, the family settled uneasily in suburban St. Louis when Tennessee was aged 7. Although he took whatever opportunities emerged for travel, visiting Europe while still in high school, St. Louis was to be his home until he was in his mid-20s.

Nevertheless, this was a disrupted childhood and adolescence, thanks in part to the father's alcoholism and his hostility toward his son. Williams twice started university but dropped out, before eventually graduating from Iowa in 1938. Between bouts of education he worked as a clerk in a shoe company, and was hospitalized for nervous exhaustion. In the meantime family tensions escalated, and the parents would eventually separate in 1948. Rose was diag-nosed as schizophrenic and confined to mental hospitals. She was subjected to a lobotomy in 1943 and subsequently never left mental institutions until her death in 1996; from his first successes in the 1940s Williams was to pay constantly for her care. He was deeply moved and haunted by Rose's fate. Her avatars appear repeatedly in his work, and she forms the basis for some of his most celebrated female characters. This sometimes works in a very direct way, for instance as the vulnerable Laura Wingfield in *The Glass Menagerie* (1945), and it is often only more obliquely apparent – she certainly forms one element of Blanche DuBois from *A Streetcar Named Desire* (1947).

Williams was very much a driven writer, someone never satisfied even with critically esteemed work and an enviable public profile, feeling all the time that his work was unfinished, what he most wanted to say still unsaid, and even published work was in need of revision and improvement. He frequently speci-fied that his writing came not from any desire for success and recognition; and that, indeed, achieving those things could ruin a writer. He said that his need to write originated in the emotional turbulence of his childhood and adolescence, speaking particularly of his 'deep South' 1940 play *Battle of Angels* as the first of his dramatic works written to 'release and purify the emotional storms of my earlier youth' (*Plays 1937–1955* 277). In fact, this was a work to which he obsessively returned, and with much revision it became *Orpheus Descending* (1957). Yet he also saw those emotional storms, and that youth, as inevitably embedded in the South. 'The stage or setting of [*Battle of Angels*] was the country of my childhood,' he wrote, and went on to recall being in the Mississippi Delta with his maternal grandfather, particularly citing 'the mysterious landscape of the Delta country, the smoky quality of light in the late afternoons when I, as a child, accompanied my grandfather, an Episcopal clergyman, on seemingly endless rounds of rural parishioners' (*Plays 1937–1955* 277).

This recalls William Faulkner's explanation of the title for *Light in August* (1932). He was attempting, he said, to depict a few days of light in mid-August in Mississippi 'when suddenly there's a foretaste of fall, it's cool, there's a lambence, a soft, a luminous quality to the light, as though it came not from just today but from back in the old classic times. It might have fauns and satyrs and the gods and – from Greece, from Olympus in it somewhere' (qtd in Ruppersburg 3). For both writers, the light embodies a set of values, a passing, a possibility, and for both the light also represents something exclusive to the South. It is a mixing of different times, times that might be personal or historical, yet contained within place. Williams's account of the origins of *Battle of Angels* is telling in exactly this combination of the familial, the personal, and the cultural, and how as a writer he needed to find the right 'synthesis' of 'all the violent symbols of my adolescence' (*Plays 1937–1955* 277). Still, synthesis implies resolution, or at least its possibility, and one of the key elements of much of Williams's work is its lack of resolution, his refusal to supply aesthetic conclusions to what are irresolvable and actual conflicts. Indeed, his compulsive revising of even published work also suggests a refusal to close off something, to let go. As he once commented, 'Finishing a play … is like completing a marriage or a love affair … You feel very forsaken by that, that's why I love revising and revising, because it delays the moment when there is this separation between you and the work' (qtd in Parker 331).

SOUTHERN CONTRADICTIONS

Both the location of the South and the gothic mode are right for this kind of irresolution. The South has been much commented on as a place of disruption and contradiction. Edward Ayers has memorably expressed this sense of the South as comprised of irreconcilable but coexistent oppositions:

> Southern history bespeaks a place that is more complicated than the stories we tell about it. Throughout its history, the South has been a place where poverty and plenty have been thrown together in especially jarring ways, where democracy and oppression, white and black, slavery and freedom, have warred. The very story of the South is a story of unresolved identity, unsettled and restless, unsure

and defensive. The South, contrary to so many words written in defense and in attack, was not a fixed, known, and unified place, but rather a place of constant movement, struggle, and negotiation. (Ayers 62)

Williams's work is certainly alive to these destabilizing contradictions in actual social terms, as well as to how they are part of the South's 'blood and culture.' As he remarked in 1950, 'There is something in the region, something in the blood and culture, of the Southern state that has somehow made them the center of this Gothic school of writers' ('Introduction' ix). He provides compelling representations of both the prosperous agrarian-based South and the cramped spaces of urban industrial modernity. The Pollitt Delta plantation in *Cat on a Hot Tin Roof* comprises 28,000 acres of land, and Big Daddy estimates his wealth at $10 million (*Plays 1937–1955* 924, 929). By contrast, the wage-dependent Stanley Kowalski rents a two-room flat in a poor section of New Orleans in which he and his wife Stella will start their family, and try to accommodate Stella's sister Blanche. In both cases, the actuality of either wealth or straitened circumstances is challenged. Blanche cannot fit her sense of an aristocratic Big House past with her present circumstances, so that what emerges is grotesque incongruity. As she remarks on seeing the Kowalski home, 'Only Poe! Only Mr Edgar Allan Poe! – could do it justice! Out there I suppose is the ghoul-haunted woodland of Weir!' (474). Big Daddy proudly reminds his family that he is a self-made man, without the inherited wealth and aristocratic past that a plantation usually implies.

While acutely alert to actual social, cultural, and material incongruities in the South, Williams typically shows these as realities and contradictions that have become internalized by his characters. They must either ignore these contradictions or acknowledge them and consequently struggle to find, if not synthesis, some means of acting in the present while accommodating their palpable presence. This is also one of Williams's own self-contradictions regarding the South; his acquired or inherited sense of the region's past – inevitably an imagined past. 'The South,' he wrote, 'once had a way of life I am just old enough to remember – a culture that had grace, elegance ... an inbred culture ... not a society based on money, as in the North. I write out of regret for that' (qtd in Leverich 54). Leaving aside the implications of an 'inbred culture,' this region and this cultural imaginary are even for him, as he implies, an unreal South bound up with inherited ancestral memory and with recollections of his childhood, of that 'smoky quality of light' before the family moved to Missouri. He is also aware that regret and nostalgia do not fit readily into the present, that they represent ghosts with which the actual present must grapple. This is one aspect of what could be called the recurring 'meta-theatrical' aspect of Williams's work: the ways in which several of his major characters are self-consciously performing, acting out roles. They do so because the imagined and the actual have become incongruent, to the extent that there is no sense any more of a 'natural' self; all is performance.

It is in effect another version of Gothic, presupposing the dislocated self and examining the consequences of this. Blanche DuBois is perhaps the most extreme and most intense representation of this, someone who senses life only as performance, as storytelling. Indeed, much of the power of *A Streetcar Named Desire* comes from Blanche's storytelling as simultaneously heroic and filled with pathos: she needs to be both admired and pitied. She can generate admiration because she upholds the Romantic's belief that the imagined life is one's own true identity; yet she also stimulates pity because the force of that imagined life increasingly renders her incapable of functioning in the actual modern world. This incongruence is brilliantly conveyed in the opening sequence of Elia Kazan's film version of the play, where we see Blanche trying to find her way through the city streets, confused in urban modernity. Since she is played by Vivien Leigh, we inevitably get the trace of Scarlett O'Hara, here displaced, in transition from the Technicolored estate of Tara to the monochrome contemporary city, a Rip Van Winkle puzzled and distraught by the modern landscape, a ghost seeking material form. Substituting actual reality for imagined possibility is essentially a Romantic gesture, and Williams himself is at heart a Romantic. So too are many of his protagonists: they are people who dream, people who can exist in reality only with difficulty or with a form of self-deception, who feel restricted and limited by actuality.

Blanche DuBois and Amanda Wingfield are major examples of this trope, but the Romantic turned grotesque is a recurring Williams type. He urges us not simply to pity such characters, but to acknowledge a kind of heroism that they enact. As he once reflected, likely with his sister Rose in mind as well as his dramatic personae, 'I have found it easier to identify with the characters who verge upon hysteria, who were frightened of life, who were desperate to reach out to another person. But these seemingly fragile people are the strong people really' (qtd in Stang 3). He insisted that performances of *A Streetcar Named Desire* should not make us feel pity for Blanche, but should require us to recognize her strength. In his character descriptors for *The Glass Menagerie* he wrote of Amanda that she was 'a little woman of great but confused vitality' in whom there is 'much to admire ... and as much to love and pity ... she has endurance and a kind of heroism' (*Plays 1937–1955* 394). For all of her self-imaginings, when objectively viewed, Amanda copes well in the modern world as a pragmatic working mother trying, by her own lights, to ameliorate the situation of her vulnerable daughter. By contrast, Blanche loses her struggle with the arch-realist Stanley, who exposes her Romantic fictions of the self as duplicitous fantasies masking what he sees as a sordid reality. For all of his actual violence toward Blanche, culminating in her removal to an asylum, his cruelest action is in stripping her of the capacity for dream, symbolically represented by his viciously tearing off the shade from the lamp and exposing her to a naked light bulb. In a way entirely characteristic of the Gothic, Williams typically explores the imagination seeking but failing to find congruence with fragmented and harsh actuality. Indeed, for the epigraph to *A Streetcar Named Desire* he used a quotation from Hart Crane's poem 'The Broken Tower': 'And so it was I entered the broken world/To trace the visionary company of love' (*Plays 1937–1955* 467).[1]

VISIONARY POETS

Poets appear again and again in Williams's work, often with an autobiographical element – and often quoting from the quintessential Romantic John Keats. Williams commented on this recurrence in 1961, with reference to Sebastian Venable in *Suddenly Last Summer* (1958): 'the archetype of the poet has become an obsessive figure, a leit-motif in my recent work for the stage, and possibly was always, since Tom Wingfield in *The Glass Menagerie* was a poet, too, and so was Val Xavier in *Orpheus Descending*' (qtd in Tischler 149). There are others that can be added, including Blanche's dead husband Allan Grey. Yet they are notably failed or frustrated poets, risking ridicule and social estrangement at the very least; and in the case of Sebastian, the probable victim of cannibals. The name 'Sebastian' is a highly loaded one for Williams, referring both to the martyred Christian saint and to the name that Oscar Wilde adopted during his despairing self-imposed social ostracism in France. Tom Wingfield, a clear relation of Tom Williams, is described as '[a] poet with a job in a warehouse,' and while *The Glass Menagerie* is his 'memory play,' it tells of loneliness, frustration, and lack of fulfillment, as well as of his ultimate escape.

Val Xavier in *Orpheus Descending*, one of the major works of Southern Gothic, is indeed the visionary poet come to our broken world, a 30-year-old mysterious stranger arriving with his guitar in a small Deep South town. The state is unspecified, although the setting in Two River County indicates Mississippi, where Madison County is known as 'The Land Between Two Rivers.' In this grotesque version of the Greek legend, Val lacks the Orphean power to revitalize, animate, and enrich our prosaic lives through art and the imagination. This was exactly the kind of power that the younger Williams had found so seductive in the writings of D. H. Lawrence, linked as it is in his work with sexual power as a defiance of death. Unpromising as it might sound, Val as a clerk in the dry-goods store could be said to have animated the small-town inhabitants. To some extent he inspires a local painter, Vee Talbot, although it could equally be said that what he actually does is intensify her frustration at small-town life. He impregnates Lady, the wife of Jabe Torrance, the store's owner. As this is revealed at the play's climax, Lady, who had thought herself barren, represents her pregnancy as a victory over death: 'I've won, I've won, Mr Death, I'm going to bear' (*Plays 1957–1980* 95). She tells Val, 'this dead tree, my body, has burst in flower! You've given me life, you can go!' (94). However, as in the legend, Orpheus cannot permanently save Eurydice from death, and here death triumphs once more. Having overheard Lady, Jabe appears – 'He is death's self,' Williams notes in his stage direction (95) – and shoots Lady dead as she shields Val from him; her last words are among Williams's most memorable: 'The show is over. The monkey is dead' (95). The revolver is empty when Jabe tries to shoot Val, and he cries out for help, shouting that 'the clerk' is robbing the store and has killed his wife. Immediately on the scene, the lynch mob is about to get a rope when one of them has 'something better,' which turns out to be a blowtorch. Val thus ends up burned to death, a fitting end for a Don

Juan, or for this Orpheus descended to hell. Apocalyptic though the ending is, Williams does offer some slight hope in the final moments of the play, when one of Val's conquests, the earthy Carol Cutrere, trades her gold ring for Val's snakeskin jacket, suggesting affirmation and some kind of continuity in the midst of this dead land.

THE LAND OF THE DEAD

Orpheus Descending was not a popular play. Neither critics nor audiences warmed to its melodramatic excess, and it closed after a respectable but not especially profitable 68 performances on Broadway. By Williams's own standards, the play was a failure. To put this into perspective, in the previous decade *The Glass Menagerie* had run uninterrupted for three years, and *A Streetcar Named Desire* for two. Indeed, the more grotesque and lurid Williams's dramas were to become, the more his audience dwindled – several later plays closed after runs of less than a week – and critical discussion of his decline as a writer intensified. Typical assessments of Williams's career represent 1962s *The Night of the Iguana* as his last major play, winning as it did the Drama Critics Circle Award for that year's best play. The year also saw Williams pictured on the cover of *Time* magazine, designated the nation's greatest living playwright. Yet in spite of its negative reception, *Orpheus* is an important play in Williams's representation of the South. As Faulkner had for his fragmented gothic narrative *As I Lay Dying* (1930), Williams borrowed from the classical tradition to represent the South as the underworld, the land of the dead. Such classical allusion, from Homer's *Odyssey* for Faulkner, from Greek legend for Williams, is itself an irony, one of the South's much-vaunted exceptionalist claims being its reverence for those classics.

In broader terms, a core question for Williams is how to act in this land of the dead, and typically it is answered ambivalently. In part he celebrates the essential vitality that Stanley Kowalski brings to this land. Williams's stage direction emphasizes this as essential to the role: 'Animal joy in his being is implicit in all his movements and attitudes,' he is a 'gaudy seedbearer,' fecund in this waste land (*Plays 1937–1955* 481). More typically, in these recurring dramatizations of Eros and Thanatos, Williams attends more to those who are analogues of the dead, those who are unable to assert life or joy. We have Amanda Wingfield's 'confused vitality'; the insulated world inhabited by her daughter; the home of death that Tom must flee to find life, a gesture strongly reminiscent of Paul Morel at the end of Lawrence's *Sons and Lovers* (Tom has apparently become a merchant sailor following his escape). There are those for whom, like Blanche with her love of Keats, life is '[t]he long parade to the graveyard' (*1957–1980* 479) – again recalling Addie Bundren from *As I Lay Dying* posthumously repeating her father's saying, 'the reason for living was to get ready to stay dead a long time' (Faulkner 114). The sentiment recurs in *Suddenly Last Summer* in Mrs. Venable's 'Most people's lives – what are they but trails of debris, each day more debris, more debris, long, long trails of debris with nothing to clean it all up but, finally, death' (*Plays 1957–1980* 111). Deeply ambivalent though they are, Tom's escape, the Kowalskis' expulsion of Blanche, and Val's puta-tive legacy testify to the possibility of rising above this death-haunted world. Nevertheless, in *Orpheus* this possibility is much more muted, both with the lurid murder of Val and the death of the pregnant Lady. Furthermore, the grotesque elements of the play are characteristically Southern. These include voodoo, represented by the silent presence of the Conjure Man, and the blues music of the Delta, both in some measure representing distorted survivals of another Southern past, the African. When Williams updates Orpheus's lyre into Val's guitar, he provides the instrument with a history, comprising the names of the great Southern musicians, Leadbelly, King Oliver, Bessie Smith, Fats Waller (35). In one of the plot revelations, it turns out that revenge is a key motive. We learn that Lady and her father had come to the South as Sicilian immigrants, and he set up as a bootlegger. Enraged by the father's selling alcohol to African Americans, the whites, led by Jabe Torrance, set fire to his property and he died in this fire. In the play's present action, Lady has found this out and is poisoning Jabe, and we discover that part of Jabe's motiva-tion for killing her is also revenge. *Orpheus* is Southern reality revealed as gro-tesque, magnified into melodramatic distortion but still bearing relation to actuality. Indeed, Williams, as he did so often, insisted that the drama needed a non-naturalistic set design, and, as he had done in previous plays, uses non-naturalistic effects and intrusions.

Sexual Repression and the Gothic

A famous eighteenth-century complaint about the prevalence of the gothic tale inadvertently drew helpful attention to the key characteristics of this bur-geoning genre: 'It has been the fashion to make *terror* the order of the *day*, by confining the heroes and heroines in old gloomy castles, full of spectres, appari-tions, ghosts and dead men's bones' (qtd in Wright 24). While Williams was far too driven ever to write formulaically, it is relatively easy to map his work onto these gothic elements, and to add the Southern twist. The gloomy old castles in which his characters are confined might have been updated to become apart-ments in New Orleans or suburban St. Louis, a hotel room, a dry-goods store in Mississippi, large plantations, big houses and the memories of them. In fact, one of his last plays, *A House Not Meant to Stand* (1981), specifically echoes Edgar Allan Poe's 'The Fall of the House of Usher.' In Williams's stage world the confinement might be psychological rather than geographical, and the ghosts that haunt his characters might be memories: memories both of the dead and of lost spaces, lost former lives, lost, repressed, or misdirected desires. Of course, Williams inevitably locates these in his South, a South itself haunted by its past, its dead, its inability to provide a coherent, stabilizing narrative. Yet he also adds violence and brutality, and violence and its varied representations are consistently there in his work. He came to consider *Not about Nightingales*, one of his earliest plays based on an incident in a prison, too violent to be performed in his lifetime. In his Foreword to *Sweet Bird of Youth* (1959) he remarked that in the 19 years since *Battle of Angels* he had written 'only five plays that are *not* violent' (*Plays 1957–1980* 153). In that Foreword Williams implies that there is a psychological reason for this violence, mentioning that he had recently started to undergo psychoanalysis. The violence that he stages reflects the violence that he sees in American life, his long-standing interest in Freud suggesting that it is the inescapable price of society's sexual repression.

In this light, the violent deaths of Val Xavier and Sebastian Venable are grotesque punishments for their sexual expression. However, as so often in Williams's world, desire itself is never straightforward, always containing the capacity to become lurid. In *Love and Death in the American Novel* (1960), Fiedler suggested that because it was taboo, the literary representation of homosexuality inevitably turned into Gothic, rendered obliquely, turned grotesque (477). While this is a seductive argument, and Williams was one of the writers Fiedler had in mind, it is not quite the full story. Certainly, prior to the raising of gay profiles in the aftermath of the Stonewall Riots of 1969, it was usual to represent gay characters indirectly. Yet however encoded it might have been, Williams's stage representation of homosexuals is actually reasonably direct. On stage there is no misrepresenting Blanche's recollection of her husband Allan Grey in *A Streetcar Named Desire*, of Violet Venable's recall of her dead son Sebastian in *Suddenly Last Summer*. Of course, these are both dead characters; they are never on stage in spite of the powerful presence they exert. The representation of major characters such as Tom Wingfield and of Brick Pollitt in *Cat on a Hot Tin Roof* is considerably more ambivalent and has been much discussed.

It is also true that the filmed versions of the plays typically resulted in an indirect representation, or in a complete misrepresentation, of the gay character, as screenplays conformed to codes of voluntary censorship. The most extreme example is the film version of *Suddenly Last Summer*. Sebastian as a sick sexual predator and possible pedophile is crucial to the play, resulting as it does in his mother's attempt to re-shape the narrative of his life, conflicting with the motivation of her niece, Catharine Holly, who wants to tell the truth about her cousin. Ironically, the Production Code Administration permitted the unobfuscated screen representation of Sebastian as homosexual on the grounds that he was, apparently, punished for this perversion – hence making *Suddenly Last Summer* seem homophobic. This is of course a misreading, but the gay character as victim does recur in Williams's drama, from the suicides of Allan Gray and Skipper in *Cat on a Hot Tin Roof* to the murdered Sebastian. There is a particular exception in Tom Wingfield, as *Glass Menagerie* is his memory play, and Williams notably reveals virtually nothing of the character's life after leaving his mother and sister.

As such, Williams has been criticized for his apparent inability to produce a 'positive image' of a gay person (Paller 2). There is certainly an element of presentism in this view, a judgment of Williams without considering the historical contexts in which he wrote. In part his negative representation may be his own form of realistic assessment of the situation of the gay man in the United States prior to Stonewall. He did after all write mostly at a time when gay men were part of an underworld, almost invariably and inevitably associated with secrecy and concealment. Tom Wingfield is the strongest example of this type, with his secret life of night-times spent 'at the movies,' deflecting the questions of his mother and his sister. However, it is more appropriate to think of this representation in the context of Williams's gothic vision, and to link it more certainly to his overall depiction of sexual desire, both gay and straight. For the Romantic, and of course for Lawrence as it had been for Whitman, desire and its free expression are healthy, expressing something natural and life giving. The gothic strain deforms this, so that one consequence of a society determined to repress the sexual is that desire comes to be associated with darkness and marginalization, and turns into a destructive force. Tellingly, Amanda bans Lawrence's work from the Wingfield home, referring to his 'hideous book' as the product of a 'diseased' mind (*Plays 1937–1955* 412). In the world that Williams presents to us, desire has become a sickness, not a source of health. Desire comes also to be associated with deceit, the furtive; but again, this is true of all sexual desire. The most obvious example is Blanche, who sees the secret sexual activities of her forebears, their 'epic fornications,' as the reason for the loss of Belle Reve, the family estate (*Plays 1937–1955* 490). Yet she too lives in a world of deception and self-deception, trying to conceal or re-script her alcoholism and her sexual dealings from others as well as from herself. Deception is somehow essential to this world. In *Cat on a Hot Tin Roof* Brick famously rails against mendacity, but for him and for many other major Williams characters, deception and self-deception are necessary conditions for existence.

Conclusion

It is important to emphasize that while Williams's plays can be staged naturalistically (and typically were in their sometimes troublesome cinematic incarnations), his aim as a dramatist was to explore psychological truths, to find a kind of deeper realism than that offered by the everyday surface. In this respect he is reminiscent of Poe, and the latter's famous disdain for mimesis: 'if an artist must paint decayed cheeses, [his] merit will lie in their looking as little like decayed cheeses as possible' (Poe 1330). The artist's job is not to reproduce the real but to look through it, under it. Again, this distortion of the real is a central tenet of Williams's Gothic. In his directions he repeatedly alludes to the need for the drama not to stage reality but, Brecht-like, to demonstrate its own theatricality. 'The scene is memory and is therefore nonrealistic. Memory … omits some details and others are exaggerated … [the interior is] rather dim and poetic,' he wrote of *The Glass Menagerie*, a play that signals its unreality through the use of 'legends' projected onto a screen (*Plays 1937–1955* 399). His 'Notes for the Designer' for the set of *Cat on a Hot Tin Roof* even stipulate what is in all likelihood impossible: 'the room must evoke some ghosts; it is gently and poetically haunted by a relationship that must have involved a tenderness that was uncommon' (*Plays 1937–1955* 880). In *A Streetcar Named Desire* we enter an interior space as Blanche recalls her dead husband, and we hear the shot that she recalls. Indeed, Blanche performs as if the world is her stage, she arranges and tries to direct her scenes, scripting her world, although it is a world increasingly detached from that inhabited by the other characters. Williams's stage world is expressionistic, not naturalistic.

In his 1948 essay 'The Catastrophe of Success,' Williams reflected on the potential damage that success might represent for the artist, transforming hunger and desire into luxury, laziness, and complacency. It is a familiar enough theme, and Williams well knew the earlier treatments of it by Hemingway and by Fitzgerald, and he quotes William James's condemnation of American 'worship of the bitch-Goddess success – our national disease' (James 23). For Williams it becomes another version of Gothic, a dark tale in which the romantic sense of possibility and achievement is replaced by self-alienation and lost desire, where security is 'a kind of death' (*Plays 1937–1955* 1048). In this essay he talks of the Cinderella story as 'our favorite national myth, the cornerstone of the film industry if not of Democracy itself' (1045). Yet what fascinated Williams was the obverse of the myth: the self becoming dislocated rather than fulfilled, life as a fractured narrative exacerbated by the unresolvable contradictions of the region that he both loved and reviled, nights of anxiety not days of comfort, Orpheus descending not Icarus rising.

NOTE

1. Williams prefaced several of his plays with quotations from Hart Crane, a poet he both deeply admired and identified with; he apparently always carried a copy of Crane's poems, and hoped to be buried at sea at the location of Crane's suicide. It is also worth noting that he took the epigraphs to his plays very seriously, considering them to be an indispensable part of the script and insisting that they be printed on the playbill for each production (see Debusscher 172–8).

BIBLIOGRAPHY

Ayers, E. (1996). What we talk about when we talk about the South. In E. L. Ayers, P. N. Limerick, S. Nissenbaum, & P. S. Onuf (Eds.), *All over the map: Rethinking American regions* (pp. 62–82). Baltimore: Johns Hopkins University Press.

Brook, P. Theatrical revolutionary: Interview with James Naughtie. *BBC Radio,* 4 May 2015. http://podbay.fm/show/482933200/e/1413532843?autostart=1

Debusscher, G. (1997). European and American influences on Williams. In M. C. Roudané (Ed.), *The Cambridge companion to Tennessee Williams* (pp. 167–188). Cambridge: Cambridge University Press.

Faulkner, W. (1985). *Novels 1930–1935.* New York: Literary Classics of the United States.

Fiedler, L. (1960). *Love and death in the American novel.* New York: Stein and Day.

James, W. (1920). *The letters of William James* (Vol. 1). Boston: Atlantic Monthly. 2 vols.

Jennings, R. C. (1973, April). *Playboy* interview: Tennessee Williams. *Playboy,* pp. 69–84.

Leverich, L. (1995). *Tom: The unknown Tennessee Williams*. London: Hodder and Stoughton.

Paller, M. (2005). *Gentlemen callers: Tennessee Williams, homosexuality, and mid-twentieth-century drama*. London: Palgrave Macmillan.

Parker, B. (1996). A developmental stemma for drafts and revisions of Tennessee Williams's *Camino Real*. *Modern Drama, 39*, 331–341.

Poe, E. A. (1984). *Essays and reviews*. New York: Literary Classics of the United States.

Ruppersburg, H. (1994). *Reading Faulkner: Light in August*. Jackson: University Press of Mississippi.

Stang, J. (1965, March 28). Williams: 20 years after *Glass Menagerie*. *New York Times*, vol. II, p. 3.

Tischler, N. M. (1997). Romantic textures in Williams's plays and short stories. In M. C. Roudané (Ed.), *The Cambridge companion to Tennessee Williams* (pp. 147–166). Cambridge: Cambridge University Press.

Williams, T. (1950). Introduction. In C. McCullers (Ed.), *Reflections in a golden eye*. New York: Houghton Mifflin Company.

Williams, T. (2000a). *Plays 1937–1955*. New York: Literary Classics of the United States.

Williams, T. (2000b). *Plays 1957–1980*. New York: Literary Classics of the United States.

Wright, A. (2007). *Gothic fiction*. London: Palgrave Macmillan.

Further Reading

As is to be expected, Williams features prominently in critical surveys and histories of US drama since 1945. Christopher Bigsby's *A Critical Introduction to Twentieth-Century American Drama Volume 2* (Cambridge: Cambridge University Press, 1984) and *Modern American Drama 1945–1990* (Cambridge: Cambridge University Press, 1992) are especially recommended, along with Thomas Adler's *American Drama 1940–1960: A Critical History* (New York: Twayne, 1994). Excellent book-length critical studies include *Understanding Tennessee Williams* by Alice Griffin (Columbia: University of South Carolina Press, 1995), *Tennessee Williams: Rebellious Puritan* by Nancy M. Tischler (New York: Citadel, 1961) and *The Broken World of Tennessee Williams* (Madison: University of Wisconsin Press, 1965).

These are explored with regard to sexuality in *Sexual Politics in the Work of Tennessee Williams* by Michael S. D. Hooper (Cambridge: Cambridge University Press, 2012) and in *Gentlemen Callers: Tennessee Williams, Homosexuality, and Mid-Twentieth-Century Drama* by Michael Paller (London: Palgrave Macmillan, 2005). *The Cambridge Companion to Tennessee Williams*, edited by Matthew C. Roudané (Cambridge: Cambridge University Press, 1997) has some excellent essays, particularly on the lesser-known plays and short stories, and it includes a helpful survey of critical material, by Jacqueline O'Connor.

Williams's *Memoirs* (London: W. H. Allen, 1976) provide important insights into his personal life, and can be read alongside critical biographies by Lyle Leverich, *Tom: The Unknown Tennessee Williams* (London: Hodder and Stoughton, 1995) and Ronald Hayman's *Tennessee Williams: Everyone Else is an Audience* (New Haven: Yale University Press, 1993). Together they show how Williams's dramas are deeply rooted in his experiences and anxieties.

CHAPTER 30

Truman Capote's Gothic Politics

Michael P. Bibler

The Southern Gothic conventions and tropes of Truman Capote's early fiction invite ready comparisons to the works of his contemporaries Carson McCullers, Eudora Welty, and Flannery O'Connor. Indeed, the lines of influence between them are clear: McCullers was an early mentor of Capote (and later claimed that he copied aspects of her writing),[1] and Capote's short story 'My Side of the Matter' (1945) is a direct response to Welty's 'Why I Live at the P.O.' (1941). However, Capote's gothicism is more than just a matter of literary apprenticeship. Throughout his career, he continued to incorporate and adapt aspects of the Southern Gothic even in works that may seem realist or observational in style, and in works that may seem disconnected from the South.[2] Moreover, recognizing Capote's evolving use of Southern Gothic elements provides important insights for understanding the complex relationship between his theories of artistic style and the politics of his writing, even when those two things might appear at odds with each other.

Gothic Uncertainty

Most discussions of Capote's version of the Southern Gothic focus on his first published novel, *Other Voices, Other Rooms* (1948). The novel follows the coming-of-age and coming-out of the queer adolescent Joel Knox, an effeminate boy sent to live with relatives in the remote Alabama setting of Skully's Landing, an isolated, decaying plantation house with a name evocative of death. The house is populated with a truly eccentric mix, including Joel's stepmother Amy, who affects an aristocratic persona that is at once delicate and domineering; Joel's paralyzed, bedridden father, who cannot communicate except by dropping little red balls off the bed; Amy's cousin Randolph,

M.P. Bibler (✉)
Louisiana State University, Baton Rouge, LA, USA

© The Editor(s) (if applicable) and The Author(s) 2016
S.C. Street, C.L. Crow (eds.), *The Palgrave Handbook of the Southern Gothic*,
DOI 10.1057/978-1-137-47774-3_30

391

who occasionally dresses as a 'queer lady' in white and eerily watches Joel from an upstairs window (67); and the wizened African American Jesus Fever and his granddaughter Zoo, who always wears a scarf to hide the scar on her neck. Joel also befriends the young tomboy Idabel Thompkins and her ultra-feminine twin sister, Florabel, who further highlight the instability of gender roles and characteristics alongside what Gary Richards calls Joel's 'gender transitivity' (31). Capote extends this sense of strangeness and difference by placing these characters within a wider spectrum of freakishness, figured most prominently by Miss Wisteria, a blond midget traveling with a freak show, and Little Sunshine, an African American hermit who lives at the now-collapsing Cloud Hotel in the remote woods.

As Joel navigates this landscape of isolation, freakishness, and uncanny fear, he gradually comes to identify with his queer cousin Randolph and ends the novel with an unambiguous acceptance of his own queer sexuality. This groundbreaking move made *Other Voices, Other Rooms* the first major American novel to offer a positive ending for an openly gay protagonist, and its queer positivity remains a central focus in discussions of Capote's engagement with the Southern Gothic, as well as the novel's interventions in post–Second World War sexual politics. For example, Tison Pugh shows how the novel combines 'gothic terror and sentimental pathos' for its gay protagonist in order to 'urge the novel's audience to a better understanding and deeper acceptance of homosexuality' (664, 665).[3] In this way, *Other Voices, Other Rooms* marks the emergence of a new genre that Jaime Harker calls the 'gay protest novel.' Foregrounding 'the suffering of the main characters,' these novels 'insisted' to their readers 'that "we" are just like "you"' (14). Although *Other Voices, Other Rooms* uses grotesque figures to expand the possibilities for making sexual and gender queerness visible, Capote destabilizes the Gothic's association with death and decay and fosters greater tolerance and understanding for gay people in a time of sexual oppression.

Thomas Fahy suggests, however, that Capote's use of the Gothic mitigates the novel's political appeal. He writes that because Joel decides to join Randolph at the end of the novel, his 'decision to embrace his own homosexuality ... seems to necessitate Joel's isolation from others' (44). Idabel gets sent away, and Joel's relationship with Zoo also does not last, in part because of the trauma she experiences when a group of white men gang-rape her in a roadside ditch. As Fahy writes, Zoo's traumatic experiences 'position her too solidly in the real world for Joel. He wants to be protected from the social realities of racial and sexual violence, not exposed to them, so he chooses instead to live with Randolph' (44). Nevertheless, Zoo's story still adds a further political edge to the novel. In Fahy's words, Capote 'confronts the reader with the horrifying details of Zoo's story not merely to condemn the practitioners of such acts but to express moral outrage over white America's wilful blindness to the problem of sexualized violence against black women' (52–3). Thus, the novel subtly denounces the violence and oppression directed at America's queer, black, and female 'others,' even as its embrace of isolation, withdrawal, and privacy as protections against violence seems to back away from taking a sharper political stance.

This apparently contradictory approach to politics in *Other Voices, Other Rooms* has frustrated some readers and critics, especially those who criticized Capote for not subsequently using his fame and fiction to speak out more directly about gay life and gay rights.[4] Nevertheless, this paradoxical nature of the Southern Gothic allowed Capote to remain politically engaged in his work without becoming too narrowly political. Throughout his career, he consistently depicted characters who, if they were not precisely homosexual, were still queer in the broader sense that they deviated from the conventional norms of gender and sexuality. His work is full of grotesque outsiders, misfits, and, in a more sinister vein, criminals and murderers. Yet, even as he sought to create a space for individuals who have been excluded or rejected from mainstream society, he always avoided the political reductiveness of social realism. That is, while the Gothic enabled Capote to generate sympathy and understanding for his characters, he never let those characters become purely representative of a marginalized group. While Joel helped forge a path for depicting gay people positively in literature, his return to the isolation of the crumbling plantation house foregrounds the idiosyncrasies of his individual character and ultimately makes him a poor figurehead for the gay rights struggle as a whole.

For Capote, the Southern Gothic thus became a way to explore the inner complexities that generate the greatest friction between a person's or character's social identity (as, for example, a homosexual, or a woman, or an African American) and his or her unassimilable individuality. Capote's early short stories collected in *A Tree of Night and Other Stories* (1949) are especially full of characters whose psychological fears, impulses, or implausible hopes separate them from society. Sylvia in 'Master Misery' literally sells her dreams in an attempt to avoid coming to terms with her fears about sex and intimacy. In the O. Henry award-winning 'Shut a Final Door,' the sadistic, self-loathing, bisexual protagonist Walter runs away from his interactions with others and his fears of his own sexuality. In this case, he removes himself physically (instead of psychically, like Sylvia) from one city to the next, and eventually to New Orleans, while being pursued by a mysterious, unnamed caller on the telephone who claims to know his secrets. Similarly, Miriam in 'Miriam,' which also won an O. Henry award, becomes haunted by a young child named Miriam too. Much like the telephone caller in 'Shut a Final Door,' the young Miriam is in many ways a manifestation of the childlike impulses and desires of the bland, somewhat repressed adult Miriam. And, at the end, the adult Miriam is nearly driven crazy by her inability to get rid of this frightening figure. All of these stories offer a critique of social and sexual conformity, but the problems that these characters face are more than purely social problems with plausible solutions. Instead, their stories play out at the point where the real and the uncanny intersect and create an atmosphere of insoluble mystery. For example, the young Miriam also claims to have lived with an old man before meeting the adult Miriam. The child cannot be only a manifestation of the return of the repressed for the adult

Miriam, because the child appears to have a history without her. For Capote, a simple psychological explanation is inadequate, and he adds this gothic twist to make it impossible for readers to resolve or explain fully the adult Miriam's predicament.

The lighter stories in *A Tree of Night* also incorporate this gothic uncertainty and grotesque strangeness.[5] In 'Children on Their Birthdays,' Miss Lily Jane Bobbitt is at once a precocious young girl and, in the way she talks and acts, a sexually wise adult woman. She also defies the segregationist logic of the town by befriending a young black girl named Rosalba, and she challenges the town's sense of religious morality by preaching the value of evil alongside the value of good. In a further gothic twist, she is hit and killed by a bus, thus maintaining her complexity instead of maturing into an adult who might have had to shed her enigmatic ways to survive in the world. In 'Jug of Silver,' the source of mystery is also a child – a young country boy named Appleseed who claims to have second sight – but a second source of mystery is the jug full of coins placed in the drugstore in a contest to see who can guess the amount inside. Appleseed makes the correct guess, and the townspeople marvel for years over how he was able to name the exact amount. Another character, the self-described Egyptian, Hamurabi, helps explain the importance of the mystery over the answer itself: 'It's the mystery that's enchanting. Now you look at those nickels and dimes and what do you think: ah, so much! No, no. You think: ah, *how* much? And that's a powerful question, indeed. It can mean different things to different people' (24). In keeping with the Gothic's emphasis on uncanny, illogical situations and irresolvable uncertainty, Hamurabi reminds us that the value lies not in the number of coins, but in the different meanings they hold for different people. And yet, like with Miss Bobbitt's delightful challenges to the sexual, racial, and spiritual mores of her small Southern town, this story also has a political edge, for Hamurabi's character implicitly defies his town's racism. It may be that Hamurabi is truly Egyptian, or it may be a ploy that lets this dark-skinned man circumvent racial segregation. Claiming to be African instead of African American allows him to move about town free of the rules and strictures that limit all the other black people. Capote's story challenges Southern racist politics even while it holds back from a more didactic critique, redirecting our attention to the gothic mystery in which Hamurabi, Appleseed, and the jar 'mean different things to different people.'

IN TENSION WITH POLITICS

Thus, the gothic situations and grotesque characters in Capote's early fiction do not exactly undercut his literary interventions in the social and political contexts of the 1940s. Rather, Capote makes sure that gothic uncertainty stays in productive tension *with* politics. As much as Capote is interested in pushing the boundaries of conformity and challenging the oppression of queers, outcasts, racial minorities, and others, he is equally interested in the intangible mysteries that lie beneath, above, and beyond the narrow categories of identity that, by themselves, fail to explain everything about a person. The Gothic allows Capote to push against social and political constraints without reducing his text's meaning to a singular moral or political message – the way, for example, the jug of silver could become merely a monetary value instead of a vessel of multiple possibilities.

This productive tension between gothic mystery and political engagement is especially visible in his second novel, *The Grass Harp* (1952). This is sometimes criticized for backing away from the pro-gay tenor of Capote's first novel, yet the acceptance of all forms of love is its central theme. The novel follows the young Collin Fenwick, who joins his spinster cousin Dolly Talbo, their multi-racial housekeeper Catherine Creek, and a small number of others as they set up camp in a treehouse outside of town. They move into the treehouse because Dolly's sister, Verena, has tried to capitalize on Dolly's homemade dropsy cure without her permission, violating Dolly's sense of privacy and autonomy. As others in the town grow angry over the group's withdrawal and occupation, they swear a warrant for the rebels' arrest, thus inspiring the elderly Judge Cool and the young man Riley Henderson to join the treehouse in solidarity, as well as the traveling evangelical preacher Sister Ida and her 15 children, who seek out the treehouse because they have been forced to leave town.

In terms of plot, the narrative is unmistakably political: the town's various outsiders withdraw from society and create a defiantly alternate world in the treehouse. When the town's prominent citizens begin harassing them, the police arrest Catherine, the one racial minority in the group, even though she has done nothing wrong. Their intolerance is likewise visible in their unjust treatment of Sister Ida on the grounds that she is sexually immoral. The novel could thus be read as a civil rights novel that challenges racial and sexual oppression in the South. However, Capote does not expand this meditation on justice to create a targeted political message, such as we see, for example, in his friend Harper Lee's *To Kill a Mockingbird* (1960). Rather, when Dolly and Verena make up, and everyone returns to their homes, Capote pulls back from the text's political edge and shifts the focus back to the subject of embracing love in its many forms.

Judge Cool provides an explanation of this theme:

> We are speaking of love. A leaf, a handful of seed – begin with these, learn a little what it is to love. First, a leaf, a fall of rain, then someone to receive what a leaf has taught you, what a fall of rain has ripened. No easy process, understand; it could take a lifetime, it has mine, and still I've never mastered it – I only know how true it is: that love is a chain of love, as nature is a chain of life. (44)

In this theory, love exists in all kinds of relationships, pushing against the town's racist, heterosexist norms, because it necessarily includes illegal, inter-racial relationships, as the Judge discusses (41), as well as gay desire, as suggested in Collin's homoerotic fascination with Riley. However, even though Capote holds back from making Collin openly gay, what looks like reticence or even closetedness should rather be understood as Capote's attempt to avoid imposing narrow meanings on his larger point about love, identity, and non-conformity.[6] Indeed, when Dolly suddenly dies of a heart attack, the novel returns to its eponymous, gothic symbol of human diversity and inclusiveness: the grass harp that collects all the voices of the dead. Instead of different types of people divided by identity categories, or by hypocritical or selfish social mores, the grass harp gathers all people into one rich harmony together. As Dolly instructs Collin at the beginning of the novel, the grass harp is 'always telling a story – it knows the stories of all the people on the [cemetery] hill, of all the people who ever lived, and when we are dead it will tell ours, too' (9). Capote uses the Gothic to incorporate more complex meditations on the human condition beyond, but never in exclusion from, the politics of a specific time and place.

THE BRIDGE OF CHILDHOOD

Capote's interest in the immaterial, unassimilable aspects of life and identity informed more than just his fiction. His early non-fiction pieces collected in his book *Local Color* (1950) are also strikingly gothic. From the hanged man in a courtyard in 'New Orleans,' to the eerily hollow landscape of 'Hollywood,' the litany of unusual, somewhat tragic loners in 'New York' and 'Brooklyn,' and the odd combinations of comedy and fear in 'Tangier' and 'A Ride through Spain,' these vignettes combine the realism of reportage with the haunting resonances of gothic fiction. As in his stories, mystery and uncertainty are central to his strategies for creating an evocative sense of the strange 'local color' of a place. In the piece 'Haiti,' for example, Capote describes attending a Vodun ceremony. At the end of the ceremony, the Houngan, now inhabited by the spirit, bangs on a door that stands as an 'obstacle' to the 'magic' behind it: 'truth's secret, pure peace.' If the door ever opens, Capote does not report it. Instead, much like the jug of silver, Capote celebrates the inconclusive mystery: 'if the door had opened, as it never will, would he have found it, this unobtainable? That he believed so is all that matters' (38).

Local Color is also one of the key spaces where Capote worked out his relationship to the South in his writing. Just as he was able to adapt and expand the Gothic to northern settings in his short stories, Capote learned how to adapt his interest in mystery, strangeness, and wonder to non-Southern locales in his non-fiction. This adaptation is especially clear in 'To Europe.' Standing on the wall of an Italian castle, Capote traces a path from the Southern Gothic of New Orleans to the old Gothic of Europe, and the realization is an epiphany: 'suddenly it was true and I wanted the trueness of it to last a moment longer … And what was this truth? Only the truth of justification: a castle, swans and a boy with a harp, for all the world out of a childhood storybook' (39). At this moment, life imitates art, and Capote regards this revelation as 'a bridge of childhood, one that led over the seas and through the forests straight into my imagination's earliest landscapes. … [T]o think I had to go all the way to Europe to go back to my hometown, my fire and room where stories and legends seemed always to live beyond the limits of our town' (39–40). The 'legends' that he encounters in Europe help him understand better his 'imagination's earliest landscapes' in the US South, adding potency to his Southern viewpoint while also enabling him to carry his gothic way of seeing beyond the South. Originally published in the same year as *Other Voices, Other Rooms*, 'To Europe' provides vital insights into Capote's sense of how he could combine the fairy-tale dimensions of the Southern Gothic with a more cosmopolitan style to consider larger 'truths' both within the South and beyond it.

Capote developed this theory of cosmopolitan style further in 'Style: And the Japanese' (1952), in which he uses a decidedly gothic term to praise the evocative style of indirect representation in Japanese theater – what he calls the 'dread of the explicit, the emphatic' (73).[7] Much like the embrace of the 'unobtainable' behind the door in the Vodun ceremony, the Japanese 'ceremony of style' became for Capote a model for embracing suggestiveness, mystery, and evocation, instead of the harsh light of exposition that we associate with journalism. He continued to hone this style in his first extended work of reportage, *The Muses Are Heard* (1956). In this book, Capote records his travels to the Soviet Union with the cast and crew of the musical *Porgy and Bess*. The show was organized in part by the US State Department as an attempt to showcase American arts and put a positive spin on American race relations during the Cold War and the civil rights movement. Capote dutifully records political conversations about racial inequality, but, as in his other writing, he does not editorialize or make those conversations the centerpiece of the work. Rather, he spends more time poking at the foibles and antics of the American and Russian individuals around him. Instead of dwelling exclusively on the national and global politics at stake in the venture, his interest in seemingly trivial matters of gossip, clothes, and romance underscores how these people are more than just their nationalities. And yet, this approach is also still political, for Capote's attention to each individual's humanity implicitly challenges the racist logic supporting segregation and the totalizing ideological structures of both communism and capitalism that shaped the Cold War.

Capote's later *roman à clef, Answered Prayers* (1987), also showcases the idiosyncrasies of the myriad characters who drift in and out, as well as the complexity of his bisexual narrator's erotic life and identity. Yet, in this case, Capote dwells on the antics of the wealthy without setting them in tension with a coherent political superstructure. For example, the gossiping women in the chapter 'La Côte Basque' tell the story of a friend of J. D. Salinger who killed himself by drinking too much whiskey and falling asleep in the New Hampshire snow. The anecdote ends with one woman absently musing, 'That *is* a strange story. It must have been lovely, though – all warm with whiskey, drifting off into the cold starry air' (149). The women ignore whatever may have driven the man to suicide, even though their longing for the warmth and beauty that make his death seem 'lovely' highlights their own feelings of emptiness and depression underneath their chatty façade. Their rapid turn from that story to the next piece of gossip further reveals their inability or unwillingness to confront those feelings. Politically, however, the grotesque story does little more than emphasize the almost amoral emptiness of the cosmopolitan elite. Perhaps because the novel remains unfinished, it lacks the sustained, if subtle, engagement with some larger political or social system, ideology, or normativizing process that, in his other works, adds a sense of depth and purpose to his Gothicism.

Like *Answered Prayers, In Cold Blood* (1965) cultivates the geographically cosmopolitan style of Capote's 'bridge of childhood' by adapting the Southern Gothic to a non-Southern setting. However, the politics of *In Cold Blood* are more apparent. The text is saturated with the gothic sense of dread and fear, not least from the randomness of the central event: the senseless murder of the Clutter family in Holcomb, Kansas, by total strangers without warning and almost without motive. Capote also links this sense of existential dread to the oppressive politics of small-town life, for the first two books describe the numerous petty grudges and rivalries that lead the various townspeople to suspect each other as the killers. Furthermore, Capote extends this sense of existential dread and uncertainty by dwelling on the two killers' lifelong feelings of being unable to fit into the national narrative of being a 'normal' and productive citizen. And, in the later sections of the text, he further compounds this sense of existential fear with the legal oppression of the state as the killers wait under the protracted threat of capital punishment on Death Row. Capote chillingly links the cruelty of the murderers to the cruelty of the state, and he often spoke and testified against the death penalty on these grounds.

Despite this political edge, the gothic element of uncertainty still dominates *In Cold Blood*. The text records the capture and punishment of these killers, but it defiantly refuses to offer a sense of completion or safety after their execution. Rather, Capote foregrounds the unexplainable mystery of why Perry Smith and Dick Hickock committed this murder in the first place. Although their motive is revealed – they believed that they could steal a substantial sum of cash from Clutter's home safe – Capote circles endlessly around the psychological and sociological factors that transformed the botched robbery into a mass murder. He offers multiple explanations for the men's ability to kill, including bad relationships with their parents, childhood traumas and sexual abuse, lack of educational opportunities and good jobs, possible physical and cognitive disabilities, and the vicious cycle of jail time and recidivism, among other things. Nevertheless, as in Capote's other writing, he never allows any one of these factors to stand out as the ultimate cause for the killers' actions. While each of these explanations is entirely plausible, Capote never lets go of the gothic possibility that these men might just be monsters, innately predisposed to murder. And in that regard, he once again raises the more frightening existential dread that *any* person might be equally capable of such a crime.

In Cold Blood and *Answered Prayers* demonstrate Capote's interest in writing a cosmopolitan style that uses Southern Gothic conventions without being anchored exclusively in the South. This trajectory reflects his frustration about being labeled strictly a 'Southern writer' – and, for that matter, a 'gay writer.' Yet, Capote never truly abandoned his biographical or literary Southern origins, and he frequently returned to Southern settings and situations, even in his famous New York novella, *Breakfast at Tiffany's* (1958). As I have argued elsewhere, *Breakfast at Tiffany's* incorporates many components of both Southern literature and gay literature.[8] Holly Golightly's Texas childhood creates an interesting friction with her urbane sophistication, and it is impossible to define her as exclusively either straight or lesbian. Also, although Holly has loudly disparaged the narrator's stories because of their rural settings, African American characters, and gay themes, these same literary elements return in the novella's climactic scenes. As Holly and the narrator ride horses through leafy Central Park, some African American children make the horses bolt; and later, a lesbian policewoman hits Holly during an arrest. Both of these events arguably cause the miscarriage that prevents Holly from becoming trapped in the life of an unwed mother. Thus, ironically, these Southern- and gay-identified literary devices enable her to leave New York to follow more global pursuits of wealth and experience. The novella subtly asserts itself as a work of both Southern and queer fiction, even as it incorporates contradictory elements that defy generic categories. Moreover, these layers of irony and enigmatic contradiction give *Breakfast at Tiffany's* a greater level of gothic complexity than Capote's first attempted novel, *Summer Crossing* (2006). Although *Summer Crossing's* wealthy New York heroine resembles Holly in several respects, she follows a more conventional path of sexual rebellion by marrying below her class. We do not know why Capote felt that the novel was not good enough to publish, but perhaps it was because *Summer Crossing* does not incorporate the mystery and strangeness of the Southern Gothic that he went on to discover in *Other Voices, Other Rooms*, and then to expand in *Breakfast at Tiffany's*.

Music for Chameleons (1980), Capote's last collection of fiction and nonfiction, returns even more closely than *Breakfast at Tiffany's* to the 'bridge of childhood' that helped him combine Southern and non-Southern styles, tropes, and settings. For example, 'Dazzle' is set in New Orleans and makes an interesting return to the Southern Gothic in that Joel's acceptance of a gender-transitive gay identity in *Other Voices, Other Rooms* becomes, in this story, the young Capote's failed wish to change his sex completely. At 8 years old in the story, Capote becomes fascinated by Mrs. Ferguson, the 'only white laundress in New Orleans,' who claims to have magical powers (52). Anxious to enlist her help to change from a boy to a girl, he agrees to steal a large rhinestone pendant from his grandmother and bring it to her. However, Mrs. Ferguson mocks him and places him under a hypnotic spell that burdens him with a lifetime of shame and trauma, both about his secret wish and about his theft.

Instead of reading this story strictly in terms of whether or not Capote really wanted to be a girl, we get a richer understanding of the text when we consider his gothic depiction of New Orleans. As an Irish American, Mrs. Ferguson deviates from traditional New Orleans literary tropes in which hoodoo, voodoo, and magic are typically associated with African Americans. Capote takes the uncanny of the Southern Gothic and renders it uncanny again in a new way. This difference further corresponds with the fact that his grandmother's pendant is a valueless piece of glass and thus not worth the trauma that Capote experiences. And, at the end of the story, Capote describes his grief at his grandmother's death as 'absurd' and 'out of proportion' because she 'was not somebody I had loved' (64). In these ways and more, 'Dazzle' immerses us in the gothic world of uncanniness, incompleteness, and the schism between our view of ourselves and how others view us. Capote manipulates the Southern Gothic to remind us that the categories we might use to make sense of ourselves and the world are always inadequate, perhaps even traumatic, because they are out of proportion with the messy realities of life, desire, and loss.

The centerpiece of *Music for Chameleons*, *Handcarved Coffins* – which Capote described as non-fiction but is, in fact, entirely fictional – investigates a series of murders committed in a Western state, once again transporting the Southern Gothic to a non-Southern setting. Capote positions himself squarely within the story as he and the detective, Jake Pepper, try to prove that the murders are being committed by the wealthy ranch owner Bob Quinn, who is allegedly trying to kill everyone who opposed his claims to expanded water rights on the river adjacent to his land. When Capote first meets Quinn, he has a flashback to a traumatic event in his childhood when his family's African American cook takes him to be baptized against his will by an evangelical preacher, the Reverend Bobby Joe Snow: 'I shut my eyes; I smelled the Jesus hair, felt the Reverend's arms carrying me downward into drowning blackness, then hours later lifting me into sunlight. My eyes, opening, looked into his grey, manic eyes. His face, broad but gaunt, moved closer, and he kissed my lips' (117–18). Quinn's religious delusions, conveyed through his frightening similarity to the preacher, add a level of gothic mystery and terror beyond the more earthly motives of power, land, and money. From this flashback, Capote gains crucial insights into Quinn's character that Jake never sees; namely, that Quinn *knows* – not thinks – that 'he's the Lord Almighty' (119). The Southern Gothic is essential to the larger meanings of this novella, which otherwise has nothing to do with the South at all.

CONCLUSION

Throughout his career, Capote adapted and experimented with aspects of the Southern Gothic in both his fiction and his non-fiction (although this chapter has not discussed his work with cinema, television, and the Broadway stage). He used elements of the grotesque to highlight the lonely individuality of his characters and subjects; and while he often wrote about queers, misfits, outcasts, and outlaws, the grotesque also allowed him to evoke the strange idiosyncrasies of characters and people at the center of society, from the small towns of Kansas to the jet-setting elite of New York and Europe. Capote also turned to the Gothic for non-linear, asymmetrical, and out-of-proportion narrative structures that helped him craft the convoluted worlds – interior and exterior – through which his characters move. Moreover, for Capote, the Gothic is not a world of only terror and darkness. Rather, he combines the Gothic with elements of sentiment, camp, and subjective reportage to create sympathy and space for those who are often excluded by society, and to create a broader and calmer sense of 'dread' for the things that cannot be represented or observed directly. Capote extends the Southern Gothic to steer readers toward the unseeable, unspeakable mysteries that add to the richness of life precisely because they cannot be categorized and explained. Finally, Capote's interests in inexplicable mysteries and truths characterize all of his writing, not just what he set in the South. As a 'bridge of childhood,' the Southern Gothic allowed him to broaden his exploration of his 'imagination's earliest landscapes' and explore the mysteries that link his Southern childhood to the rest of the world.

Because of his interest in multiple meanings and unexplainable truths, Capote never used his writing to make explicit political commentary. However, he still used his various depictions of freakishness, isolation, cruelty, and violence to push against prescriptive ideological norms and social mores. From implicit demands for greater acceptance for sexual and racial minorities to a biting critique of the cruelty of capital punishment, Capote consistently invites his readers to consider the larger social implications of his writing. At the same time, his constant return to the indeterminacies of the Gothic keeps readers and critics from pigeonholing his work as narrowly committed to a single political message or dogmatic way of thinking. For Capote, the mysteries of the Gothic add to the political energy of his work precisely because they push readers to open their minds to wider possibilities beyond what they already know or what makes them comfortable. This interchange between the Gothic and the political thus opens opportunities for readers and critics to get a better understanding of Capote's conscious engagement with the politics of the twentieth century. And, because his gothic uncertainties always make his descriptions mean 'different things to different people,' his evocative style continues to inspire readers to consider the relevance of his work to their own time and place.

NOTES

1. See Clarke 98, 177.
2. I am lucky to have read Jason Barr's work in progress on Capote's uses of the Southern Gothic throughout his career. Although I have not consciously referenced or borrowed from his work in this chapter, I have still benefited from Barr's insightful readings of Capote's fiction and non-fiction.
3. See also Mitchell-Peters.
4. See Christensen 46.
5. Many critics have discussed Capote's alternation between darkness and light in his early work. See, for example, Garson.
6. For a discussion of Capote's different approach to gay politics and queer-phobic violence in 'The Thanksgiving Visitor' (1967), see my article 'How to Love Your Local Homophobe.'

7. For further discussions of Capote's style, see Anderson 48–81; and Nance 216–39.

8. See my article 'Making a Real Phony.'

BIBLIOGRAPHY

Anderson, C. (1987). *Style as argument: Contemporary American nonfiction.* Carbondale: Southern Illinois University Press.

Bibler, M. (2007). Making a real phony: Truman Capote's queerly Southern regionalism in breakfast at Tiffany's, a short novel and three stories. In A. Jessica, P. Michael, & A. Cécile (Eds.), *Just below South: Intercultural performance in the Caribbean and the U.S. South* (pp. 211–238). Charlottesville: University of Virginia Press. Print.

Bibler, M. P. (2012). How to love your local homophobe: Southern hospitality and the unremarkable queerness of Truman Capote's "The Thanksgiving Visitor". *MFS: Modern Fiction Studies, 58*(2), 284–307. Print.

Capote, T. (1987). *Answered prayers.* New York: Plume. Print.

Capote, T. (1993). *The Grass Harp.* New York: Vintage International. Print.

Capote, T. (1994a). Dazzle. In *Music for chameleons* (pp. 51–64). New York: Vintage International. Print.

Capote, T. (1994b). *Handcarved Coffins. Music for Chameleons* (pp. 67–146). New York: Vintage International. Print.

Capote, T. (1994c). *Other voices, other rooms.* New York: Vintage International. Print.

Capote, T. (2004). Jug of Silver. In *The complete stories of Truman Capote.* New York: Vintage International. Print.

Capote, T. (2008a). Haiti. In *Portraits and observations: The essays of Truman capote* (pp. 30–38). New York: Modern Library. Print.

Capote, T. (2008b). Style: And the Japanese. In *Portraits and observations: The essays of Truman Capote* (pp. 72–73). New York: Modern Library. Print.

Capote, T. (2008c). To Europe. In *Portraits and observations: The essays of Truman Capote* (pp. 39–44). New York: Modern Library. Print.

Christensen, P. (1993). Truman Capote (1924–1984). In E. S. Nelson (Ed.), *Contemporary gay American novelists: A bio-bibliographical critical sourcebook* (pp. 46–59). Westport: Greenwood Press. Print.

Clarke, G. (1988). *Capote: A biography.* New York: Simon and Schuster. Print.

Fahy, T. (2014). *Understanding Truman Capote.* Columbia: University of South Carolina Press. Print.

Garson, H. S. (1992). *Truman Capote: A study of the short fiction.* New York: Twayne. Print.

Harker, J. (2013). *Middlebrow queer: Christopher Isherwood in America.* Minneapolis: University of Minnesota Press. Print.

Mitchell-Peters, B. (2000). Camping the gothic: Que(e)ring sexuality in Truman Capote's other voices, other rooms. *Journal of Homosexuality, 39*(1), 107–138. Print.

Nance, W. L. (1970). *The worlds of Truman Capote.* New York: Stein and Day. Print.

Pugh, W. W. T. (1998). Boundless hearts in a nightmare world: Queer sentimentalism and Southern Gothicism in Truman Capote's other voices, other rooms. *The Mississippi Quarterly, 51*(4), 663–682. Print.

Richards, G. (2005). *Lovers and beloveds: Sexual otherness in Southern fiction, 1936–1961.* Baton Rouge: Louisiana State University Press.

PART V

Monsters, Vampires, and Voodoo

CHAPTER 31

Southern Vampires: Anne Rice, Charlaine Harris and *True Blood*

Ken Gelder

Timur Bekmambetov's 2012 film *Abraham Lincoln: Vampire Hunter* – an adaptation of Seth Grahame-Smith's 2010 'mash-up' novel of the same name – certainly did something unusual to the 16th President of the United States. As a boy, Lincoln realises that his father owes money to Mr Bart, a slave trader who also turns out to be a vampire. Soon afterwards – the year is 1818 – Mr Bart kills Lincoln's mother, Nancy. A mysterious figure, Henry Sturges, encourages Lincoln to become a vampire hunter, telling him that the slave trade has made vampires stronger than ever: 'Vampires have been in the New World for centuries, slaughtering native tribes and early settlers. But when the Europeans arrived with their slaves, the dead saw a sinister opportunity. They built an empire in the South.' After a long and rigorous training regime, Lincoln goes off to battle an old vampire called Adam, who owns the Eden plantation near New Orleans. A black American slave tells Lincoln, 'There's a war coming. A war for the soul of the country.' As his political career begins, Lincoln is dismayed to see that other politicians want to appease the vampires and other slave owners. However, his speeches begin to inspire the Union cause: 'Our nation was built on the backs of slaves,' he tells his audiences. 'The demon of slavery is tearing our nation apart.' When Lincoln is elected President in 1860, the Southern slave states form a Confederacy and, urged on by the vampire slave traders, they begin what becomes the Civil War. Lincoln momentarily gives up vampire hunting – 'I would not fight with an axe, but with words and ideals' – but when vampires make their way into the White House, he retrieves his axe and arms the Union with silver bullets. In a prolonged finale, Lincoln kills Adam, the Confederate vampire soldiers are defeated and all the vampire slavers are forced out of the country: 'Our enemies have made their exodus,' Lincoln proudly announces, 'some back to Europe, some to South America

K. Gelder (✉)
University of Melbourne, Melbourne, Australia

© The Editor(s) (if applicable) and The Author(s) 2016
S.C. Street, C.L. Crow (eds.), *The Palgrave Handbook of the Southern Gothic*,
DOI 10.1057/978-1-137-47774-3_31

405

and the Orient. They've seen that America shall ever be a nation of living men, a nation of free men.'

The connections that are mobilised here between vampires, race and slavery in the American South can make even the most preposterous fantasy narrative meaningful at a national level. For the Lacanian critic Slavoj Žižek, in fact, *Abraham Lincoln: Vampire Hunter* is nothing less than revelatory, much more so than films that earnestly attempted to chronicle the real historical predicament of Lincoln around this time. Žižek contrasts Steven Spielberg's 'big feel-good "high quality"' film *Lincoln* (2012) with 'its obviously poor cousin', agreeing that the former 'whitewashes' Lincoln by over-emphasising 'healing and unity' (63). In *Abraham Lincoln: Vampire Hunter,* however, Lincoln's discovery that 'vampires will help the confederate army if the South regularly delivers to the vampires black slaves as the source of the blood they need for food' is certainly 'ridiculous', but it also draws stark attention to a truth that Spielberg's film glosses over. '[T]his ridiculousness', Žižek claims, giving his usual Lacanian spin to Bekmambetov's film, 'is … a symptom of ideological repression or, even stronger, psychotic foreclosure: what is excluded from the Symbolic returns in the Real of a hallucination, and what is excluded is class struggle in all its brutality' (64). Putting aside the odd slippage from race to class in this passage, Žižek is certainly right to notice that *Abraham Lincoln: Vampire Hunter* 'hallucinates' the realities of slavery in the antebellum South by literally demonising the slave trade and Southern secessionism. The problem with the film is that it eventually re-invests in the myth of Lincoln in much the same way as Spielberg does. In *Abraham Lincoln: Vampire Hunter*, Lincoln defeats the Southern armies and expels vampires from the Union, putting the issue of slavery to rest; which means that there is no sense in the film that the legacies of slavery, like racism itself, persist in the United States as a sort of undead thing that unleashes trauma and violence over and over again.

This chapter will look at two Southern American fantasy novelists – Anne Rice and Charlaine Harris – whose novels play out, in one way or another, exactly these kinds of connections, putting their vampires in the framework of a legacy of slavery and plantations, the Civil War and race.

INTERVIEW WITH THE VAMPIRE

Jason S. Friedman has in fact identified Anne Rice's *Interview with the Vampire* (1976) as a 'plantation gothic' novel (192), although strictly speaking this only applies to the first section where Louis tells the story of how he became a vampire. Louis begins the account of his life in 1791 when, as a young man (and before he is turned into a vampire), he is a French Catholic slave holder and the owner of an indigo plantation in Louisiana called Pointe du Lac. The slavery system was already deeply unstable by this time: in the year Louis begins his story, around 100,000 slaves had risen up against their owners on the French-owned colony of Saint Domingue, 'burning down 180 sugar plantations and hundreds of coffee and indigo plantations' (Censer and Hunt 124). As Robin

Blackburn has noted, the slave revolt in Saint Domingue – coming in the wake of the French Revolution and ending with Haiti's independence from French (and white) rule as the world's first black Republic in 1804 – 'aroused the most intense alarm amongst the possessing classes on both sides of the Atlantic' (155). Advocacy for the abolition of the slave trade and slave emancipation certainly increased in some places in the wake of this revolt, but support for the slave trade also increased. In *Interview with the Vampire*, Louis's brother Paul urges his family to 'sell all our property in Louisiana, everything we owned, and use the money to do God's work in France' (Rice 7). In fact, indigo plantations – like Louis's – were struggling financially by the 1790s; one of the effects of the slave rebellion in sugar-producing Saint Domingue was a rise in the number of sugar plantations on the mainland. In lower Louisiana, Adam Rothman notes, sugar plantations also 'promised to reverse the declining fortunes of indigo growers around New Orleans' (75). A neighbouring French plantation in *Interview with the Vampire*, owned by the Frenieres, produces sugar. For the vampire Louis, the South is deliriously attracted to this slave-produced substance: 'This refined sugar', he says, 'is a poison. It was like the essence of life in New Orleans, so sweet that it can be fatal, so richly enticing that all other values are forgotten' (Rice 41). In this plantation gothic novel, sugar is a bit like blood, bringing both life and death; the South is addicted to it.

When Louis's brother dies and is buried in the St Louis cemetery in New Orleans, the slaves at Pointe du Lac 'talk of seeing his ghost' and – when these visions of a guilt-ridden plantation owner begin to cause unrest – 'the overseer couldn't keep order' (10). Grieving, Louis takes to the streets, where he meets the vampire Lestat. It turns out that Lestat 'wanted Point du Lac' (15); no commentator on this novel, so far as I know, has noted that the Lestat turns Louis into a vampire precisely in order to gain control of his plantation. The two things – becoming a vampire and relinquishing the plantation to Lestat – are explicitly tied together. 'We went at once to the plantation the next evening', Louis says, after Lestat drinks his blood, 'and I proceeded to make the change …. [T]here were several acts involved, and the first was the death of the overseer. Lestat took him in his sleep. I was to watch, and to approve' (15). Later, Lestat attacks and kills some runaway slaves and encourages a reluctant Louis to do the same. Soon, Lestat becomes interested in the Frenieres' sugar plantation, killing more slaves. The young Freniere manages the plantation for his family, but the promise that sugar might reverse the fortunes of plantation owners is not yet realised: 'Its fragile economy, a life of splendor based on the perennial mortgaging of the next year's crop, was in his hands alone' (42). When Louis curses Lestat for killing the young manager, Lestat angrily replies: 'If I didn't like the life of a Southern planter, I'd finish you tonight' (45). Louis, then, is the instrument through which Lestat literalises his ambition to own, and expand, his slave-owning properties; as in *Abraham Lincoln: Vampire Hunter*, vampires in the South are organically connected to plantations, sugar and blood, and black slaves are the source of both their labour and their food.

As his narrative moves towards the end of the eighteenth century, Louis reflects on the slaves who live on his – and now Lestat's – plantations, giving them a distinctive cultural identity and tying them to the Saint Domingue slave revolt a few years earlier:

> In seventeen ninety-five these slaves did not have the character which you've seen in films and novels of the South. They were not soft-spoken, brown-skinned people in drab rags who spoke an English dialect. They were Africans. And they were islanders; that is, some of them had come from Santo Domingo. They were very black and totally foreign; they spoke in their African tongues, and they spoke the French patois; and when they sang, they sang African songs which made the fields exotic and strange, always frightening to me in my mortal life. They were superstitious and had their own secrets and traditions. In short, they had not been destroyed as Africans completely …. the slave cabins of Pointe du Lac were a foreign country, an African coast after dark, in which not even the coldest overseer would want to wander. No fear for the vampire. (49–50)

The links here between slavery, Louisiana and Saint Domingue are more or less historically accurate, with the plantation slaves cast as French-speaking Africans who maintain their 'secrets and traditions' – meaning, in the novel, that they practise voodoo. In his important book *Slave Religion: The 'Invisible Institution' in the Antebellum South* (1978), published just a couple of years after *Interview with the Vampire*, Albert J. Raboteau wrote:

> From the early days of French Louisiana, the voodoo cult was associated with slaves imported from the French West Indies. Voodoo originated in the relation of Africans, but the most immediate catalyst to the growth of the cult in Louisiana was the emigration of slaves and free blacks from the island of Saint-Domingue at the time of the Haitian Revolution. (75)

In a much later novel in Rice's vampire chronicles series, *Merrick* (2000), Louis and Lestat have to deal with a voodoo priestess in New Orleans who is also a powerful witch. But in *Interview with the Vampire*, voodoo – as the earlier passage notes – does not trouble the vampires. Some of the slaves plan a revolt against their new masters, but 'the power and the proof of the vampire was incontestable, so that the slaves scattered in all directions' (Rice 57).

To literalise the metaphor of the Southern plantation owner as a vampire preying on his slaves is both preposterous and, in an obvious sense, entirely appropriate. The master/slave relationship also structures the relationship of one vampire to another, as if it is endemic to the species. 'I am not your slave,' Louis tells Lestat. 'But even as he spoke I realised I'd been his slave all along' (84). Lestat says: 'That's how vampires increase … through slavery. How else?' (84). This is why the early part of *Interview with the Vampire* – the part of this Southern vampire novel that chronicles the origins of Louis's vampiric life – has to begin on a plantation. Rice's vampires then reproduce enslavement as a routine matter of self-definition. In one sense, her vampires enjoy the privileges of masters, free to prey on anyone they want and to go wherever they please. In another sense, the very fact of *being* a vampire severely limits their options; in particular, it limits their capacity to go anywhere other than where they are taken by other, older vampires. Commenting on William Faulkner, Taylor Hagood writes: 'The two cities most often associated with him are New Orleans and Paris' (71). Interestingly, this is also true for Rice's *Interview with the Vampire*: Louis leaves New Orleans for Paris, to try to discover, in effect, the origins of vampirism – and slavery. As Barbara Eckstein remarks, the novel's connection with Paris is significant: that city 'keeps alive the particular colonial foundations of New Orleans' by placing it in the framework of the 'circum-Atlantic and third coast – that is to say, Gulf Coast – territory of French and Spanish colonialism and the slave trade' (150–51). Louis returns, disillusioned, to New Orleans at the end of the novel, as if he is himself enslaved to it. New Orleans, however, is different from the slave plantations. Although traces of plantation slavery flow through it, the city is much less Manichean than the plantations themselves. It is defined instead as a cosmopolitan trading port, a mixture of very different races, of people who do indeed seem able to travel around freely:

> There was no city in America like New Orleans. It was filled not only with the French and Spanish of all classes who had formed in part its peculiar aristocracy, but later with migrants of all kinds, the Irish and the German in particular. Then there were not only the black slaves, yet unhomogenised and fantastical in their garb and manners, but the great growing class of free people of color, those marvellous people of our mixed blood and that of the islands, who produced a magnificent and unique caste of craftsmen, artists, poets and renowned feminine beauty. Then there were the Indians, who covered the levee on summer days selling herbs and crafted wares. And drifting through all, through this medley of languages and colors, were the people of the port, the sailors of ships, who came in great waves to spend their money in the cabarets, to buy for the night the beautiful women both dark and light, to dine on the best of Spanish and French cooking and drink the imported wines of the world. (Rice 39)

John Blassingame has noted the 'radical difference between the treatment of slaves on the [Louisiana] plantations and their treatment in New Orleans', not least because slaves could be both more mobile and more anonymous in the city (2–3). In the earlier description of New Orleans, however, slaves are not anonymous at all, but spectacular: they stand out. On the other hand, unassimilated African slaves are one group among many others, mixing with 'free people of color', native Americans, colonising Europeans (French and Spanish) and other European immigrants. This is therefore a *post*-slavery description. The emphasis now is not on the master/slave relationship or on unassimilated African traditions, but on cultural diversity, as Louise McKinney has noted:

> Into Rice's novels go the habits and manners of clannish nineteenth-century Creoles, the exoticism and seemingly foreign cultural traits of African slaves and

immigrants from colonial St. Domingue, as well as the idiosyncratic practices and rituals of New Orleans' Roman Catholics. Rice uses to her advantage certain Gothic flourishes – the element of ever-present architectural decay, simultaneously the proliferation and rot of the city's abundant tropical vegetation, and the presence of hideous insects and scuttling rodents – to act as the backdrop for her supernatural beings. (131)

New Orleans has been immensely important to Anne Rice, who has literally imprinted herself on the city: taking up 'the cause of the antebellum homes' (McKinney 132), purchasing old Southern properties such as St Elizabeth's Orphanage or the St Alphonsus Catholic school (which Rice attended) and restoring them. Eckstein has also commented on Rice's 'devotion to historic preservation' in this city, 'specifically [the] preservation of Catholic sites significant to her own New Orleans Catholic girlhood' (153). Lafayette Cemetery No. 1, in the Garden District of New Orleans, was particularly important to Rice: once a part of the Livaudais plantation, the vampire Lestat hides in one of its tombs. When Louis returns to New Orleans at the end of *Interview with the Vampire* – in the present day – Lestat is not far away, living in a 'doomed house' on St Charles Avenue. Louis thinks nostalgically about the early days of slave plantation Louisiana and 'of all the things I'd ever lost or loved or known' (Rice 334); full of melancholy, he leaves Lestat soon afterwards, but feels 'that I might never leave New Orleans' (336). The end of the novel captures both the post-slavery aspect of contemporary Southern American life and the sense that even a modern vampire – as mobile and anonymous as he might otherwise be in this city – is never quite able to escape the spectres of his slave-owning past.

SOUTHERN VAMPIRE MYSTERIES

Writing about Southern vampires in the wake of Anne Rice, the Mississippi-born Charlaine Harris began the first of her Sookie Stackhouse novels, *Dead Until Dark* (2001), by both acknowledging and literally distancing herself from Rice's powerful influence. Harris's novels are set in a fictional small provincial town in northern Louisiana called Bon Temps, not far from the actual town of Shreveport. Working as a barmaid at Merlotte's in Bon Temps, Sookie – the narrator – desperately wants to meet a vampire: 'But rural northern Louisiana wasn't too tempting to vampires, apparently; on the other hand, New Orleans was a real center for them – the whole Anne Rice thing, right?' (Harris 1). There are 13 novels in Harris's immensely popular Southern Vampire Mysteries, which ended in 2012 with *Dead Ever After*. The novels were also adapted for television in a seven-part HBO series, *True Blood*, which ran from 2008 to 2014, created and produced by Alan Ball. New Orleans features occasionally in the Southern Vampire Mysteries, but it is no longer a 'real center' for vampire activities. Instead, the novels both provincialise their various encounters with vampires – Bon Temps is much less cosmopolitan than New Orleans and much more 'redneck' – while at the same time opening those encounters out right across the neighbouring Southern states: Mississippi, Arkansas and Texas. The cosmopolitan world of Anne Rice's New Orleans is to do with mixing together racialised groups of people, some of whom – like the African slaves from Saint Domingue – remain unassimilated. Charlaine Harris's novels, on the other hand, are not so directly interested in racialised identities; instead, they mix together a rather dizzying array of different supernatural species, although the question of assimilation – who assimilates, who remains separate from everyone else – is interestingly now much more prominent.

Most of the (human and supernatural) residents of Bon Temps in Harris's novels are white; in contrast to Rice's New Orleans, this small Louisiana town makes very little space for racial difference. In *Dead Until Dark*, Sookie notes that '[b]lacks didn't come into Merlotte's much' (151); the town's funeral director, Mike Spencer, only buries white folk, not 'people of color' (39). Lafayette is a minor character in *Dead Until Dark*, and the very small role that he plays in the Southern Vampire Mysteries is cut short when his murdered body is discovered at the beginning of the second novel in the series, *Living Dead in Dallas* (2002). Sookie remarks that another waitress at Merlotte's bar 'had never gotten along with Lafayette, whether because he was black or because he was gay, I didn't know … maybe both …. But I'd always kind of liked Lafayette because he conducted what had to be a tough life with verve and grace' (211). It is not clear whether Sookie is referring to Lafayette's ethnicity or sexuality here; she is in fact repelled or embarrassed by examples of flamboyant male homosexuality in the novels. Even so, non-white racialised identities in the Southern Vampire Mysteries are indeed often attributed to minor characters who do not last very long. There is only one native American in *Dead Until Dark*, a bartender called Long Shadow, who works for the powerful vampire Eric Northman. When Sookie reveals that Long Shadow has been taking money from Eric's bar, the bartender 'savagely' attacks her, but is quickly killed by Eric and Sookie's vampire lover, Bill Compton: 'there was gunk, black and streaky', Sookie tells us, 'and the absolute horror and disgust of watching Long Shadow deconstruct with incredible speed …. Even the gunk began to vanish in smoke. We all stood frozen until the last wisp was gone' (205–6). In her book *Reconstructing the Native South* (2011), Melanie Taylor talks about 'the entrenched southern repression of … Indian histories and survivors' in Southern American fiction by writers like William Faulkner, who had little to say about native American dispossession (34). Yet in this scene in *Dead Until Dark*, the brutal removal of native Americans – think of the Southern support for Andrew Jackson's 1830 Indian Removal Act – is graphically literalised, as the novel's only native American character (cast by Sookie and the white vampires around her as untrustworthy, 'savage' etc.) vanishes from its pages.

Harris's Southern Vampire Mysteries spend just a moment literalising Native American dispossession. On the other hand, they spend a considerable amount of time legitimising the possession and ownership of property by white settlers. Unlike Rice's *Interview with the Vampire*, these novels do not (quite) place Southern plantation histories and slave ownership at the source of their vampire chronicles; this is something the *True Blood* television adaptations are much better at doing, as I shall note later. However, the novels do return to a defining moment in Louisiana's settler history: the Civil War. Perhaps surprisingly, very few commentators on either Harris's novels or the *True Blood* series have remarked on this. Nevertheless, the vampire Bill Compton's Civil War experience becomes the first point at which the novels become historical and genealogical.

Not long after he arrives in Bon Temps, Bill is asked by the locals – and particularly by Sookie's grandmother, a member of 'The Descendants of the Glorious Dead' who calls the Civil War 'the War of Northern Aggression' – to give the townsfolk a much-needed first-hand history lesson. (As he delivers his address, a boy in the audience says, innocently enough, 'He's so white.') It turns out that Bill fought as a Confederate solider in the Civil War, defending Louisiana's right to secede from the Union and remain a slave-owning state; by the 1860s, in fact, almost half Louisiana's population was enslaved. Bill's family is from the Old South, arriving and settling in Louisiana just a few years before the Stackhouses: 'My folks were here when Bon Temps was just a hole in the road at the edge of the frontier' (46). The Comptons and the Stackhouses are the earliest of white settlers, but they are also tied to Louisiana's slave economy. Sookie's grandmother asks Bill if her husband's 'great-great-great-great grandfather' Jonas had ever owned slaves. 'Ma'am,' Bill replies, 'if I remember correctly he had a house slave and a yard slave. The house slave was a woman of middle age and the yard slave a very big young man, very strong, named Minas. But the Stackhouses mostly worked their own fields, as did my folks' (47). This is smallholder slavery, not plantation slavery, but it still implicates both families in the slave economy of pre–Civil War Louisiana. Bill arrives in (or returns to) Bon Temps precisely in order to claim what he sees as his rightful inheritance. 'That's why I came back,' he tells Sookie's grandmother. 'The land reverted to me, and since things have changed in our culture toward people of my particular persuasion, I decided to claim it' (47). After her grandmother is murdered, Sookie similarly takes possession of Old Southern property, her grandmother's antebellum house: 'It was my house, now,' she proudly announces. 'The house and the twenty acres surrounding it were mine, as were the mineral rights' (133). *Dead Until Dark* brings together a vampire and a (mostly) human waitress, two quite different species. Nevertheless, since they both come from old Southern slave-owning families, they have something important in common. And since they both take possession of antebellum Southern properties, they place themselves at both the end and the beginning of a long genealogy of Southern American settler domination.

It is not too far-fetched to suggest that Bill's vampire aspiration to 'mainstream' – that is, to assimilate, to join the rest of America – might well be understood in terms of his position as a landowner and Confederate in a secessionist Southern state. In her book *Gothic America* (1997), Teresa A. Goddu writes about the Southern Gothic in the following way: 'The South's oppositional image – its gothic excesses and social transgressions – has served as the nation's safety valve: as the repository for everything the nation is *not*, the South purges contrary impulses. More perceived idea than social reality, the imaginary South functions as the nation's "dark" other' (76). The vampires in Louisiana, Mississippi and so on in Harris's Southern Vampire Mysteries and in *True Blood* certainly capture this sense that the South is everything that mainstream America is *not*; and the question of how willingly and effectively vampires like Bill can assimilate into that mainstream gives these fantasy narratives much of their energy. In *True Blood*, the most exaggeratedly Southern vampires – like Russell Edgington, the King of Mississippi – remain utterly secessionist, violently opposed to assimilation. Edgington is also homosexual; another reason why he is cast here as 'the nation's "dark" other'.

Of course, the vampires in Harris's novels and the *True Blood* series are for the most part not dark at all. Quite the opposite, in fact: their untanned preternatural Southern whiteness almost glows (another thing they have in common with Sookie). This is one reason why so much of the commentary on these texts therefore turns not to racial issues, but to issues to do with sexuality or gender; as if race is invisible as a category here. The chapters collected in Brigid Cherry's *True Blood: Investigating Vampires and the Southern Gothic* (2012) barely mention antebellum slavery and the Civil War; nor do they have anything much to say about race and racialisation. There is just one exception, Victoria Amador's 'Blacks and Whites, Trash and Good Country People in True Blood', an essay that pays tribute to Sookie's grandmother, who 'represents Southern hospitality and tolerance' and regards Bill Compton as 'in many ways the ideal, old-fashioned Southern gentleman', someone whose 'old blood and fine manners … transcend many other issues of class, race and "ethnicity"' (Amador 132–3). It would be difficult to find a more cheerful apology for the ideology of white Southern American secessionism.

Amador's essay concludes that '[r]ace in the American South and in *True Blood* is slowly transmuting into an ordinary aspect of life like gender, central to the action only occasionally' (127). Putting aside the conflation of an actual place with a fantasy narrative here, this perspective is both peculiar and not at all uncommon: it may very well underwrite Harris's Southern Vampire Mysteries, for example (but not the *True Blood* series, as I shall argue later). The downplaying of the significance of race, racial difference and racial discrimination in America – as if it is 'central to the action only occasionally' – only makes sense in the framework of a perspective or point of view that has often been called the 'post-racial'. In November 2008, just a few months after *True Blood* premiered on HBO, Barack Obama was elected President of the United States. Although he was America's first black president, Obama is nevertheless also sometimes linked to 'post-racialism'; that is, to a sense that expressions of racial difference are now anachronistic, displaced and over-ridden by the larger national/communal imperative to be 'American'. Obama's much earlier and often-cited 2004 keynote address to the Democratic National Convention makes this post-racial aspiration clear: 'There is not a Black America and a White America and Latino America and Asian America: There's the United States of America' (see e.g. Nilsen and Turner 1).

I have suggested that Harris's Sookie Stackhouse novels might very well play out the kind of 'post-racial' vision of the South that is no longer especially interested in the realities of racial difference, making it easier for the novels to take Southern whiteness for granted as the privileged, property-inheriting signifier, and making it easy in turn for commentators on the novels to more or less go along with all this. Yet under Alan Ball's direction, the *True Blood* television series – as it adapted Harris's novels to the screen – decided to challenge this vision. It did so by keeping Lafayette alive and turning him into one of the series' main protagonists; and it did so again by turning a fun-loving young white woman in the novels called Tara Thornton – a friend of Sookie's, although she appears only occasionally – into a major character, a volatile, disaffected black American.

Both Lafayette and Tara work at Sam Merlotte's bar, where the patrons are – as Sookie had already noted – mostly white. For the critic Tara McPherson in her essay 'ReVamping the South: Thoughts on Labor, Relationality, and Southern Representation' (2011), *True Blood* is in fact 'a kind of workplace drama' and its 'engagement with labor is firmly rooted in the working class and in a pronounced resistance to performing unfulfilling labor' (347). There is little in the television series to suggest that Lafayette and Tara are 'working class', however; and Lafayette is hard-working and reliable, turning up regularly at Merlotte's kitchen (with a couple of exceptions). Lafayette is also a drug dealer and a prostitute; but again, there is no sense of his 'pronounced resistance' to these tasks, and in fact he becomes remarkably successful, driving expensive cars and so on. Deborah Mutch has noted that 'Lafayette's homosexual encounters in the first season are exclusively with White men' (174), but the series does not suggest that he is exploited by his lovers. (He is powerful enough, in fact, to threaten to expose one of them, a Republican senator.) However, because Lafayette has been dealing vampire blood, Eric Northman captures and punishes him, chaining him up in a dungeon and putting him to work on a large grinding wheel. This is one of a number of moments in the *True Blood* series where images of enchained slave labour are explicitly referenced; something that would be impossible to do in Harris's novels. Justin D. Edwards and Agnieszka Soltysik Monnet suggest that Lafayette 'embodies the history of the civil rights movement ... in the US and, more specifically, in the American South' (6). Yet this kind of reading massively overburdens this character, who in fact never expresses the aspirations of civil rights (he humiliates redneck whites in Merlotte's bar because of their homophobia, not their racism) and who is in any case socially atomised. Lafayette is Tara's cousin in *True Blood*, and he often works hard to calm this prickly character down. It is Tara who plays out a 'pronounced resistance' to unfulfilling labour, as we see in the first episode of the first season when she is sitting in Supersavers reading Naomi Klein's *The Shock Doctrine*. It is not long before Tara quits, calling the white manager a 'pathetic racist'; 'Fuck this job!' she says, as she walks out. Her sensitivity to racism and racial discrimination becomes a defining feature, making her life – as the seasons of *True Blood* unfold – increasingly difficult.

Tara is a constant reminder of race as an issue in a (fantasised) American South that aspires to be post-racial by calling for vampires to 'mainstream' or assimilate, trying hard not to openly discriminate, and so on. In season one of *True Blood*, Tara says: 'People think that just because we've got vampires out in the open now, race isn't an issue no more .... Race may not be the hot issue it once was, but it's still a button you can push on people.' When she introduces herself, she notes that she is 'named after a plantation'; interestingly enough, Tara is the name given to the antebellum mansion in Margaret Mitchell's epic Civil War novel, *Gone with the Wind* (1936), owned and doggedly defended by Mitchell's feisty white Southern heroine, Scarlett O'Hara ('No one was going to take Tara away from her .... She would hold Tara, if she had to break the back of every person on it'; Mitchell 603). In *True Blood*, on the other hand, Tara does not own any property, having walked out of her alcoholic mother's makeshift home. It is, incidentally, worth comparing the representation of Tara's mother Lettie Mae (who abuses and dispossesses her daughter) with Sookie's grandmother (who generously provides for her daughter and allows her to inherit her house and land); when Lettie Mae gives a dignified speech at the grandmother's funeral, Tara reminds her, 'You hated her guts.'

Tara is Sookie's immediate and radical opposite in *True Blood*, a homeless black American woman who drifts in and out of a white Southern woman's inherited antebellum house. Sometimes she is there as an invited guest; in the second season of *True Blood*, however, she squats in Sookie's antebellum house for a while, helping (under the influence of a maenad) to desecrate it. When Lafayette and Tara dutifully clean Sookie's house after the grandmother's murder, it is difficult not to see them in the role of house slaves. It is in fact Tara in *True Blood*, not Sookie's grandmother, who asks Bill whether he had ever owned slaves before the Civil War. Sookie is sufficiently linked to vampires – as white Southern property owners – to be romantically drawn to them, Bill and Eric in particular. Yet Tara is hostile to all vampires, regarding their mainstreaming ambitions with deep suspicion and recognising that, deep down, they only want to enslave and control humans. Her worst fears are realised when the vampire Franklin kidnaps her, takes her to the King of Mississippi's antebellum mansion, ties her to a large bed and systematically rapes and abuses her (telling her that she smells 'like spice'). When Tara finally escapes, running across the property in her white nightdress, she looks like a runaway slave.

Tara is a pathologised register of racial discrimination in *True Blood*, perpetually disaffected, angry and intolerant, unable to commit to relationships. She is – if I can recall my earlier discussion of Anne Rice's *Interview with the Vampire* – a resolutely *unassimilated* figure. Victoria Amador's chapter on *True Blood* misses the point completely when she writes that Tara's 'conflicted nature is due more to her impoverished upbringing and alcoholic mother than to her race' (127), a conclusion that simply refuses to acknowledge the structural work that racialisation performs in the television series. Discussions on various internet sites have been much more forthright about Tara's racialised identity in *True Blood* than most academic commentaries. A blog called *Racialicious* recognises the stark racial contrasting of Sookie and Tara, but complains that Tara's 'strong and angry' character is a racial stereotype for black Americans (Tami); while a post on *InSol: Womyn of Colour Collective* enjoys the 'impoliteness' of the way Tara asks Bill about his slaves, noting that it immediately exposes 'white privilege' (Isislight).

A series of events in the first and second seasons of *True Blood* intensifies these issues in important ways. At one point, Tara's mother visits a voodoo priestess, Miss Jeanette, to exorcise the 'demon' that makes her drink so much and abuse her daughter. The exorcism seems to work; not long afterwards, Tara visits the voodoo priestess ('I knew you'd come') who gives a fairly accurate diagnosis of her character and puts her through her own exorcism ritual. For a moment, it seems that Tara has been cured, losing all her 'hate'. However, when she discovers that Miss Jeanette is in fact simply a pharmacy shop assistant, her mother's faith – 'Just because Miss Jeanette ain't real, doesn't mean she can't help you' – offers no consolation. Season two begins with the discovery of a murdered black body in a car: not Lafayette's (as in Harris's second novel in the Southern Vampire Mysteries series) but Miss Jeanette's, the voodoo priestess. The murderer turns out to be a maenad, a wealthy white woman called Maryann Forrester who lives in a huge mansion; one that might rival Scarlett O'Hara's Tara in *Gone with the Wind*. It turns out that Tara had summoned Maryann during the voodoo ritual. Maryann diagnoses Tara just as Miss Jeanette had done; then, taking on the role of a generous and nurturing mother, she invites Tara into her house. Here, Tara meets a troubled black American man called Benedict – or 'Eggs' – and she falls in love.

In her essay on *True Blood*, Tara McPherson writes that 'a new form of representing and understanding race (and region) in the United States is emergent, one signalled by a whole range of cultural shifts from the first black man elected U.S. president to a spate of popular television series featuring mixed-race casts' (343). Yet the narrative about Tara and Eggs living in the opulent mansion of a wealthy and powerful white woman – and increasingly falling under her spell – disturbs this blithely optimistic post-racial perspective on American popular culture. Everything is provided for them and they seem to have nothing to do: far from being put to work, they are encouraged to give themselves up to leisure, and pleasure. Nevertheless, as Maryann's hold over them increases, they find themselves unable to leave; they do her bidding; and soon they are enslaved to her. 'I don't wanna be blacking out!' Tara cries, aware that significant parts of her waking life are no longer under her control. When the maenad moves into Sookie's antebellum house she brings Tara and Eggs with her, replicating the white plantation owner/black house slave relationship and spreading her influence across the town. Maryann's death eventually releases Tara and Eggs (and everybody else), but Eggs later confesses that – under the maenad's influence – he killed a number of victims, including the voodoo priestess. Clutching a knife, Eggs approaches Andy Bellefleur, the town's incompetent redneck police officer, wanting to confess his crimes. Sookie's brother Jason, who has recently undergone paramilitary training, thinks that Eggs is about to attack Andy. He draws his gun and shoots him dead.

This is a scene that must surely resonate with American audiences; it certainly affects Jason, who is haunted by the shooting, and Tara, who is distraught. So far as I can know, however, no commentator on *True Blood* has mentioned it. Still, I write this chapter in the wake of the 2014 race riots in Ferguson, Missouri, following the fatal shooting by police of a black American man, Michael Brown; and not long after the April 2015 South Carolina shooting (in the back) of black American Walter Lamar Scott by a white police patrolman. The shooting of unarmed black men in particular by white police officers – where police will often claim that their victims were acting 'suspiciously' or 'aggressively' (e.g. in the 2013 shooting of Michael Ferrell in Charlotte, North Carolina) – is, of course, an all-too-familiar event in the United States, and hardly restricted to the American South. In *True Blood*'s representation of this event, Eggs is armed but is intending to confess his crimes, not commit one. (Andy later admits to Tara, 'He was innocent.') Afterwards, far from being investigated and indicted after Eggs's murder, Jason goes on to *join* the police force, identifying himself as Andy Bellefleur's loyal, enthusiastic deputy. McPherson's view that popular television series in America increasingly feature 'mixed-race casts' might be true; but the romance between Tara and Eggs is not mixed race at all. Under the maenad's spell, these two characters are made to behave in raw, 'primitive' ways, beating each other up and making brutal love. Yet when that spell is broken, a white wannabe police officer makes sure that they have no future together. Not long afterwards – early in the second season – Tara is, as I have noted, kidnapped and raped by the vampire Franklin. After she escapes, Franklin comes for her again and confronts her outside Merlotte's bar. Jason sees them together and assumes, this time more correctly, that Franklin is going to attack Tara; he draws his gun (with a wooden bullet) and shoots the vampire in the back, killing him. The scene both reflects Jason's earlier shooting of Eggs and is its exact opposite. It releases Tara from enslavement and exploitation at the hands of a cruel white vampire linked to the secessionist King of Mississippi, and is about the closest Jason ever gets to atonement.

Later on – at the beginning of season five – Tara (after she sacrifices herself to save Sookie) is turned into a vampire by Eric's progeny, Pam. As it goes about the business of systematically wrecking the lives of each of its central characters, *True Blood* makes sure that Tara finally becomes the thing that she despises most of all. The television series then literalises the master/slave relationship that we saw earlier with Lestat and Louis in Anne Rice's *Interview with the Vampire*, as Pam puts Tara to work in her vampire nightclub and Tara is obliged to obey her every command. 'This is not your house,' Pam tells Tara when she momentarily asserts herself. 'It is mine. You work here, got it?' Tara's reply – 'Yessum … Missy Pam' – puts her right back into the plantation/house slave's position, subordinated and reluctantly obedient; precisely recalling her earlier relationship with the maenad, Maryann. 'So I'm basically your slave,' Tara says to Pam, just before she makes one of *True Blood*'s most insightful anti–post-racial observations: 'The more things change, the more they fucking stay the same.' Becoming a vampire in *True Blood*'s American South can certainly mean domination and power if characters are white; but if they are black, they are just as enslaved as they ever were.

BIBLIOGRAPHY

Amador, V. (2012). Blacks and whites, trash and good country people in true blood. In B. Cherry (Ed.), *True blood: Investigating vampires and the Southern Gothic*. London: I.B. Tauris.

Blackburn, R. (1988). *The overthrow of colonial slavery, 1776–1848*. London: Verso.

Blassingame, J. W. (1973). *Black New Orleans, 1860–1880*. Chicago: University of Chicago Press.

Censer, J. R., & Hunt, L. (2001). *Liberty, equality, fraternity: Exploring the French revolution*. University Park: Pennsylvania State University Press.

Eckstein, B. (2006). *Sustaining New Orleans: Literature, local memory, and the fate of a city*. New York: Routledge.

Edwards, J. D., & Monnet, A. S. (Eds.). (2012). *The Gothic in contemporary literature and popular culture*. New York: Routledge.

Friedman, J. S. (2007). "Ah am witness to its authenticity": Goth style in postmodern Southern writing. In L. M. E. Goodlad & M. Bibby (Eds.), *Goth: Undead subculture*. Durham: Duke University Press.

Goddu, T. A. (1997). *Gothic America: Narrative, history, and nation*. New York: Columbia University Press.

Hagood, T. (2015). Cosmopolitan culture: New Orleans to Paris. In J. T. Matthews (Ed.), *William Faulkner in context*. Cambridge: Cambridge University Press.

Harris, C. (2001). *Dead until dark*. New York: Ace Books.

Isislight. Where are your manners?: Racism and rudeness on [*sic*] *True Blood*. InSol: *Womyn of Colour Collective*, 6 Sept 2010. https://wocinsol.wordpress.com/2010/09/06/128/

McKinney, L. (2006). *New Orleans: A cultural history*. Oxford: Oxford University Press.

McPherson, T. (2011). Revamping the South: Thoughts on labor, relationality, and Southern representation. In D. E. Barker & K. McKee (Eds.), *American cinema and the Southern imaginary*. Athens: University of Georgia Press.

Mitchell, M. (2008). *Gone with the wind*. New York: Pocket Books.

Nilsen, S., & Turner, S. E. (2014). *The colorblind screen: Television in post-racial America*. New York: New York University Press.

Raboteau, A. J. (2004). *Slave religion: The "invisible institution" in the Antebellum South*. Oxford: Oxford University Press.

Rice, A. (1976). *Interview with the Vampire*. New York: Ballantine Books.

Rothman, A. (2007). *Slave country: American expansion and the origins of the Deep South*. Cambridge, MA: Harvard University Press.

Tami. True blood. Tired stereotypes. *Racialicious – The intersection of race and pop culture*, 24 Sept 2008. http://www.racialicious.com/2008/09/24/true-blood-tired-stereotypes/

Žižek, S. (2014). *Trouble in paradise: Communism after the end of history*. London: Allen Lane.

Further Reading

Cherry, B. (Ed.). (2012). *True blood: Investigating vampires and the Southern Gothic*. London: I.B. Tauris. This is an interesting, enthusiastic collection of essays on aspects of the HBO television series, but it unfortunately has very little to say about the series' important engagement with Southern histories of plantation slavery, the Civil War and the Confederacy, and questions of racial difference and discrimination.

Eckstein, B. (2006). *Sustaining New Orleans: Literature, local memory, and the fate of a city*. New York: Routledge. This book gives a brief but very perceptive and useful account of Anne Rice's *Interview with the Vampire* and its engagement with histories of New Orleans, voodoo and the slave trade.

Friedman, J. K. (2007). "Ah am witness to its authenticity": Gothic style in postmodern Southern writing. In L. M. E. Goodlad & M. Bibby (Eds.), *Goth: Undead subculture* (pp. 190–216). Durham/London: Duke University Press. This interesting essay looks at Anne Rice as well as another Southern vampire novelist, Poppy Z. Brite. Its focus is on Southern *goth* (rather than *gothic*) writing, which is more directly supernatural and 'metaphorical'. Interestingly, the essay argues that *Interview with the Vampire* 'seeks to undermine a dehumanising construction of slavery that the southern gothic has helped propagate' (202).

CHAPTER 32

Voodoo and Conjure as Gothic Realism

Anne Schroder

Southern Gothic resonates with the history and legacy of slavery. Throughout the Americas and the Caribbean, the experience of enslaved Africans and their descendants provides subject material for a wide range of narratives from these regions. The horrors of the Middle Passage, the auction block and life as somebody else's property readily conjure up a nightmarish and well-established gothic imagery of torture, incarceration and loss of selfhood. However, as Teresa Goddu points out, any attempt to depict the factual reality of slavery strains against the limitations of the Gothic as a genre of pure fiction (Goddu 139). A set of representational strategies associated with the unreal, the Gothic nevertheless offers an index through which the manifestations of slavery—past and present—can be articulated. Advocating a continued use of gothic vocabulary as a gateway to the phenomenon of slavery, Goddu conceives of this as a process of 'allying the gothic with reality' that necessitates a rethinking of the relationship between 'gothic narrative' and 'gothic history' (139). Her refusal to capitalize the term enables an orthographic distinction in a discussion where gothic reality contests gothic sensationalism to produce gothic realism as an alternative literary mode.

Voodoo activates both a Gothic and a gothic register. In the dominant cultural traditions of the United States and the wider North Atlantic, voodoo is often an unambiguously negative term that is wholly relegated to the realm of Gothic. The very word instantly conjures up images of evil cults, superstitious followers in trance-like states and victims possessed by magic spells. Indeed, the *Oxford English Dictionary* defines voodoo as 'a black religious cult … characterized by sorcery and spirit possession', and in literary works such as George Washington Cable's *The Grandissimes* voodoo appears as a dark undercurrent that can never quite be grasped although it informs the lives of the characters.

A. Schroder (✉)
University of Surrey, Guildford, UK

© The Editor(s) (if applicable) and The Author(s) 2016
S.C. Street, C.L. Crow (eds.), *The Palgrave Handbook of the Southern Gothic*,
DOI 10.1057/978-1-137-47774-3_32

For Afro-diasporic communities, however, the gothic reality of slavery and its aftermath has contributed to a worldview that expresses itself through voodoo and its related Caribbean forms of obeah, myalism, pocomania and Santería, as well as the hoodoo/conjure found in the American South. These practices serve as a way of preserving, reconceptualizing and reinforcing a sense of identity and community through a belief system originating in an African past, but shaped by the encounters and experiences in the New World.

William Faulkner famously declared that '[t]he past is never dead. It's not even past' (Faulkner 85). In Faulkner's world, the past haunts the living remorselessly as the figures of the dead continuously intrude into the present, refusing to be laid to rest while equally refusing to be anything but wholly lost to the people who mourn their absence. Caddy is the missing centre of *The Sound and the Fury* just as the corpse of Emily's lover in 'A Rose for Emily' embodies a past that is quite literally dead but not buried. Faulkner's succinct articulation of 'the past' as an undead phenomenon, however, fails to address the fact that it is no singular unified category, but a disparity of collective as much as personal experience. The particular past that is invoked in Faulkner's works represents what Wilson Harris refers to as 'that dismantled Southern racial protocol or privilege', while the very nature of the South constitutes a field criss-crossed by 'European, African and pre-Columbian hidden antecedents' (Harris 95, 92). Within this complex and heterogeneous fabric, the violent history of slavery has created a set of material and imaginary structures that converge around a specific brand of Southern and Gothic/gothic consciousness and sensibility.

CONJURING THE GOTHIC

Charles W. Chesnutt's *The Conjure Woman* (1899) is a collection of short stories all featuring the three characters of John, Annie and Uncle Julius. Set on a former slave plantation in North Carolina, the stories can be read individually, but form an interconnected whole through their sophisticated exploration of conjure as a device, as a structuring principle and, most significantly, as a way of affecting material reality. The conflicting perspectives of the three central characters reflect the intersecting power dynamics of race, gender and privilege that shape their understanding of a world where conjure becomes a way of obtaining agency. The opening tale, 'The Goophered Grapevine', introduces us to first-person narrator John and his wife Annie, a white couple who have left their native Ohio to seek a warmer climate in what John proprietorially calls 'one of our own Southern States' (1). Looking around for an appropriate place for pursuing his grape-cultivating business, John finds the ideal spot where 'labor [is] cheap, and land [can] be bought for a mere song' (1). The plantation in question once contained a vineyard, and the mix of old vines and new saplings bear a few grapes that John instantly views as 'the undisputed prey of the first comer', establishing the grapes as a contested site of material value (3). This 'first comer' turns out to be an elderly black man whom John and Annie encounter in the yard, sitting on a log eating the grapes with evident relish.

John assesses the stranger and concludes that he is 'not entirely black' (4). Revealing his propensity for racial classification, he goes on to note that '[t] here [is] a shrewdness in his eyes, too, which [is] not altogether African' (4). Shrewdness in a black man—even if he is not 'entirely' black—is obviously not something that John considers a desirable character trait, but he nevertheless decides to engage the man in conversation. Julius McAdoo (Uncle Julius) was born and raised on the plantation and is a fount of local knowledge, a fact that John acknowledges in most of the subsequent stories and that leads him frequently to consult Julius on matters of business; that is, how best to expand his property and increase his profits. In 'The Goophered Grapevine', Julius warns the couple not to buy the plantation as the old vineyard is conjured: 'Well, I dunno whe'r you b'lieves in cunj'in' er not,—some er de w'ite folk don't, er says dey don't, but de truf er de matter is dat dis yer ole vimya'd is goophered … cunju'd, bewitch' (5). This information is conveyed with 'such an air of confidential mystery' that his interlocutors are drawn into Julius's orbit of storytelling and narrative command, and he now takes over the first-person narration in a magnificent act of conjuring up the past realities of slavery for the two Northerners (5).

This pattern is repeated throughout Chesnutt's *The Conjure Woman*. John begins the story, Julius takes over and recounts a specific tale of conjure that happened during the time of slavery, while John finishes off by telling us how the story has affected Annie and himself and brought about a change in the current situation on the plantation. In 'The Goophered Grapevine', Julius explains how the former master hired the local conjure woman, Aunt Peggy—another recurring character in the collection of stories—to put a goopher (or conjure) on the grapevines to prevent the slaves from eating the crops. The conjure woman 'could make people hab fits, er rheumatiz, er make 'em des dwinel away en die', and the slaves duly stop helping themselves to the fruit (6). When Henry, an elderly new field hand, arrives and nobody remembers to tell him about the goopher, the inevitable happens and he seeks out Aunt Peggy to get her to reverse the spell. Having paid her generously, Henry can now not only eat the grapes, his lifecycle is curiously tied to the lifecycle of the grapevine itself: every spring when the sap rises, Henry grows youthful and strong, and when the leaves fall from the vine in the autumn, he loses his suppleness and energy in a naturally occurring pattern of repetition. The vineyard is eventually ruined when the plantation owner is tricked or, as Julius puts it, 'bewitch' by a 'Yankee' who has come south to educate white people in the art of raising grapes (11). Destroying the roots of the plants, the white 'conjurer' from the North thereby kills Henry, whose life is deeply intertwined with and inseparable from that of the vineyard through the conjure that has been put on him.

'The Goophered Grapevine' serves as a frame for the rest of the stories. Not only introducing the structure and themes of the collection as a whole, it stages a contest between John, who wants to buy the plantation, and Julius, who does not want it to revert to mere 'property' once again. This initial battle is won by John who makes his purchase despite Julius's warnings, and it places the white couple on the plantation, ready to hear the rest of Julius's stories of slavery and conjure. The following tales continue the pattern of dispute between the two men while developing the notion of conjure as an act of transformation that mediates between different life forms or states of being. 'Po' Sandy' and 'The Conjurer's Revenge' present a man turned into a tree and another into a mule, while 'Mars Jeems's Nightmare' recounts a white master's ordeal after being transformed into a black slave. Each story, however, works its magic around a specific object or person in the present over whom both John and Julius are seeking to assert power: an old schoolhouse that John wants to tear down but Julius wants preserved is the site of conflict in 'Po' Sandy'; in 'Mars Jeems's Nightmare' Julius manages to get the couple to re-employ his grandson whom John has just sacked; and 'The Conjurer's Revenge' concludes when Julius tricks John into buying a friend's decrepit horse despite his resolve to acquire a mule. Using tales of mystery in the past to gain an advantage in the present, Julius occasionally succeeds in stemming, or even reversing, the flow that has instated John as the newest incarnation of a profit-seeking 'master' of the plantation (Hemenway 101–19; Edwards 88–92).

Chesnutt's *The Conjure Woman* tales are firmly grounded within the gothic canon. Treating conjure as part of the supernatural as well as setting the stories on a plantation both during and after slavery, Chesnutt reinforces the traditional link between American Gothic and slavery—as identified by Leslie Fiedler as early as the 1960s—and elucidates the parallels between past and present race relations in the South (Fiedler 140–46). Constantly juxtaposing and merging the 'real' horrors of slavery with the 'unreal' conjure elements, Julius's stories lay claim to both gothic narrative and gothic realism through their ambiguous truth-value. Throughout, John is amused by the black man's store of supernatural plantation legends, which he receives with all the superiority of knowing that they cannot possibly be 'true'. As Julius describes men being turned into various animals and objects by the transformative powers of conjuring, John views the dualism inscribed in the stories through the prism of race and informs the storyteller that 'your people will never rise in the world until they throw off these childish superstitions and learn to live by the light of reason' (Chesnutt 52). Annie, meanwhile, is moved by the descriptions of an economic and social system that effectively converted human beings into commodities to be bought and sold, traded and swapped, lost or won in a game of cards or hired out to the highest bidder. Her responses to stories that blur the boundaries between human, animal and 'thing' reveal an understanding of how slavery—as much as conjure—erases the possibility of a clear subject/object distinction.

The tales illustrate the complexities of the nature and meaning of conjure. Sometimes used for good and sometimes for evil, conjure serves a range of purposes and works on both white and black characters. The common denominator that defines conjure throughout the stories, however, is that it constitutes a transaction between individuals, and Julius always conscientiously tells us precisely what Aunt Peggy is receiving in return for her services as she 'neber lack ter wuk fer nobody fer nuffin' (80). The conjure woman works for whoever pays her, regardless of race or the rights and wrongs of the outcome that the conjure is designed to accomplish. In 'The Goophered Grapevine' the goopher initially constitutes a curse that strikes down anyone who eats the grapes, but it becomes a more ambiguous phenomenon in the metamorphosis of Henry as the goopher ties him to the vine. The personal benefit that he derives from living through the phase of youth again and again is appropriated by the white master who owns both Henry and the vineyard. Never missing an opportunity to make a profit, the master devises a scheme whereby he sells his slave when the latter is at the height of his powers, only to buy him back cheaply when he starts to wane so that the procedure can be repeated the following year. Henry's fluctuating value on the open market, then, is a monetary manifestation of the conjure that ultimately serves to augment his master's wealth and enable his acquisition of another plantation, despite resulting from an act associated with the 'primitive' belief system of the slaves. Already in this opening story, the line between 'childish superstitions' and 'the light of reason' that John is so keen to uphold breaks down immediately. For Julius's stories do not position conjure in opposition to a worldview based on scientific rationality that John purports to represent; rather, they delineate a reality governed by the structures of greed and ruthless self-interest, where conjure forms part of an everyday strategy of survival within this system.

Voodoo and the Caribbean

In 1938, African American anthropologist and novelist Zora Neale Hurston published an account of her travels in Haiti and Jamaica. Her travelogue *Tell My Horse* announces the focal point of the study through a subtitle clearly intended to kindle the potential reader's interest: *Voodoo and Life in Haiti and Jamaica*. Privileging the term voodoo over 'life', the text promises stories of the mysterious Caribbean cults that have long thrilled the Western imaginary through sensationalist tales of superstition and nefarious goings-on. Indeed, the *New York Herald Tribune Books* review quoted on the back of the 1990 Perennial Library edition describes the content as 'spine-chilling supernatural grotesquerie'. Selected as part of the paratext, which also, more soberly, classifies the work as 'Black Studies/Anthropology', the *Herald Tribune* deploys a distinctly gothic discourse to convey the nature of Hurston's account, and the reader turns to the text itself with excitement and anticipation.

Tell My Horse seems to deliver on its promise from the outset. On the very first page, Hurston launches into a discussion of Pocomania, a Jamaican version of voodoo that 'boils down to a mixture of African obeah and Christianity' (3, 4). Describing the followers of Pocomania as a 'cult' with 'barbaric rituals', Hurston, however, instantly defuses the obscure magic inherent in this loaded and gothic terminology as she adopts a conversational tone to address the reader, explaining that Pocomania is a central part of life in Jamaica, 'so perhaps we ought to peep in on it a while' (3, 4, 3). The notion of 'peeping in on' barbaric rituals sets up a tension between the supposedly disturbing phenomena that we are about to witness and the cavalier manner with which Hurston is prepared to treat these as commonplace occurrences. In the subsequent explanation and depiction of various Pocomania ceremonies, she wholly abandons the gothic mode by portraying a joyful celebration of the Christ Child and a 24-hour-long festivity known as the 'Sun Dial', characterized by singing, dancing and 'baptisms at sacred pools in the yard' (4, 5). These familiar Christian elements thwart our expectations of primitive and menacing Otherness, and Hurston emphasizes images of light, brightness and transparency in noting that the 'Christ must day' ritual is lit up with a multitude of candles, while the 'Sun Dial' takes place 'in the open air' (4). Rather than encountering a catalogue of unspeakable actions shrouded in darkness and mystery, then, we are introduced to a form of worship that does not appear to differ so very substantially from our own.

Hurston proceeds to interweave social observations with information pertaining to the customs surrounding the dead. Explaining that Jamaicans view death as a transition from one condition of being to another, Hurston records the elaborate rituals and animated talk about the much-feared duppy during a 'Nine Night' vigil that she is invited to attend. A duppy is the life force of any living human, released from its earthly constraints at death and apt to hurt the living if the necessary burial rites are not carried out to keep the duppy with the body in the grave. Although the talk concerns the serious matters of life, death and evil-doing, the vigil itself is a celebration that brings people together around food, drink, singing, storytelling and bursts of uproarious laughter. And this discrepancy between dark subjects and the light-hearted tone in which they are discussed defines Hurston's own text, where form and content are curiously at odds with each other. Indeed, the 'confusing mix of modes' leads Roger Luckhurst to declare that it is 'considered a great embarrassment of a book, even by Hurston's admirers' (Luckhurst 101).

Armed with camera and notebook, the anthropologist and recorder of folklore—so often identified as a source of gothic narrative—gathers information through her methodology of 'talking and asking questions' (Hurston 34). Describing her activity as 'collecting', she stresses the need for authenticity and 'the real thing': 'If I do not see a dance or a ceremony in its natural setting and sequence, I do not bother' (22, 23, 22). This conscientious approach to her fieldwork and awareness of the importance of context establish her credentials as the objective social scientist, but are undermined by her informal narrative voice, her disregard for context, setting and chronological sequence, and the scant attention she pays to seemingly unexplainable phenomena. She is in conversation with a medicine man one evening, and he demonstrates how he can make the deafening chorus of frogs on the opposite mountainside fall silent with a mere gesture of his hand. Hurston simply reports this in her matter-of-fact way and moves on to the more mundane matter of jerked pig. Mixing the everyday with the fantastic, the seamless and free-flowing textual fabric of *Tell My Horse* rejects the gothic mode in favour of a slippery form of representation that treats the mysterious as *part of* rather than separate from the mundane, and so locks the gothic elements of its content to a more realist form that captures everything through the prism of the ordinary.

Hurston's study follows a tripartite structure. This takes us from the opening section 'Jamaica' through 'Politics and Personalities of Haiti' until we finally get to the promised 'Voodoo in Haiti'. Making us wait a good 100 pages for the subject that has such prominence in her subtitle, Hurston shrewdly paves the way for an exploration of voodoo that both delivers and negates the horrors of the Gothic. In 'Politics and Personalities of Haiti', she sketches the continuing bloodshed, violence and corruption that have swept the island nation, and makes it clear that all of these evils have their source firmly in the human realm of greed and self-seeking rather than the supernatural: 'In the past, as now, Haiti's curse has been her politicians' (74). This is part of the context for voodoo in Haiti. Borne out of the world's only successful slave revolt, the country remains the poorest in the Western hemisphere; Hurston observes how 'the peasants of Haiti are so hungry' while the men of influence are planning another trip to Paris (80, 74).

The section entitled 'Voodoo in Haiti' continues the meticulous descriptions of innocuous ceremonial gatherings. Only too aware of 'the fantastic things that have been written about Haitian Voodoo by people who know nothing at all about it', Hurston dismisses 'the stereotyped tales of virgin worship, human sacrifice and other elements borrowed from European origins ... that paint ... the Haitian as a savage' (83–4). Despite this disavowal, she includes one unequivocally and unashamedly gothic passage in her discussion of voodoo, and this pertains to the secret societies that are supposedly responsible for turning human beings into zombies. Informing us that she has come across an 'authentic' zombie, the social scientist substantiates the truth-value of this case by simply stating that she can 'see and touch' her (182). If seeing is indeed knowing in Hurston's text, then her subsequent portrayal of the nefarious nocturnal activities of the dreaded Secte Rouge lays no claim whatsoever to their being witnessed and therefore 'real'. A sudden shift from the present to the past tense in the middle of a chapter signals a change in register, and the words on the page now convey gothic narrative rather than anthropological observation: 'The night was very dark but starry. Only a homemade lamp ... fought against the blackness. Members came in like shadows from all directions ... parting the rustling leaves so skillfully that there was no sound' (211). The section goes on to record how the Secte Rouge practises cannibalism and roams the countryside at night in search of victims, who are hunted and bound with lengths of cord made from the intestines of previous victims. As Hurston finally allows the Gothic to intrude into her travelogue, she does so by signalling the supreme artifice of this part of her narrative as the Gothic spectacularly erupts into the 'real' and creates a chasm between the excessive and fantasized depiction of the Secte Rouge and the rest of *Tell My Horse*. Moreover, she still exempts voodoo from the domain of the Gothic by insisting that the Secte Rouge is a criminal organization that 'is outside of, and has nothing to do with Voodoo worship' (208).

'REAL' ZOMBIES

Harvard ethnobotanist Wade Davis wrote about Haitian voodoo in the 1980s. Having been commissioned by two US medical experts to locate and bring back—if it exists—the drug that Haitians use to turn people into zombies, Davis's mission brought him into close contact with the voodoo societies of the island nation, and his subsequent book *The Serpent and the Rainbow* is a record of his time there. A narrative charting the search for 'real' zombies inevitably raises the spectre of the Gothic, and Davis constructs his text around a careful negotiation of the pitfalls and advantages of allowing the gothic mode to affect and direct his account of a scientific expedition to prove the existence of zombies.

Like Hurston, Davis opts for a tripartite structure, with each part divided into chapters. The first part, 'The Poison', follows his initially unsuccessful attempts at tracking down the zombie powder and ends as he is poised to return to the United States with a jar of the 'real thing' in his suitcase. In the second part, 'Interlude at Harvard', laboratory tests confirm the zombifying properties of the drug, while the third section, 'The Secret Societies', sees Davis back in Haiti seeking to understand the context for zombification as a phenomenon deeply ingrained within Haitian society. The structure reflects the logic and chronological progress of Davis's journey of discovery, and his narrative is as linear and transparent as Hurston's is slippery and disorientating, or so it would seem. For as a piece of creative non-fiction, Davis's text brings together the two radically different genres of scientific and novelistic writing, and in so doing blurs the boundaries between the real and the unreal.

The Serpent and the Rainbow presents itself as medical and social science. Offering an explanation of the mystery of zombies based on pharmacology and the inner workings of the voodoo communities, the author's credentials as a Harvard scientist allow him to speak from a position of authority, and his methodology combines the disciplines of botany and anthropology that constitute his own area of expertise in ethnobotany. The narrative is peppered with passages summarizing Davis's research into botanical and ethnographic literature, grounding the zombie quest in a scientific framework of knowledge production based on the principles of Enlightenment rationality. Despite this commitment to a rigorous pursuit of 'truth', Davis's account reads like a swashbuckling page-turner of an adventure story. The scientist-cum-intrepid explorer draws on the conventions of the detective story and the thriller in his manner of building suspense, foreshadowing and employing setting as a way of creating dramatic effect and moving the plot along. By using such literary techniques, Davis ruptures the linearity and transparence of his written testimony, which now reveals itself as artifice rather than pure realism.

The gothic novel has a long tradition of blurring the distinction between the real and the unreal. Horace Walpole's *The Castle of Otranto* is presented as a historical document in the form of a found and translated manuscript, while Edgar Allan Poe's *The Narrative of Arthur Gordon Pym* claims to be a real travel narrative but is, in fact, entirely fictional. Davis's narrative sits uneasily between scientific and novelistic discourse: the two cannot be kept apart, but move into each other as the literary devices governing the structure and plot development break down any clear-cut relationship between fact and fiction. This process of doubting Davis's scientific findings has only been amplified by the emphatic rejection that his zombie poison has later received at the hands of the established scientific community. Now largely discredited, the pharmacological explanation of zombies that we find in *The Serpent and the Rainbow* is nevertheless only part of the story. Perhaps the most compelling aspect of the text is Davis's struggle to find an appropriate way of writing about voodoo. Wanting to meet the expectations of a Western audience reared on sensationalist accounts denigrating and vilifying voodoo, Davis is simultaneously at pains to demonstrate that this other set of beliefs and practices grows out of the violent history of slavery and reflects a worldview that has as much cohesion and integrity as our own. With these dual considerations shaping the text, Davis brings us back to the tension between gothic narrative and gothic reality.

On arriving in Haiti for the first time, Davis takes in the sights and 'feel' of the capital city of Port-au-Prince. The people seem 'gay, careless, jaunty' as they flow rather than walk along the streets, 'exuding pride' and 'a rakish charm' that give the whole city a 'raw elemental energy' (45). This imagery is strikingly reminiscent of stock depictions of the racial Other as joyful and carefree yet potentially menacing in his explosive primitivism, but it does inscribe a dualism that, according to Davis, is the key to the nature of Haitian voodoo. Highlighting one particular sight as 'a clue' to the country, Davis notices a man—perfectly sane and happy—dancing with his own shadow in the afternoon sun (45).

Later that same night, Davis attends his first voodoo ceremony. A commercial undertaking staged for paying tourists, the service features invocations of the *loa* (or spirits), the tracing of symbolic designs on the ground, drumming and dancing, and, crucially, the all-important spirit possession where the *loa* arrive to take control of the devotees. The audience watches as a tiny woman suddenly acquires the strength to lift grown men and 'swing them about like children' and breaks a glass with her teeth, swallowing shards of it (49). Following this display, the *loa* drop an acolyte onto the open fire at the centre of the *hounfour* (voodoo temple), where she remains for some time until, leaping out, she picks up a red-hot lump of coal and carries it around in her hands and mouth, again for a considerable length of time. Back at his hotel, the sleepless Harvard scientist tries in vain to process what he has just witnessed: '[t]here was no escaping the fact that a woman in an apparent state of trance had carried a burning coal in her mouth for three minutes with impunity' (50). Mentally reviewing the scholarly literature on various faith groups ritualistically exposing their flesh to fire, Davis smiles to think how 'Western scientists have gone to almost absurd lengths to explain such feats', and can only conclude that he has 'no experience or knowledge that … allow[s] [him] either to rationalize or to escape what [he] ha[s] seen' (51).

The ceremony constitutes Davis's first encounter with voodoo. Before he can even begin his investigation of zombies, he is confronted with the inexplicable phenomenon of possession, and the limitations of a Western system of knowledge production form one of the main thematics running through the text. As he gradually 'solves' the problem of *how* people become zombies, Davis turns to the question of *why*. Unlike Hurston, who sees the construction of zombies as criminal activity completely unrelated to voodoo and perpetrated by secret societies like the 'evil' Secte Rouge, Davis believes that these same societies are an integral part of voodoo culture and that they convene as judicial councils to pass judgment on individuals whom their members have accused of a crime. The act of zombification, then, constitutes a de facto death penalty where the person who has transgressed the norms for social and economic behaviour is condemned to a fate worse than a fate worse than death and forced into endless backbreaking labour for a 'zombie master'.

Davis's attempts to understand why people are turned into zombies lead him to consider the parallels between ceremonial possession and zombification. Both scenarios re-enact and re-configure the experience of slavery through two very different forms of possession: the zombie's loss of mind, memory and identity transforms it into mere labour power for its new owner, while the individual subject is effaced and supplanted by the spirits for the duration of the possession ritual. The link back to slavery and Davis's contention that zombies are real and spirit possession inexplicable position his text on the threshold between the supernatural and the mundane, between gothic narrative and gothic reality. Adding his perspective to other studies and literary texts on the subject of voodoo and conjure, Davis's demonstration of the limitations of North Atlantic notions of 'reason' and 'science' leaves open the question of how we should view and approach the structures of other systems of ordering and making sense of the world.

CONCLUSION

Chesnutt's *Conjure Tales* revolve around the notion of transformation and the unstable boundary that divides human beings into white masters and black slaves. His treatment of the master/slave dialectic as a subject/object binary expresses the affinities between conjure and voodoo as a shared ontology for the dispossessed, where those who were possessed as slaves in the past may find new forms of identity and empowerment by invoking the figures of the dead in the present. Hurston's travel text is similarly preoccupied with transitions from one state of being to another through its extensive discussions of the *loa*, duppies and zombies that form the ever-present backdrop to the fabric of life in the Caribbean. The slippery relationship between the living and the dead is central to Davis's search for zombies and his attempts to understand what happens during the possession ceremony. Both zombies and those possessed by the *loa* are transformed into empty vessels, but zombies lose their selfhood permanently, while the voodoo devotees return as subjects when the ritual ends and the *loa* leave. Hurston describes the creation of a zombie as a transformation from master to slave, as no one is safe once they are laid to rest in the cemetery, and her vision of how the zombie toils endlessly on a plantation highlights the link between the zombie and the slave and reminds us of Chesnutt's 'Mars Jeems's Nightmare'.

Davis, Hurston and Chesnutt represent three very different approaches to voodoo and conjure. What brings them together across their disparate textual genres, however, is a shared commitment to demonstrating that the demonized and ridiculed belief system developed by slaves and their descendants has an internal coherence and integrity that are inseparable from an understanding of the violence that the institution of slavery inflicted on its many victims. Conjure and voodoo provide the dispossessed within the Afro-diaspora with a meaning-making system that disrupts, subverts and contests the Enlightenment rationality that continues to underpin the economic structures of slavery and post-slavery exploitation and domination. As a competing ontology, voodoo and conjure are tied to the categories of power, agency and possession as these relate to ideas of the human subject. Here, the past in the present and the dead among the living are features of gothic realism, not gothic narrative, as the literatures of the South continue to mediate and negotiate the relationship between the Gothic and gothic through the history and legacies of slavery.

BIBLIOGRAPHY

Chesnutt, C. W. (2000). *Conjure tales and stories of the color line.* New York: Penguin.

Davis, W. (1985). *The serpent and the rainbow.* New York: Simon and Schuster.

Edwards, J. D. (2003). *Gothic passages: Racial ambiguity and the American Gothic.* Iowa City: University of Iowa Press.

Faulkner, W. (1996). *Requiem for a Nun.* 1950. London: Vintage.

Fiedler, L. (1960). *Love and death in the American novel.* New York: Anchor Books.

Goddu, T. A. (1997). *Gothic America: Narrative, history, and nation.* New York: Columbia University Press.

Harris, W. (1999). *Selected essays of Wilson Harris: The unfinished genesis of the imagination.* London/New York: Routledge.

Hemenway, R. (1974). Gothic sociology: Charles Chesnutt and the Gothic mode. *Studies in the Literary Imagination, 7*(1), 101–119.

Hurston, Z. N. (1990). *Tell my horse: Voodoo and life in Haiti and Jamaica.* 1938. New York: Harper & Row.

Luckhurst, R. (2015). *Zombies: A cultural history.* London: Reaktion Books.

FURTHER READING

Deren, M. (1975). *The Voodoo Gods.* Herts: Paladin. Print. This is a study of the intricate structure and function of the range of deities in voodoo.

Herskovits, M. J. (2007). *Life in a Haitian valley.* Princeton: Markus Wiener Publishers. Print. Widely regarded as one of the first serious anthropological records of Haitian voodoo practices.

Hurston, Z. N. (1970). *Mules and men.* New York: Harper & Row. Print. A collection of African American folk tales and hoodoo practices in the American South.

CHAPTER 33

Nothing 'So Mundane as ghosts': Eudora Welty and the Gothic

Sarah Ford

When asked by Alice Walker in an interview if she had ever been called a gothic writer, Eudora Welty responded 'They better not call me that!', but then admitted 'Yes, I have been, though. Inevitably, because I'm a Southerner' ('Eudora' 137). She had a particular version of the Gothic in mind, however, as she explained: 'When I hear the word I see in my mind a Gustave Dore illustration for "The Fall of the House of Usher". Anyway it sounds as if it has nothing to do with real life, and I feel that my work has something to do with real life' (138). Welty's explanation points to the use of the term 'gothic' to denigrate narrative works by suggesting that their use of the supernatural or the grotesque renders their subject too far from 'real life' to matter.

Ellen Glasgow, in being perhaps the first to use the term 'Southern Gothic', indicates just this worry in a 1935 article when she asks the 'novelist of the Southern Gothic school' to 'deal as honestly with living tissues as he now deals with decay' (359). Welty, however, is able to explore those 'living tissues' in part through her use of gothic tropes. Although she wrote only one true ghost story, 'The Purple Hat', her other works are indeed infused with gothic motifs, from crumbling family mansions and damsels in distress to ominous signs and the practice of conjure. That the characters of her story 'Asphodel' picnic in the ruins of a Southern colonial house is emblematic of her fiction, where characters must exist with a past that keeps asserting its influence on the present. Welty does not, however, become fixated on the decay that Glasgow found offensive in Southern fiction. Instead, Welty rewrites gothic conventions, challenging the racial and gender dynamics at play, and using the decay, the grotesque and the darkness to animate her characters' lives. I will show how Welty rewrites the racial colouring of the Gothic in her depiction of African Americans in *Delta Wedding*, and how she rewrites the gender dynamics of

S. Ford (✉)
Baylor University, Waco, TX, USA

© The Editor(s) (if applicable) and The Author(s) 2016   433
S.C. Street, C.L. Crow (eds.), *The Palgrave Handbook of the Southern Gothic*,
DOI 10.1057/978-1-137-47774-3_33

the Gothic in her allusions to Edgar Allan Poe's 'The Raven' in *The Optimist's Daughter.*

In her essay 'Some Notes on River Country', Welty explains that she has never seen in the lost towns between Vicksburg and Natchez anything 'so mundane as ghosts', but has felt 'a sense of place as powerful as if it were visible and walking and could touch me' (*Eye* 186). Her attribution of the power of the past coming back as a 'sense' and not literally as a 'ghost' signals Welty's light hand with gothic devices. Her hauntings are woven into the fabric of her characters' lives, her grotesques are exaggerations of the average, and her sense of the unknowable is often more mysterious than downright terrifying. Nonetheless, the 'sense' of a place imbued with a past occurs repeatedly in her fiction. Most readers of her work attribute this haunting sense to the 'Southernness' of her writing; as she noted in her response to Alice Walker, Gothic and Southern are often conjoined. When the term 'Gothic' is modified by the adjective 'Southern', critics are typically pointing to the heightened use of the grotesque in the works of writers such as William Faulkner and Flannery O'Connor.[1] Charles Crow explains that 'grotesqueness, which involves distortion to the point of the monstrous, is a quality that overlaps with the Gothic, but neither is necessary or sufficient for the other' (129). Alfred Appel, the first critic to identify Welty's work with the gothic genre, argues for a distinction between grotesque and the Gothic. He seemingly prefers the grotesque, echoing the negative connotations of the Gothic, and contends that while 'Gothic writers do not convince us that they are dealing with models of significant reality', grotesque is 'heightened realism' (74). Given this distinction, Appel then argues that Welty's only gothic works are 'The Purple Hat', 'Clytie' and 'The Burning'. Crow also restricts Welty's connection to the Gothic. Offering a close reading of 'Clytie', he finds that 'the compassion Welty evokes toward her characters typically qualifies her stories' Gothic effects' (130).

Both Ruth Weston and Susan Donaldson take a more expansive view of Welty's use of the Gothic, and both focus on gender. Although Weston takes issue with the phrase 'female Gothic' coined by Ellen Moers, because, she argues, 'all forms of the Gothic' investigate issues of gender and power, she nonetheless focuses her analysis on the depiction of women in situations of enclosure and escape, as well as offering readings of Welty's use of gothic settings and spatial devices (*Gothic* 2). Weston's book-length study covers almost all of Welty's oeuvre and demonstrates the pervasiveness of Welty's use of the Gothic. Donaldson focuses her article on Welty's early short story collection *A Curtain of Green*. She compares Welty's depiction of eccentric female characters to William Faulkner's and investigates the ways in which Welty's women who are in the spotlight are not the damsels in distress that the gothic plotline would suggest they should be. They are spectacles, but not unwilling ones. Donaldson asks, 'what happens when one essentially tries to take control of the spotlight and aggressively seeks the gaze of onlookers?' (576). One effect is that the attention is shifted to the observer and the activity of looking, so that 'Welty makes spectacles that are often so outrageous and boundary-breaking that we are never quite sure what we are looking at or where to place ourselves as spectators' (583). Donaldson's reading of this uncertainty points again to Welty's light touch, in that readers are not horrified or filled with terror; they are instead made uneasy. This early collection of stories shows Welty already playing with the conventions of the Gothic in creating women who may be grotesque, but who are not necessarily victims. Weston's argument also follows this line, as she ends her book with a chapter on the female hero in Welty's later works.

My reading will build on these earlier readings by expanding our view of how Welty both uses and rewrites gothic tropes. My intention is not to define any Welty work as 'gothic', in that few of her works have at their core the intention to scare the reader.[2] Instead, I will argue that Welty uses gothic motifs for various effects in many of her narratives, following Weston's view of the pervasiveness of the Gothic in her work. My interest, then, is not gothicism as an identity but rather as a tool, echoing the way in which critics have discussed mythic intertexts in Welty's work.[3] Welty employs myth but she does not write myth. She uses gothic devices, although she rarely writes a truly gothic tale.

DELTA WEDDING

Welty's 1946 novel *Delta Wedding* includes characters who talk to dead relatives, several mentions of local ghosts, a lost girl who seems as much spirit as human, a deadly whirlpool, family members who seemingly replicate former generations, a creepy, abandoned and perhaps haunted house, and scenes of African Americans practising conjure. If the Gothic is a list of ingredients, enough of the ingredients are present to make this a full-fledged gothic novel. However, in keeping with Welty's preference for haunting that is a sense rather than an actual ghost, all of these gothic tropes are relegated to the background. The narrative is told almost exclusively through the points of view of the white female members of the Fairchild family and is generally kept on the comic end of the spectrum, focusing on the details of a wedding. The narrative then exists in a tension between this happy surface and the undercurrent of darkness glimpsed in the traces of the Gothic, creating not terror in the reader, but certainly an uneasiness about the blindness of this family and the future of the fragile world they have created.

Even in the glimpses, though, the gothic tropes do not carry their conventional meanings. Welty instead plays with the connotations that typically provide a kind of shorthand for readers, such as the equation of African American characters to the darkness of the Gothic. Many critics have traced the history of what Toni Morrison calls the 'dark, abiding, signing African presence' in American literature and have found that the issue of race is central to the American rendition of the gothic (*Playing* 4).[4] In *Delta Wedding*, on the narrative's surface the African Americans play the typical gothic role of the Other to highlight and establish the whiteness, or more precisely the fairness, of the Fairchild family. Simply their existence on the margins of the text signals their difference. Morrison explains, 'Even, and especially, when American texts are not "about" Africanist presences or characters or narrative or idiom, the shadow hovers in implication, in sign, in line of demarcation' (*Playing* 46). Yet Welty does not simply leave these characters on the outside of the narrative. In a 1977 interview, Morrison called Welty 'fearless' and claimed that Welty writes 'about black people in a way that few white men have even been able to write' ('Talk' 47). The portrayal of African Americans in *Delta Wedding* is indeed 'fearless' because they do not remain dark, gothic shadows. They intrude as embodied agents.

The white narrators do not note this intrusion, however, because they cannot easily access the motives and desires of the African American characters. David McWhirter even calls the African American characters 'secret agents' because they are figures who 'can't and/or don't want to be known, don't want their stories told, and won't be made to tell them if they don't want to' (119). Nevertheless, I have argued elsewhere that the reader can discern their agency in their laughter, which punctuates the text, and Donnie McMahand claims that the reader can 'decipher the signs of their bodies' (166). Another avenue that critics have not yet explored is their use of conjure.

Working against that surface othering of African American characters are the glimpses we have of African American women employing conjure. We would expect that the practice of 'dark magic' would further confirm the gothicism of the black characters. Robert Hemenway explains that this is typically the case in depiction of conjure: 'conjure is irrational, supernatural in its animism, a magic of the night, in many ways terrifying' (112). He finds in his reading of Charles Chesnutt's *The Conjure Woman* that Chesnutt rewrites the conjure so that it has 'positive effects' and acts as a 'source of redress for an enslaved people', as the 'omnipresent evil' in his stories is not conjure but 'slavery itself' (112). Welty's rewriting of the gothic colouring of conjure is not as sharply critical, but she does depict conjure positively as empowering to African American women and, strangely enough, even to their white counterparts.

The active practice of conjure is part of the separate religious culture of the African Americans in *Delta Wedding*, as exemplified by the young girl Pinchy, who throughout most of the narrative is wandering about the area, attempting to 'come through'. Although not specifically spelled out in the text, the implications of coming through suggest that it is a religious experience that signifies a young girl's maturation.[5] Pinchy succeeds in this on the eve of Dabney's wedding, of which the white characters take note primarily because the servants' celebrations delay the rehearsal dinner. At the wedding, Pinchy is dressed 'all in white' and stands at the front of the other servants, 'where the circle had its joining, making the circle a heart' (*Delta* 300). Pinchy's coming through echoes Dabney's wedding, creating a doppelganger effect. The white women, however, pay little attention to the doubling.

Other instances of African American religious activity are more blatant, and other African American characters seem to have more agency. Partheny, for example, has quite a lot of power for an African American woman in this historical context, although readers must consider her role as a conjure woman seriously to see it. Early in the novel the white matriarch Ellen is summoned by Sylvanus to help Partheny. Ellen immediately understands the reasoning, asking Sylvanus 'Has she had a spell?' and acknowledging Sylvanus's worry that he will get into trouble with 'Mr. Troy' the overseer if he stays with Partheny instead of showing up for work (254). When Ellen arrives at Partheny's house, Partheny explains that the spell is over but that she had been 'mindless' (166). She had been 'standing on Yazoo bridge wid des foot lifted' when Troy stopped and told her not to jump in the river and 'make good white folks fish you out!' (166). Taken on its own, this incident suggests Partheny's weakness, as she needs Ellen and Troy's help. Brannon Costello even labels Ellen's care of her 'paternalistic' (28). Partheny's 'spell' leaves her 'mindless' and weak, so that Barbara Ladd and Donnie McMahand both read her description of her behaviour as attempted suicide. Partheny's status as conjure woman, nevertheless, suggests that the spell may be part of her vision-seeking, much like Pinchy's wanderings in her attempt to come through. So Partheny's standing on the bridge might have been misinterpreted by Troy as an attempted suicide or Partheny might have been about to jump into the river due to the power of her spell instead of the desire to kill herself. Other incidents give us a more complicated view of Ellen and Partheny's relationship.

Partheny was Ellen's nurse when the oldest Fairchild children were little, and out of all of the white characters Ellen alone seems to understand Partheny's powers. Ellen asks Shelley to take a cup of broth to Partheny and to ask her if she knows where Ellen's garnet pin is. The explanation that Ellen gives Shelley for asking Partheny is that 'she came and cooked for your papa's birthday and I had it on my dress' (*Delta* 213). This reasoning, however, does not make much sense, as Ellen would have taken the pin off at the end of the evening, long after the dinner was over and Partheny was gone. Shelley's wording of the question amplifies the seeming silliness: 'maybe you might have seen it floating around somewhere—if maybe you could send word to her where you think it might be. Where to look' (217). Ellen's question only makes sense if she is trying to tap into Partheny's power to locate the pin. Partheny pretends to look around her house, but Shelley spies the undercurrent of conjure: 'this was a lowly kind of errand, a dark place to visit, old Partheny was tricky as the devil' (219).

In first losing and then searching for the garnet pin, Ellen is not simply missing a piece of jewellery. The pin was a gift from her husband when they were courting and throughout the narrative represents female sexuality. Ellen tells the beautiful lost girl in the woods that she was looking for the pin; the girl's red glass buttons suggest that she stands in for the lost sexuality of youth.[6] And when Laura finds the pin, she quickly loses it again in her baptism in the river, which is described as an awakening into womanhood. Partheny understands the pin's significance to Ellen and seems sympathetic: 'I don't know what could have become of Miss Ellen's pretty li'l garnet present, and her comin' down agin, cravin' it, who knows. Sorry as I can be for her' (220). She then substitutes a different but fitting gift.

Partheny gives the girls a 'little patticake' to take to George, with the instruction to 'eat it tonight at midnight, by himse'f, and go to bed' so his wife will then return to him (220). The ingredients, 'a little white dove blood in it, dove heart, blood of a snake', clearly point to Partheny's practice of conjure, a practice that makes her feel powerful: 'giving them all a look of malignity, pride, authority' (220). When Shelley asks how Partheny knew that Robbie had left George, Partheny simply replies, 'ways, ways' (220). Although the cake does not make it to George, it still works its magic, as Louise Westling explains: 'the patticake ends up being eaten by those who need it: Troy and Robbie, the outsider members of the two pairs of lovers, and also by the black girl Pinchy who is undergoing some sort of sexual and spiritual initiation' (36). Partheny's conjure is not treated in the narrative as a malevolent force or dark gothic energy. Although it remains in the background, it exerts power, helping both the African American characters, as Pinchy comes through after eating the patticake, and the white family, as Troy and Dabney are married and George and Robbie are re-united. Partheny may not find Ellen's pin, but she helps to bring about Ellen's deep romantic wish that George's marriage to the lower-class outsider Robbie will prove a happy precedent for Dabney's marriage to the outsider Troy. Partheny's agency with respect to the family is clearly demonstrated at the wedding. She shows up early, dressed in a traditionally royal colour, 'clothed from top to bottom in purple'; she throws the other women out of Dabney's room with 'Git out, Nothin'; and she takes the role normally given to the matriarch to dress the bride (*Delta* 299).

Reading Partheny as powerful but not evil and the practice of conjure as beneficial helps us to read the more enigmatic conjure woman in *Delta Wedding*, Aunt Studney. Her very name, a version of the only response she makes to white people, 'ain't studyin' you', signals her desire not to associate with the family (26). Her mysterious presence intrigues Laura, the city cousin visiting for the wedding. Laura remembers that Aunt Studney always carries a 'big sack', but Roy tells her 'nobody knows what she's got in the sack' (267). When Laura asks where Aunt Studney lives, Roy answers, 'back on our place somewhere. Back of the Deadening' (263). The 'Deadening' is literally the area where the trees were burned off to make the land available for farming, but the word figuratively hints at Aunt Studney's link to the supernatural. She is connected to sexuality as well when Roy declares that Aunt Studney's sack is 'where Mama gets all her babies' (263). As Peggy Prenshaw points out, Aunt Studney shares this link to sexuality with Partheny, 'high priestess of erotic love', so that they both 'appear as keepers of women's mysteries' (57). Perhaps this association with women's sexuality is what allows these conjure women to be beneficial to the white women despite the vast power difference between them. Whether Aunt Studney is in the end as positive towards the family as Partheny remains, however, difficult to discern.

Since Aunt Studney refuses to use language to connect to white people, we are left with interpreting her actions and thus with deciding the motives of the conjure that she performs in Dabney's future house, Marmion. After Roy tells Laura about Aunt Studney, they follow her into the abandoned house, jumping over a dead bird to enter. Marmion was built as a Southern mansion by the children's grandfather, with a double staircase in the entry, a large chandelier, and a piano at the base of the stairs. No one has ever lived in the house, because the grandfather was killed in a duel before it was finished and, in true romantic style, his wife 'died broken-hearted very soon' (209). The house, then, has the requisite background of a haunted mansion, and the mysterious Aunt Studney may play the part of the ghost, or at least the witch. As the children explore the house, Aunt Studney stands in the centre with her bag until 'all at once Aunt Studney sounded too—a cry high and threatening like the first note of a song at a ceremony, a wedding or a funeral, and like the bark of a dog too, somehow' (265). The children then notice bees everywhere and, assuming they came from Aunt Studney's sack, Roy asks her, 'Why have you let bees in my house?' (266).

Aunt Studney is performing some kind of ritual, but it is unclear if it is meant for good or evil. Laura cannot decipher whether that cry is for a funeral or a wedding—a crucial distinction. Aunt Studney could certainly be declaring a funeral and cursing the house. The Fairchild daughter is marrying the overseer, a man who claims that he has the Delta figured out because 'it's just a matter of knowing how to handle your Negroes' (183). And the Fairchild family's wealth, which allows grand weddings and elaborate houses, depends on African American labour. Cursing the house would make Aunt Studney the epitome of the gothic priestess of dark magic seeking retribution. And yet, given the re-writing of the gothic connotations in relation to Partheny, Aunt Studney's actions could have a different meaning.

After the bees are let loose, Laura notices Aunt Studney's behaviour with the sack and realizes that 'Aunt Studney was not on the lookout for things to put in, but was watching to keep things from getting out', suggesting that Aunt Studney has the power to unleash other creatures or perhaps spells into the house, but she chooses bees, which have the positive connotation of fertility (266). Earlier Laura also notices that Aunt Studney hovers over her bag 'like an old bird over her one egg' (265). If the egg and the bees signal fertility and Aunt Studney's cry is that of a wedding, her conjure may be a form of blessing for the new marriage. That Aunt Studney's actions can even possibly be interpreted as beneficial certainly challenges the gothic connotations of conjure as evil. The reader is ultimately not allowed to know why Aunt Studney might be blessing the family, but despite her independence she makes an appearance at Dabney's wedding along with Pinchy and Partheny. Through the depictions of Partheny and Aunt Studney, Welty re-writes the conflation of African Americans with the Gothic and makes that 'dark, abiding, signing Africanist presence' at the margins of the text powerful without its necessarily being evil.

THE OPTIMIST'S DAUGHTER

In *The Optimist's Daughter* Welty performs a different kind of re-writing, focusing this time on gender and targeting a more specific allusion, Edgar Allan Poe's 'The Raven'. Poe's use of rhyme, alliteration and repetition creates the gothic tone for his poem's subject of a man grieving his lost love and imagining that a raven croaking 'nevermore' means that he will be forever trapped in his sorrow. Poe explains in his essay 'The Philosophy of Composition' that his decisions in writing 'The Raven' were not just logical but inevitable. If 'Beauty is the sole legitimate province of the poem', then it follows that the appropriate tone is 'Melancholy' and the topic must be 'Death', which leads Poe to his 'obvious' subject: 'the death, then, of a beautiful woman is, unquestionably, the most poetical topic in the world' (678–80).

Welty's rewriting of 'The Raven' in her own scene of bereavement with a bird challenges the natural order of Poe's Gothic. In *The Optimist's Daughter*, Laurel Hand has returned to her hometown in Mississippi for her father's funeral. The experience causes her to confront not just her father's death, but also his choice to re-marry, her earlier move from her hometown to pursue a career, and finally her mother's death years before. After her father's funeral, Laurel returns to her family home alone, only to find that a chimney swift has got into the house. Characters in *Delta Wedding* acknowledge the folk superstition that a 'bird in de house mean death!' and in *The Optimist's Daughter* the connection of the bird to death is clear (Trouard 248). Maybe even too clear. Dawn Trouard complains that the bird's meaning is over-determined and makes a list of ideas that the bird equals in the narrative, such as 'bird = Laurel', 'bird = death' and 'bird = freedom' (240).

If the chimney swift, however, is a re-writing of Poe's raven, its presence during Laurel's night of remembering points to Welty's play with the gender dynamics of the Gothic. Laurel discovers that a bird has taken refuge from a storm: 'the bird touched, tapped, brushed itself against the walls and closed doors, never resting' (*Optimist* 962). Welty's language echoes Poe's, as the raven is described several times as 'tapping' on the chamber door and then later repeating 'nevermore' ('Raven' 58–61). Welty exchanges Poe's male narrator for the female Laurel and has her shut the door against the bird instead of letting it in, but the uncanny sense that something is wrong is the same. Laurel asks, 'What am I in danger of here?' as her heart is 'pounding' (*Optimist* 962).

As the bird continues 'beating against the door' throughout the scene, Laurel retreats from her parents' bedroom into an adjacent smaller room, which her mother had used as a sewing room. This small room has the opposite connotations of closet-like rooms in the gothic tradition. Anne Williams explains that in the architecture of the Gothic, 'dungeons, attics, secret rooms, and dark hidden passages connote the culturally female, the sexual, the maternal, the unconscious'; these places not only hold secrets, but also 'dark female "otherness"' (44). Although the sewing room is certainly a female space, instead of the terror associated with secrets hidden in a dark room, Laurel remembers 'firelight and warmth' (*Optimist* 964). She is comforted by the quiet and finds her mother's desk. This 'secretary' would be expected in a typical gothic novel to house disturbing secrets, but instead the desk has, as Laurel discovers, no key to keep her from reading her mother's papers. Ruth Weston proposes that the mother's desk being 'exiled' to the sewing room suggests 'the confinement of the madwoman in the attic' ('Feminine' 85). However, even with the gothic structure of the scene, the import is reversed, and the room will give Laurel insight instead of fright.

With the allusion to Poe, this insight is unexpected. The obsession with the death of a beautiful woman leaves Poe's narrator helpless and distraught. He asks the raven if his lost Lenore is in Heaven. The raven's anticipated answer of 'nevermore' leaves the poet anguishing over never seeing Lenore again. Welty's character Laurel, however, discovers that in going through her mother's desk, she is able to bring her mother back to life. She finds in the 'pigeonholes' of the desk the letters her father wrote when her parents were courting and a present of river stone her father had given her mother. When Laurel looks through a book of photographs, something remarkable happens. Her mother begins speaking: 'the most beautiful blouse I ever owned in my life—I made it' (*Optimist* 966). Throughout the rest of the scene Laurel's memories are interspersed with her mother's voice telling stories. When Laurel, for example, remembers that her mother taught school, she hears 'I rode [our horse] to school. Seven miles over Nine Mile Mountain, seven miles home' (966–7). And as the storm rages outside and Laurel feels the house 'shaking after a long roll of thunder', she hears her mother say 'Up home, we loved a good storm coming, we'd fly outdoors and run up and down to meet it' (971). The gothic setting is overturned by a voice from the past that is not haunting but comforting. Unlike Poe's gothic vision where the beautiful woman must die to be the subject of poetry, the woman here is remembered by another woman as very much alive, even after her death. When Laurel recalls her mother's painful last five years as an invalid and the anger that her mother expressed in being helpless, she is still letting her mother speak. Rebecca Mark argues that Laurel 'is saving [her mother's] life by telling her story in a way that shows not only empathy and compassion but deep understanding of the incredible complexity and depth of passion, anger, love that was her mother's life' ('Wild' 347). Although Poe's narrator is left with a raven that 'still is sitting, still is sitting' (61), Laurel frees the chimney swift the next morning.

CONCLUSION

The family home in *The Optimist's Daughter* and the abandoned Marmion in *Delta Wedding* become sites of haunting because they are places with the sense that Welty felt in River Country of a past powerful enough to become visible. The patticake Partheny bakes, the bees Aunt Studney lets loose and the bird trapped in Laurel's home are different to the 'mundane' ghosts with which Welty did not want to be associated in eschewing the gothic label. They function like ghosts, though, in hinting at a world beyond the ordinary one, a world just as real and just as significant for Welty's characters. Although this other world may not evoke fear or terror in the reader, the uneasiness that the glimpses of darkness cause serves to signal that Welty is summoning the presence of the Gothic. In incorporating elements of the Gothic, however, she revises the standard connotations, making the damsel in distress into a spectacle or heroine, the conjure woman into a force for good and the beautiful woman alive again. Welty makes the Gothic her own tool and, in these rewritings, makes it speak to 'real life'.

NOTES

1. See Botting 160–61.
2. For a discussion of the reader's visceral response to traditional Gothic, see Clemens.
3. See Mark, *Dragon*.
4. For a discussion of American Gothic and race, see Goddu.
5. When asked in an interview about the meaning of the phrase 'coming through', Welty responded, 'It is just a term that meant that you would get religion' ('Seeing' 255).
6. See Graham-Bertolini for a reading of the lost girl as a 'phantom of the younger Ellen' (102).

BIBLIOGRAPHY

Appel, A., Jr. (1965). *A season of dreams the fiction of Eudora Welty.* Baton Rouge: Louisiana State UP.

Botting, F. (1996). *Gothic.* New York: Routledge.

Clemens, V. (1999). *The return of the repressed: Gothic horror from the castle of Otranto to Alien.* New York: State University of New York Press.

Costello, B. (2004). Playing lady and imitating Aristocrats: Race, class, and money in *Delta Wedding* and *The Ponder Heart. Southern Quarterly, 42*(3), 21–54.

Crow, C. (2009). *History of the Gothic: American Gothic.* Cardiff: University of Wales Press.

Glasgow, E. (1935). Heroes and monsters. *Saturday Review of Literature, 4*(May), 3–4. Rpt. in J. E. Bassett (Ed.), *Defining southern literature: Perspectives and assessments, 1831–1952* (357–360). Cranbury: Associated University Presses, 1997.

Goddu, T. A. (1997). *Gothic America: Narrative, history, and nation.* New York: Columbia UP.

Graham-Bertolini, A. (2013). Searching for the Garnet pin: Confluence as narrative technique in Eudora Welty's *delta wedding. Eudora Welty Review, 5,* 95–108.

Hemenway, R. (1974). Gothic sociology: Charles Chesnutt. *Studies in the Literary Imagination, 7,* 101–119.

Ladd, B. (1988). Coming through: The black initiate in *delta wedding'. Mississippi Quarterly, 41*(4), 541–551.

Mark, R. (1994). *Dragon's blood: Feminist intertextuality in Eudora Welty's the Golden Apples.* Jackson: UP of Mississippi.

Mark, R. (2003). Wild strawberries, cataracts, and climbing roses: Clitoral and seminal imagery in *the optimist's daughter. Mississippi Quarterly, 56*(2), 331–350.

McMahand, D. (2013). Bodies on the brink: Vision, violence, and self-destruction in *delta wedding.* In H. Pollack (Ed.), *Eudora Welty, whiteness, and race* (pp. 165–184). Athens: University of Georgia Press.

McWhirter, D. (2013). Secret agents: Welty's African Americans. In H. Pollack (Ed.), *Eudora Welty, whiteness, and race* (pp. 114–130). Athens: University of Georgia Press.

Morrison, T. (1993). *Playing in the dark: Whiteness and the literary imagination.* New York: Vintage Books.

Morrison, T. (1994). Talk with Toni Morrison. Interview by Mel Watkins. In D. Taylor-Guthrie (Ed.), *Conversations with Toni Morrison* (pp. 43–47). Jackson: UP of Mississippi.

Poe, E. A. (2004a). The philosophy of composition. In G. R. Thompson (Ed.), *The selected writings of Edgar Allan Poe* (pp. 675–684). New York: W.W. Norton.

Poe, E. A. (2004b). The Raven. In G. R. Thompson (Ed.), *The selected writings of Edgar Allan Poe* (pp. 58–61). New York: W.W. Norton.

Prenshaw, P. (1979). Woman's world, man's place: The fiction of Eudora Welty. In L. Dollarhide & A. J. Abadie (Eds.), *Eudora Welty: A form of thanks* (pp. 46–77). Jackson: UP of Mississippi.

Trouard, D. (2003). Burying below sea level: The erotics of sex and death in *the optimist's daughter. Mississippi Quarterly, 56*(2), 231–250.

Welty, E. (1942). *The eye of the story: Selected essays and reviews.* New York: Vintage.

Welty, E. (1984). Eudora Welty: An interview. By Alice Walker. In P. W. Prenshaw (Ed.), *Conversations with Eudora Welty* (pp. 131–140). Jackson: UP of Mississippi.

Welty, E. (1996). Seeing real things: An interview with Eudora Welty. By Jan Nordby Gretlund. In P. W. Prenshaw (Ed.), *More conversations with Eudora Welty* (pp. 248–261). Jackson: UP of Mississippi.

Welty, E. (1998a). In R. Ford & M. Kreyling (Eds.), *Delta Wedding. 1946. Eudora Welty: Complete novels* (pp. 89–336). New York: Library of America.

Welty, E. (1998b). In R. Ford & M. Kreyling (Eds.), *The optimist's daughter. 1969. Eudora Welty: Complete novels* (pp. 881–994). New York: Library of America.

Westling, L. (1992). Food, landscape and the feminine in *Delta Wedding. Southern Quarterly, 30*(2–3), 29–40.

Weston, R. D. (1987). The feminine and feminist texts of Eudora Welty's *The Optimist's Daughter. South Central Review, 4*(4), 74–91.

Weston, R. D. (1994). *Gothic traditions and narrative techniques in the fiction of Eudora Welty.* Baton Rouge: Louisiana State UP.

Williams, A. (1995). *Art of darkness: A poetics of Gothic.* Chicago: University of Chicago Press.

Further Reading

Fuller, S. M. (2013). *Eudora Welty and surrealism.* Jackson: UP of Mississippi. Fuller seeks to counter the reading of Welty's work as strictly regional by arguing for an interdisciplinary approach. He examines the influence of the Surrealist movement on Welty's works, specifically *A Curtain of Green, The Wide Net, Delta Wedding, The Golden Apples* and *The Bride of Innisfallen,* and finds that 'ambiguity in figural representation characterizes swaths of Welty's fiction' (49).

Gygax, F. (1990). *Serious daring from within: Female narrative strategies in Eudora Welty's novels.* New York: Greenwood P. Gygax offers a feminist reading of Welty's work focusing on four texts: *Delta Wedding, The Golden Apples, Losing Battles* and *The Optimist's Daughter.* She borrows from narratology to study Welty's narrative techniques, such as point of view.

Kreyling, M. (1980). *Eudora Welty's achievement of order*. Baton Rouge: Louisiana State UP. Kreyling traces the order or unity in Welty's works through a study of her technique. He examines history context in *The Robber Bridegroom*, point of view in *Delta Wedding* and *Losing Battles*, mythological patterns in *The Golden Apples*, monologue in *The Ponder Heart* and resolution in *The Optimist's Daughter*.

Marrs, S. (2005). *Eudora Welty: A biography*. New York: Harcourt, Inc. In this extensive and authoritative biography, Marrs details Welty's life, family and experiences, placing Welty's photography and written works in the context of the events of her life.

Woolf, S. (2015). *A dark rose: Love in Eudora Welty's stories and novels*. Baton Rouge: Louisiana State UP. In her examination of Welty's works, Woolf finds a persistent focus on love in its various guises. She argues that in each work the beauty and promise of love are tempered by a dark counter-story of loss and loneliness.

CHAPTER 34

Talismans of Shadows and Mantles of Light: Contemporary Forms of the Southern Female Gothic

Peggy Dunn Bailey

The literary Gothic is the language of trauma; it records and reveals wounds and losses so profound that their repression, or abjection, seems necessary but is impossible. Gothic writers who reveal the role that gender plays in trauma experienced by women write Female Gothic texts. While some contemporary Female Gothic texts are superficially quite different from the primarily late eighteenth- and early nineteenth-century British novels that Ellen Moers examines in *Literary Women* (in which the term 'Female Gothic' was introduced in 1976), they combine a focus on forms of suffering and anxiety that Moers links specifically to 'female experience' with a more explicit awareness than Moers articulates of the role of cultural ideology in women's trauma. Southern Gothic fiction by women often exhibits the Female Gothic's tell-tale focus on women's trauma within the context of the Southern Gothic tradition. Southern Gothic literature is fueled by the need to come to terms with foundational trauma (often both individual and cultural), the violation or loss of that which is essential to identity and survival but often irretrievable. Southern Gothic literature is characterized by obsessive preoccupations—with blood, family, and inheritance as well as the construction, destruction, and/or blurring of the boundaries of gender, race, and class—and the compulsion to talk (or write) about these preoccupations. Themes of family/blood as destiny and the centrality to identity of 'place' (geographic and socio-economic) abound in Southern Gothic texts.

There are dialects of the literary Southern Female Gothic, discernibly different forms that are nonetheless prone to borrowings and exchanges. The

P.D. Bailey (✉)
Arkansas's Public Liberal Arts University, Arkadelphia, AR, USA

© The Editor(s) (if applicable) and The Author(s) 2016
S.C. Street, C.L. Crow (eds.), *The Palgrave Handbook of the Southern Gothic*,
DOI 10.1057/978-1-137-47774-3_34

445

Supernatural Gothic is replete with witches, vampires, and ghosts; intriguingly, along with this emphasis on the supernatural is an unrelenting focus on the primal power of material, bodily reality—specifically blood (inherited, transmitted, spilled, and/or taken)—to determine identity and fate, especially for female characters. An example of the Supernatural Southern Female Gothic in contemporary literature is Anne Rice's *The Witching Hour* (1990), which begins the Chronicles of the Mayfair Witches. While the theme of bloodline as fate appears as frequently in the Realistic Gothic as it does in the Supernatural, the Realistic Gothic tends to expose more directly the *cultural* determinants of trauma and to reveal the inscription of identity through broader, social models of gender, class, and ethnicity. In *Bastard Out of Carolina* (1992), Dorothy Allison re-writes the Female Gothic from the perspective of a twentieth-century, 'white trash' Southern girl. The Supranatural or Romantic Gothic is formed by the impact of Romantic characteristics on the Gothic. The most visible of these Romantic characteristics are a predominance of oracles and/or the oracular mode; the depiction of Nature as sentient and capable of direct, personal intervention in human life; an investment in the concepts of liberty, equality, brotherhood, and sisterhood; and an emphasis on the revolutionary power of the mind to participate in the creation of 'reality.' A novel of epic proportions that traces the socio-political history of nineteenth- and twentieth-century Cuba via fictional family histories that illuminate modern-day Cuba's 'three origins' (Spanish, African, and Chinese), Daína Chaviano's *The Island of Eternal Love* (2006, English trans. 2008) is a Supranatural Southern Female Gothic text. It features not one gothic heroine but several, and in its depiction of a house that haunts the most recent of these heroines, it provides a fresh metaphor for the Gothic's longstanding insistence on the inescapability of the past and of the primal power of place, bloodline, and *home* to shape identity and destiny at the same time that it emphasizes the transformational power of art, storytelling, and love.

CHRONICLES OF THE MAYFAIR WITCHES

One does not become a witch; one is born a witch. Anne Rice's Chronicles of the Mayfair Witches abound with evidence in support of such an essentialist assertion. The first of the Chronicles, *The Witching Hour*, is a Female Gothic tale just short of 1000 pages in length and marked by supernatural occurrences, beautiful, powerful, sensual, and doomed characters, and expressions of forbidden sexuality (most notably, incest). It features a familiar spirit who appears and attaches himself to a different Mayfair witch each generation and an ancestral mansion—home to dark secrets and acts of imprisonment and violence—in a lush Southern environment (the Garden District of New Orleans, Louisiana). The site of devastating epidemics, fires, floods, and hurricanes, New Orleans is also the port city through which legions of Africans (the ones who survived the passage) entered into a life of enslavement in the New World, and enslavement literal and metaphoric is a recurrent motif in this novel, as it is virtually any gothic text. Whether imprisoned in dungeons, attics, jail cells, convents, or more comfortable and even opulent environments, the most haunted—and, ultimately, doomed—characters in the Gothic are those who are enslaved by forces both internal and beyond their conscious control. While other characters or events may be their avatars, these forces—presented as inherited predilec- tions, affections, capacities, and desires—are more intransigent than any jailer, for bloodline and family history are utterly impossible to change via act of will, and they dictate, far more often than many would be comfortable owning, one's thoughts, actions, motivations, and desires.

Most of the tale consists of flashbacks, fittingly provided—given the pre- dominance of found manuscripts (letters, wills, deeds) in the Gothic—by centuries-old documents created and held by an order of scholars of the super- natural, the Talamasca. Through these documents, the reader of *The Witching Hour* is immersed in narratives of generations of the Mayfair witches, begin- ning with the 'simpleton' Suzanne, the 'cunning woman' and midwife who summoned the spirit Lasher to one of the ancient stone circles of Scotland in the seventeenth century (ironically, alerted to the possibility of such an action by the books of a lascivious 'witch hunter' who enjoyed his work—and Suzanne's body), and ending with the thirteenth witch in the line, Rowan, whose inherited desire and ability to heal physical ailments manifest themselves in neurosurgery guided by instinct as well as medical training. However, her lack of knowledge regarding her family history combined with her belief that she is powerful enough to control the spirit who has manifested itself to—and through—generations of her family (a belief that goes back at least as far as the third witch, Charlotte, whom Rowan resembles in both body and spirit) sets the stage for this Mayfair witch to accomplish not her will and desire, but Lasher's; it will be Rowan who quite literally gives birth to monsters.

Rowan's very name suggests the ultimately self-defeating nature of the 'born witch' in this Female Gothic text. Named for the tree believed to ward off witchcraft, Rowan, like many of her maternal line, possesses a prodigious will and a powerful mind; a physician with decidedly metaphysical abilities (mind and body 'reading' of a sort that defies scientific explanation), her capacity for healing is linked to a powerful ability—and sometimes desire—to destroy (via conceptualizing the blood vessels and rupturing them, telekinetically). While the preceding description may superficially bear little resemblance to the Female Gothic heroine as she appears in the original Female Gothic novels of the eighteenth and nineteenth centuries (a motherless, vulnerable young woman facing the threat, if not the reality, of confinement and/or violation), a closer examination of Rowan's character and situation at the beginning of the novel reveals the viable possibility of reading her as a Female Gothic heroine. She is, indeed, motherless. Having been taken as a newborn from her biologi- cal mother, Deirdre, whose catatonia rendered her metaphorically absent long before her actual death, Rowan has recently lost even her adoptive mother to cancer when the novel opens. While not a teenager, as so many of the late eighteenth-century gothic heroines were, Rowan is still young; despite her keen intelligence, professionalism, and wealth, she is vulnerable and alone—until Deirdre's death triggers the series of events that brings Rowan home to New Orleans. This gothic heroine's enslavement pre-exists her awareness of it; it takes the form of her inherent difference from other, 'normal' people, her seeming isolation, her compulsions, and the supernatural abilities that she utterly refuses to acknowledge as such. Her violation arguably begins the night that the spirit Lasher first appears to her, immediately after her mother's death. Although Rowan is no Radcliffean—ulta-virtuous, always chaste—heroine, she is imprisoned by bloodline, inheritance, and family history.

Rowan is the thirteenth witch in a long line of witches born with an extra set of chromosomes; the Mayfair witches are thus essentially different from other human beings—a race or even a species apart—and a close examination of Rice's text reveals something much more significant than gothic fantasy in the pages of *The Witching Hour*. 'Indeed,' as Frank A. Salamone, a professor of anthropology and sociology, writes, 'Rice's treatment of witchcraft as an innate tendency bound with physiological characteristics, in her telling genetic, bears a close relationship to anthropological treatments of the subject' (48–9). Salamone examines the ways in which Rice, in the *Chronicles*, 'illustrates a grasp of basic anthropological principles: the ambiguity of "reality," the relativity of good and evil, the role of perspective in understanding and interpretation, the interaction of nature and nurture, and the conflict and dependence of humanism and science,' and identifies in the study of literary texts such as Rice's the formation of 'a promising subgenre of the emerging but still nameless field of work stemming from the *rapprochement* between literary studies and anthropology' (37). His comments on Rice's 'treatment of a matrilineal/ matrilateral descent system' and her representation of the 'descent of witchcraft through the mother's line …, found in most African witchcraft' (49) are especially appropriate to this study of forms of the Female Gothic, for a version of this 'representation' reappears in Chaviano's Supranatural Southern Female Gothic text, *The Island of Eternal Love*.

Rowan, like her foremothers in Rice's novel and in the Female Gothic, is prone to victimization, especially victimization of a sexual nature, even though her education, wealth, and personality blind her to this fact. She becomes the sexual prey of a supernatural predator, Lasher, who has a deliberate agenda. Lasher 'seduces' Rowan as a prelude to repeated rape; his goal is full, material embodiment and reproduction. Despite Rowan's image of herself (as a hyper-competent, brilliant neurosurgeon, and sexually liberated woman whose pleasure comes on her own terms), and despite her claim that she is 'a doctor first and foremost[,] only a woman and a person second' (Rice 697), Rowan's femaleness has everything to do with the horrors that happen to—and through—her. For Lasher requires a female vessel and vehicle for his full entrance into material reality, and his gifts (virtually limitless wealth, supernatural knowledge, erotic pleasure, *himself* as a powerful, virtually indestructible ally) come at a steep price; once a witch sees and acknowledges Lasher and his power, she is his as much as, or more than, he is hers.

BASTARD OUT OF CAROLINA

On first glance, Dorothy Allison's hyper-realistic, semi-autobiographical narrative of grinding poverty, family violence, and childhood sexual abuse might seem to have little in common with the opulent, supernatural world that Rice's Mayfair witches inhabit, but *Bastard Out of Carolina*, like *The Witching Hour*, is fundamentally a Southern Female Gothic text.[1] It explores the themes of family/bloodline as destiny and the importance of place. In Rice's supernatural universe, one's identity as a witch is a matter of blood rather than choice or even practice, and the beautiful, sensual, and fabulously wealthy Mayfairs are literally a race, class, and/or (with their extra set of chromosomes) species unto themselves. Allison's Boatwright clan exhibits the theme of family/blood as destiny as well. Their status as 'poor white trash' is also a matter of inherited identity, a compound of race and class that determines perception (by self and others) and therefore behavior and response, and this inherited identity is rooted, as Allison demonstrates throughout the text, in the family's physical, geographic environment. Readers who proceed from *The Witching Hour* to the other chronicles learn why the original summoning of Lasher took place in an ancient stone circle in Scotland, but southern locales—from the south of France, to the Caribbean island of St. Domingue (now Haiti), to Louisiana—are home to and for the majority of Rice's Mayfairs, certainly the central 'legacy family' of First Street in New Orleans, and some of these characters—especially the female Mayfairs who try to resist Lasher's 'gifts'—experience home simultaneously as refuge and prison, sanctuary and purgatory. Allison's Boatwrights seem tied to the Southern home-place as well, so much so that this home-place is presented in the very title of the text as the source of identity: Ruth Anne (Bone) Boatwright is the 'bastard' *out of* Carolina, and the adverb followed by a preposition underscores the novel's revelation that Bone's identity—and, it seems, her destiny—was created by and through the culture out of which she came as well as the family into which she was born.

Bone is the narrator of the novel and a quasi-fictional representation of author Dorothy Allison's younger self. Bone grows up poor in mid-twentieth-century Greenville, South Carolina, a place that she says was, in 1955, 'the most beautiful place in the world' (*Bastard* 17). Writing of the same place and time in her memoir/performance piece *Two or Three Things I Know for Sure*, Allison describes 'home' in more gothic terms; she emphasizes the connection between fertility and decay, attraction and repulsion: 'Everything was ripe, everything was rotting …. That country was beautiful, I swear to you, the most beautiful place I've ever been. Beautiful and terrible. It is the country of my dreams and the country of my nightmares' (*Two* 6–7). Unlike the rental houses into and out of which Bone's stepfather moves the family throughout her childhood, her larger home is a complex mix of geography, socio-economic condition, and emotional associations.

Although it contains hints of the supernatural in its characterization and narrative—for instance, the 'women's magic' (*Bastard* 44) of two of Bone's aunts and her Uncle Earle's propensity to liken an especially fertile female family member to a 'vampire' (128)—Allison's text exhibits its Realistic Southern Gothic heritage via its emphasis on the inscription of identity through cultural models of gender, class, and ethnicity. It further signals its kinship to the Realistic Gothic tradition—the tradition of Faulkner, O'Connor, and Tennessee Williams, the latter two with whom Allison explicitly aligns herself as a writer in a 1994 interview ('Moving' 81)—through its reliance on literary grotesques. Allison's grotesques are far from the sexually alluring and glamorous witches-by-birth and vampires of Rice's Supernatural Gothic; they are the 'bad poor,' the 'poor white trash' often spoken of as a race apart, perhaps not even fully human (Wray and Newitz).

Allison's Bone Boatwright is a contemporary Southern version of the original, eighteenth- and nineteenth-century Female Gothic heroine. She is young and vulnerable; the novel ends when she is a few weeks shy of her 13th birthday. She has been raped by her stepfather, Daddy Glen, and Allison's depiction and placement of the brutal scene support Laura S. Patterson's claim that Glen's rape of Bone 'represents rage against a matriarchal community' (41). As a further form of betrayal, Bone has been abandoned by her mother, Anney, who has left her and (re)joined her husband, Bone's rapist. Bone leans against Raylene, the aunt who, in Anney's absence, performs the role of nurturing mother, and 'the night close[s] in around [them]' (*Bastard* 309). Before the final scene fades to black, however, Bone thinks empathetically of her mother, identifies with her, reaches toward understanding and connection. She knows that she is the daughter of a mother who was also young and vulnerable. In fact, Bone's narrative suggests that this female vulnerability may very well be inherited, passed from mother to daughter, a cultural reality of trans-generational female suffering that calls into question, as the Gothic so frequently does, the optimistic rhetoric of self-determinism. Bone's mother did not, like the mothers of earlier gothic heroines, die and leave her child vulnerable; believing that marrying a man was the only way to redeem her child from 'illegitimacy,' she lived in a way that helped make her so.

Attempting to explain her choices (to stay with Glen, to return to him time and time again), Anney says to Bone, 'I just loved him so I couldn't see him that way. I couldn't believe. I couldn't imagine' (306). Her words suggest powerlessness, inability (she 'couldn't see,' 'couldn't believe,' 'couldn't imagine') rather than active choice. She sounds very much as Bone describes her during this devastating moment between mother and daughter: 'Bones seemed to have moved, flesh fallen away, and lines deepened into gullies, while shadows darkened to streaks of midnight' (306). Anney sounds broken, beaten, and old, and she looks like a decaying corpse. Supernatural monsters are not required for gothic fiction or for gothic reality; human predators can do such violence that their victims are, essentially, the walking dead, and inherited modes of thinking and living can so blind and enslave that not even the thought of an alternative to the horror occurs to the victim living a gothic reality.

THE ISLAND OF ETERNAL LOVE

Thankfully, alternatives—and even antidotes—to enslavement, victimization, and horror do exist, and sometimes they manifest themselves in supranatural ways. In a 2010 interview with Silvia Viñas, Daína Chaviano discusses her writing style and explicitly identifies *The Island of Eternal Love* as a gothic novel. Viñas asks Chaviano, 'How is your writing style different from Magical Realism? Is it in any way similar?' Chaviano responds:

> I know very little about magical realism for one reason. The few novels I know, classified as such, have not given me much enthusiasm. … Critics tend to think that if a ghostly element is placed in a Caribbean setting it must be magical realism, but I could have placed that plot in the Scotland of Mary Stewart. Maybe then they would have understood that this is a Gothic novel. In fact, I've said elsewhere that the novels of *The Occult Side of Havana* series [of which *Island* is a part] belong to what I call 'Caribbean gothic,' a term I've used to classify my own books, because no critic has managed to do it. (2)

As a dialect of the Southern Gothic, the Caribbean Gothic offers scholars invaluable opportunities: to see the familiar Southern Gothic preoccupations from a different perspective, to recognize new versions and embodiments of those preoccupations, to enrich—perhaps even revise—what we mean by Southern and Gothic. For Cubans, the southernmost regions of the United States are 'the North,' and Chaviano's novel, as well as her comments on it, alerts us to the existence of a branch of the Southern Gothic family tree that is remarkable for its incorporation of the characteristics of the Supernatural *and* the Realistic Gothic, and for its affirmation of the possibility of light dispelling the gothic shadows of the past. Chaviano's novel is a Supranatural, Romantic Gothic text that is insistent in its focus on life and reality not as a matter of antagonistic contraries but of potential and revolutionary unions—of past and present, blood and history, family and culture, art and lived experience—and on the possibilities of revision and transformation.

The Island of Eternal Love is the only one of Chaviano's novels to be translated from Spanish into English, and the title refers to the author's native Cuba. The novel is divided into six parts: 'The Three Origins,' 'Gods Who Speak a Honeyed Tongue,' 'City of Oracles,' 'Passion and Death in the Year of the Tiger,' 'The Season of the Red Warriors,' and 'Chinese Puzzle.' Individual chapter titles are taken from the boleros that echo throughout the text and serve to reflect or comment on characters' experiences and states of mind, as well as to suggest thematic threads connecting characters, times, and storylines. The boleros are intimately associated with the supernatural. For example, they accompany the appearance of Amalia, the woman in the darkened Miami nightclub who mesmerizes the contemporary heroine, Cecilia, with her detailed stories of the generations of three families whose lives intertwined in Cuba; by the end of the novel, Cecilia has no choice but to accept the truth—she has been conversing with a ghost.

Cuban music represents Cuban identity throughout the novel, and music is also associated with spiritual forces and, as previously noted, supernatural events in the narrative. Identifying a few of the ways in which this association is demonstrated allows readers to begin to grasp the intermingling of bloodlines, cultures, times, and characters that marks this complex tale. In a nineteenth-century Cuban brothel, a woman plays the drums and chants a song to the African goddess Oshùn, and, possessed by this powerful spirit, a former slave, Caridad, and her young daughter Mercedes (who was listening and observing without the adults' knowledge) become purely creatures of sexual pleasure. Mercedes seems destined—by forces both external (cultural attitudes regarding gender, race, and class) and internal (her 'possession')—to live the rest of her life as a prostitute until a brave young man, José, falls in love with her, and a violent encounter that almost leads to her death triggers instead a type of exorcism. When she recovers from her physical and psycho-spiritual wounds, she emerges as a new creature, with a new 'history' (constructed in part by the loving José); she is re-born as José's wife and the mother of a baby girl (Amalia). The brothel out of which Mercedes emerges is run by a character called Miz Ceci, whose real name is Cecilia. The contemporary Cecilia's mother had been enamored with *Cecilia Valdés*, the nineteenth-century Cuban novel by Cirilo Villaverde that inspired the zarzuela of the same name. *Cecilia Valdés* reveals the ways in which colonization creates dynamics of race, class, and gender that interact to forge identity and destiny; notably, the title character finds herself enslaved by these dynamics. The contemporary Cecilia's mother had only *thought* she was naming her baby girl after a character in a work of art. She was tapping into a parallel 'reality'; not one played out faithfully in her own daughter's life, but one with marked similarities to Mercedes's life, with one remarkable difference: Mercedes is rescued, freed by love and, as readers may later discern, spiritual intercession. Art (the novel/zarzuela *Cecilia Valdés*) was not simply reflecting 'real life,' and 'real life' was not simply imitating art; instead, they were both narratives—with implications and connections to other narratives of which even their authors were unaware.

Other elements of *The Island of Eternal Love* that demonstrate the link between music and the supernatural and speak to the novel's gothic heritage include a recording studio that is named The Imp (run by José and Mercedes) and the appearance in the text of Rita Montaner, the great Cuban singer known for her performances of zarzuelas (including *Cecilia Valdés*) and her enchanted silver shawl, Mexican Blood. The Imp is named for Martinico, a mischievous and quarrelsome spirit who first appears in the novel when he attaches himself to Angela, a young woman in Spain. When Angela sees Martinico and the imp begins manifesting its restless energy, her mother takes her to a Priestess, who diagnoses the girl as suffering from the Evil Eye and attempts an exorcism (35–7). However, Angela's mother knows at least part of why her daughter is behaving so strangely: 'all the women in her family, since time immemorial, had been shadowed by a certain impish creature named Martinico,' who is, essentially, a legacy: 'The wife of the firstborn son inherits it' (37). Angela's father is devastated: '[H]is daughter's blood was contaminated with the family's supernatural curse' (38). Like generations before them, Angela's parents flee their home, attempting to escape the 'curse,' but Martinico follows Angela and her family across the Atlantic to Cuba in the nineteenth century, where it/he continues to appear to women destined to join the family. Readers learn that Angela is Amalia's paternal grandmother, and at the end of the novel the contemporary Cecilia, after meeting Miguel, Amalia's grandson, sees Martinico.

As for 'Mexican Blood,' the great singer Rita Montaner informs the young Amalia that her shawl's name derives from its essence; it is made of pure silver, which Rita notes 'flows from the earth there [in Mexico] as blood does from the people' (213). Furthermore, Rita tells Amalia, the shawl is 'bewitched … [w]ith a spell from the time when the pyramids were covered with blood and flowers. "If the mantle of light comes in contact with a talisman of shadows in the presence of two strangers, they will love each other forever"' (214). The 'talisman of shadows' is the amulet that Amalia is given at birth by her mother, Mercedes, to protect her from the Evil Eye (the same amulet that Cecilia discerns hanging around the mysterious woman's neck in the bar in Miami in the late twentieth century). Meanwhile, the young Pag Li (Pablo), on an errand for his Chinese parents who run a laundry in Cuba, comes to the 'wrong door' with his laundry delivery. Amalia's amulet falls from her neck; Pablo bends to retrieve it, and his fingers brush 'Mexican blood.' Amalia and Pablo marry and have a daughter, Isabel, who gives birth to a son, Miguel, who carries in his blood Cuba's 'three origins.' At the end of the novel, Cecilia and Miguel, guided by the ghost of Amalia, meet. Nevertheless, as a Female Gothic heroine, Cecilia must traverse some rough terrain before she reaches home, or—more to the point in this Supranatural Gothic text—before home reaches her.

Cecilia is an orphan haunted by the past and obsessed with a mysterious 'phantom house' that appears on different dates at different locations in Miami, a house that becomes her 'Holy Grail' (186). Cecilia, dubbed by a friend 'Saint Cecilia of Havana in Ruins' (92), only thinks that she is 'indifferent to her [cultural] past' (91); she is, in fact, mourning it and living the life of an exile in modern-day Miami:

> She had left her country escaping many things, so many that there was no longer any value in remembering them. And as she watched the crumbling buildings along the Malecón disappear into the horizon—in that strange summer of 1994 when so many fled the island on rafts in broad daylight—she swore she would never return. Now, four years later, she was still afloat. She wanted nothing to do with the country she'd left behind, but she still felt like a stranger in the city that housed the largest number of Cubans in the world after Havana. (6)

Although she works as a journalist, socializes with a couple of friends, and takes a lover, she is haunted by a terrible loneliness: 'The worst part was that feeling of perpetual loneliness. Her scant family, except for a great-aunt who had arrived thirty years earlier, still remained on the island; the rest of her companions—with whom she had grown up, laughed, and suffered—were scattered throughout the world' (32–3). Cecilia's interpretation of the exodus from Cuba as a veritable diaspora is suggested even more directly near the end of the text, right before she solves the mystery of the phantom house:

> Her family was practically extinct, her friends dead or dispersed throughout the world. Several of them had committed suicide, weighted down by life's complications. Others had drowned in the Strait of Florida, attempting to flee. Many were exiles in unlikely places: Australia, Sweden, Egypt, the Canary Islands, Hungary, Japan, or any other corner of the planet where there was a piece of earth to land on. (357)

Cecilia's feelings about Cuba—specifically Havana—are decidedly conflicted. She wonders how she could 'hate something and long for it at the same time' (221). When she thinks or speaks of her original home, the familiar gothic language of attraction and repulsion, desire and loathing is clearly evident: 'She recalled her old city, her lost country. She hated it. Oh, God, how she hated it! It didn't matter that her memories filled her with torment. It didn't matter that the torment now resembled love. She'd never admit it, not even to her own shadow' (291). For better or worse, Cuba is in her blood, and she imagines it very much as a living, complex organism with its own genetic makeup. In an early conversation with Roberto, a man who would become her lover, Cecilia tells him that he is not Cuban if he was born in Miami. Roberto disagrees, insisting that he was 'born here [Florida] by accident,' and Cecilia observes, 'It was as if the genes of the island were so strong that it took more than one generation to disavow them' (144). As much as she tries to 'disavow' her heritage, it will not let her, and more than one oracle is required to help her understand this truth.

Female oracles abound in *The Island of Eternal Love*. Amalia is the first, and she appears in the very first line of the novel, even though '[i]t was so dark that Cecilia could hardly see her' (5). Yet she does see her, and after speaking with her, and even communicating telepathically, Cecilia still seems utterly unaware of the significance of Amalia's appearance and her message:

> [Cecilia] suspected her blood carried the genes of her grandmother Rosa, who had ended her days confusing everyone and everything. If she had taken after her grandmother Delfina instead, she might have been a clairvoyant, knowing beforehand who was going to die, which airplane would fall from the skies, who would marry whom, and what the dead had to say. But Cecilia had never seen or heard anything that other people couldn't also perceive. And thus she was condemned. Her birthright would be premature senility, not the powers of an oracle. (25)

Readers might realize, or suspect, how wrong Cecilia is, but she remains (perhaps willfully) unaware until virtually the end of the novel; the reason for this lack of awareness is her disconnection from her inheritance—familial and cultural. Thinking again of her grandmother Delfina, who 'became the local oracle' after predicting the devastation that Castro (whom she christened the

Grim Reaper) would bring to Cuba, Cecilia muses, 'Once more Delfina had foreseen what no one else was able to anticipate, and ever since then her doubters recognized that she had a mouth that was close to God' (91). Her hunger for family and home heightened by Amalia's stories, Cecilia finally seeks out her great aunt Loló, Delfina's sister. When she asks her great aunt if she (Loló) 'see[s] things too,' the old woman replies:

> I told you, I'm not like my sister. She was an oracle, like that one at Delphi. I think Mama had a premonition when she gave her that name. Delfina could speak with the dead whenever she felt like it. She would summon them and they would show up in droves. *I can speak to them, too, but I have to wait for them to appear.* (96; emphasis added)

Cecilia is more like her great aunt than she realizes.

Other female oracles include Guabina, of whom Cecilia hears in one of Amalia's stories, and Gaia, who has seen the phantom house and whom Cecilia realizes she knew years ago in Cuba. Guabina is the 'seer' whom Angela consults when she is in distress over her Pepe's (José's) behavior and his plan to bring Mercedes (a prostitute) into his parents' home for sanctuary. Guabino has a 'spirit messenger,' a 'mute, scar-crossed Indian, assassinated centuries ago' who appears to warn her of impending danger (183). She also has an altar to Catholic and African saints, and when Angela alerts her to José's plan, Guabina appeals to Obba, the 'mortal enemy of Oshún,' the only deity who 'would be able to help her snatch a victim [Mercedes] away from that ghost' (180). The specificity and placement of Guabina's appeal to Obba—which comes immediately before Mercedes's wounding and the exit of the 'cold that had inhabited her for years' (183)—suggest that Guabina's intercessory prayer is successful. Gaia, named of course for the Greek goddess of the earth, has seen the phantom house, and Cecilia consults her near the beginning of the narrative. It is Gaia who helps Cecilia understand the significance of the house and the dates of its appearances. Gaia tells Cecilia that 'the house is a symbol. I've already told you that these phantom mansions revealed certain aspects of a place's soul' (185). With the knowledge that the dates of the house's appearance are significant dates in Cuba's history, Cecilia asks Gaia, 'But which place? Miami or Cuba?' Gaia encourages her to shift her focus: '[W]e need to find out who's occupying it. Usually it's the people who move from one place to another. I think the house is following the impulses of its inhabitants. That's the link we have to look for: the people' (185). When Cecilia combines the descriptions of the inhabitants with an old photo that she sees at Loló's and focuses not just on when the house appears but where, she realizes that the house has been coming nearer and nearer *to her*, and that the inhabitants are her parents and Delfina (the oracle). Cecilia cannot go home again and thinks that she has no wish to; so home has come to her, not to herald her death (as it might in some gothic narratives), but to startle her awake psycho-spiritually, to herald her transformation from St. Cecilia of Havana in Ruins to a woman who knows herself, embraces her heritage, and finds the antidote for the terrible loneliness that has haunted her.

In this Supranatural Gothic text, Nature, like the ghosts of ancestors, is quite capable of direct intervention in life. While 'The Three Origins' refers to 'the three principal ethnicities that make up the Cuban nation—Spanish, African, and Chinese' (*Island* 3), the term also appears in the first tale that Amalia tells Cecilia. 'Wait for Me in Heaven' is the story of the beautiful Lingao-fa, mother of Kui-fa and grandmother of Pag Li (Pablo), who hangs herself rather than be made to marry another man after her husband's death. Mei Lei is the servant entrusted with young Kui-fa's care. When the child becomes 'gravely ill' and '[n]o doctor could find the cause of her illness, ... Mei Lei didn't lose her head. She went to the Temple of the Three Origins' (19). Mei Lei makes her prayer and her offerings to heaven, earth, and sky, and Kui-fa begins to recover. The Three Origins are 'sources of happiness, forgiveness, and protection,' and Mei Lei teaches Kui-fa 'to keep in harmony with these three powers. From that time on, heaven, earth, and water were the three kingdoms to which Kui-fa directed her thoughts, knowing that in them, she would always find protection' (20). When Kui-fa, Siu Mend (her husband), and their young son survive a horrific raid and successfully make the perilous journey from China to Cuba, where Siu Mend's grandfather, 'a *mambi*, as the Cubans called the rebels who fought against the Spanish army,' lives (85), the family fully believes in the Origins' protective power.

Other characters in the novel experience (supra)natural intervention as well. The spiritually receptive Angela (Amalia's Spanish paternal grandmother) does not see only the imp Martinico; while journeying with her family through Spain on their way to the coast to board a ship for Cuba, Angela meets and converses with Torrelila, a local fairy spirit:

> According to legend, she was a spirit older than the village itself, and she had resided in a spring for centuries. ... Some old women believed she was related to the Galician *mouras*, who also emerge to comb their hair on [Saint John's Day]; others maintained she was a cousin of the Asturian *xanas*, denizens of creeks and rivers. ... In any case the fairy of the foothills wore a lilac-colored tunic, unlike her northern relatives, who dressed in white. (100–1)

Angela speaks with the fairy, who tells the girl about other nature-spirits in the area who 'have been here since long before people arrived' (105).

As if on cue, the next time Angela enters the woods, she encounters none other than the great god Pan; she offers him honey, which delights him. They even have a brief philosophical/theological discussion. Angela asks him, 'Isn't there only one God?' Pan replies: 'There are as many as humans want. They create us and they destroy us. We can endure loneliness, but not their indifference; it's the only thing that makes us mortal' (109). Martinico appears, and Pan informs Angela that she can 'get rid of it,' and he can help her (110). Nevertheless, Pan can do only one thing for her: rid her of the imp or give her

Juan, with whom she has fallen in love at first sight. Angela chooses love, and Pan tells her that although he could do only one thing for her, he can offer one of her descendants 'whatever he wanted ... twice,' whether that descendant knows anything about the pact between them (Angela and Pan) or not (110). Pan makes another appearance in the narrative when he plays the flute at Amalia and Pablo's 'wedding' (a mystical union that takes place in nature) and grants Amalia's wish that the love between her and Pablo will last 'beyond death' (273–4). After their marriage, Amalia and Pablo establish a music store that they christen Pan's Flute. At the end of the novel, Cecilia sees Amalia 'dancing with a boy who looked like Miguel, with slightly more Asian features' (394). Pan's second intervention in the life of one of Angela's descendants (again, Amalia) is brief and marked simply by the sound of his flute. Pablo, who had been imprisoned for political reasons (the descendant of a *mambí* could not sit quietly by while an oppressive regime held power), is released, but Amalia clearly sees what the 20 years in prison have done to him. 'In a moment of delirium,' as Pablo weeps and embraces her, 'she yearned to renounce the blessed serenity of death and become a spirit, caring for the souls of those who suffered. In the distance, she thought she heard a delicate sound, something like a flute, hidden in the brush' (365). Years later (a year after her physical death), Amalia will begin to care for one of those suffering souls in a dark nightclub in Miami. In *The Island of Eternal Love*, Nature is alive, sentient, and intimately involved in human life, both the site and source of great spiritual power that can manifest itself materially.

Another aspect of the novel's Supranatural/Romantic Gothicism is discernible in the ways in which the ideals of liberty, equality, and brotherhood/sisterhood are reinforced and promoted. Characters as diverse as Pablo and his *mambí* great grandfather, who comes to comfort and guide him in/through death, and Delfina, Cecilia's oracular grandmother who warned everyone about 'the Grim Reaper' (Castro) and who comes to comfort and guide her grandchild into life, believe in these ideals; the storylines themselves underscore the theme of connection and community as the antidotes to tyranny and enslavement. The novel directly engages the Cuban struggle for independence in a number of ways (from Pablo's political activities and subsequent arrest to the historically important dates on which the 'phantom house' appears), but no discussion of Cuban independence would be complete without mention of José Martí, and Chaviano certainly incorporates the nineteenth-century Cuban hero into her narrative. Not surprisingly, given *The Island of Eternal Love*'s supranatural identity and Chaviano's focus on the importance of art, she emphasizes Martí's spiritual beliefs as expressed through his poetry. Near the beginning of Part Three, 'City of Oracles,' Cecilia attends a lecture. An old woman reads from 'several texts in which Martí spoke of the soul's return after death to pursue its evolutionary apprenticeship.' It is no shock to the reader of Chaviano's gothic novel to find such a statement, for, by this point in the text, more than one spirit has 'returned' to accomplish something. However, Cecilia is 'astonished.' She had not before considered 'the apostle of Cuban independence' as 'practically a spiritualist' (141).

When the old woman at the lecture quotes from one of Martí's poems, the novel's investment in liberty and equality as well as the significance of some of its 'ghosts' snaps into focus even more clearly: 'Then she quoted from a poem [by Martí] that seemed to attribute her country's suffering to the law of karma, as if the extermination of the indigenous people and the killings of the black slaves demanded a purge, a reincarnation of those souls in the future' (141). After completing the novel, the reader may begin to form a theory. What if Chaviano is showing us that 'reincarnation' can take the form of family? Children, grandchildren, great-grandchildren inherit the genes of their ancestors and, as the Gothic suggested long before the human genome project verified the suggestion as scientific fact, these descendants can inherit much more than physical traits. Perhaps they can inherit drives and desires (for example, for freedom) and, after a generation or two, perhaps they can find a way to fulfill them. Amalia's great-grandmother, Dayo (renamed Damiana), is brought from Africa as a slave; Dayo's child, Kamaria (renamed Caridad), experiences legal emancipation only to find herself in a brothel with her daughter. However, that daughter, Mercedes, as has already been noted, does escape enslavement and, interestingly enough, her escape/rebirth is communicated spiritually to Guabina, the woman who makes an intercessory prayer to an African goddess on Mercedes's behalf. Guabina receives this communication from her spirit-messenger, a scarred Indian who had previously come to warn Guabina of impending danger but who never re-appears to her after Mercedes's deliverance. The spirits of the enslaved and slaughtered do come back in this Southern Gothic text, but they do not all come back in their original forms; nor do they re-appear solely to demand justice for themselves. In *The Island of Eternal Love*, even most of the ghosts and spirits are committed to the fight for liberty and equality.

The Romantic concept of the creative and transformational power of the mind is also discernible in Chaviano's text. Near the end of Part Four, after a break-up with her lover, Roberto, and thinking yet again of her island home from which she is in exile, Cecilia is alone, desperately ill, and undergoing a dark night of the soul during which even nature seems to weep: '[i]t rained for three days and three nights' (264). She senses her grandmother's caress and, 'acting on impulse,' picks up a book. She reads one line: 'Our minds carry the power of life and death' (265). She proceeds to lower her alarmingly high blood pressure and temperature—with her mind—and, after three days and nights of illness and desperation, essentially comes back to life (265–6). Nurtured by Amalia's stories, Cecilia's paradigms are beginning to shift; she has begun to recognize that the source of her pain and loneliness is not truly external at all; she has been alienated from her own nature, and a large part of this alienation has to do with her disavowal of her heritage. By the final part of the novel, Cecilia realizes that '[s]he couldn't lie to herself. That country [Cuba] *did* matter to her—as much as her own life, or even more. How could it not, when it was a part of her?' (368–9). Cecilia has begun to re-integrate and to acknowledge the transformational power of her own mind. Still in

Miami, she is nonetheless home because the 'phantom house'—her family, her cultural past, her ancestral home—has found her. Her external reality has not changed (with the significant exception of Miguel's entrance into it, thanks to Amalia); her mind has.

Those who read beyond the last page of the novel encounter Chaviano's acknowledgments. In the final paragraph of those acknowledgments, Chaviano writes:

> I would also like to extend my thanks—from this world to the next—to the late Aldo Martinez-Malo, executor of the estate of singer Rita Montaner (1900–1958), who, one day long ago, in a gesture characterized as 'unusual' by those friends who witnessed it, draped my shoulders with the legendary diva's silvery shawl, a relic that she loved to show off but would never allow anyone to touch. (396)

Chaviano wonders whether her contact with the garment 'brought [her] such strange visions of the past' (396). Beyond the boundaries of the gothic narrative proper, Montaner's shawl, with its powerful linkage of cultural wealth with cultural suffering and identity, functions as 'a mantle of light,' passed from one Cuban artist (Montaner), whose artistry reflects and keeps alive her cultural heritage, to another (Chaviano). Chaviano certainly wears this mantle of cultural identity and revelation as she pens a Female Gothic text utterly infused with the foundational preoccupations of the Southern Gothic and ending with supranatural enlightenment.

NOTES

1. The following paragraphs on Allison's *Bastard Out of Carolina* appear in earlier form in 'Female Gothic Fiction, Grotesque Realities, and *Bastard Out of Carolina*: Dorothy Allison Revises the Southern Gothic,' published by the author in *Mississippi Quarterly* 63.2 (2010): 269–290.

BIBLIOGRAPHY

Allison, D. (1992). *Bastard out of Carolina*. New York: Dutton.

Allison, D. (1994). Moving toward truth: An interview with Dorothy Allison. Carolyn E. Megan. *Kenyon Review, 16*(4), 71–83.

Allison, D. (1996). *Two or three things I know for sure*. New York: Plume.

Bailey, P. D. (2010). Female Gothic fiction, grotesque realities, and *Bastard Out of Carolina*: Dorothy Allison revises the Southern Gothic. *Mississippi Quarterly, 63*(2), 269–290.

Chaviano, D. (2008). *The island of eternal love*. 2006. (trans: Labinger, A.G.). New York: Riverhead Books.

Chaviano, D. (2010, May 7). Hispanista: Interview with Daína Chaviano. Silvia Viñas. *Uptown Literari*. www.dainachaviano.com. 5 May 2012.

Ellen, M. (1985). Female Gothic. *Literary women: The great writers*. 1976. New York: Oxford UP.

Patterson, L. S. (2000–2001). Ellipsis, ritual, and 'real time': Rethinking the rape complex in southern novels. *Mississippi Quarterly 54*(1), 37–58.

Rice, A. (1990). *The witching hour*. New York: Alfred A. Knopf.

Salamone, F. A. (1996). The anthropological vision of Anne Rice. In G. Hoppenstand & R. B. Browne (Eds.), *The Gothic world of Anne Rice* (pp. 35–53). Bowling Green: Bowling Green State University Popular Press.

Wray, M., & Newitz, A. (1997). Introduction. In M. Wray & A. Newitz (Eds.), *White trash: Race and class in America* (pp. 1–12). New York: Routledge.

FURTHER READING

Botting, F. (1996). *Gothic. The new critical idiom*. London/New York: Routledge. Provides a helpful overview of the history and forms of the Gothic, with a useful chapter devoted to 'Homely Gothic' (i.e., American Gothic literature).

Crow, C. L. (2009). *American Gothic. History of the Gothic*. Cardiff: University of Wales. Surveys the evolution of the American Gothic from its origins to the contemporary 'post-American' world; contains a Works Consulted section that includes primary and secondary texts of crucial interest to scholars of the Gothic.

Hoppenstand, G., & Browne, R. B. (Eds.). (1996). *The Gothic world of Anne rice*. Bowling Green: Bowling Green State University Popular Press. Identifies and examines the gothic elements in Rice's fiction.

Paravisini-Gebert, L. (2002). Colonial and postcolonial Gothic: The Caribbean. In J. E. Hogle (Ed.), *The Cambridge companion to Gothic fiction*. Cambridge: Cambridge UP. Traces gothic emanations in a variety of texts from and about the Caribbean.

CHAPTER 35

Shadows on the Small Screen: The Televisuality and Generic Hybridity of Southern Gothic

Brigid Cherry

The set of texts that constitute Southern Gothic television is fluid and potentially encompasses quite different kinds of programming, although it is not a term that is often employed in marketing or critical discourse (except as an occasional synonym for horror). Programmes range across the horror, supernatural romance, thriller or crime series. However, this does not mean that particular programmes cannot be identified as Southern Gothic or that the elements of Southern Gothic cannot be identified within them. There are examples of programmes that are both geographically located in the Southern states and are narratively and thematically linked to their literary antecedents. Reception is important in this respect. In his account of postmodern Southern writing, Jason Friedman argues that since 'popular and critical imaginations conceive, as products of the deep, dark South, all manner of horror and brutishness', all Southern writing, whether it incorporates gothic conventions or not, 'is always already construed as Gothic' (193). Although it would be plausible for a programme set in the South to avoid associations with Southern Gothic (there are several comedies, for example), Friedman's point could be addressed to television. Might the Southern television series too be always already gothic? Historically, Southern Gothic writing has had a presence on television through telefilms and plays for television of literary works by Tennessee Williams and Flannery O'Connor. Yet it is only with the recent flourishing of horror and supernatural romance in popular culture that Southern Gothic programming—often developed specifically for television—can be identified.

These gothic texts do not present a homogenous or straightforward generic category. As Teresa Goddu argues, the gothic genre within American literature is 'extremely mutable' and 'transgressive' (5). The problem of applying any

B. Cherry (✉)
St Mary's University, Twickenham, UK

© The Editor(s) (if applicable) and The Author(s) 2016
S.C. Street, C.L. Crow (eds.), *The Palgrave Handbook of the Southern Gothic*,
DOI 10.1057/978-1-137-47774-3_35

genre label aside, however, the notion of Southern Gothic television immediately sets out lines of inquiry, in terms of aesthetics (what are the televisual qualities of Southern Gothic) and of textuality (how might it be defined in terms of content, narrative and theme). And of course, the term also indicates—however loosely—a connection with Southern Gothic as we understand it as a literary form or movement, and a further avenue of inquiry concerns Southern Gothic television's relationship to the Southern Gothic novel. It is primarily these areas that inform the account of Southern Gothic television in this chapter.

THE SOUTHERN GOTHIC ON TELEVISION

To consider the literary forms of American Gothic and Southern Gothic already implies 'a regional sense of place' (Blanco 22). As Goddu reiterates, 'the American Gothic is most recognizable as a regional form' (3). Regionality, then, is crucial here. As a case in point, the television series *American Gothic* (1995–96) may locate itself through the series title in relation to the national form of Gothic (and Helen Wheatley's analysis of it in her book *Gothic Television* follows the same line), but its setting (a small town in South Carolina) and themes (the dark undercurrents, secrets and taboos within the central family) locate it within a regionally Southern tradition.

In fact, much of the programming set in the South makes connections to the Southern Gothic form.[1] Some of it can be considered as extending the tradition of Southern writing, with its creators and showrunners (the person, often a writer-producer, with overall creative responsibility for a television series) drawing on their own experiences of the South. *True Blood* (2008–14), about humans, vampires and other supernatural beings in the small town of Bon Temps in Louisiana, is based on the Sookie Stackhouse novels by the Southern writer Charlene Harris and is adapted for HBO by Southerner Alan Ball. *True Detective* (2014) is created and written by Southern novelist Nic Pizzolatto, and focuses on murder and corruption in the coastal plains area of Louisiana. *The Walking Dead* (2010–), based on the comic book written by Kentuckian Robert Kirkman, follows a small group of survivors in rural Georgia after the zombie apocalypse. The Southern Gothic television series is not always overtly Southern writing, however. Often, by dint of their being set in the South and evoking the milieu of the Deep South with its macabre, violent or grotesque overtones, such series contain Southern Gothic tropes even though they are not rooted specifically in Southern writing. These include *The Vampire Diaries* and its spin-off series *The Originals* (2009–), a paranormal romance featuring vampire brothers and the woman they love in a town in Virginia; the third series of *American Horror Story*, subtitled *Coven* (2013), depicting a society of witches in and around New Orleans; the aforementioned *American Gothic*, focused around the battle for the life and soul of a young orphan; and *Carnivàle* (2003–05), a Manichean battle set in a travelling carnival in the Dust Bowl of the 1930s.

It is widely recognised of course that Southern Gothic literature is not inherently tied to the spectral, whether supernatural or horrific; the monsters of

Southern Gothic are often grotesque examples of humanity. And while similar cases can be identified in Southern Gothic television, it is often alongside monstrous or supernatural characters (sometimes indeed in the same character), frequently in a way that highlights their grotesqueness. Thus many Southern Gothic series also incorporate supernatural elements and monstrous, inhuman figures familiar from the horror genre, or they suggest demonic, supernatural or occult phenomena at work in the worlds of the series. Some examples fall into the category of the supernatural romance: *True Blood* and *The Vampire Diaries* are populated by vampires, witches, fairies and werewolves. Others, *American Gothic* and *Carnivàle*, incorporate ghosts and demonic entities as might be found in cosmic horror; *True Detective* overtly anchors its police procedural narrative in Cajun folklore and nihilistic horror in the vein of H. P. Lovecraft. *The Walking Dead* and *American Horror Story Coven* are organised around the more explicit conventions and tropes of the horror genre—shocks, scares and visceral imagery, and traditional monsters including zombies, Frankenstein-like creatures and serial killers.[2] All these series, though, remain rooted in the grotesque and draw heavily on the legacies of Southern Gothic writing and the history of the Southern states. There is therefore a generic hybridity to these series, with elements of horror, the Gothic and Southern Gothic, that creates a particularly vivid and emotionally affective visual surface. This generic hybridity is itself gothic. In discussing *True Detective*, it is significant that Scott Wilson refers to the hard-boiled crime genre being 'conjoined' with Southern Gothic (153), bringing to mind the grotesque imagery of the freak show and the uncanniness of the doppelganger (also seen in the fourth series of *American Horror Story*, *Freak Show*, itself containing many Southern Gothic characters). And as Wheatley explores within her broader engagement with television Gothic, many of the defining elements of Southern Gothic are similarly conjoined with the spectral and visceral imagery.

Although she sets out the ways in which television is an ideal medium for the Gothic as a genre and as a mode, Wheatley's account does not overtly engage with a specifically *Southern* Gothic. While she analyses the series *American Gothic*—a text, as already mentioned, that is certainly close to Southern Gothic in its settings and concerns, drawing on many of the literary tropes—Wheatley discusses it solely in the context of spectrality and the ways in which advances in television technology facilitate a televisual style that is ideally suited to gothic texts in general and American Gothic (from which the TV series takes its name in counterpoint to its Southern Gothic milieu) more particularly. Wheatley concludes *Gothic Television* (204–5) by stressing that it is not a completist account she offers, but rather a series of starting points for further study. The lack of specific engagement with Southern Gothic is not an oversight in the context of Wheatley's overall thesis—an understandably broad historical account of television Gothic—but it does leave something of a lacuna when thinking about television programmes that evoke the tradition of Southern Gothic writing. It is this I take as *my* starting point, addressing this absence with a further account of Southern Gothic television.

Televisuality

Landscape and climate are among the strongest contributors to Southern Gothic televisuality. These may recall the characteristics of the classic, European gothic (the plains surrounded by vertiginous mountains of the gothic sublime are visualised in *Carnivàle*, for example when the carnival makes camp and sets up its tents and fairground rides on a flat valley floor overlooked by rocky hills), but they more often depict the landscape of the Deep South, emphasising the qualities of its light, heat and lush vegetation. Location and setting are stressed in the titles of *True Blood*, for example, with its images of bayous, foliage, water and wildlife. Such depictions of landscape visualise heat and humidity; they are often shot in hot, rich tones of yellows, reds and oranges, even at night via the use of neon lighting; and they have a liquid quality, often literally including bodies of water, drops of condensation or sweat.

Thus the most striking visual aesthetic in *True Blood* comes from landscape and climate. Running counter to the expected mood and tonal qualities of the Gothic (dark, dank, cloudy and cold environments), sun, light and heat become a visual focus; moreover, they signify passion, perversity and other uncanny appetites (boys messily eating berries, women writhing and dancing in a sexualised way, religious ecstasy), predation, danger, death and decay (time-lapse footage of a dead fox, a Venus flytrap). There are gothic spaces in *True Blood*—the dungeon under Fangtasia or Bill's decaying antebellum house with its crawl space—but although the vampires are associated with the night, they are also inextricably linked to the sunlight. The vampire queen of Louisiana Sophie-Anne has decorated the inside of her New Orleans mansion with trompe-l'oeil paintings of windows and ceiling lights open to the midday sun. In a perverse reversal of the heroine Sookie, she reclines by a swimming pool, wearing a bikini, pretending to sunbathe. Sookie herself, who is a love interest for vampires, werewolves and other creatures of the night, is an inveterate sun lover. When she is about to become a victim of the serial killer in season 1, the pursuit is through a graveyard, but it is in brilliant sunshine (see Ruddell and Cherry for further detail).

In her discussion of Southern Gothic, Victoria Amador lists 'the pungent odours' among the 'banalities of real southern life', alongside 'the maddening humidity' and 'the barely tameable landscape' ('Gothic Louisiana' 164). Although olfactory (and tactile) qualities cannot be directly incorporated into the televisuality and soundscape of the television series, odours, along with tactile sensations of light and heat, can become affective viewing experiences. Anna Powell, in her Deleuzian account of horror cinema, reminds us that film has haptic qualities, inducing physical sensations, and there are ways in which the quasi-filmic qualities of many of these Southern Gothic series replicate these affects. The heat is palpable in shots of Bon Temps residents cooling themselves with fans or having a cold beer in Merlotte's. Stacey Abbott, responding to Karen Lury's point that the closeup is suited to the intimate visuality of television as a domestic medium, argues that closeups in gothic television produce 'a horrific form of spectacle that is intricately bound to notions of intimacy' (32). Moreover, as Amador stresses, these elements are irrevocably tied into the culture of the Deep South:

> Through juxtapositions of the familiar and un-familiar, Southern Gothic texts readily establish macabre tonal strategies already associated with the Southern states and made more threatening by their conjunction with the banalities of real southern life. ('Gothic' 164)

In *True Blood*, heat is similarly signified through closeups of beads of sweat trickling down necks as Bon Temps residents sit in the church to hear Bill Compton's talk on his experiences in the American Civil War ('Sparks Fly Out'). There is a link here to vampirism itself, with sweat replacing the blood droplets that might otherwise signify the vampire bite, but it is also intimately tied in to the history of the South. The Descendants of the Glorious Dead keep the memory of their ancestors alive, but they are joined by the vampire who lived through those events and knew their kin. It is telling in this respect that this is the moment when many of the residents accept 'Vampire Bill' as a member of their community.

Open spaces under a broad sky or dappled sunlight through the trees of the bayou make the heat and humidity visual in other Southern Gothic series too. The vampires in *The Vampire Diaries* can move around freely during the day thanks to magic rings, for example, allowing sunlight to be potentially ever present. Pivotal burial scenes in *American Gothic* and *Carnivàle* take place under a blazing sun. The survivors in *The Walking Dead* are depicted as sweaty and grimy; they frequently pause in their work to wipe away the sweat. In *Coven*, Fiona takes the pupils on a field trip and as they walk through New Orleans she shades herself from the sun's rays with a parasol. In *True Detective*, the investigation, the search for clues, the apprehension of suspects and violent acts of all kind take place under the full sun or in rooms cast in yellow light as if it were daylight. In each case, the sunlight contrasts strongly with the narrative events that are being depicted: in *The Walking Dead* the work is often killing and defending the community from the 'walkers', the zombies of the series; in *Carnivàle*, the dead woman becomes a tormented spirit trapped in a ghost town; in *True Blood*, Sookie is a telepath thanks to her fairy blood and is shunned, feared and othered by the inhabitants of Bon Temps; in *American Gothic*, digitally treated time-lapse photography is employed to show a tree newly planted in commemoration of the dead to grow alarmingly quickly, accompanied by cries and screeches on the soundtrack; in *True Detective*, the yellow that predominates is not only sunlight but signifies the 'Yellow King'. Cohle espouses the philosophy that life is a dream in the locked room of the mind, and there is a monster at the end of the dream—a monster he finally encounters in the maze of 'Carcosa', a cavernous, almost subterranean space (in fact the ruins of an American Civil War–era fort that could be a stand-in for the gothic castle) where sunlight enters only tangentially through roots and brickwork. In these television series, the bright sunlight serves only to conceal the grotesqueries and horrors of the world. The everyday is thus rendered uncanny.

The frequent use of certain shots and camera techniques also constructs disorientating visual effects that further emphasise the tactile sensations as well as the underlying horror. These include frequent use of high-angle shots (which suggest that the characters are subject to fate or swallowed up by the narrative or setting), Dutch angles and use of a fish-eye lens. High-angle shots are employed in *Carnivàle*, for example, when Scudder burns his face with acid; and Dutch angles are used in the vision sequences in *American Gothic* when Gail re-visits her childhood trauma. *American Horror Story Coven* makes extreme and excessive use of such techniques, throwing the viewer into a warped and bizarre world. When Fiona walks with the coven through New Orleans, the angles of the buildings in the famous French Quarter lean away from the centre of the screen, taking on the look of a German Expressionist film. This becomes even more extreme when the witches are voyeuristically observing the young men working in the next-door garden from their balcony: the characters standing on the balcony look as if they are about to slide off the screen down a 45-degree incline. In a sequence showing the exiled witch Misty in her shack in the bayou after she has healed the Frankenstein-like monster Kyle, the image rotates slowly through a 90-degree angle, the wall of the shack seeming to lie on its side, and then to a direct overhead shot, effectively turning the world upside down. When the nineteenth-century French socialite Delphine is forced to become a maid and wait on the witches, she is shot with a fish-eye lens as she pushes a trolley down the corridor, emphasising her grotesqueness and alienation in the modern world (she is a notorious serial killer who tortured and murdered slaves). Similar shots permeate the series, lending the whole a disconcerting feel. These stylistic devices skew the image, destabilising the characters and the worlds they inhabit, explicitly connecting the visuals to the experiences and emotional affects of the Gothic text.

Admixtures

Discussing *Interview with the Vampire*, Ken Gelder describes New Orleans, the heart of Southern Gothic, as 'a place in the New World which is nevertheless somehow older and more decadent than Europe, simultaneously "primitive" and sophisticated, a "mixture" of all kinds of peoples' (110). The important point here is not just the conjunction or overlap of past and present, but its simultaneity. The character of Delphine in *American Horror Story Coven* is based on the historical figure of Madame LaLaurie; in the series she was made immortal by witchcraft and chained in a coffin until being dug up in the present day. The character of Marie Laveau, the witch who cast the spell, is also a historical figure, the Voodoo Queen of New Orleans. The characters' immortality permits simultaneity. In a scene that again employs a high-angle shot skewed at a 45-degree angle, Delphine and Fiona sit on a bench outside Delphine's old house (now a morbid museum dedicated to her heinous crimes; Delphine is angered by what she sees as misrepresentation on a tour of the house). The shot emphasises and exaggerates the historical plaque on the wall above them, bringing it into the foreground of the image. In her list of banalities outlined earlier, Amador includes 'the uneasy truce between the races', a factor already suggested in the depiction of the racist Delphine as she is made to serve the black (that is, African American) witch Queenie. In such a way, the televisuality emphasises the identity of the American South, not just its geography and climate but its particular concerns, its history and its relationship with the past (in the example just mentioned, the shadow of slavery and racism).

In respect of history and identity, the Southern states are a complex site of contradictions (to borrow a phrase from Amador). The concept of mixing is central here too. It is not just the past and present that mix, but people—and specifically races. The idea of admixtures in this context relates to Adrian Parr's discussion of national trauma, drawing on the work of Deluze and Guatteri:

> The past is not so much a tangible terrain, a demarcated and identifiable space, or a monumental time that acts as a warning or reminder both in the present and for future generations, but an admixture of times that affirm the present and future and in so doing encourage a more nomadic subjectivity that identifies with a variety of subjectivities. (143)

The trauma to which this admixture relates is slavery, culminating in the Civil War (seen in the 'bitter nostalgia' offered by scenes from *True Blood* and *The Vampire Diaries*). For the South, and thus for Southern Gothic, the mixing of peoples and thus the admixture of race is a continuing anxiety. Southern Gothic television series can thus be read as admixtures of history and identity.

As already discussed in the analysis of the Descendants of the Glorious Dead scene in *True Blood*, past and present always come together in the form of the vampire. Flashbacks depicting the lives of vampire characters in earlier times are a common trope of vampire texts (as indeed they are with the immortal characters in *Coven*). Both *True Blood* and *Vampire Diaries* make frequent use of these, but they are not used solely in order to fill in character backstory. They often represent admixtures of past and present. In the scene from *True Blood*, an elderly man in the audience asks Bill about Tolliver Humphries, his great-grandfather, who served in the same regiment as Bill and died in action. Bill remembers the man and talks vividly about how he died, sacrificing himself in a futile attempt to save the life of a fellow soldier. The televisuality of the series affords the opportunity to depict the events as a flashback, bringing them into much sharper focus. The dead are not simply memorialised, they are brought back to life, albeit for a moment. The elderly man is given comfort in finally learning some details of his family history. Bill tells him that Tolliver's action was precipitated by believing it ordained by God, and moreover gives the man comfort when he tells him that God did indeed look after his descendants. A close shot shows the emotion on the man's face. This connection to the past is as true for the vampire as it is for the human descendants; the mayor of Bon Temps has searched the archives and found an old tintype of Bill and his family taken before he went to war. The past is brought alive for Bill just as he bought it alive for the descendant. A closeup shows the emotions that these memories evoke as Bill blots away his tears. These shots emphasise the emotionality as past and present overlap and blur in the sharing of experiences.

A similar blurring of past and present, although using a different narrative technique—the depiction of re-enactment rather than flashback—is employed in the Founder's Day episode of *The Vampire Diaries*.[3] The Founder's Day celebrations in Mystic Falls take the town back to the Civil War era with men wearing Confederate uniforms and women dressed as Southern belles, while the town square and floats are draped in Confederate colours. The use of re-enactment, more even than the flashback, provides a sense that past and present overlap. Elena, the heroine, dresses in a crinoline for the event. This performance of history is made complex since Stefan, her boyfriend and one of vampire brothers of the series, was turned—like Bill Compton—during the war and is thus anchored in it. He is unchanged in both the past being re-enacted and the present enacting it. The frock coat, brocade waistcoat and cravat that he wears for the event break down the distinction as to whether this is the present day or a vampire flashback to his earlier life. The scene also makes reference to Katherine, Elena's ancestor and her doppelganger, as well as the vampire who turned Stefan and Damon. Wearing nineteenth-century dress, Elena is indistinguishable from her past 'self' and it is clear from their look that Stefan and Damon see Katherine, the woman they both loved. Further, Katherine, stealing Elena's present-day clothing, becomes interchangeable with Elena, masquerading as Elena to passionately kiss Damon and stab Elena's father. She—as in the Elena/Katherine gestalt—is if you will her own ancestor and descendant.

In this way the Civil War and Confederate mise en scène is a significant element of these Southern Gothic series. It is worth noting that in *True Blood* the church is also decorated with the Descendants' banner and swags of fabric around the lectern that display the colours of the Confederate flag, as well as the flag itself. Southern identity is written into the scene, as well as the flashback scenes of Confederate troops in their grey uniforms (and in his white suit with waistcoat, bow tie and shoulder-length hair, the descendant of Tolliver Humphries is in every way the Southern gent). However, this sense of identity is complicated by the fact that Bill calls the Union flag by its pre-war nickname of 'Old Glory' and describes himself as a patriot who will not put himself before it. This linking of Old Southern identity with the original Old Glory that was hidden in a quilt when Tennessee seceded from the Union also places Bill in a liminal position, reflecting his already liminal position as a vampire.

As Victoria Amador points out, while Charlene Harris's *Southern Gothic Mysteries* fail to address issues of race in the South, *True Blood* associates vampirism with race ('Blacks and Whites'). There are major black characters in the series and thematic material engaging with issues of gender and race, as well as slavery. In the episode 'Nothing But the Blood', Lafayette—a gay black man—is chained to a rotating wheel in the dungeon at Fangtasia, the vampire bar. He is naked to the waist and the chain is attached to a thick leather collar around his neck. When he is cowering behind the wooden post splattered with blood after (the very white, Nordic) Eric kills one of the other 'slaves', it only serves to recall images of the whippings that recalcitrant slaves might have received. Racial tensions surrounding slavery re-emerge in the present too through Delphine in *American Horror Story Coven*. She is appalled, distraught and then angry at learning that there is a black president; conflicts around race are structured through the positioning of Delphine as personal maid to the tough and streetwise Queenie, who will not tolerate being called slave by Delphine.

The opposition of Fiona and Marie (and Queenie, who changes sides later in the series) also gives the terms white and black witchcraft additional meanings. Marie tells Fiona that all witchcraft derives from black peoples, from Africans and the Arawak people of the Caribbean. 'Everything you got, you got from us,' Laveau says, and tells her that slaves took it with them to Salem where they taught it to (racially) white witches. Queenie, who complains about 'growing up on white girl shit like Charmed and Sabrina the Teenage Cracker' (from this she assumed that [racially] black witches did not exist), crosses the boundary between the white coven of the school and the world of voodoo. She is a descendant of the slave witch Tituba who sparked the Salem witch trials, and describes herself as a human voodoo doll (she can inflict harm and injury on herself that is experienced by her victim). This itself is a significant, and potentially abject, blurring of the boundary of the body and self.

Body—and appearance—are also significant in respect of gender. Patricia Yaeger (138) argues that 'the beautification of the white female body—the southern belle—is work designed to attract southern men, but it also emphasises the grotesque', the grotesqueness of the female figures in the Southern Gothic of Flannery O'Connor being wrapped up in the culture of Southern womanhood. It is a culture of beauty that requires all kinds of grooming practices to form and shape the body in such a way that it can appear socially decorous. These practices of beauty are sites of violence. We see this enacted explicitly in *Coven*, in which Delphine (in her original time) keeps slaves caged and tortured in her attic, where she bleeds them for her beauty rituals. Like a vampire, specifically Countess Báthory, she paints her face with fresh blood in an attempt to retain (or regain) her youth. Violence and suffering underlie the beautification of the Southern woman, but here that is also tied to race and violence towards the black slaves that serve the white woman.

INTERTEXTS

As this example also illustrates, there are several ways in which the Southern Gothic series presents itself as an admixture of texts. To consider Southern Gothic television is also to consider its links to Southern Gothic literature. Thomas Leitch, discussing the *Southern Vampire Mysteries* and *True Blood*, suggests that adaptation is a relevant context in terms of the shared tropes and conventions of Southern Gothic television. He argues that Southern Gothic adaptations sidestep 'the dead end of fidelity studies by envisioning different contexts that generate a different set of questions' (331), as Delphine's beauty rituals do with respect to O'Connor's work. Leitch sees these works 'as an intertext designed to be worked through, like a window on their source text' (30). Literary adaptation is thus an important concept here, but Southern Gothic television's intertexts are much wider and more varied. Such intertexts include, for example, the dry dusty landscape of *Carnivàle*, the dust bowl of the South during the Great Depression and the migration of 'Okies' west to California. Central character Ben Hawkins is from a farming family who have lost their land, his mother dying from black lung in the first episode. *Carnivàle* invites comparisons to photographs of the people of the South during this time. The dress, mannerisms and faces of the Carny folk, posed against the bleak landscape and impoverished communities, recall the work of Walker Evans, the Great Depression–era photographer whose imagery has been described as the depiction of Southern Gothic.

Carnivàle is also an intertext of Flannery O'Connor's *Wise Blood*, seeming to draw directly on her literary themes. In the episode 'Damascus, NE', Ben is a version of Hazel Motes, the grandson of a travelling preacher who now spreads the word of anti-religion. In parallel to Motes, Ben is the son of carnie performer who led (fake) healing and revival meetings. Like Motes, Ben takes this role on himself (the Carnies hold fake services to raise money when they are forbidden to operate their carnival) and is forced into wearing his father's suit, much as Motes is compelled to dress in a preacher's garb. Moreover, Ben's father Hank Scudder reminds us of the preacher Asa Hawks, who has (ostensibly) blinded himself with lye in order to escape worldly pursuits. Scudder, in a flight from his past life, burns off his face with acid (shown via the overhead shot mentioned previously). With his visions (seeing Scudder's act of self-mutilation being one), Ben not only has 'wise blood' (like Motes), but seeing and not seeing become additional intertexts: Lodz, the blind mentalist with his milky white eyes; and Brother Justin, the minister who self-flagellates; and even Management, the mysterious figure behind the curtain who speaks only to Samson, the dwarf—there is a conjunction in these figure of Enoch Emery with his mummified dwarf that he keeps under the sink.

Intertexts are thus an important factor in (re)creating Southern Gothic for the small screen. In series such as *American Gothic*, *True Blood* and *True Detective*, evil and violence reside at the heart of the community. *True Detective* exposes the corruption in the run-down, post-industrial town of the fictional Erath, and it is not inconsequential that the real Erath is regarded as the heart of Cajun Country. Rape, murder and child abuse are also the small-town secrets in *American Gothic*: Caleb's sister and father are murdered by the sheriff, who once raped his mother and is Caleb's true father; Caleb's elder sister was emotionally traumatised by witnessing the rape, and his mother committed suicide after giving birth to him; it is implied that Buck also killed the parents of Caleb's cousin Gail, with whom Lucas is intent on consummating a relationship. In the episode 'Ring of Fire', Gail seeks to learn about her parents, who died in a fire when she was a child, but learns instead that her father abused her. Characters are frequently grotesque. The sanctimonious Maxine Fortenberry and alcoholic Lettie-Mae in *True Blood*, the cowardly minister Gabriel, the volatile 'redneck' Merle Dixon and the sociopathic 'Governor' in *The Walking Dead*, the revival tent preacher Joel Theriot with his Elvis sideburns and the scarred killer Childress in an incestuous relationship with his half-sister in *True Detective*, all work as intertexts of the literary Southern Gothic; Amador ('Blacks and Whites' 134) says that Mrs Fortenberry is reminiscent of Ruby Turpin in O'Connor's 'Revelation'. These examples, and many others like them, illustrate Peggy Dunn Bailey's point that:

> The Southern Gothic is fueled by the need to explain and/or understand foundational trauma, the violation or loss of that which is essential to identity and survival but often irretrievable. Southern Gothic literature is characterized by obsessive preoccupations—with blood, family, and inheritance; racial, gender, and/or class identities; the Christian religion (typically, in its most 'fundamentalist' forms); and home—and a compulsion to talk (or write) about these preoccupations. (269)

Bailey suggests that 'the high visibility and popularity of Gothic texts that feature supernatural characters and events' in contemporary Southern literature (she mentions Anne Rice's *Vampire Chronicles* and Charlaine Harris's *Southern Vampire* series) 'have tended to obscure the legacy of the non-supernatural Southern Gothic'. Counter to this, I would argue that the very visceral admixing of Southern Gothic literary intertexts with the tropes of horror and the supernatural amplifies rather than obscures such a legacy. While some of the series discussed are adaptations from literary sources—as *True Blood* and *The Vampire Diaries* are from novel series and *The Walking Dead* is from a comic book—*American Gothic*, *Carnivàle*, *True Detective* and *American Horror Story Coven* are all original productions for television. However, all these series draw on the history, concerns and identity of the South, as well as the themes of Southern Gothic and grotesque writing, as intertexts. The Civil War, slavery, the dustbowl, the writing of Flannery O'Connor—all these and more are central to the continuing popularity and vibrancy of Southern Gothic television.

Notes

1. Other series that incorporate elements of Southern Gothic, but which length does not permit discussion, include *Justified*, *Treme*, *Dexter* and *Nip-Tuck*.
2. While the zombies depicted in *The Walking Dead* and *Coven* resemble the contemporary popular culture form initiated by George Romero, significantly those in *Coven* are linked to the Voodoo form through the character of Marie Laveau, who raises them by African witchcraft.
3. Flashbacks are used elsewhere in the series, as when Katherine is shown turning Stefan at the Founder's Ball in 1864.

Bibliography

Abbott, S. (2012). TV loves fangs: The televisuality of HBO horror. In B. Cherry (Ed.), *True blood: Investigating vampires and Southern Gothic* (pp. 25–38). London: I. B. Tauris. Print.

Amador, V. (2012). Blacks and Whites, trash and good country people in true blood. In B. Cherry (Ed.), *True blood: Investigating vampires and Southern Gothic* (pp. 122–138). London: I. B. Tauris. Print.

Amador, V. (2013). The Gothic Louisiana of Charlaine Harris and Anne Rice. In D. Mutch (Ed.), *The modern vampire and human identity* (pp. 163–176). Basingstoke: Palgrave MacMillan. Print.

Bailey, P. D. (2010). Female Gothic fiction, grotesque realities and Bastard Out of Carolina: Dorothy Allison revises the Southern Gothic. *The Mississippi Quarterly, 63*(1/2), 269–281. Print.

Blanco, M. d. P. (2012). *Ghost-watching American modernity: Haunting, landscape, and the hemispheric imagination*. Oxford: Oxford University Press. Print.

Friedman, J. K. (2007). "Ah am witness to its authenticity": Gothic style in postmodern southern writing. In L. M. E. Goodlad & M. Bibby (Eds.), *Goth: Undead subculture* (pp. 190–216). Durham: Duke University Press. Print.

Gelder, K. (1994). *Reading the vampire*. London: Routledge. Print.

Goddu, T. (1997). *Gothic America: Narrative, history, and nation*. New York: Columbia University Press. Print.

Leitch, T. (2007). *Film adaptation and its discontents: From gone with the wind to the passion of the Christ*. Baltimore: John Hopkins University Press. Print.

Lury, K. (2005). *Interpreting television*. London: Hodder Arnold. Print.

Parr, A. (2008). *Deleuze and memorial culture: Desire, singular memory and the politics of Trauma*. Edinburgh: Edinburgh University Press. Print.

Powell, A. (2005). *Deleuze and horror film*. Edinburgh: Edinburgh University Press. Print.

Ruddell, C., & Cherry, B. (2012). More than cold and heartless: The Southern Gothic Millieu of true blood. In B. Cherry (Ed.), *True blood: Investigating vampires and Southern Gothic* (pp. 39–55). London: I. B. Tauris. Print.

Wheatley, H. (2006). *Gothic television*. Manchester: Manchester University Press. Print.

Wilson, S. (2014). The nonsense of detection: Truth between science and the real. In *True detection* (pp. 146–163). San Bernardino: Schism. Print.

Yaeger, P. (2000). *Dirt and desire: Reconstructing southern women's writing, 1930–1990*. Chicago: University of Chicago Press. Print.

Further Readings

Cherry, B. (Ed.). (2012). *True blood: Investigating vampires and Southern Gothic.* London: I. B. Tauris. An edited collection with papers exploring gothic and Southern Gothic approaches to *True Blood*, including folklore, gender and sexuality, landscape, religion and race.

Connole, E., Ennis, P. J. & Masciandaro, N. (Eds.). (2014). *True detection.* Schism, An edited collection of papers on *True Detective*. While not specifically focused on Southern Gothic, it presents a range of approaches that explore the generic hybridity of the series.

Thompson, C. M. (2012). The grotesque and the post-apocalyptic South: Ourselves and our ghosts. *American Popular Culture*, November 2012. Online. Commentary on *True Blood*, *The Vampire Diaries* and *The Walking Dead* that engages with the figure of the zombie, as well as Southern Gothic themes.

CHAPTER 36

The Southern Gothic in Film: An Overview

David Greven

In her study of the construction of Southern culture in travel writing after the Civil War, Rebecca C. McIntyre provides us with a template for the enduring image of the South as a gothic domain:

> Besides the grotesque, travel literature after the war used gothic and medieval imagery in descriptions of southern scenes. Postbellum travel writers turned the swamp into a dismal landscape of an imaginary medieval past ... 'gothic aisles dim with the incense of a thousand creepers and mosses' ... [and fashioned] ruined tapestries out of the tangled vines of a Louisiana bayou. These cathedrals of gnarled trees and streaming moss helped satisfy the nearly insatiable appetite of Americans for an ancient past. Even though imaginary, such 'ruins' made an acceptable substitute for the crumbling castles and gothic towers of Old World landscapes. (54)

McIntyre's analysis illuminates the ways in which the South has been represented since the latter half of the nineteenth century, the opportunistic and arbitrary nature of this construction. The Gothic South has not only held an undeniable appeal, but has also been useful to US self-identity as historically rich and continuous. The concept has its roots in certain features, customs, specificities, and contingencies related to the Southern region, its history and peoples, but is also a national fantasy.

Artists working in the mediums of literature and film of the twentieth century found this idea of a Gothic South both fascinating and fertile. The extraordinary creative flowering that occurred in twentieth-century Southern literature—the works of authors such as William Faulkner, Thomas Wolfe, Carson McCullers, Flannery O'Connor, Eudora Welty, Truman Capote, Tennessee Williams, Katherine Anne Porter, and others—sprang from the dark, rich soil

D. Greven (✉)
University of South Carolina, Columbia, NY, USA

© The Editor(s) (if applicable) and The Author(s) 2016
S.C. Street, C.L. Crow (eds.), *The Palgrave Handbook of the Southern Gothic*,
DOI 10.1057/978-1-137-47774-3_36

of these stylized images of the region. The writers collectively imagined the Southern Gothic into being. The focus of this chapter is the deployment of this concept in American film from the classic Hollywood era to the present. I will also touch on twenty-first-century television narratives, which bespeak both the prominence of television representation since the 2000s began and the enduring fascination of Southern Gothic, in particular season one of HBO's *True Detective* (2014).

SOUTHERN GOTHICISM

Before turning to cinematic examples, I want to take a moment to consider the 'gothicism' of the Southern Gothic. In her book *Gothic Subjects*, Siân Silyn Roberts discusses the transformation of the British Gothic into an American idiom. What was at stake in the early British Gothic of the eighteenth century was 'the definition of the individual and its claims for moral authority' (4). In contrast,

> the American gothic novel ... takes the individual in a rather different direction by questioning its field of application in a diasporic setting. By detaching identity from geographic origin, consanguinity, or exemplary political status, works of gothic fiction imagine Americanness as an ability to change, adapt, travel, and even subsume individual difference and cultural particularity beneath forms of mass collectivity. [American innovations of the British gothic produce] 'gothic subjects.' By this I mean a constellation of different narrative personas whose mutability and adaptability make them ideally suited to a fluctuating Atlantic world ... [marked by] the fluctuations of the market, immigration, accident, chance, circumstance, and opportunity. (7)

The Southern Gothic, as scholars such as McIntyre have shown, was an opportunistic construction that reflected anxieties about American newness in the face of mounting pressures and desires to create a stable and hegemonic American identity. Indeed, the development of Southern Gothic demonstrates the continued adaptation of the traditional Gothic discussed by Roberts for the American idiom well into modernity and beyond.

My analysis proceeds from the position that the Southern Gothic is politically Janus faced. On the one hand, Southern Gothic, even within its galleries of grotesques and lurid situations, has had the capacity to speak for the marginalized. Most notably, the sub-genre has been able to explore, on occasion, issues of feminism, race, and religiosity in critical and reflective ways. Works such as *Dark Waters* (André De Toth, 1944) and *Hush, Hush, Sweet Charlotte* (Robert Aldrich, 1964) offer surprising feminist critiques (for an extended reading of *Hush, Hush* and feminism, see Greven, 'Bringing'); African American filmmakers have challenged the status quo while innovating the genre; and films such as *The Night of the Hunter* (Charles Laughton, 1955) and *Wise Blood* (John Huston, 1979) have examined the psychosexual underpinnings of religious fanaticism. Further, if the South is always the 'Other' America, Southern Gothic works give this Other America a voice and a prominence. On the other hand, many—too many, in the end—Southern Gothic works exploitatively and simplistically relegate the South and its denizens to the category of degenerate and menacing otherness. This chapter will attempt to make sense of both, and equally strong, strains of the Southern Gothic. I will offer an overview of the history of Southern Gothic films and consider what the sustained preoccupation with the South *as* gothic tells us about attitudes toward this region and the reasons why film and Southern Gothicism have enjoyed so fertile a partnership.

A POLYGLOT AMERICA

In a 2015 essay on the Southern Gothic in film for the British film journal *Sight and Sound*, Nick Pinkerton establishes the artistic imperative behind the sub-genre's emphasis on the grotesque, the decayed, the ruined, and so forth:

> The specific designation 'Southern Gothic', however, is connected to a new social criticism and a flowering of the arts in the South that began in the early 20th century, in the years immediately following the 1917 publication of H.L. Mencken's essay 'The Sahara of the Bozart' (a hillbilly corruption of Beaux Arts) ... [Tennessee] Williams, authoring a spirited defence of [Carson] McCullers's sophomore work, *Reflections in a Golden Eye*, which had been criticised for its excessive grotesquerie upon its 1941 publication, ventured to describe the local 'Gothic school' to which he and McCullers had been consigned: 'There is something in the region, something in the blood and culture of the southern state that has somehow made them the center of this Gothic school of writers'. Defining the unifying attribute of work in this school, which he compared to the contemporary creations of the French existentialists, Williams singled out 'a sense, an intuition, of an underlying dreadfulness in modern experience', going on to praise McCullers's novel as 'conceived in that Sense of the Awful which is the desperate black root of nearly all significant modem art, from the *Guernica* of Picasso to the cartoons of Charles Addams'. (45)

Pinkerton's emphasis on Williams's comradely defense of McCullers is apt. Southern Gothic film, as does the closely related literary tradition, proceeds from the basis of 'an underlying dreadfulness,' but one that is less about 'modern experience' than it is about something inherent within the South, at least as perceived by the purveyors of Southern Gothic.

In film terms, the sub-genre encompasses a wide range of 'Souths': the Appalachia of *The Night of the Hunter* and *Deliverance* (John Boorman, 1972), based on James Dickey's novel; the titular locale of *The Texas Chainsaw Massacre* (Tobe Hooper, 1974); the bayous of southern Louisiana in *Dark Waters* and *The Skeleton Key* (Iain Softley, 2005). Of Hooper's film, one critic pertinently observes:

> The film is deliberately designed to create a sense of panic and hysterical anxiety, as if the relentless Texas heat has finally driven everyone insane. Its atmosphere creates a sense of disruption and dislocation that occurs on a variety of levels simultaneously ... [reflecting] the crippling double blow of Vietnam and Watergate. (Magistrale 157)

Southern Gothic works maintain an unusually close, visceral relationship to the land, both in its material authenticity and its stylized aspects.

A wild, polyglot America emerges from the Southern Gothic film tradition that, in its weird specificity, seems like an alternative version of the nation, especially given the general emphasis on the Northern states in the nation's self-presentation. If the South is always the moribund and morbid underside of the nation, left behind and forgotten even if preserved in the amber of nostalgia, Southern Gothic films challenge this status, constituting a mythopoeic realm far livelier than and more threatening to the stability and sameness of mainstream American life (at least in these pop-mythic terms).

One of the first classic Hollywood films to represent the sub-genre is the 1941 *Swamp Water*, directed by the great French filmmaker Jean Renoir, his first movie made in the United States. Starring Walter Brennan and Walter Huston, it was based on the novel by Vereen Bell and shot on location in Georgia's Okefenokee Swamp. The film concerns the vindication of an innocent man, Tom Kagan, wrongfully accused of murder. Ben Ragan, searching for his lost dog, encounters Tom, a fugitive from prison, in the swamp. When the townspeople discover that Ben has befriended Tom, they try to force him to give Tom up; eventually the real culprits of the murder for which Tom was convicted, a pair of nefarious brothers, meet dubious ends (one left to drown in the swamp, the other set adrift) while Tom is finally exonerated. As Colin Davis writes, the 'film has a strange beauty' that transcends its conventional plot. Of particular importance is that Renoir does not create a realistic swamp setting, but rather uses the swamp in a manner that is 'primarily allegorical.' A 'wild, inhospitable space,' the swamp 'represents one pole in the oppositions between culture and nature ... More fundamentally,' the swamp evokes death, a place from which no one returns, which makes the escaped convict Tom Kagan's ultimate emergence from the swamp more than 'the reestablishment of justice,' a 'return of the dead' (15–16). These uses of the swamp atmosphere, metonymic of the Louisiana bayou setting endemic to Southern Gothic film, crucially render the swamp as a dreamlike, mythic realm that defies reality, an alternative and symbolic space, a geographic atmosphere and mood rather than locale.

The 1944 *Dark Waters* demands a much fuller analysis than I can provide here and deserves to be better known. The director, André De Toth, makes eloquent use of the Louisiana bayou setting as metaphorical of the dark, tangled motives of the conmen, but also of the treacherous labyrinth of the heroine's mental anguish. The survivor of a shipwreck that killed her parents, the heroine is a traumatized young woman who seeks refuge in her as-yet-unmet aunt's bayou mansion; once there, however, she gradually discovers that the strange people who welcome her to the mansion are not members of her family at all but conmen (and -women) impersonating her family members. The charlatans attempt to drive her insane so that she will not reveal their stratagems. The plot of the film evinces what is, in my view, one of the most radical aspects of the genre, its critique of the hystericization of women. It should be noted that Joan

Harrison, who worked with Alfred Hitchcock before branching out on her own, was a co-writer and producer of the film, which may account for its notably feminist sensibility (Hanson 10). Equally notable is that the film depicts a non-stereotyped African American male character who works with the heroine to discover the truth about her dubious faux-family. In a chilling moment, she discovers his dead body one night on the grounds of the estate after he is murdered by the charlatans. What is striking about this moment is its quiet horror; she stumbles over him in the dark just outside the property, where his body has been tossed. The moment indicates an enduring post-Reconstruction era death drive, the continued reification of black subjects as commodities (the dead man was a servant for the original family, fired by the imposters) that can be simply discarded. Moreover, the film suggests a parity between the modern independent woman and the black man alike, menaced by the same sinister forces of greed and corruption that target them both as vulnerable and negligible outsiders.

While some important 1940s films begin to develop the cinematic Southern Gothic, the sub-genre really comes into fruition in the 1950s. *The Long, Hot Summer* (Martin Ritt, 1958) reflects Faulkner's impact on American popular culture. Filmed in Clinton, Louisiana, this film features several Method actors and is loosely based on three Faulkner works: the 1931 novella 'Spotted Horses,' the 1939 short story 'Barn Burning,' and the 1940 novel *The Hamlet*. Another author whose works successfully translated into film and stage adaptations was Carson McCullers. Her 1946 novel *The Member of the Wedding* was made into a famous 1952 film version directed by Fred Zinnemann. Her most gothic work, *The Ballad of the Sad Café* (1943), was made into a cerebral 1991 film by the British actor Simon Callow. While not fully successful, it does boast a powerhouse performance by Vanessa Redgrave as Miss Amelia, a masculine woman who essentially runs her small town and agrees to marriage with the tough guy Marvin Macy, only to kick him out of their marital bed on their wedding night. Amelia falls in love with her cousin, a dwarf named Lymon who manipulates her into caring for him. At the climax, a horrific boxing match occurs between Amelia and Marvin, who has returned from prison to seek revenge on Amelia. Just when Amelia is about to land a triumphant final blow on Marvin, Lymon, like a winged fury, flies off his perch with a shriek and knocks Amelia down, allowing Marvin to win the match. Lymon, wildly in love with Marvin, helps him to trash Amelia's house and titular café and to steal her money. The film ends as it opens, with a haunting shot of the lonely, ravaged older Amelia, her once short-cropped blonde hair now lengthy and white, forlornly staring out of her window. The film, as the novella did before it, emphasizes two key dimensions in the importance of Southern Gothic: the figure of the grotesque—Cousin Lymon, the malevolent dwarf; the ogress Amelia—and its potential queerness.

To return to the 1950s, the rise of the cinematic Southern Gothic was spurred on by the massive popularity of film adaptations as well as stage productions of the works of Tennessee Williams. One of the greatest American playwrights, Williams crafted a highly stylized and idiosyncratic world of lyrical language, grotesque situations and characters, and a doom-laden atmosphere. While Southern Gothicism informs the film version of *A Streetcar Named Desire* (Elia Kazan, 1951) and other works, it is with the 1959 film adaptation of Williams's *Suddenly, Last Summer* that the particulars of the sub-genre really come into play. As with McCullers's work, *Suddenly, Last Summer* foregrounds the grotesque and the specter of homosexual desire.

Directed by Joseph L. Mankiewicz from a screenplay by Gore Vidal (Williams was listed as the co-screenwriter, however), *Suddenly, Last Summer* is, like so much of Southern Gothic and also Williams's works at their most intriguing, centered on powerful female characters. Set in New Orleans in the late 1930s, *Suddenly, Last Summer*'s plot revolves around the fate of the heroine, Catherine Holly (Elizabeth Taylor), a beautiful and emotionally troubled young woman who has been institutionalized after a nervous breakdown. Her breakdown occurred after a trip with her cousin, Sebastian Venable, to the Spanish town of Cabeza de Lobo, where Sebastian mysteriously died. Catherine wants to tell the story of how and why Sebastian died, but his rich patrician mother, Violet Venable (Katharine Hepburn), wants to have her lobotomized instead. An innovative young surgeon, Dr. John Cukrowicz (Montgomery Clift), investigates the story to determine whether Catherine should indeed be lobotomized; Violet attempts to bribe the state hospital to ensure this outcome.

While some critics have found this film homophobic, it is better understood as a commentary on homophobia, in my opinion. When Catherine finally gets to tell her story, it is a grisly one. Sebastian used both his mother and Catherine as 'bait' to lure the young impoverished men who then became his sexual conquests. In a grotesque cannibal orgy, the starving children and young men of the Spanish beach town descend on Sebastian and devour him as Catherine watches. The Southern Gothicism of the narrative stems from this hideous, and climactically revealed, 'secret' to the mystery surrounding Sebastian's death.

The film primarily evokes the elements of the sub-genre, however, in the mise en scène of Violet's mansion and in her outré characterization. To meet with the surgeon and give him a tour of her home, Violet, in an ethereal white outfit, descends from a height like a *deus ex machina*; following her stroke after her poet son's death, she had an elevator built inside her home. Her garden, through which she guides Cukrowicz, is an overgrown, lush, and frightening realm inhabited by ravenous Venus flytraps and presided over by a large, looming statue of a hybrid creature, an angel with outstretched wings and the face and body of a skeleton, of the kind associated with Spanish cemeteries. Such touches ensure that we see Violet as the true monster. What is especially interesting for our purposes is that, in a feverish version of the pathetic fallacy, Violet's fearsome garden reflects her equally fearsome and obsessive personality. The sense of enclosure and claustrophobia endemic to the Gothic takes on a lurid character here that typifies the Southern Gothic, in which nature assumes a twisted, sinister form that mirrors the madness, entrapment, and hopelessness of the characters.

SAVAGE SOUTHERNERS

While many films of the 1960s—*Reflections in a Golden Eye* (John Huston, 1967), based on McCullers's 1941 novel; *Toys in the Attic* (George Roy Hill, 1963), based on the Tony Award–winning play by Lillian Hellman; *This Property Is Condemned* (Sydney Pollack, 1966), adapted from Tennessee Williams's 1946 one-act play—extended the previous decade's investments in the Southern Gothic, it was a 1970s film that created the template for the contemporary version of the sub-genre that has remained remarkably consistent well into the twenty-first century. Directed by John Boorman, *Deliverance* is a 1972 American film based on James Dickey's 1970 novel of the same name. Burt Reynolds, Jon Voight, Ned Beatty, and Ronny Cox play four Atlanta businessmen who travel to Georgia's fictional Cahulawassee River Valley for a canoeing trip. This is the film famous for its 'dueling banjos' scene between Cox and Billy Redden, playing the inbred and apparently mentally retarded 'Lonnie,' a remarkably talented banjo player. The Voight and Beatty characters are ambushed by two malevolent hillbillies, an episode that contains the film's infamous male rape scene, punctuated by the command 'Squeal like a pig!' uttered by one of the hillbillies as he rapes Beatty's character.

Deliverance is notable for the vivid visual style that Boorman, who also directed *Excalibur*, characteristically brought to it. He creates an expressionistic natural space charged with malevolence, refining the Southern Gothic aesthetic in a bold manner. In one particularly memorable shot, the men discover the dead Cox in the water, his body hideously contorted and entwined within floating logs and branches. However, the movie's lurid demonization of the Appalachian peoples (those who live in the general area fictionalized by the film continue to report the cultural aftershocks of this demonization) and its predictable gender politics (it is no accident that it is the heavyset and therefore less conventionally masculine Beatty character who is sodomized by the hillbilly villains) make this a vexing work. Its construction of wilderness space as a testing ground for masculine bravado is an outgrowth of its reactionary gender politics, just as its depiction of the regional populace, alternately eerie and unsettling (the banjo-playing boy) and horrifically amoral (the hillbillies), is an outgrowth of its reactionary cultural politics. For what the film seeks to establish is that the effete, socialized businessmen can only achieve their titular deliverance once their essential gendered strengths have been tested in the crucible of nature.

The demonization of poor rural whites foregrounded in *Deliverance* is perhaps the chief mainstay of the Southern Gothic film. Devoid of contextualization, works in this sub-genre typically offer its rural, impoverished grotesques as representatives of Southern culture and peoples. Innumerable post-Deliverance films have followed its model of a fundamental savagery in Southerners that extends to its landscape and of a regressive, primordial quality to the region and its denizens. It is telling that the extremely well-made, thoughtful, and mesmerizing stand-alone first season (2014) of the HBO miniseries *True*

Detective, created by Nic Pizzolatto, both indicates levels of profound political corruption in the South and concludes with a confrontation with a villain revealed to be the embodiment of the degenerate Southerner, inbred, misogynistic, and given to spouting messianic messages. I will touch on *True Detective* again later.

Angel Heart (Alan Parker, 1987) takes the familiar tropes of the Southern Gothic—cruelty and corruption in the Louisiana bayous—to a genre-bending level, intermixing film noir and horror. Indeed, its villain Louis Cyphre (Robert De Niro) is ultimately revealed to be the devil himself, as his name already adumbrated. In the final shots, an elevator carries the protagonist down to hell. Nevertheless, most Southern Gothic villains are not as elegant as Louis Cyphre.

The number of pathological hillbilly-cum-redneck-cum-mountain-man-cum-lawless-outsider Southern villains in media far exceeds the ability to enumerate them here. Martin Scorsese's 1991 remake of the 1962 film *Cape Fear*, directed by J. Lee Thompson, is a case in point (and one of the worst films of a great director). The re-make depicts its antagonist Max Cady, originally played by Robert Mitchum and here by Robert De Niro, a super-fusion of myriad degenerate Southern villains. In the original version, Mitchum's Cady stalks the lawyer Sam Bowden (Gregory Peck), who testified against him in court after seeing Cady assaulting a woman; in the re-make, Bowden was Cady's defense attorney, who suppressed evidence in order to make sure that Cady would be put away for rape. De Niro's Cady boasts jailhouse musculature and a body covered in tattoos of wrathful biblical quotations. Evangelista, a critic who more positively values the re-make and De Niro's performance than I do, comments:

> Speaking with a thick, ignorant-sounding hillbilly drawl, De Niro is muscled and crass, braying obnoxious laughter at a movie theatre while puffing up mushroom cloud-like cigar smoke. By the end of the film, he's mutated into something akin to a slasher movie monster—his face burned and scarred as he violently tries to kill everyone.

The original *Cape Fear* is subtler and more effective, drawing a brilliant contrast on the level of acting styles and star personae between Mitchum and Peck and submitting the idyllic model of the white all-American family of the 1950s and 1960s to a chilling series of threats. Scorsese's version considerably heightens the class-based critique of Cady's sustained program of revenge. Yet the re-make emblematizes the Southern Gothic film's penchant for pitting an uneducated yet bible-spouting, pathological rural masculinity against an educated, effete one.

Many Southern Gothic films reflect the troubling legacy of both slavery and Reconstruction-era lynchings (a practice that endured into the twentieth century, as the harrowing case of Emmet Till attests). Certain films, such as the famous *To Kill a Mockingbird* (Robert Mulligan, 1962), the movie adaptation of Harper Lee's hugely popular novel, and *Intruder in the Dust* (Clarence Brown, 1949), treated this anguished aspect of Southern history with care and sensitivity. However, more often the subject has prompted sensationalistic treatment. *Mandingo* (Richard Fleischer, 1975), long relegated to the category of exploitation flick, is set on an antebellum plantation and revels in scenes of sadomasochism and illicit inter-racial sex. The film does have its defenders, however, such as Robin Wood and Pinkerton most recently. Indeed, I would argue that it is a far more thoughtful and progressive film than Quentin Tarantino's self-consciously sensationalistic *Django Unchained* (2013), which treats similar subjects with far greater bombast.

Mandingo illuminates the gender and sexual politics of American slavery, focusing on, on the one hand, the sexual exploitation of slaves (both female and male) and, on the other, the exploitation of the male slave body, put to pugilistic use in murderous boxing matches notable for their unrestrained violence (indeed, the violence is encouraged) and resulting in death. *Django Unchained*'s most effective sequence occurs in a posh private club in which, after drinks are poured for wealthy clients, two slave men are forced to wrestle one another until one of the men kills the other as the patrons watch. This brutal sequence extends *Mandingo*'s critique of the exploitation of the slave male body.

Yet *Django Unchained*, redolent of the director's characteristically cartoonish and grandiose style and themes, largely turns its slavery narrative into a primitive revenge fantasy in which the chief villain—the one who its titular hero most torturously kills—is the house negro figure rather than the plantation master himself, dispatched by a supporting character. An infinitely better film and also one more evocative of the gothic genre, Steve McQueen's *12 Years a Slave* (2013), an adaptation of Solomon Northup's memoir, makes use of the uncanny, alien strangeness of the antebellum Southern slavery plantation to suggest an alternative realm in which those in power inflict violence on their human possessions with impunity. In this manner, it evokes Harriet Jacobs's stunning 1860 novel, a fictionalized account of her own experiences, *Incidents in the Life of a Slave Girl*. In a stunning night-time scene, the plantation master (Michael Fassbender) takes Northup (Chiwetel Ejiofor) out onto the plantation grounds to interrogate him about possible sedition. The eerie setting and the homo-erotic intimacy between the men—the master has his arm tightly coiled around his slave, holding him close to his body—heighten the sense of menace and unpredictable violence. The film unflinchingly depicts the harrowing violence in which slavery was rife when the master forces the unwilling Solomon to whip the sexually exploited young slave woman Patsey (Lupita Nyong'o).

Most Southern Gothic films focus on black/white relations in contemporary times, yet in an alternately lurid and ahistorical manner. In *Black Snake Moan* (Craig Brewer, 2006), a Mississippi bluesman (Samuel Jackson) keeps a woman (Christina Ricci) hostage as he attempts to cure her of nymphomania. *The Skeleton Key*, an atmospheric but ideologically troubling film, revises the history of lynching in the South by making black victims of the practice the villains. Servants accused of corrupting the minds of their young charges, Mama Cecile (Jeryl Prescott) and Papa Justify (Ron McCall), swap bodies just before they are lynched with the white children to whom they have taught hoodoo rituals. This film evinces a pattern of representation that I call 'the victim-monster,' in which the abused and violated become the truly monstrous oppressors and horrifying entities (I discuss the victim-monster trope in my book *Ghost Faces*). Such works indulge in stereotypes while bizarrely revising and repressing historical trauma. As one critic sternly observes:

> For a film to engage with Southern gothic, it must first invert or eliminate a sense of realism; the cartoonish subversion allows the American filmmaker to re-define questions of class, race and gender in an unapologetic and largely exploitative way. Further, it presents an arena in which directors and screenwriters can present cultural stereotypes and racialized violence in a consequence-free environment. (Crank 212)

The Southern Gothic film has, however, provided African American film-makers with opportunities for dazzling innovations of the sub-genre. In particular, *To Sleep with Anger* (Charles Burnett, 1990) and *Eve's Bayou* (Kasi Lemmons, 1997) defy the constraints of the mode and explore issues of class as well as race. Burnett's film, about the effects of a trickster/conjure figure (Danny Glover) on a middle-class black family, enlarges the concerns of the African American Gothic genre, traditionally focused on the issue of slavery. Cunningham writes:

> Slavery, however, is an afterthought in *To Sleep with Anger*; while slavery is the vessel that brought conjure to the South, the 'peculiar institution' has little bearing on the film. The haunting in *To Sleep with Anger* is done not by a slavery-ridden South, but a postbellum black South steeped in traditions, particularly a continued adherence to conjure. (124)

Several important works of the Southern Gothic film demand much more extensive analysis than I can provide here, especially Charles Laughton's extraordinary *The Night of the Hunter* and John Huston's 1979 film adaptation of Flannery O'Connor's 1952 novel *Wise Blood*. Like *Night of the Hunter*, Huston's adaptation of *Wise Blood* offers a powerful critique of religiosity, a troubling and inescapable aspect of Southern culture. Often treated in the sub-genre as yet one more indication of Southern looniness, religiosity is given the serious scrutiny it demands here. *Wise Blood* is also notable for being a successful film adaptation of O'Connor's deeply elusive literary art. These works give us much to consider both cinematically and in terms of the potentialities of the Southern Gothic in film, one of the most complex, frustrating, and irresistibly compelling archives of American moviemaking.

TRUE DETECTIVE

In terms of the contemporary Southern Gothic, one particularly acute work demands attention: season 1 of the HBO series *True Detective*.[1] To begin with, *True Detective* stunningly catalogues, in visual terms, the hallmarks of the

contemporary South as they reflect modernity and as they evince the strong-
hold of an archetypal past. In addition to Pizzolatto's mesmerizing scripts and
the great performances of its two leads, the series owes its power to the direc-
torial flair of Cary Joji Fukunaga, writer and director of the brilliant 2009
Mexican American adventure thriller film *Sin Nombre*. As one critic writes of
Pizzolatto's series, its

> fretful perspective is masterfully amplified by [its] title sequence—which consists
> of repeated superimpositions of individual characters over a vast landscape, the
> latter rendering the former increasingly inconsequential—and the show's dilapi-
> dated terrain of social institutions on the wane, from religion ('a language virus
> that rewrites pathways in the brain [and] dulls critical thinking') to the ubiquitous
> petrochemical industry, whose refineries and manufacturing plants provide the
> series' contaminated backdrops. (Griffin)

A key factor in the series, its Louisiana setting, was a last-minute decision. The
first season was initially going to be filmed in Arkansas, but Pizzolatto chose
to film in Louisiana, a less-expensive venue due to the state's attractive film-
tax incentive program. (No doubt the Arkansas setting would have proved
distinctly interesting.)

In addition to the series' visual design, its depiction of its distinct, often
antagonistic, yet strangely connected heroes, Louisiana State homicide
detectives Rust Cohle (Matthew McConaughey) and Marty Hart (Woody
Harrelson), creates a new template of American masculinities. The series inge-
niously manipulates the temporal scheme of its narrative, oscillating between
scenes set in the present and from years beginning in the mid-1990s. Pizzolatto
was, like horror filmmaker Wes Craven, a literature professor (at places such as
the University of Chicago, the University of North Carolina at Chapel Hill,
and DePauw University), and this shows in the highly literary particulars of
Cohle and Hart's obsession-making case, central to the narrative and spanning
17 years, which concerns a young murdered prostitute named Dora Lange
whose corpse is discovered in Vermilion Parish, Louisiana in 1995. Her head
and long tresses, adorned, as if crowned, with deer antlers, have been inserted
into a complex circular lattice of twigs within an immense tree—a welter of
symbolic images. The case eventually leads to revelations that a powerful family, the Tuttles, who run a series of Christian schools in the state, are hazily
involved in a strange cult that combines the mask and masquerade culture of
New Orleans Mardi Gras, Christianity, and literary works by Ambrose Bierce
('An Inhabitant of Carcosa,' 1886), Robert W. Chambers (a series of tales
known as *The King in Yellow*), and H. P. Lovecraft. The show 'begins to explore
Cajun Mardi Gras and revival-tent religion. Cohle, a Texan, notes that the area
they're investigating has a winter festival that goes "heavy on the Saturnalia, a
place where that Santeria and Voodoo all mashed together"' (Young).

While the series deserves extensive scrutiny, for our purposes I want to draw
our attention to the finale, which proved to be extremely controversial. (This
controversy seems like a harbinger of the critical abuse heaped, unfairly in my

view, on the second season, set in Los Angeles.) Many viewers, critics and audience members alike, criticized the show for its lack of a twist ending and for its in-your-face indulgence in Southern Gothic stereotypes. The killer, a bastard son of one of the Tuttle family men, turns out to be an obese, dirt-covered, sweating ogre who lives in a sprawling, dilapidated, maze-like lair—his version of the mythic shadowy realm Carcosa, in which 'death is not the end'—with his half-sister, whom he incestuously molests and well-nigh imprisons. While I do not find the finale to be on a par with the rest of the series, I do believe that it was unfairly scorned. I propose that the depiction of the villain Errol—scarred of face, called 'the Green Man' and the 'Spaghetti Man'—is self-conscious and deconstructive, a kind of art-installation piece titled 'Southern Gothic Degenerate Hillbilly Villain.' Alerting us to the deconstructive aspect, Pizzolatto writes a comic, quizzical scene in which Errol watches Alfred Hitchcock's comic suspense thriller *North by Northwest* (1959), specifically the scene in which Cary Grant's Roger O. Thornhill, a Madison Avenue ad man mistaken for a government agent, confronts the villain, James Mason's British-sounding Vandamm, at an auction, which Thornhill humorously commandeers in order to escape the villain's henchmen. Errol bizarrely speaks in an arch mock-British, P. G. Wodehouse accent, and addresses and treats his incestuous half-sibling with mock courtliness.

To my mind, the series seems to be calling attention to the cheesiness of the Southern Gothic's typical recourse to villains of this type, and the imitative performance that ensues from the viewing of the Hitchcock film adds to the sense that Errol merely puts on a series of roles—a series of masks in keeping with his Carcosa mythology. When he confronts Cohle in his spectral realm, he hisses, 'Take off your mask.' On the one hand, this line speaks to the diegetic issues of the plot, but it also alerts us to the put-on nature of the entire narrative's exploration of Southern types, emblematized by its shifting and telling landscapes, noir-archetypal leading men, and wide range of personae ranging from mock-messianic preachers, mentally limited child molesters seeking redemption, wild-eyed heroin-addicted petty yet murderous criminals spending their lives in solitary, and good-ol'-boy cops.

CONCLUSION

Overall, Southern Gothic has a penchant for the stereotypical that reinforces mainstream understandings of the Southern region as moribund and even monstrous, in a cartoonishly vivid manner. At times, as I have tried to suggest, the Southern Gothic film has been capable of much more, such as the surprising feminist critique that it provides at times, the deconstruction of American masculinities in such works as the original *Cape Fear* and *True Detective*, and, much more rarely, the opportunity for a resistant African American cinema. One must explore the sub-genre with discretion and a certain apprehension, but some valuable works can be discovered with committed sifting.

NOTES

1. While not exactly Southern Gothic, the 2010 indie film *Winter's Bone*, an adaptation of Daniel Woodrell's 2006 novel, deserves careful consideration. Written and directed by Debra Granik, the film stars Jennifer Lawrence as 17-year-old Ree Dolly, a teenage girl in the rural Ozarks of the central United States. Entrusted with her young brother and even younger sister, Ree also looks after her mentally troubled, silent mother. To prevent her family from eviction when her father, due in court for his drug-trafficking crimes, goes missing, Ree must appeal to the distant, threatening, locally powerful relatives who killed him for snitching to the police. This film offers a strong feminist take on the regional Gothic. It climaxes in a stunning sequence in which formidable older women connected to the powerful patriarch who ordered her father's execution help Ree cut off the hands of her father's corpse, buried in distant icy water, so that she can submit the hands as evidence that he has been killed, thereby ensuring that her father did not renege on his bail and that her family can keep their house. The film crosses *Antigone* with the regional Gothic and creates a new feminist myth from the fusion.

BIBLIOGRAPHY

Crank, J. A. (2011). An aesthetic of play: A contemporary cinema of south-sploitation. In A. B. Leiter (Ed.), *Southerners on film : Essays on Hollywood portrayals since the 1970s* (pp. 204–217). Jefferson: McFarland. Print.

Cunningham, P. L. (2011). The haunting of a black southern past: Considering conjure in to sleep with anger. In A. B. Leiter (Ed.), *Southerners on film : Essays on Hollywood portrayals since the 1970s* (pp. 123–134). Jefferson: McFarland. Print.

Davis, C. (2012). *Postwar Renoir : Film and the memory of violence*. New York: Routledge. Print. Routledge Advances in Film Studies ; 16.

Evangelista, C. Compare/contrast: Cape fear (1962/1991). *CutPrintFilm* | Movie Reviews. N.p., n.d. Web. 13 Aug. 2015.

Greven, D. (2013). Bringing out *Baby Jane*: Camp, sympathy, and the 1960s horror-woman's film, *Jump Cut: A Review of Contemporary Media*, No. 55, Fall 2013. Accessed on 3/3/2016. http://ejumpcut.org/archive/jc55.2013/grevenWmHorror/index.htmlhttp://ejumpcut.org/archive/jc55.2013/grevenWmHorror/index.html

Greven, D. (2016). *Ghost faces*. SUNY Press. New York

Griffin, T. (2014). Episodic disorder: Tim Griffin on true detective. *Artforum International,* 52.9, 133. *Biography in Context.* Web. 8 Aug. 2015.

Hanson, H. (2007). *Hollywood heroines : Women in film noir and the female Gothic film.* London /New York: IBTauris. Print.

Magistrale, T. (2005). *Abject terrors : Surveying the modern and postmodern horror film.* New York: Peter Lang. Print.

Mcintyre, R. C. (2005). Promoting the Gothic South. *Southern Cultures, 11*(2), 33–61. Print.

Pinkerton, N. (2015). Southern Gothic. *Sight and Sound, 25*(5), 44. Print.

Roberts, S. S. (2014). *Gothic subjects : The transformation of individualism in American fiction, 1790–1861* (1st ed.). Philadelphia: University of Pennsylvania Press. Print.

Young, Adrian Van. (2014). Santeria and Voodoo All Mashed Together. *Slate* 4 Mar. *Slate*. Web. 14 Aug. 2015.

FURTHER READING

Frye, S. (Ed.). (2013). *The Cambridge companion to Cormac McCarthy*. Cambridge: Cambridge University Press, Print. Cambridge Companions to Literature. The contributors analyze film adaptations of many of McCarthy's most well-known novels, such as *Outer Dark, Blood Meridian, All the Pretty Horses*, and *The Road*.

Shaw, B. (2010). Baptizing Boo: Religion in the cinematic Southern Gothic. *The Mississippi Quarterly*, 63.3 4, 445. Print. The special issue focuses on 'The South in Film.' Shaw's article discusses the films *The Apostle* and *Sling Blade*.

INDEX

Note: Page numbers with "n" denote notes.

© The Editor(s) (if applicable) and The Author(s) 2016
S.C. Street, C.L. Crow (eds.), *The Palgrave Handbook of the Southern Gothic*,
DOI 10.1057/978-1-137-47774-3

The manufacturer's authorised representative in the EU is Springer
Nature Customer Service Centre GmbH, Europaplatz 3, 69115 Heidelberg,
Germany. If you have any concerns regarding our products, please
contact ProductSafety@springernature.com

Printed and bound by CPI Group (UK) Ltd, Croydon, CR0 4YY

23/04/2026

02095592-0016